Book
Ballantine Books
1993 by Allan Cole and Christopher Bunch
ly Shapiro

served under International and Pan-American Copy-
tions. Published in the United States of America by
oks, a division of Random House, Inc., New York,
ously in Canada by Random House of Canada Lim-

ngress Catalog Card Number: 93-90151

8056-8

in the United States of America

r Edition: September 1993
rket Edition: July 1994

6   5   4   3   2   1

THE FAR KINGDOMS

Once in a blue n   he
door into another world, and a grand quest
beckons . . .

"As for epic fantasy . . . my pick is the glorious
swashbuckling of Allan Cole and Chris Bunch's
The Far Kingdoms."
—Faren Miller, *Locus*

"*The Far Kingdoms* by Allan Cole and Chris
Bunch is well written, neatly plotted with a few
nice twists, and absolutely riveting. This was the
field's page-turner of the year."
—Scott Winnett, *Locus*

"A thoughtful and well-crafted epic fantasy."
—*Publishers Weekly*

"An excellent fantasy adventure."
—*Science Fiction Chronicle*

"*The Far Kingdoms* is that rarity, an intelligent
fantasy novel written by adults for adults."
—Norman Spinrad

"*The Far Kingdoms* is a richly drawn epic fantasy
novel about a voyage of discovery . . . If you ever
wondered what lay beyond the edge of a map,
you'll want to explore this unforgettable fantasy
world."

—*Sense of Wonder,*
B. Dalton's Science Fiction,
Fantasy & Role Playing Newsletter

THE FAR KINGDOMS:
Chosen by *Locus* for their 1993 Recommended
Reading list of Fantasy Novels.

By Allan Cole and Chris Bunch
Published by Ballantine Books

The Sten Adventures:
STEN
THE WOLF WORLDS
THE COURT OF A THOUSAND SUNS
FLEET OF THE DAMNED
REVENGE OF THE DAMNED
THE RETURN OF THE EMPEROR
VORTEX
EMPIRE'S END

A RECKONING FOR KINGS
A DAUGHTER OF LIBERTY
THE FAR KINGDOMS

THE FAR KINGDOMS

Allan C
and
Chris B

A Del Rey
Published b
Copyright
Map by She

All rights r
right Conve
Ballantine B
and simultar
ited, Toronto

Library of C

ISBN: 0-345

Manufactured

First Hardcov
First Mass M

DE
RE

A Del Rey
BALLANTINE BOO 10 9 8 7

for
Jason Cole
and
Elizabeth Rice Bunch

The
First
Voyage

CHAPTER ONE
The Courtesan

KING OF FIRE.

King of Water.

Queen of the Muse.

I, Amalric Emilie Antero, put quill to linen on this, the second candleday of the Harvest Month, in the tenth year of the Time of the Lizard. I swear on the heads of my descendants all I write is true. I beseech thee, My Lords and My Lady, to look with favor upon this journal. Fire, light the way through dim memory. Water, nourish the fruit of my thoughts. Muse, look with kindness on my poor skills and grant me words worthy of the tale I tell. The tale of my travels to the Far Kingdoms.

And what I found.

AS I REREAD those lines I could hear Janos' laugh. It was a deep drum of a laugh that could warm a cold night or turn a fool's words to stone. I heard it loud, as if he sat next to me, instead of from a distance of over forty years. The laughter mocked me. Not for writing this history. He approved of histories and all books of knowledge. He thought them more sacred than any holy cedar grove, more telling than the mirror of any Seer. Yes, he would have approved, even if this account sometimes paints him in an ugly light. Which it shall. It shall. For have I not sworn to tell the truth? Janos was Truth's most ardent worshipper. Even when he lied . . . Especially when he lied.

The mockery, I am sure, was for the traditional opening spell I penned, calling on fire, water, and the Muse to assist me in my endeavors.

"It's a silly custom," he would have said. "What's more, it is

3

also a waste of your energies and your substance. It's like curing a nest of warts, and then not having anything left over for important things like a demon in your skull. A knotted thread's as good as thrice-blessed toad skin for a wart, and much less expensive, besides."

Then he would have slapped me on the back and filled our wineglasses to the brim. "Just start the book, Amalric. It'll come to you as you go."

Very well, then ... It began with a woman.

Her name was Melina, and she was the most exquisite courtesan in all Orissa. Even after all these years, my loins stir when I remember her. She had large, dark eyes a man could lose his soul in and long, perfumed waves of black hair to cover him with if he were accepted into her embrace. She had the form of a goddess, with golden skin, hennaed lips, red-tipped breasts, and silken thighs that promised the most welcome harbor any voyager of the flesh could imagine. In short, I was a man of exactly twenty summers, and I lusted for her with all the blind, unreasoning youthmust that hot-blooded age carries. If she had satisfied that lust, I would not be telling this story. Instead she held me transfixed in her professional thrall with nothing more than promises.

I was on a rare bit of business for my father the day I entangled myself in her net. A ship bearing goods from the west had just disgorged its cargo into one of my father's warehouses and it was my duty to oversee the accounting. This did not mean I was to interfere with my father's excellent slave clerks. I was there as a "presence of authority," as my father put it. This meant keeping the bribes allocated to the port officer, city tax collector, and Evocators' tithingman to a sensible level. I had a purse of gold and silver coins to slip into greedy fingers, and had been warned that if I paid out all of it profits from this voyage would be slim. The voyage had been long and with much incident, including a storm that had caught and battered our ship just off the mouth of the river that nourishes our city. It was tricky business, and I was amazed at the time that he'd entrusted it to me. But my father was trying to encourage me during a time of youthful confusion. He saw merit in me that I did not see in myself.

The port officer was green but overly cautious to make up for this failing. As we went from crate to bundle to barrel to jar and toted up the value, I saw a look of craft mar his youthful eyes as he envisioned a bribe equal to a year's wages. As his appetite sharpened, my mind raced for a solution. My gaze fell on a broken bundle of fabric. I groaned, ripped it open, and let the rich cloth spill onto the dusty warehouse floor. I shouted for the ship's captain, ignoring the startled look on the port officer's face. He must have thought I'd gone mad. But the look turned to amazement when the captain arrived and I showed him the offending cloth and cursed its poor quality.

"You are either a fool who has been taken by a great cheat," I berated him, "or *you* are that great cheat in the flesh." I swore the cloth was of substandard quality, and even a dimwit could see it would rot within a week in Orissa's moist river climate. And if this was so, what of the other goods? "Damme, captain, look at me when I speak!"

The captain was an old hand and caught on quickly. He moaned regret and swore ignorance. I sent him away to contemplate my father's wrath and turned back to the port officer. His smile was weak when I apologized, and the smile grew weaker still as I expanded on that apology—slipping him a single coin for his bribe—to include the obviously diminished value of the cargo. He did not protest, but gripped the coin tightly and fled before I came to my senses and said that it was too much.

The city tax collector took no thought at all—he owed my father many favors—so he was happy with a rare trinket from the west to pleasure his much younger wife.

Believing myself a new master of commerce, I awaited the tithingman from the Evocators' Council. This was one test that I'd feared. In those days there was great animosity between my family and the Evocators. I was swaggering with thoughts of minor revenge when the wizard's arrival was announced. But the sorcerer who showed himself quickly pricked that thinly stretched silk. Prevotant was known as one of the fattest, greediest Evocators in Orissa. He was notorious for both his poor skills as a wizard and his frightening talent for skinning a merchant of his purse. The moment he saw me, he chuckled in glee that one so young and stupid was all that stood between him and fortune. His chuckle was echoed by a shrill chittering from the Favorite clinging to his shoulder.

In that time there were still a few, usually older, Evocators who kept a Favorite to assist them in casting spells. Part animal, part demon, they could change their size at will from twice that of a man to even smaller than the scaly thing curled around Prevotant's neck. The creature's chittering grew wilder as it stirred itself into a boiling broth of excitement. Most Favorites were high-strung and sometimes difficult to control, but I could see that this creature was as hysterical as a much-beaten dog. Instead of soothing it with a soft word and stroking its leathery hide, Prevotant cursed and gave it a stinging blow. The Favorite squealed in pain and anger but subsided. Still, I could see it was brooding, for its skin had turned from black to pulsing red. It worried at a bloody sore with small, sharp teeth.

"Perhaps he's hungry," I offered, thinking to ingratiate myself. "I could send for a morsel to tempt him."

The Favorite chirped, but Prevotant shook his head, flapping his jowls from side to side. "Never mind him. Let's get to the business at hand." He puffed up his girth and fixed me with a fierce stare. "I have reports of sorcerous contraband hidden in your cargo."

My good sense fled before his charge. It was an old ploy at the docks, especially among the Evocators' tithingmen. My father would have dismissed it with a laugh. I knew this. My father had always made a point to mention these small confrontations and conquests to aid my education. But *knowing* and *doing*—ah, now, there's a great divide. My face, that great betrayer of redheaded folk, turned as fiery as my hair.

"But . . . But . . . That's not possible," I sputtered. "We ordered all precautions taken. *All* precautions!"

Prevotant grimaced and pulled some scribblings from his stained robes. He examined quill scratches, keeping his hand cupped to hide them from my view. He shook his head, gloomy, then replaced his notes. His Favorite snatched at the pocket, receiving another blow. "Nasty beast," the Evocator hissed, then he shifted his attention back to me. "Nonetheless," he said, "these charges are serious. Serious indeed." He gazed lovingly at my father's goods. "I have no choice, but to . . . but to . . ."

But I was gaping, numb. His head gave an impatient jerk, and he stared at me, hard. *"But to—"*

Light belatedly dawned. "Oh. Oh . . . Right!" I grabbed my belt and gave the purse a great shake. His eyes widened at the rattle, and his face glowed as he counted his new wealth. A burst of chatter from the Favorite hinted at the deep emotions at play. He absently pinched the creature in rebuke. As for me, I'd realized my error the instant I'd acted. Now Prevotant knew what I had, and all I had was his to take. Disaster lay on one side, humiliation on the other, as I groped for wit. And the bargaining began.

"Well, *yes*," he said at last, "there are certain things I *should* do. Some would say, am *required* to do. But I would need assistance. Ten colleagues . . . or more."

I shook the belt again, angry that I had no choice but to plunge on. "But, you . . ." I said, wearily joining his game. *"But you—"*

"—Don't necessarily have to go by the book," he answered. "I've learned to trust my sweet nature in these matters." He eyed the purse, but I kept my hand in place.

"I could do it myself," he said, willing that hand to free the gold. "Except that would require . . ." He looked over the cargo again. "My masters wouldn't permit me to tithe you less than . . . three coppers for every tenth weight?"

I sighed. "Then I must depart at once to my father's house to bring news of his ruin." I patted the purse. "The tithing you ask will take all this—and more."

Prevotant looked pained. His jowls sagged. But I saw the eyes of his Favorite glint, and its tongue flicked at me, tasting for fear. I held my nerve, betraying nothing. The Evocator broke first.

"I have it," he said. "I'll perform a simple purification. But to be safe, it must include the whole warehouse. The tithe for that is set at one copper per hundred weight."

He lifted a hand. "However . . . there's still only my Favorite and myself to perform the enchantment. There's a great deal of work and prep—"

I slipped the purse from my belt and gave it to him. The Favorite hooted greedily as his master swiftly tucked it away.

"I'll have it done in no time," he said, briskly. "No time at all."

I sent a slave to fetch his things from his litter, and in a few moments he'd set up a tripod with a brass bowl of hot coals dangling beneath it, and was tossing pinches of various dusts and molds and powders into the bowl. A ghastly smell arose, but there was no smoke. His Favorite leaped to the floor, jumping about and shrieking protests at what lay ahead. I'm sure it would have fled if not for the long, slim chain Prevotant clutched in his fist.

The Evocator had chosen a narrow aisle between crates of wooden toys to place the tripod. It was to help direct the force of the enchantment, he said. He waddled down the aisle dragging the Favorite behind. It fought all the way, squalling like a child and choking itself on the chain. "Stop," Prevotant hissed. "You'll only make it worse."

He eased himself to one knee and scrawled a circle on the floor, then a square encompassing that. He shortened his grip on the chain and pulled the Favorite to him. Its little teeth snapped frantically at his fingers, but he finally got it by the neck and hurled it into the circle. The creature was still for a few moments, stunned by the fall. Prevotant nodded. "Good. And if you give me any more trouble I'll have you skinned for shoes." The Evocator puffed back to his feet and strode to the tripod. He motioned for me to join him, and I complied.

"I need the presence of an owner," he explained, "or the purity spell will not be lasting."

He dug out another pouch from his kit. "I want to make it good and strong," he said. "I like to see a satisfied client."

There were people scattered about the warehouse, clerks and loaders and prospective customers getting an early look at the goods. "Shall I clear the place?" I asked.

"No need. There's little danger." He dropped a fat fistful of what appeared to be brown shavings into the bowl. There was a wet hiss as they fell on the coals. I looked closer and once again noted there was no smoke.

He began abruptly. "Oh, demons who dwell in darkness," he intoned. "Beware! Be-ware!" There was a hiss as he shook more brown stuff on the coals. And I saw the coals begin to lose their glow, as if the heat were being sucked from them.

"Fire to Cold. Cold to Fire. I summon flames to seek you out. Beware, demons! Be-ware!"

He emptied the rest of the pouch into the bowl. There was a flash, and the pile of coals collapsed in the center, gray and dead. A ghastly howl came from the creature in the chalk prison. The circle was alive with leaping flames. The Favorite gibbered in pain, dancing and jerking about as the fire seared it through. The fire's touch left no mark on its hide, but there was no question it felt the heat. Its howls of anguish were very real. The creature suddenly shrank until it was the size of a pebble, even though its screams resounded as loudly as before. I jumped back as the pebble became dog size, then bulked until the Favorite towered out of the circle that enclosed it, small teeth now big, glistening fangs gnashing in agony. But size was no escape, for the flames leaped even higher, enveloping all but the howl. Prevotant shouted, "Be-gone!"

The Favorite was stricken mute, mouth gaping and ghostly through the flames. Silence settled. But I soon heard a ticking, then another. Then it was as if the roof had opened to let in a storm of insects. Whole clouds fell dead from the rafters and walls: winged things, boring things, crawling things. The thick, dry rain stung my flesh as they fell. I heard another stirring, which became a scurry and a scratch that doubled, then doubled again, and the floor became a sea of fur and scales as rats and lizards fled the warehouse. There were cries of alarm and disgust from the men and women scattered about the place.

"Nothing to fear," the Evocator said in a normal voice. "The spell is perhaps a bit strong, but at least you'll be rid of vermin, as well." Before I could answer, he flung up his hands, shouting, "Finit!" A *woosh*, and the fire vanished. With a start, I saw the coals in the tripod glow into renewed life.

The Evocator hauled on the chain, dragging his Favorite across the chalk boundaries. It was normal size, but still furious from its treatment. "Now, there's a good job done," he said to me, jerking viciously on the chain. "I only need to—" Both of us jumped as the Favorite snarled and shot up to half man size. It jerked on the chain, and Prevotant yelped as the leash slipped from his grasp, cutting soft flesh.

"Here now," he thundered, "what's this all about? Stop it at once." He waddled forward, fist raised. The Favorite snarled again, and the snarl became a snap, snap, snapping of hysterical teeth. It cowered as Prevotant approached, but its size did not diminish and its skin flashed with angry colors. The Evocator gave it a furious kick. The beast shrieked and leaped over its master. The Evocator whirled, cursing and shouting for it to come back. The Favorite closed its ears and bounded across the warehouse like a dog dosed under the tail with pepper oil. A richly dressed woman screamed and leaped back into the company of her slave retainers. Her scream drew attention, and the Favorite veered and shot past her, scattering the woman's slaves and leaving a bloody bite on the woman's arm.

Prevotant's anger turned to panic. "Come back to Daddy," he pleaded in high soprano. "Daddy has some tasty treats . . . Please come back." But the Favorite ravaged on, shredding bundled goods with its teeth, ripping crates open with its claws. My men tried to pin it in a corner, but it drove them back, growing even larger and charging forward. Then it was ravaging through the cargo again. The chaos must have sharpened my wits, for I saw not only that the damage was minimal, but that in that damage was my own escape from the Evocator.

"Ah, ha!" Prevotant shouted, as the Favorite turned and raced back toward us. "Now you'll listen to reason." But it shrank and dodged between us. I saw my chance and quickly tipped the tripod over. The smoking coals tumbled among the crates of wooden toys. Now it was the Evocator's turn for hysteria. He rushed over and began beating at the small flames with the hem of his robe. "Help me," he cried, "or all is lost." He had visions of this warehouse—and then the whole riverfront—going up in smoke. I strode casually up, gentled him aside, and stamped the fire out.

I left him there, mumbling stunned apologies, while I fetched the warehouse overseer, got a net, some long sticks, and a few husky slaves. It wasn't long before we netted the Favorite, who was now tired and frightened, and brought it to its master. Prevotant looked at me with sheep's eyes. I ignored him, gazing coldly about at the ruin.

"Please let me set it right," he said.

I held out my hand. "You can start with my father's gold," I retorted.

This shocked him. "So much?" It was barely a whisper. But he gave me back the pouch just the same.

"And, that's just to start with," I continued. "Once I've tallied the score of this day's work . . ." I shook my head. "I doubt you have the means for repayment. I'll advise my father to seek recompense from the Council." I only meant to put the fear of the gods in him. I really didn't expect to collect more. I figured the debt my father's bookkeepers would conjure up would keep him humble for years to come. I was about to go into my own dance of "Buts" and "On the other hands," when he raised a finger for silence. He looked about to see if anyone was watching.

"Perhaps I have something here that will soothe the young gentleman," he said, all oiled charm. He dipped into his robes and plucked something out. He gave me a leer. "You will see it's very special," he said.

He handed me a card. It was white and bordered in rich red. In the center was the seal of the hetaerae guild: the blatantly naked form of Butala, the harvest goddess, with exaggerated breasts and pudenda. Beneath it, in gold leaf: *Melina will dance tonight for her special friends and benefactors.*

I knew who she was, as did every other man in Orissa. Melina was one of perhaps no more than a dozen beautiful women who were at the very top of the pleasure trade. They were all well-spoken and educated in the refinements of civilization. Great men, rich men, handsome men, heroes, wooed them as much for the pleasure of their company as for the pleasures of their flesh. And in that final hot, rutting goddess of a skill they had no equal. A man would do much for the love of Melina. Especially a very young man with little to offer but his youth.

I gaped. "How did *you* come by this?" It was not possible that a man like Prevotant would be asked to join such exalted company, even if he were an Evocator.

Prevotant dismissed my implied insult with another leer. "Do you really care?"

I looked at the card again. Butala was no longer alone. Now she reigned over an elaborate orgy. As I stared the naked figures began to move, coupling and uncoupling in more ways that I had ever imagined.

"I was going to sell it," the Evocator whispered in my ear. "It would bring a fancy price, no doubt."

I looked at her name again, heat rising, the letters growing larger until they filled my vision. "Melina," came the harsh whisper of the Evocator. "For you?"

I took the card, forcing a casual air. "Oh, I suppose it might be of interest." I put it in my jerkin.

"We have agreement, then?" Prevotant asked.

I hesitated but felt the card burn at my breast. Already I was in her spell. I had to see this woman for myself. I nodded. Prevotant chose to take the nod as a formal seal, shook my hand, and with much babbling, fled the warehouse with his little fiend chattering on his shoulder. But his leer stayed in my mind after he left, and I felt a little silly for accepting the card. Instead of taking the recovered gold and going straight home to triumph, I went to a tavern and drank and gamed with my friends until it grew late. Brandy fumes mixed with youth to blow my first hesitations away. Why should I let river slime like Prevotant affect me one way or another? Besides, wasn't he an Evocator? And weren't the Evocators the bane of the Antero family? Why, if I went, I'd be snapping my fingers under all their noses in the name of my family. Wouldn't I?

I slipped away from my companions and went out into the night to hire a litter. The slaves carried me away through narrow streets. When they finally set me down, the moon was at her full height. The building the invitation drew me to had nothing to distinguish itself except general shabbiness. In fact, the whole street was a neighborhood of tenements, shops, and taverns for the lowest of the free classes. Lizards and pigs fought in mounded rubbish over scraps of offal. I entered the tenement, doubt of a different kind nagging. Inside, the dark was suffocating. I pulled fire beads from my pocket and whispered an enchantment; they glowed into dim life. The interior was more forbidding with this small bit of light. I could see dark forms hunched here and there, and smaller creatures scuttled from my path. But I plunged on, climbing rickety stairs, stepping with care over broken steps and snoring bodies.

The brandy fumes curling in my brain began to dissipate in this squalor. I eased my rapier in its sheath. This was a place of thieves and witches, and I wondered again at my judgment. Then I heard faint sounds of music wafting down the stairs, and laughter. On the last landing was an enormous door. Floral incense floated through, pushing aside the tenement's miasma of poverty and too many failed spells. I pulled the chain. Bells chimed. Then footsteps, and the door swung open, creaking on its hinges. Light spilled onto the landing, and I flung up a hand to shield my eyes.

"How may I assist you, gentle sir?" came a deep voice. My stylish costume was a badge of class and wealth.

"I have . . . an invitation," I said, rubbing my eyes to hasten vision. "I have it here . . . someplace." I was nervous as I groped for the card in my jerkin.

My eyes suddenly adjusted. My heart lumped into my throat when I saw the enormous black spider perched across my greeter's face. It had an obscene, bulbous body, with jagged bands for legs and huge red eyes that stared back at me. The spider spoke. "Welcome, gentle sir."

I buried panic. The spider was an elaborate tattoo, a totem. My greeter was a tall, skeletal man, with a long, narrow face and pale skin that rarely saw sunlight. He wore rich, brocaded clothing with the red waist sash of a Procurer—a manager licensed by the hetaerae guild.

"The hour is late," the man said. "But you are most fortunate. Melina has yet to dance." He motioned. "This way, if you please." I entered a broad, well-lighted foyer, carpeted with thick, colorful rugs from the western lands. The music and laughter were louder. The man looked over his shoulder. "My name is Leego, young sir. If there is any way I can assist you this evening, you have only to mention my name to a slave."

I found voice. "That is most kind of you, Leego," I said. "May Butala always smile upon you."

Leego nodded, then flung wide two large doors. "Greetings to our new guest," he bellowed. Feminine shrieks of pleasure and laughter met his announcement. I was surrounded by a dozen of the most beauteous creatures I had ever seen, all quite naked. Now, I was not an inexperienced youth. I'd played tickle and slap-a-belly with many a pert, young household servant and tumbled in the hay with female cousins at my father's farms. In recent years, I'd disported myself with enough tavern wenches and half-coin hetaerae to worry my father that I was poised for self ruin. But I had never, ever been confronted with so much lusciously available flesh. Each women seemed lovelier than the next. One was tall and shorn of all hair. She had legs and arms long enough to wrap around any man's girth. Another had flowing blond hair and was small enough to twirl into any imagined position. Some were lush, others slender. And they all giggled and pressed themselves against me, burying me in jiggling flesh and tugging me deeper into the room.

Someone asked my name. "Amalric," I croaked. "Of the Antero family." I heard a buzzing as my name was whispered around the room, and then I found myself sprawled among thick, perfumed pillows, a goblet in my hand filled with heady spirits and a naked woman to tempt me with candied delicacies from a silver tray. Fearing any moment someone would shout fraud and drive me out of this paradise, I peered about, trying to behave as if this experience was trifling.

No one was paying me the slightest attention. There were about twenty other men in attendance. Rich men, important men, older men, laughing and talking amongst themselves. Like me, they were lying on thick, richly brocaded pillows and tended by Melina's naked servants. The room was large, with vaulted ceilings, and was pleasingly lighted. Soft music stirred the silken curtains that covered an arched entryway to one side. Beside the entryway was a large, golden statue of Butala. Her form was more slender than the traditional image, more inviting of caresses. Rugs from the western lands covered the floor. I had never seen weavers' art like these. Erotic figures curled and blended together. The walls were ablaze with murals depicting wild orgies in every imaginable setting, from forest glens to the pleasure rooms of the gods and goddesses. A heady incense burned in a copper brazier. It produced the thick red smoke wealthy hetaerae used to inflame a man's imagination. For me it was entirely unnecessary. My imagination was already as white hot as a swordsmith's furnace. The woman into whose charge I had been given lifted a slice of honeyed peach to my lips. I obediently opened my mouth.

Then I saw Melina—and my mouth snapped shut. I have already described her great beauty, her charm, her intelligence, and her skills. But those are poor, weak words that cannot begin to illuminate the sensuous creature I saw that first time. She was lounging across a low, gilded couch on the far side of the room. The couch was raised on a rug-covered pallet. Unlike her slave girls, she was fully clothed—maddeningly so. She wore translucent pantaloons the color of hearth coals and a sheer blouse of the same shade, with a form-fitting, equally transparent jerkin over it.

The buttons were of rare, worked stones. Her feet were bare and quite small, with red painted nails and gold anklets. Her hands were slender, with long, delicate fingers tipped in red. Each finger bore a glittering ring. Expensive bracelets jangled at her wrists. Long black hair tumbled to the curve of her waist. She toyed with it as she listened to a plump man sitting on the floor next to the couch. He was middle-aged and dressed like a wealthy merchant. A half-dozen other men were also favored enough to sit close to Melina.

I hated every man in that room. I could see that each only pretended interest in his companion's conversation. The laughter was false, the talk chattering bravado. In reality all they could think of was Melina. Their eyes kept flickering toward her, greedy, devouring. The naked flesh of those lovely slaves was nothing to them. Just as it had become nothing to me. I had eyes only for the flash of those gold limbs beneath the sheer material of Melina's costume, the red-tipped breasts and the red glint of henna between those silken thighs. The nakedness of her women intensified my desire to glimpse more—much more—of Melina.

Then my heart stopped. The hatred was forgotten. Melina idly lifted her eyes. They met mine. I felt as if I had been struck by a heavy, padded club. I had never in my life seen such dark mystery. Those eyes were slightly bored at first; then I saw—or prayed I saw—a spark of interest. Full, hennaed lips parted. A pink tongue flicked across them. She looked me up and down. Leego came forward to refill her goblet, and I saw her whisper and point. She was pointing at me!

I thought my heart would burst at such good fortune. Then I began to worry. Had I somehow become ugly? Had I been cursed with warty features by some witch hiding on the awful staircase? Had a bat shit in my hair? I reflexively touched my head and realized what had caught her interest. It *was* my hair. In those days, before the winter of age, my hair was as bright as an Evocator's torch. I was one of the very few men and women in Orissa with red hair. Until this moment it had mostly served as a source of humor to my friends, as had the pale skin that displayed my every emotion. Leego whispered. My name, I supposed. She laughed. I felt my skin turn the color of my hair. I was mortified, sure that, once again, my hair had transformed me into a jest.

To cover my embarrassment, I turned to the slave girl and accepted the peach slice. My mouth was so dry I could hardly chew, much less swallow. Then the music stopped, as did the chattering voices of the men. I heard the sweet sound of strings being plucked. I turned back to see that Melina had raised herself into a sitting position. In her soft lap was a lute. Her lovely fingers touched strings, and the most melodious sound emerged. But it was nothing compared to her rich voice when she lifted it in song.

Melina sang a tale of long ago. It was the story of a young courtesan, sold into the guild by her impoverished family. The girl fell in love with a handsome captain, off to the wars. He promised he would make her his wife when he returned. But he died in battle. The young hetaera grew in beauty and her skills were acclaimed. Many men came to her doorstep with rich gifts and richer promises. She gave herself to them, as was her duty, and accepted their gifts. But there was not one she could ever love. For there was that secret place only the handsome captain had ever touched, a place where no other man would ever be permitted to venture.

When the song was done I could barely hear the applause of the others. I felt tears scalding my cheeks. I ached for Melina and the torment she must be suffering. For I immediately made her the heroine of that song. And I burned with the need to comfort her and take the place of that handsome captain. As did every other man in the room.

Melina, as I have said, was wonderfully skilled.

Her charming smile of thanks singled each of us out. She leaned forward as if to speak, and the room was silent. Instead, a graceful arm stretched out. A perfect finger pointed to Butala. An old woman, draped in a rich red robe, emerged from the curtained entryway beside the statue. She wore a golden, tasseled sash about her waist. She was one of the hetaerae guild's Evocators.

"Greetings, my lords," she said in a voice oddly youthful for such withered cheeks. "All praise Butala."

"All praise Butala," we responded in the traditional return chant. "May our loins be strong, and the wombs of our women fertile and deep."

I glanced over my shoulder and saw with great disappointment that Melina was gone. The Evocator's words brought me back. "You gentlemen will be pleased to know I have just cast the bones, and the omens are favorable: tonight will be a most special evening. Butala is pleased with the worthiness and piety of the gathering. She has signaled to me she will permit Melina to reveal a sacred dance few have been fortunate enough to witness."

"All praise Butala," we all chanted. The voices of the other men were as thick as mine. The Evocator slapped her hands together. The statue of Butala moved, a graceful swivel of the torso, arms splaying wide, head going back. A rich, colored liquid spurted from the statue's breasts. Two slave women ankled forward, burnished hips swaying. They caught the liquid in a large golden bowl. In a few moments it was brimming, and the twin fountains stopped. The women passed among us, offering the bowl to each man. When it came to me I obediently bent my head, smelling a thick, pleasing, musky odor. I drank. The liquid went down smooth and sweet, lighting a warm fire in my belly. The warmth spread, and I felt my blood stir and all my senses snap into full, clear life.

Another clap from the Evocator, and a thick cloud of red smoke burst from the incense brazier. It smelled of roses and violets, and my flesh tingled in anticipated pleasure. The curtain of billowing silk parted. We saw nothing in the dark alcove except stringed instruments and pipes abandoned on the floor by the never-seen musicians.

The Evocator clapped again. "Oh, beautiful Butala," she intoned, "grant us music as sweet as your womb." She crooked a finger at the instruments. "Play," she commanded. We sat in gaping wonder as the instruments rose from the floor. Pipes and harps and dulcimers alike swayed gracefully. Two small gilded drums danced on either side. Strings were plucked by invisible fingers. Small, padded hammers coaxed beauteous sounds from the dulcimers. Pipes fluted visions of woodland bowers. Drums *tat-tat-tat*ted the rhythms of love.

Melina came out of the gloom like a ghost from the mountains of the gods. Torches flared up on either side, lighted by invisible hands. Her naked flesh shone pure gold. We saw the startling perfection of her smooth body for so quick a moment one couldn't be sure it wasn't the sacred drink and our imaginations. Suddenly Melina was covered from toe to crown with writhing shapes of many colors. She stood quite still for one, two, then three heartbeats. We saw images of men and women coupling, other figures in playful chase, women embracing other women as lovers, handsome boys doing the same, and wonderfully twisted combinations of both sexes. Melina turned in a slow pirouette, body alive with other scenes of living erotica.

The music shifted and Melina began to dance. First a slow, swaying shuffle, hips rotating, arms weaving, long, firm legs moving gracefully. Melina's dance quickened, as did the music and spirit forms at play on her body. She kicked and twirled and shook her breasts and hips until I thought I would go mad with lust. I felt the heat rise in the other men. The room became stifling with our must. When we could bear no more, Melina stopped. She held a pose to make a sculptor weep. The images were gone, and we could see her in all her glory. My eyes fed on her like a starving man, on her lips, breasts, and smooth, shaved vulva outlined in henna. Then the alcove went black. We turned to look at one another, mouths dry, eyes aching in their sockets . . . our balls as hard as stones.

"Well, gentlemen," said that wondrous voice, "did I please you?" Our heads swiveled. There, lounging on the couch, was Melina, dressed in pantaloons and jerkin as before. Only a slight sheen coating her body hinted that she had danced that incredible dance.

"All praise Butala," we shouted. The applause was deafening. Men tumbled forward to praise her art. There was a loud and constant jangling of coins and the clink of rare gems as gift after gift was flung at her feet. Leego floated among the men, smiling, patting them on the back, and coaxing even more gifts. I couldn't help myself. I jumped to my feet, hands fumbling for the only gift I had: my father's fat purse of gold. I muscled through the crowd around her, elbowing my competitors aside as if my strength were twice that of a normal man. She lifted her eyes to meet mine and I stood before her. I saw a glint of pleasure. Sensuous lips curled in smile. I dropped the purse on top of the other gifts. The sound of its fall was pleasingly heavy.

"Ah . . . it is my handsome young man with the fiery hair," she said. Her voice was warm and welcoming. But her hot perfume rose to smite me dumb. All I could do was nod.

"Amalric Antero, it is not?" There was no music as lovely as my name upon those lips.

I bowed. "At your service, my lady," I said.

She laughed at my stiff formality. But it was not meant to be unpleasant. Still, I flushed. Melina's white, perfect teeth gleamed. "Oh, do please call me Melina. All my gentlemen friends do. My *very* close friends, that is." Her fingers touched my hand and I trembled at that touch. "And I can see as well as any diviner, young Amalric, you and I are destined to be . . . close friends."

I'm not sure what I stuttered. But she giggled as if I were the greatest wit of all Orissa. "Tell me," she said, "is your hair real? Or is it some clever cosmetic the young bravos of Orissa now affect?"

"It's quite real, I assure you, my—uh . . . Melina. Upon my honor."

"Perhaps I shouldn't take your word for it," she teased. "After

all, there are more interesting ways of proving it, young Amalric."
The glint in her eyes told me it was not my sprinkle of chest hair
she hinted at. "I could also learn if it is true what knowledgeable
women say about redheaded men and their ardor."

If I was dumb before, now my tongue had been ripped out. I
wanted to shout to the gods to let me prove it now. Now! I would
show her true ardor. Not the fraudulent love these—these beasts
offered. Before I could recover, Leego pressed forward. With him
was a middle-aged man of distinguished bearing. I recognized him
as one of my father's wealthiest competitors.

"If you please, my dear Melina," Leego said, "I want to introduce a very special admirer of yours."

The man stepped forward, his eyes eager. Before I could hear
the exchange I started to rush away. I knew this was the man chosen to enjoy Melina's favors that night. The gift he had presented
would beggar mine and those from most of the other men in the
room. If I don't leave now, I thought, I'll kill him where he
stands.

Melina's voice stopped me. "One moment, Amalric."

I turned, afraid to lift my eyes, because I knew they would betray my feelings. But I couldn't help it. I had to see her once
more. For the first time I noticed the color of her eyes. They were
as green as stones from the hot forests of the north.

"What is it, Melina?" I husked.

"You will come again, won't you? Please promise me you
shall."

My answer was hot, unguarded. "I would lay my life down as
a gift, fair Melina," I said, "to win another invitation from you."

She did not answer. If she had I'm sure I would have slit my
throat for being such a fool. Instead she kissed one of her perfect
fingers and laid it against my hand. "I'll be waiting, Amalric," she
whispered. "My handsome, redheaded man."

I don't remember how I got home. But I felt so godlike after
those words, I'm certain I must have discovered the power to lev-
itate.

AFTER THAT NIGHT I went to see Melina at every opportunity.
Which meant anytime I had weaseled enough coin to buy a suitable gift. Leego made it very clear I would be unwelcome without
one. I blamed him for this, not my fair Melina. I was certain she
wanted me for myself, not for something so crassly material as
gold. What could he know of the higher feelings that beat in both
our breasts? He was a Procurer, after all, interested only in the

profits the hetaerae guild said was his right. And I knew he must be the most greedy individual of his money-grubbing trade.

I tried desperately to ignore Melina's wild swings of mood. One moment only *I* seemed to matter. The next I would be dust at her feet. I wallowed in her humiliations, the rich gifts she scorned, the cold looks, her ostentatious displays of affection to other men. I put my gifts at her feet with the others. Bore her scorn. Bore her jokes at my expense. Bore Leego's increasingly mocking manner.

I spent all I had. Then I sold my possessions. I lied to my father and begged sum after sum. When he refused me, I borrowed from my friends so heavily they began to avoid my company. For soon as I would despair, Melina would become warm, casting long haunting looks, stroking me and petting me until I was on fire with desire. She would praise me loudly to the other men, make a trinket I had delivered into a treasure trove, or complain she was weary and ached from her work—I dared not imagine *how* she came by those aches and pains—and beg me to massage her. Many a time I was her slave and worked her limbs into suppleness. She would groan under my hands as if lit by passion. She would turn slightly and allow my hands to brush against her secret places. Then she would send me away with promises burning in her eyes. So I always returned, richly laden and eager. This time, I would think, she'll fall into my arms and beg me to carry her away like that brave captain in the song. That moment never came. Because as sure as the sun king lashes his chariot into motion each dawn, the next greeting would be as cold as a slave seller's heart.

This went on for month after humiliating month. I became pale and thin in the fevered pursuit. When I slept, the sleep was so troubled that I awakened as exhausted as before. It was in that time that I began to have a strange dream. A nightmare that came with increasing frequency as the days of my obsession passed. Even now as I recall it to write these lines in this journal, the dream leaps to life, leaving me as shaken as it did so long ago.

But I swore I'd tell this tale. And tell it all, despite any pain I might relive . . .

I was not fettered, but rose when he beckoned as if I wore manacles and he was the keeper at the end of the chain. I stepped awkwardly across the boat's thwarts and then lunged up onto the slime-thick dock carved from living stone. My feet dragged, as my mind screamed: Strike out. You cannot go up those stairs. You must not.

The water beside the boat was thick, heaving, a dark, viscous substance. I could hear the hiss of the great river beyond as it rushed through the black gorge the boatman had brought us through. I could also hear baying. It came from above, from the ruined, cursed city on the gorge's plateau. It was not the howling of jackals, or even direwolves. Far above, far outside this river-dug cavern, in the city, in the shattered amphitheater, in the gods-hammered stones, the creatures sat in patient rings. Up there in the moonless night, those creatures that bayed like hounds bore no semblance to anything seen on this earth. The thought came that they might have been men, once. Men who had struck a dark bargain.

The boatman took one of the torches that guttered on either side of the arched stairway and beckoned once again. In the flare of the burning pitch I saw his arm clearly, muscles flexing, jumping: an arm that was twisted like an olive tree that had fought its way up to sunlight through arid stone. But there was no sunlight in his world. I knew his body's contortions had come from the rack, from the fire-hot rod. He turned, satisfied that I was following, and went up the worn stone steps, steps that many had stumbled up, crying aloud in their pain. But no one had ever come down again. No one but the masters. Or this man or his comrades.

I knew this. I knew not how.

He wore only black breeches. On his back I could see the marks of the lash, old and new. I knew he prided himself on those lash scars. On my own back wounds throbbed and I felt the searing, shame, struggle and moment of pride not yet yielding.

I, too, had been tortured.

Somewhere above, someone was waiting. A great drum began, its boom drowning the dark howls from the ruins on the midnight plateau above.

The steps ended.

We entered in a great chamber, stone arches lifting into blackness. A king's welcoming chamber. It was empty, except for the man and myself. He beckoned once more. I heard the shatter of a cymbal, perhaps only in my mind, as I stared full into his face. It was riven by a thousand sins, a thousand eagerly sought pains. His nose had been broken, then broken again before it had healed. His lips had been shaved away, and his ears were cropped. His face was sliced by a smile, crooked, black teeth leering. One eye gleamed black. The other was a gaping socket. But something moved within that socket. A tiny red, writhing fire. A fire that saw more than the solitary eye that peered at me.

"Yes, Amalric, my prey, my enemy, my friend, my reward, his intended partner and ambition," said his voice. "We are almost there. This is what you wanted. This is your weird. This is what your brother could not embrace. Come ... Come ... It has been too long and He is waiting."

He laughed, and the laugh was joined by a great boom from the darkness, from beyond. That roar came from someone who could find no pleasure except in lashing pain. It rose, echoing the now mad baying from the nightmares in the damned city beyond, then it buried their joy and became its own cacophony.

I smiled and walked forward, my arms open, welcoming the dark comradeship to come.

I awoke, trembling and perspiring, more exhausted than when I had come to my bed. At first I feared the dream might be an omen or a curse in repayment for my obsession with Melina. But to accept this, I would have needed to confront myself and see the folly of my ways. So each time it returned I pushed the dream from my mind and fell to scheming once again for money or presents for Melina.

Finally, the day of reckoning came. Spurned by my friends, mocked by my enemies, and in danger of being disowned by my father, I sat in my room reviewing the meager possessions yet unsold. I was to see Melina that night. One of her slaves had brought the invitation to my house. She had written at the bottom of the card in her own, dear hand: *Come early, my love. So we might steal a few precious moments alone.* Hope burned bright in my breast and my loins, then dimmed as I realized I had nothing of value to sell for her giftprice. I thought of rushing to the river and throwing myself to the demon of the currents.

I seriously considered creeping into my father's strong room and stealing the gold that would be required. Then I was appalled for even thinking such a thing. To steal from my father? What devil has possessed you, Amalric? How could you have allowed events to come to such a pass? This must stop. This must end. Besides, what if she spurns me once more, after I steal from the man who gave me life and was so generous and understanding of such a useless son? It would be impossible to bear.

But I *must* have her, I thought. I *must* make her mine. Yes ... but, how? An evil plan rose. It disgusted me to even think it and I hurled it away and flung myself onto the bed where I buried my head from the betraying light that streamed in from the balcony.

A bird cried outside, and I swore it called, "Melina . . . Melina . . . Melina." The evil idea crept in again. If I could borrow enough money, I knew of dark places in Orissa where it was reputed that certain potions and spells could be purchased, with no questions asked and without the chit of permission from an Evocator. I would buy a love spell.

I understood this was not only evil but illegal, as well. I knew very well it was strictly forbidden to give a love potion to a hetaera. The whole courtesans' guild system might collapse, making a mockery of the sanctity of Butala. The penalties prescribed by the Council of Evocators started with dismemberment and grew quickly worse. And you will shame your family, I thought. Think of the terrible shadow your family already suffers under for angering the Evocators once before. Think of the awful disappointment for your father.

I tried. I really did. But all I could think of was Melina's lips and breasts and thighs that had been denied me so long. These hot thoughts were further fueled by the vow I had taken after our first meeting. I had been with no other woman since that time.

Lust won the toss. Risking life and my family's honor, I rushed out to put my plan into action.

CHAPTER TWO
Janos Greycloak

BY DUSK I was pacing back and forth outside Melina's door. I had a bottle of spirits in my pocket, spiked with a black-market love potion; its guaranteed enchantment was fixed in my mind. I was waiting for dark . . . and courage. The moon was a sliver over the tenement when I saw Leego exit the building and stroll off, whistling a merry tune. I knew he'd be ensconced in his favorite tavern for some hours. A few moments later I was up the stairs, pulling on the bell chain, and then a servant was leading me to Melina's bedchamber.

"It is your redheaded slave, my fair Melina," I sang out as I entered, my voice as bold as you please, despite the frantic beating of my heart.

"Oh, my dear, dear Amalric," she said when she spied me. Her face was so dazzling when she greeted me, I thought perhaps I had been a fool to think I needed a potion. "I have been so bored," she said, sprawling across a mighty bed that seemed to have been built to pillow a legion. "I am sick of potbellied old men with skinny legs."

I plumped down. She was dressed only in a rough, carelessly draped half robe. She was direct from her tub and looked like a fresh-scrubbed milkmaid with knowing eyes. As she raised her head to pillow it on an arm, the robe fell open. I saw the flash of a tender breast, pink-tipped nipple, and as she lazily tugged the robe closed, the vee of softness between her thighs, the paradise I so longed for that I was willing to risk all.

"Then let me take you away from all this, Melina my love," I said, in false lightness.

"You would make me your wife?" she said. Her voice was mocking. But only a little.

Now I was all seriousness. "I would pledge anything to make it so," I said fervently.

"I don't think you'd welcome a hetaera as the mother of your children," she laughed.

"Then you don't know me, Melina," I answered. "For I love you more than any man has a right to love. I fear the gods will grow jealous if they realize just how great my feelings are for you."

Melina sighed. "You are very sweet and very kind," she said. "But you will come to your senses some day, and find some deserving woman of your own class."

"Never," I said, as hotly earnest as only the very young can be.

"Besides," Melina said, "you are too young to afford me. Now, don't pout. Because you know what I am saying is true." She patted my hand. "Please don't spoil these few hours we have together. My back is so tired and I need those strong young hands of yours to soothe it." Melina gave me a naughty wink. "And . . . afterward . . . if there's time . . . Who knows? Possibly this will be the night I learn if you are *truly* a redheaded man."

My heart sank. Despite the tease, actually *because* of the tease, I understood for the first time that night would never come. I know now that I did intrigue, possibly even arouse her. Curiosity is a powerful aphrodisiac, and Melina was honestly wondering about the exotic color of my hair. I know it also excited her to have such a young man a willing slave to her slightest whim, sexual or otherwise. But it would never go beyond that. She would take me for everything I owned, including my honor. Then she'd cast me aside.

I forced cheer. "First, I have a small gift for you," I said.

Melina squealed. "Oh, how lovely. I do hope it's unusual. Please. Please. Let me see."

I drew the bottle out of my pocket. Her face fell.

"What's that?"

"Oh, this is nothing. Just some old brandy from my father's cellar. I thought we might sample it . . . and then I can show you my gift. It is a very rare thing . . . I promise."

Melina became excited again, acting like a girl. She sat up in the bed, legs so carelessly crossed I almost lost my nerve. I fetched two goblets from the tray and poured. Melina took a goblet from my hand. She sniffed at it, curling those exquisite nostrils. "Mmmm. Delicious," she said. She drank it down in one swallow. Then she lounged back on her pillows, flinging those perfect legs wide, as if by accident. "Now, show me my present," she said.

"Do you want more brandy?" I asked.

"No. That's enough. There's nothing more disgusting than a hetaera who enslaves herself to drink."

"How do you feel?" I asked, anxious.

"I feel fine. Why do you ask?" Her voice was sharp, irritated.

"Oh ... nothing." What in the name of the gods had gone wrong? Had the back-street witch defrauded me? Then I remembered I was supposed to chant the rhyme the witch had given me. But in my anxiety, the words had fled my memory.

"Well? Where is that present you promised?" Melina pressed.

My memory returned. "My heart is thy heart," I intoned, mimicking the deep drone of an Evocator's voice. "My image fills thine eyes. In darkest night, I am the candle to light thy womb."

Melina frowned. "What prattling is that? Some silly love doggerel from the taverns?"

Before I could stumble a lie for an answer, Melina gasped. Those green eyes were staring at me. Her pupils were wide and possessed. She licked her lips. "Butala, praise thy name," Melina moaned. "Amalric, you are so handsome and young you make my heart break. I'll warrant you can pleasure a woman like a great stallion. Plunging and plunging all the night long."

"Uh ... uh ... uh," was my eloquent response.

"Oh, by the gods ... take me now! Take me!" She flung off the robe and hurled herself into my arms, ripping at my clothes with sharp-nailed fingers. "I'll do anything to please you," she groaned. "Take me. Any way you want it. My lover. My handsome, redheaded Amalric man."

Passion gripped me as if I had swallowed the potion, as well. I ripped away my clothing and flung it carelessly to the floor. A small voice tried to shame me, but a cock has no honor, so I swatted the voice away like a river gnat. Melina sprawled back, lust flush coursing up her chest and reddening her slender throat, legs splayed wantonly, the shaved slit of pleasure begging my entrance.

"Oh, quickly ... quickly, please," she groaned, grinding her hips as if she had gone mad under the moon.

I fell on her like a victorious soldier, grasping the soft white mound of her bottom, then thrust into the hot, silky place I had dreamed of for so long. Imagining myself that stallion she'd spoken of, I reared back to thrust again. A bellow of pure, hot rage rang from behind me. "Get off her, you son of a lizard bitch!"

Hands encircled my throat, and with a heave, I was torn from the gates of paradise and flung across the room. Even in the throes of interrupted passion, my gymnast training took over in midflight. I twisted as I hit the floor and sprang to my feet. I stood, chest heaving, in shameful nakedness, red pubic hair finally answering Melina's question, but hardly in the manner I had dreamed.

"Don't hurt him, Leego," Melina begged. The Procurer stood there, dirk drawn, pale lips a rictus through the spider mask.

"I love him so," Melina continued. "Don't let him leave. I must be with him. Always with him."

Leego's answer was a shout. I heard many footsteps running for the room. He came toward me. I didn't fear him. I was more than enough man to make him eat that dirk. But I was in the wrong, an enemy trespassing in another man's bedchamber with a woman I had no right to. There is only one thing for any man to do, when he finds himself in this situation. In one quick motion, I scooped my clothes and sheathed rapier from the floor, then ran for the window.

I plunged through head first, Leego's voice ringing. "You'll pay for this, Amalric Antero. You'll pay."

Fear jogged memory as I sailed through that window. It was at least sixty feet to the hard, crippling ground. Just in time I snagged out with a hand and caught a sewer pipe. Momentum carried me in an arc, and I slammed against the tenement wall. In some insane instinct of modesty, I kept my grip on my clothes. For a heart-thumping instant, I struggled to hang by the pipe with only one hand. I steadied myself, slung my clothes and rapier over a naked shoulder, got a good grip on the pipe, and slid for the ground. I remembered to kick away at the last minute, and I landed a few slimed inches away from the soil pit the sewer pipe emptied into. Inside the tenement I heard thundering boot heels coming down the stairs. A big lizard lunged out of the darkness. I kicked it, and it hissed, perhaps mistaking my naked form for that of an odd pig on two feet. I sprinted away into the night. Before long the sound of the voices and pursuing footsteps faded away.

I PADDED INTO the tavern in bare feet, belting my rapier about my filth spattered finery. My mind was swirling with guilt and confusion. I badly needed to get my bearings before I slunk home like the cur I had proven myself to be. I barely noticed the few dangerous-looking men whose eyes glittered when they spied me. I also saw a few soldiers in crisp uniforms, lolling in their seats. The tavernkeep, a small, ratlike man, eyed me suspiciously. "Wine, my good man," I croaked. "No water. Better still, forget the wine. Make it brandy."

"Get a coin up first, young sir," the tavernkeep snarled. "I'll not be cheated by one of your kind again."

Impatiently I reached into my pocket, then realized my purse was gone. The tavernkeep nodded, knowing. His hand reached for a club beneath the counter. I tore a button off my jerkin. It was of fine, worked bone from a distant port and valuable enough to buy a good share of the tavern. "Take it out of this," I said.

I sensed a presence bulking near. I turned to see one of the soldiers, a sergeant, I noted from his rank badge. He was an older man, with an honest face. He seemed worried. "Would you like to come and drink with us, gentle sir?" he asked. "A bit of company is a good thing in a place like this." He nodded at the toughs scattered about the room.

"I thank you kindly," I answered, "but I really prefer to be alone. I have . . . difficulties to consider."

He looked at my ruined clothes, guessing at the nature of my difficulties. "I hope no one was injured," he said.

"Only my pride, sergeant," I assured him. I motioned to the tavernkeep. "Buy these worthy men a drink as well," I said. "Take it out of what I gave you." I felt the rough boards beneath my bare feet. "And while you are at it," I continued, "I'd be pleased to buy some shoes."

The tavernkeep didn't like this. He was hoping to keep as much of the button's value as possible. "Get him some boots," the sergeant snapped. "And if I learn you've troubled this young gentleman, I'll have your license." The tavernkeep cursed, but went to fetch the boots.

"Are you certain, gentle sir," the sergeant said, "that you will not pleasure us with your company?"

"Again, I thank you," I answered. "But, no. Brandy and my thoughts are the medicine I require."

The sergeant rejoined his companions. I clasped the brandy goblet the tavern keeper had fetched and drank it down. I motioned for more and tied on the leather scraps Rat Face brought me. Then, as forlorn as any twenty-year-old can be, I returned to my drink, staring into the depths of the chipped goblet, contemplating my sins. They were legion, beginning with the love potion itself. I had cheated Melina into behaving in a manner that she had clearly not intended. Her naked form, wriggling for the mounting, rose in my mind. The vision was not erotic, but shameful. The moment came that hopefully visits at least once in every human life. My perspective spun. I had been taken. Skinned, and gutted, the object of a fraud like those perpetrated by the mean-eyed shills in the market place. I do not use the word *victim*, because like the targets of the bazaar swindlers, it was my own greed that delivered me up. I, Amalric Emilie Antero, had aided and abetted Melina and Leego with complete enthusiasm. No one had cast a spell on me like the potion I had fed Melina. I had lusted for her and had been willing to pay any price—the respect of my friends, or the love of my family. I had made a roaring fool of myself in the process.

Wind rattled the tavern's shutters, and I felt as if I were in my home, in front of the altar of my long-dead brother. I even felt his ghost enter the dingy shack. Halab had been the family's golden child, and his fate at the hands of the Evocators still cast a long shadow over the Anteros. Although my real memory of him was that of a three-year-old dazzled by a dashing hero adult brother, I thought I could see his face most plain by the tavern door. Halab was smiling. He hoisted a thumb, encouraging me to move on. The vision vanished, but I felt a bit of worthiness return. It was only a small bit, but it was a seed I could nurture. I determined to redeem myself. I would change my ways, starting with making my long-overdue maiden expedition as a merchant. "Finding Your Tradewind," tradition called it. My father had been urging me to take up my duties with increasing impatience. But I had always been a test of that fine, old gentleman.

The door banged open, and three men entered. They were big men, hard men, with a look about them that made the other rogues nervous. One glanced at me, then whispered to his companions. They got drinks and retired to a corner. I returned to my thoughts.

I was the youngest child by far of my father's first and only marriage, with brothers and sisters in their thirties and forties. So I tended to willfulness; spoiled from skin to seed, questioning just to question, my critics said. My bodyslave, Eanes, said I was plain redheaded stubborn, with a temper to match my pate.

I was a bright but lazy student. It didn't help that the tutor who survived my mischiefs the longest was a didact, living on a false reputation. He was not only boring, but frequently completely and insistently wrong. To fight boredom, I challenged him every chance I got. In our studies of anatomy, for instance, he claimed a man's body infinitely superior to a woman's. I hooted at his premise. My sister, Rali, was the physical equal of most of the men of Orissa. "But that is different, young master," he said.

"Why is it different?" I jeered. "Rali is a woman. A beautiful woman, many say. She is also a great warrior, who could take your head off with a swipe of her sword." I slashed the air with an imaginary blade in illustration.

"One exception does not refute a fact, young master," my tutor insisted. He was getting angry, rising to my goad.

"My sister is not one exception," I prodded. "She's only one of her regiment of woman. Heroines for all Orissa. Explain that."

The tutor sputtered, then pounded on the anatomy tome. "Facts are still facts," he shouted. "It is well known women's bodies are inferior. Their teeth are proof enough to start with."

"What's wrong with their teeth?"

"Women have fewer teeth than men." He opened the book to show me the page where it said so. "You see . . . Men have thirty-two teeth; women never more than twenty-eight."

I saw a young housemaid going past. "We'll see about that," I said, rushing to catch her. I coaxed her into the room with soft words and promises of a few coins for her trouble, and then got her to open her mouth. I counted, and the number came to thirty-two. The same as a man's. My tutor stormed out, refusing to admit he'd been wrong. I spent the remainder of the day with my friends at the gymnasium, a place I fled to frequently as the years passed and I became more skilled in irritating my teacher and his successors.

As I sat staring into my brandy, it occurred to me my father had given me an education despite myself. He could have punished me when the teacher complained. Instead he had always encouraged me to question conventional wisdom, to find the truth of a thing by personal observation. It was a gift, the gift of allowing me my own thoughts and opinions. Tears of shame stung my eyes. I sniffled them back and sipped at my brandy. It was time, I thought, to put away my childish ways and make my father proud. He needed me to take up the burdens of a merchant's existence. Every time he was forced to travel, he returned woefully weary from his efforts. It took him longer to recover with each passing year. My older brothers were no help. They were stiff, formal men, better at managing the farms or the account books. They also possessed few traits necessary for a merchant. They disliked strange people and things, and distrusted any whiff of risk-taking.

They were my opposites, for I always took delight in the mysterious flavor of Orissa's docks, with all the strange tongues and costumes swirling about the unloading ships. Geography was also one of the few areas of study that held my interest. Old charts and tales of daring Findings thrilled me until I reached an age when to admit such a thing would be considered childish by my peers. I even accepted my tutor's view of the world we lived in, although it was conventional, and I have already illustrated my healthy distrust of the conventional. The earth was shaped like a great black egg, he said. The sun, nurturing light and fire, was set in motion by the gods for our benefit. Only the known lands and the sea separating them were gifted with this light. All else was a vast darkness ruled by jealous sorcerers who plotted to bring us under their sway and finally extinguish the sun, plunging us into the cold gloom, leaving us at the mercy of alien gods. My teacher said that once all had been light, that our ancestors possessed great knowledge of all enchantments. But they grew slothful and decadent, he said, losing respect for tradition of family, city, and their Evocators. When the wizards of darkness threatened, they were unprepared. But our gods took pity and kept this small beacon of hope safe from total barbarity. Over time, we regained some of the knowledge. And our ships took sail again, pushing back the darkness with every successful Finding. But there was a limit to our future, he taught. And that limit had nearly been reached.

There was one story—a fable, really—that particularly interested me. It was the legend of the Far Kingdoms. A place, the tale went, where descendants of our Old Ones lived on, a place where the sun shone amid a black wilderness ruled by sorcerer enemies. The princes and Evocators of the Far Kingdoms were said to be kind and wise beyond all imagination. It was a place where wine and song were always sweet. Every purse was fat with gold, and every heart at ease. If only we could join with them, the tale continued, all our enemies would be swept away and the world would once again bask in eternal light. It was a pretty tale that had stirred me greatly once upon a time. But I had put it away with my child's toys once I was old enough to strap on a rapier and convince myself I was a grown man.

I gave a harsh laugh as I considered the last, and once again swore an oath to change my ways. I drained my brandy to seal the bargain. I turned to order one more for a nightcap and noted with a small stir of alarm that the atmosphere had changed. The soldiers were gone, as were the original patrons. Only the hard men who'd entered after me remained. They were eyeing me openly, sniggering amongst themselves, and jabbing one another with their elbows. I saw that the tavernkeep had disappeared, as well. I felt a prickling. Something was about to happen—especially if I remained and dared the fates. I rose from my seat, nonchalant, and made my way to the door, pretending no interest in the three men. If they followed, I thought, at least outside there would be room to fight.

It is not an old man's boast that I was a fine swordsman then. Although I was not the best in Orissa, I was good enough to give the best pause. I had fought two duels, drawing first blood each time. I was also fleet of foot from all those years of escaping my teachers to the athletic fields. If necessary, I would show my heels and speed away like a wind demon.

As I exited, I heard chairs scrape as the men got up to follow. Before I could quicken my pace, two dark figures bulked out the night. Scrabbling for my rapier, I saw the spider totem on one of the men's faces. Leego! Behind me, the three brigands from the tavern closed the trap. But my blade was coming clear, and I would show them all a thing or two about respect. Then I was a fool once more as my rapier's ornate guard caught on a button. My weapon clattered to the ground, and I stood there grinning like a monkey, my fighting arm outstretched, empty fist curling, uncurling. An arm had me in a throttlehold, and I kicked back and heard a yelp of pain. But there was no time to gloat, because strong hands grabbed and held me as Leego rushed forward and slammed a fist into my belly. My gymnast's stomach absorbed the blow, and I could tell from Leego's sudden grunt that he'd hurt himself.

I took no satisfaction from his pain, because a moment later Leego was pressing his knife against my throat.

"Don't be a fool, Leego," I said, my temper easily winning the struggle with common sense over my tongue. "If you murder me this night, you'll be a prime candidate for next year's Kissing of the Stones." I was speaking of the spring planting rite, when the Evocators make sacrifice by crushing a victim between two immense stones. Criminals are favored for this annual gifting of the gods.

Leego laughed, his breath foul in my face. "There is no protection for you in this place, young sir," he rasped. "No witnesses to whatever I choose to do with your worthless life." He pressed harder with his blade. I felt a sting, then wetness as blood flowed.

"On the other hand," he continued, "your reputation is protection enough for *me*. Everyone knows you frequent the dark side of town. They know your wild habits. Your extravagant spending and dishonorable debts. If I slit your throat, people will believe footpads responsible. Or a wronged moneylender. No, my friend, your class is no shield to you here. And you will be no man's better with your guts greeting the morning sun."

He laughed again and slapped my face. Once, twice, then once more. Hard, stinging blows that did me no real bother—except he was building his rage for what was to come next. Behind him, in the mouth of a dark alley, I saw a large, dark figure making water on the side of a building. One of Leego's thugs, I thought, pausing to empty his bladder before he joined the fun. "The only reason I haven't killed you yet, young sir," Leego continued, "is that I am torn between revenge and profit. What you did to Melina has cost me many a fat purse. I'll have to send her far away now. And spend a fortune curing her of the effects of that potion."

"Piss on your money, Leego," I said. "You have taken more than enough from me these last months. And I've seen nothing in return."

Leego slapped me again. "That's what happens to a boy who comes to play a man's game," he snarled. "You keep thinking you have some choice in this matter," he said. "You don't. The choices are mine. If I decide to favor profit, you shall provide me with all the money I require. What would the Council of Evocators say if I reported this matter? Feeding a love potion to a hetaera is a great crime. I can imagine well how happy it would make the Evocators to have an Antero in their power."

"I have no money, Leego," I said, weary. "You and Melina have taken it all."

"Your father will provide, young sir," Leego laughed. "He wouldn't want his little darling in the hands of the Evocators."

"Then you might as well kill me," I answered. "For I will not ask my father for even a tenth of a coin. And if he tries to give it to me just the same, I shall refuse it."

"Oh, I don't think it would work out quite that way," Leego said. "I know men. Especially rich men. Still . . . profit is not necessarily my motive in this. For I despise you and your kind, Amalric Antero. You and your soft, spoiled ways. Thinking you're better than other men, just because you were born in a fine bed." His blade slashed across my chest. My jerkin and shirt fell away, baring tender flesh. "Killing would be so much more pleasurable," he said, drawing his blade across that flesh. I felt blood streaming down. "A nice, slow death. Then I'll cut off your face and that red hair. Your cock and balls, as well. No one will even know it is you."

My temper got the better of me again. I spat in his face. He reeled back, a great gob of spit hanging on the spider totem. Then he shrieked and leaped forward, his knifed plunging at my breast. Before he could strike, the dark figure by the alley bounded to us and knocked Leego aside with a powerful blow.

"Begone, jackals," the man thundered, and I saw a long sweeping flash of steel as he drew his sword.

One of my captors released his hold, and I bent, dropping to my knees. One man sailed over my head. The other jumped away and grabbed for steel. He slashed at my rescuer, who parried the blade with ease, then struck back to spill the man's guts in the muck. I scrabbled for my rapier in the filth and came up with it just as a man thrust at me. I ducked under his guard and skewered him through the throat. Then I was up on my feet, shoulder to shoulder with my rescuer, as our enemies re-formed and came at us. There was no sound but the clash of steel, harsh breathing, and gasps of effort. Leego leaped up, urging his men on. For a moment, we were almost overwhelmed. Then my new friend drew a long knife and charged, sword and dagger cutting this way and that. Someone got behind him, but I speared that man through the back, and I heard the whistle of lungs emptying. Suddenly the men were running, bowling Leego over in their panic to escape my demon rescuer. I started after them, but my friend stuck out his foot, and I tumbled face forward into the mud.

By the time I rose the man had Leego pinned to the ground with a heavy boot across his throat. I plucked fire beads from my pocket, held them high, and whispered the enchantment that brought them to life.

"Bring them closer, lad," the man said. "I need some light on my work."

I could see him clearly now. He was a soldier, I noted, an officer. He was quite tall, heavily muscled and darkly handsome, with a jagged scar above his beard marring those good looks. His teeth glittered as brightly as his sword.

"Please, sir," Leego begged, "there's only a small misunderstanding. I'm sure I can make it right." He squealed as my friend trod harder against his windpipe.

"What's his name?" the soldier asked.

"Leego," I answered. "He's a Procurer."

The man took this in, then leaned over my nemesis. "Look closely at my face, Leego," he said. "I want you to remember it well." Leego gurgled and nodded. "My name is Janos Greycloak, you whore's son," the man went on. "*Captain* Greycloak, to be more precise. I overheard your conversation with this gentleman, so I am witness to your threats."

"No harm meant," Leego croaked. "It was only business, kind Captain."

"Well, if business includes blackmail," Janos said, "then let me warn you: If you accuse this man, I shall stand with him and humbug your every charge. If murder is your true intent, let me make myself clear. If anything happens to him, I shall find you, Leego, and you will beg for something so merciful as murder."

"I shall not harm him, good sir," Leego shrieked. "I promise by all that is holy."

"Don't blaspheme," Captain Greycloak said. He stepped back as if to let Leego rise. He sheathed his sword. As Leego came to his elbows, that boot crushed down again. The captain pinched Leego's ear between two strong fingers. Leego howled. "To make absolutely sure we have a bargain," the captain said, "I shall take something of yours."

His knife slashed and Leego screamed. Captain Greycloak held Leego's ear in his hand, blood dripping across the spider face. The captain shook it, scattering more blood like rain. "If this young gentleman has trouble with you in the future," he said, "I shall give this stump to an old warty witch I know. She specializes in particularly odious curses. Do you understand my meaning?"

"Yes, my lord," Leego whined.

"Out of our sight, then," the captain said.

Leego fled down the street without looking behind him. When he was gone, the captain looked at the lump of bloody flesh in his hand. He laughed, hurled it away, and wiped his fingers with odd fastidiousness on his breeches. "As if I had coin for witches," he said.

"Captain Greycloak," I said, "I shall always be at your service for this night's work."

"I'm glad to hear that," he said, "for I have suddenly developed a powerful thirst." He clapped me on the shoulder and led me back to the tavern. "You would do me a great honor, gentle sir, if you would address me as a friend. And my friends—an unfortunate few, I fear—call me Janos."

"Then Janos, it is, sir," I said with fervor. "And you must call me Amalric. What's more, if I have any buttons left to trade with the tavern keeper, I will buy a river of brandy to bless this friendship." Light-headed with relief, I trooped into the inn to make the rat-faced tavernkeep a richer man.

Soon, we had finished one goblet of brandy and were well into a second. I had been musing on the fact that I had just sent one man to his death, and most likely the one I'd lung-stabbed would not live out the night, yet I felt neither guilt nor shame, unlike the ballads pretend. Thinking further on the brawl outside, honesty shamed me into confessing aloud I did not consider myself worthy of rescue.

"The argument," I said, "was over a dishonorable act on my part. I did not deserve your interference."

"Don't be so hasty in flailing yourself, my friend," Janos answered. "I know quite a little of men like Leego, and I strongly doubt at any moment in your dealings you ever had the upper hand."

"I was a fool," I said. It felt cleansing to say those words aloud.

Janos nodded. "I suspect you were," he said. "It usually happens when a man thinks with his cock instead of his brain." He laughed. "However, I *did* overhear one thing that intrigues me. Something about a love potion. Applied to his prize whore." His eyes sparkled with what I thought was amused interest. Later I learned that his interest in these matters was far from casual.

I blushed. "I fear what you heard is true. It was a terrible sin I committed, and I regret it deeply."

"Oh, don't be a prudish fellow. What's there to regret? The doxy and Leego got their money's worth out of you, I'll warrant."

I made a complete and full confession, starting with the moment Melina and I first met and ending with my flight from her bedchamber. Janos was a remarkably easy confessor. He was sympathetic without being syrupy. He interrupted only to ask a detail—one that always seemed to bolster my side—or make a jest to lighten my spirits. It was like talking to a much older brother, although I realized he couldn't be much more than five years my senior. When I was done he poured the last of the brandy, then turned the bottle up to signal it would be our last.

"In my unworthy opinion, Amalric," he said, "this is a tale that began sadly and ended happily. You learned a lesson most of us don't come to until a late age, if ever. Forget the woman. Forget your imagined humiliations. I assure you it will make a wonderful story to tell your sons when you are an old man. At least tonight, you acquitted yourself well. So be done with it."

I thanked him, although I was not convinced my sins could so easily be washed away.

Janos raised his goblet in a toast. "To the new Amalric Antero. May his future adventures be half as sweet." Our goblets chinked together, and we drank. As we lowered our glasses I caught Janos eyeing me thoughtfully across the table. "I think my own fortunes changed this night, Amalric," he said, quite sincerely. "For did I not meet a redheaded man? And is that not one of the luckiest signs the seers can find in their crystals?"

"For your sake," I said, "I hope so. It is not so lucky for its possessor, I fear."

Janos laughed, that rich boom of a laugh I spoke of before. "Now that is a riddle worthy of the greatest Evocator," he said. "Much more so than how many demons can gambol on the head of a pin. If the Omen portends well, does that mean the Omen will also *end* well?"

Even writing from this distance, with all the events that have passed since we first met, I still do not know the answer to that riddle. I doubt I will until the night the Dark Seeker comes to carry off my soul.

My spirits lifted as I pondered his riddle. At long last, a friend with wit. Then, defeated, I shook my head. "Even if it were not late," I said, "I doubt I could unravel your puzzle. Indeed, it is a riddle whose answer may be as impossible to divine as . . ." I searched for comparisons, and one popped up like a light. "As finding the Far Kingdoms." I laughed, but I laughed alone. Janos was staring at me, excitement in his eyes.

"What is it?" I asked.

"Why did you say that?" he asked.

I was confused. "You mean . . . about the Far Kingdoms?"

"Yes." His voice was abrupt, prodding.

"I . . . really can't say. Except it was on my mind just before Leego's thugs arrived."

Janos peered closer, and I suddenly felt rather stupid.

"It's that kind of silliness on my brain that's kept me from my responsibilities," I said, a bit hot. "Forgive my babbling."

"If you knew *me*," Janos said, "you would realize when it comes to aimless chatter, there is no man the master of Janos Greycloak." I laughed as he drew me toward the door. "We'd best go quickly, my friend," he said, "or we'll soon be wrecked on the shoals of more brandy and babbling."

We went out into the night. Down the street I saw a torch flare, and thought once more of the Far Kingdoms. Then the thought was gone and only night remained.

CHAPTER THREE
The Finding

I WOKE THE next morning feeling bleary, my mind stuck like a dying fly in the dregs of last night's wine. Then I smelled the clean sharpness of the spring wind whispering in my chamber's window, and the haze vanished. With some surprise I also realized that for the first time in many days I had not been troubled with the terrible dream of the one-eyed man. I went from my bedchamber to the anteroom, washed, then knelt and whispered the ritual prayer to the hearthgod. The hand mirror—no matter how close I held it—told me I would not need to be shaved this day; so I began to put on the clothes laid out for me.

Then I caught myself. "Eanes!" He entered the chamber soundlessly, his face carefully made up in polite, if only slightly interested concern—the expression I later understood to be the mask bodyslaves quickly learn to wear for survival. I indicated the clothes he had laid out: the shirt was plain; the breeches were of a sober color; the jerkin was of poor quality; and the cap could have been worn by an elder. "Is this what you think happened?"

A smile flickered, then vanished. "I think nothing, m'lord. But since you said my presence would not be required when you went out last evening; and you returned escorted by two soldiers not far from dawn; *and* I found wine and earth stains on your clothes, which were scattered as if the Month of Winds had been prematurely in your chambers; *and*—"

"Enough!"

"As you wish, sir."

"I had some unexpected encounters was all."

"I have never heard *her* called that, before."

I chose to ignore his words. My teachers had repeatedly cautioned me from childhood that I was overly familiar with slaves and the lower classes—just as I was guilty of showing insufficient respect to my elders and superiors. But it is impossible for anyone with bowels to play the lordling to a small, balding slave whose first service was carrying you from your father's arms to the waiting Evocator at the naming ritual.

"But I thought," Eanes continued, "you might wish your dress for this day to be . . . shall we say of a hue that would not offend an eye that is bleeding, nor a parent still below stairs who heard the clatter as you reeled in?" Eanes might have been surprised I did not pale; but I had need of my father today: there was a debt to repay, and thanks to Melina and my own foolishness, I did not have the means. I walked into the wardrobe and carefully chose my costume: breeches of green, with a matching flat cap worked with gold threads; a flower-embroidered belted tunic; ankle boots, since the weather appeared balmy; and a short cloak. Remembering the last night's embarrassment, I chose a simple rapier, one without curlicued quillons, slung it from a baldric set with the family seal, and considered myself in a mirror: my image was just as I wished to appear—a sober young heir, but not one in mourning; a young man who, though sprightly in his air, was not the type to consort with whores of any pricing, or their pimps.

"I see," Eanes said. "So she left you empty pursed once again. And you are planning to go out and about. I assume you will not require my presence."

"I may not have paid much mind to my tutors, but I recollect the one—I disremember if it was the fellow who somehow fell into the harbor or the one whose robes ended up mysteriously on fire—who told me the story of the savant who prided himself on the excellence of his predictions; and while boasting to his students of this talent one day, he kept walking along a cliff edge some yards after the solid land had come to an end. And so the babbler died, to the great cheers and relief of his tortured students. The reality is I shall be infinitely pleased to have your company, even if I fear senility is setting in. We will be going out shortly."

"Yes, noble Amalric, my never-to-be-sufficiently-praised owner. I will be ready. Although I must add—you were correct when you said you paid little heed to your teachings. Consider the fable whose moral you so twisted. In truth, after the tragic death of that poor wise man, several of his students killed themselves, despairing that they would no longer benefit from his guidance. And, considering the day looks as if it threatens rain and storm, and I have more than a hint of chill—caused by my waiting up deep

into the night, worrying about my poor master, stumbling drunkenly through some filth-strewn alley and stalked by evil
cutthroats—you should learn from the shamed suicides of those
students, and meditate long that I shall not be with you forever."

As usual, the end-scoring favored Eanes.

FOUNTAINS FLASHED IN the gardens in the center of our villa, and
our tame birds rainbowed colors from limb to limb of budding
trees. My father was sitting at a long table, a plate of fruit and a
glass of well-watered wine for breakfast beside him. He was surrounded by his factotum, Tegry, plus an array of scrolls, tablets,
minions, and lackeys. I seated myself at the far end of the table
and waited. Father noticed me, but let me sit without greeting for
several long minutes. He pressed his signet to a document, and its
bearer left. Father held up his hand and the next man respectfully
waited a few yards away.

"Have you eaten?" he asked me.

"I have not."

"No doubt you have no appetite."

"Nossir. I mean, yes, I do."

"Hmm. I would have guessed from the commotion I was told
you produced, arriving home in the last turning of the glass, that
all you could stomach would be a brandy and milk." He did not
let me answer. "I assume you want something. And I further assume I can predict what it will be, even given my slender powers
for prognostication." I looked down at the table, then nodded.

"This will be the third time—" Tegry began.

"I think I am aware of my son's requests and can even remember the quantities. I have no intention either one of us should
waste time listening to another plea for gold that will be wasted
gilding some strum—" My father stopped himself. In spite of his
feelings, which I saw then as anger but now realize was closer to
disappointment, he would not shame me in front of a slave.
"Amalric, I feel you should consider further before making your
request."

I looked up at him. "The money is not for . . . her. But to repay
a debt."

Tegry looked at me. "A moneylender, Lord Antero."

My ears burned. "A debt of honor, Tegry. Perhaps you will
have the word translated into a tongue you understand." Shutters
dropped over Tegry's face an instant before my father scowled at
him.

"A debt of honor," my father said slowly. "Very well. I will not disgrace the request—nor you for asking. Tegry! See to it."

"Thank you, Father."

"Don't get up. You have not eaten yet. Learn a bit of wisdom—every meal you miss now, your body will remind you of many times in years to come." My father lifted his hand, and a house-servant approached me. "Now, Tegry," he continued, as if I had suddenly become invisible, "I have been pondering on the ivory from Laosia, and decided either the J'hana family are fools, or else they think we are. In either case I want a courier dispatched not later than midday, with these instructions . . ."

TEGRY HANDED ME the purse, his expression as untroubled as if there had been no unfriendly words spoken in the garden. I had been told often enough such behavior bespoke competency, but still could not understand a man with clerk's ink for blood, gold and silver for bones, and a profit statement for a mind. I shivered in the dark coolness of the villa's anteroom. I stopped at the altar and took up a pinch of sand and was about to reflexively deposit it before the portrait of my brother, Halab, as we all did each time we left the house. Then I looked closely at the picture: the painting was warranted not only to be accurate, but a simulacrum, its pigments made from Halab's most valued possessions; and the creator vowed all the rites had been followed and the painting was sympathetic to Halab's shade. I sprinkled the sand, wondering: was this enough? There had been no corpse to be found, not even a shard of bone, when the Trial ended. Did this sand give Halab's ghost peace? Or was he still going to and fro in this world, never to find surcease? Again, I shivered: I hoped when I died—and hoped that would not be for eons—I would not be unshriven, unburied, unrevenged if my death was not natural.

Eanes was waiting near the inner gate. He saw my expression and recognized it: Halab . . . his death . . . what should have been . . . and what was never to be . . . still hung heavy over all of us. I was very glad to feel the warmth of the spring sunlight.

"YOU ARE PLANNING on enlisting, Lord Amalric," Eanes inquired, sounding honestly worried. "I know it is traditional for young men who have been worried in affairs of the heart to consider such drastic measures, but I must counsel against it. *Imprime*, my health would not stand up to campaigning, even the gentle games of war our army has been fighting of late. So your armor would be unpolished all too often and you would be forced to eat cold rations. *Secun*, the two men I met who *did* join over a woman swore they could not remember the frail's name once they recovered from their mustering drunk. *Tert*, they also swore they were branded fools, since everyone else had agreed to wear the helm either to escape debt or vengeance, or else to eat more often than once a day. *Quat*—"

"Four," I said, "I am not joining, I am selling you for catapult fodder. Seal your lip. We are here on business." The two sentries at the barracks gate saw my dress and realized they were being approached by a nobleman. They saluted, crashing their pike butts against the cobbles.

"I am seeking Captain Janos Greycloak, of the Magistrates' Own Guards," I said.

One of them frowned, then remembered. "Oh. The Lycanthian. He's with Second Cohort, sir." He glanced up at the sun. "Most likely they'll still be at the butts. He works his men hard."

The soldier gave me instructions. As we went through the maze of barracks, I puzzled over what the soldier had said. A Lycanthian? In Orissa's service? Especially serving in the elite unit responsible for the safety of the Magistrates? Thinking back, although I had paid little mind the night before, I *did* recall a trace of an accent on his tongue; but it was quite unlike what I'd heard from the few Lycanthian traders I'd encountered.

I saw the boil of dust and the swirl of arms from the end of the parade field. There were thick logs buried vertically in the ground that could be used for targets or practice enemies. There were two such butts behind my family's villa, where the weapons teachers hired by my father had taught me. There came a bellow of *"Stand,"* and the dust settled, revealing perhaps fifty paired-off soldiers. They carried bucklers, wore leather jerkins with high necks, leather greaves, and leather helmets. In time of war the leather would be reinforced with iron or steel plating in strategic places and, if the battle was to be intense, chain-mail corselets, as well. One man of each pair held a short stabbing spear, the other a sword. The spear blade was covered with a guard, and the swords were clipped into their sheaths. To one side was Janos Greycloak. Unlike the others, he wore a full-face helmet with nosepiece, and an unusual leather jerkin that had a full-length sleeve on the left; and that sleeve was armored with close-set steel plates, with a partial breastplate/shoulder guard on the same side. In his right hand, Janos carried the long, slender sword I'd seen him use so effectively, and, like his soldiers, he held a buckler in his left. The man who'd shouted at the soldiers I also recognized—the older sergeant who'd advised me on the brandy the night before.

Janos saw me and nodded, but did not greet us. He walked forward into the center. "That was smartly done," he said, but there was little real praise in his voice. "Fit for any parade soldier. Sergeant Maeen?"

"Sir!"

"If you will step out and, as if you were mired in honey, strike at me with your spear."

The heavy man did as he was told. He'd barely begun a lunge when Janos ordered a stop.

"A parade ground is a parade ground," he said, in a conversational tone. "War is something different. I shall teach you many ways besides the ones you learned as mewling recruits. None of them are wrong, if you survive the encounter, and none of them are right if the spear thrust casts your ghost to the winds. Here are some things that may be done." As he spoke he moved slowly, like a man under water. "Take the spear thrust on your shield, turn the shield aside, and strike. Or strike the spear itself behind the haft with your sword . . . and perhaps you may break it. Yet another device, if your enemy oversteps his balance—thank you sergeant, just so—is to sidestep him, and then strike directly over or under his armor. But as you do so, do not forget your enemy has someone beside him, and if you become too intent on your target it will be your death that is harvested. A good trick—and this is one which will never be taught to young gentlemen—is to carry a handful of dust in your fist and cast that in your opponent's face before he can attack. If you are quick enough you may be able to duck low and hamstring him with a slice, although that is a very risky undertaking. Another undertaking of risk, less so if you are very strong, is to parry the spear with a sword slash, then thrust with your buckler as if it were a weapon. I have seen men blinded by the boss on a shield who were then cut down at leisure. The most important thing you will learn is to never watch the shield, never watch the sword, but watch the eyes of the man you are fighting. They will *always* betray his next move."

Janos stepped back. "Now, Sergeant Maeen will have you perform the same evolution. But this time without the one-two-three—and this time there is no required parry or attack. Sergeant!" His order triggered new roars from the sergeant, and dust cycloned once more. I determined not to mention either of the two duels I'd fought, sure that Captain Greycloak would think them nothing but the formal, pecking challenges of young cocks in the farmyard. Hamstringing . . . throwing sand . . . blinding . . . no. Even though I'd taken them most seriously at the time, as I assumed had my opponents, those two affairs of honor which had been settled with the first dribble of blood had not been real battles.

Janos watched the drill without comment or expression, then walked over. "Good morning, my friend," he said. "You see, I am already subverting these fine soldiers from being mannequins. How is your head this morning?"

"That's the first thing everyone's asked me," I said. "I didn't think I was *that* drunk."

"We never do," Janos said. "How may I be of service?"

I took the purse from Eanes and handed it to him. "Please accept this poor recompense for my unbroken bones—and reputation."

Janos hefted the purse, then handed it back. "Thank you, but there's no reward required for booting a hyena away from a sleeping victim."

"I—I wish you would take this," I said carefully. "In all seriousness, the shadow of my debt to you is overlong."

Janos nodded thoughtfully and took the purse; then he turned back to the mock fray. *"Stand."* His roar made the sergeant's appear to be a mousesqueak. "This gentleman," he said, without preamble, "has for some unknown reason decided to favor you." Janos tossed the purse to Maeen. "The cohort will have meat for even-meal tonight," he announced. "And one skin of wine to be shared between two."

There was a ragged cheer; then silence slammed down like a curtain as Janos' face become ice. "I did not," he said, in a calm voice, "give any of you leave to speak. By all rights I should be shamed, and return this money to your patrician admirer. But I shall not. You appear to have great wind in you. That is very good. Sergeant, run them to the top of Mount Aephens. You remain at the base. Run them up and down until you weary of the sight of them." Mount Aephens was three leagues distant and nearly a league high, rough brush, deep ravines, and rugged stone. "Since they are to be glutted tonight, fasting through the noontide will be good for them. That is all." A few moments later the elements of the cohort trotted away, Maeen bellowing some arcane chant as they disappeared.

"You must never," Janos said, rejoining us, "let soldiers think you are trying to buy into their graces." Then he stopped and smiled apology. "My pardon. I have been playing magister all morning and have trouble shedding the cloak."

He sheathed his sword. I'd noted with some interest that his blade was long and narrower than the conventional army weapon, and sharpened on both edges. Even more curious was that the blade was rippled; obviously made of the finest watered steel; yet the guard was simple and plain. Surely a captain, even one fresh in Orissan service, could afford a bit of gold, silver, or fancywork to boast his rank. He carried his scabbard slung across his back, so that his sword's handle protruded at an angle over his right shoulder. Very unusual, but I had seen such an arrangement before, on a barbarian from the frontiers beyond Lycanth. When I'd asked about it, the fellow had told me the design not only made it easy to draw on foot or horseback, but also did not get mixed up between his legs and trip him when he was drunk. Like that barbarian, Janos also wore a dagger mounted for a left-hand crossdraw on his belt: a practical weapon with a blade that appeared no more than a forearm in length, unlike the great tapering poignards street bravos carried. Like his sword, its pommel, grip, and guard were bare of decoration. I made note that if my plan was carried to completion, I would see that Greycloak was armed in a manner befitting a retainer of the Antero family—thus proving I knew even less about real weaponry than I thought.

"Let me sluice the dust from my face and change into walking-out dress," Janos said. "There's a wineshop I know of that has decent pressings for a soldier's pay. If you would care to join me?"

I would, indeed.

THE INN WAS not unknown to me: it was a favored trader's shop, located not only close to the central market, but at the riverbank; a suspicious merchant could watch his stock being loaded or offloaded and still negotiate yet another contract. I tossed Eanes a quarter-coin, and he joined the other slaves in a nearby arbor waiting their masters' bidding. We found a table, and a waiter brought wine, water, and a plate of pickled octopus tentacles, oil-cured olives, and cheeses. Both of us watered our wine liberally—I did not want Greycloak believing I was a complete sot.

"This morning, at mess," Janos began casually, "I mentioned I'd met you last night, although without describing the interesting details. One of the officers said you were planning a journey. What he called—Finding your Tradewind? He said it as if this were a custom I should be aware of, which I am not."

I kept my face calm, but promised a sacrifice to our hearthgod and also whichever god ruled over chance encounters. This was as if I were one of the city's mummers, and the fellow across from me was reciting the words as they'd been rehearsed—giving me my cue. I explained: Finding a Tradewind was not a law or a ritual of Orissa, but a custom, just as Janos had described it. When a merchant's son closed on his majority, it was customary for him to lead a trading expedition. The expedition would consist of the young man, any associates or friends he thought necessary, an Evocator, of course, and a small military escort for safety's sake. He was supposed to seek out new lands, new riches, and new customers, just as his merchant father and father's father had done. This custom was meant to guarantee that Orissa would remain the trading queen of the known world for another generation—until the young man raised a son himself and sent him out to Find his own Tradewind.

Janos listened intently as if I were all that existed in the world. I must have sounded hesitant: explaining something you have always taken as a commonplace is very difficult, but I wanted to be clear and concise, for the other purpose for my seeking out Captain Greycloak was to test him, to see if I wanted him as the commander of my own guard. I knew few soldiers, and those I did were more suited for the wineshop and ceremonials than a sudden ambush by raiders. It was traditional for the army of Orissa to be used as a recruiting station for Findings, and for full-scale merchant expeditions. Not only was the burden of the soldiers' wages alleviated while they served a merchant, but an officer and the men he chose would also be given bonuses dependent on the expedition's success.

After I'd finished my carefully chosen exposition Janos thought a moment, then asked, "This has been going on for how long?" I didn't know, precisely, but my father had told me of his father's father's father's Finding, so as far as I knew, forever.

"A puzzlement," Janos said. "Each year someone—or several someones—go seeking new worlds. Yet the charts I've seen in Orissa still have great areas that are marked as unknown outlands. Are these Findings kept secret, familiar only to you merchants and your rulers?"

All merchants have trading secrets, and any new discoveries would be held close as long as they were profitable; but I told him that wasn't the complete story: the journey, in truth, would not be into completely unknown lands, but almost certainly to the west, to cities and regions familiar to Orissans. Perhaps a daring young man might chance traveling a distance to the south, if not as far as into the realm of the Ice Barbarians. That was what my father had done on *his* Finding. But he had been regarded as a wild man, or so I'd heard the merchants of his generation say when drink loosened their memories. For many young men the journey was expected to be as much an exploration of fine wines and the willing maidens of other cities as anything else. It was also a test, of sorts: a man who returned from his Finding having shown an ability to get along with his father's customers, or having found a few new markets or goods, or who survived without being so ludicrously cursed with ill luck that he was ambushed by bandits— this man would be feasted and praised. There *was* some danger: I would not have sought out Janos if the Finding was nothing more than a celebration of beautiful scenes, women, food, and drink. But I dwelt on the romance, not jeopardy, being the true son of Orissa's most silken-tongued merchant.

"I understand, now." Janos turned his goblet in his fingers. "So then, your Finding will be in which direction?"

I stared. Either I hadn't explained clearly, or else a Finding was something completely alien in the world he came from. "Why, west, of course."

There was a pause. Janos looked at me, then smiled, and the sun came out once more. "Yes. As you say: of course." He drained his goblet. "Perhaps we should find something more substantial than these morsels before we drink any more. A good way for an outlander such as myself to suddenly not have to worry about promotion beyond captain is to be found stumbling through the streets before the sun lowers. My treat."

He clapped me on the back, dropped coins on the table, and we went out. He had said nothing . . . and his face had shown less. But I felt I had somehow failed a test.

I REMEMBER ORISSA as beautiful in that bright spring day as we wandered the winding lanes; Eanes, for once, not trying to parade his wisdom and walking some five paces behind us. Orissa was much then as it is now: a farm could still be found beside a smith's forge, and a free peasant's shack just behind a sprawling villa such as my father's. There were fewer people then, so the land was more open. The great city and its suburbs and outer district censused no greater than three tens of thousands free, and the same number slave. No fool had yet proposed a Grand Plan for the city, as has been mentioned recently, to turn Orissa into a nightmare of orderliness such as Lycanth. The rolling hills that rose to the Magistrates' Citadel were rainbows, each house or shop painted or stained as its owners saw fit. Many shades of reds, blues, golds, and even purples made Orissa the beautiful artist's palette it was. A visitor from the west had once said that Orissa looked like a magpie's nest, undignified in its chaos of hues. My father had eyed him with barely concealed scorn and wondered if he thought Orissa would still be marveled at as the Queen of Cities if, like Lycanth, its buildings and streets were gray and black, or if they were shamefully left in their common stone or wood colors. That was what the great hairy not-men of the northern tropics did, to conceal their lean-tos in the jungle. As did the barbarians of the ice who tried to pretend their great bare stone monoliths showed the virtues of simplicity rather than a lack of imagination and courage to shout splendor to the envious gods.

Eventually we found ourselves on the Street of the Gods. Coming down the middle of the street, behaving as if there were no other traffic, was a Master Evocator—his name was Jeneander. In front of him were staff-armed, naked servants, their bodies shaved bare; and behind him was his retinue of journeymen, adepts, and secretaries. I turned away, not making obeisance, as if suddenly entranced by the shabby tabernacle that honored some fruit growers' deity. From the corner of my eye I saw Janos knuckle a mark of respect; then he turned in the same direction I was facing. He laughed, a barely audible chuckle.

"Even here in Orissa," he murmured, "superstition calls it the worst of luck for a Evocator to cross your path. In some places I have visited, seeing such a man or woman would require you to return home and go immediately to bed—or face the worst of nameless fates."

I nodded and said something such as yes, I supposed even the most rational of us had *some* superstitions; but I did not tell him the real explanation. It was not superstition at all, but cold hatred: for the Evocators and their magic had murdered my brother.

CHAPTER FOUR

Dance of the Far Kingdoms

WE WERE DAWDLING through a sculpture garden near my villa before I broached the subject again. We had been talking of nothing, talking of everything, each taking the measure of the other. Finally I was comfortable enough with my new friend to comment on something that had been troubling me for a time. "I saw your look of disapproval when I said I would journey west in my Finding," I said.

Janos stopped in his tracks, made a musing sound, and stroked his beard. His actions gave me yet another reason to find the altar of the godlet who ruled over face hair: beard stroking seemed a wonderful device for a canny man to use to consider his words before they tumbled out. "My apologies," he said. "I thought I was more capable at the graces of civility than I evidently am. You appear to have some of the talents of a seer."

"There's no magic to it," I said. "I am only someone who grew tired of being thought a rich fool. You should see all the flies that buzz about when you have a wealthy father, all saying how wise you are, how handsome, how your games are the best to be played, how you should be the captain of the team. Even how your lovemaking is the most head-spinning they have ever encountered. And could you spare a bit of your purse for a few days, Amalric, my friend?"

Janos nodded. "The best way to live, and I wish it were possible, is to live honestly. All we need do is find a world where everyone about us is equally as virtuous. And thick-skinned. I confess that I did disapprove of what you plan for the Finding of your Tradewind. Because I was judging your actions by what *I* would do were I in your place."

"What *would* you do, friend Janos? If you were magically transformed into Amalric Antero?"

"First, I would endow a certain Janos Greycloak with riches to indulge himself beyond his wildest dreams, so he'd never again have to dance attendance on fat old fools. Then I would seek my Tradewind—to the east. And if I lived, my Finding would not only make me rich, and give me knowledge and power beyond that held by the most hoary Evocator, but ensure my name would be remembered from this day to the ending of history."

"Ah," I said, grinning. "You would seek out the Far Kingdoms."

"Just so."

I started to laugh, for I had thrown out the goal as a jest; I then saw his face was darkly serious. "You believe such a place exists?"

"I do not believe. I *know*."

"Oh." I could feel the shutters of my mind close, just as it does when a respected tutor announces there are worlds beyond our own, or when a sage begins drooling like a goat in heat over an empty-headed strumpet.

As a boy I had eagerly listened to the tales of the greatness of the Far Kingdoms, located in the distant east, well beyond the ken of man. Most tales agreed that it lay across the straits of the Narrow Sea, beyond the benighted Pepper Coast, in uncharted territory. If a man could survive such a hazardous journey—which, all agreed, no one alive could, since we were a far cry from the giants of earlier days—he would find himself in a land of fabled wealth and wizardry. I had always considered—even when I had told some of the tales myself as a sprat—the Far Kingdoms were suitable for philosophers' examples, peasant dreams, or the fictions of the bards. In the past, hearing such a statement as Janos had just made, I would have politely smiled, chatted on for a while, made my excuses, and then left—determined to find another officer to accompany me on my Finding. But now, hard on my new course of honesty, I pressed on.

"I have always believed, as did my father—and, for that matter, all the *educated* men I've encountered—that the Far Kingdoms was a dream. Just as some peasants believe there was a Golden Age before us, when men were all heroes, women were all virgin-whore-mothers, all things were free for the asking, and so forth."

And Janos asked, "What would convince you a dream is, in fact, real?"

His comment gave me a jolt, which I hid, as I suddenly remembered another dream: the dream of the man with one eye in the river cavern—the nightmare that had plagued me since meeting Melina. It was as if the spring day had suddenly turned chill. Then I forced my mind away from that dream and pondered Janos' question. "I don't know, really. And I'm not trying to sound like some savant creaking about whether a man dreams he is a butterfly or a butterfly dreams he's a man. Pain? I've bled in dreams. That they seem to continue on forever? I've dreamed most of a life on occasion."

"I will offer three arguments, but not as the logicians teach us to do," Janos replied. "I'll start with the most crushing. This." He lifted a thin chain from around his neck and handed it to me. A device dangled from it: a small, broken statuette of a dancing maiden, her arms stretched above her head; perhaps one of her hands had once held a twisting scarf or veil. The statuette had been broken at the woman's hips. It might have been made of silver or some other semiprecious metal; but it was badly tarnished now. The workmanship, however, was exquisite: the maiden's face was alight in happiness, and, I thought, if I could put a jeweler's pane on the figurine, I would be able to distinguish every detail of her face and arms. "A pretty," I finally said. "But I've seen equal craftsmanship in the shops of our metal-crafting masters."

"Touch it." I did—and the statue came to life. The chain seemed to vanish, and the half woman danced on an invisible platform before my eyes. Instead of tarnished silver, her skin was soft ivory and tipped with crimson; her hair was black, her sheer gown violet. I took my finger away, and once more I was holding a dirty, shattered figurine.

"*That* I have never seen or heard of," I admitted.

"Nor anyone else in these lands," Janos said. "I have consulted priests and Evocators, and none of them know the spells necessary to make such a bauble. In fact, one fool told me it violated all of the laws of thaumaturgy—so it must be black sorcery. He ordered me to give it to him so that he could 'purify' it. I took it back and told him what he might well face if he mentioned the statue to anyone."

"Where did you get it?"

"My father gave it to me as a gift on my first birthing day. It was not broken then. When I was six he told me where it came from. My mother said it had cost him three war mounts—stallions whose lineage went back to the Horsegod himself."

"Your father said it came from the Far Kingdoms?" I guessed.

"Yes."

I was silent, thinking again of those peasant tales of the mysterious eastern lands beyond. How great sorcerers ruled and how they could even make battle magic that could stand against the strongest counterspells. How the streets and statues were solid gold. Here was hard evidence of some master wizard's work; something the most adept Evocator of Orissa would herald as his lifetime achievement and deem worthy of a king's wedding gift.

"How was it broken, if I may ask?"

Janos's face was still. "This is not the day for such a tale," he said.

I changed the subject. "Your first premise carries weight," I said, handing the maiden back to Janos. "But just to be stubborn I must bring up the counter that no one knows of every conjurer in the world. Not just ones from still undiscovered cities, but those whose weird it is to live in solitary haunts—in jungles or mountains."

"True. But not that powerful a rejoinder. My second and third arguments have less substance, and I cannot give you anything to hold in your hand. But hear them out. You've heard them call me a Lycanthian. But I am not, even though I spent years in their service. In truth I come from another land, across the Narrow Sea from Lycanth, in Valaroi. A land of high mountains and small glens. Kostroma."

"I have never heard of it," I confessed.

"No. You would not have." He started to elaborate, then changed his mind. "Not far from my family's stronghold was a traders' route. They paid tribute to my father, and he provided soldiery to keep them safe from those without law. Where they paid tribute, they held a bazaar. This would be twice, sometimes three times a year; and for us, those fairs were as big an excitement as the Day of Sowing. My father would sometimes invite one of the traders to our home. He would feed and guest the man lavishly. Not just out of courtesy, but because this was the only means for our out-of-the-way land to learn of the world beyond. Among the stories they told were of the Far Kingdoms."

"I must interrupt you here," I said. "Surely you aren't telling me you trust the word of traders? We are renowned for swearing a yard of goods was custom-woven for a high priestess' mystery, if it means we can knock the price up a copper or two."

"Nevertheless," Janos said, "it was most interesting listening to their tales. And not one of them ever said he had visited the Far Kingdoms. Nor did any claim to have even seen their border posts. But *all* who had traveled to the east had seen their trade goods. Luxury items that had passed from hand to hand, their price increasing at each step. Sometimes they would even cautiously show such a bauble to us, something that would be well beyond the modest profit my father's herds earned: lutes that when strummed by a stable boy would make him seem a fine troubadour; a gown, or even a veil, that would turn the most coarse serving wench into a dazzling seductress. And there were other things—like my little dancing maiden—that were even more marvelous. Incantations beyond any we knew of; and to this day they are still beyond any I have ever encountered in my travels."

I said nothing: Janos may have thought this second premise but idle gossip, but it wasn't to the son of a merchant prince. We, too, had heard of—and sometimes seen—devices that struck wonder into our hearts, even if none were as exotic as Janos' tiny dancer. And it would be claimed that they were from the Far Kingdoms, which always produced guffaws all around. Since it was known that there were wizards of great power hidden in the lonely places, these goods were generally ascribed to one or another of them. But why, I suddenly wondered, was it considered more logical to believe in a sorcerer hiding in a swamp, a conjuror in a jungle, an enchanter on another mountaintop, rather than to theorize there might be a single source for these fineries?

I asked Janos the same question. "That's easy to answer," he said. "Since when does any man or woman like to think that there is a person or place more gifted, more civilized, than where they come from?"

I nodded. "Yes. Certainly my father has reminded me often enough that when I go afield I should not brag loudly on the wonders of Orissa. Boasting like that, even if it's true, gets nothing but resentment from bumpkins, even if they pretend to be awed as you boast. Your argument is doing better than I thought it would, Captain Greycloak. What is your third premise?"

"Perhaps we should find another wineshop before I tell it to you, since it seems to slide more easily down the craw with lubrication. And rightly the tale should be told only when everyone is somewhat pickled, and it is a stormy midnight outside."

"A ghost story? I'm partial to them," I said.

"Ghosts? I don't know. You can call them what you want. But this is a tale that happened to me personally."

We found a shop with its own arbor and an agreeably smiling maid to serve the shop's fine vintage.

"There were times," Janos said, "when our aruspex would

dream the moment had come to sacrifice a particular animal, one that would be chosen from my family's own herds. Mostly the entrails would reveal nothing, but on occasion the diviner would see something terrible. At that time he would order a curfew. All men and women, girls and boys of our valley would have to be inside from dusk to dawn. The flocks would be abandoned, the watchtowers unmanned for as long as four nights.

"Our people would huddle at fireside, shutters or curtains drawn tight. Sometimes . . . rarely . . . there would come a thunder, the same thunder a cavalry patrol makes outriding in a swift patrol. There were those who swore they could hear the creak of harness and even the clatter of hooves against the cobbles as the patrol crossed one of our few paved squares. But at dawn there would be no hoof marks in the roadway. Nothing at all."

"What was out there in the night?" I wondered. "Or was it just thunder? The gods know I convinced myself often enough, lying awake as a boy, that I heard all manner of demons in the street outside our villa, or sometimes on the roof just above my balcony, where they were waiting to pounce. But I'd like to think that I would have been foolish enough to slip out unnoticed to see those ghost horsemen."

"I did just that." Janos half smiled, a smile of approval for my imagined audacity. "I let myself down from my bedchamber with a rope I'd stolen from the guardroom earlier that day, when the prophet shouted his latest warning."

"But of course the horsemen didn't materialize that time," I guessed.

"That was not what happened at all. I'd cleverly listened to all the tales and carved a small map of the area around our citadel. On it I'd marked where the riders had been reported most frequently. One such place was a narrow pass, about eight spearcasts—we measured things in that way in Kostromo, which would have been about one-third of a league—beyond one of my father's byres. I hid myself in an olive tree below the pass. The moon was just past half. Then I waited. I don't know for how long. Being perhaps eight or nine, probably I would have slept, in spite of my excitement. The noise woke me. Just as the herdsmen had said, I heard crashing horses' hooves."

"But you saw nothing."

"Nothing in the pass," Janos said, looking down into his goblet as if it were an oracle's pool, giving him a vision of the past. "But I saw something—two somethings—ride to the hilltop overlooking that pass. Two riders. Men, I thought them to be. They wore armor—or at any rate I saw the gleam of plate and spears. High-roached helms. Even their mounts seemed protected, since I saw another moonflash from one steed's head. The position they took was exactly the one I would order now—if I were leading a patrol into unfriendly territory—overlooking the pass so my main force would not be ambushed. The hoof thunder grew louder, and passed. As the sound cleared the pass the two outriders galloped down to rejoin the others. The sound of their passage died away then. They were riding to the east—where legend tells us the Far Kingdoms lie. I fled back to the castle, and to my bed, as if I were pursued."

"And next morning, when you returned?"

"Nothing was there. No hoofprints in the soft ground on the hilltop, no markings in the pass. No sign that a scouting band, riding far beyond their frontiers, had passed."

"A dream," I said, disappointed that Janos' tale hadn't included a bloody skull, a disappeared peasant, or a flock that stampeded over a cliff in panic.

"No doubt," Janos agreed. He glanced at the sundial just outside the arbor. "And my new dream is that I am watch officer this night, and I have barely time to return to the barracks and bolt on all the finery I must wear to clank around my post.

"I have enjoyed this day, my friend," he said, taking silver from his belt pouch against my objections. "And you have convinced me there can be no such thing as the Far Kingdoms. Perhaps we can meet again another day? Perhaps I can help you plan your Finding, since I have made some minor travels to the west." And he was gone.

I stayed on, ordering another pitcher of wine—partially because I was curious as to which one of us the barmaid had been smiling at, partially to muse on what he'd told me. Because somehow, in spite of what Janos had said about his being converted to logic, I felt, somewhere out there, far to the east, the brooding darkness and gold that was the legendary Far Kingdoms.

I SAW JANOS several times over the next few weeks when he was off duty. Freed of Melina's entrancement, I was readying myself for my Finding, talking to older traders and collecting tales from travelers and seamen at the docks, just as I had when I was a boy. But this time I knew what I was looking for. My father seemed to note my new earnestness with some degree of approval, since I found myself subjected to his ironic criticisms less and less. I was also gathering all the tales of the Far Kingdoms, attempting

to make sense of them. There was none to be made: for every
story that the Far Kingdoms had enchantments that bade horses to
fly, were others saying their Evocators had spells so powerful that
no dray animals at all were needed: objects and men flew through
the air of their own accord.

Some of these tales I related to Janos. He listened politely, but
skeptically. It was almost as if he were not that interested. In fact,
he was behaving just as I do today when I am offering a parsimo-
nious tailor a shipment of brocade that's priced somewhat beyond
what he was prepared to pay. "I agree, sir, that perhaps this cloth,
no matter how rare and fine, is highly priced. It took me two
weeks of the most bloodcurdling bargaining before I myself could
afford it." Or: "Of course, this material requires care in its working, and is intended for the most discriminating of wearers." And
so on and so forth, until the poor wight would contemplate murder if I refused to make him the sale.

ONE EVENING JANOS asked me to dine at an open mess with his
fellow officers. I was honored: the Magistrates' Own regarded
themselves as among Orissa's social elite and invitations were
much prized. Besides, there was something I was almost certain I
wanted to tell Janos, and something I wished to ask. All that remained was how to present the matter. Janos accompanied me
back to my father's villa, where I washed and changed into
matching black velvet breeches and vest, a red silk shirt with a
wide lace-edged collar, knee boots, and a full-length hooded
cloak. I told Eanes he need not accompany me—there would be
more than enough servitors present.

As we walked through the twilight streets toward the barracks,
I chanced asking Janos why, if he was so intent on seeing new
worlds, he was serving in the Magistrates' Own Guard? Certainly
it was an honor, but its duties kept it for the most part
watchguarding the Magistrates, Evocators, and the great public
buildings of Orissa, which was hardly adventurous. Janos agreed:
it *was* a dubious honor, but he'd had no choice. When he had
shown up at the barracks wanting to enlist, the minute they'd
heard his mother's name, he was doomed.

"They would never consider dishonoring the Kether family, no
matter how tenuous my claim to the name, by making one of
them serve in a unit like the Frontier Scouts, which actually might
have to smell blood or wave a sword in anger. Which was my ini-
tial request. Instead, I'm a captain with the Magistrates' Own. An
intellectually stimulating post if ever there was one. Did you

know that it's against the social graces to discuss war, the unit's policies, religion, or women at mess? Horses, dogs, and hunting, around and around, around and around. If I hear one more tale of how someone's pack of hounds exhibits almost oracular abilities at finding game, I may be forced to tell the tale of how I once lived on dog for a month when I was manning a watchtower for the Lycanthians in the South. Not bad, actually, larded with bacon and baked with yams," he said meditatively. "Oh well. There's never been a soldier who didn't cry woe and doom at every opportunity. It's his right, issued with his practice sword and brass-polishing cloth."

The Magistrates' Own mess was splendorous: the plates were silver, as was the service; the goblets were crystal; and each table was covered with fine linen. In the center of the tables were the regimental trophies, and the honors of war hung from the high rafters and lined the walls. Janos excused himself, then returned in full dress—short, soft, leather boots, shoulder cloak, and brocaded skirt and tunic. Over it he wore a sleeveless jerkin, padded and worked to look as if it were armor. Instead of his usual sword, slung over his shoulder, Janos wore a belt with a shoulder harness. A conventional short sword and dagger hung from it. He carried a highly polished open-face helmet with a great, waving plume atop it. The other officers wore similar garb.

Stewards with wineglass-laden trays passed through the crowd. One of them stopped in front of Janos. He hesitated, then shook his head. "I'll have water with my meal."

I heard a low, knowing laugh. I puzzled . . . Janos was hardly an ascetic. Then I recollected something my father had told me when I was in the depths of adolescent despair, vowing to cut myself off without a coin and join the army. He'd chuckled kindly and asked what unit I would be joining. Perhaps the Magistrates' Own? At that time, enamored of their dash and splendor, I'd sulked out a "possibly." He'd told me what it cost to be in the regiment: a young subaltern's wages would barely suffice to cover his mess bill—his wine, his brandy, and the levies for special dinners. The Magistrates' Own was only for the wealthy; it took, by some estimates, as much as ten thousand silver pieces a year to maintain the proper standing, when one considered the dozen or more different styles of uniforms required, the half a dozen chargers, the personal servants even beyond those allocated, and so forth. I remembered that Janos had mentioned poverty twice today.

I understood his plight: once I had joined a boys' fencing team, made up of other merchants', Evocators', and Magistrates' sons. No one thought of coins; but there was one boy, a year younger than myself, whose father had made some bad investments, so the young man's tunic was not new at every occasion, and he had but one foil, and that one secondhand. It was embarrassing, although I don't remember either my friends or myself saying anything. The boy was competent, I remembered, and then tried to think what had happened to him? I couldn't recall—one day he'd just not been there.

Janos could not afford wine. Very well. I called the steward over and made certain there would be no offense to the customs. In a few moments the head steward announced to the room that the wine this evening was a humble offering from Amalric Antero, in honor of being a guest of such noble soldiers. Goblets were filled and I was toasted. I caught a sidelong glance from Janos, but only a momentary one.

We ate after another round, far better than I thought soldiers ever dined. I thought of the sergeants and spearmen in the barracks outside, and remembered that once before I'd bought viands for the regiment. A dish of meat for the common soldiery, which suggested that normally they ate as commoners did. This was wrong—Father told me a trader either ate what his clerks did, or else dined privately at home. No one loved ostentation from a rich man—or military officer—unless it was shared with all.

Meal complete, the high officers excused themselves. Now the evening would belong to the lower ranks, grain, and grape. More wine was drunk. Wine and brandy. The evening promised nothing but boring befuddlement and a thick head on the morrow. I was trying to pace myself, not wishing to shame my family by crashing nose first into the sweet tray. Others, however, were taking no precautions. Voices were getting louder, jests were growing cruder, laughter was more boisterous. Then I heard, in a momentary lull, the clear statement, "Of course, half-breeds aren't *completely* worthless. Their women are sometimes spectacular, like mongrels can be. And their soldiers can be brave, although I suspect they run just as fast from a battle as to it."

There was the silence of the crypt. Everyone looked at Janos: his face was pale against his waxed, curled beard, a hard death mask. The officer who had spoken wore the stylized shoulder cops of a captain. Someone tried to break the silence with the beginnings of a jest; three words from his mouth and he stopped.

Janos beckoned to a servitor. He took the silver serving tray from the man's hands and drew his dagger. He put it on the tray so that its hilt faced out. Then he beckoned to a subaltern. "Convey this to Captain Herron. Tell him that it has a sister, which belongs to Captain Janos Kether Greycloak, of Kostroma and Orissa. They belong together. In one hour, at the butts."

I knew this challenge would not result in a duel to the pinking, as had mine. There would be at least one corpse in the sand this night. The young officer, as pale as Janos, walked to the other captain, extended the plate holding the dagger, and repeated Janos' words. Herron did not take the dagger. Instead, he flushed, and, staring down at the ground, muttered, "It was but a joke."

"Inform the honorable captain I failed to see its humor. Perhaps our meeting outside will educate me. Or perhaps the captain would like to apologize," Janos said, slightly bending the protocol of an affair of honor by speaking to, no matter if indirectly, the offending party.

Again, leaden stillness. Finally, Herron spoke, still mumbling, "I wish to apologize for any offense my chance remark may have caused Captain Greycloak."

Janos took three deep breaths. "I accept," he said. "And the matter is forgotten. The invitation is withdrawn, Herron." I noticed, as did everyone else in the room as the dagger was returned and sheathed, that Janos had deliberately neglected to call Herron by his rank, or to refer to him as a brother in arms, equal, or whatever term would suggest true forgiveness. Herron's cowardice would be remembered for a long time. Or so I thought his behavior to be back then, when my blood ran as red as my hair. Now I know what grounds a man fights on and what soil a fool can blithely choose for his own killing floor.

Janos began to reach for another wine goblet, then caught my eye. "Perhaps," he said, his voice low, "you would care to walk out with me? The air here has become thick." Without waiting for a response, he moved toward the cloakroom. I followed. Outside, he pulled his cloak over his shoulders and looked down at the lighted barracks windows below us.

"You see how it is," he said, as much to himself as me. "If I continue in this cage, pacing, snarling, and measuring the strength of my bars, sooner or later there will be a death. Perhaps that of a boor like Herron, perhaps my own. This city and this parade-ground emptiness cannot hold me much longer. Come on!" He started down the hill, and I went after him.

"Where are we going?"

"Who knows," Janos said. "I need the company of men, not popinjays. Men . . . and women. Perhaps the riverfront."

I shrugged. Why not? I, too, had been bored by the formalities in the mess, and thought them just as empty as any of my fathers' guild banquets.

Our path led us past one of the city's gates. As usual, except in times of great danger, the reinforced portals of ironwood were open; only the elaborately wrought iron of the twin gates of the outer sally port were barred. Through them we could see, not far off in a field, the roar of flames from a fire reflecting off the canvas of many tents. We could hear shouts, laughter, the whine of flutes, and the thudding of drums.

"Guard," Janos challenged one of the sentries. "Who lies beyond?"

"A tribe of Ifora, Captain. They cannot enter the city at night because—"

"I am aware of the reasons, soldier. Open the gates. Their company suits me well tonight."

I knew as well as Janos why the tribesmen were not permitted into the city. They were one of the many dangers a trader must accept, and so my father had explained their barbaric culture quite thoroughly. The Ifora were nomads, wandering tribesmen from the southern deserts. They were known as cunning thieves able to slip past the guards of any caravan that entered their territory and remove what they willed. Or, if their numbers were great or the caravan's masters stupid, they would massacre all of the men and absorb the women into their own tribes. They were also noted for bravery, implacability to their enemies, and for rare talents as torturers. They came north into civilized grounds infrequently, and then only to trade their elaborately woven rugs, fine woolen cloth from their goats, and exotically worked silver jewelry. No city would allow them inside its gates: the Ifora considered it their sacred duty to relieve people like us, whom they considered sickly weaklings, of whatever possessions they desired, and by whatever means—be it by stealth or by sword—and with no regard for subsequent events such as arrest and trial.

I thought of saying something to Janos: So he'd missed his chance to risk his neck in a duel; did he have to find another opportunity for a severed weasand? But being young and too timid to chance anything that might smack of that very timidity, I said nothing. Besides, all these tales of piled skulls and screaming women being carried off into the bowels of the desert—I was curious as to exactly what monsters the Ifora were. I loosened my rapier in its sheath, sorry that I hadn't brought a dagger and a mail shirt under my formal garb to accompany it. I also wished I'd reminded Janos when he strode forth that he was only carrying the traditional short sword of his unit, instead of the double-edged razor he preferred.

A great bulk of a man loomed out of the shadows as we drew near the encampment. "Orissans . . . no. Not come. Not welcome. Be hurt. Get kill." Janos spoke to him in a fluid torrent of words. The hulk growled and answered him in what sounded to be the same tongue. So this was another of Janos' accomplishments—he was familiar with the Ifora. I should have guessed—although somehow I sensed this night he might have been just as willing to walk into their den if they'd been deadly strangers. The two of them rattled back and forth. The monster laughed, as a bear might. Janos turned, indicating me. More words. A grunt. Janos frowned, then spoke again. The brute laughed once more.

"Take out your sword," Janos said. "Press it to your forehead and give it to him." I hesitated, but obeyed. The man accepted the weapon, turned, and bellowed something into the encampment. A moment later, a tall, imposing man wearing rich robes came toward us. His skin gleamed in the firelight, as black as the night. Flanking him were two sword-bearing guards, both fair skinned, as was the mountain who'd stopped us.

"This," Janos said quietly, "will be their *Ham'u*. Chief. The Ifora believe that the darker a man's skin, the more blessed by the gods he is. Since they are predominantly light complected, a black man is automatically considered noble. If he or she can lead, that man or woman will be destined to rule the tribe. The belief comes from long ago, when the Ifora were what they call barbaric. Their slaves revolted and took over, showing them how to conquer the desert. That was the beginning of their greatness." I blinked, the jeopardy forgotten for a moment. None of this had been told me by my father, nor had I heard any of it in the grotesque tales from other merchants of their encounters with the tribesmen.

The black man greeted Janos, who bowed. I took the hint and did the same. Janos drew his sword, touched it to his forehead, and gave it to the chief—the *Ham'u*. The black man repeated the motion and returned it. Janos spoke once more, indicating me. The *Ham'u* took my rapier from the guard, did as he'd done with Janos' blade, and gave it back. We bowed once more, and the *Ham'u* stepped aside, beckoning us into the camp.

"We are now the honored guests of the Ifora. From now until dawn three days hence we are their blood kin. During that time they will offer us their best and, if we have been pursued by enemies, they will ravage them as if one of their own had been wronged."

"What happens if we're still here after the three days?"

"Eh," Janos said, moving his hand from side to side in the universal signal for 'perhaps this, perhaps that.' "We would have to talk some more. And at least they would give us a running start."

We were led into the center of the camp, where the fire roared. The ground was paved with rugs, and pillows were high-piled for seats and backrests. Behind them large barrel-vaulted tents stood, made of some red-dyed animal skin. There were fifty or sixty men and women lying around the fire. I was presented to a man, who bowed as if he had just met the king of the world and found me a seat. He waved his hand, and a maid a few years younger than myself came out of the shadows. They spoke; she giggled and bowed to me. Then she went into one of the tents and came out with a wide-mouthed bowl. I took it, and looked to Janos for guidance. He was already sprawled on a pillow nearby, a pair of young women nestled beside him.

"Drink it."

"What is it?"

"Just drink. I'll tell you afterward. Drink deeply, or you will offend." I obeyed, and the back of my head exploded. The world shimmered around me. My stomach rose up, protesting. But somehow the drink stayed down and spread warmth, warmth becoming fire, fire becoming a hot rainbow, and I thought it best if I sat down. Rapidly. The girl took the bowl from me as I collapsed.

"The drink is *depsh'*," Janos said. "Fermented milk from their mares, fermented blood from their cattle. This is then combined with certain shrub blossoms their *Ham'u* takes to ensure the clarity of his vision. You might think they know distillation, given the impact. But instead the *Ham'u* recites an incantation over the mixture, and it takes on its present form. I have as yet been unable to persuade one of them to teach me the chant," he said. "If I could learn that, I would have no need of an army, a sword, or someone to sponsor me in the travels I want to make."

One of the two women next to him held out an identical bowl to Janos. He drained it and cast it over his shoulder. "One of the great commodities the Ifora have is their daughters. Even though they despise the weaklings of the watered lands—as they call everyone but another Ifora—they think it a great blessing for their young women to become courtesans for a time. They return laden with silver, which is used to purchase goats or horses, and they marry, greatly honored. How rich a marriage they make depends on their success in their previous profession. This is a young woman's destiny, unless the auspices read when she is a year old indicate she will be either a chief or a councillor, which is a supreme blessing; or a woman of the camp, which they consider somewhat of a disappointment. The woman beside you is, by the way, the daughter of the man who the *Ham'u* chose as worthy of the honor of being your host. Her name is Tepon."

It may have been the *depsh'*, or perhaps I was becoming acclimatized to unsettling events here, beyond Orissa's walls, but instead of frowning at what most Orissans would consider the deepest depravity, I turned and smiled at the girl, who, encouraged, moved closer, allowed a bit of her robe to slip open. I smelled roses and musk.

Tepon smiled. Her lips were rouged, her breath sweet, and her teeth were filed into pretty needle points that added exotic spice to her looks. I took another drink of *depsh'*. The girl spoke to me, her voice soft and musical. I shook my head. I didn't understand.

"She thinks the color of your hair is beautiful. Like a desert sunrise," Janos translated.

I made some inane response. Then the reality of the situation struck. "Janos, my friend. I assume that the Ifora are human?"

"Indeed."

"Then this guesting must have a price. Unless they are entranced by my hair and your vocabulary."

"There is a price," Janos started, and then a man stood, tapping on an elaborately carved clapper. A flute piped, then another. Thumb-cymbals tinkled. A great drum boomed rhythmically. "Ah," Janos said. "I know this one. The price is low."

He stood, unpeeling one of the girls who'd become curious about what was under his tunic, and drew his short sword. He cast it up, spinning, and caught it by the handle. "No," he said, "I need a real sword, not an ornament," and he threw the blade, burying it to its hilt in the ground. He shouted in Ifora, and from out of the darkness a great curved scimitar was pitched to him. Janos cast, caught, cast again, the blade spinning, catching firelight, sending sparkles into my eyes. The *Ham'u* rose and began a rhythmic chant. It may have been the herbs in the drink, or it may have been my imagining, but I understood, most clearly, the story Janos was enacting as he danced, slowly, then faster; and now he was wearing only the kilt. It was the story of a great warrior who was defeated by evil and sorcery, forced to flee from his tents into the depths of the desert, where not even the bones of the wild ass could be found. He wandered for a time. There were evil beings of the dry salt marsh who attempted to slay him—and here Janos's blade flashed in a series of arabesques— but he defeated them. He was lost, abandoned, staggering, about to die, and the god of the desert wind took pity. The two maidens who'd been with Janos were beside him, their bodies moving, firelight and silk, next to him, touching him. He gained strength and the tale went on: And the spirit of the wind fed him and nourished him and bore him back across the trackless sands to the tents of his enemy. Suddenly Janos danced alone, his sword a blur, as if he were fighting an invisible foe. Finally, the warrior triumphed, and his opponent lay dead before him. All the riches of the man belonged to him now. But instead, the warrior chose another path. He chose to return to the desert. And to the embrace of the desert wind.

Janos stopped as the chant ended. There was nothing but the crackle of the flames. Then a thumb-cymbal tinkled once, twice, three times. A sudden wind gusted through the camp. Janos bowed. To the Ifora? To the wind? To the dance? I knew not. The two women approached him and took him by the hand. They led him away into one of the tents.

A bowl touched my lips. I drank deeply. I lay back, against Tepon's body, her fingers moving tenderly over me. For some reason, this felt to be the time.

"Janos!" My voice was not loud.

"I hear."

"Will you accompany me? To the Far Kingdoms?"

Laughter boomed from nowhere. "Of course! Of course! I thought you would never ask."

And there was nothing more except Tepon, the tent that suddenly blossomed around us, and we were alone, and her body, and firelight.

I woke some time after dawn. I was naked except for my cloak wrapped around my waist. There was an inquisitive goat staring at me from less than a foot away. I lay on rocky ground in the flaring sunlight. Tepon's head was pillowed on my stomach. The great drum of the night before was now in my head.

And I was destined for the Far Kingdoms.

CHAPTER FIVE
The Evocators

MY SISTER TRAMPED in from the exercise yard, undid her cuirass, and dumped it on the floor. "If you love me, brother, dear," Rali groaned, "fetch a drink before I perish." I hastened to the fireside where I had set a strong, spiced punch to brew. I lifted the iron jug from the ashes with tongs and poured out a steaming, aromatic goblet. It was my sister's favorite drink. She grinned as I handed it to her. "Such a devoted brother," she said. "Unselfish, as well. Anticipating his sister's smallest whim, with no thought of any reward." She took a long drink.

"Don't tease me, Rali," I begged. "I've barely slept since our talk last week."

"Oh, please don't complain to me about your sleeping habits," she said with a laugh. "You've probably slipped another love potion to some doxy and she's been ferreting about your bed all this time." My sister crossed the room on those fine, long legs of hers, kicked off her sandals, and settled on the couch. "Come rub my feet," she commanded, "and by and by, I shall tell all."

I rushed to do her bidding, anxious to learn on which side of the ledger my sister was going to write her name. If she was opposed, there was little chance my father would agree to Janos' scheme to seek the Far Kingdoms. If her vote was yea, and she further agreed to smooth the way with our father, there was a small chance he might bless the plan and fund my maiden expedition.

Rali sighed as I coaxed the knots from her tired feet, and took another drink. "This soft life will be the death of me," she said. "Every day is the same. Up at daybreak to drill and train my women. Administrative work until dusk, and then I share a drink

64

and a roasted joint or two with Otara. By day's end I'm so weary with boredom, it's a small miracle if I have energy enough to give Otara a tumble. A situation she has been quick to deplore of late."

Otara was her lover of many years. She was a small, motherly woman of delicate beauty who doted on my sister and would fight to the death to keep her from harm. Not that Rali was likely to require help. She was tall, with long, cabled muscles and narrow hips. Rali was some ten years my senior and in her fighting prime. Swift as a direwolf in an attack and twice as deadly. She was equally skilled with sword, javelin, and her strong, ram's horn bow. But no one would ever mistake her for a man, nor did she ape men in her manners. Rali had a pleasing form and was willowy and delicate in her movements, although soldier plain in her talk. When I was small and still allowed in her bathchamber, I remember how struck I was at the smooth, milky color of her skin where the drill-field sun did not touch. Where my hair was fiery red, hers was the color of pale straw, and her eyes were as clear and blue as the seas.

"What I need is a good fight to get the blood up," Rali continued, as I rubbed at her sore feet. "Or at least a hard march with some purpose, other than training. An enemy to cow. A city to besiege." She raised the cup to her full lips and drank more. "But I haven't much hope such a thing will soon come to pass," she said. "The Magistrates are fearful of letting us march very far from Orissa. I think they believe a barbarian horde would be conjured up to ravage the city in our absence."

Rali was a captain in the Maranon Guard. In those times it was composed of five hundred warrior women, women who had taken a vow to Maranonia, the favored female deity of war. They forswore marriage, motherhood, or any of the "normal" functions of women in our culture. The guardswomen were highly trained and devoted to the defense of Orissa. Few were man haters, although all preferred other women as sexual partners.

"May I fetch you another cup of punch?" I asked. "Or something to eat? I could tote your bathwater, if you wish. Or any other errand suitable for a brother bent on groveling for his sister's favor. A sister as beautiful as she is wise. As soldierly as she is tender. As—"

"Stop before I throw up," my sister laughed. "All right, Amalric. You win."

I changed my foot rubbing into a light stroke. "Oh, speak to me, sibyl," I intoned. "Tell me what is in thy heart." Rali was stricken by a fit of giggles. Not from my cleverness so much as my skilled tickling of her feet. I had found her weak place when I was a small child and she was a green recruit.

My sister was one of the few people I had ever felt completely at ease with. There was no secret I would not confess to her, no sin she would not forgive. But she never took advantage of this trust by prying. I valued her advice above all others. It was for this reason, I suppose, I had stayed away from her during those months I was afflicted with Melina. I was too much in rut to want to hear good sense. But when I had finally come to her, Rali's words were similar to Janos'. She told me to tote the incident up to experience. "I'm not saying to go forth and sin no more," she'd said. "But I *am* saying, next time you might try sinning less expensively . . . and publicly." Then she'd fixed me with those clear blue eyes and asked what I intended to do next. "It is time I sought my Finding," I had answered, "and join our father in the business."

"Noble words, dear brother," she'd responded. "But I wonder if that is really what you *want* to do. I've suspected for some time your recent behavior might have a deeper cause than youthful folly. Perhaps you don't view the prospect of a trader's life with joy." I realized once again how perceptive my soldier sister was. Perhaps I *was* fighting a stodgy future, to be forced into the company of men who cared only for money.

"You see it exactly," I had cried. "If I am to be a merchantman like our father, I want to do much more than just take over the family business. I want to make my own mark and be more than the son of a rich man, living off our father's youthful deeds."

"How do you plan to accomplish this? Or, have you given this thought?" she'd asked.

I told her about the Far Kingdoms and my desire to make them the object of my Finding. And I told her of Janos. She'd listened closely, offering no opinion until I was done. Then she'd said, "I won't say nay. And I won't say yea. In fact, I will offer no view at all at this time. However . . . What I will do is to ask about. And when I have learned more, especially more of your *new* friend, Janos Greycloak, I will give you my decision."

Now it was time for the decision she'd promised. Although I joked and tickled, I awaited the outcome in agony. My sister pulled her feet away and sat straighter in the couch. "Fetch me another drink, please," she said, "and I will tell you what I have learned." In a moment she had her wish, and I sat there, barely able to breathe.

"You will forgive me, dear Amalric," she said, "for I went at this in an unkindly fashion. Rather than investigating the worthiness of your Finding to start with, I first sought evidence your friend is a scoundrel." A raised hand stopped my protest. "You must admit, your company of late has been questionable young men as well as women. For all I knew, Janos Greycloak was just a new, best friend." I bowed my head, admitting the truth.

"To begin with," she said, "I had a few quiet words with some of my acquaintances in the Magistrates' Own Guard. My conclusion is Janos is not only an excellent soldier, but a skilled leader and organizer." My breath *whoosh*ed in relief. "Don't be so quick," Rali warned. "All is not lightness. Captain Greycloak, it seems, is also a man who has earned his share of enemies during his short time in the Guard. But I think most of it is because of jealousy. Also his confident manner would anger many of those rich whoresons who lead their soldiery from a favorite tavern."

I broke in. "There is also his ancestry, and the time he spent in the service of the Lycanthians."

"I realize that," my sister answered. "But in an odd fashion, these facts end up speaking well for him. Janos' mother was an Orissan, a member of the Kether family. She had a reputation as a hotheaded maid with a stubbornly romantic streak. Janos' father was a prince from Kostroma, who paid a rare trading visit to Orissa, where he met the young Kether woman. They fell in love. It was quite a scandal at the time. Especially since Janos' mother defied the wishes of her family and ran off with the dashing young prince. I believe they are both dead now. Although no one knows the circumstance."

This partly explained Janos' reluctance to tell me much about his parents. "How he came to serve the Lycanthians," my sister continued, "I do not know. Although I suspect he needed some means of earning his way after his father and mother died."

"He is quite poor," I said. "It was my impression he is using all of whatever savings he has to maintain himself in the Guard."

"Exactly so," my sister said. "He obviously viewed it as an investment. So he could meet the right people to further his career."

"And I am that right person?" I asked, worried once more. Had I been played for the fool again?

My sister patted my hand. "Don't be so quick to judge where I'm going," she said. "He may be poor, but I do not think money is his goal."

"He said that himself," I said, a bit hotly, sorry I hadn't defended him a moment ago.

"It seems the Kether family—or what is left of it—stewed for quite some time when Janos showed up in Orissa. They believed he would soon pay a visit, and make blood demands for assistance. They would have refused him, of course. Their view was he had no call, since his mother's direct line no longer exists. Her father, it is said, died of a broken heart after his daughter shamed him by taking up with a barbarian prince."

"But he didn't go, *did* he?" I said with satisfaction.

"Actually, he did. After a time, he called on his uncle. But to that great skinflint's relief, Captain Greycloak was not only respectful, but made sure his uncle understood he had no intentions of attempting to cash in on family connections."

"Well, good for Janos," I said.

"Yes. It does tend to show his intentions are honest. Unfortunately, it did nothing to stem the flow of coin from his purse." Rali finished her drink and set the goblet on a table. "To make sure of my impressions," she continued, "I went to visit him myself."

I was startled. I sat there, tense, waiting. "Well?" I prodded.

My sister laughed. "I think your friend is mad, bad, and dangerous to know." I frowned, puzzled at her comments and laughter. "Especially for women," she said. "He knows how to speak with a woman, to compliment her mind rather than her appearance. And he looks you straight in the eye, weighing your every word, as if each were a treasure. We had a lovely talk. Near the end he made it known—in a subtle, gentlemanly way—he would have loved nothing more than to bed me!"

"What?" I almost shouted this, angry at Janos for insulting my sister.

Rali only laughed harder. "Oh, you should see your face. Together with your hair, you could light an arena at the dark of the moon. Don't be so protective. Especially when it isn't necessary. As I said, he was very gentlemanly about it, only hinting. Quite flattering, actually. As a matter of fact, if I were ever to consider bedding a man—disgusting thought that it is—your friend would be an early choice. He is *most* attractive. If it weren't for that scar, he would be almost too handsome."

I was soothed, happy. "Then you approve of Janos?"

"I do, indeed. He is a good soldier. A practical soldier. And I believe he would do all he could to make sure you returned safely from your Finding."

"What of the venture itself?" I asked. "My plan to seek the Far Kingdoms."

"I think it is insane," my sister announced, becoming serious.

"But I think you would regret it the rest of your life if you did not go."

She leaned forward, intent on what she was going to say. "In a way, I'm jealous of you, Amalric. A jealousy that makes me angry at all men. When I was a girl, I dreamed of such adventure. But I quickly learned my sex doomed me at birth. I could marry and bear children for some pig of a husband who would command every moment of my time. I could be a concubine, which considering my tastes, would be an equal hell. Although even that would have been denied me, since I am the daughter of a noble family. Thank the gods I was born with the Antero gift for athletics and a loving father *and* mother understanding enough to allow me to enter the Maranon Guard. Believe me, I prefer this boredom to any other offered to my sisters in this city."

"So you will press my cause with our father?" I asked.

"I will. But for a reason much deeper than satisfying a youthful wanderlust. If you are successful, you will strike a blow for the entire Antero family. And we can end these whispers about us that emanate from the Council of Evocators. Halab will not be revenged. But at least our poor brother will sleep in peace."

"I thought I saw his ghost the other night at a tavern," I said. "The night I met Janos. He smiled at me. And raised his thumb in encouragement."

"An excellent omen," my sister said. "Halab's ghost must have suspected what was going to happen."

A long silence fell. It was always thus when Halab's name was mentioned. It had been his bad luck to lead the family into the path of the Evocators. It was his worse luck to be born with an Evocator's talent. As a child, he was seer enough to frighten the maids with predictions of unwanted pregnancies that proved true. Rali confessed once that Halab had known in advance our mother was to die, and spent six months in silent mourning before that event came about.

I remember only a few boy's tricks he played to amuse or soothe me. I had had a pet ferret I carried everywhere. It lived and dined in my pocket and slept by my pillow at night. My pet sickened and died. This was shortly after my mother's death, so the loss was an awful blow for one so young. I mourned so deeply I grew ill myself and almost died of a fever. But Halab dug the ferret up from the garden grave I'd buried it in. I remember wakening to his chants. He was sitting on the floor by my bed, dangling the withered corpse of the tiny beast over a blue flame licking up from a copper bowl. I smelled the odor of putrid flesh burning.

Halab sprinkled a powder into the flame, continuing his chant, and suddenly the awful odor became wondrously sweet. Then he breathed on the dead animal, twirling it about by its tail.

He placed it on my chest and put my hand on top of the cold body. "Breathe on it, Amalric," he said, his voice so gentle I can hear it across time. I breathed. And I felt the cold turn to warmth. Then a stirring. Then a squeak. And my pet's nose poked out between my fingers. I gave a loud cry of joy as its masked face appeared next, little eyes bright with life. They say my fever broke an hour later. Within a week I was jumping about as pesky as ever, my little ferret in my pocket.

To this day, when I think of that time, I don't know whether to smile or weep. We all loved my brother and were in awe of his gifts. I realize now that for my father, the awe was tempered by trepidation. My brother was intent on becoming an Evocator. He wanted the knowledge only they could teach. But his desire for these powers went at cross purposes to the politics of the times. My brother was an idealist, a romantic who saw his gifts being used to benefit the people of Orissa. He dreamed of curing the ill and easing the plight of the poor and enslaved.

The Council of Evocators, however, was intent on maintaining its influence over Orissa. No Magistrate, regardless of the importance or antiquity of his family, could act without its blessing. No merchant, craftsman, shopkeeper, or courtesan could ply his or her trade without paying the mandated tithe. My brother was honest and open in his ambition. It was only with great reluctance that the Evocators agreed to consider accepting him into their company. They tested him more thoroughly, my sister told me, than most. And they were rude in their questioning, as if he were of low or questionable birth.

The Evocators rejected him, saying he had failed. But Halab was not to be discouraged. He demanded the ultimate test: Trial by Ordeal. The entire city, I was told, was abuzz when that day approached. My brother had refused to accept the wisdom of the Council and chose to take his case directly to the gods. The details of the trial were secret, but all knew that failure meant death. He entered the temple that day—and never returned. The Evocators sent word he had died. But there would be no corpse for the family to honor. No rites performed to ease his passage. Halab's ghost was doomed to wander a cold limbo world between this life and the next.

It was a high price we all paid for Halab's dreams. My brothers complained of it frequently in private. But they were meek men who crept around the shame. My father also never spoke of it publicly. Not out of fear for himself, but for his family and the generations to come. I do know he hated the Evocators. It was a hate he shared with my sister and myself.

Rali stirred on the couch. She smiled at me, but I could tell from the weary tilt of her lips, her thoughts had roamed the same gloomy woods as my own. "Give me a week," she said. "You know how Father dotes on me. But I'll still need time to work my daughterly wiles."

"Take Otara with you when you visit," I advised. "He always enjoys her company."

"Oh, I will. I will. But you must promise me one thing, darling brother," she said.

"Anything. Name the mountain, and I'll climb it. The desert, and I'll cross it. The treasure, and I'll steal it."

"Can you stay out of trouble?"

"Much more difficult," I said. "But I'll try my best . . . I promise."

"I AM NOT inclined to favor this expedition," my father said. His words caught me unprepared. Rali had laid the groundwork well, and I had been certain he would approve.

"You must, Father," I pleaded. "I doubt there shall ever be such an opportunity in my lifetime. Please, you must give me your blessing."

"There is nothing I *must* do, Amalric," my father replied. "Except pay my tithes to the Council of Evocators, my taxes to the Magistrates, and a gold coin to the Seeker, to make my passage to the other world painless and swift. These things, I *must* do. Favoring a foolish voyage by a hotheaded stripling of a son is fortunately not a requirement of my existence."

"Forgive me for using that word, Father," I said, chastened. "But please tell me what I can say to convince you. Is it the goal itself you find unworthy? Do you doubt the existence of the Far Kingdoms?" My father only looked at me. Not angrily, not sternly, but with great weariness. He did not have to use words to answer. I remember my father being very old at that time, although I am much older now than he was on that day of confrontation. His hair was white, close cropped like a helmet, in the manner of his generation. He had a small, neat beard—also white. His face was lined and his skin leathered from exposure in his travels. His hands were larger than most and spotted with age. But I realize now Paphos Karima Antero—the patriarch of our family—was only a few years past his prime, and the great age I recall is more a view from my own, very tender years. He seemed so *wise*, then. I suppose I viewed him a bit like a god. So when he fixed me with that look, my heart sank and I felt small and unworthy. For I saw it was *myself* who was lacking. *I* was the reason the journey to the Far Kingdoms was not to be.

Except for the crackling of the fire in the stone hollow behind my father's desk against the chill only he felt, there was no sound in the room as I considered how to plead my cause. "I know I have been a grave disappointment to you, Father," I said at last. "My conduct has been unforgivable. To say I am deeply and truly sorry would be such a weak repayment for my sins that no apology—no matter how abject—should weigh the balance in my favor."

My father continued his steady, testing gaze.

"This may appear like a sudden, wild enthusiasm on my part. And considering my past history, I would also reject my plan, if I were a father with such a son. But, I beg you, sir, to look into my heart and see the truth that lies there. I desire nothing more than to please you. To wipe away all thought of suspicion of my future motives. To be worthy of the Antero name, so my father can speak proudly in the marketplace." I fell silent, not sure how to proceed.

"Is that all you have to say?" my father asked, voice harsh.

"No, sir. I also wish to make clear that no matter what your decision, I shall accept it without complaint, and I shall do my best to accomplish whatever Finding you deem worthy for one such as me. However, before you firmly shut the door, sir, please consider this. For most men my age, a Finding is only an excuse to travel and pleasure themselves at their fathers' expense. No new ground is ever broken. Knowledge of the world is not expanded. And our trade routes still bump against the same forces that keep Orissans from achieving their true purpose. Your generation was the last to push those bounds back, sir. You, yourself, dared to redraw the maps with your Finding many years ago. And much of our knowledge of the furthest western regions comes from your later trading expeditions. But you must admit, the tradition of Finding One's Tradewind has become a mockery in these days. It is an excuse for the sons of the rich to spend their fathers' money on foreign luxuries and women and wine, out of sight of prudish Orissan eyes. And they return with nothing but a firsthand knowledge of the best taverns and sporting houses in the civilized world."

"You propose to be different?" my father said, dryly.

"Yes, I do, Father. For this reason, I ask for no more than a tenth of the funds usually allotted. This is to be a *real* Finding, sir. I will not purchase a fancy wardrobe to impress the courtesans. Nor do I request coin for an entourage of my friends as is the current custom. Nor do I desire any of the luxuries such caravans usually carry: fine tents and carpets and pillows to ease the passage; wines and delicacies to soothe the pallet after much barbarian fare; slaves to do all the labor; or women to relieve our passions when local pleasures are denied us. I intend for this expedition to be as lean and professionally equipped as I can make it. And with such a small expense there is a good possibility it will be profitable, even if we do not reach our goal. I further believe, sir, that I was most fortunate in meeting Captain Greycloak, a man whose presence doubly assures success in any such venture."

"What if I approved the Finding, but to a different destination?" my father asked.

"I would do the same in all things, sir," I answered. "Except I would not do it so well, because I would not have Captain Greycloak in my company. I would be disappointed, to be sure. But proving to you my worthiness, Father, is more important to me than avoiding disappointment." I stopped, then. For no other arguments presented themselves. I braced for his rejection. Begging Halab's ghost to help me take his refusal well.

There came a tapping at the door. My father's servant, Tegry, poked his head in. I saw a small grin of pleasure on his features. It grew larger when he spied my obvious discomfort. He was chuckling to himself, no doubt, that I was finally to get proper punishment for my actions.

"What is it?" my father asked, testy. Tegry's grin vanished. My father's tone was dangerous.

"You asked to be informed, master, when Captain Greycloak arrived."

I was dismayed. Obviously, my father had asked Janos to attend my final humiliation. I tried not to be angry because this would be a rudeness to Janos as well. "Send him in," my father said. "And bring us some wine. None of that vinegar from the marketplace, mind you. Fetch a good bottle from my cellar." My gut wrenched as Tegry shot a nasty look in my direction and disappeared to do as he was told.

My father's actions were very puzzling. What he said to me next was more puzzling still. "For once, I do not quarrel with the company you keep. And I did not rely alone on your sister's evaluation of Janos Greycloak. Captain Greycloak seems to be an excellent soldier to command the military side of such an expedition ... if it is approved. I was impressed enough with him, as a matter of fact, to invite him here to personally tell him I find no fault in his character. It would be rude to do otherwise."

I heard Janos' boot steps in the hallway, and I wanted to slink away like an incontinent mongrel who had just fouled his favorite spot by the fire. "Come in, my good captain," my father called with loud cheer when Tegry announced Janos. "Thank you for being so prompt in answering my request."

Janos had dressed with care and made a fine impression as he entered and bowed low. "It was my own great pleasure in your kind invitation that brought me so swiftly, Lord Antero," Janos answered.

"Here, none of that," my father said. "We should speak as equals, if you are to lead my son's expedition to the Far Kingdoms. Call me Paphos, sir ... if you please."

My jaw was polishing the hardwood floor. My head was spinning with first confusion, then sheer joy. Tears sprung to my eyes, and I felt a lump in my throat threatening to become a great sob of relief. I wanted to fling myself at my father's feet and babble my thanks.

My father smiled and gave me a wink. "Pour us a little of that wine that Tegry has fetched, Amalric," he said. "I want Janos' opinion of it."

I poured and passed the goblets around. Janos gave me an odd look, but I turned away so I wouldn't make a complete ass of myself. I barely heard the conversation that ensued over the next hour. The exchange must have been pleasant, as well as to Janos' credit, for there was much laughter at my father's jests and respectful silences when he related some of his favorite adventures.

I kept wondering—what had I missed? A moment before my Finding had been denied. Now it had been heartily approved and was being blessed with toasts of my father's best wine. In other words, where had I gone right? What had I said to change the notoriously stubborn mind of one Paphos Karima Antero? Then I understood, at least partly. His refusal had been a test. It wasn't *what* I had said that won the day, but the heartfelt passion of my defense. It was a ploy I have used many times myself since that day. It has served me well.

"There is one matter we need to be absolutely certain of from the beginning," I heard my father tell Janos.

"And what is that, sir?" Janos asked.

"In my experience, one of the greatest causes for an expedition's failure is that a clear line of authority and responsibility is not drawn."

"Your wisdom is much greater than mine," Janos said. "So I would not presume to argue such a thing. Especially since my own small experience bears your words out as complete and total truth."

"Good," my father said. "Then you will not quarrel with my first and only rule. In all matters relating to the safety of the expedition, you will be in charge. My son will in no way interfere with your dealings with the soldiers.

"However ... In all matters of business, of budget, or of trade, my son's word is law. It is *his* Finding. *His* expedition. And he shall answer to me at the end for success or failure. Is this agreed?"

"Without the slightest hesitation, sir," Janos said.

My father turned to me. "Amalric ... If there is to be argument about this, now is the time. You don't want to leave it until you're in the desert and a horde of demons comes charging over the dunes. So ... Do you agree as well?"

I was still too gripped by emotion to do more than nod vigorously and croak my acceptance.

Janos broke in. "If I may be so bold, sir," he said, "I have a small proviso of my own."

His words rocked me. What was he doing? My father had already agreed. Why was Janos pressing for more? I was certain my father would cancel his approval on the spot.

"And what would that be, Captain?" I heard my father answer, amazed at the jovial tone of his voice.

"I only want to know your opinion of our ultimate goal, sir. For I must warn you, that I will risk anything we have won, once we near that destination. But, if you think it is only a fable we seek ... now is the time for us to part company."

That's torn it, I thought. My father was not a man for fables. I was getting my way, I thought, only because he thought there was a good chance of profit in the voyage. It didn't matter what the goal was, as long as there was a chance for trade along the way. And now all his good will would be dashed by Janos' ultimatum. Still, I was curious how he would react. I remembered it was a question I had asked ... and gotten no answer.

I expected to see fury in my father's face. Instead, it was gentle, reflective if anything. "That's fair," he said at last. "I would want to know the same if I were in your boots." He refilled his glass and sipped. "We share a common dream, Captain," he said at last. "The Far Kingdoms have held me in their spell since I was a child."

He must have heard me gasp, for he turned his head and gave me an odd, twisted smile. "I've never told anyone this," he said to me. "But I once sat where you sit now, son. Pleading with my own father to go on such an expedition to the east. He refused me. And I have regretted it every day since that moment."

I stumbled for words. A moment ago, in my thoughts, I was accusing my father of being a profit-hungry merchant, with a soul too small for fables or dreams. "But . . . How could he? Everyone knows you were a great voyager. Why, many of our trade routes would not exist if it weren't for you."

My father waved the praise away. "Anyone could have done the same. This is not humility speaking, for the gods know I am not a humble man. The fact is, few young men set out on really important Findings in my day. So it was easy to stand out in so small a company. I saw then Orissa's world was shrinking, not expanding. And it has only grown worse since our victory over Lycanth. Now it takes small effort to be a rich man. We only have to ply the nice, safe ports of the past. Which is why there have been so few important explorations since my time. And this is the reason I give my blessing. If Orissa does not seek, then soon it will not exist."

"Then you *do* believe in the Far Kingdoms?" I asked.

My father hesitated for a long moment. Then, "Let me put it this way . . . I prefer to believe. There must always be a place for seekers to seek. We are all born with the curse of a yearning heart. And if the answer is only an extra crust of bread snatched from our brethren, then what is the point of it all? So I give you my blessing, son. And you, too, good captain. Seek the Far Kingdoms. Find them, if you can. By the gods, if the Far Kingdoms *do* exist, I will go to my grave a happy man, knowing an Antero breathed their air." He raised his goblet to his lips and drank it dry. "Is that answer enough, Captain?" he asked, briskly.

"More than I could have ever asked, sir," Janos answered, his voice as respectful as I would ever hear it. "I thank you."

"No thanks required," my father said. He turned to me. "It is settled, then. Now, all that impedes you is permission from the Council of Evocators."

My heart gave a jolt. I had forgotten about the Evocators. No trading expedition was permitted without their approval, and that approval could not be won unless money and promises of more money exchanged hands. Even this was no guarantee that the omens would be favorable. Especially for a venture like this, a venture I had boasted to my father was far from the ordinary Findings of my peers. There would be a casting. How the Evocators would read those bones was always in doubt. Especially for an Antero.

My father read my face and refilled our glasses. "Let me see how I can help you," he said. "I have a few debts owed that are far past repayment. Meanwhile . . ." He lifted his goblet. "To the Far Kingdoms!"

"To the Far Kingdoms," we echoed. As we drank I looked across my goblet at Janos. He was smiling, but the smile seemed uncertain. At least I wasn't the only one worrying about the Council of Evocators.

IN THE DAYS of my Finding the budgeting of an expedition was done by what we merchantmen called the Rule of Three. One part of the cost went to equipment, the second to the men of the party, and the third for the gods. Profits of a successful expedition were divided by the Rule of Four: two parts for the merchant and backers, one part for the members of the expedition or their survivors at home, and the final part was once again for the gods. The Evocators collected the gods' coin, and it was the joke at the time that the eldest Evocator threw all the coins into the air. Whatever stayed up remained with the gods. Whatever fell to the floor was for the Evocators.

Unfortunately for the purposes of true accounting, neither rule was completely accurate. The cost of just securing an appointment before the Council could add up to a small river of silver as the merchant slipped "gifts" to Evocator clerks and priestly aides. An even more princely "gift" would have to be given to one of the members of the Council to champion the merchantman's cause before his colleagues. There was no getting around this, although it was rumored many had tried, been caught, and then banned from all trade for life—assuming the Evocators had been kind enough to leave the errant trader a life to suffer.

Next came lengthy and expensive purification rites, and then a Casting of the Bones by one of the supplicants. A good omen was not necessarily assured, even if that small river of coin were a flood. For sometimes an ill omen was so powerful it was impossible to deny. But a bad omen *was* guaranteed if the merchantman was niggardly in distributing the "gifts." As for the four rules of profit division, a wise merchant sweetened the part collected by the Evocators with more handfuls of silver—privately disbursed. This was to get past another Orissan law, which stated that every object borne by the returning expedition must be tested for spiritual purity. It was also a given, and no amount of "gifting" could circumvent this, that anything that advanced sorcerous knowledge automatically belonged to the Evocators. Any book, talisman, powder, or potion that met this definition had to be immediately turned over to the Council. The penalty for breaking this law was death.

Since my Finding was for the explicit purpose of mapping a route through the mysterious and deadly barriers—some physical, some sorcerous—that so narrowed our world at that time, a great deal of attention would be paid to this law. The Council of Evocators would require brassbound guarantees if it was to permit our expedition to the legendary Far Kingdoms.

But my father was an experienced and masterful hand in such things. In the art of wooing the Evocators, Paphos Karima Antero had few masters. Despite his unpopularity with the Council, he was so knowledgeable in negotiating the crooks and alcoves of its administrative maze, he rarely failed to win his way and at a better price than most. A stroke of a quill in a ledger book or its absence can sometimes have powerful results. So as I worried over my future from the perspective of a youth looking up at an enormous mountain that must be mastered, my father went to work—dropping a word here, a purse there, and cashing in old favors owed.

Finally the day came. It was early summer, a time of morning mists and warm afternoon suns. The scent of orange and budding rosemary pleasured the air. The sunlight seemed exceptionally bright. We waited in the gardens behind the Evocators' Palace. We wore the pure white robes of supplicants and were freshly scrubbed and anointed with purification oils. Our innards were growling with emptiness from the three-day fast and purging required for the rites. My tension was heightened by my father's last words as we left the house. "Be on your guard," he'd warned. "Do exactly as you are told . . . and nothing more. The destination you chose for your Finding has aroused the interests of our enemies. They will be watching and listening closely."

Janos was unusually silent as well. I glanced over the head of the small clerk whose charge we were in and saw him nervously fingering his beard. He saw me, and the frown on his face turned to a quick grin. "Nothing to worry about," he said. "The worst they can do is tell us no." I thought of Halab and did not answer.

A slave came running down the steps. "They are ready for you, masters," he said. The clerk tugged at my sleeve. "Put this on, sir," he said, handing me a long bit of red cloth. "Tie it tight and do not remove it until you are granted permission." As he handed a second blindfold to Janos, I breathed a prayer to our hearthgod and wrapped the cloth about my eyes until there was no more light. The clerk led us stumbling up broad stone steps and into the palace.

The place was a whirl of scents and odd noises: a mixture of perfumes and sulphur, jangling chimes and *tap tap tap*ping of hollow wood on stone. As we moved from room to room the air grew cold, then warm, then suddenly cold again. There were constant whispers, dark sibilants hissing from every corner. There came a *whoosh* of dry air as a large door opened, and we entered a room that smelled of shed lizard skin. A tug on my sleeve halted me.

"You may remove the cloths, gentle sirs," said a harsh voice. It was not the clerk's. I untied the blindfold and entered a world of gray stone and dirty yellow light. A robed figure stood before us. It was the Evocator Janos and I had encountered in the streets some time before.

"I bid you welcome, gentle sirs," he said. "My name is Jeneander. I am to be your guide on this reckoning day."

I stood mute for a moment, then felt Janos' elbow in my ribs. "Praise the gods you are to be our light," I intoned, and quickly took a purse from my robe and pressed it into Jeneander's eager hands. It disappeared as quickly as a sea lizard plucks a gull from the air.

Jeneander leaned closer and whispered, "I will leave for a few moments. Refresh yourselves with this in my absence." He passed us a small, oilcloth-wrapped bundle. "I am pleased to announce one of our most promising young Evocators has found favor with your proposed expedition," he said loudly. "He will be here presently to join in the Casting. You may know of him. His name is Cassini."

I buried a groan. "Good fortune continues to smile on us," I managed to reply. We exchanged bows with Jeneander, and he slipped away to prepare for the ceremony. I hastily unwrapped the bundle and found several large hunks of black bread drenched in wine. "But what of our fast?" I whispered to Janos. "I thought all food was forbidden?"

Janos chuckled and snagged a chunk of bread. "I have learned, my dear Amalric, there are as many shadings to that word as there are coins in a rich man's strong room." He wolfed down the bread. "Eat up. I believe our new friend was more worried about our food-starved wits than a minor bit of blasphemy." I ate, gobbling down the bread with gusto. Immediately my mood shifted, and I began to see things in a clearer light.

"Who is this Cassini?" Janos asked. "I thought we had a choice of the Evocator the Council will require to accompany our expedition."

"Sometimes," I said. "Sometimes not."

Janos eyed me. "From your expression—artfully guarded, I hasten to add—I got the impression you know of this Cassini."

"Dear me," said a voice. "It's only midday and already I hear my name being bandied about." We both turned to greet the speaker. He was a tall man—about my age—with not much flesh on his bones, and a soft, spoiled mouth. The Evocator's robes he wore were richly embroidered for one so young, indicating his family's wealth.

"Ah, there you are, Cassini," I replied. "I was just about to describe your charming personage to my companion ... Captain Janos Greycloak."

At my introduction, they bowed to one another. "Cassini and I were once comrades of the athletic field and tavern," I explained to Janos. "There were many who mourned the day he got the Calling and left us to our childish pursuits." Janos understood from the wag of a guarded finger, I was not among those who'd mourned. "We did not know each other that well, which was my misfortune and his good luck."

Cassini stepped forward, a prissy smile on those soft lips. "Then you are not disappointed that I have chosen to join your Finding? Please be truthful, my friend, if I can call you that."

"Oh, absolutely not," I lied. "Curse my seed if I should ever entertain such a thought."

I turned to Janos. "Our journey has been blessed from the start," I said. "For in Cassini you will find a studious and pious Evocator and a most amiable companion."

"Not so overly pious that I object to those morsels in your hands," Cassini said with an artificial laugh, pointing at the remains of the crust-and-wine feast. We had the good sense to blush and quickly rid ourselves of the evidence.

"Welcome to our ranks, good sir," Janos said. "I feel almost as if the Casting had been performed and we were already on our way, with a good omen lighting our path. May I ask what in particular allowed you to find favor with our efforts?"

"Why, the goal, of course," Cassini said.

"Then you are not among those who question the existence of the Far Kingdoms?"

"I wouldn't go that far," Cassini answered. "There is not yet enough evidence to make up my mind to the matter. However, the effort itself is certainly worthy. No matter what the truth turns out to be, I would be honored to carry the news back to my elders."

Janos nodded, showing he understood. From the gleam in his eye, I saw he understood more deeply than Cassini intended. For Cassini was a young man of favored birth, but little talent. I doubt, in fact, if he had a tenth of the talent of my brother. Wealth and family connections had won him membership into the Evocators. But now his career was stalled—perhaps permanently. He badly needed a great success to shake off the torpor. In the Far Kingdoms, he saw his chance. Janos realized Cassini was acting out of private desperation, for there was an edge to the Evocator's tone, a forced calmness to his manner, betrayed by shifting feet and fidgeting hands.

"You were right in thinking there is much to be gained from this expedition," Janos said. "But I would be doing you a disservice if I did not point out there is grave danger as well. No one has gone where we intend to go ... and returned to tell about it."

"I am but an empty vessel for the gods to fill, or break," Cassini said. "Knowledge of their design is its own reward." The usual uncomfortable silence followed this sticky, false modesty, broken by Jeneander's return.

He greeted Cassini with a smile. "Now the third adventurer has joined us." He motioned. "Come. The Council awaits."

We followed through heavy curtains down a long passageway lit by fire beads dangling from the heads of old gods and the fanged beasts who were once their Favorites. They cast eerie shadows on the walls: horns and long teeth and sharp talons. The passageway spilled into an immense dark cavern of a room. Jeneander led us to a stone platform raised several feet off the floor. It was ringed by great torches that guttered, smoked, and sparked. We stood there blinking for long moments, trying to get our bearings. I cannot speak for Janos, but my own heart was full of dread. It gave a hard jolt as a great voice rang out, "Who are these mortals who stand before us?"

"Seekers of the way of Orissa, my lords," Jeneander answered.

"And who attests to their piety and worth?"

"I do, my lords. I . . . Jeneander bring them before you."

"Who shall speak for them?"

Silence. Then I felt Janos' toe jab my heel. My wits returned to some manner of order. "I speak for them, my lords," I answered. "I, Amalric, son of thy daughter, Emilie; son of thy son, Paphos Karima Antero."

I could see more clearly now. Just in front of the platform was bare stone floor. It was graven with sorcerous squares, triangles, and mysterious numbers and symbols. The whole was enclosed in an enormous circle, outlined in pure gold leaf. The Council of Evocators sat on the other side of the circle in all its black-robed and gold-sashed glory. There were ten of them, and they sat on thrones of carved emerald. The wall above was a swirl of color and smoke and writhing shadow forms. The speaker sat on the center throne. He had a wrinkled, hawklike visage, as if someone had carved that bird of prey from an apple and then let it shrink and dry. His hair and beard were gleaming white and spilled down as if they had not been cut for years. His eyes were smoldering yellow and seemed to pierce my soul. It was Gamelan, the eldest of the Evocators.

"And what is the nature of your quest, Amalric, son of Emilie, son of Paphos Karima Antero?" Gamelan asked.

"We seek the Far Kingdoms, my lords. For the greater good of Orissa and the glory of her gods."

There was a pause as the Evocators whispered among themselves. I did not know if this was the usual practice, but saw from Cassini's worried look it was not. Finally Gamelan spoke. "There is one among you who is a stranger, but who was born from the womb of a daughter of Orissa."

"I am that man, my lords," Janos answered. "Janos, son of Kether; son of Prince Greycloak of Kostroma."

"We have heard you have some interest in the Evocator's art."

Fear seized my heart. What was the purpose of this question? Who was spreading tales about my friend? There seemed to be no safe answer. Seers are all knowing, so if Janos denied it, he was impugning their power. But if he admitted it, Halab's way might lie ahead. "It is true," Janos answered swiftly, "I have a small talent, but none of it comes from wizardry or witchcraft, I assure you. As a soldier amongst the barbarian Lycanthians I was forced to rely on my own Orissan-blessed wits. I have had some success with the boils and foot rot that afflicted my men. And I once cured an arse wound inflicted on my sergeant."

I thought I heard stifled laughter amongst the Evocators. But it

must have been my nervous imagination, for was not laughter unseemly amongst such an exalted group? "Once I kissed Orissa's
gates," Janos continued, "I quickly threw away what little I had
learned. I believe that even the curing of boils is foolhardy without professional counsel. And when I learned just moments ago
that one of the most skillful young Evocators in all the realm was
to accompany us on our journey, I immediately promised a fat
lamb for the god who chose to smile on us."

I could almost feel Cassini preen, his ego spreading like a pea-
cock in its mating dance. From the nods amongst the Evocators I
could see that Janos' answer had found favor. "Very well, then,"
Gamelan said when the whispering had ceased. "The time has
come to cast the bones. Are you ready, Amalric Emilie Antero?"

"I am ready, my lords," I answered.

Jeneander stepped up to me and opened an ornate box. It was
divided into two compartments. On one side were two thick
chunks of what appeared to be the thigh of some creature. On the
other were the fragments of a human skull. But which to choose
first? My hand hesitated, then some power seized it and drew it
to the left. I took the thigh bones from the box. I clutched them
in my right fist, and with my left struck my breast five times as
I intoned, "Oh, great Lord Te-Date—god and protector of all
wayfarers—I summon thy vision for our holy quest to the Far
Kingdoms." I tossed the bones into the golden circle. Then I drew
out the skull fragments, struck my breast thrice more, and completed the incantation. "Bless us great Lord Te-Date with thy wisdom. And in these bones reveal our fates." The fragments gave up
a dry rattle as I cast them beside the others.

A silence followed that knows no equal in the world of men.
A cold darkness crept in until only the glowing circle could be
seen, but my scalp prickled and burned as if I were near a great
heat. My tongue grew as dry as lizard scales, and my eyes became
hot, tearless holes. The thigh bones moved. They rose from the
floor, and the sound of their scraping against the stone injured my
ears with unnatural loudness. They hovered for a moment, then
moved slowly together until they touched. At the click of their
touching, red smoke and sulphur clouds erupted. An unreasoning
terror gripped me, and I wanted to flee, but a great force held me.
The cloud swirled and sparked and took form. A great beast
emerged from the cloud, snarling and roaring and rattling its talons. It towered over us on two massive legs, lashing its sharp-
spined tail. The beast was horned, with fiery red eyes and
blood-dripping teeth the size of my forearm. Its scales were the

green of a corpse from the river. The demon turned this way and that, looking for its enemy. It spied me. As I looked in those eyes I thought I had never seen such evil.

It shrieked and leaped forward, and I heard a long gasp in the chamber as it bounded over the barrier of the gold circle. Once again I tried to bolt, but I was as pinioned as a victim staked for sacrifice. The demon's jaws gaped, and I was nearly overcome by a hot breath that smelled of all the dead and foul things of this world and others beyond. The beast leaned forward to take me with those massive teeth. Suddenly there came a heavy drumming *boom* that thundered through the Evocators' cavern. The demon stopped. I was inches from death. The *boom* sounded again, jarring my bones.

The beast turned, its horned head arcing back toward the golden circle. I saw the head jolt as the beast spotted something. It gave a shriek that turned the air white hot. It leaped forward, taloned paws coming up to do battle, and I could finally see its enemy. A naked, unarmed man stood where I had cast the skull fragments. But he was like no manner of man I had seen before—or since. He was not tall, but thick and powerfully built, with stubbed columns for legs and arms. His chest and back were densely pelted, and his face was a jut of heavy beard. His jaw was slung forward and dark holes for eyes glared from under a sloping brow, armored with bone. The man roared at the demon and stamped a foot upon the stone. *Boom.* The chamber shuddered. He slammed down the other foot. *Boom.* Again and again came the challenge. *Boom. Boom. Boom.* All three of us knew our hopes rested upon that naked, weaponless man.

He leaped to meet the demon's charge and gave it a blow with his fist that rocked the room. The beast staggered backward, and the man bared yellow fangs and braced to jump for its throat. A groan burst from my lips as the demon spewed fire and smoke from its mouth, blinding our champion. The man stumbled and the demon was on him, teeth crunching bone. The beast gripped the man between its jaws, shook his body in a shower of gore, then hurled the corpse to the stone. The demon lifted its horned head and trumpeted conquest. As my ears rang with the sound of its awful joy, I knew our dreams of the Far Kingdom had been dashed.

My heart surged into my throat as I saw the corpse of our champion come to life. The naked man rolled to his feet. There was not a sign of a wound upon his flesh. He stamped once, and the *boom* rocked us again. The demon jolted, fanged jaw gaping in surprise. Then it recovered and lashed out with its sharp-spined tail. But our champion hurdled the blow and struck the demon in the chest. There was a loud, dry crack of bone collapsing, and the demon howled in agony. The man bounded upward and gripped the beast by the neck. He wrapped those columned arms about the demon and gave a mighty wrench. There was a scream and snap, and the man leaped away as the demon tumbled to the floor. Our champion turned to us. Raised his hands high in victory and gave out a great bellow. There came a rush of white, sweet-smelling smoke ... and he was gone.

The smoke parted and became a window to a distant place. The image took my breath away. I saw green forest, silver streams, and a rugged plain the color of mustard in bloom. Beyond that, hunched upon the horizon, was a mountain range. It sat upon the land like a big-knuckled fist. There were four squat peaks in the range, with a curved fifth that made the clenched thumb. The peaks were of black volcanic rock, dusted with snow. Snow drifts picked out each digit of the fist. The valley between the thumb and forefinger rose smoothly upward—passage through that black range.

A passage to ... my thought was completed by Janos' whisper of awe ... "... the Far Kingdoms." I was uplifted by that truth. I was light as a kite and yearned to fly to that distant land and see for myself. A land no one in the known world had walked before.

A shriek rent the image, and it was gone. I gaped as I saw the demon rise, unblemished and strong as before. Across from it stood the naked man. He stamped his booming challenge, the demon roared its return, and they charged across the circle at one another. But before the combatants could meet, they vanished. The golden circle was empty.

I blinked as the black gloom was swept away. I turned to look at Janos. His face was bloodless above the beard, but his eyes were alive with inner fire. He looked at me as if to speak, then shook his head. Cassini stirred beside me. I turned and our eyes met. His were as alive as Janos', but it was greed and ambition that fired them. I'm not sure I realized that then. Perhaps I am coloring my memory. I do remember I felt joy ... and uneasiness.

"Praise be Te-Date," Gamelan said, from across the chamber, "protector of the weary traveler."

"Praise be Te-Date," we all murmured in return.

"The omen is clear," Gamelan said. "Your expedition has equal chance of success or failure."

"But at least we know the goal is worthy, holy one," Cassini said. It was his right as our Evocator to reply. "The omen portended the Far Kingdoms lie just beyond the black mountains that look like a fist."

"Do not let your wishes cloud your reasoning powers, young brother," Gamelan admonished. "The vision was of mountains—not of what lies beyond." Cassini hesitated and I feared in that pause our chance might be lost. The omen said neither yea nor nay. The final decision still rested with the Council of Evocators.

"May I speak, lords?" Janos asked. Gamelan nodded, giving him permission. "You say there is grave danger ahead, with the outcome of the expedition in doubt?"

"So speaks the omen," Gamelan agreed.

"But was there any danger for Orissa? Will anyone be threatened, or suffer if we fail?"

"Only your families," Gamelan said. "For failure will mean certain death. In that, the omen was plain."

"Every man here is willing to risk it, my lords," I broke in. "In our hearts we all know great glory can come of this. Glory for our dear Orissa—flower of all the civilized world."

The Evocators considered at length, then exchanged a few whispers. Finally, Gamelan turned to us. "Permission is granted," he said. "All praise Te-Date."

"All praise Te-Date." Our reply was a shout. In my mind the image rose of the fisted mountains and the snowy passage that led through them. And for a moment I thought I saw a glimmer. Just a flash of golden light where the thumb and forefinger met. A flash where the Far Kingdoms awaited.

CHAPTER SIX
Lycanth

THE GODS SHOULD have set the scene more carefully: the day was sunny, the cloudless sky a soft blue, and a gentle breeze, tangy with salt, blew off the sea below us. Against this gentle backdrop rose Lycanth, a most inappropriate city to see on such a day. The weather should have been dark, with storm clouds scudding across the sky. An icy wind should have keened like lost souls; and the sea should have been a gray and white maelstrom. This was the nightmare panoply that Lycanth deserved.

It has changed much since then, so let me describe it thoroughly. Lycanth was built at the end of a peninsula, a peninsula whose tip hooks like a crooked finger. In that crook is one of the greatest deep-water harbors known. I heard a sage say the peninsula once had a volcano at its end; when it erupted, aeons before man broke his chains and escaped from Godhome to settle the earth, fire fought with water; but the sea, as always, was the victor. The harbor is the crater of that volcano, a volcano many Orissans wish would return to life, because Lycanth has been the cause of many deaths and sorrow for our city. The crater is steeply cliffed, and there is but one way down from the peninsula to the harbor—a gently shelving passage that might be a lava slide that solidified. The passage has been smoothed by man and time until it is as regular as a sculpted ramp. Around the harbor and down the peninsula's neck, the men who became known as Lycanthians built their city.

The peninsula is narrow, so where we built Orissa as a sprawl across rolling hills, the Lycanthians built upward, and tall buildings stretched toward the sky—buildings that looked to have been carved from a single stone by a dark giant. The sun would shine for only a few moments each day in the streets below the buildings. Janos had told me these buildings were warrens, crowded with apartments and workplaces. The higher the floor, the more expensive the dwelling. But the eye barely noted these stone towers at first. It was drawn to the brooding sea castle at the tip of the peninsula. From here the two Priest-Kings of Lycanth, the Archons, ruled—together with their council of sorcerers. In that castle were their treasure vaults and, far below, Lycanth's dripping dungeons and torture chambers.

The castle appeared impregnable. But it had been taken once, a battle that began in treachery and at night, and ended in fire and sword. It had fallen to Orissa twenty years before I was born in the final battle of the Second War of the Cities, when we regained our freedom from the occupiers whose heavy heel had been at our throats for five generations. Once the victory was in hand, however, instead of obliterating Lycanth and all Lycanthians from this world, we made an honorable peace. Our Magistrates reasoned that were there no Lycanth, another power could well rise up, one just as likely to be hostile. Or else, if unoccupied, the cursed land could provide a footing for anarchy. We were also unwilling to hold Lycanth as a vassal state—there is little profit in a garrisoned and hostile land. That was why the sea castle still loomed on its promontory. If the city was to be allowed to stand, common humanity and dignity before the gods required Lycanth to be able to defend itself against the pirates that swarmed the Narrow Sea. All we required was reparations for the damage done to Orissa, sacrifices to the ghosts of those killed during the two wars, and death gifts made to their survivors. There was one other requirement: a permanent reminder of their error in considering Orissa a city of fat merchants and powerless gods. So we ordered the destruction of the immense wall they'd built across the neck of the peninsula. We forced the secrets of the wall's protective spells from the sorcerers, and our mightiest Evocators combined powers in a massive enchantment of dissolution and decay. Their purification before undertaking the ritual filled more than a year, and the Spell Saying itself occupied a month. Three Evocators died in the enchanting, and even when it was finished, legions of Lycanthian war prisoners were required to clear the rubble, and in some cases topple still-standing stones.

As we drew closer to Lycanth, Eanes beckoned to me. I cantered back to him. Eanes, along with Sergeant Maeen and the ten guardsmen who'd volunteered to accompany Janos on my Finding, rode in a great ox-drawn charabanc, together with our baggage and the chests that contained our gold and silver. Janos, Cassini, and I were on horseback.

"Why," Eanes wondered, pointing at the still-blasted barrens where the wall had stood, "don't the Lycanthians build out here, now that their great battlement's been turned into anchor weights? Or are they afraid of forest spirits?"

"A good question, my friend," Janos said. "And there is a reason. Lycanth thinks it is shameful that their wall was torn down, and I have heard men growl that one day the wall will rise once more. So the statute limitations go no farther than this barrenness and no Lycanthian will build beyond, for fear he might be thought to approve of their defeat."

"We should have sold their men to the Ifora," Cassini said, "taken their women for our pleasure, turned the city stone from stone, and sowed the ground with salt. My skills do not extend far into prognostication as yet, but I feel in my bones, that we shall be troubled by Lycanth again."

"Harsh words," Janos said. "I am not sure I agree with you as to whether Lycanth should have been blotted out. Across the Narrow Sea, in Valaroi, what you suggest is the way wars are fought, and I have seen the results. But you are correct that Lycanth wishes to regain her old powers. When I was in their service I heard such talk constantly. And if they do, once again they will strike at Orissa. The Lycanthians have long memories for anything they consider a wrong. I found it necessary to guard my tongue closely—just as we must from this point forward. All of us may be Orissan, or in Orissan service, but stressing those facts will make us few new friends. Not here in Lycanth, nor, most likely, across the Narrow Sea in Valaroi. I do not know how long a reach Lycanth has in those parts, although I helped garrison many of those watchtowers we've seen for the last two days. We shall travel as anonymous traders, appearing to owe no allegiance to anyone. It is far safer."

He stopped himself and grinned, a bit shamefaced. "My apologies, Lord Amalric," he said, quite formal. "I meant, of course, that I would recommend such an appearance of neutrality to you . . . but the decision is certainly yours."

I laughed, taking no offense. Cassini might disapprove, but I refused to run my Finding as if it were as rank-bedazzled as any army. "Any one of us who thinks he knows a better way had better speak up, or else we stand no chance of reaching the Far Kingdoms. We will travel without banners or bugles, as you advise." Janos nodded, still looking a bit shamefaced.

Eanes chuckled and said very quietly, for my ears only, "I have heard that no lion eats carrion happily."

WE HAD MADE a quick, if cautious journey. The caution was especially necessary because of the amount of coinage I was required to carry. If my Finding had been a commonplace one, we would have had need for little cash, and whatever was necessary for trading and expenses could be drawn from local banks on my father's letter of credit. But since our voyage was to begin in Lycanth, this was not possible. The city was not only a longtime military foe, but a bitter trading rival as well. My father's most hated enemy, a clan named Symeon—now headed by its youngest, and my father swore most evil, son, Nisou—was Lycanthian. They had not only betrayed us in private third-party trading agreements, but, he was sure, used their knowledge of our trading practices to hire local raiders and ambush several of our caravans. He'd advised me to be most cautious when we were in Lycanth.

The journey had been without incident—except for the witch. The road had been narrow and rutted, running under huge, gnarled-branch trees. We were all nervous, since this would be a perfect place to be raided. Suddenly there was a woman in the middle of the road, blocking the way.

She was naked, but no man would feel lust stir his loins, not without a potion distilled ten times beyond the one I'd given Melina. I thought she was fairly young; but I was not sure, since she was filthy, as if her last bath had been the fluid in her mother's womb. Her blond hair scraggled around her face. Before the drivers could pull at their reins, she lifted one hand, palm toward us, and the oxen stopped as if they'd been slammed between the eyes with the butcher's hammer. I could hear the whispers from the soldiers, silenced by a mutter from Sergeant Maeen. She lifted her other hand: from it dangled a bit of rope. "A tribute . . . a love gift," she chanted.

"We pay no one, mother," the driver said.

She waved the rope. "Tribute . . . or this rope . . . this string . . . this yarn . . . dangling loose, dangling limp . . . brave soldiers . . . dangling limp, dangling loose, and none of you will be able to honor your women . . . dangling loose . . . dangling limp . . ." The soldiers stirred and their protests were audible, in spite of a barked command from Maeen.

Cassini slid from his horse and walked forward. He glanced up at where the sun shone through branches . . . then, smiling gently

. . . at the witch, "Ah woman, ah woman, you see that tree . . . you see that shadow . . . the shadow of that tree is that tree . . . that tree's roots reach deep, deep into the soil . . ." he chanted. "Like that tree you shall stand, you will stand, stand you must . . . and you will not be seen by any traveler . . . and the next by shall be an axe to that tree, as an axe to *your* tree."

The woman was a stark statue. I could see her lips try to move.

Cassini made a cruel laugh and said, "You may speak, you may speak, you have my blessing, oh tree."

"Your pardon, your pardon," the words came. "I knew not that there was one with Power among you. I beg forgiveness."

"Not from me, oh tree," Cassini said. "Beg pardon from these men you called brave soldiers."

"Men of iron, men of iron, you are like iron when you love, the rope is gone, the string is gone, the yarn is gone, it was never woven . . . you are iron, you are steel."

"We thank you, woman," Cassini said. He walked back to his horse and remounted. "Amalric," he asked, "is there a reason we cannot leave her to her fate?" A wail keened from her lips.

"You are tree, oh tree," the Evocator snapped, and there was silence. I looked at the petrified woman. No. There was no reason. I took three gold coins from my purse and dropped them in the road.

"She can go free," I said.

"You have heard, oh tree," Cassini said, reluctant. "You shall be free, but you shall stand, you will stand, stand you must, until the shadow of that tree you became no longer touches you."

I nodded to the drivers, and they tapped reins against the backs of the oxen. They guided the charabanc around the witch, and we continued on. I turned as we rounded a bend and looked for the last time back at the woman, standing in the middle of the road as if she were one of the figures of doomed men in a frieze along the Street of the Gods.

Janos rode up beside Cassini. "An interesting spell."

"It is," he agreed. "A simple one . . . and it helps immensely if there is a simple mind for it to work upon."

I puzzled: Cassini did not make sense; spells worked the same on all, Magistrate to peasant, lord to slave . . . Did they not? My thoughts came back to the present as the wheels of the charabanc clattered and my horse's shoes rang.

We were no longer on the dirt track, but on a stone-paved road. There was a log barrier across the road, and, beside it, a low building. Out of the building ran five soldiers. They stopped beside the road and stood to attention. They were smartly dressed, clean, and handled their weapons as if they were familiar with their use. One of them, I guessed their officer or sergeant, shouted for us to stop. Customs.

"Who are your passengers?" the man asked.

"Lord Amalric Antero. A merchant of Orissa. And his retinue."

A scowl flickered on the man's face. "Pass . . . wait." He walked to Janos and looked at him carefully. He started to say something, then stopped, and stepped back. "Pass. Welcome to Lycanth," he said, his tone as welcoming as the one used to the tax collector.

The charabanc moved on, and I kicked my horse forward until I rode close to Janos. "What was that all about?"

"The fellow recognized me," he said. "He was about to question me as to what a Lycanthian officer was doing in the retinue of an Orissan slimeworm. Then he thought better—perhaps I'm a spy, returning from an assignment."

"So he would not have heard that you left the Lycanthian Army."

"Sometimes Lycanthian soldiers are discharged or even drummed out dishonorably to begin a secret assignment."

Now I blush at my naïveté, but on that day I actually gaped and asked, "Lycanth does things like that?" To Janos credit he merely nodded soberly, instead of showing any scorn for someone so innocent. Buildings rose up around us. We were in Lycanth.

WE FOUND AN inn and began our final preparations. The soldiers were told nothing about our direction of travel and certainly not of our dreamed goal of the Far Kingdoms. Their duties would be to guard our gold and give any assistance needed. Eanes was to be our majordomo, and Cassini would be charged with gathering charms and other magical supplies, such as our wind spirits. I was to secure a ship to carry us across the Narrow Sea to the most distant Valaroian port Janos was familiar with. Examining his chart, I was once more shocked by how little was known about this region: our intended destination, the port of Redond, was but two finger-breadths east of Lycanth across the sea; just east of the port was the Pepper Coast, of evil rumor. All else was a mystery: there were no markings on that portion of the map, no cities, no demarcations for tribes or nations; and beyond the Pepper Coast was a great mountain range that Janos had sketched on the map. It was a mountain range known but to him, since his homeland of Kostroma lay somewhere in its fasts.

"There are stories I heard in Lycanth," he'd told me, "that claim the Archons have secretly sent explorers east, beyond Redond, beyond even the Pepper Coast. But I never found a man who truthfully laid claim to having been on such an expedition, so I discounted the tales."

Sergeant Maeen was in charge of securing our weaponry, guided by Janos, so that we would not appear ostentatiously Orissan. The rest of our supplies—horses or mules, provisions, tenting, and the like we would buy or have made in Redond.

Janos told me privately he had other matters to arrange to assure the success of our expedition—matters that someone of my station would be unwise to involve himself in. He said I was not to take alarm at his irregular comings and goings, or some of the people he might be doing business with. It was well he warned me; if he hadn't, I would have bellowed for Maeen and the Lycanthian watch when I first saw the man shamble into the inn's courtyard. I have learned over the years that the man or woman to be wariest of may have the features of a god or goddess and the benevolent manners of a holy one; whereas the real saint may have the outward semblance of a monster. But Greif looked the villain he was. Eanes was the first to notice him. He whistled softly and asked me to take note of the man below us. "Surely," Eanes said, "he is rich. Mothers must reserve his services months in advance to frighten their babes into good behavior." Greif was but an inch or so taller than me, but twice the mass. He had the solid, heavily built body of a porter or brewer. But if he'd worked either trade, the reasons for his discharge were obvious: Greif's ears had been cropped—a sign here, as in Orissa, of a thrice-convicted thief. His arms were misshapen, bent. At first I thought he'd been crippled, then I saw, below the rolled sleeves of his soiled silk finery, the seared scars that came from the rack's bindings.

I shouted down, asking him his business. He said he was seeking a Captain Janos Greycloak, a man who once served Lycanth. His voice was a mellow bass that might have served a prayer caller well. Eanes asked his name.

"Greif."

"Well chosen," my bodyslave murmured. "And your business?"

"Private . . . with the captain," the man said.

Janos came out of his chambers onto the balcony. "I am Greycloak. Who sent you?" The man did not answer—at least not verbally. Instead his hand moved in front of him, secretively, in three fast motions.

"Up here, fellow," Janos said. "Eanes. We'll have wine." The villain may have seen the torture chamber—but he was hardly a cripple. He went up the stairs like I'd seen great apes from the north scramble up their cages in Orissa's gardens. His tunic flipped up momentarily, and I saw the sheath of some hidden weapon. Janos called him into his chamber, where they stayed for two hours. Then Janos came out and asked me for a double measure of gold coins. I hesitated, liking little any business with this Greif, but realized I was being foolish. Certainly, in the days to come we would no doubt be dealing with villains who would make us fondly remember Greif as a saintly virgin.

I HAD MY OWN troubles to grind my teeth about, because what I'd thought to be a simple matter of hiring a ship was turning into an elaborate negotiation. It was a long, sleek ship, fitted with what a dockside idler told me was a lateen sail, which was now furled around a yard that had been lowered to the deck. The large, sweeping, two-man rudder was mounted on the ship's side, and its bow curved up to a gull's beak, surely a good omen for something I wished to cleave the seas smoothly and rapidly. It was partially decked at the bow and stern, although the quarters would be cramped. The ship was either new or exceptionally well kept. Of greatest interest to me, since I feared my stomach would be tender on my first sea passage, it had an outrigger along its left side, hung from two graceful curving beams. I found my way from deck to deck across the three ships between it and the dock. A man was waiting for me. He looked as I imagined all sailors to be—barefoot and bareheaded, wearing a shapeless wool waistcoat and knee breeches.

He noted my dress and nodded respectfully. "My lord. You wish passage?"

The man introduced himself as L'ur, master and owner of the *Kittiwake*. Before he even addressed himself to my opening bid, he insisted on showing me around his ship. I knew little about ships then; but now I know a great deal, strictly perforce, about the damnable inventions, owning far more of them than a man could count in a day. I frankly think it quite adequate to call a ship a boat, the bow the pointy end, and the stern the arse, and have done with all of the nonsensical labels seamen use. Finally we returned to the rear of the ship, what he called the quarterdeck, and he sent for vile wine. I watered mine heavily. He said he'd considered my wishes and that he would be honored to convey us to Redond. He named the price . . . in gold . . . in advance. I hope

I kept from sputtering his resinous swill over his deck, and told him I merely wanted to charter his little plaything, not purchase it outright. He smiled as if I were jesting and mournfully spoke of the dangers of the Pepper Coast.

I asked him what were the dangers, *specifically*? His gloomy list was impressive: he mentioned rocks that changed their locations from voyage to voyage; great whirlpools; sea monsters; pirates; lee cliffs with nary a landing safe to beach on; storms blowing up from a clear sky, no doubt brought on by some great and evil Evocator somewhere on the Pepper Coast; stars not consistent in their courses, so no navigator could be sure of his location. After piling up this fearful heap, he said, "My ship is fast. And I will hire the most skilled men possible, men able to work a sling or a ballista as well as furl a sail. And I hope some of your retinue know which end of an arrow is to be nocked."

That was how it began. Each day I would travel to the docks, and we would bargain and lie, back and forth, to and fro. By the time we had struck a deal for ship and crew—about twice what I'd offered, half on departure day, half on arrival at Redond—I was willing and, I think, able, to strap all fourteen of my party on my back, plus our money chests, and *swim* to that damned-of-the-gods Valaroi. Nothing, I should add, has changed the way seamen do business, from that long-ago day to this.

THE DAY BEFORE I finally wore L'ur out, something most odd happened. Greif was waiting when I came back to the inn. He was carrying a closely tied bag, which held some of the "preciouses"—his word—he'd secured for Janos. I offered to accept them, but he refused—Captain Greycloak had insisted that Greif would be paid by, and answer to, only him. I thought of snapping back that I was Janos' employer, and certainly there should be no secrets from me, but realized I was tired from the endless haggling with L'ur. Out of common politeness I offered Greif wine. He accepted and we found a corner of the inn's common room.

"This is passin' strange," he said. "Me, comin' from a foundlin' shelter, drinkin' with a merchant prince. None that I grew with'd believe it." He laughed in pleasure, showing black teeth. "Th' wine's e'en sweeter knowin' I'm doin' service f'r an Antero."

"How did you know my family name?"

"One a' th' soldiers said. To his mate. Not knowin' that m' ears might be trimmed, but pointed right, they hear as well as any. But don't worry. Any secret Greif knows, when it's a friend, he keeps. I learned about bein' mouthy." His hand caressed the rope burns on his arm almost fondly. I wished Janos would come—this man's presence made my skin crawl as if I were lice ridden.

"You've heard of my family?" I asked.

Greif nodded, then turned in his chair and lifted his tunic. My stomach curdled. I'd seen lash scars before, white and twisted on a man's back—but never this deep. The whip must have cut to the bone. "One time," Greif said, turning back and pulling his tunic down, "m' luck had turned, an' I agreed t' do a job for Nisou, Master Symeon. Yes. Yes. I saw th' look a startlement. The Symeons. Even a street scut like me's heard of your feud. Anyway, it wasn't he who paid, but me. A dozen's dozen. He used the whip his own self. He's got his own cells below th' buildin' th' Symeons have for their clan home. I don't know if I screamed or not. Prob'ly I did. Most do, when there's metal wove into th' whip leather." He smiled and licked his lips, as if recollecting a lover's embrace. "Then he had me thrown int' th' bay. I wasn't expected t' live. But I did. Swearin' there'd be another time. Another place. Knowin' I was jus' blatherin', to keep from passin' out. So maybe this, helpin' you, in whatever you're plannin' is a getback against th' Symeons. Jus' a bit. An' a bit here, a bit there . . . I've seen mice take an entire loaf like that."

He drained his wine, and I signaled for more. Greif went for the jakes. I looked about the common room. The few people in it were more interested watching Greif's stumble than in me. I bent and felt the bundle he had for Janos, like a child trying to determine what he would receive on his birthing day by fondling its wrappings. Some bottles . . . a box . . . some other things that rustled, like dried plants . . . some packages that held round seeds . . . and then I cut myself. There was a gleam from the blade—it'd punctured the linen the bundle was wrapped in. I quickly tore a bit away. The blade was curved. It was a tiny sickle, the miniature of what a peasant uses to cut wheat. But it was made of gold—and I knew without looking, there would be arcane lettering on the blade itself. This scythe was intended to cut herbs and other plants—but not for a cook or a chambermaid. These plants would be used for enchantments. By an Evocator.

I wondered what Janos Greycloak wanted with the forbidden tools of sorcery. I wondered what the other items in that bundle were and thought I might know. I remembered the question that Gamelan, eldest of the Evocators, had asked Janos back in Orissa, and how Janos had turned the question aside with a jest, not answering. But I did not tell Janos what I'd seen when he arrived near simultaneous with Greif's return from the privy. The question would have to be posed much later, in private, because the penalty for a non-Evocator possessing or using spellbinders' implements could be anything from imprisonment to banishment to death.

THAT NIGHT, FOR the first time in months, I dreamed my nightmare once more. I could not remember what it had been before, but from that time on, the face of my keeper, leading me out of the boat to my doom, was Greif's. But in my dream one of his eyes was gone, and something like a worm or a light squirmed out the socket at me.

THE NIGHT AFTER that another horror came upon us, but this one was very real. I'd noticed the moon was full as I went upstairs toward my chamber. I was readying myself for sleep when the baying started. I grabbed my rapier and went out onto the balcony. Two guttering torches at the gates showed me the creature crouched in the courtyard's center. It had come from no womb on this earth, but only from an Evocator's incantations. Imagine a hyena, a hairless hyena starved nearly to death, and with the face of a man.

The creature spoke—in the voice of a man who might have come straight from the Archons' dungeons. "You are summoned," the being screeched. "You are summoned to the castle. All men, all women, who are not Lycanthian. You are summoned. In one hour. The oracle has named this for the time. You are ordered to appear. All of you. It is the order of the Archons. You must obey. You are summoned. Let those who disobey find the death, the death of burning, the death of water, the death of crushing, the death of falling. This is the voice of the Archons. One hour."

The being loped out of the courtyard, down the cobbled street toward another inn. I turned and saw Janos, his face stone. "This means a death," he said. "I was afraid they would sniff us out." He nodded to me. "You must order everyone dressed. No one is to carry a weapon, not even an eating knife. We must be in the square before the sands run out of a glass . . . Or else we shall *all* die."

THE STREETS OF LYCANTH were eerie: here and there were torches carried by bewildered foreigners; silent patrols of Lycanthian soldiery stalked through the streets, refusing to answer all questions except to repeat that the Archons must be obeyed. The high buildings were dark, as if no one was behind the windows, but now and then I caught the flash of a white face as it chanced a look out, then ducked back behind curtains.

Janos had returned hastily to his chamber while I gave the orders. I heard the crashing of something being smashed, then nothing. I had to shout three times before he came out. Now, as we walked through the streets, I heard him stop by Maeen. Then he moved up to Eanes, and I heard him ask, in a whisper, if he could read. Eanes may have been frightened, but had enough self to snap that of course he could, not being a barbarian from Lycanth.

Then he moved up to me. "Here," he whispered, handing me a bit of metal. "Learn this. Recite it at the proper time. You will know when. I have given one to Maeen and to Eanes as well."

"What about Cassini?" I whispered back. Our Evocator was walking a few yards in front of us.

"He has nothing to worry about," Janos said. "The cloak of equals will extend over him." He handed me a cap, used by the servitors to keep dust from their hair. "Pull it on. We need to light no watch fire for *them*."

Ahead of us was the castle. Over its main entrance—the gate lowered and the portcullis raised—was a great flare, roaring flame, without fuel or support. I heard part of a whisper from one of the soldiers. "Stink ... sorcery ..."

"On your life," Janos hissed. "Say nothing, and think nothing bad about what is happening."

It was now light enough for me to look at what I held. It was a shard of highly polished brass. Now I understood the crash I'd heard—the brass was part of the reflector for one of the room lamps in our quarters. Scratched on it by a knife point were words:

> *I am mirror*
> *I am not seen*
> *I think as you*
> *My mind is a wall*
> *Feel nothing*
> *Think nothing*
> *What you see is what you are*
> *What you see is what we are*
> *I am mirror*

As frightened as I was, I still wondered: first the bundle of thaumaturgical objects, and now this incantation. Did Janos

Greycloak fancy himself an Evocator? But there was no time for further thought; soldiers closed around us as we went through the gate and into the huge open courtyard.

At the far end was a stand, a stand like a great podium. On it stood two men; their bodies shimmered, and they appeared to be taller than men should be. Each of them wore the diadem of Archon. I shuddered ... This was an evil. Common men, let alone outsiders, were never supposed to lay eyes on Lycanth's Archons, their Master Evocators. I heard a soldier whisper a prayer and the thud of the blow as Maeen struck him. We were formed into lines by Lycanthian soldiers. There were perhaps three or four hundred of us in the square. Dressed or half-dressed, none of us wore the garb of Lycanth. Men and women, nobles and slaves, children and ancients. Some of us were crying; some of us were drunk and trying to appear brave.

Then another creature appeared between the two Archons. I heard a voice, from nowhere, from everywhere.

"There is evil, there is evil, there is evil abroad this night
Evil for me, evil for Lycanth, evil that must be ended
The vision is clear, the vision is clear
This is the hour
This is the hour
Seek, our messenger, our inquisitor, our lover."

The third creature—I now saw it was the ghastly messenger that had summoned us here, a being created by the blackest of spells—leaped down from the sand. It bounded toward us, and somehow I knew what its new role would be: finder. I could hear sniffing as it came. I knew this was the time.

I am mirror/I am unseen ...

The creature moved down our ranks, slowly. As it approached me, one of our soldiers fainted. I heard his body thud against the flagstones.

... Feel nothing/Think nothing ...

The demon was in front of me. I dared not look down. I felt its loathsome muzzle touch my bare leg and barely kept from writhing.

What you see is what you are ...

I did not fall. The hound was gone. I heard a puzzled whine from down the row, but did not chance a look. The beast sounded exactly like one of my own dogs, knowing that what he sought was close, but still somehow hidden. There came the scratch of claws ... coming back toward me.

What you see is what we are ...

Again, the beast passed on. This time it broke from our ranks and trotted to an open space between us and the Archons. It sat on its haunches and then howled at the setting moon. Once. Twice. A third time. Someone came out from the crowd toward the seeker, summoned by the baying.

It was a young woman. Even now I can remember how comely she was. She was very young—perhaps she was even a virgin. She wore only nightclothes. At another time, someone might have felt the stirrings of lust. But not now. Not here. Lycanth had chosen its victim. She walked to the beast. It was as if her feet wanted to run, to flee. But the spell would not let her. Her lovely face was contorted in horror. There came a shimmer in the air in front of her, a shimmer like that hanging around the Archons. The shimmer became a dagger—not large and with a slightly curving blade. The maiden herself might have used one like it in her kitchen if she were a commoner, or one of her slaves would have sliced her morning fruit with it if she were noble.

Very slowly the woman took the blade. She turned the blade toward her. Then she made the first cut. The spell she was under allowed her to scream. None of us could run, could even turn our eyes. She cut again. And again. To this day, her screams still hang in my mind. It was near dawn before she could not scream anymore, and they let her die. The demon vanished, and there was no one standing on the Archons' podium.

We turned and stumbled out. There was nothing in the square, lit by the dying torches, except the sprawled body of something that had once been very beautiful.

"THAT IS THE custom in Lycanth," Janos told me later, when I was able to talk about it. "When the Archons or their diviners descry a doom or an evil descending on the city, sacrifice is made."

"No doubt it is always an outsider."

"Not always," he said. "I have seen natives of the city, even a young Evocator once, choose themselves. Those who offer themselves to save Lycanth are mostly young. Mostly handsome. Sometimes those who make the choice have spoken out against Lycanth. Or are hereditary enemies of the city. Or merely stand out. That was why I asked you to wear the cap. Perhaps those reasons are why the ... the creature who must not be named ... stopped by our party. But perhaps not. Perhaps the woman harbored greater secrets and greater feelings than any of us. And that . . . that was not the worst death I have seen the Chosen One find."

I hesitated, about to ask him how he knew to write the counterspell, but decided against it. It was not a question to be asked aloud in Lycanth.

IT WAS TIME to go; our ship and crew were provisioned and ready. We would leave in two or three days, on a neap tide. Evidently Janos had found all he needed from the black market, since I did no longer see Greif about.

Janos, Cassini, and I were in one of the city's weapons shops, choosing suitable instruments for the journey, weapons that would not shriek of our origin. I eyed a beautiful rapier of watered steel, which had a jeweled and golden guard and pommel and a gold-threaded grip. Next to it lay a matched dagger. The smith murmured that an Evocator had cast a spell of invincibility on both weapons. I asked the smith if I might handle them. Both seemed to float in my grasp. But not being an experienced warrior, I turned to Janos to see what he wanted me to carry. He himself already had his weapons—the same he'd carried the day I met him on the drill field in Orissa.

"Carry what you wish," he said. "No man should have his individual weapons dictated before he goes into battle, unless the commander has specific reasons. But those two, handsome as they are, would not be my personal choices. First is that it is not advisable, particularly in a small party, for officers to be easily recognizable. Hence you do not wear a long crest, gold workings on your armor . . . nor jewel-like curlicues on your blade. There is nothing that makes a soldier lose heart so fast as seeing his commander fall. I also have known waterfront toughs to assassinate a man solely because they lusted for his sword. As for those enchantments . . . can you imagine any man heading for battle, whether he's a peasant armed with nothing but a brass-bound club or a great lord, whose weapons have not been blessed by someone? An Evocator, a witch, a local sorcerer or . . . or an Archon? Plus the field of battle itself swirls with spell and counterspell, even more thickly than the dust raised in the struggle. I have always felt that battle spells and weapon talismans tend to counteract and hence negate each other. But that's just my feeling, or maybe cynicism. Lastly, the rapier may be well built, but consider this broadsword, instead."

He indicated—and the smith was quick to hand it to him—

another sword. It was built like a claymore, but shorter and its grip intended for but one hand. "Sturdy. Double edged. Also of ondanique construction. You could probably do what I'm about to show you with either blade—but the more slender one could take a cast." He took the blade tip in one hand, the grip in the other, and bent the blade into an arc, his muscles bulging. I knew the steel must snap—but instead, it curved into a near semicircle. Janos let it ease back and nodded to the smith. "No magicking here, Master Kanadis. Just the finest of metallurgy."

"You have found me out." The smith grinned. "I share your skepticism about sorcery's place on the battleground, although I would be the last to deny an Evocator's blessing before the fight. I have, however, hired an Evocator to place a charm against rusting on this—and all my other watered-steel blades—so they may be used aboard ship, for instance, without the owner having to spend all his waking hours cursing and scrubbing with an oil-soaked rag."

"A sturdy sword," Janos continued. "Better than the rapier for travel, since you will find yourself using that sword for everything from a tent stake to a brush cutter to a spit, although I will speak most harshly to you in the event I see you thus distempering the metal. And these simple, straight quillons will serve to stop an enemy's slash, yet not bind as ... as some other weapons I can think of might do." I reddened a bit. I thought Janos had forgotten my performance as less than a master of the duello down at the riverfront in Orissa.

"Here is a knife to match," Janos said, passing me a rather modestly worked scramasax—a single-edged knife with a fairly long and broad blade grooved on both sides. "This will be your copse, carcass, or thief cutter, which you will keep always beside you. The sword you will find uncomfortable, and tend to leave by a campfire, or tied to your saddle, especially just before you need it. And this dagger can be your salvation. All else you'll need is a small knife for cutting your meat, which you may pick out over at the cutlery section.

"Do you agree, Master Kanadis?"

"I do."

"Two men who know better than I have spoken," I said. "Although sometimes I feel less the master of this expedition than its sponsor, as if I were an old dodderer infatuated with a vapid simperer."

"And all of us whores appreciate you," Janos said, with a laugh.

"One more thing," he said. "While we're on the subject of, er, ostentation. Your hair. I've known great chieftains who are proud of their locks, and dare an enemy to shear them. I have admired them. From afar. Especially during a battle. We will be traveling through regions whose peoples think it blessed by the gods to hunt down a flame-headed man and pitch him off the nearest cliff to ensure a beneficial harvest or perhaps just better weather the next day."

I considered. Janos had a smile on his lips, but it went no higher. I remembered the castle courtyard and the hound. "When we return to the inn, I shall have Eanes shear me like a young lamb," I promised, and reached for my purse to pay the smith.

Cassini, who had listened but said nothing during our exchange, bought the exotic rapier and its companion.

"DO NOT HAND me the mirror," I begged Eanes. "Just tell me what I appear to be." My hand stroked at the emptiness where my hair had curled in waves to my shoulders.

"Perhaps," Eanes said thoughtfully, "a galleyslave."

"Or a thief intended for the Kissing of the Stones," Janos put in helpfully, peering around the corner.

"A criminal," I moaned. "A condemned man."

"You're too harsh, my master. You could also pass for a holy man who's taken a vow of celibacy."

"Definitely that," Janos said. "Possibly even a castrato."

"I think," I said, "I shall go next door to Evocator Cassini's chambers, and ask him if he could prepare a small spell that delves into the arena of baldness."

"Too late for me," Eanes said, patting himself on his shiny pate. "But beware it doesn't turn back on its caster, as so many incantations do."

"I am starting to believe," I said, "that being thrown from a high cliff is better than listening to either of you. Janos. This was your idea. You may buy me a brandy . . . no, several brandies . . . below stairs."

I rose and picked up my new sword. I was still getting used to its heft, more than a bit heavier than the rapiers or short swords I carried in Orissa. Eanes carefully gathered up the cloths he'd laid around my chair before he began his barbering. He shook them into a leather bag.

"You were clever enough to not let any of his locks fall on the carpet?" Janos asked, most serious.

"I was, Captain. Just as I have been since I was named his bodyslave, back when he was a mewling infant. Careful with hair, careful with the trimmings from his nails, careful with the down from what he wishes will be a beard one of these years, even careful when he was a disgusting pup and vomiting in all directions like a fountain. Although there have been times I would have gladly sold a bit of my master to some evil witch, provided she would include civility and common sense in whatever spell she planned to cast over him."

"Good," Janos said, still serious. "But do not dump the cuttings down the jakes, please. Carry them out to the main sewage ditch, where you may be sure the water flow is constant."

Eanes' smile evaporated, and he became as serious as Janos. "I shall do as you say," he said. "And I know not whether you've any premonition, but just being in this city of dead stones and cursed souls makes me constantly think all our doom is just around a corner."

All of us crossed fingers. Eanes gave a heavy sigh. "It is so bad," he said, "I am even looking forward to the ocean, where I will be forced to hold Lord Amalric's head over the side when he pales, and inform him that puking to windward is not blessed. Thanks be that I myself have a stomach of the most solidly cast iron." He picked up the bag and went out.

"To the best of my knowledge," I said, "Chatterbox Eanes has never been on any boat in his life, except perhaps one in a garden pond."

Janos smiled a bit. "He reminds me of my own nurse. Scuffling, whining, complaining, worrying, but always—"

A scream curdled the night. Janos and I were out the door onto the balcony. His sword was already in hand, I scrabbled mine out. We clattered down the stairs into the courtyard. The two watch soldiers at the gate were peering out, their weapons ready. Other soldiers pelted out from their chambers, buckling on their gear.

"Eanes," one of the soldiers shouted, pointing down the street. The watch had been ordered to let nothing lure them from their posts. "He just went—"

I didn't hear the rest, as we rushed out into the street. Janos grabbed one of the torches from its stanchion as we went. At the end of the street, I saw three men struggling. We hallooed and charged forward. One of them broke away and darted off into the blackness. The other paused long enough for me to see his arm strike across the chest of the third, who collapsed. Then there was no one in the cobbled street but the sagging body of a man.

It was Eanes. We turned him over. He'd been slashed twice—once on the arm, cutting it to the bone, and then across the body, deep into his body cavity. But he still lived.

"Call Cassini," I ordered to Janos. He shouted for the Evocator and his healing herbs. I could hear feet running toward us.

Eanes' eyes opened, then found me. "They . . . didn't get it. I did not let them," he gasped. "They wanted . . ."

"Be silent." Janos knelt beside me. He held out a small leather bag—the bag carrying my hair clippings. My bowels clenched. It could not be. They thought the well-dressed little man was carrying a bag of coins.

"They said . . . they wanted what had come . . . from you . . . that I would be rewarded if I yielded it over. And if I didn't . . ." Eanes sucked in air, air that was no comfort to his ripped lungs.

"Hold on," I said. "Cassini is powerful. He has potions and spells. You'll be all right."

Eanes shook his head. "No," he whispered. "One boon, master. One last boon." I knew he was dying. "Free me," he managed. "Let me die a free man."

That was no boon—it was my fault he would die here on these rough cobblestones in this damned city. But that was all I could do. I tried to find words; but I'd had never freed a slave before. Janos spoke.

"Say the words after me," he ordered. I echoed him.

"I . . . Lord Amalric Antero, of Orissa, do declare this slave Eanes, Eanes of . . . of . . ."

"Of Mangifera," came the whisper.

"Of Mangifera . . . a free man. He now owes no man homage . . . save those superior to him by station or duty . . . he has the right to property . . . to wife . . . to children, who shall be free as well . . . he has the right to his own life . . . to his own death . . . I, Lord Amalric Antero, do declare . . . willingly and openly . . . here, under the sight of all gods . . . I will have no claims . . . now or forever . . . on this man, his children, his family, or his soul."

Eanes' lips parted, in what might have been intended as thanks or as a smile. Then his gaze changed, and he saw through me, saw beyond me. Saw nothing. His body was suddenly quite heavy.

I could not see his face through the blur. Someone took the body from me. Janos helped me rise. Then I remembered: I scraped up a handful of dirt from between the cobbles and let it sift down on Eanes' body. Now his ghost would not wander the earth. And, I promised, I would fulfill the rest of the duty, so that he would be blessed by the Dark Seeker, and avenge his murder. But at the time I felt no anger. Just a great sorrow, and a great shame, for in all those years of service, I had never asked my most faithful servant, and my truest friend, just what his homeland was.

Janos put an arm around my shoulders. "We mourn later," he said, his voice harsh. "We sail today."

WE PACKED HASTILY. I fumbled with my possessions, knowing that for the first time in my life, I had no one to remind me what hairbrush went where, which tunic should be folded in what manner, and so forth. When I realized my thoughts, I cursed myself yet again for selfishness. A man had just died, and all I could think of was whether my pomade had been corked properly and packed in the correct trunk. Sergeant Maeen detailed one of his soldiers to help, but I fear he was of little assistance. At least I had the courtesy not to snarl.

I sought out the innkeeper and paid our reckoning. He vowed he knew someone who knew the Orissan ceremonies, and that he would have Eanes' body burned after the ritual, as our beliefs dictated, so no magus could rouse the dead earth and animate it to be serving flesh. Janos had said he was to be trusted in this, so I did not bother mentioning that the Antero family has a long memory, and it would be a black matter indeed if he did not keep his promise. I think he looked into my eyes, however, and *knew*.

When we gathered in the courtyard, Janos brought us into line and gave each of us a small tooth, gold mounted and hung on a chain. He told us they'd come from ferrets and would make us hard to kill. I remembered my pet ferret and how Halab had brought it to life. Perhaps this would be a good omen on a journey that appeared plagued from the beginning. Cassini frowned—any charms should have come from him, rightly—but did not say a word, and he slipped his amulet over his head as quickly as the rest of us.

Janos stood in the middle of the courtyard, staring at the one tooth remaining. Perhaps he was wondering if it would have saved Eanes if he'd given it to him two hours before.

IT WAS LONG after dawn before the *Kittiwake* sailed out of Lycanth's harbor. It took time to raise L'ur, for him to find the sailors we'd hired, for him to find a waterfront witch to cast an evidently satisfactory prophecy for the journey. A heavy summer fog still hung across the harbor when we finally let go our lines, and four sailors manned the sweeps to row us far enough out to rig a sail for the light breeze coming off the land. Our prow pointed toward the open sea. To one side was the monstrous sea castle of the Archons and, across the narrow harbor mouth, the watch tower, claws on the curling, grasping rocky hand of the harbor that seemed reluctant to let us go.

I turned back to look at Lycanth as it vanished into the mist. The mist lifted, and I saw the dock we'd just left. There was someone standing there . . . so motionless, I thought him at first to be just one of the pilings. Then I recognized him, even though the distance should have been too great for my eyes to make out such detail. But I knew. I knew.

The man watching our departure was Greif.

CHAPTER SEVEN
The Archons' Tempest

IN THE DAYS that followed I had rueful revenge on Eanes. The sun was bright, the wind brisk, and the seas high. The *Kittiwake* charged through those seas like a living thing, great sail straining for more speed. For once one of Eanes' prophecies didn't come true. I was as healthy at sea as on land. I thought of him often as waves broke over the ship, wetting us all to the skin. The soldiers were permanent fixtures at the sides, heaving their guts into the spume, to the vast amusement of Captain L'ur and the other seamen. Among the gut spewers was Cassini, which gave Janos *his* private pleasure. Seasickness, Janos laughed in my ear, did not seem vulnerable to a conjurer's ways. It was a good joke at the time—for I had never felt so healthy in my life. My strength swelled with each passing league as we beat our way toward the port of Redond. My blood was alive with adventure, and all thoughts of Greif's dark figure vanished. As for Eanes: I promised myself I would learn from his death, although I was not sure yet what lesson should be drawn. Privately, I dedicated the expedition to him—promising a fat ewe as a sacrifice when we returned— and put him away in my chest of tragedies, along with Halab and my mother.

It is common for every voyager heading for new lands to pay small attention to his fellow travelers in the beginning. Each sight is so new and different, the ways and doings of his companions are overshadowed, so I cannot say with accuracy what the other members of the party spent their days doing. I remember Cassini being permanently sick. I remember the grumbling seamen, although I believed the grumbling minor. I don't remember much of our soldiers, except that Sergeant Maeen separated them from the seamen and kept them busy with small tasks and training. I remember Janos keeping mostly to himself, poring over charts and mysterious scraps of documents.

In the beginning I saw other ships—all from a distance, since L'ur was a properly wary captain who never tempted a pirate. But I wondered at them, as all lubbers wonder, guessing from whence they came and where they were bound. It came to me they could be seeking no landfall as wondrous as the country I sought, and laughed at their puny expectations. Once we were well out into the open sea, we saw no ships, for few dared this journey, and those who did traveled as cautiously as we did.

The seas were alive with all manner of creatures. There were fish that flew out of the water; turtles with backs broad enough to carry several men; insects with bodies as big as a man's head and long, spindly legs that carried them swiftly on the hunt from kelp bed to kelp bed. I saw a creature twice as long as our craft that spewed water from a hole set in the top of its head. It fled our approach. Later I saw two immense birds, or things that looked like birds, with vast, leathery wings and long, sharp beaks. They alighted on a dark shape drifting in the waves, crying out in delight and tearing at its flesh. As we drew closer, I saw it was the corpse of one of the spouting beasts I'd seen. There were several spears in its side.

On another day a sea lizard broke surface. It was huge and old with long trails of barnacles streaming from its side. At first the men said this was lucky. But it followed us, and they grew wary, casting dark looks back. It trailed us for a long time, and the looks became curses before the sea lizard disappeared. But the men did not forget.

Just after that the seas changed color and shape as we entered a region of great depths. The sailors whispered that there was no bottom here and an angry god dwelt in the vast reaches—a god whose name no man had heard and lived. The captain laughed at the talk, mocked it as superstitious blathering, unworthy of a true sailor. But I caught a hollowness in the mockery and saw him finger his talisman. He did nothing to stop the whispers.

Despite the fears of the seamen, nothing in particular occurred during our voyage across the deep. But I understood their nervousness. In the time we traveled in those waters, we saw never a living thing—no fish, or sea lizards, or even a wayward bird. It was as if we had come upon a watery desert. So when a seaman spotted another sail one day and gave the cry, we rushed to the bulwarks rather than hastily preparing to take flight. L'ur made the excuse of checking his position and buying fresh food and steered for the stranger, with the two-hands-clasped flag of friendship flying from our mast. The ship was lateen rigged like our own, but with three sails. It stayed its course as we closed, making no attempt to tack nearer or to flee. We cried out that we were friends. No one answered. As we came within a spearcast of the ship and could see its decks clearly, we realized there was no one to answer. The ship's sails drew taut and the snap and crack they gave in the wind echoed eerily. We saw with a jolt that the rudder had been shipped. Who was steering, and how? "Wizardry," I heard a seaman hiss.

L'ur barked orders to pull away, but it was too late to prevent us from skimming closer to the strange ship's side. The deck was spattered with a terrible gore, fresh gore—with red blood pocking the deck and more blood dripping down the mainmast. But there was not a corpse to be seen, much less the sobs of wounded men. We fled in terror, L'ur screaming and the seamen dashing about to do his bidding as if the Dark Seeker had loosed his hounds. The *Kittiwake* leaped away from the ghost ship, and when we had sailed a great distance, L'ur hove to for consultation.

Some of the men said it was the work of an evil wizard. Others said it was men. The men they imagined were half pirate, half demon, who crept up on innocent seamen to make a meal of their flesh or to carry them away to eating pens. At Janos' urging, Cassini stilled his quaking guts enough to give a little speech about kinder gods and gentler men. There was little passion to his talk, so it was unconvincing, less from Cassini's illness than his own fear. He seemed to be trying to come to terms as to what manner of things he would encounter, and be expected to overcome, as the expedition continued. He could see how little his words meant, so he called for a sacrifice to the gods of this region. This started a quarrel. Some said we should sacrifice to our own gods as well, so as not to make them jealous. Some said we should make sacrifice *only* to our own, or they would abandon us permanently. There was only a small pig to kill—the ship's mascot. Cassini wisely stayed with his first judgment, placating the near rather than the far. The pig squealed as he cut its throat, and he bled it into a copper bowl engraved with arcane symbols.

"That'll do no good," I heard a man say.

"We'll need a better gift than that," another said.

"It's just our poor pig," someone said quite near.

"That's all our luck he's killin'," came a grumble.

I heard someone say, "It's the redhead who's to blame. Everyone knows red hair's bad luck on a ship." Janos' hand gripped my elbow, and I gave no indication I had heard. As he pulled me away I heard a final comment. "It oughta be him, 'stead of the pig. That'd change our luck."

"I see what you meant about my red hair," I groaned. "It's always been a curse to me."

"It's foolish to mourn a thing you were born with," Janos soothed. "I wouldn't be surprised if there are kingdoms with nothing but redheaded people, and it is the poor black-haired fellow who's cursed."

"What should I do?" I asked.

"Don't trouble yourself. We're only a few days out of Redond. Why stir a pot to boil, when a simmer does no harm? Besides, we have our own men, good, loyal Orissan soldiers the seamen would not dare challenge." He eyed me, grim despite his words. "But keep your knife ready. In case someone comes at you in the night."

Cassini completed the sacrifice, pouring the blood and a mixture of sorcerous ingredients on the seas, and calling to the gods in a loud voice that we were peaceful men who would soon be quit of their kingdom. We set sail again, and the spirits of the men seemed somewhat eased. The muttering ceased, although my hair still drew looks. The crew became almost cheery as we entered a region everyone said was always blessed with steady winds. L'ur changed course to make a straight run for Redond, speeding over the waves like the fish with wings. That afternoon the wind died.

L'ur told his men not to worry, it was only a temporary lull, and reassured them about the well-known reliability of the winds in these parts. We remained becalmed all that night. In the morning we leaped up, ready for the fresh winds of the new day. They never arrived. The late afternoon winds failed as well. Nor did the night breezes bless us with their kiss. The following morning the sun dawned close and hot. Our heads ached as the still day wore on. The seamen's horny feet blistered and stuck to the deck, skin coming off if they pulled too hard. There was not a cloud in that blazing sky to give us hope of fresh winds rushing in over the horizon.

L'ur came to me in the late afternoon. "It's time you got your Evocator to get out the wind spirits," he said. "I've never had need of 'em in these parts, and would have advised we keep 'em for a nasty bit just off Redond." He looked up at the cloudless skies and shook his head. "Somethin's cursed us, sure," he said. "And I think we ought to get off quick."

I huddled with Janos and Cassini. One paid a dear price for a good bag of wind spirits, making many old witchwomen a handsome living in the ports where they plied their trade, capturing errant wind spirits in a sorcerous sack, then selling them to sailors for use when the wind failed. The bags were so costly, however, they were used only in emergency. We all agreed that an emergency had come.

Cassini made quite a ceremony of it, chalking a pentagram on the deck just behind the beaked prow. He purified the area around the pentagram, sprinkling ashes made of rare spices and the cremated parts of equally rare creatures. He donned his best robe and fetched the sack containing the wind spirits. All of us gathered as he lifted his hands and cried out to Te-Date in a loud voice. He summoned the wayfarer's god for half an hour, and then spent most of an hour more praising Te-Date's name and enlisting his sympathy for our plight. The heat was intolerable, but no one complained, fearing to interfere and cause failure. We bore with his long exaltation, propping up our fellows who had been overcome by the sun. I remember well that blazing sky and Cassini's sonorous words beseeching it. Not one small cloud paid a visit.

Finally, the moment came. Cassini laid the bag on the deck, gripped the drawstring, and gave a hard tug, stepping back quickly to avoid the blast of the emerging wind spirits. There are tales of men being killed by the fury of their escape. There was no fury on that day. Instead of a great cloud rushing to the skies to spawn the winds, a sickly gasp belched from the sack. It collapsed on the deck, a poor, flat, dead thing with no hope for us. Cassini stood there in dismay, mouth agape, a fool decked in Evocator's robes. The crew shouted in surprise.

One of the men brazenly tramped into the sacred pentagram and picked up the bag. I did not know his name, but he had the cropped ears of a man who had paid a price for thievery. He looked at the seal dangling from the string and hooted in angry disbelief. "I'm knowin' this mark," Crop Ear shouted, "and its maker's a great cheat. Sells her spirits right cheap, she does. Puny things that won't make a spit of a cloud." He turned to me and shook the sack at me in accusation. "The Redhead's a tightfist, boys," he cried. "Rather make our women widows than pay fair price for fair merchandise." The crew bellowed anger, ignoring L'ur's pleads for calm. Some of them put hands on their knives and shouted for my red scalp to appease the gods.

Janos barked an order, and suddenly Sergeant Maeen and the soldiers were there. Swords scraped from their scabbards, and the crew fell silent. Janos leaped on a keg. "Hear me well, men of *Kittiwake*," he shouted. "If one of you lays a hand on this man, I will order our soldiers to slay you all. We are close enough to Redond that lack of your seaman's skills—such as they are—will not stay our hand, I promise you." Maeen clanged sword against shield to punctuate the remarks. The soldiers did the same, and the ringing of war metal against war metal made the crew cowards. They crept back in silence.

"The wind will come, when the wind will come," Janos said. "We have plenty of food and drink and only the heat to bear. Te-Date will bless us soon. He is obviously busy now with the distress of others who are in *real* danger. But he will come to us by and by. Has he not been called by a great Orissan Evocator? Te-Date would never ignore such a blessed one. Now, go about your business and leave us be."

"You heard 'im, you whoresons," L'ur bellowed. "There's plenty to do to bide the time. And if you can't find work, I'll find somethin' for you."

The sailors dispersed, and L'ur set some of them on the buckets, heaving in seawater and flooding the decks to cool us off. I looked for the crop-eared man who'd accused me, but didn't see him. Janos jumped down from the keg and went to Cassini, with me just behind him. The Evocator's face was white, and his eyes shifted warily as we approached.

"What did you do, man?" Janos growled anger, dropping all customary respect for an Evocator. "I gave you good money and plenty of it. I even directed you to the best place to buy wind spirits. Why did you ignore my words?"

Cassini shook his head. He had no answer.

"I'll tell you what you did," Janos said. "You thought you'd buy cheap and pocket what was left over. You thought you had talent enough to sniff out the good among the cheap. Am I right?"

Still Cassini did not answer. I saw from his look that Janos' remarks had struck truth. I also saw a flush at his throat and knew guilt struggled with anger. This would not do. Cheat or not, fool or not, we needed Cassini. Orissan law and the power of the Council of Evocators had put him in our company, and there he must stay until we were home.

"I am sure it was only an error, Janos," I said. "Perhaps he took a wrong turn in seeking the address."

Cassini grabbed at it. "That's it," he said. "I was sure I went to the right place. And I paid full price. I am sorry for my error."

"Don't think too hard on it," I said. "All of us will make errors on this journey. And please forgive Captain Greycloak for his temper. The weather is trying on us all."

Janos saw what I was about and quickly changed tack. "You are right," he said. He turned to Cassini. "Please forgive my rudeness . . . and stupid accusations. My blood was up."

"There is nothing to forgive," Cassini said. "All is forgotten." The three of us smiled and went to choke down a little food. But I knew from the tightness in Cassini's smile that Janos' intemperate words would *not* be forgotten.

The winds Janos promised did not come, and the days passed in stifling misery. While the *Kittiwake* drifted, its sail slatting limp and lifeless, we lay in whatever shade we could find, panting like dogs. One day as I sat under an awning, sharing a jug of well-watered wine with Janos, my mind turned to that first night we had met, when Leego and his dogs trapped me at the tavern.

"Consider this, Janos," I said. "Perhaps my hair *is* lucky. Through it I fell into Melina's clutches, which is ill fortune on the surface. But the gods are wondrous indeed in their workings, for without that ill fortune I would never have met you and set out on this journey. And the meeting itself was of the greatest luck imaginable. For if you had not sought an alley to relieve yourself, Leego would certainly have killed me."

I meant this as a bit of a tired jest, but Janos did not favor it with a smile. Instead, he frowned, struggling for a moment with some inner turmoil. I was astonished at what he finally said. "I'm ashamed to say that meeting was no accident," was his reply. "I think it is time I confessed what really happened." He took a long pull of the wine. Then, "Maeen came to get me after you refused his safe company. He said there was a young man of noble birth who seemed intent on daring trouble. My honest response to this was laughter. For what do I care about rich men's sons?"

He looked at me, but I made no reaction, for I was confused at this belated confession. "But then I thought, perhaps here is opportunity," he continued. "As you know I was seeking support for an expedition since I arrived in Orissa. I did not know if you could be the man to help, but I thought it wise to gamble."

"So you were waiting outside the whole time?" I asked.

Janos nodded. "I should have come out of duty or honor, at Maeen's first word, but I'm ashamed to admit I did it for selfish motives."

I was charmed by this admission. It made Janos seem more human. I didn't doubt for a moment that after this time our friendship bloomed from honest ground. Otherwise, why would he confess? It did him no good to shine an ill light on his own deeds. I have learned since my youthful reasoning powers were poor protection, for men and women do many things for many motives. And although I now believe Janos *was* my friend, he could not help but play on my weakness. For he was a creature of his obsession.

I poured more wine, new interest making me forget the heat. "Thank you for that," I said. "It takes a strong man to admit a failing."

Janos laughed ruefully. "I have more failings than strengths, my friend," he said. "But I appreciate your words just the same."

"You are a most curious person," I said. "My sister called you mad, bad, and dangerous to know. And my sister is not often wrong. Tell me about yourself, if you would. All I know are the rumors of the marketplace and the few hints you've dropped. How is it you find yourself here with me? Awaiting the winds from a lazy god."

Janos's face darkened. At first I thought I had offended him by prying. His next words shook me. "Damn all the gods," he said, voice hoarse. "They never come when they're wanted. And arrive only when disaster is complete. Do not depend on the gods, Amalric. For they are as cunning and mean as any demon."

I was too amazed at this blasphemy to speak. Janos rushed on. "Let me tell you what happens to those who trust in the gods, instead of setting their own course. As you know, my mother was the daughter of an Orissan noble, and my father was a prince of Kostroma when they were joined. When he returned to his homeland with his bride, his father had died and the populace was waiting to anoint him king. This was a heavy responsibility and there were brothers who could have taken the load, but the people wanted him . . . and with great reluctance, he accepted."

"Why would one be reluctant to be a king?" I wondered.

"For many reasons, as you shall see if you live long enough. But in Kostroma a king's lot was especially difficult. For a king of Kostroma was responsible for the city's luck. It was the law when calamity struck, and all hope was lost, it was the king who was required to lay down his life for the kingdom as the ultimate sacrifice. My mother's family was partly correct in viewing Kostroma as a land of barbarians. But my family was much more civilized than their imaginings, of course, and in the few years I was given with my parents I had all sorts of skilled tutors to make up for any lack in innate civilization."

"Forgive me for tearing at a tender scab," I said, "but I had heard your parents were dead. Does this story have something to do with that?"

"All of it," Janos said. "Kostroma had many enemies, but my father used his wits to keep them divided and his warrior skills to keep them from our fields. Then one day news came that a great horde was advancing on our lands. I do not know who they were or are, for I was too young to know more than they were a dangerous and particularly evil enemy. My father sent out scouts, and they came back with reports of such vast numbers, he knew all was lost. Kostroma was doomed.

"So my father donned his priestly robes and took up the standard of our god, our protector. He advanced alone to the field outside our city where the enemy host was formed, set down the standard, and called upon our god to accept his sacrifice and save the city. Such was our bargain with that god. I will not speak his name, because my hate might give him life.

"The enemy charged, my father between them and the city. He cried again for help and stood his ground. A horseman laughed and lopped off his head with a single blow. His body tumbled and the horseman impaled his head on swordpoint and led the army through the city gates. They killed all who fought them and carried off those who surrendered to sell as slaves. My mother was one of the dead. In a way this was fortunate, for as a final humiliation to Kostroma, all the princesses were thrown to the horde to be tormented.

"I did not learn until later what went on in the city, for I was with my father that day. Although I rose barely to his waist in height, I was a prince and knew I must stand by his side in the sacrifice. When he fell I struggled to raise that standard myself. I remember how heavy it was. How scared I was. But I knew if I raised it and called the god, he would come quickly and put everything right. Someone rode for me, shouting and waving his sword. I struck at him with the standard, but he knocked it away and plucked me off the ground and into the saddle."

Janos' eyes were tormented. "After the battle I was put in the slave pens."

"But you escaped," I cried. "You must have, or you wouldn't be here to tell the tale."

"No," Janos rasped. "I was marched for many a league, almost dying from weariness and thirst. Eventually we came to Redond and their slave market, where a buyer for the Lycanthian army bid on me like I was one of my father's lambs."

I gawked, a little amazed at myself for not shrinking away from someone who had just revealed that he came from the lowest caste. I looked again at the dark-bearded man with the scarred cheek and saw only my friend. "How did you survive? You must have escaped, and returned to your home. Yes, this is what must have happened."

Janos shook his head once more. "No. I stayed. And as for Kostroma, it no longer exists. Our enemies razed it and scattered the stones. Only beasts dwell there now."

He lifted the dancing girl from beneath his shirt. "I have only this to remember my father by. It is all I have left to keep his memory close. And that of my mother's. It had been broken on that day and was now so tarnished, no one saw any value in it and took it from me."

Janos drained his cup and motioned for more. I hastily refilled it, anxious to hear the rest of this strange tale. "I was slave to the soldiers for many a year," he said. "At first I toiled in the kitchens, or cleaned the latrines. I was a nasty lad with an evil temper and I kept a sharp knife close for anyone who tried to make me his bum boy. My gift for languages was discovered. An army had been raised to fight near where Kostroma had been and I knew the dialects, so I was taken along. From that time on, I traveled whenever the army went out. I was well trained as a killer and treated despicably. But I was encouraged to test my language skills, so over time I came to know many peoples and many cultures."

"How did you come to be free, then?" I asked.

"The Lycanthians are an evil lot and I despise them all," Janos answered. "But they have one custom in which they are superior to the Orissans. Lycanthians allow slaves to buy their freedom. From there they can advance to any point in society. That is what I did. I saved my coin, did all I could to earn . . . or steal more. And finally I had enough to purchase my freedom. I always intended to return to my mother's homeland. But pride kept me away a few more years. Pride, and more."

He fingered the dancing-girl necklace again. "This is what kept me from going mad all those years," he said. "I dreamed of the Far Kingdoms on countless nights, imagining it to be a wondrous place, where all my suffering would cease. I envisioned it a place set above the dwellings of the gods. A place where no one is slave to another, and all words are spoken in kindness. Wherever I went, whatever I did, the goal of finding the Far Kingdoms motivated my actions. It was a boy's imaginings. But it hardened into something much more. I swore in my lifetime I would see it for myself. So I stayed with the Lycanthians, and rose to captain in their ranks. Once again I set aside funds, until I had enough to finally quit the city."

"Dreams would not have kept *me* from going mad," I said. I spoke with great assurance, for I could not imagine myself a slave to another man.

"You would be surprised, my friend," Janos said, "what a person will do for just one more breath of life. As for madness, perhaps I am. But, as I said, any sanity I do possess I owe to my dream. I studied languages. I examined people so I could see them from every direction as well as into their hearts. And you will not be amazed to know, for I have seen your looks when I practiced in my quiet corner of this ship, that I developed an unseemly interest in the Evocator's art. I spoke with shamans in distant villages, studied the habits of barbarian priests. I hope you will still call me friend when I confess I have a small knowledge of wizardry and have pored over ancient texts."

"I guessed as much when you gave me the ferret's tooth," I said. "And although I know the Evocators say it is evil for common men to practice their skills, my own view of those whoresons is so dismal the sin you admit seems slight to me." I said this boldly, but an honest shiver in my guts remembered Janos' lie when questioned by the Evocators. I prayed there would be no discovery of that lie.

I covered my uneasiness with a laugh, and I refilled our goblets. I toasted, "To new friends and old enemies," I said. Janos' cup clinked against mine.

"What of the winds?" I asked, circling back to the beginning. "When do you think they will come?"

Janos shrugged. "When we're the least ready," he answered. Then he turned over and slept.

The next morning we awoke to find the ship mired in a vast bed of seaweed. It stretched beyond view in every direction. When we saw how we were caught, some began to despair of ever escaping. The smell of decay was overpowering. But not so overpowering as the feeling that we were being *watched*. The feeling grew into certainty when a sailor cried out, and we saw two huge eyes poking up from the seaweed. The eyes were no more than a ship's length off our port bow. We came to know those eyes well. They were yellow and shot with roped veins of red. As they observed, there was a constant bubble and moil beneath the surface, as if the creature were feeding. The captain ordered one of the crewmen to climb atop the mast to see if he could make out more of the creature from the heights. As he climbed, the creature's eyes rolled slowly back, following him.

Just before he reached the top, an enormous, purplish cable of flesh shot out of the water. The sailor screamed as the tongue—for that's what it was, and covered with small, sharp teeth—wrapped around him and plucked him, howling with fear, from the mast. He wriggled and fought as the tongue pulled him down into the water and to the still-unlimned creature. There came one more burbling scream as he disappeared. There was a small struggle, and blood welled. The eyes went back to their task . . . watching us.

Night slashed down, as black a night as I had ever seen. We could not see the creature's eyes, much less ourselves, but we knew we were still being watched. I heard men weeping. I heard frightened whisperings. I heard someone shout, "It's the redhead the fiend wants!" Janos had Sergeant Maeen assemble the soldiers. From their voices they were as frightened as the sailors. Maeen calmed them, steeling them against the night. But we did not know in which direction the most danger threatened—from the watcher in the sea, or from our own kind.

I fell into a troubled sleep. It was a dream of strange voices, but no images. There were constant whispers, whose nature I could not determine, but I knew they were discussing my fate. A ghastly light crept in. The light grew into blue flames that leaped higher and higher, as if fanned by wizardry. I wanted to run, but my limbs were heavy stone columns. There came a shout that hammered my soul, and the two Archons of Lycanth burst out of the flames. "Arise the winds," one of them called, and his voice was thunder.

"From the north and the south," the other cried, "east and west. Gather ye winds. Gather." His voice was lightning.

"Seek the redheaded one," the thunderer commanded. "And the one known as Greycloak. Find them on the seas where no wind blows."

"Blow foul, blow fierce," the other said. "Then fiercer and fouler still. Blow, ye winds. Blow." A black cloud exploded out of the flames, and the Archons were gone. The cloud was bristling with black forces, swirling this way and that. Then I could see the Archons in the cloud. They were pointing at me! *"Blow ye winds, blow!"* came their great shout. The black cloud howled toward me.

I bolted awake, dripping sour sweat. It was morning. I looked about, still shaken from my dream, and saw the other men were

rising from the deck. They were smiling. I felt a cool breeze fan
my cheek, the reason for their smiles. Janos clapped me on the
back. "Our luck has returned," he cried. "The winds are back."
The seamen leaped to obey Captain L'ur's commands. Soon the
lateen stirred in the gathering breeze. I ran to the side and saw
that the watcher was gone—and the wind was parting the floating
mass of seaweed. There came a boom as the sail filled, and the
Kittiwake leaped forward. I heard the men cheer, but I did not feel
the same joy. For looming up on the horizon was the great cloud
of my dream, if it was a dream and not a vision of our fate. My
answer came as the cloud turned black and fierce and filled the
sky. Janos shouted, but his words were whipped away as the wind
went from stiff breeze to a demon storm that lifted the seas and
smashed them against the ship. The cries of joy turned to screams.
A line snapped and lashed past, scarring the deck. I dropped to
the planks to escape the wind's blast. A body slammed into mine,
and I grabbed and held the man down as the wind fought to tear
him away. I saw, as he found a secure hold, the man was Janos.

A great hand lifted the ship and flung us forward. The *Kittiwake* buried itself in a wave, and we all nearly drowned as the
seas poured over us. She struggled up, and I felt weightless as she
flew across the waves. We clung to whatever holds we had found
for hour after hour as the storm raged without stop. Many times
we were underwater so long, I prayed to the gods for gills like a
fish. Somehow we always emerged, as the *Kittiwake* refused to
surrender to the Archons' winds. We were, Captain L'ur gasped in
my ear, far beyond Redond, in unknown seas. Ahead must lie the
cursed Pepper Coast! No one dared lower the sail, and perhaps
this saved us. Or perhaps the pig's blood Cassini had offered was
enough to appease the local gods, because the lateen held as if
woven by sorcerous threads and kept us flying across the seas.

A fist hammered my shoulder, and I turned to see Janos pointing. I looked up, I heard a dry *crack*, and the mast split just above
the step. If it gave, all was lost. Janos was pulling at me, screaming words I couldn't hear. I knew their intent—somehow we had
to save the mast. We struggled forward. I believed Janos had gone
mad, for he seized a thick length of line and began wrapping it
about the mast. I thought it a useless reinforcement that would
only hold for a moment or two.

This time I heard his shout, "Help, me, Amalric!" Thinking
these were my last moments of life, I did as he indicated, wrapping lines around the growing split in the mast. Janos tore an iron
marlinespike from a rack and pushed it through the rope. He fum-

bled in his pocket and pulled out an object that dangled from the end of a string. I realized that it was a ferret's tooth, the tooth meant for poor Eanes. Janos wrapped the necklace about the spike, closed his eyes, and chanted mightily, stroking the tooth as he chanted. The mast gave another *crack*, and the sail gave a terrible clatter. But before it could give way, I felt the rope lines harden and tighten under my hands, until they became as strong as new forged steel, and the mast held firm.

We collapsed on the deck, exhausted. More hours passed, but now the winds were diminishing. Janos and I stumbled up to take stock. We spotted L'ur struggling alone to get the rudder back into its post. We fought our way to his side, dodging flailing lines and loose cargo. I heard a roar in the distance and turned to see land. Ragged reefs lifted fangs through the white-crested stormsurf. In the gray light I could see the shore beyond. A wave lifted and hurled us toward those reefs. We braced for the wreck. As if alive, the *Kittiwake* shook herself in the water, heeling as she struck. Seas torrented over us for an eternity. Just when I thought I could no longer hold my breath, the seas rolled back.

The ship was stranded, hard aground on the highest reef. Another wave rolled in, but now the storm was weakening, and the wave foamed harmlessly around our keel. Janos and I hoisted ourselves upright. I almost laughed, for his gape at still being among the living must have been a twin of my own surprise. I heard men crying out and turned to see how I could help. Amazingly, Maeen and the soldiers seemed to have survived, and the number of seamen did not seem much fewer.

"Over there," Janos gasped, pointing. Three of our seamen must have been flung from the ship when she struck. They were wading through waist-high surf toward the rocky beach. One of the men, I noted, was Crop Ear. He seemed stronger than the others and strode vigorously forward. One of his companions, weak and bleeding, grabbed him for help, but Crop Ear swatted him off and pushed on.

Janos gave a sudden groan. "Ah, the poor bastards." I saw the reason for his lament. Hundreds of dark figures scuttled along the beach toward the wading seamen. They were waist high to a man and seemed to be composed of hard shell and sharp spines. At that moment the sun broke through the stormy skies. The figures were not creatures at all; they were miniature men, savages really, armed with tridents for spears and wearing shields and armor made of some species of thick-shelled beasts. Scores of them plunged into the surf for the seamen. Crop Ear bellowed alarm and tried to flee. In moments they swarmed over him. Soon they had Crop Ear and the other seamen spread-eagled on the shore. One of the small warriors leaned in and cut a long strip of flesh from Crop Ear's wriggling, squealing body.

The savage held up the strip of bleeding hide. He shouted a challenge at the ship, then raised his head and swallowed the flesh whole, like a cormorant taking a fish. He whirled around and plunged back at Crop Ear for more. There was nothing we could do but watch as the savages devoured our comrades alive.

CHAPTER EIGHT
The Warrior in Amber

JANOS BELLOWED, "FOLLOW me." I saw him grab a fishing net. I could see it was snagged, and wondered why my friend wanted to go fishing when we were all about to be eaten by those fearsome folk on the shore. He bellowed again, breaking my coward's death grip on the rail, and I stumbled to help. The net came free, and Janos threw it over his shoulder and leaped onto the railing. "Come on," he shouted. He plunged over the side. I didn't think, but vaulted after him. I followed him, splashing and bounding across the reef and into the shallows—knowing he was mad, but I was madder still.

Janos was screaming at the Shore People. The words were unintelligible at first, then I realized they were in Trader's Tongue. " 'Ware the ghosts!" he was shouting. " 'Ware! These be evil men. 'Ware the ghosts! 'Ware!" Then we were among the enemy. They must have thought we were mad as well, for instead of falling on us like sensible little savages, they stood back, gaping, shields and spears drooping. "Evil men ... 'Ware the ghosts!" Janos kept shouting, and they parted ranks and let us through. I saw frightened faces, stunned faces, even a few grateful faces blur past. Every stride we took and every shout Janos gave made them believe they faced a terrible threat, and we were not that threat. As we sprinted for the knot dining on our comrades, Janos unslung the net. "Back," he shouted. "Get back. 'Ware the ghosts!"

The little men leaped away in shock as Janos hurled the net into the air. It spread its wings like a mountain bird and floated down and down. The savages held their breaths, watching it fall, and I knew they were calling on their own gods to aid the net. A sigh rose as it settled over the corpses. They were safe from the ghosts.

Janos whirled about, and when he saw the warrior who had challenged us when we were aboard ship, he assumed the man was one of the leaders. "Thank the gods you slew these men," he said with great emotion. "Please tell us what deities bless this place and we will make immediate sacrifice. For we are men of Orissa, known to all the world for our piety." I heard the word Orissa echo through the crowd. There were gasps of recognition, but amazement as well. The warriors had heard of our river kingdom, but we were evidently the first to come among them.

The warrior leader goggled at Janos. His shell armor gave a dry rattle as he shifted, unsure. "These Lycanthians were your enemies?" he asked. I heard more rattling as the other warriors crept closer.

"To be Lycanthian is to be an enemy of all civilized folk," Janos chanced. There were mutters of angry agreement. "But these men you killed were worse," Janos said hotly. "They were either demons in men's skin, or possessed by demons. It is because of *them* that we find ourselves wrecked on your shores, and begging your hospitality."

He half turned to me, still speaking in the tongue of the traders so all could understand. "We are most fortunate to come among these people, my lord. I fear your aged father would soon be weeping for his youngest son if they had not witnessed our plight. And joined in disposing of this, this—" Janos spat at the bodies. "—Lycanthian filth!" I looked at the net and saw Crop Ear grinning back at us. But Janos was urging me to join in this desperate game quickly. Most of the warriors seemed confused, open to suggestion. But I still saw doubt. A few were even eyeing us speculatively. If they were our rescuers, then what price could they exact for our salvation?

"The crimes of the Lycanthians are known to all," I said, then made my face solemn. "But not all *these* men were evil. Do you not see, Captain Greycloak, who lies among our enemies?" I pointed at the only body that quickly caught attention—Crop Ear.

Janos caught my ploy. He stared closer at the net, and all the warriors stared with him. When he saw Crop Ear, he gave a low moan of sorrow. "Why it is our brother, the Holy Crop Ear." He stifled a sob. "Poor Crop Ear. And he was so kind to homeless children, and starving widows."

"This man was not evil?" the warrior said, alarmed. "But . . . he is Lycanthian. It is plain to see by his costume."

"Yes, of course he is," I said. "But he is one the gods blessed with knowledge of his own people's foulness. He came to Orissa many years ago, and performed so many acts of charity and other pious deeds he was purified by our greatest Evocators. Since that time, he has become a hero among us and an example for our children."

The warrior still wasn't convinced. He pointed at the scarred reminders that Crop Ear was a felon many times over. "Why does he carry those marks?"

"They were self-inflicted," I said. "The Holy Crop Ear wanted the gods to let him bear the burden of the sins of the innocent."

I heard sympathetic noises from the ranks. The warrior chief was so crestfallen, Janos dared to step closer, shrinking his form—by craft, not wizardry—to not bulk large over the man. "Do not mourn, my friend. You could not know." He cast an arm out toward our wrecked ship on the reef. "These Lycanthians seized us at sea. By sorcery, I assure you, not by arms, for our soldiers would have soon overpowered the pirates. They plotted to use our ship, with us as their slaves, to spread their foul influence wherever they could. For some reason, they chose to come here to commit their first black deeds."

The mutterings in the ranks grew louder, proving Janos had correctly guessed that pirates and Lycanthians had clashed with the Shore People more than once. "But our own Evocator, who was ill at the time, or else they could not have trifled with such a powerful wizard, joined with the Holy Crop Ear to thwart them. For all of us had heard of the goodly folk of the Pepper Coast, and how you have suffered at the hands of the Lycanthians. When the storm caught us, we thought we were blessed. If we were to die, at least these demons would be stopped. But the storm wrecked us on your shores, and those men"—he jabbed a disdainful thumb at the bodies—"tried to escape into your lands, where they could cause great misery. The Holy Crop Ear tried to stop them. But, alas . . ." He shook his head. "It was an easy mistake to make, my friend. I am sure he would forgive you."

The warrior chief removed his helmet and wiped a tear. I heard a few soldierly noses being blown. My merchant's instinct nudged. It was time to close the sale. "Certainly, he would," I said. "And I can see that great good will come from all this. For now we Orissans and the Shore People have finally come together. All our gods are sure to bless such a joining. And there can be much profit as well, for both our people. Friendship and trade will blossom on these bountiful shores."

I lifted my hand in formal greetings. "I am Amalric Emilie Antero. Son of Paphos Karima Antero, the greatest merchant prince in all Orissa. And in his name, I offer you the friendship of our noble house."

The warrior, too, raised a hand. "I am Black Shark, shaman and chief of the Shore People. Welcome, men of Orissa. Welcome." As his hand dropped, he thrust a chin at the corpses. "And we owe you thanks as well for capturing their ghosts. We did not know they were demons when we began to eat them."

"Think nothing of it, Black Shark," Janos said. "Now, if it wouldn't be too much trouble . . ." He pointed at the tattered *Kittiwake* and our forlorn comrades, who peered out at us from the wreck. "Perhaps we could organize a party to fetch those people ashore?"

Black Shark smiled. It was meant to be gentle, but was spoiled by the filed teeth.

"Don't forget the cargo," I said.

"Right," Janos said. "Could you take off the cargo as well?"

"It will be done before the tides turn," Black Shark said. He barked orders in their native tongue, and while I was congratulating myself for being alive, the cannibals of the Pepper Shore laid down their weapons and swarmed out to the *Kittiwake* to help our friends. True to his word, Black Shark plucked everyone off and salvaged our gear before the tides covered the reef. By nightfall they had helped us erect shelter in their village, which was hidden in a nearby cove not far from the mouth of a river, and Janos, Cassini, Captain L'ur, and I were sitting about a driftwood fire, sucking the meat out of roasted crab claws.

The human toll had been light; except for Crop Ear and his poor sailor friends, only one other fellow was dead—and he was a sailor as well. Black Shark and his people had easily accepted our assurances that these Lycanthians—L'ur included—were of that new and astonishing breed, Reformed Lycanthians, like the Holy Crop Ear. The soldiers had suffered only small injuries, and Sergeant Maeen was tending to them as we sat by the fire and reconsidered our future. But I was not totaling my good fortune as I sat there finishing my meal. Instead I gloomed into the fire, contemplating disaster. "Can you build another ship?" I asked the captain.

"Aye," he said. "It can be done. Nothin' like the *Kittiwake*, a course. But it'll be a sound craft. Got a whole forest of pepper trees about, and that's prized timber for ship building. I'll not have time to age the wood, but it's more'n sturdy enough green for our needs."

"I'm sorry about *Kittiwake*," I said. "But I'll make it up when we get back." L'ur smiled, relieved, which had been my intention. I needed his full support. "How long will it take to build a new ship?"

"Two, maybe three months," L'ur said. "These be per'lous waters—as we've all witnessed. So we must take a care in the buildin'. The new craft'll need to be better'n just seaworthy if we're to make Redond."

"That is not so long a trial," Cassini said. Under the circumstances he seemed oddly cheery. "We'll be home soon enough, with all of Orissa to praise our names."

"How can you say that?" I cried. "We've been wrecked before I've even *begun* my Finding."

"Oh, I think the oracle was clear when it foretold our troubles," Cassini said. "But it also hinted at success. And here we are, on the Pepper Coast, where no Orissan has ever gone. You said yourself the trade opportunities are fabulous. The captain has just spoken of the worth of the timber. And there'll be precious metals and we've seen wonderful animals and birds to delight the people at home. You've *found* your fortune, my friend, Amalric. There is no need to search further."

"But ... the Far Kingdoms ... they're lost to us," I said. "I can't guarantee my father will fund another expedition. And I doubt your superiors will approve another."

"No," Cassini said. "I am sure they won't. To go further, they'll say, would be to defy the oracle. But don't you see? We no longer have need of the Far Kingdoms."

I didn't answer. Yes, there was much profit to be had on these shores. Exclusive profit and fame of sorts for the Anteros. Although our journey had not been completed, this was the first new area opened to Orissa in many a year. But this meant nothing to me. All I could think of was the flash of golden sunlight that beckoned from beyond the black fist. Beckoned me still to the Far Kingdoms.

"You can keep your gold, Cassini," Janos rasped. "And you can keep all the huzzahs from the good folk of Orissa. I, for one, intend to go on."

Although I knew he was behaving like a fool, my heart jumped into the light when I heard Janos speak. "It is not for you to decide, Captain Greycloak," Cassini said. "This expedition cannot continue without my blessing, even if it were possible. Which it most definitely is not."

Janos was so angry, I thought he was going to draw his knife. I quickly broke in. "Hold on, Janos. And you, too, Cassini, if you please. There's no need for hard words between us. Just as there is no need for a quick decision. Why don't we consider for a few days . . . when our condition will be clearer."

"I have no need for further clarity," Cassini said, refusing to let it drop.

"Oh, you don't, do you?" Janos retorted. "Well, let me ask you this. How do you propose we feed ourselves for three months?"

Cassini began, "The Shore People—"

"Manage quite well, thank you," Janos interrupted. "And they have a little extra to spare, besides." He indicated the remains of the roasted crab. "But these are fisherfolk. Actually, not even that. They live on what they can pluck from the rocks, or dive for beneath the surf. They plant a little grain here and there and harvest a bit of fruit and nuts. But that is not near enough to feed us all for three months or more."

"We have our supplies," Cassini protested.

Janos snorted. "Dried goods. And a few treats from home. But that was just to stretch things. We were going to live off the land, remember? And don't say we can do the same here, because we can't. With all of us added to their numbers, the shore's bounty will soon become scanty. And you will notice the fruit and nuts don't grow in orchards, but are scattered thinly about the forest— which is the way of all life in these climes. Plus hunting will make scarce return as well after a month or so. The Shore People will soon find us poor guests. The presence of the seamen might be borne, because they can help with the fishing. But the three of us, and the soldiers, are hardly famous hunters who can provide more than we would consume. Mark my words, they'll kill us rather than face famine."

"How can you know all this?" Cassini sputtered. "We have only been here a few hours. It is not possible to make such an assessment."

I leaped in before the quarrel could continue. "I asked you both to let a few days pass," I said, making sure I spoke with force. "This is still *my* Finding. Financed by my father. And I insist on that time to contemplate."

"I won't—" Cassini began, but I cut him off with an impatient wave of my hand.

"I trust you enough to know you will do what is best at the time," I said. "So leave it be."

Both men remained quiet after that. Cassini drew into a corner of the tent to brood, while Janos went outside to count the stars, perhaps. Or consult with Maeen. I stayed by the fire with L'ur, realizing now was not a good time to reason further with my friend. L'ur fell quickly asleep after the argument, and there was a smile pasted on the sleeping face. He mumbled things, like "board feet." And "mind the mast." A happy craftsman, contemplating the work ahead. Ah, well, at least he had a goal: to build a ship in three months. L'ur was the only happy man that night.

After a time my own thoughts drove me out. I found Janos hunched on a rock, listening to the lonely surf pound the shore. I made no greeting, but sat beside him, haunted by my own thoughts. "Thank you ... for the delayed decision," Janos finally said, with effort. I made no answer, because the reprieve was false. When the time came there would be few choices for the picking. Then he asked, "I wonder what your father would say, if he were here?"

"Go back, I expect. My father usually takes the long view."

"Not always," Janos said. "He still regrets listening to his *own* father, and not seeking the Far Kingdoms himself, long ago."

"He had no choice but to obey," I answered.

Janos sighed. "Your father is a much better man than I will ever be. He said it would make him happy if he went to his grave knowing his own son achieved what had been denied him. For me, that would be *no* satisfaction at all." He gave me a grim smile. "I would curse him because I was not first."

"What will you do," I asked, "if ... our worse fears come true?"

Janos hesitated, then, "I'd rather not think on it just now," he said. "But I must warn you. I will not give up easily. Give me half a chance and I'll carry this expedition on my own back if I have to."

"Be careful with Cassini," I warned. "He can do us much harm."

Janos patted his knife. "Not as much as I can do him," he said. His words chilled me. This was not meaningless angry talk, to be forgotten on the morrow.

"You won't hear an Antero defend an Evocator," I said. "But you should know that Cassini is only trying to put a happy mask on our failure. He *needs* a victory. He's practicing what he'll say in Orissa. Remember, his own career is at stake here."

"Careers be damned," Janos snarled. But he seemed to instantly regret the outburst and fell silent for a moment. Then he asked, "What about you, Amalric? What of your own career?"

"I feel much as you do," I said. "Yes, there are riches here. And yes, I could put a happy mask on as well and boast of this success before all Orissa. But . . ." My voice trailed off.

A bark of harsh laughter from Janos. "You've been bitten as well, haven't you, my friend? Afflicted with the Far Kingdoms disease. Before long, you'll be sorry we ever met." The moon broke from behind a cloud, bathing Janos in an unholy glow. "There is no cure for this malady," he said. His finger stabbed out. "Except one." I didn't need to look. He was pointing east to the Far Kingdoms.

Black Shark came to us the next day. He wore no armor, but instead was dressed as a common man in a plain, brown tunic of bark cloth. The only mark of office was a shaman's eye daubed on his forehead. He was nervous, humble, almost, if such a fierce man could ever be humble.

There was no preamble. "I have come to ask a great boon for my people," he said. "We have no right to ask it. For our trouble is of our own doing. An unpardonable sin committed by us long ago."

I could not imagine what sin might trouble cannibal folk, but I made appropriate noises about the great service they had performed for us, and promised we would do what we could. Black Shark turned to Janos. "You have shown much skill with ghosts," he said. Cassini coughed at this, but Black Shark didn't appear to notice. "We thought that skill might help us."

"Please go on," Janos said. "Although I must beg your understanding that it was his"—he motioned at Cassini—"enchanted net I threw. However, as outsiders we might have a clearer view of the causes of your misfortune."

Black Shark was pleased by Janos' modesty. He called for pillows of sea grass and shells brimming with some heady liquid for our refreshment. We settled down to hear his tale. "It was in my grandmother's time," Black Shark began. "She was a young woman and had not yet delivered her first child. We were a happy people then, and the sea blessed us with its bounty, and the forests delivered much fruit as well, so there was always plenty for the Shore Folk to eat and drink their fill. The world was a kindlier place in that time, and our enemies were few. Then one day the Shaman, who was her father, called the people together in this very place"—Black Shark's hand indicated the spot where we sat—"and warned them there were ill omens bubbling in the village cooking pot. The odor was not right, he said, and when he poked into the pot with a stick, a two-headed seal pup came to the top.

"How it got there, no one could say. But they all agreed it could not have been placed in the pot by one of us, because who would wish such a thing on their own folk? People were afraid and cried out for the Shaman to tell them what they must guard against. He could not say, for the bad magic in that foul pot had confounded his powers of vision. People fell to guessing what manner of ill to expect. Some said it would be a fierce storm that would leap upon us. Others said we should see to our weapons, for it could only mean an attack from our enemies—the Dalree—who dwell not many leagues from here."

Black Shark gave us a look of deep sincerity. "You should know you are most fortunate to have come to our shores," he said. "The Dalree are evil folk who care nothing for a stranger's life. They are fierce men and will not even honor those they have killed by eating their flesh."

Cassini coughed again. It might have been a laugh. I refilled Black Shark's shell, so he wouldn't notice any rudeness.

"But it wasn't the Dalree we had to fear, although my grandmother said precautions were taken and offerings made. The tide returned and departed many times over until even the Shaman had nearly forgotten the omen. One morning, just before the sun drove the fog spirits from the beach, the village heard a loud thundering. It was the storm, they thought, come at last. Not the Dalree. Everyone rushed out to shriek, wail, and whirl about as the Shaman had instructed. This way, he said, the storm would believe its brother was attacking us, and would seek out others to make miserable. Such as the Dalree."

Out of the corner of my eye, I saw Cassini nod in appreciation. Rare approval from an Evocator of Orissa. "But there was not a cloud in sight, and my people soon realized the thunder was not the drumming of a storm. And the sound didn't come from the sea, but from the land at our backs."

Black Shark gestured, and we all turned to look at the high bluffs beyond a stand of trees. "To the east," he said, "just past those bluffs, there is a canyon. An abyss with no known bottom. And behind that canyon, there is a cliff so steep, that not even a devil could climb it. From thence, my lords, came the sound.

"The Shaman ordered the warriors to gird for a fight, and he sent a party of our bravest men to learn the nature of the threat.

When they came to the abyss, they saw no one about, and the thunder had ceased. Everyone marveled at the mystery and made ready to return. Before they could, alas, the drumming started up again. They saw nothing at first, then one of them gave a shout and pointed to the cliff. They saw metal flashing from atop that cliff. The cliff, as I said, no man could climb. But there were men there just the same—as that flash of metal will witness. Men, and horses as well."

Janos leaned forward, brow furrowed in concentration, and I suddenly remembered the tale he had told of his own childhood encounter with ghostly horsemen. Black Shark noticed. "You know of men like this?"

"I am not certain," Janos said. "Were they armored?"

"Yes, they were armored. Both the men and the horses they sat astride. The helms were oddly shaped, the witnesses said. Like this . . ." With a finger, Black Shark traced a high-roached helm in the air. Exactly like the helms Janos had described.

"What happened?" I asked.

"Nothing at first," Black Shark said. "They seemed to be just watching, or at least that is the way it was reported later. Most of the men had sense to know sorcerers when they saw them, so they flung themselves on the ground and made abasement. Then they fled before their presence could anger those mighty horsemen. But, alas, one man was not so wise. My grandmother said he was one of the older warriors, who was jealous of the success of the younger men. Instead of abasing himself and fleeing—as would have been proper—he shouted a challenge. One of the warriors looked at him, and he took insult and flung his spear."

Black Shark moaned at the folly. "The cliff was too high for this to be a threat," he said, "but this was no obstacle to the gods who hate the Shore Folk. The man's horse took fright and reared, and the sorcerer fell into the abyss, which was too deep for his companions to retrieve the corpse. They rode off without giving him proper burial. And his bones lie there to this day, a curse on all our lives."

Moved by his own tale, Black Shark sniffled, then drained his cup. "Our luck fled that day," he continued. "All trade ceased, and only pirates, or Lycanthian thieves came to these shores. And do you know—" He leaned closer, voice lowered for a heartfelt admission. "—terrible lies have been told about us. And there are many who fear us because of those demon-whispered lies."

"You don't say?" Janos answered, betraying not one sign of mockery. "Such gentle-natured folk as yourselves?"

Black Shark nodded sadly, eyes red from drink. "It isn't right, but what can we do? We have no luck."

"What if we retrieved the remains of that warrior?" Janos asked. "You could build a shrine and bury his remains beneath that shrine to put the wizard's ghost to rest."

Black Shark's eyes welled with tears. He was almost too moved to speak, but his nod was pitifully eloquent. "That is what . . . we hoped . . ." he choked.

Janos looked at me and then Cassini. "What do you say, my friends? How can we deny these good people?"

THE MOON HID its face that night as they led us through the forest. It was unnaturally quiet. We heard no buzz of flesh biters nor even the cough of a hunting direcat. It was as if all the forest creatures had learned of our quest and were in hiding. Black Shark and his men took us as far as the bluffs. Then he begged our forgiveness and drew a whip of sea grass from a pouch. He lashed us lightly with the whip, one by one, so any offense we committed would not be blamed on the Shore People. They slipped away into the night. Cassini looked after them, an odd gleam in his eye. "The whipping will do no good," he said, voice low, "if those wizards are powerful as he says." He opened the pack he brought with him and drew out the things we had spent all day preparing.

"Then you give credence to his tale of the curse?" I asked.

"I would be a fool if I didn't" was his only answer. Janos grunted. I knew *he* believed. The description of the Watchers on horseback was too close to what he had witnessed as a child. We stripped to the skin and blackened ourselves with charcoal dust so as to avoid any evil eye that might fall upon us. Cassini whispered a spell to further trick any ghosts. We slung the bundles of grass rope over our shoulders and climbed up the steep slope of the bluff. I was proud of my comrades that night. Janos moved ahead, silent as a panther, marking the way. Cassini followed, brave as you please, a gold disc held ready to turn back any spell hurled our way. His long bout with seasickness and his general hatefulness had made me forget, in our days at the gymnasium, Cassini had a well-earned reputation as a brave man. As for me, I won't say I was brave, but merely too young and stupid to know fear.

Atop the bluff was a broad, rocky plain. But instead of a jumble of boulders and sharp stones to test our feet, the ground under us seemed as smooth as wizard-cast glass. The way became easy, and we moved at a faster pace. We could barely see a hand before our face, but we could sense that great cliff Black Shark had described bulking near. The gods must have smiled, for the moon suddenly brightened behind its cloudy veil, and we came to a jerky stop with the abyss yawning at our very feet.

"We must be insane," I whispered, "to attempt this at night."

"Enter darkness *from* darkness," Cassini whispered back. "That is the rule."

"At any rate," Janos said in a normal voice, that made us jump, "we'll soon settle the argument over whether a ghost can or cannot see at night."

"Shush," Cassini hissed. "He might hear."

"I'd almost rather he did," Janos said, "If we creep up on him, he's sure to think we're his enemy." But this came as a whisper just the same. Cassini motioned for the bulky pack I carried. I upended it, and a thick bunch of dry weed tumbled out. Cassini uncorked a flask he carried on a string tied about his naked hips and slowly poured a foul-smelling liquid on the weed. He whispered an enchantment, and I saw something glow deep inside the mass of weed. A flame flickered, and as it burst into a roaring flame, Cassini quickly kicked the whole mass over the side.

We watched it fall, but instead of diminishing from our view, the fire grew larger until it seemed to fill the rift from side to side. Then it bounced, exploded into black, greasy smoke, and came to rest. Apparently the abyss was not so bottomless after all. I peered down. My stomach gave a lurch, for bottomless or not, it was still a great distance. Janos uncoiled his rope. "I'll go first," he said, to my relief.

"What if this isn't the right spot?" I asked. Janos merely pointed. Beyond the fire I saw my answer in a flash of metal. It must be the warrior.

Going second was small consolation. We had to tie all three ropes together, and it was still short by at least the height of three men. But before I could comment, Janos looped our lifeline about a boulder and swung over the side. He quickly slid down, reached the end, kicked away from the side, and dropped. I heard him whisper a chant and saw the glow of light beads. I followed, my hands slipping on the sweat Janos' grip had left. It should have been easy. I was skilled at such things, as I mentioned before, but I was no more than a third of the way down when hopelessness struck me. I looked down, and suddenly the light on the canyon floor seemed immeasurably far. The gap of three men's height suddenly became twenty, then a hundred. The surface of the rope turned to slime, and I plunged down at a great speed. I kicked out to slow my fall, but the rock my feet shattered into pebbles and dust.

Janos shouted, and his shout gave my fingers strength until they bit through the slime, and I came to a jolting stop. My hands burned with the heat of the fall, and my body felt like it had been gripped by a great weight. Then I realized my eyes were closed and opened them. First I saw Cassini's face peering down, pale in the moonlight, eyes wide. Oddly, his face did not seem that far away. Then I looked down. I was the same distance from the bottom as I had been before the fall.

"It's only in your mind," Janos called, anxiously. "A spell left by the warrior's friends."

I wanted to cry out: What do I do? I am no sorcerer. Cassini emptied a pouch over the side, and I saw the glitter of magic dust floating toward me. Soon I will be safe, I thought, but as the dust descended I knew it would not reach me until it was too late. The feeling of hopelessness caught at my gut again, and I felt my fingers slipping. I heard a voice, just at my ear. "Amalric," it whispered. "Do not fear."

"Halab?" I cried, for I thought it was my brother.

"Light as the air," the voice said. "Quick as a falcon, on the hunt."

The helplessness fled, my fingers found their grip, and then the dust was falling across my shoulders. I broke out of the spell like a drowning man kicking his way to air. I swung down the rope as easily as a tree dweller. At its bitter end I dropped the rest of the way and came lightly to my feet. Janos put a hand on my shoulder. "Are you all right, Amalric?" he asked. For a moment I thought his voice was the one that had whispered in my ear. "Take a care," Janos said. "Cassini's coming down." And now there seemed to be no similarity at all. I stepped aside as Cassini dropped beside us. Now it didn't matter whose voice it was, for the spell was broken, and we were all safe on the floor of the bottomless abyss. There was no time for self-congratulation, for the silence was broken by the splash of falling liquid. A long moment later we heard another splash, then another. The sound came from where the ancient warrior had fallen. No sooner had we puzzled this out than a most wondrous odor arose, sweeter than any flower, richer than any courtesan's perfume. We walked tentatively toward the sound and scent.

The warrior's body lay broken across a large, flat stone. His corpse could be clearly seen in the light of Cassini's purifying fire. Janos muttered something, and although I couldn't make out his words, I knew he was reacting to the shape of the armor and helm the corpse was wearing. It was exactly as he had described the horsemen of his childhood. The warrior had been a large man, taller even than Janos, with wide shoulders and thick chest. He had a beaked face, like a bird of prey, with deep-set, still-open eyes that seemed permanently set to peer into vast distances. There was a sword strapped to his waist, and a broken spear lay to one side. His body shone a deep, earthen brown, as if he had been daubed with many layers of paint.

Cassini pointed upward, and we saw a thick drop of heavy liquid form on a rock that hung above the corpse. It gathered into a bead and splashed down on the warrior. As it broke, the sweet odor rose again, and we watched in fascination as the drop spread across the warrior, leaving a brown trail like heavy oil. Janos motioned us closer, and we could see that the body had been covered and preserved by the liquid falling over many generations. The man grimaced up at us, his look as painfully fresh as the moment he'd died.

"I've seen insects preserved like this," Janos said, "but only in old forests. The local people said they were trapped in the sap running from the trees; they sell them as talismans when the liquid dries. It's called amber, I believe." Janos touched the preserved body, curious. "A warrior in amber," he mused.

"I don't see any trees here," I said. "Only stone."

"It is obviously a spell his companions cast," Cassini said, "to preserve their comrade from the elements. Since he could not be properly laid to rest, they did what they could to comfort his ghost."

Cassini filled a gourd with coals from his purifying fire and shook it over the corpse. Sparks and smoke showered as Cassini moved around the stone, chanting soothing words to placate the warrior's ghost. He promised a handsome shrine, with many gifts from the Shore People to honor him. In the shadows I heard a long sigh. The warrior's eyes seemed to glitter, then went blank. We took this as acceptance, and the three of us lifted the corpse free of the killing stone. He came up so easily, I nearly fell. The body was lighter than a child's, empty of all the fluids and flesh that give a living thing weight. As we laid the warrior on the canyon floor, a purse fell and shattered, spilling its contents. There were a few old coins, pierced for trading stock; a whetstone for the sword; and what appeared to be a roll of writing linen. My hand reflexed for it. "Wait," Janos warned. But one finger touched before I could snatch my hand back. A corner of the linen crumpled into dust.

"I'm sorry," I said. No one heard me.

"It looks like some type of map," Cassini said.

Janos' eyes lit with excitement. "Can you reconstruct it?"

Cassini didn't answer, but excitement gripped him as well. He fished in his pack for a small vial of black fluid and an herbalist's knife. He shook a few drops of the liquid in the blade's measuring trough, then sprinkled a pinch of the linen dust over it. I couldn't hear the words of his enchantment; he said them so quickly and smoothly, you could see he had long practice at this sort of task. I remembered all young Evocators were put to work in the library, turning scraps of scrolls or manuscripts into dozens of duplicates each day.

While he worked, I glanced at the pouch the map had fallen from, marveling that the leather it had been cut from had also been preserved by the amber. I saw something on its face that I took at first to be discoloration, then realized it was too regular. I leaned closer, but did not touch the pouch, having learned my lesson. Worked into the leather was an emblem: a serpent coiled across a tooled star. I saw bits of pigment clinging to the emblem, blue on the serpent's coils and yellow on the star, which I realized was actually a sunburst. I pointed it out to Janos, and he scrutinized it as carefully as I had.

"A family crest," I hazarded.

He shook his head. "Not likely for a soldier serving in an organized formation. I would guess it is the crest of those he Watched for. Perhaps a prince, perhaps a sorcerer, perhaps a king. Perhaps that is the emblem of the Far Kingdoms themselves."

I was about to wonder as to the certainty of his words when Cassini announced that the spell had begun to work. He breathed over the mixture. A speck of goo congealed to another, and that small lump bonded to its brother as well. In a moment we could see a sliver of linen begin to grow, and Cassini quickly dumped the knife's contents onto the mother roll. There came a crackle and a hiss as if a fire were being fed, and the roll of linen began to move. In a blink, all traces of antiquity fell away, and the linen spread out before us as fresh and white as the day it was made. The quill scribblings had turned into deep lines of black ink, glistening as if just dipped up from a bottle.

Cassini lifted the light beads, and the three of us leaned forward to see. It was a map, as he had guessed. But it was a most unusual map, for where a human mapmaker would mark perils such as swamps, canyons, or thick jungle, the linen was blank. What was marked were mountain peaks, each crag carefully delineated; rivers that could be seen from the air; and certain high points where a Watcher might have his post. "A map," I murmured, "meant for birds."

"Or," Janos said, "men who can fly, or at least transport themselves from peak to peak with magic."

There was the outline of the Pepper Coast, as if this marked the limits of the Watcher's area of concern, then the map sprawled east. At the easternmost edge of the map was a great lump of a mountain range, a big, black fist knuckling up from the linen.

We heard a sigh, and we spun to see the warrior's eyes all a-glitter again. He seemed to be looking at me. I'm sure the others felt the same, but for a moment I believed that long-dead warrior was trying to speak to me. Then I heard a terrible rattle from his throat, as if he had been clinging to life all these years and was only now being released. The eyes went blank again, but now his rictus grimace was more like a smile.

Janos spoke, voice rough. "Is that omen enough for you, Cassini? What more do you need?"

Cassini was silent, but I could feel the tension building and saw great emotion twitching at the muscles in his face.

"Well?" Janos prodded. "Do we still return home? Or do we go?"

FOUR DAYS LATER we marched east. We left L'ur and his crew in the company of Black Shark's people, who had vowed eternal gratitude for our releasing them from that ancient curse. He even sold us small asses to help carry our burdens and assigned some of his people to go along as hostlers and guides, "until the ends of the world, if you so wish." Furthermore, after the Shore People built the promised shrine for the Warrior in Amber, they promised to help L'ur construct a new ship to take us homeward when we returned.

L'ur himself was now a firm friend of the Antero family. If we met disaster and did not return within six months, L'ur held a note to my father with a pledge of payment for all the time he would have waited, as well as for a replacement of the *Kittiwake*. I had no doubt L'ur would wait, and it wasn't just because of the small fortune I had pledged. He had become as gripped by the fever as any of us when I unrolled the map to the Far Kingdoms.

"For the first time in my life," the old sailor said, "I wish to the gods I had been born a walking man."

CHAPTER NINE
Nomads at World's End

THE RIVER LED inland through rolling countryside that the eye sought hard to fill with farms and villages and people, but there was little sign of humanity in that wilderness. We passed close to a few hamlets; their ragged settlers watched us pass without smiles, without gestures. Our soldiers grew rapidly tired of shouting ribaldry at the few nubile women we saw, for the bawdiness was treated as if it had never occurred.

"All the people," Janos observed, "have the same look as some of the poorer folk in the hills near where I grew up. They see any man with a sword, no matter how tightly it's sheathed, as their enemy. You may recollect what I said once before," he continued, lifting his voice to Cassini, who was walking not far from us, "about what war is like on this side of the Narrow Seas? The look in those people's eyes says more than I can about their lives."

Cassini shrugged. "The strong have always battened on the weak, and always shall. Nature and the gods dictate, man follows."

After a time, we saw no more inhabited villages. Once or twice Janos identified an overgrown weedy patch of secondary growth as where a village, or a farm estate, might have stood years earlier. The climate was a bit warmer than Orissa, perhaps, and it rained more frequently. But the rain drifted softly, like a mist, and came as welcome relief to the heat of the day. We held to an easterly direction, by compass and, from time to time, the sorcerous "map" Cassini had fashioned from the Watcher's tailisman. Even though it showed but peaks and occasional features of the landscape, it was still valuable, and we were able to keep our journey on its proper course.

There were many things of interest to me, and it was not just because I was with the first civilized men—civilized *Orissan* men, I should say—to see this land, but also because this is when I really began to view things through the eyes of my own people. Although honesty directs me to admit that as a merchant's son, I *also* saw much gold being heaped into the Antero vaults. Here there was a fish whose delicate white flesh could be smoked. There was a fruit of glowing green/purple, whose taste exploded in your mouth. A minor spell against decay and corruption, and those could become the latest savory in Orissa. A seed that was as fiery as any dried and ground pepper any of us had tasted.

After a march of five days, the worst problem we had encountered was a persistent fit of sneezing that seemed to set upon all of us just at dusk. We were traveling as if strolling through a park—a park set aside for our private enjoyment. Then, after about a week more, things began to change. I was walking beside Cassini and thinking idly of how easy the way had been for the past hour, as our route wound over low hills, following a series of shallow ravines. He halted, abruptly, and Sergeant Maeen, walking just behind us, had to double-step to avoid running into him. Cassini paid no mind; his eyes were blank and staring . . . looking far into nothingness. I pulled Cassini out of the line of march and beckoned for Janos, who quickly was beside us. I feared our Evocator had become suddenly sorcelled in an unknown manner. But such was not the case, for Cassini soon brought himself back to full awareness; he peered around, realizing that the entire party had stopped and was looking at him.

"This land," he said, without preamble, "was as the Shaman of the Shore People said. I felt the souls of thousands of people, some who lived on these hills, some who traveled this way, traveled on this very road whose ruins we are pacing." I nodded, involuntarily, realizing why our path had been so easy. Of course we were on a long-forgotten, ruined road. "In that vale just beyond," Cassini said, "which you cannot see from here, there was a famous inn . . . at a crossroads. Many stayed there. It was a happy place."

"What happened?" Janos asked.

"Death," Cassini said. "Death and blood. So much blood, for so many years, that those who lived fled, fled or gave up their spirits in hopelessness."

"Who brought the death? Where did it come from? What was it? Steel . . . or sorcery?"

"I think . . . both," Cassini said slowly. "Sorcery is what I feel most strongly, echoing from these hills. Who brought it? I do not know. Where did it come from? I do not know that, either."

Then he returned fully to normal. "Enough," he said. "I do *not* do Seeings as if I were some witch putting unwashed peasants to awe at a Planting Time fest. You. Soldier. Bring me some wine. And check the ties on my boot when you return. I fear I am developing a blister." Cassini was a cold man, even for an Evocator.

An hour later one of the asses brayed and reared, his pack spilling across the ground. The pack was small, but quite heavy, since it contained the thick canvas bag with half of our gold. The pack thudded to the ground and ripped, coins rolling away into the greensward. Maeen shouted at the animal's master, but he shook his head—vowing he'd done nothing to spook the creature—and pointing out that he had been nowhere near the animal when the pack fell. The other Shore People chimed in that he was telling the truth.

"Then you are doubly to blame," Maeen roared. "For you tied your hitches so poorly this morning when you packed the animal that the rope must have worn and broken. You are doubly an ass, and your animal should be leading you, rather than the opposite." The Shore Man stammered that the rope must have been old, but Maeen would have none of that.

I walked to where the pack and its cargo were scattered and picked up the rope. It was quite new . . . L'ur had taken it from the wreck of the *Kittiwake* to make up our pack frames. I examined the end of the rope: it had been *cut*, cut cleanly, in fact, as if a very strong man with a very big, very sharp knife, had slashed it. I took the rope to Janos, who also showed it to Cassini. Janos told Sergeant Maeen that was enough. Have the ass repacked and continue the march. None of us said anything, but our thoughts were clear. I was remembering that tiny golden scythe that Janos had secured back in Lycanth, which now rode in his pack. I knew it could be used not only in the cutting and preparation of magical herbs and such, but to work spells from afar. Certainly there were *other* golden scythes like it, and wizards to wield them. I thought again of the Choosing in Lycanth, and how close that creature had come to me. Then I thought of the Archons tempest; that thought made me look back over my shoulder, and although I saw nothing to warrant it, I shivered.

Minor annoyances increased as we traveled: we were attacked by swarms of black mites whose bites stung like fire; an increase in minor accidents made it seem that all of us were suddenly in the throes of boyhood gangliness; and at dusk, the mysterious fits of sneezing returned.

The problems came to the fore the night we found the ruins. A low pass had made it easier for us to follow close along the river. The river suddenly shallowed and spread out for two spearcasts over visible shoals. It did not seem logical, since I could see in the distance that the river returned to its normal, gently flowing character. As a child of a river city, I thought I knew what I might find, and sharpened my gaze. I surmised that aeons ago this river had been channeled. I called for a halt while I wandered through the brush looking for more evidence. Without much trouble, I found what I was looking for: the river "banks" were carefully mortared stone walls, and those walls were nearly thirty feet apart. Janos was beside me, evidently puzzling at the U-shaped construct.

"Built by man," he said. "But for what end?"

"A set of locks," I explained. "At each end there would have been wooden gates—allowing a boat to enter and either rise up, or be lowered to a new level to continue its course. Over there"— and I pointed to the shallows—"would most likely have been the overrun when the locks were not in use. When it was abandoned, time would have passed, and the river, impatient with its bonds, would have burst through the overrun to find a new bed."

All of us were silent, imagining these locks filled with boats laden with trade goods, waiting for passage along the river. The width of the lock showed that the country had once been fully as prosperous as Cassini's vision had told us.

Janos had Maeen send out scouts, and they returned quickly with more signs of civilization. Further up the river, one man found a winding path. It would have been a tow path, I guessed, so boats heading upriver were not dependent on muscle, wind, or the energy-draining spells necessary to move heavy-laden craft. A few feet away, hidden by a screen of vines, was a building with thick stone walls and narrow-slitted windows. The great beams that held the roof were still in place, though black with age. In front of the building was a smaller, circular structure.

Now it was Janos' turn to be the expert. "A barracks," he said. "The small building would have been for customs and the on-watch guards. We can take shelter here," he said. "The canvas from the packs will stretch over the old beams for our ceiling." He ordered a halt for the night, even though it was two hours before dusk, and detailed two of the Shore People who'd claimed great experience with nets, poisons, and piscatorial spells to catch something fresh for dinner.

I stood in the middle of the bustle, lost in thought. I was not then, and certainly am not now, one of those fools who believe man has a right to throw up his houses and businesses wherever he pleases; but I recognized then, and have felt the same since, that there is something sad and frightening about ruins. Here man was once, and then he vanished: by choice or by threat, who could know?

Then another, even stranger thought struck. I mentioned this quietly to Janos. "In which direction do you think the soldiers were guarding? Were their enemies ahead of us, to the east? Or was this to prevent some threat from behind?" Janos shrugged and did not bother to guess.

We heard a cry of pain, then angry voices, and the sudden clang of a sword against a shield. We ran into the center of the ruins. A scattered fire . . . an overturned cookpot . . . two soldiers with swords ready. Janos shouted, but the two men circling each other, eyes probing for an opening, paid no heed. His hand blurred in that violently quick motion I remembered from outside the tavern in Orissa, and his broadsword flashed, knocking away both blades of the soldiers. They came back to their senses, and there was a babble of ". . . bastard knocked over . . ." ". . . laughed . . ." ". . . clumsy ape . . ." and a bellow for silence.

"Enough!" Janos roared. "Drop the swords, both of you!" Steel clattered to stone. "Lifting arms against a brother! How dare you? You know the penalty. Banishment if there is no harm, death if there is an injury! This is—"

A calm voice interrupted. "This is sorcery, Captain." We turned. It was Cassini.

"We are cursed," he said, in his customarily abrupt way, and he did not pay attention to the reaction to his statement. "Small curses," he went on, "have been dogging us for some days. The sneezing . . . those mites that appear at the least convenient times . . . how all of us have been too quick to anger without provocation."

"Who cursed us?" a soldier growled in spite of Maeen's glower. "Th' damned Shore People?" And scowls were turned against our small companions.

"I think not," Cassini said. "But there must be a casting, and a counterspell. Now, this night. Each of these curses is small, such as an Evocator can cast from a distance, and easily maintain without a drain on his strengths."

"But they can kill," Janos said quietly. "Lione, if that first sword slash had landed, we might well be saying the words for Cherfas as well."

Now it was my turn. I felt a slight flicker of pride as the orders came easily. "Well spoken, Evocator. Again, we have realized how lucky we are that you chose to accompany us and be our shield against evil." My compliment was not truly felt, of course. But I knew the men would need maximum trust in Cassini for a ceremony to work smoothly. "Captain Greycloak," I went on, formally. "Send a man . . . two men . . . to the river and fetch back our fisherman. We shall not chance anyone outside the camp this night. Also, post sentries in the correct manner. Evocator Cassini, all of our resources are yours to cast this counterspell."

Cassini preened just long enough to put my teeth on edge, then began ordering people here and there as he made his preparations. An hour later, as night fell, the surprisingly simple ceremony was performed. Cassini had two soldiers bring a cloakful of clay from the riverbank. We were formed in line, and each of us was commanded to take a handful of the clay and, while Cassini prayed in an unknown tongue, to shape the clay into a figurine. After that he told us to cut a bit from a garment or trapping and work it into the figurine. He cautioned us to *not* use spittle, fingernails, or anything that was a true part of our bodies. He led us out of the barracks into the brush, where a low fire of greenwood had been prepared. He drew a circle around the fire and told us to put our dolls inside that circle. We then formed a second ring, with the orders to focus all of our attention on our doll and to try not to think of anything but the figurine and how it looked exactly like us. Perhaps one or another of the soldiers might have jested about the less than artistic sculptures we laid down; but all of us were frightened—both of these spells and magic itself. I fancied I could feel forces of the night curl around us as Cassini lighted the fire and began chanting as the smoke rose.

> "Smoke shall build
> "Smoke shall climb
> "Choke the eyes
> "Choke the mind . . ."

He softly cautioned us not to break our concentration until . . . until he clapped his hands three times, and as ordered, we spun, turning our backs on the dolls and the fire. Without looking back,

we then walked back toward our campsite. I heard Cassini continuing his chant from behind us.

> "Now we sleep
> "Now we stay
> "Now you seek
> "Now you find.
>
> "Circle shall hold
> "Circle shall reach
> "Circle shall gather
> "Circle shall hold . . ."

An hour later he rejoined us and told us that we should eat and
then sleep. It would do no harm to go out in the bushes for natural
calls, but none of us should go down to where the remnants of the
fire smoked. We should make as little noise as possible, but we
should relax and not worry. The counterspell was cast, and all of
those annoying spells should be drawn toward those figurines.

The soldiers and the Shore People seemed relieved, and they,
having put their trust in Cassini and his sorcery, felt these problems were over. I took Cassini aside, and Janos joined us. I promised the Evocator a bonus for this night's actions when we
returned to Orissa. I asked him if these curses were indeed tied to
those dolls out in the night. He said he was sure—since none of
them were particularly cast to be lethal, none required much of a
counterspell to fool. It was better, he felt, to divert the spells and
allow them to run on rather than to break them completely. "This
will, I hope, keep our enemies happy believing that we are still
plagued by their spells and do not require more stringent attention."

"Our enemies," Janos asked. "From where?"

Cassini looked unsure of himself. "At first, I thought these incantations came from Lycanth, where we know we have enemies,
from the Symeon clan to . . . to others.

"Indeed, I *did* feel emanations from this direction. But I also
felt something else. Something . . . neither of you are Evocators,
so I cannot use the terms of my craft . . . something like a great
rolling wave, a flood perhaps. Coming from the east."

Janos and I were jolted. "But . . . none of us have been beyond
this point, that I am aware of," I said. "Except perhaps one or another of the Shore People."

"It makes little sense," Cassini agreed. "And what I found more puzzling was . . . this flood, this presence, perhaps, I did not feel to be evil. At least, I felt no especial threat to any of us. It was . . ." and he fumbled for words, ". . . as if there were some great, invisible force above us, a force that . . . that . . . ah, I do not have the words," he said. "Think of a great fish in a lake, knowing of the tiny perch around him. He is not hungry at present, but sees those little fish. And perhaps, in an hour or a week, when he *is* hungry, he might look at them more closely." Cassini shook his head. "That is the best comparison my mind allows."

We agreed to set a careful watch that night, less concerned with intruders than that one of our men might become curious, investigate the scene of Cassini's casting, and spoil all of the work. Janos, Cassini, Sergeant Maeen, and I would be the guardians. Cassini took first watch, which started at once. Janos told me later that he chose the Evocator because everyone would still be awake, and Janos would not have to worry about the sorcerer's competency. Maeen followed, then I was to stand guard, and then Janos would take the final watch in the always hazardous predawn hours.

I was sleeping soundly when Maeen tapped me awake for my watch. I took my weapons and found a station just inside the barracks door where I could look out into the starlit night without being seen. Periodically I left the building and walked around it, to ensure no one was creeping up on us. It was very peaceful and very still. The sound of the river was soothing. I felt refreshed by my sleep, and as if a weight had been lifted by Cassini's art. I realized I had been as nibbled by those minor sorceries as any of my men. I looked back at the pass, perhaps a sixth of a league behind us. My eye was drawn to a rock formation on the hillcrest. Then the rock moved and became two men. Two men on horseback.

I should not have been able to see that distance with the degree of clarity my mind told me I was. But I swear now I could see they were both wearing plate armor, strange for such a poverty-crushed land, and helmets with high crests. My mind heard Janos' hushed description from that sunny afternoon under an Orissan wineshop's arbor. *"Even their mounts seemed protected, since I saw another moonflash from one steed's head. The position they took was exactly the one I would order now, if I were leading a patrol into unfriendly territory, overlooking the pass . . ."*

I started to shout the alarm, then stopped myself. The day had ended with enchantments, and everyone was frighted. I had heard stories from old soldiers who were friends of my father about young sentries who swore a bush became an attacking enemy and then changed back to a bush when the watch commander was alerted or a spear was thrown. Then I noticed there was nothing on the hilltop; the horsemen were gone; obviously it had been an illusion of the night. Still, when I woke Janos for the last guard, I waited until he was fully alert and told him about my mirage.

Janos tugged thoughtfully at his beard. "So," he said after a while, "Cassini's great fish may have several senses. We could, if we wished, go to the hilltop after the sun rises. The best that could happen is we would find actual horse droppings and hoof-prints, to prove someone human is watching us in this country. But if we do not find such signs . . . well, either you imagined it, or . . ." Janos snorted. "I think we should not say anything, or do anything at all, my friend. If there were Watchers atop that bluff . . . are we even sure they are aware of us? Assume yes. Are they necessarily our enemies? No one in Kostroma ever reported these ghostly guardsmen to do them physical harm. And . . . even if they are aware of us, and assume they know all from their leaders' great wizardry, is it not unlikely they intend us no evil? We did, after all, provide last rites as best we could for one of their fellows. Soldiers of any race . . . or even ones who were never birthed by human loins must certainly appreciate honors such as that. Even considering that we did remove that talisman."

I found a smile at that one. "Friend Janos, you are now starting to sound like one of a pair of dullards playing odds and even. If I had one stone in my fist last time, should I have the same number this time, and should I say I have one, two, or none. Perhaps I should do the same thing, but no, my friend will know I did the same, and three casts ago, that was my plan, so this time I should . . ." I let my voice trail off. Janos was chuckling.

"Thank you. I *was* making myself as confused as a room of scholars wondering whether the mirror is the reflection or the reality. Whether these Watchers mean us good or evil, or if they are as little concerned about our existence as that satiated great fish will no doubt make itself clear in time."

"Should we consult Cassini?"

"I . . . propose we do not. Let us see how the situation develops." I thought that Janos Greycloak was more worried about this new unknown than he let on; but then, he *was* the one who had seen them once before as a boy.

Two nights later, higher up the river as it began to shallow and narrow into tributaries leading off into the hills, the Watchers were seen again. This time by three men—Sergeant Maeen, a soldier, and one of the Shore People. Again, they did nothing but sit their horses and then vanish. Cassini insisted on casting an interrogatory spell, trying to find out who these Watchers were and whether their presence presaged good or evil for us.

"Cast a spell in their direction," Janos muttered. "How intelligent. If they were not aware of us before, they certainly are now."

Cassini's spell produced nothing. From his wizardry, these Watchers could be nothing else but a natural illusion—an unusual sort of mirage. Janos also had a thought on this—that the Watchers might well have armor beyond what could be seen with the eye. Cassini followed this bit of possible imprudence with something I *knew* to be dangerously arrogant. The next day, he found the highest hilltop in sight, and, carrying a flaming torch to its top, "claimed" the land for Orissa. By this I do not mean he professed physical rights to the land for himself or for our city—even in those days none of us, not even an Evocator, possessed such insolence. The ceremony, which consisted of prayers and then the planting of seeds brought from our city, was intended to tell the beings physical and invisible of Orissa and its people. The ceremony went on to request, although I thought it sounded more like a demand, that just as all beings from and of this land were entitled to respect and honor and protection under the real and Evocatorial laws of Orissa, so our party "requested" equal justice and consideration.

I did not think such a ceremony wise at any time, and am grateful I have succeeded today in banning it from use when Orissans travel abroad. I certainly did not think it apt in this strange country, with its sorcerous "waves," its unknown people and customs, and most of all those spectral Watchers. But neither Janos nor I could say anything. If I ordered Cassini not to perform the ceremony here or elsewhere, he would unquestionably report me to the Council of Evocators when he returned. And they would, without a doubt, put the most selfish and even treasonous interpretation on what an Antero meant by such a command. Since this was yet another problem I could not solve, I tried to put it from my mind.

Cassini's conceit, in spite of his performance with the counterspell, was annoying everyone. He seemed to think he was in charge of the expedition, and that it was the duty of all members to make certain their Evocator was comfortably fed, clothed, and kept safe. As our journey grew wearisome, I found myself thinking how much I would be willing to take my chances without the purported benefits of an Evocator's cloak on my Finding, and how cheery I might become if something incapacitating happened to Cassini.

The river shallowed, then became spotty pools and marshland. We found ourselves standing around a rather picturesque pool from which a spring bubbled.

"This is the first time I have ever followed a river from its outlet to the headwaters," Janos observed. "Does this, O Evocator, entitle me to some special blessing?" Cassini smiled thinly, but said nothing. If the other members of the party were not getting along with Cassini, he and Janos were almost to the point of open enmity. Fortunately neither of them was foolish enough to spark a feud on this foreign shore, although I feared there would be some confrontation when we returned.

We camped at the spring that night. Janos and I spent some time discussing how we would navigate from this point—the Watcher's relict showed little detail of what we surmised were the long, barren leagues ahead. We used two landmarks behind us that also appeared on the Watcher's "map" and set a compass direction from there that we felt would lead us most directly to the next landmark. I had discovered a hidden talent: I understood maps and liked drawing them. I had been keeping careful track of the terrain thus far, and even if we were forced to double back I was sure we could quickly return to this spot, and not repeat our previous wanderings that sometimes had led us into marshes or up blind or torturous canyons.

After dinner the man who spoke for our drivers sought me out. He said this was as far as the Shore People had contracted to go, and tomorrow they and their mounts would turn back toward the coast. I started to lose my temper and was proud that I caught myself in time. I told the man that he and his brothers had contracted for our *entire* journey, which had barely begun. That was not true, he said. They agreed they would travel with us to the end of the world. This spring—this place where the river stopped—was the end. So I asked, pointing into the distance: what then, is beyond the spring? Or that grove of trees near the rise? The man shrugged: the answer was obvious. He said that *must* be another world, for it is known to all this one ends at the spring; and that world most certainly belongs to some other tribe. He smiled and said he was sure that tribe would look with favor upon such good men as ourselves. You will meet new friends, he said, and perhaps you can acquire new beasts of burden from them.

The argument began, and I quickly backed away from moral issues and concentrated on rewards. There had been some sort of misunderstanding—my fault or theirs did not matter. Now I offered them a chance not only for glory among their own people—glory that would travel back with me to my own homeland—but riches. I had already promised gold and now I doubled the amount of that offer. I told them that when we returned to the Pepper Coast, they could have their choice of any of our weapons or clothes, save only the most personal. That interested the man; but it would be very difficult, he said sadly. Very, very difficult. I increased my offer: we would have L'ur and his skilled sailor/shipwrights build new and superior huts for them before we left. And, since I would swiftly return from Orissa to begin developing this new trading area, they would be rewarded with costly gifts from Orissa when I came back. He still shook his head: very, very difficult. Spices that would make their fish soar in flavor. Ah? A glimmer of interest, then: sorry, but it remains very, very difficult. I took gold from the chest and gave each man two pieces as evidence of my intent. We are very grateful. But . . . I must think . . . Perhaps . . . if we did agree to continue . . . but, no, that would be very, very difficult. New nets and even boats for their fishing. Nice, but still, very difficult. Imagine what your wives, your concubines, your daughters will have for clothing, colors and silks of the finest. Ah?

It was after midnight when I finished. The man, who'd been joined by the other Shore People, sat thinking. Then he said, "You have honored me . . . you have honored us greatly. Black Shark was very wise in deciding you are a valued friend."

"Then you will continue with us?"

"The journey . . . it will be very, very difficult." He smiled then and tapped me on the shoulder, a sign of respect for an equal. "But what is life without the very, very difficult . . ."

Exhausted, I went to bed, the campfire guttering into ashes; but I was elated, and perhaps the honeyed, diplomatic tongue of Paphos Karima Antero had also been granted to his increasingly respectful son. I slept, feeling proud. But I woke feeling a fool. Sometime before dawn the Shore People had vanished. Their tracks led west, back toward the coast and their homeland. At first I was angry. They had agreed, hadn't they? Janos was trying to keep from laughing as he explained that there were certain peoples who could not say no, and they would use any evasion . . . to avoid it.

"Such as 'very, very difficult,' " I said bitterly.

"Such as 'very, very difficult' to prevent having to reject someone bluntly and make them into an enemy," Janos replied.

So much, I said, for my honeyed tongue; and so much for the gold pieces I'd given them. "Actually," Janos said, "you did quite well. I guess you did not notice, but they left the asses—and their harness. Perhaps the gold paid for that. Or perhaps it was your, ahem, honeyed tongue."

We could waste no more time on my embarrassment. We laboriously loaded the asses, a task the Shore People had made appear simple but took *us* nearly half a day; we continued on, learning how to be drivers as we went. For some time afterward it was common for someone, just within my hearing, to look solemnly at a friend and announce, "Things are very, very difficult." I pretended not to hear.

The land grew drier and drier: rolling grasslands were interspersed with rare copses of trees around increasingly muddy springs and then rivulets. For a while we could use these groves to lead us to water, but then we saw more and more thorn trees with no moisture around them; their roots must have reached down into the underworld for moisture. We were not, however, in jeopardy or danger, and that was due to Janos' experience. He taught us to follow the antelope and to stake out their water holes at dawn and make clean, swift kills. We ate the animals and then turned their stomachs into waterskins: the hides were green and smelled—but they held water. The patient asses brayed, but accepted the additional burdens. Our sandals and boots were wearing thin, so Janos announced that it was time for us to learn to walk as the gods intended—barefoot. He said we must save the footwear for rougher terrain. Cassini whined so much at this, we found it easier to make new soles for his boots from green skin every two or three days rather than force him to travel barefoot. The lessons continued as we went: there was game to be speared or, better yet, netted; arrowheads were removed and replaced with hand-carved, blunt, fat tips of wood. These were for the plump, flightless birds around us: the tip would stun a bird long enough for the hunter to wring its neck, yet the arrow would not travel through the quarry and be lost in the brush. We were taught that it is generally unwise to eat a new fruit or berry if the sap is like milk, and also that red berries and fruit are sometimes dangerous. If you think a plant or a fruit is edible, cut it and rub it on your arm; if your arm blisters, do not eat. Besides water holes, we found that some tall trees have reservoirs in their hearts, saved from the annual rains.

If what I have just written implies that my Finding had suddenly been turned into a bleak fight for survival, that was not my intention. Despite the difficulties, we ate well, we had enough water, and we were healthy, if dirty.

As we traveled, the sun arced overhead and the air seemed to glow in dry silence. The world was mostly brown, but the occasional green leaped out to the eye as if it were in relief. There seemed to be nothing ahead of us but more and more of this prairie, a prairie I did not realize was turning to desert. There were animals besides antelope: packs of wild doglike creatures, hunting families of direwolves that would trail us for a space until they decided there were no stragglers who could be easily dragged down, and several species of large direcats: we saw them frequently lolling about, their cubs climbing out of their mothers' pouches to frolic. The cats offered us no threat, and we made sure to stay well clear of their dens and retreats. Once we saw, just at dawn, a great black-maned lion atop a rearing crag. Suddenly beside him were two of the mounted Watchers. The lion seemed not to be aware of them. One of the Watchers stretched out a gauntleted hand, armor glittering in the rising sun, and stroked the great cat's head. The lion preened like a pet . . . and the Watchers were gone.

Finally the baked-summer-day dream came to an end. Now we were in real desert; the ground rolled up and around us, searing rocks and sand broken by ravines filled with dry brush. Even though we had several compasses to keep us from trusting a single lodestone whose power might have vanished, and my mapmaking had continued as best it could, given the shortage of identifiable landmarks, we became unsure of our course. Janos said there was no help for it, but we must hold our current heading. When we came to the next landmark on the talisman map, a mountain range that appeared to be quite distant, we would locate ourselves exactly. We must not, he said, start doubting in our compasses or our common sense, else we could find ourselves wandering in tight circles about this desert and, ultimately, our own arseholes. We knew we were not the first men to traverse this desert, which was comforting, because of the caravan tracks we encountered. We followed them, which made our holding to our compass directions more difficult, but there was no other choice—not only did the tracks follow the easiest terrain, but they led us from water hole to solitary well to oasis.

Then we saw the makers of the tracks. Far on the horizon we spotted a line of mounted riders. Nomads, Janos guessed. They appeared not to see us, although all of us thought that doubtful. His guess was confirmed when we crossed their track some hours later and found not only horse but goat droppings. Janos said he doubted that the Watchers traveled in such groups or that they brought their own mutton along.

"It is a pity," I said, "these people aren't blood kin to the Ifora, and we could renew old ties. I thought that woman—Tepon, it was—*quite* charming. Even if she did file her teeth."

Janos grinned. "When you come to do your memoirs, friend Amalric, and you describe this stage of our journey as arduous, perilous, and filled with dangers at every step, you should not mention your last statement. It's hard to be dying of thirst and have your mind bedded in your groin at the same time. As for the Ifora, I should tell you that when I first made their acquaintance I had a mounted patrol of fifty Lycanthian cavalrymen at my beck, and there were but twenty of them. That was a ratio I tried hard to maintain. A commonality I have found among all desert folk I've encountered, is that they tend to be capricious at best and, if they feel you possess something of interest, capable of astonishing cruelties."

"So let us hope we went unseen," I said. Janos nodded, dropped back to Sergeant Maeen, and gave him instructions for the men to be fully alert at all times.

The next day there were two riders on either side of our course. At first I thought them to be the ghostlike Watchers, but they maintained their course hour after hour, riding about a league to either side of our party. Cassini announced that he sensed spells being cast, spells that did not "feel" like they emanated from any of the previous sorceries. Janos, too, said he felt something. The old traditional prickling of his thumbs, I asked? He shook his head: different; it was as if he felt someone looking over his shoulder.

At dawn we saw more riders behind us, and people on foot in addition to the two that flanked us. They also held their distance. We tried to keep our pace steady, both to conserve energy and to avoid showing fear. About midday the party doubled . . . to twenty. Janos told us to be doubly wary.

The attack began as a blur. If I had not chanced to be looking in that direction, I would not have seen it. Movement . . . and then one of the asses reared, screaming, two arrows sticking out of its flank. Screaming, and a shout of agony, and a man staggered out of the column, a third arrow buried deep in his thigh. We were attacked—and the nearest bowman was half a league distant! The next few moments were a shout of orders . . . me ordering the men to flatten and not to let the asses bolt . . . Janos and Maeen bellowing for the soldiers to put on chain mail immediately . . . shouts from the wounded man . . .

I had Cassini by the arm. He was gaping at these arrows from nowhere. "Dammit," I was shouting. "A counterspell . . . and quickly!"

Cassini's mouth opened and closed like he was a beached fish. His eyes . . . and most likely his mind . . . were blank.

Janos heard my shout and understood. "Uncertainty," he ordered. "The wizard is suddenly unsure."

Cassini looked bewildered, then he got it. He stammered a phrase, his words growing more fluid as his memory brought the spell back to him. Another flight of arrows blurred out of nowhere, but this time buried themselves in the sand, short of us. There were six of them this time.

"Good," Janos said. "Again. The next flight should be still farther away." Then he bethought himself. He pulled one of the arrows from the sand and handed it to our Evocator. "A better spell: Brother speaks to brother."

I saw Cassini's sunburned face redden still more. "How can you—"

"Do it, man, or we die here!"

Cassini took the arrow in both hands and put it to his lips. He whispered words I could not make out, but they became a chant. Then he snapped the arrow cleanly in half. Expecting what I should see, I glanced at the other arrows that had attacked us . . . they were broken, as well.

"Good," Janos approved. "Broadcast that spell now. And broadcast it wide."

Cassini obeyed. I do not know what effect it had, but there were no more flights of arrows. Janos started to say something else, then caught himself, and worded what might have been conceived as an order as a vague thought, the thought of a man who knows little of magic: "Now, Cassini, can you put something between us and them? Invisibility?"

Cassini had recovered enough to curl a lip. "That would require too much power, and be too much a drain on my senses. I can do something easier . . . and better."

He picked up a handful of sand, then allowed it to slip through his fingers; then he prostrated himself, muttering all the while. I looked back at the nomads and saw small dust devils rising, swirling, just knee high between us and them. Cassini, emboldened by promises of success, ran to the ass carrying his equipment and began sorting out gear, to build and bind his spell. Our soldiers were now in full mail, baking in the sunlight, but much safer from another attack. I remembered the wounded man and went to him, but he was dead. I beckoned to Janos, who walked over, looked down, and nodded, grim. He also noticed that one of our pack animals was dead, although it had suffered only a slight arrow wound.

"A spell on the arrows," I guessed.

"Probably not," Janos said. "More likely venom of some sort on the arrowhead. The desert breeds many killers from vipers to scorpions. There is no need to waste substance coming up with a bit of sorcery when nature provides an even swifter killer whose efficacy does not wane with distance."

Cassini had powders and potions out, and pentagrams and symbols drawn in the sand. The dust devils were larger, lifting fifteen feet in the air.

"Good," Janos said. "The sandstorm will at least keep us safe from further attack. Although with those others out on the flanks, it will be hard to escape. Impossible, most likely, since I would think those men know where we are going ... Now I must heal two wounds."

He turned to the soldiers, who knelt or sprawled in positions of defense. "Very good," he said. "You moved swiftly. I feel I chose well for my men." I, in turn, searched their faces and was surprised to see none of the horror or borderline panic I had expected. Their expressions showed anger and traces of worry. Evidently this death, even though it had been aided by sorcery, was not that much of a shock. Perhaps this was what was meant by the phrase "a soldier's lot."

"On your feet," Janos ordered. "We will be moving, and moving fast. Sergeant Maeen, detail two men to each ass to make certain they do not bolt if we are attacked again. And have the dead ass's pack broken up among the other animals. We will say the words for our comrade when our Evocator finishes his protective spell."

Cassini had evidently completed his work. Janos walked over to him as he repacked his gear. "My apologies, Evocator," he began. "I did not recognize you were already making your plans."

Cassini stared at him coldly. "You said once you had an interest in sorcery," he said. "Quite an interest indeed, to be familiar with a brother-speaks-to-brother incantation. Such a familiarity in Orissa might require an explanation to the Council."

"Freely offered here," Janos said, trying to sound light. "I recollected that once, when I served Lycanth, such a spell was cast by my regiment's own sorcerer, when we were occupying a foreign city and being stalked by assassins from the rooftops."

I waited to see how much of a fool Cassini was. The Evocator eyed Janos. "Your memory," he said coldly, "works most expeditiously in moments of danger."

"So I have been told. May I give you a hand relashing your equipment? We must travel fast."

After the death ceremony over the dead soldier, I asked Janos what, exactly, were our plans. "Assuming," he said, "that this part of the route is like the others, we should strike a source of water, whether a well or an oasis, within two days at the most. I would propose if we have not been able to lose the nomads by then, we keep them from the water until they are forced by thirst to retreat."

"You do not think they'll have been discouraged by Cassini's magic and just give up?"

"Not a hope," Janos answered. "All that showed was we are travelers with power, which means that we have something worth taking. No. The battle has only begun." I prayed Janos was wrong.

We moved all night, following the stars and the track. At dawn I thought my prayers might have been answered, since there was no sign of our followers. Janos, however, looked even more worried, but refused to tell me why. Two hours later we saw, ahead of us on the horizon, a shimmering green that was not a mirage; it was an oasis. We reached it an hour before dusk. It was beautiful, blue ponds reflecting through low brush and shade-beckoning trees. Our eyes ached for this place, for color beyond the browns we were stumbling through.

We were only two spearcasts from entering it when the ululation began. The nomads had beaten us to the oasis. An arrow shower, launched by muscle and not sorcery, arced out of the brush and landed a few yards from us.

Janos barked orders. "You men. Move the asses into that hollow. Sergeant Maeen, take charge of them. Cassini . . . Amalric . . . hold here with me. They will almost certainly be sending out an emissary."

I wondered how Janos could make such an assessment from a few arrows that buried themselves far short of our party. "Sheath your weapons, until I tell you otherwise," Greycloak went on, before I could ask. "When they come out, look proud, and defiant, not beaten. Our enemies want us alive."

Cassini asked how Janos could know this. "The arrow launch

was meant to intimidate, not harm. So those nomads wish us either for slaves or for sacrifice. Most likely the former, since no desert dweller wastes real substance on invisible gods unless forced."

Three men came out of the brush that ringed the oasis. They were dressed approximately the same: baggy knee breeches and tunics, with flowing hooded cloaks. Curving swords were sheathed at their waists. Two of them carried reversed spears, with a white cloth tied between them. The other spread his hands out, palm open. They approached. I prepared to make the same symbol of peacefulness. Janos shook his head. "No."

He raised his voice. "Stop!" The three did. "How can you proclaim peace," he demanded, in Trader's Tongue, "when you have already killed one of us, and send arrows against us when we have shown you no enmity? Do you think us fools?"

The man in front laughed sharply and answered in the same tongue, although brokenly, as if he spoke it but seldom. "I do not see you as fools, no. I see you as . . . perhaps lambs. Lambs who have lost their flock, and are wandering through this wasteland, in danger from wolves and eagles. I . . . I am the shepherd, who offers safety and shelter."

"No doubt purely from the goodness of your soul," Janos said.

The man lifted his shoulders slightly. "No one does anything completely from benevolence," the man said. "Else he would be a god. The shepherd offers the lamb safety, and the lamb provides its wool and, in the end, its flesh so the shepherd may protect yet another generation. It is the way."

"How kind of you," Janos said. "But . . . perhaps there is something wrong with my vision. You speak of being a shepherd . . . and I see nothing but three cackling carrion crows, stinking of dung while they prate of honey." He pretended not to notice the hiss of anger as he continued. "Nor are we lambs." Then his sword whipped out—and the slaver jumped back, his own hand going to his blade. "Lambs do not have fangs like this," Janos said. "Perhaps the desert sun has addled your senses, and you do not see you are challenging wolves." Janos turned to me. "Do you wish to accept this jackal's offer, and wear chains?" he asked, still in the trading tongue.

I did not need to answer. "Nor I," Janos went on. "Never again." Cassini seemed to hesitate. "Evocator," Janos said, "you will not be included in his kind offer, but rather sacrificed to add to their shaman's power."

Cassini covered his hesitation. "I stand with you, of course."

"And I can speak for the soldiers," Janos finished. "You must take us with the sword, corpse eater," he said to the slaver. "And in the taking you will bring sorrow to the tents of your people."

The nomad held up his hands in acceptance. "You have spoken bravely. Perhaps tomorrow . . . or the next day . . . you will croak differently when your water is gone. Or perhaps my lions of the desert will not allow me to be merciful and wait until you have come to your senses." The three backed to the oasis and disappeared.

"Cassini," Janos snapped, "a few words of the protective spell. Immediately!" Cassini had barely begun a mutter when an arrow shot from cover, aimed directly at Janos. I could see, as if we were all in amber, the arrow wobble as our Evocator's spell caught it. Then Janos stepped to one side and his free hand shot out, a blur, and then he held the arrow. He broke it, cast it aside, and turned, stalking back to the hollow. We followed.

Janos gathered the men and explained what had happened. One or two of the soldiers looked as if they might have reached a different decision if consulted, but hid their looks as quickly as Cassini had. Then the three of us withdrew to make plans.

Janos said, "They might wait until we all collapse before they make their move. But it is unlikely they would have that much patience. More probable is they will let us bake our brains for two or three days, and then attack. They certainly will *not* strike now, when we are fully alert. Warfare becomes more bloody the greater the number of soldiers on the field. When few fight, and many die, *all* lose in the long run. That is why nomads fight from ambush or with a sudden, unexpected raid."

Cassini furrowed his brow. "If that is true, Captain . . . then isn't it likely that when they do attack, if we can stand them off and hurt them, they might give up?"

"Exactly," Janos said. "Which is why we will pretend to be running out of water before dusk, and become increasingly feeble hour by hour. We shall drink only after dark, and all of us will husband our strength. If necessary, if they try to wait on us, we can kill the asses and drink their blood and stomach fluids."

It was not an idea, nor quite a vision that struck me then. But a certainty. "The slavers think," I began slowly, then more rapidly as my thoughts coalesced, "we are city dwellers or maybe farmers, correct? If they have sold us short, can't we use that arrogance against them? Sort of . . . sort of like no one takes a runner seriously if his oil is rancid or the robes he sheds at the line are tattered or dirty?" That particular example was one I'd been guilty of and rued ever since.

Janos bared his teeth. "I would wager you are holding up a mirror to their thoughts. And I agree. Continue. You hold the speaker's glass." Even in that fearful, sun-blazed moment, I admired Janos' ability to hold his tongue, rather than burst out with the obvious ideas that were occurring.

"This night," I said. "You, me, Sergeant Maeen, one other. Each man with someone to guard his back, as I've seen you train the Praetorians."

Janos was taken aback. "But the others—"

"No. Let the others play roles as sheep, so there can be no possibility of mistake. You, Evocator, must stay with them. We need a spell like you cast before . . . Uncertainty. Or something like it." I remembered what Janos had said in the armorer's shop about sorcery on the battlefield, but thought this might be different. My plan bore no more semblance to battle—if it worked—than the slavers' attack on us in two or three days would.

"Better than uncertainty," Janos suggested, "can you manage a spell that might suggest terror at the right moment? Such as a peasant might feel when a lightning storm strikes in midsummer out of a clear sky?"

"Once I am aware of what, exactly, Lord Antero's plans are," Cassini said with acerbity, "I can come up with devices fully as subtle and sophisticated as any you have, *in your own field*, which *I* would never have the temerity to interfere with."

Janos held back the urge to snap a retort. "Very well. Four of us, eh? The best time will be . . . just after moonset, which will give us a sufficient amount of time before dawn. Tinderboxes . . . we'll scrape tar from our animals' packs, soften it in the fire, and smear our bird arrows with it. Once inside the oasis, we will take brands from their own fire to light their deaths . . ." And his muttering became inaudible as he filled out my plan.

WHEN THE MOON went down, the four of us crept out, equipped as Janos had planned, plus we each carried short, thrusting spears. Sergeant Maeen had chosen the hot-tempered Lione as our fourth, saying his quickness to violence was exactly what we needed here.

In the oasis three fires still burned, indicating the nomads' camp; at least there was no danger of our becoming lost. We circled until we were a quarter arc away from our camp, then we struck for the oasis. The place was parklike, with thick brush and palms stretching up, but with little grass or vines to trip and snare. We found one of the winding paths that travelers had worn between the water pools and the open areas suitable for campsites, and padded toward the nomads. Janos had told me to keep my gaze away from their fire, to avoid losing my night eyes, but it was hard. It also became difficult to see objects between us and fireglow the closer we got to the camp. I stumbled in mud and nearly fell into one of the pools, but the sergeant steadied me. Then his hand forced me down, into a kneel. I saw a bulk ahead of us that was not one of the palms but a sentry. Another bulk closed on it, and I heard a "Hunh!", just the sound of a man who's been punched below his lungs. Janos let the sentry sag down, and I saw steel glitter as he pulled his dagger out of the body.

Now we were on the fringes of their camp. Janos waved us up. We crouched, hidden by brush, and looked at the camp. There were two tents that looked as if they could hold ten men or so each. That would be, I guessed, where the nomads slept. Stretched out on the ground, between the banked fire and the tents, were sleeping men and women. I saw the gleam of metal and followed the chains from person to person. The slavers had already found part of their "flock," evidently. There was a half-awake man guarding the slaves, and another guard as well, who stood outside a small conical tent. I guessed it would belong to the nomads' leader.

I shuddered as if a chill wind had blown across my soul and felt my invisible being wandering in a dark desert, a desert filled with great beasts I would rather have slaughter me unknowing than show their ghastliness openly in my final moment. Cassini's spell was working.

Maeen and Janos nocked war arrows, while Lione and I uncovered our tinderboxes, blew sparks into a low flame, and held our tarred arrows into them. Flame . . . and Janos hissed. Bowstrings twanged . . . just as arrows hit with that solid and most final thunk. The sentries dropped without cry. Lione and I loosed our fire arrows at the tents, and Maeen and Janos quickly followed suit. Then we rose and charged.

Baldly written on white linen, these events might make me seem guilty of being either suicidal or a lie maker. Nothing could be further from the truth. Imagine yourself a desert nomad, sleeping peacefully, and perhaps dreaming of how you are about to reap a rich harvest of foolish merchants out there in the desert. Then screams . . . flames . . . raw fear shatters down at you . . . you seize your sword . . . and stumble out of your tent . . . and are confronted with four howling demons. A spearthrust coming out of the night, dropped, then blood-dripping swords slashing, constantly moving, like desert dust devils with deathsteel in one hand, gouting fire from torches taken from your own fire setting your tents ablaze. Now, with those terrible facts in front of you, might you not do as those slavers did? Might you not also drown out our howls with your own screams and pelt away into the night? And might not the gruesome sight of six of your comrades' disemboweled corpses lend speed to your feet as you fled into the desert?

I was beside that conical tent, sword ready for the killing lunge, when the flaps came open; I thought it fitting that the nomad chieftain meet his death at my hands, but as I braced to strike, a woman stumbled out into the firelight. I now thank the gods I was not then the warrior Janos or Maeen were, nor the warrior I myself became later. I was slow enough in launching my attack to catch myself, and my sword tip went wide. The chief's concubine, I thought, and then I saw, in the fire flicker, the silver that cuffed each of her wrists and stretched between. Another poor captured being, destined for slavery.

The woman was young, and she wore the puffed shirt and baggy trousers of a man. Her black hair dropped in waves to her shoulders. I noticed, as if we were standing in the midday sun and I had a god's time to appreciate, that she wore gold and the sparkle of gems at her throat. She was also quite beautiful.

"Who are—" we each asked at the same moment, or at least I guessed we did, because the woman spoke in an unknown tongue. I said something about "rescuers," and she seemed to understand. She looked beyond me; I turned and saw the rest of our soldiers run into the firelight. Among them was Cassini. The slaves were on their feet now, and Janos and Maeen moved among them. Maeen had found keys and was unlocking their chains. Janos preferred the direct approach and used his great blade to pry the chain links apart.

The woman saw something and walked past me, paying no heed to the bloody sword in my hand. She walked to one of the nomad bodies that lay faceup and bent over it. I recognized the man—he was the band's chieftain. Very deliberately the woman spat in his face, laughed harshly, and said something else in her own language.

"Janos!" He freed the last of the captives and came to me. He pulled firewood from a pile and tossed it into the flames; they roared up. The captives seemed bewildered.

Janos tried Trader's Tongue. Only one man seemed to understand, and that very slightly, so Janos began motioning, trying to make his signs universal, as he spoke.

"You are free"—casting aside one of the chains—"we must go

on . . . we travel east"—tapping chest and indicating—"you must come with us . . . slavers will return . . . tomorrow"—motioning to the other darkness and arcing his hand like the sun rising—"with more men . . . more weapons"— again, the chain, and then fingers spread, spread, spread again, showing numbers. "Come with us . . . you are free."

The men and women looked at each other, hesitant. No one moved. Finally, the beautiful woman stepped forward; she walked up to me and said a word I did not understand. Then she repeated it, this time in the patois. This time I understood; the word she used was *free*. She said it with great relish. Then she turned back to the others and shouted a few sentences. The freed captives found their tongues and babbled. Then one, then two, then five walked to Janos. The others were suddenly silent. They looked down at the ground, then sat. Janos tried again, but none of them rose. He even seized one man by the arm and dragged him to his feet. But the man went limp and let himself collapse. Janos was angry, seething . . . as if he might kill someone . . . or as if he might cry.

Maeen broke his building rage. "Sir. Captain Greycloak. It's false dawn. We must be moving."

Janos forced calm. "I should have remembered," he said to the captives. "There were people like you when I was . . . what I was. Men who would rather live in chains than die free."

Then it was as if they did not exist. He shouted us into motion. We must return to our camp and get the packs onto the asses. The nomads *would* be back—almost certainly with reinforcements. We must be gone when they came, deeper into the desert. We looted the camp, leaving only foodstuffs for those who had decided to remain in slavery. All else we burned. We drove their horses out in a different direction, hoping to provide a false trail. We dared not take them with us—the nomads might know exactly where every water source was, but we did not. And we did not want to land-mark our direction of flight with a line of carcasses. Then we marched out. As we moved out of the oasis, in the first red flush of real dawn, the woman caught up with me and tapped my chest and asked something. It took a moment before I realized what she wanted to know.

"Amalric," I answered. She touched her own chest.

"Deoce."

Then we went on into the desert, the last flames from the no-mads' camp lost in the glare of the rising sun.

CHAPTER TEN
Deoce

DURING THE NEXT few days, Deoce and her companions had cause to regret their rescue. The desert nights were so cold, our bones ached, and the days so opposite we begged for the comfort of night. It was impossible to keep the fast pace Janos desired, so we were grateful the slavers had evidently decided not to follow. And as the sun beat down and the asses bawled their misery, and we wished for tears enough to weep, we realized only a fool would pursue us. For we were all clearly doomed, as would be anyone who followed. Still, there *were* beasts about—although I cannot attest they were of this world. At night we heard them howling for the wetness of our blood; during the hot day we could sense them snuffling, just out of view, on our scent.

On the third dusk of our ordeal, Cassini's divining rod finally gave a weak twitch, and we all fell to the sand and began to scrabble and dig like dogs. I growled with satisfaction like the others when my fingers found wet sand. I scooped up the wetness and stuffed it into my mouth, sucking eagerly on the grit, spitting it away when it was dry, and grabbing up another handful. When I was nearly satiated I looked up, munching on sand as if it were sweet sherbet, and saw Deoce. Her face was filthy, and when she grinned at me, sand clung to her teeth. She laughed at my own look, and when I laughed back at her own poor state, she found greater amusement, laughing even louder.

Deoce had a lovely laugh. I can hear it now as I write these words and struggle for descriptive powers. It wasn't musical or bell-like, or any of those "winds in a sacred grove" comparisons. She laughed from the toes up, a deep, heartfelt laugh that tickled the spirit of anyone in her company. Soon we were all laughing, and it took little encouragement from Janos to get the men busy widening and deepening the hole and helping the animals get a drink.

I am not saying we were as good as new that night, or even re-freshed, but our spirits were much lighter. When one of the beasts howled, Lione mocked it with a howl of his own, and soon all the men were howling, until the only sounds we heard in the desert were our own.

Deoce sat near me as we ate, and after a time we attempted conversation. She pointed at me, said my name, and gestured about. She repeated my name, but this time with a question to the tone. "Ah," I said. "You want to know where I come from." I pointed west. She frowned at this and shook her head, as if this was not possible. So I nodded, firm, and pointed west once again. As she thought on this, I spoke her name, and gestured about as she had. Where did she come from? She pointed south and flashed her fingers at me several times, indicating much distance. I raised both hands in a question, pointed south again, then back to where we had encountered the nomads. "What happened?" I asked. "How did you come into their company?" Deoce shook her head, puzzled at my meaning. So I pointed at her wrists, mimed manacles and chain, and again lifted my hands in question. Her lovely eyes cleared as she understood. She chattered heatedly in her own language, then frustrated, she made walking motions with her fingers in the sand. Her face took on the look of blissful in-nocence, and she hummed as if she hadn't a care in the world. She was acting out the beginning of her journey, making motions to indicate many companions and a strong guard. Then she sud-denly took the part of the nomads, face crafty, evil, lurking. And I realized the nomads were lying in ambush when her party went past. Then she mimed a leap forward, made noises of battle, took on the roles of soldiers waging a fierce fight, and then threw her arms about herself to indicate her capture. She tapped both wrists to indicate the manacles and made motions of walking again. This time with a look of terrible despair. She sighed, acted out a stifled sob. Deoce pointed east. This was the direction the slavers were taking her. She made motions of a purse full of coin exchanging hands. I understood she was to be taken to some far place to be sold.

Even in the baggy trousers and puffed shirt, with a thin line of sand about her lips, Deoce was a remarkably beautiful woman. She would have fetched a handsome price for that nomad chief-tain.

We were silent for a time, as each of us struggled to think how to continue our conversation. "Perhaps I can help, my friend," Janos said. I hadn't heard him approach and looked around with mild surprise. He handed me a small, wooden writing box and crouched by my side. "I have some experience in these matters, if you recall."

"I'm not sure that you can help," I said. "Our languages seem to have no similarities that I can grasp."

Janos laughed. "I told you once before, my dear Amalric, that the best dictionary is one that you can bed."

I was shocked at this suggestion. "Oh, come, now, Janos. I wouldn't take advantage of the girl. She is obviously from good family. As good, or better than my own, I warrant. And she is clearly a virgin. It would be wrong for me—"

"It would be wrong for you to act as if you were home in peaceful, *dull* Orissa, just now, Amalric. This is life. *Real* life." He gestured about the wilderness. "Take it as you find it, my friend. Or you will regret it the rest of your days."

I wanted to protest, but Amalric turned to address Deoce. "My friend thinks you are a most lovely woman, lady," he said in our tongue. "He believes you are a princess. And, perhaps you are. Amalric is almost a prince, so you would make a good match."

Deoce frowned a little at the mystery of his words, but she smiled and nodded as he spoke, chattering back in her own language. She pointed at the writing box, and Janos opened it to display clean pads of linen and writing implements. Deoce laughed and drew them out, quickly catching on to his intent. She plucked at her sleeve, said a word, then repeated that word . . . slowly . . . and wrote it down on the linen. She handed it to me, motioning for me to do the same. "Sleeve," I said. "Slee—"

"Don't be so single-minded, my merchant friend," Janos admonished. "She obviously means the whole garment. If you go on like that, you'll be all night discussing small parts of clothing. From stitch to cuff to collar."

"You think she means the whole shirt?" I asked, feeling foolish.

"Count on it," Janos said.

Deoce was looking back and forth as we debated. She seemed impatient. She tugged at the front of her shirt and said the same word she'd said before and pointed at that word on the linen. "Shirt," I said. "Shirt." I wrote the word down. Deoce clapped her hands in delight. She grasped a leg of her trousers. "Trousers," I said. And Deoce repeated after me . . . "Trou-sers."

Janos got up. "It gets even more interesting," he said, "when you get past clothing . . . to anatomy."

I blushed like fury, sure Deoce could understand the tone of his comment. I turned, thinking of some way to apologize for my friend's lusty remarks, but found a look of wonder on Deoce's face. Her fingers rose, tentative, and touched my hair, my face. She said a word. I didn't need a dictionary. The only word it could be was . . . red.

As Janos strode into the darkness he called back, "I don't know why you thought you had to use a love potion on the fair Melina, Amalric. That fiery hair of yours is potion enough for most women."

Deoce patted my hand for attention. "Me-li-na?" she asked. "Melina?" She made motions for me to write the word on the pad.

I shook my head. "Let's leave Melina for another lesson," I said. "Much later."

Gentler country greeted us at the end of the next day's trek. We found a creek slashing through a narrow gully, with trees and brush forming a thin line on either side. Later, the creek grew into a stream, with thicker vegetation to soothe us. The water came from a great solitary butte, which lifted from the plains. The maps showed the butte with a heavy X marked in its center, possibly and hopefully indicating a place to rest. We were all too trail weary to question the logic of finding comfort in such a place. Even with water tumbling from the rocks, the butte seemed as desolate as the plain. Janos put Maeen and his men at the ready in case the butte was occupied, and as the sun dipped for its dark coverlets, we struggled to the top.

A marvel awaited. The butte was hollow in its core, with thick walls to protect everything within from the outside elements. The crater was filled from wall to wall with trees and flowering plants, with streams crisscrossing it. We could see animals drinking by those streams, and in the dying light the sky was alive with thousands of birds calling and swooping through dense clouds of fat insects.

Deoce gave a small cry of amazement and pointed to one of the pools of water scattered about this pocket paradise. We all looked and saw a half-dozen slender antelope playing in the water. Among them were two tigers. The tigers were splashing about and rolling on their backs, kicking claws in the air in mock combat like kittens. They paid no attention to their natural prey. A wonderful feeling of peace and joy spread, and I had a sudden urge to race to join them in play. Deoce drew smile lines on her face and said something in her language. I smiled back into the sparkling eyes. "Happy," I said. "Very happy."

"Happy," she repeated. Then added, "Yes ... Happy. Deoce ver-y happy." It was her first full statement in Orissan.

Darkness and caution kept us from going further that night. It was too far and the footing along the crater's rim was too dangerous. In the morning Maeen sent Lione and a few men to scout the area to make sure no enemies lurked about. There was little conversation while we waited; all of us were content to loll about and study the place at our ease. Deoce and I spent several hours adding words to our dictionaries, pointing out different creatures and flowers and trees.

Lione returned just before nightfall. He and the other men were grinning and joking, behaving more like gamboling lambs than soldiers. "The only trouble we'll have here, Cap'n," he said to Janos, "is gettin' up enough foolishness to leave." He painted a wonderful picture of their day's adventure. There was life aplenty: animals with hooves and paws, fur and scale; blunt-toothed grazers and fanged flesh eaters; shade trees, fruit trees; and every variety of flowering plant, with accompanying sippers of nectar. "Near as we c'd figger," Lione said, "only thing missin' is men. No sign of people ever bein' about. Oh, yeah. One other thing. Big thing, really. Those tigers and deer we saw playin' yesterday?" Janos nodded. "It's like that all over the valley. Things that oughta duck and hide walk 'bout bold as you please. An' things that oughta be stalkin' and killin' pay never no mind."

"But how do they eat?" I asked the question for all of us.

Lione's eyes grew wide with wonder as he considered how to answer. "That's the craziest thing. It was peaceful like I said, all day. But just 'fore we got back, everythin' changed. Deer spooked and bolted. Tigers bolted a'ter 'em. Same with th' other critters. Things that make a good dinner started lookin' for a place to hide, an' things that kills and eats for a livin' went lookin' for 'em. But oddest damn thing, was the hunters seemed to take on'y what they could eat ... 'n' no more. Then, all of a sudden, th' whole commotion stops. An' things got all peaceful like before." He scratched his head, a silly grin pasted to his face. "Now ain't that th' damndest thing you ever heard of?"

I looked at Cassini, a little uneasy at this peacefulness. "A spell?"

Cassini thought, then shook his head. "I have no *feeling* of another ... presence," he said. "But I do have a sense of ... wellness? Yes. That's it. Wellness. But what its source is, I cannot say. Although I suspect all the spells I have been casting to assure our safety have finally come together to protect us." He gestured at the thick walls of the crater. "Possibly the structure of this place has helped to concentrate my spells."

Janos snorted. "So all these creatures suddenly became tame when you stood upon the rim? Blessed in the presence of the Master Evocator? Come now, Cassini. If that is the explanation, then I think your superiors back in Orissa had better start rewriting the sacred texts."

Cassini's face darkened. "Enough of this," I broke in. "Instead of questioning and arguing, I suggest we all just enjoy what we have stumbled upon. We can rest here and recuperate for as long as it is necessary. That is all I, for one, care to know."

"Here, here," Lione broke in. Maeen, who had been hovering at his side, glowered at him. "Sorry," Lione said. "Di'n't mean to poke my nose where it don't belong. But I b'lieve Lord Antero has a sensible suggestion. There's plenty to enjoy. Come the morrow, you'll see for yourself."

The next day we got ourselves, our belongings, and the animals to the bottom while the dew was still fresh on the ground. It was the sweetest air I ever breathed, and the music of the songbirds was sharp and clear. Everything that Lione warranted was true. We barely set up a real camp that day, but freed the asses of their burdens, and they bawled in delight, rushed off to a nearby pond, and plunged in with much kicking and splashing. Two big lizards, each three times the length of a man, came out of the water to watch them play, smiling toothy lizard smiles with mouths that gaped wide enough to swallow the asses whole. The asses ignored them, somehow knowing they were safe, and a bit later we were among them, shedding civilization along with clothes, acting like fools as the cool waters washed away the grime of the long trek.

I dived deep, swimming like the river rat I was, feeling all that coolness caress my belly and flanks. The water was so clear, I could easily make out the limbs of my comrades churning about, as well as the fat bodies of the lizards, with their stumpy, powerful legs. To one side I saw a shaded inlet leading away from the pond. I came up for air, dived down again, and swam along that watery avenue edged with gentle, moss-covered banks. Every Orissan child is joined to our great river practically at birth. Toddlers play in currents that strong men might fear in other parts. I was no different, and I had always particularly enjoyed swimming underwater, holding my breath as long as I could, to seek out the many wonders that dwell there; so I had gone some distance down that avenue before I felt the need to emerge for breath.

I kicked lazily, rising slowly to the surface. But as I rose, I saw slender limbs near the bank. Instead of surfacing, I swam closer and saw those legs were the shapely limbs of a woman. They were light nut brown, rising to a delicate smear of black where they joined. Above them was the flare of hips and a narrow waist. I had not a thought or care in my mind as I let myself rise, immensely enjoying the view. I broached the surface, opening my mouth to drag in a breath, and I heard a giggle, then a splash, and I drew in water instead of air. Gasping and choking, I stumbled toward shore, trying to clear my lungs and my eyes at the same time. I heard more splashing as someone waded for the bank. By the time I could breathe and see again, the owner of those limbs was not in sight. Not that I had any doubt to whom they belonged.

Deoce's face peered out through dangling willow branches. "I see Amalric," she cried. I caught a glimpse of a shapely breast tilting up through the willows. She saw me looking and pulled the branches closer. She made a face. "Amalric see Deoce, too." She laughed. "Make Amalric happy, yes?"

"Very happy," I answered, for the first time *really* appreciating Janos' ideas on language. She pointed, and I looked down to see that I was standing naked in water that came only to midthigh. "Deoce *very* happy. Amalric nice."

As I gawked, her face disappeared. A moment later a much-patched, long-tailed shirt came sailing out of the willow. I pulled it on; the shirt came to my knees. "Amalric come talk Deoce, now," she called out. I climbed out and found her sprawled on the embankment. She'd washed and mended her costume so well, it was hard to imagine that not long ago it had been nearly reduced to rags. She patted the ground beside her. "Talk to Deoce," she said. My lady ordered. I could only obey.

My hopes were dashed, however, when as soon as I sat, she displayed the writing box. "Deoce learn very more . . ." She frowned, searching. She muttered an impatient mutter and grabbed a dictionary from the box. She stuck a pretty little pink tongue out at the pad, then searched its pages. "Aha," she cried, stabbing her finger at a squiggle. "Deoce learn very more . . . words." She smiled at me, eyes twinkling. "Yes?"

"Absolutely," I said. Remembering Janos' advice on anatomical lessons, I took a small toe in my fingers. "Toe," I said. "Toe." Deoce dutifully repeated, "Toe." She scratched in the dictionary and handed it to me to put the Orissan word beside her own. I let my hand trail up further. "Leg," I said. "Leg." Her eyes widened as she caught my intent. Then they crinkled at the edges. She gave a low laugh. "Leg," she repeated. My hand rose again. "Knee," I said. "Knee," she returned, but I felt muscles flex as she prepared to snatch the object of my exploration away. Instead of going further in that direction, I touched her arm. "Arm," I said. She gave me an odd look as I changed my tactics. "Arm," she replied, cautiously. I leaned close to her, and she did not draw away. "Kiss?" I asked, and I moved my face closer still. Her reply was a whisper. "Kiss?" Our lips brushed, and I trembled at the softness I found there. I put my hand on the back of her neck to draw her nearer to drink more deeply of those lovely lips. I felt a small hand on my chest, pushing gently away. I obliged, gasping a little. "No more kiss," she said, but I noted her voice was husky, and I saw a flush of passion rising from her neck. "Amalric teach Deoce words. Not kiss," she said.

I nodded and picked up the dictionary, my mind stumbling for balance. Deoce noted my confusion and patted my hand. "Kiss nice," she said. "Make Deoce happy." She straightened her costume and sat up, prim. "Teach kiss later," she said. And as my hopes leaped upon my features again, she laughed. "Very later," she said. Then, "Maybe . . ."

THAT NIGHT, JANOS called a meeting of the expedition leaders. "I think it would be wise," he said, "for us to agree to certain things. How long we are going to stay here, for instance. And how we are going to behave during this stay."

"I know how anxious you are to move on, Janos," I said, "but we need a rest before we strike out again. I doubt the journey will get any easier, and the better shape we can get ourselves and the equipment into, the better chance we'll have against what is to come."

"I will not quarrel with that," Cassini said. "However, your mention of behavior is puzzling."

"I am speaking of the pact the creatures who live in this crater seem to have made," Janos said. "I think we should follow their *rules*, if that word applies, and limit our hunting as they do."

Cassini glared. "What makes you think dumb beasts can make such an agreement?" he scoffed. "The peacefulness you see is for our benefit, and our benefit alone."

"Do you still think this is your doing?" Janos asked, not troubling to hide disgust in his tone.

"What other logical explanation can there be?" Cassini said. "Since the moment we left Orissa, I have been casting spells to assure our safety and well being. Plus we have the powerful blessing of the Council of Evocators. Thus far, both these things have kept arrows from piercing our flesh, and found us water in the middle of a wasteland. Now, they have given us respite."

Instead of a heated retort, Janos considered Cassini's words. "Help me, my learned Evocator," he said, and both Cassini and I were surprised that there was no mockery in his tone, "see the wisdom of your logic. Without revealing any deep secrets of your craft, how is it you choose a spell? And how is it you know what that spell's ultimate effect may be?"

"It is very simple," Cassini said, "for those who are blessed with an Evocator's powers. We study all the spells that have been written, under the wise tutelage of a Master Evocator, and commit those spells to memory."

"But there must be countless spells," Janos said. "Even for an Evocator, wouldn't it be difficult to memorize them all?"

"Certainly," Cassini answered. "And just as there are Evocators with greater or lesser degrees of power, so it is that some are better at memorizing. I, for one, have an excellent memory. This is not a boast, but an attribute pointed out by my first teacher when I was accepted by my brother Evocators. However, for those not blessed, and even I find it hard to recall absolutely everything, we merely have to go to the archives where all spells are kept."

"When you travel," Janos pointed out, "you can't carry a library."

Cassini tapped his forehead. "I keep it here," he said. "Which is one reason you are fortunate, Captain, that I asked to be included in this expedition."

"Yes, I can see that we are," Janos answered. "However, I just want to get one thing straight. The spells you use, then, are recited from rote. Wisdom, as they say, passed down over the ages in ancient texts?"

"Exactly," Cassini said. "We know they work, because they have *always* worked. It does not matter why. For it is not possible for men to ever understand such a thing. Only the gods can know why."

Janos stared at him. Cassini flushed, realizing where the conversation had taken him. But just to make sure, "Then we can't say the whys of this small paradise we have found," Janos said. "Or am I missing something?" Cassini sputtered, but found no answer. "So we do not know," Janos pressed on, "if the peace we find here is the doing of men, or the doing of . . . beasts. True?"

"True," Cassini answered, hating it.

"Then I suggest we do not second-guess the gods," Janos said. "I suggest we abide by the rules we found here, just as if they were handed down by the gods themselves."

"I think it's the safest thing to do," I said, jumping strongly in on Janos' side. "Besides, if Janos is in error, there can be no harm. And we can't possibly say what will happen if he is correct."

"Very well," Cassini said, teeth gritting. "We'll do it your way."

"We'll *all* keep the hours?" Janos pressed.

"Yes," Cassini said. He rose before Janos engaged in more verbal trickery, and stalked away from the fire.

"Is it not amazing, my friend," Janos said, "to learn something so basic as sorcery has no laws whatsoever—except the rules the sorcerers make to keep all knowledge to themselves?"

"I suppose that is just the nature of things," I said.

"Do you really think that?" Janos asked.

I started to answer, then shook my head. "Who can say? I drove my own teachers to near madness with such questioning when I was a boy."

"And now that you are a grown man?"

"I am not Cassini," I said. "There is no need for games. Say what is on your mind. For I can see from your agitation that you are bound to."

Janos laughed at my foresight. "Oh, don't we all love to hear ourselves talk?" he said. "There must be a small demon of self-admiration that dotes on the sound of our own voices." He sipped sweet water from a gourd and passed it to me to drink. "I *do* have my own theories, as you have guessed, and they go much beyond Cassini's prattling that a thing works, because it has always worked."

I nodded for him to continue. "I believe there are certain principles underlying the whole thing," Janos said. "One, is that like produces like, and it follows that an effect resembles its cause. Another is that things formerly in contact will continue to act on each other, no matter how great the distance. One example that illustrates both: if an Evocator chooses to destroy someone, he tries to get something personal, a lock of their hair, for instance. Such as was tried on you in Lycanth. He then makes a likeness of the enemy, with the hair as part of the makings, and then attacks the likeness—by burning, for instance. If this is done correctly, the enemy will suffer greatly, and sometimes even die."

"Black magic," I muttered.

"That is an example of the *Evocators'* laws," Janos said. "*They* divide sorcery into black and white. Good and evil."

"You don't think there is a difference?"

"Not at all. For the one trying to destroy his enemy, the sorcery is a good thing. White, in other words. For the target, why, it is most certainly black. I think the only difference is where you stand."

"Why do you trouble yourself with such things?" I asked. "Why not leave well enough alone?"

"It is a means to an end, I suppose," Janos said. "I became interested when I was a slave, so I guess that further means I was anxious to seize some control over a life that another could snuff out on a whim."

I shook my head. "Is this healthy? Better yet . . . is it wise?"

"Neither, I suspect," Janos said. "For another theory of mine is that every spell cast must have some effect on its caster. So eventually, after many spells, the sorcerer should be aware his own substance is being harmed. The trouble is, sorcery is such a seductive science—for science I believe it will be some far-off day. When one is faced with a goal that cannot be denied, then anything may be risked."

I thought of the love potion and Melina and could not help but agree. "What do you hope to achieve by this study?" I asked.

"To reach my goal," Janos said, his voice soft. "And nothing more." He looked deep into the fire. "There will be wiser men in the future, Amalric," he said. "Men who will ferret out all the laws . . . be they sorcerous or what we call natural. Why does a river flow down from a mountain instead of up? Why does a stick placed on a rock lift an object you could not budge with brute muscle? How does a divining rod find water? How is it possible to catch the wind spirits in a leather bag, and then let them loose later to fill the sails? Perhaps I am a fool, but I reckon there are laws that govern these things. And wouldn't it be elegant, my friend, if they were all the one and the same? That there is no difference between the natural and spiritual?"

"Do you really think so?" I asked, amazed.

A chuckle from Janos. "No. It would be too easy. But if you should live so long to meet those distant thinkers, do not be surprised if at least some of what I say proves true."

That was the end of our conversation, but I have thought about his words many times since that short time we dwelt in paradise. One thing I remember clearly, however, is that I felt a sudden surge of hope when he told his views. If there *were* rules, I thought, if there were laws of sorcery any man or woman could learn, this might be a great boon to all. If that day ever came, I mused, would it break the hold the Evocators have over common people such as myself? Such as they had over my brother? At that moment, a thought bubbled up: Janos might be onto something as worthy as this Finding itself. I heard Deoce laugh at a nearby camp fire, and the thought fled.

The days that followed went swiftly and were among the happiest in my life. We fell easily into the graceful ways of the crater. We swam and frolicked with the animals, dined on fruits and nuts, and killed for flesh only during the appointed period when hunter and hunted returned to their customary roles. Our skin was soon scrubbed of all the embedded grime of the trek, and the hollow places created by our ordeal filled with new, healthy muscle.

Deoce and I grew closer. She was lovely before, but under the peaceful influence of our new abode, she became strikingly beautiful. Her limbs were more shapely, her skin and hair glowed with health, and her eyes were flashing beacons that filled in the gaps when language failed. Our companions pretended to ignore us as we strode hand in hand about the lush crater. There was many a quiet brook and soft, green glen that invited our presence, and during that interlude we probably visited them all. We continued our language lessons, but they went more swiftly now, and in a short time both of us became so adept at jumping from her native tongue to my own, it was as if it were just one language.

I learned Deoce was a princess, as I suspected. Her mother was the chieftain of a small but wealthy principality named Salcae. In her clan, Deoce said, men, being better with details and smaller things, controlled the tents and the hearth, except in time of war, when everyone fought. The women were the scouts, the leaders, the war captains. For political reasons her mother had betrothed Deoce to a nobleman from another clan. She was on her way to be married when her party was ambushed by the slavers.

At first I was greatly upset when told of the impending wedding. But Deoce quickly put my mind at rest when she explained that the "nobleman" was a boy of less than six years, and since she had been in the company of strange men for so long without proper chaperoning, there was no chance she would be considered suitable marriage material. However, my self-concern turned to anguish for her when I heard this.

Deoce chuckled when she learned the reason for my dismay. "It only means now I won't have to marry a little boy," she said. "In my own clan it is not so important to be a virgin. It is only important to ... other people. People like"—she shuddered—"the slavers. They were going to sell me as a harvest sacrifice." She gave me a grim smile. "If I were not a virgin, at least I would have had a better chance of staying alive."

She looked at me, thoughtful. I wondered what was going on in her mind. Then she sighed. "In some ways," she said, "it was easier when our ... words ... were fewer."

"In what way?" I asked. But she just shook her head and said, "Never mind." Despite my question, I knew her meaning. If anything, I had become an overly courtly suitor since that day on the embankment when I tested her with a kiss. Our newfound ease in speech drew me much closer to her than mere lust would have. As we sat chatting, I realized we had become fast friends. We became even faster friends a bit later, when she quizzed me about her journey and I felt enough trust to tell her the nature of my mission.

"The Far Kingdoms?" she cried when I named our goal. "Do you really mean to find them?" Her eyes were so full of enthusiasm and awe, I was gladder than ever I had chosen such a course.

"The gods willing," I said.

"I am sure they must be," she said, "or you would not have come so far already. Among the Salcae it is said that once our people, and the people of the rest of the world, are joined to the Far Kingdoms, all violence will end. No more banditry, or war."

"No more war?" I laughed. "Now that is a pretty thought. But, I fear, my lovely Deoce, war is a permanent affliction, and has nothing to do with the dark forces that are said to be battling the enlightened folk of the Far Kingdoms. Sorcery it may be. Evil sorcery, at that. But killing is the nature of all things. It does not need help from the forces of the dark."

Her answer was a wave of a hand to the spring that bubbled up from the roots of a large tree. Beneath that tree, a hyena fled, howling mock fear before the onslaught of a fat young monkey. "It is not so here," she said. I had no rebuttal.

Then, out of nowhere, she said, "I must see this for myself. I will go with you."

"That is not possible," I said, alarmed.

"What do you propose to do with me?" Deoce asked. It was a sensible question I had avoided for some time. "You cannot send me back to Salcae. You cannot turn back—not when you are so close; so there is no way I can join a trading caravan, for there is no such thing in this desolate land. You can only go forward. It seems reasonable, then, that you supply me with weapons—I am a skilled warrior, as all women are in Salcae—and let me travel with you as a companion, rather than another burdensome bit of baggage."

Once again I was left without rebuttal. I laughed, and she started to take offense, until I explained she reminded me of my own sister, Rali, who had a soldier's way of striking at the plain truth of the matter. "You would like my sister," I said.

"I am sure I *will*," I thought I heard her say, but she spoke so low, I wasn't certain. "Pardon?" I said.

She opened her mouth to answer, then shook her head. "Oh, Amalric," she said, "are the men of Orissa *all* like you?"

"I don't know what you mean."

"Enough," she cried. "What does a woman have to do to collect that kiss you promised?"

With that she flung herself on me. She was small, but her weight carried me back to the ground, and her mouth crushed against mine. I was momentarily startled, but only momentarily, as eager female flesh squirmed against my own, and the fire I had kept damped so long exploded. We dragged at each other's clothing until there was nothing between us. I rolled on top of her, her legs splayed wide, hips thrusting to meet me, and I plunged into her like a wild man. I felt resistance, heard her groan in what I thought was pain, and I tried to pull back. But her hands gripped my buttocks and pulled me into her harder. The resistance gave way, and madness overtook me again, and I rode her on and on, our hips slamming together, our mouths and hands going at one another like a fury.

We made love all that night. In the morning we bathed, devoured a quick breakfast, then crept far away from our companions, where we made love until exhaustion overtook us. As the days went by our passion only intensified, as did our love. And there was no longer a question that she would accompany us on our journey. I tell you now, if I were a Master Evocator I would cast a spell so powerful it would take me back to those days with Deoce in the peaceful wilderness of that mysterious crater. I would live there with her until the end of our appointed time in this world.

I don't know how many more days we lingered, for I was too bemused with Deoce to keep count. But when it ended, something precious was lost that I have never been able to find in all my long life.

It was just after the hunting period, when all the creatures reverted to their normal natures and ate. We had scrupulously kept our part of the bargain during our stay in the crater. That day we had taken two antelope and a few fish. We roasted and ate with gusto and set the remaining meat out on drying racks. Janos and I were sprawled on a bank, basking in the last sunlight, contented after our meal. Cassini was restringing his bow. One of the antelope had fallen to his arrow, to his enormous satisfaction. It was odd that an Evocator should take such delight in the things common men must do to win their daily sustenance, but Cassini strutted after a kill as if he were the most manly of hunters.

I heard Deoce give a delighted cry and raised myself up on my elbow. She was standing beneath a sprawling fruit tree pointing up into its branches. "Look at the monkey," she called. "It's marvelous."

I strained for a glimpse and spotted it perched on a branch, gnawing on ripe fruit and scolding Deoce. It had an amazing coat: the creature's fur was a blaze of many colors—green and red and blue and gold, all swirling about in the most remarkable pattern. "I've never seen its like," Janos said. We rose to take a closer look.

Out of the corner of my eye, I saw Cassini rise as well, his bow clutched in his hand, but I thought nothing of it. We joined Deoce beneath the tree. The monkey leaped about, flinging itself from branch to branch. We laughed at its antics. "Just the size for a fancy hat," Cassini said.

I turned, puzzled. "What do you—" To my horror, I saw that he had the bow drawn and an arrow nocked.

Janos shouted, "Cassini. No!" At that instant Cassini loosed his shaft. For a moment I thought it would miss, for the little creature was in midleap from one branch to the next. But good fortune rarely smiles on man or beast in such moments, and we watched helplessly as the arrow sped true. It buried itself in the creature's breast; the monkey gave a cry of pain and terror so like a manchild's, you had to believe Cassini had just committed murder.

The monkey plunged to Cassini's feet. He picked it up, face lit with victory. "I didn't even use a spell on the arrow," he boasted

Deoce stood there, eyes wide, mouth open in a tragic *O*.

"Damn you, Cassini," Janos shouted. "You broke the agreement."

Cassini shrugged. "So what? It was a silly bargain. And now I have the material for a lovely hat to shade my head." Janos raised his fist, as if about to strike. I saw Deoce clutch the haft of her knife. In my own breast I felt hot fury pouring out, and if I'd had a weapon at hand, I would have attacked. Then a great revulsion struck me, and I turned to spew my guts. But a terrible scream sounded: a tiger howling for blood. Someone cried out in terror, and we whirled to see men fleeing for their lives, a tiger bounding hot on their heels.

Janos raced for them, picking up a firebrand from the camp fire as he ran. He flung it into the tiger's face, and the beast howled, leaped over the men, and disappeared into the trees. But no sooner had that danger passed than we heard other roars of fury.

"What is happening?" Deoce cried. She yelped in pain as a missile was hurled from the tree, striking her a stinging blow on her arm. That missile was followed by a dozen others, and then scores of hard objects were raining out of the trees. We couldn't see our attackers, but we knew them by the angry monkey cries. Hundreds were massing, so many, the trees bent under their weight. We could hear the other beasts of the crater calling for revenge. In the pond I saw the two big lizards swimming toward shore. They were joined on the embankment by a pack of hyenas. In moments the bank swarmed with carnivores gathering for the attack.

"Flee for your lives," Cassini shouted, and ran for the camp. At that moment the skies opened up and a great deluge fell. The rain was so heavy, it was difficult to draw a breath; but to our relief, we saw that it had stymied the animals as well. Our new enemies took cover. We knew, however, the respite would be brief. When the storm was over, they would renew the attack. There was no hope our band could stand against the united forces of the crater.

There was no conversation; no discussion of what we should do next. As the lightning and thunder crashed and the rain poured out of the heavens, we jammed our gear into our packs, quicklashed them to the asses, and fled.

Deoce and I stopped at the top of the crater. We turned for one last look at the place where our love had blossomed. But there was nothing to be seen in the storm's fury. Janos came up behind us. He put a hand on each of us, a hand of comfort. The three of us stood there for a long moment, the rain beating down on our forlorn figures.

Then he said, "It is time to go, my friends. Come." The three of us turned and stumbled out of paradise.

CHAPTER ELEVEN
The Wasteland

WE FLED THE valley into a wasteland: for leagues the land stretched, flat and studded with rocks and flint and shale. The only plants we saw were gray, twisted trees that reached low along the ground like old men's fingers. We saw no wildlife, and the only water we found was brackish and so deep, we had to dig for hours before the slightest moisture trickled out.

We were forced to wear our tattered footwear once more, and all too soon their soles were cut through. We wrapped rags around our feet and cut canvas socks to ease the burden of the poor beasts who bore our goods. Cassini must now have rued his insistence on having boots made before we entered the valley: his last pair wore through in less than a day, and there was nothing to make new ones from. Not that anyone would have made them for him anyway—no one was speaking to the Evocator beyond the necessities of duty. Our anger grew as he found it increasingly hard to cast his spells around the relict, and we depended more and more on navigating by the sun and taking star readings after nightfall for the next day's navigation.

We spoke to one another less and less, and then through sun-cracked lips, as if all of us were growing to hate each other. At least there was no conflict between Deoce and myself, although we had so little energy, we rarely made love. There were mutterings from some of the men, especially Lione, about the privileges of the rich, and how I was doing less work than any of them. They chose not to notice that I had made myself the expedition's cook—not because of any particular talent or feeling for the art, but simply because I knew the truth of what my father had told me as a boy. "If you carve yourself the largest piece of the pie, you must also have done, and be seen to have done, more of that day's labor than anyone else." Not that cooking was an onerous chore, requiring nothing more than putting water, some smashed corn, and dried vegetables and spices in a pot and shredding a bit of dried meat into the "soup." No one—yet—mentioned killing the asses for food.

Another great absence we noted was the Watchers'. I did not know whether to be relieved, fearful, or concerned that we had lost our way. Even though we did not know whether their purpose was maleficent or benevolent, we had grown used to seeing the speck on the horizon or mesa top.

Then one night we made a dry camp, mechanically chewed what dinner we could stomach, and tried to sleep, each man curled into a hip hollow he'd dug. I lay on my back, with my hand outstretched to touch Deoce. It was not hot, not cold; the sky was very clear and very dark, and the stars seemed especially close. Then I thought it grew hazy, as if a sandstorm was rising, but I did not move. I was asleep, and I dreamed.

My dreams must have lasted all night, because when I woke, I felt sore in every muscle, as if I had not slept at all. Deoce seemed just as tired: there were dark circles under her eyes. I was foolish enough to mention her haggardness, and she snapped at me, then apologized. Everyone in the party looked as wrung out as we did. Wordlessly, we all began reassembling our packs for the day's journey. Janos broke our stupor suddenly and ordered us all to assemble around him.

Without preamble, he began, "Cassini, I dreamed last night." I expected a sarcastic retort from the Evocator, but Cassini just nodded, as if he knew just what Janos was talking about.

"I think," Greycloak went on, "that all of us did. Am I correct?" Surprised nods, grunts, agreement from all of us. "I could tell you my dream exactly, but we cannot waste too much time on details. In short, my dream told me that this region we are marching through, this blasted heath, comes not from the gods, but from something else. I dreamed that this was once a fallow, peaceful land, with cities and towns, even greater than what Cassini's vision told him of the river and the land beyond the Shore People's borders. This land was shattered, and destroyed. Destroyed in but one week. The people were killed or driven away, I do not remember that well. The water sank far beneath the ground, and even the hills and mountains were crushed, as we might crush an anthill beneath a boot. Yes? Is my dream your dream? I shall let our Evocator finish, then. What caused this destruction?"

Cassini's face was even more haunted than anyone's. "A spell," he whispered. "A spell or a web of spells, cast by Evocators with powers far beyond those I could even dream of, far beyond the sorcery that tore down Lycanth's great wall or the Archons' tempest we barely survived. Not only was this land obliterated between the setting and the rising of the sun, but enough of the spell's power lingered on, so that this land shall never again be fruitful."

Janos asked, "Can you tell us where this spell came from?"

Cassini shook his head. "Only that your dream was right, and it was cast by men . . . or by creatures who once were men, and not gods."

"From th' Far Kingdoms," one of the men muttered. His name was Sylv. "An' we're walkin' down their throats like roebuck follyin' th' net trail into th' killing ring."

"No," Cassini said flatly. "I sensed then, and still do, great magic from the east—from where our talisman shows the Far Kingdoms to be. But this is not from that direction . . . but from everywhere . . . and nowhere."

Janos came to his feet. "So if this spell yet lingers on . . . and to use your own words about the killing floor, Sylv, we had best move ourselves beyond spear reach, even if that spear might be a sorcerous one."

Quickly spoken by both of them, and we did pack quickly and continue moving. But the men's fears were not assuaged. We began seeing more and more dark looks, looks of anger and fear and guilt, looks that broke away when one of the four expedition leaders noticed them. Janos began marching close to the two asses containing our water supply, and Maeen stayed close to the ones with our treasure. I asked Janos if there could be a mutiny, and he told me no. "Not yet," he said. "They are too tired; no one has died; and, most importantly, none of them see a place to flee to. The most likely would be the five we rescued from the slavers, since their homes would be closer. But they are still beaten down from their capture. No. No one will murder us in our sleep. Yet."

The next day, Cassini lost his magic. His shouts woke me just at dawn, and I ran to him, thinking that perhaps a desert serpent had sought him for warmth. Cassini was sitting with the cloak he used for his bedding, his face as blank and terrified as an infant who's had his first nightmare and wakes knowing nothing but terror.

"I . . . I do not have my spells," he said. "I . . . my mind is wiped clean!" He could barely talk, and it took some time to find out just what he meant. He'd awakened and determined to cast a simple spell that might wipe out the fleas that were living in the lining of his cloak. "But I could not . . . cannot . . . remember the gods to use in the incantation, or the incantations themselves, or even what symbols might be drawn . . . I cannot, in fact, remember *any* symbol except the circle, and the lowliest dolt knows that to be magical."

"Then we are naked," Maeen said, before he caught himself. I do not think that anyone else heard him, but they did not need to. If Cassini *had* lost his powers, that would mean all the little spells, from those that meant a leak in our waterskins would seal itself to whatever protective words he'd cast to shield us from outside sorcery, were gone. We *were* naked. Even worse was that, without the words, the Watcher's relict, our map, was useless. I was very grateful that at least we'd had some warning, and Janos had begun relying on secondary, if less dependable, forms of navigation. With luck our path still continued toward the still-unseen mountains and the five peaks and the pass through them that I had begun thinking of as the Fist of the Gods. We marched on, despair settling deeper.

I waited until Janos was separated from the others, then fell back to walk beside him. I chose my words carefully. "You told me once you had a small knowledge of wizardry," I began. "If I come up with a scheme to occupy Cassini, perhaps send him off with a soldier to scout in front of us on some pretext—" I broke off, as he looked at me, and I saw that his expression was as drawn as Cassini's.

"I, too, my friend," he said. "I, too, have lost what little words I might have known. But I said nothing. Not only because of the laws, but . . ."

He was silent, not needing to say more. If the men knew that both Janos and Cassini had lost their "powers" at the same time, they would know the loss could come from only one thing— another Evocator, a wizard who must be our enemy and was even now casting about this wasteland to find and destroy us. I saw Lione looking at us with suspicion, and forced a bright expression and a laugh I knew was hollow. Janos did the same.

It was as Cassini had feared; without protection a myriad of annoyances came on us: Deoce and I found ourselves snarling at one another over nothing, and making up became words forced and unfelt. I caught myself making a list of everyone in the expedition, and just how incompetent, evil, and malicious each of them was, and how none of them belonged on my Finding. Then my loathing turned inward: how dare I have the temerity to seek the Far Kingdoms? Did I not think that better men had already tried and died? Did I not think that anything as powerful as the Far Kingdoms would also have powerful enemies, enemies we must pass through to reach the realm? If the Far Kingdoms existed at all, which my self-demon told me was a ludicrous thought at best. We should turn back, turn back now. Perhaps we could return to the river and to our friends the Shore People. Or . . . But what would it matter if we were captured by slavers in the desert? At least we would still be alive, wouldn't we? And if they chose to kill us, why would that matter? Our scatter of filthy, reeking bodies was best suited for the dung heap, anyway. The thoughts wound on and on, head swallowing tail, and the circle continuing. But we continued on . . . or rather I should say that Janos, with my assistance, forced us to keep marching, promising, threatening, cajoling for another step, another league, another day. Deoce proved that she was the daughter of a strong queen and took as great a hand as Janos or I in driving the men by any means conceivable.

Sickness came next: a lethargy, a fever, an ache in the limbs, a weakness. Two men—Sylv and Yelsom—became so sick, we had to make sledges for them from blankets and spears and let them be dragged by the asses. Yelsom died a day afterward. Now we were all sick to a greater or lesser degree. At least, I told myself wryly, no one now has enough energy to plan mutiny. But that spell remained over us—neither Cassini nor Janos could recollect the slightest detail of wizardry—their implements, tools, and herbs remained unknown curiosities to them.

Two days travel after we buried Yelsom, the land around us changed. Instead of being almost flat and stony, it became sandy. We saw a touch of green from time to time, low scrub brushes. I thought I saw an animal—a tiny antelope, perhaps—dart from cover to cover. I would never have dreamed I would be glad to enter a desert, but I was. I hoped that we had been through the worst, and the desert would become greener, would become watered lands, and finally we would see the ground start to rise toward the mountains.

Our route was a bit more circuitous—the land was deeply pitted. Now I learned more about how to navigate on land. We would approach such a pit, trying to keep to the compass heading Janos had determined to follow. Then we would strike a course 90 degrees away from our intended heading, keeping track of our paces. Once we were clear of the pit, we would resume the original course until past the hole, turn another 90 degrees, and walk back the same number of paces, and then take up the correct direction once again. It was quite maddening.

Some of these depressions were shallow, others were as deep as fifty spearcasts. I wondered what could have made them? Perhaps what I'd heard was true—the shooting stars that brightened Orissan summer nights were not signals from the gods, but rocks from beyond; real rocks that might have fallen from Godhome onto earth. But why should there be so many of them, here in this desolation?

As I was musing over this, we found the first body. It took a moment for our lead man to determine what it was, and then he shouted for Sergeant Maeen. It hurt every bone, but I managed to stumble to the front of the column, as did Janos. We gathered around what had been an antelope, or so I guessed. It was not a complete body, but the sun-blackened skin of some sort of four-legged creature. It was about ten feet from another pit. Maeen saw another skin, further on. It looked as if it had been torn apart. By a hunting cat, perhaps? But the cat would have devoured the skin and left bones, I thought. We went on. At least this meant there would be more water now, and fresh meat if we could net or trap one of these creatures. We found other pits and other animal skins. I remembered what they reminded me of—grape skins tossed aside after their juices were sucked out. The next body we saw was that of a man; he, too, had been killed in the same manner: there was no sign of any bones, but the man's skin lay mummified on the ground, skin from midchest to the feet; his head was also missing. The man would have been about my size and of normal shape; so much for the tales of men with heads in their stomachs—or perhaps we had not traveled far enough to meet them. There were no traces of clothing or weaponry, so we could not tell if we were looking at the body of a savage or a savant. Janos suggested we close up the marching order and move carefully past brushy areas. Again, perhaps a great cat had seized the man and ripped off his head. No one had a better theory.

We were skirting another pit when suddenly the ground gave way beneath us; then we were sliding, scrabbling frantically in the collapsing sand, but sliding toward to the bottom of the pit. I saw one of the asses . . . one that carried one of our treasure chests . . . tumble, braying in panic, gold coins spilling, cascading down . . . a soldier floundering, trying to climb back to solid land . . . Cassini shouting in panic . . .

Something came out of the bottom of that pit. A black nightmare. I never saw ... or my mind refused to admit it had seen ... all of the creature. There was a huge, pulsing abdomen ... a wedge-shaped head on a turreted neck ... jaws that were razor scimitars flashing on either side of a pursed mouth ... claws scrabbling at the sand, digging, digging, digging away, making the sand slide us down, down toward death. Cassini lost his footing, fell, and began to roll. The ass's bray became a scream, became silent, and Cassini stopped himself, legs splayed wide on the sand, then he began sliding again, very slowly. He was shouting for help, screaming.

Janos, too, had slipped into the creature's trap and was sprawled a few feet above the Evocator. He fought himself up, to his knees ... Cassini's hand implored him, stretched out ... Janos started to move ... and then stopped. We all became part of some horrible tableau, frozen in this bit of time. Then I was leaping, once, twice, my feet digging in, and I was below Cassini and buried to the knees in the sand, his slide broken against me, and then both of us were tottering. Somehow I steadied myself ... standing ... afraid to look back, afraid to see how close to the terrible thing we were, not balanced enough to draw my sword, shouting to Cassini to crawl, man, crawl, and he was scrabbling upward, I wading after him, and I thought I heard a great hiss from behind me, like the creature was being cheated, and from the lip of the hole spears came down, arcing just over my shoulder, and the hiss became a shrill, and I was staggering up, sliding back down ... and Janos was beside us, somehow able to walk in this dry mire, and then we were out of the creature's den, diving away from its edge. Deoce and Maeen ran up, stringing bows, each of them holding arrows in their bow hands. But there was nothing to shoot at.

The sides of the pit were still sliding, as the sand resought the cone's natural perfection. There was nothing at the bottom of the pit. No creature, no ass, no treasure chest. I thought I could see a gleam that might have been a few of the coins. Unless the creature had power to make itself invisible or was a demon from some unknown hell, it must have reburied itself. I had time to think of each of the pits we had passed, each housing such a monster, and refused the abominable thought. Then we realized one of the soldiers—Aron—was missing. We never saw his body, and I ordered our party to march on before the creature in the pit had time to drain his juices and cast his body among us. Cassini was glowering at Janos, who avoided his gaze; but still we marched, on and on.

That night I woke and saw a bulky form that could only be Janos sitting just beyond our party. I rose silently and joined him. "By rights," he said softly, "you should reduce me to the ranks and put Sergeant Maeen in charge. I failed today."

I had just about enough of what I perceived to be Janos' complete inability to recognize his own humanity and flaws. "The mighty Greycloak, afraid," I said as sarcastically as I could manage. "The stars fall from their courses, the earth shudders, and there is blood on the moon. As if a damned great monster like that would not have sent shudders through any of the heroes of old."

"It wasn't fear," Janos said, and I knew he spoke the truth. "No one who is a soldier can allow his fear of death, which we all share, to paralyze him as I was."

"So you let yourself wish Cassini dead. Dammit, I have *no* idea what sent me after him, considering the number of times I've wished him to contract some dread plague."

"My feelings for Cassini also had nothing to do with it. And I will add now that no matter how much we dislike him, we *cannot* do without him. We will need all of his Evocatorial skills to enter the Far Kingdoms, and I feel we are very, very close now."

"Then what?" I asked, impatient.

"As I said, the Far Kingdoms," Janos went on. "The thought came on me, just as I saw Cassini floundering like some beached carp, how imbecilic it would be for me to die ... here ... now ... within reach of my life's dream. To achieve that dream, I would have let Cassini be sucked of his juices."

I should not have asked, but I did. "Suppose, Janos, that it had been me, there? Slipping into those jaws. Would you have still played statue?"

A long silence, and I began to grow angry. Then, "I do not think so, my friend. Or perhaps, I hope I would not have. No. I would have helped." But the questioning note remained.

I returned to my blankets and Deoce and tossed and fretted over what had happened. As my memory flees back to that night to coax words for the lines required to describe my youthful thoughts, I realized now that I felt hurt—betrayed by my friend. But I can also see from this great distance what I could not understand then. For I can look ahead, whereas the young Amalric could not. In the days that followed, Janos' attitude toward me made a subtle shift. He seemed ... easier in my company, somehow. As if a barrier had been lifted and a strong bond formed. And that bond was this: until that day I had been Janos' friend, there was no questioning that; but he had not really been mine. After the pit Janos Greycloak was *truly* my friend—or, as much a friend as he could be to any man or woman.

The next morning Janos showed me the figurine of the dancing girl. I gasped at the sight of it: she gleamed as if a silversmith had been working long hours with his polishing rouge, and even more startling, the figurine had partially re-formed. Before, it had been broken off at the hips, and now it was complete down to the ankles. The woman's hand now held a silvery feather, and the scarf I'd thought to be part of the original casting was gossamer and . . . *alive*. At that moment I had no doubt we were closing on the Far Kingdoms!

A day later Deoce was first to notice that the horizon was a darker blue. We prayed that blue meant we were approaching mountains. If that was what they were, they seemed to be many leagues and days distant from us. The question was whether we had the strength to reach them. I thought we did not. The best I could imagine was that we might find another oasis, one with game and fish. We must rest and recover—the sickness was getting worse. Perhaps, if we could stop moving, the curse that dogged us might pass on, and Cassini's powers would return.

Lione was walking at the head of the column; I was about a spearcast behind him. The ground had become low rolling hills. I came over one crest—just ahead of us, no more than a few minutes' walk, opened a narrow valley: a great cleft in the ground that looked as if a giant had dug both hands into the soil and pulled them apart. I saw, just below the vertical rim, deep green that could only mean well-watered trees. I shouted to Lione, who was pacing on straight for the cleft, as if he intended to walk into it. He looked at me, puzzled, then came back.

I asked him, "Why didn't you shout when you saw it?"

"Saw what?"

I thought the soldier was being obstinate, then realized he'd been stricken by the sickness. I motioned. He turned, and it was as if a veil was lifted. "It . . . it . . . wasn't there. I . . . just saw . . . hills," he managed. "I *was* about to come back and say I thought we should take another heading."

Maybe someone intended him to think that, I considered. Trying not to look like a war party, but with bows and spears ready for use, we moved slowly toward the cliff edge. By the time we reached it, two men and a woman were waiting. Since the woman was in front, I thought her to be their leader. They held out empty hands, palms up. All three of them were dressed as if for a festival, in colorful, loose, silk-looking garments. None of them appeared to be armed. The woman spoke a sentence. I did not understand it—but yet I did, much like one half remembers a familiar face or a dream on sudden wakening. Deoce drew her breath in surprise. "They are speaking my tongue," she said. Then, in her own language, "Are you of my people?"

The woman smiled and chattered, and then I could pick out a word here, a word there. Deoce was frowning, trying to follow. She held up a hand, and the woman stopped. "The language . . . is not quite mine," she said, carefully finding the exact phrases. "She speaks like old people . . . no, that is not the word . . . like wise men say my people spoke once, long years gone."

Deoce introduced us: the two men were Morning Fog, their shaman, and Harvester; the woman, Dawnhope, and she was their chieftain. She addressed me, speaking slowly, and I could now pick out the sense of her remarks, so similar was her language to Deoce's. "We have been seeing you for two days. We hoped you would see us." I understood her words, but not their meaning, and begged her to explain further. With Deoce's help, she did, and I learned why Lione had not seen the valley. I was told there was a mighty, protective spell cast on the valley. No one intending harm or evil could see the Rift, but would sight only more rolling hills—hills they would be impelled to turn away from without knowing why.

Cassini heard the translation. "There are indeed great Evocators in this land," he said, half in fright, half mournfully, and I felt a flicker of sympathy. Cassini was like a man whose life and work depended on keen vision, but who'd been suddenly blinded. It was a flicker of compassion, but no more. I still remembered the paradise he'd lost for us. Besides, I was now busy with the standard greetings and small-present exchanging common to any traveler meeting a new, friendly people. We were invited to share their land and home for as long as we wished, and were asked only to follow their customs and laws, which, Harvester, their Giver of Laws, said were no more than common sense and hardly onerous. I reserved judgment—the Shore People felt cannibalism was a perfectly natural custom. But I felt no threat or challenge yet from these friendly people. They led us to the cliff's edge, where a carved stone stairway zigzagged down the rock face to disappear into the trees below. I could see the gleam of a lake down there and smell fragrant wood smoke. Nearby, a small waterfall ran down the rocks to the valley floor. We blindfolded our asses, who found strength to bray protest until they smelled the water, and started down.

We had gone but a dozen steps when I heard a shout from Cassini and whirled, hand touching sword. He stood mazed, tottering, as if about to faint. One of the men steadied him, but Cassini seemed not to notice. "My powers . . . my magic . . . they have returned!" I looked quickly at Janos, and from the smile beaming through his beard, knew Cassini was not deluding himself. The Rift Tribe had powerful Evocators indeed if their spell could not only blind enemies who were physically present, but mask the eyes of sorcery as well.

All of the tribe was waiting in the village, which was made up of several central buildings, a feasting area, and cottages flung, seemingly at random, around the main gathering places. There was a feast prepared, but I'm afraid none of us did it service and might even have shamed our hosts. We were taken to huts, and men and women of the tribe offered us fresh clothing. Other members of the tribe helped our sick undress and put them into waiting hammocks. These nurses told us they already had potions and remedies ready to treat them. It was obvious we were not the first to encounter the Rift, nor the first to stumble across that horrible wasteland.

Deoce and I bathed in the lake, changed, and feeling like the walking dead, forced ourselves to the feast. Only a few of us— Deoce, Janos, Sergeant Maeen, and Lione among them—were around the great circular table. I ate but little, feeling I might become sick if I stuffed myself. Lione and Maeen *did* get sick, but our hosts paid no mind. Finally, staying awake became too torturous, and we made excuses and tottered to our huts. I remember little of the next few days, beyond waking, eating, bathing, and making sure my men were taken care of.

But eventually I returned to my usual self, and in a shorter time than I would have thought. Again and again in my life I've been reminded how much punishment this animal body can absorb and recover from, and never cease to marvel how some beings can let life slip away so easily. Here in the valley was the first time I observed this. One of the men we'd rescued from slavery died, and then a second. In spite of the best incantations and herbs provided by Cassini and Morning Fog, the sickness seemed to cling to our people and keep them enfeebled. Only Janos, Cassini, Deoce, Sergeant Maeen, and I had not fallen ill, and Lione refused to admit he had been taken by the disease.

As I recovered I began asking about the Rift Tribe. There were perhaps two hundred of them living in this valley. They tended to live long, peaceful lives. New blood came to the tribe as wandering refugees or, very occasionally, traders who decided to retreat from the world. The people cheerfully gave up their huts and moved in with friends because of the new stories they would hear of the world beyond. The tribe's people lived on the crops planted farther up the valley, where the forest was thinner. They used long, hollowed gourds for piping to run water from springs or creeks to their fields. They hunted the abundant game as carefully as any herdsman decides which animal can be slaughtered without impairing the herd. Once they had kept goats, but they had died a generation ago. Cattle and horses they remembered but dimly from long ago in the past, and they seemed a bit fearful of our asses, who, being the sturdy creatures they are, had recovered instantly from their travails.

The Rift Tribe had come to the valley many generations ago. In their homeland, they had been caught between two great warring peoples and were doomed. But they had a great wizard, Morning Fog told me. "Powers great . . . very great . . . more than me . . . more than your shaman . . . he came from the Far Kingdoms. You have heard of them?"

I could barely restrain my excitement. I called for Deoce and Janos to make sure I would miss none of the questions I now had, and Morning Fog did his best to answer them. Yes, the wizard had been from the Far Kingdoms, a great man who had chosen to leave his world of gold and silk to help others who were not so strong. He had happened on the tribe fortuitously, just after that war began. He volunteered to lead them west, away from the destruction and death that would come. Janos interrupted—did Morning Fog know how distant the Far Kingdoms were from the tribe's homeland? He did not. Nor did he know just how far the tribe had traveled under the Evocator's guidance before they came on this valley. "The tales say it was a long, terrible journey." He shrugged. "But since when is *any* journey not a danger-filled saga, when told around the fire at night?"

I had a question that seemed a bit irrelevant: the refugees and traders he'd told us about earlier, had any of them come from the Far Kingdoms? No, Morning Fog said. In fact, there had been no travelers from the east since before he had been born.

"What," Deoce wanted to know, "do your tales of the Far Kingdoms say? Are they men or gods? Are they good or evil?" That took the rest of the day, as Morning Fog ran through the tribe's legends, and then into the evening, as other older tribesmen and -women were consulted. There was not much we had not already heard about this land of fabulous magic and enormous wealth. There were only two items of note: *all* of the Rift Tribe's legends agreed—the Far Kingdoms were beneficent. Why else would that Great Evocator be as saintly as he'd been? The problem—and Morning Fog said this was most certainly the source of our magical troubles—was the lands around them, what the Rift Tribesmen called the Disputed Lands. It was these kingdoms that had caught the Rift men and women in the nutcracker of one of their perennial wars.

As for who the Watchers were—no one in the valley had heard of or seen them, and were frightened when we described those ghostly sentinels.

"So, we will travel again into darkness when we leave," Janos muttered.

"You do not have to leave," Morning Fog told us. "There are many young women in our tribe who lack mates. It is legend among our people that this, too, is a gift from the Great Evocator, to ensure that travelers who would most likely be male would not upset the balance if they decided to stay on." It seemed as if all of my men had found companions, even if most were able to do little more than sip broth and have their fevered brows wiped. And it was also clear that the customs of the tribe were quite open about sex—the tribeswomen changed their partners frequently, and sometimes visited, in pairs, with a particularly attractive—or potent—man. Two of them asked Deoce if, to use their phrase, she wanted to "walk in the moonlight" with them. Deoce pretended to be shocked, but I think she was flattered. Even Cassini was seen to slip into the shadows once or twice with one of the women, further proof that despite my opinion, there *had* been a human or two in his ancestry over the centuries.

Most astonishing was Janos' behavior. He was like a stag in rut. There was a constant stream of women, sometimes singly, sometimes in groups, giggling their way toward the cottage he slept in—although it would appear he had little time for sleep.

As for myself, I needed no one but Deoce. She was constantly inventive in her love, always fiery, but sometimes coy, sometimes brazen. I busied myself with regaining my strength, even making myself walk, then run a league around the valley rim each day. Then I began running up—and then down, far more painful—the great staircase leading to the outer world. It was a strange time, I knew even then. I felt like we were in a great dome, if one can picture a dome with a glass roof. Above and beyond the Rift, even though the desert sky shone harsh blue every day, it felt like there was a great storm raging—a great storm we must reenter.

I took Cassini, with the relict, to just below the cliff top several times, and had him chance the spell. Now the Watcher's talisman worked perfectly. Again, we saw the Fist of the Gods, and now there were fewer of those enigmatic landmarks between where the talisman thought we were and the pass.

I grew increasingly anxious to move on. There was reason for my concern—the season was growing late, and the autumn would be approaching. If the talisman and the vision back in Orissa was correct, we would have mountains to cross before reaching the Far Kingdoms, and we did not need to add snow, ice, and storms to our already lengthy list of adversaries. But my men recovered most slowly. I did not wish to winter over, no matter how charming and kindly these Rift people were. At last, I reached a decision. I would split the party. I would leave the sick here. Sergeant Maeen would remain in charge of them.

That left just four. I intended to push on, traveling as fast as we could, for the Fist of the Gods. We would cross the pass; and if the Far Kingdoms lay within reach, return to the Rift. If my men were healed by then, and if we had encountered no obstacles, we would march onward, in the path of the first reconnaissance. If not, I accepted we would have to winter here with our friends. I knew from what the soldiers had said that small scouting parties frequently could move faster and more secretly—hence, more safely—than larger groups. But I had also heard tales of how vulnerable such a small party could be, if surprised by enemies.

I also determined that Deoce would stay. Now, many years later, I see I was being foolish—she'd already proven her toughness surviving the slavers and her tenacity in the wasteland. But . . . but if she were to die, to die because of *my* probable foolhardiness in pushing on with only a few . . . I would never forgive myself. She raged when I told her. What did I think of *her* feelings, if I were to be abducted . . . or worse? What would she tell my father when she went to Orissa? How would he be even polite to her if she, daughter of a chief and granddaughter of a great satrap, had let her true love disappear into the wilds? I noticed, while she tore at me, both of us were now assuming we would return to Orissa and remain together. I thought I was being clever when I cut through her angry diatribe and proposed marriage. She almost struck me. Instead, she ordered me out of the hut. I could sleep where I would, with anyone I pleased. And as far as marriage . . . to the hottest and sandiest of afterlives with you, Amalric

Antero. Most of the village had heard our argument, and I found myself greeted with mock sympathy and concealed smiles. I found a small vacant hut, and, brooding over the complexity of women, continued my planning.

Nothing she had said changed my thinking, so it would be Janos, Cassini, and me. I wondered just how I would broach the subject to our Evocator, and did not see a way. He might be as eager for the Far Kingdoms as I was—or had been at one time, anyway. But he might well see such a three-man push as suicidally insane. Besides, he was hardly a boon companion on the road when he could force the soldiers to act as his bodyslaves, and now he would have to carry his own weight. Finally, the man was not a soldier—I now considered myself, especially after the foray into the slavers' camp, to be as competent as the least of Maeen's soldiery.

So, it would be just Janos and me. During the past few days, when I'd struggled with my plan, I'd hardly seen him. He'd been busy with his concubines and, I rather guessed, those mysterious supplies he'd brought from Lycanth. Now, I sought his cottage. From inside I heard chanting and then moans. I waited until silence had fallen, plus an appropriate few minutes for recovery before I tapped on his doorpost.

"It is?"

"Amalric. Your sometime leader."

"Enter, my friend."

Not knowing what to expect, I did so. I could not have imagined what was within. Incense hung thick in the large main room. All the furniture had been moved out. Hanging on the walls were three parchment scrolls with symbols I did not recognize. The floor had been covered with white sand. "Drawn" on it, with red-colored sand, was a pentagram, inside a triangle, which was inside a circle. There were seven people in the room. Six of them were women, and the other was Janos. Janos wore nothing but a thin red robe. Five of the women wore nothing but red cords around their waists. They knelt at each corner of the pentagram. They were holding down—actually using no real force—the sixth woman by hands, feet, and hair. She was naked. None of them, except Janos, seemed aware of me. I could understand why the sixth was oblivious—she was returning from that far place we go in orgasm, and the sand and pentagram around her hips was roiled. The others seemed entranced, as if taking part in some experience impossibly transcendent.

"It is over, my friends," Janos said softly, and the women's expressions returned to normal. They helped the sixth one to sit up, and someone brought her some wine. They recognized and greeted me. None of them seemed to be even slightly aware of the somewhat bizarre circumstances.

Janos led me to another room. "I fear the remains of our pleasures might prove a bit distracting," he said dryly. "What brings you here?" he wanted to know. "I would have thought you and Deoce would have been ... finding your own heavens by this hour."

I didn't tell him Deoce and I were currently not recognizing each other's existence. I *did* tell him of my decision. He reached up and touched the figurine of the dancing girl that hung against his naked chest.

"Interesting," he mused. "A small party, intending to spy out the land. Amalric, sometimes I think you would have made a better Frontier Scout than a rich merchant."

I thanked him and informed him that I wanted to leave within a day or two, as soon as we assembled dry provisions and weaponry.

"Ah," he said, and it suddenly appeared to me as if he had lost interest in our quest, lost interest in everything except whatever he was now occupied with. "Yes. We should go. But we should choose the hour, and day of our leaving carefully. Perhaps," he said, his voice sounding most vague, "perhaps we should have our Evocator cast runes, for the most propitious time. Or, perhaps it might be wiser that we *do* wait until the men are well. Consider this, Amalric. Neither of us have become ill, but that is hardly a guarantee we will not. I would hate to be back of beyond and fall prey to whatever ailment has been dogging us. I think my friends in the other room would be far better nurses than you."

I started to snap something, but stopped myself. "I see." I stood. "It would appear I caught you at a bad time. We will talk further on this. Tomorrow." Trying not to appear angry, and certainly failing, I left.

I might have grown angrier, had I chance to brood, but Deoce was waiting for me in my bachelor's hut. It matters not what was said, nor what tears were shed. Lovers mending a quarrel are only of interest to the two star-struck ones, and either boring or disgustingly sentimental to everyone else.

Janos was waiting for me at dawn, when I stumbled out to make my ablutions. He apologized profusely. He had no idea what had gotten into him, except, well, perhaps if I remembered his friends, I might forgive him. Of course we would make the scouting expedition. It was a brilliant plan. We could realize the dreams of our life after traveling just a few hours and a few leagues, or so he hoped. We would leave this day, if I wished. Assuming I still wanted a fool and a sloth for company. I laughed. As if I myself had never been confronted with and rejected a good idea at an ... inappropriate moment.

Now I could sense the Far Kingdoms, taste their perfume, and feel their riches run through my fingers like a crazed miser with his bags of gold.

Two days later, carrying light packs and dry provisions, Janos Greycloak and I struck out for the Fist of the Gods.

CHAPTER TWELVE
The Fist of the Gods

OUR MARCH LASTED longer than the few hours and leagues that my friend had led me to believe. Janos laughed and said this was a valuable lesson for me, one any good leader of soldiers should learn. You must never tell a ranker *any* distance is greater than five leagues, to avoid ruining his spirit. Five leagues at a time, he told me, and you can conquer the world.

We traveled fast, much faster than we had even at the beginning of our journey when we struck out from the Pepper Coast. But we moved as circuitously as possible, skirting open areas if we could; and if we could not, we carefully checked for signs of danger before leaping from cover to cover. Our night camps were fireless—our cooking was done with dry wood at midday, and the food eaten cold for supper that night and breakfast the next morning. Our travels were also slowed by my insistence on mapmaking. For Janos, it would be enough to discover the Far Kingdoms. I must be able to return time and again, and, more importantly, instruct my traders as to the routes they would follow.

The rolling hills became foothills, leading toward the mountains in the distance, mountains that never seemed to be any closer. Cassini had reluctantly taught Janos the spells necessary to evoke the Watcher's talisman, and we took our first "sighting" three days' travel beyond the Rift. That was our first mistake. The talisman showed we were exactly on the route we wished, and the Fist of the Gods lay directly in the line of march. But it was less than two hours after the incantation that I suddenly felt someone . . . or something, was looking for me. It was a feeling, I realized, that had been with me since before the Shore People had abandoned us, and even Cassini's spell on the river had not shaken it.

The only time it had been absent was in the Rift. I felt I was thinking foolish thoughts, and so Janos was the first to bring it up. He, too, had the sensation. At first, he compared himself to a rabbit, somehow realizing a hungry hawk is soaring overhead, or Cassini's idea of a great fish drifting in its pool. Then he corrected himself—he did *not* feel that the Searcher, if it was anything beyond a figment, was necessarily evil. But neither did he feel any benevolence. Whatever it was, was just . . . interested in us.

It was that day we saw the Watchers again. Two of them sat astride their mounts on a hillcrest not far away. When we saw them, we were just coming out of a grove of trees. I might have continued on, ignoring them as we had earlier, but Janos stopped me. Without a word, he motioned me down, onto the ground, hidden by some brush.

"You are a deer," he whispered. "Think like one." I thought he was sun-touched, but did my best, not sure what he meant. I knew little about the life of a stag, so remembered the ones I'd seen on the trail and tried to think of their possible concerns. My thoughts kept straying to the horsemen on the hillcrest, and somehow I knew this was not good; although *not* to think of the Watchers at this moment was like telling someone not to think of the color red. A few moments later Janos tapped me to sit up. He indicated the hillcrest—the Watchers had gone.

"I do not like this," he said. "We do not know what, if any, intent the Watchers have. Nor do I know that we are their targets. But I fear the worst—we have not seen them lately; but just after we used the talisman, they reappear. I am hardly forgetting the relict belonged to one of them, and like will always attract like, in sorcery or in life. We must use the talisman as little as possible, if I am correct. We do not wish to draw any attention to ourselves now."

I personally thought it to be too late and hardly coincidental that the Watchers appeared on a hill athwart our route just before we passed; but Janos' caution could do no harm. From that moment we exerted even greater care when we moved, and for the next day or so afterward, tried *never* to show ourselves on the meanest skyline, to make sure we crossed any stream using rocks rather than leave prints in the muck of the bank, and never to choose the natural and easiest path.

We encountered ruins. The first was a circular stone fort. It had not been abandoned, but had fallen by storm—the huge timbered gate had been torn away and lay many feet from the entrance. All timbering, whether roofs or support beams, was charred. The fort had been put to the torch by its conquerors. Now I understood why Janos had insisted on Cassini's potential importance—I would have liked to have known whether the soldiers who held the post were taken in fair battle or by sorcery. However, since neither vines nor weeds had overgrown the outpost, and the battle looked to have been fought many years ago, I felt the presence of a wizard on that grim day. At least it was clear from the dimensions of portals and stairs that this land had been settled by people of human size, rather than giants. We did not use the ruins for shelter, but passed on quickly.

That fort might have been a border outpost, since the ruins became more common. I asked Janos how long it had been since war came to these hills. He said he did not know exactly, but he thought not in his lifetime. Outside one burned village we heard baying, and saw, across a hill, a pack of dogs chasing a multistriped antelope. The dogs were of many varieties, which indicated they were feral, not truly wild. A farming tribe, such as these people would have been, do not abandon their dogs willingly. Next I found, just inside one ravaged hut, a small, hand-carved horse, the sort of thing a father might carve for his son. No child will ever abandon a plaything unless it is ruined—or unless he is dragged away from it. I felt soldiers had come to this hamlet and taken away everything of value, including its people. No one had time to flee, unlike our friends of the Rift. The Disputed Lands, if we had indeed entered them, were well named.

We slept not far beyond the village that night, and were wakened by the sound of horses' hooves. We shrank down against the ground, hoping we were invisible. From the sound, there would have been many riders—Janos flashed the fingers of one hand three times. I thought I saw plumed helmets against the night, less than a spearcast away, but was probably deluding myself. The next morning, when we cautiously investigated, there were no droppings or prints where the riders had passed.

"Now the Watchers ride in groups, like half-company patrols," Janos said. "We *are* close."

An hour or so later, we entered a thick forest whose trees climbed far overhead, long uncut. We lost sight of the sun and depended on our compass for direction. By nightfall we were still in the depths of the wilderness. We slept uneasily. Not only were there strange sounds from unknown creatures hunting or being hunted in the blackness, but I felt closed in by this, the first real jungle I'd been in. Once I heard wing beats as some huge night bird flew overhead. The next morning we ate hastily and hurried on, forcing our way through the vines and thick brush.

Quite suddenly the forest came to an end. We stood on the outskirts of a great plain, a rugged plain now turning brown as the Month of Smokes drew near, but whose grasses earlier would have been as yellow as mustard in bloom. There was the green of forests, and the silver of running waters.

Beyond was the mountain range. There were four peaks in the range, and a fifth that twisted like a huge thumb. We had reached the plain that stretched to the Fist of the Gods. It was yet too early for snow, and we appeared closer than in my vision, so I could tell there were striations in the peaks beyond just black volcanic rock. But by all that is holy, I thought, we had *found* the Fist of the Gods. Beyond lay the Far Kingdoms.

I turned to Janos as he looked at me. Both of us went a little mad for the next few moments—mazed shock, imbecile gape, then both babbling, neither hearing the other. Silence.

"We found it," I said.

"We did."

"Did you really believe we would?"

Neither of us met the other's gaze or made an answer—perhaps there had been too much sorcery and danger and disappointment on this Finding for us both really to maintain self-confidence. Then the solemnity was broken and we were looning around like a pair of prize fools. Eventually we collected ourselves.

"Damnation and ice," I said. "I should have found space in my pack for a flagon to celebrate."

"We do not need it, Amalric," Janos said. "That stream up ahead will taste better than any vintage. We can make camp there, and I estimate we are no more than three or four *honest* days' travel to the foot of the pass."

"Three days in the mountains beyond that, perhaps," I murmured, "through the pass, and . . ."

"And the Far Kingdoms will lie beneath us," Janos finished.

We shouldered our gear and started toward that stream. I could have flown or floated the distance. No longer did I feel where the wilderness's thorns had snagged my skin or my stubbed toes and worn soles. We had done it. We had gone where no Orissan or Lycanthian had ever gone. I knew in that moment not just that we had made history, but we had changed all history to come. Once we saw the Far Kingdoms on the far side of that pass, and if we returned safely—which I was certain we would—nothing would ever be the same again.

I noted a pair of Watchers far distant to the side, away from the direction we would travel in, but paid little heed.

We were less than a dozen yards beyond the treeline when the trumpet blast sounded. From a copse a few spearcasts away rode three horsemen. Then from around its side rode another twenty. These were not Watchers—we could hear the calloo of their shouts—shouts exactly like Orissan hunters yelp when the boar breaks cover and they couch their spears and go after it. Nor were these cavalrymen dressed in the immaculate parade-ground armor of the Watchers, but instead in the practical, steel-reinforced leather of earthly soldiers. I saw men rise up in their stirrups, drawing bows. Three arrows thudded into the ground just yards in front of us, and we turned and were running. We darted back into that wilderness, and I have never been so glad to see brambles, tangles, vines, and strangling bushes as in that moment.

I needed no guidance from Janos now to think like a startled hare, ground squirrel, hedgepig, or badger being run by hounds or hunters. Behind us, as we tore our way through the brush, vines trying to hold us back as if we were in a small child's nightmare, we heard horses crashing into the forest fringes, shouts, orders, and commands. Now they would lose time, dismounting and following us afoot, or perhaps going back out and riding around the forest to lay an ambush. Neither course mattered—the two of us could hide in these thickets for years, until they brought up entire armies to comb for us. And we could outwait them here in these woodlands, which were now as precious to me as my own bedchamber had been when winter's storms roared.

My spirit soared and sang. We had seen the Fist of the Gods. Now all that we needed to do was lose our pursuers, return to the Rift, and then, moving with great cleverness, reassay the journey. Our men would have recovered by now, and Sergeant Maeen and our soldiers were more than able to stand off any cavalry patrol we were unable to elude.

There was nothing that could stop us. We would enter the Far Kingdoms before winter.

OR SO I thought. But when we returned to the Rift, we found only Deoce and Sergeant Maeen waiting. The others had abandoned us.

Janos and I had traversed the foothills and the rolling country without real incident. There *had* been patrols on the land looking for us. All of them were composed of very material, very real soldiery. They were competent, Janos assessed. But using his woodcraft skills, we were able to slip past them easily. Plus, Janos supposed, they were seeking a much larger party—we would be taken as the party's outriders or scouts. We refrained from using the talisman for a back plot, instead using my carefully drawn map that Janos had muttered at as a waste of time.

Then, safely in the Rift, I felt my world totter, seeing the wreckage that bastard Evocator had wrought. No one said anything while I raged. Janos stalked off, black faced, toward the lake.

I found control and asked what had happened. Just two days after Janos and I had left, Sergeant Maeen had fallen ill. Cassini must have seen that as his chance. That night, strange smokes and colors had come from his hut.

The next dawn he had announced, somberly, that evil had struck Janos and myself. We had fallen into the hands of an enemy. He was not even sure we still lived.

I cursed Cassini with all the foul oaths I could think of. Then I said, "Deoce, what did you do? I am sorry he brought you false grief."

Deoce shook her head. "I did not grieve, Amalric. I knew you were alive and unharmed."

"How?"

"Believe me . . . when . . . if you ever pass beyond . . . I will know. I will know."

I did not ask further. "So after Cassini announced his lies?"

Deoce had tried to argue, had asked Morning Fog to cast bones to confirm her own feelings. Morning Fog had found no indication we had come to harm. But neither had he found signs of our well-being. So, Cassini said, the party must immediately retreat—back to the Pepper Coast . . . and then Orissa.

At this point I thought Sergeant Maeen, who was nearly recovered from his bout with the sickness, would burst into tears. "I trained them," he said brokenly. "I thought I knew those bastards. I thought . . . I thought they would stand firm."

They did not, especially when Cassini announced that his spell indicated that we had left signs . . . signs that would leave a trail back to the Rift for our enemies. No matter that the Rift leaders had said this could not happen. Panic set in—within a day they had gathered supplies, packed the animals, gone up the stairs and out of the Rift, heading west.

"I cursed them," Deoce said. "But I am not an Evocator. I asked Dawnhope to curse, too, but she said her people could not. That would kill the big spell, and they would be as naked as we were, out in that waste."

"P'raps th' bastards'll die in the desert," Maeen growled. "Or be eaten by th' pit creatures."

"No." It was Janos. He had come back and appeared to be quite under control. "No, that will not happen. I have my own prediction. Anyone fleeing the Far Kingdoms has little to fear, beyond the normal treacheries of this land. Somehow I feel Cassini will make it all the way to Orissa."

"Then we shall deal with him there," I said grimly.

"If we are able. But that is not of great concern," Janos said, and I saw his eyes shining like they did when he first told me of his grand dream. I knew his meaning. We had failed, true. But this was only the first time. There would be another, and another, and yet another if needed. I extended my hand, and Janos clasped it.

We *would* return, by the gods—and the Far Kingdoms would be ours.

The
Second
Voyage

CHAPTER THIRTEEN
Heroes and Liars

WE SPED INTO Orissa's main harbor two months later, a stiff, late morning breeze at our backs. Despite the hour, there was no one around to admire L'ur's skillful handling of the *Kittiwake Two* as he came about in a feisty wind and brought us to dock. I scanned the riverfront for familiar faces, but there was only a derelict or two to return my gaze, and an old fisherman repairing a net.

"I see you have only slightly exaggerated the grandeur of Orissa, Amalric my love," Deoce said dryly. "The teeming harbor, the broad avenues, the hustle bustle of the marketplace." She glanced about the empty riverfront again, then turned to Janos. "Tell me, Janos, is it always this crowded, or did I only arrive on a particularly busy day?" Janos shook his head, as puzzled as I.

"I don't understand," I said. "Normally we'd barely be able to hear one another over the babble."

Deoce laughed. "There he goes again, trying to turn the head of the pretty barbarian girl." She deepened her voice to mock a man's. "Yes, my dear, I am a great man in my own country. A rich man. With a fine villa and many servants. Now, if you'll only tarry in my tent a moment or two longer . . ." She pinched me for the frown I wore on my brow. "There, there. Even if you are poor, I'll love you just the same."

"Believe me, Deoce," Janos said, enjoying her joke, "our friend is not poor. Take my word for it."

"Oh, I *will*, Janos. I will," Deoce said. "But in future, please spare me descriptions of"—she flung out her hand to take in the empty riverfront— "*teeming* harbors."

I leaped from the ship and strode over to the old fisherman. "Where is everyone, grandfather?" I asked.

He peered up with rheumy eyes, his gnarled fingers tying knots in the net as he considered me, my costume, and my two companions. "You're in bad luck if you're set on unloadin' today," he said, nodding at the *Kittiwake Two*. "Fact, you'da been in bad luck yesterday, and the day afore yesterday, and the day afore that as well." He shook his head at our imagined misfortune, loving every moment of it. "And mark my words, tomorrow it'll be just the same. Maybe after that, things'll be back t' normal. Although there's lots of folks bound to be in line ahead of ya. Lots of 'em."

"We'll be fine, grandfather," I said, "although I thank you for your concern. I only want to know what has happened? Where did everyone go?"

"You look Orissan," the old man said, "so I guess you musta been away a long time if you don't know." He eyed Deoce, letting his beady gaze linger a moment. "She ain't Orissan," he said. His gaze jerked away just as Deoce's temper began to boil, and came to the coin I held out. He whisked it away and resumed his knot tying. "Thankee for that," he said. "I got a powerful thirst that needs tendin'. Now, for your question, young lord. 'N my answer. There's big doin's. Been big doin's, four, maybe five days, now. Most folks've got sick heads from all the celebratin'. Only reason I ain't got a sick head, is I run outa coin. Drank my purse flat empty, I did."

"And what are these big doings in celebration of, my friend?" Janos asked.

"You boys musta been gone for a spell," the old man said. "Didn'tcha know we went and found the Far Kingdoms?"

I exchanged glances with Janos and Deoce. "That *is* amazing news," I said.

The old man wheezed laughter. "Not by half, it ain't," he said. "Why, us Orissans're on top all the way now, for sure. And the Lycanthians'll be swallowin' our wake. 'Course, we didn't actually set foot in 'em, but it's close as dammit, I tell you. Close as dammit."

"And who is the hero who came so close?" I asked, barely keeping an edge out of my tone.

"A young Evocator," the old man said. "Fella wasn't worth much before, I hear tell. But he sure is worth somethin' in folks' eyes now. His name's Cassini. Maybe you heard of him?"

"Yes. I have," was my only reply.

"Well, Cassini is probably the biggest hero Orissa's ever had," the old man continued. "He got back a few months ago. The powers that be kept a lid on it for a while, till they'd heard the whole story. But it weren't no use. Whole city was buzzin' with it. I mean, we all thought the Far Kingdoms was just a suckling's story, right? But now we know it's true. Pretty soon we're gonna go back, and we'll be shakin' hands with the folks in the Far Kingdoms. Then there won't be nothin' to stop us. Yessir, there's glory days ahead for Orissa. And I'm just glad I lived long enough to see it. From here on out, we're all gonna be rollin' in gold and pleasures."

The old man grinned, displaying blue gums. "Anyway, they decided to make a big announcement. Which they done. And the Evocators and Magistrates declared a whole week of feastin'. Which we're almost at the end of right now. This aft'noon, in fact, every citizen who ain't too drunk's supposed to get together at the Great Amphitheater. Cassini's gonna get some big honors. Plus, he's probably gonna get to lead the next expedition. Which they're settin' up right now. And they're gonna go at it right, this time. No little stuff, with just a coupla soldiers. But a big force. And I tell ya, nothin'll stand in our way. Yessir, it's a proud time to be an Orissan."

Sudden urgency hammered at my temples. "We had better hurry to my father's house," I said to Janos and Deoce. They did not question me, but as we started away the old man called, "Who might you be, young lord? Give me a name to toast when I cash your kind gift at the tavern."

I whirled back, the game playing done. "I am Amalric Emilie Antero. At your service."

The old man looked at me, gaping. Then he hooted. "Amalric Antero. That's a good un. But I wouldn't try it on anybody else, young lord. Because the Far Kingdoms was *his* Finding. 'Cept, old Amalric never made it back. He and the rest are deader'n fish stink. Cassini seen 'em get it."

It was no surprise that Cassini had declared us dead. He'd already tested his lies on Sergeant Maeen and Captain L'ur; and he'd had many weeks to rehearse before he arrived in Orissa. On our own journey home, I'd agonized over my family's reaction to his grim news. Worry had put wings on our feet. Loyalty had also aided our speedy return, for L'ur had given Cassini's tale as little credence as Sergeant Maeen. When Cassini showed up, he agreed to carry the Evocator to Redond—but no farther. There the good captain had waited, keeping the bargain I'd struck on the Pepper Coast.

"It didn't ring true the likes of Cassini would be the only one to make it," he'd said. "I told him, 'I'll stick by young Antero, sir.

And Cap'n Greycloak.' Cassini didn't like it, but there weren't much he could do, seein' how he needed me to get him a berth on a fast ship to Orissa."

Now, as I rushed to my father's villa, all my hatred for Cassini came to a boil. The hatred proved well-founded: I discovered my father lingering near death, and my sister, Rali, was in a torment when she saw me, fearing the shock of even good news would push him to the other side. She went in to prepare him for my resurrection, and in a while she returned to lead me to his room. I was shocked at the sight of him lying weak and ghastly in his bed. His frame had shrunk to that of an old man's, and his flesh was waxen and hung loose from those frail bones. But his eyes, set deep in that death mask, were alive with delight when he saw me. "Thank Te-Date, you are safe," he gasped. I was so overcome, I flung myself to my knees and nearly wept. "Do not cry, Amalric," my father comforted. "An hour ago I felt the Dark Seeker's presence. I was tempted to let him carry me away; instead, I drove him off. But if I had not—" He put a shaky hand on my head. "—I would never know this happiness."

He coaxed me up and patted the bed beside him. I saw color returning to those pale cheeks. "Come, tell me your adventures, son," he said. "Did you find the Far Kingdoms?"

"No," I said. "But I saw the black-fisted mountains. And I saw passage to the other side."

"I knew it," my father said. "All those years I dreamed. Now I know those dreams were more than a fool's delight."

I sat with him for a short time, giving him a brief account of our adventures. But of them all, he was most delighted by the news that I had returned with my future wife. He gripped my hand. "No matter what lies ahead, Amalric," he said, "treasure her above all things. And you will die a happy man." His grip relaxed, his eyes closed, and for a moment I feared he might have died. But I saw the smile on his face and a gentle fluttering of his beard. He was asleep. I crept out of the room to join the others.

My sister was torn between fury at Cassini and joy at our safe return. "The bastard's stolen all the credit," she was saying as I entered. "It is *you* who is the hero, Janos Greycloak. You, and my brother."

"The question," Janos said, "is how to reply. To tell the truth, I don't much care for the hero's mantle. It is too heavy, gives more discomfort than ease, and is too easily ripped away."

"But they are preparing for the next expedition as we speak,"

I said. "And it is a hero they want to lead it. Right now, that hero is Cassini."

"He's a liar," Deoce said. "Challenge him for the harm his lies have done. Then kill him. This is how we women of Salcae would deal with such a man."

Rali laughed, and it was a joy to hear again after all the time that had passed. "I *like* her, Amalric. She's much too good for you." Then, to Deoce, "We are not so different in Orissa, my dear Deoce. However, Cassini is an Evocator. You cannot challenge an Evocator to a duel. An unpleasant death would be the smallest penalty you'd face."

Deoce made a face. "Now I know for certain men rule here," she said. "No woman of character would allow such a law to stand."

Janos slammed down a heavy fist, rocking the table. "As *should* no man," he said. "But it would be too easy to kill him, and then be cheated out of what I desire the most. The Far Kingdoms will be mine, dammit. And no other's."

"Then let us confront him," I said. "The people will gather soon to do him honor. Let us go there and show them we not only live, but that it was no thanks to that lying coward who abandoned us and urged others to abandon us as well."

And that is what we did. I convinced Rali and Deoce to guard the villa in case all did not go well. I ordered horses saddled, and, still dressed in the rough clothing of our journey, we rode for the Great Amphitheater. Now the streets were more crowded; and I realized that although the old fisherman hadn't believed me, he must have told others about the young fool claiming to be Amalric Antero. People looked up to see the men riding past, and some of them recognized us. "Isn't that Greycloak?" I heard people ask. "And isn't that Lord Antero, himself, beside him? It's true, then. They *are* alive!"

Someone called out, "Where are you bound, Captain Greycloak?"

Janos shouted back, "We're off to confound a great liar." His words and the news that our presence was no rumor spread, and a large crowd gathered in our wake, shouting encouragement and cursing Cassini for a liar. Soon we came to the Great Amphitheater. A strong guard rushed to bar our way, alerted by the noise of the crowd. The captain of the guard raised his spear and shouted for us to stop.

"How dare you say such a thing to a citizen of Orissa," I shouted back. But my protest wasn't necessary. As soon as the man saw Janos, he lowered his spear in amazement. "By Te-Date, it *is* Janos Greycloak," he called. "Alive as the day his mother birthed him." He strode up to Janos. "I knew no Evocator could have accomplished such deeds." To his men, "Didn't I say that, lads? Didn't I say only a soldier could have done what he said he'd done?" The other soldiers cheered. The guard captain clapped Janos on the leg. "Get in there, man," he roared. "The Far Kingdoms are for all of us. Soldier and citizen, and not for the damned Evocators." We dismounted, tossed the reins to the guardsman, and went through the gates; the crowd poured after us.

It was not pleasant to be Cassini that day. I imagine him, now, moments before our entry. Every space in the Great Amphitheater was taken. The heat would have been intense from all those thousands gathered to cheer his triumph. But it was unlikely Cassini would have felt the heat. He would have been well rehearsed for the honors ceremony and would have labored many nights over the humble hero's speech he planned to deliver. As he waited patiently through the many introductory speeches, he would have basked in all the admiration. This was the culmination, the highest point in his life—a life that, he recently feared, would be unappreciated. He would already have begun to dream of the triumphs that would soon follow. He would lead the next expedition to the very portals of the Far Kingdoms and would return with even greater glory. Yes, for a short while, Cassini knew what it was like to be the man of the hour. Then we appeared, and the last of the sand ran out.

Jeneander, that old fraud, was poised to introduce his protégé when we entered. He stood on the broad center stage of the amphitheater, his voice and image magnified many times by the special spell that was cast by 112 Evocators when the first stone was set in place. Clustered about him were dignitaries from all walks of Orissan life. In the two most favored seats were Gamelan, oldest of the Evocator Elders, and Sisshon, his counterpart with the Magistrates. In the center, on the hero's throne and with a hero's garland on his brow, was Cassini.

Jeneander was in middelivery when the crowd that had followed us in roared our names, and all heads in the Great Amphitheater turned. Then the whole place became madness. There were shouts and screams and sudden, wild brawls. I heard my name being chanted, but, mostly I heard them cry out for Janos. Janos. *Janos.* I saw Cassini, standing dumbfounded next to Jeneander, fear a raw wound on his face. He was frozen in his humiliation, but the men

about him were coming to life. Some escaped association by fleeing the stage. Others began to berate him, although I could not
hear what they said over the noise of the crowd. Gamelan was the
first Evocator to find his senses. He hurried to Jeneander and
Cassini, threw his arms about them, lifted his head to the heavens,
and cast a spell. Smoke and fire billowed, and they were gone.

Then a thousand arms lifted us, and a thousand more passed us
across the arena floor to the center stage. I was the first to be set
on his feet. I had just time to catch my bearings, and then Janos
was beside me. He looked around, a little bewildered, a soldier
uneasy in the presence of so many civilians focusing on him. I
pushed him forward, guessing the point on the stage where our
images would be cast up like giants. From the sudden silence of
the crowd, I knew I had guessed right.

"People of Orissa," I said. I heard the words explode out and
wash back, rocking me by the sheer force of their sound. "You all
know me, for I am one of your own."

The crowd chanted my name. "Amalric. Amalric. Amalric."

They grew quiet when I raised my hand. "If you do not know,
I am sure you have all heard of my friend, here."

There was wild cheering as I presented Janos. I pushed him forward, sensing the people felt a close kinship to Janos. I whispered
to him, "Speak to them. They want to hear you."

Janos' eyes were glazed. "What should I say?"

I prodded him again. "Just tell them the truth."

It was the last time Janos ever suffered the malady of actors.
His form suddenly straightened, and all fear and confusion
dropped away. He stepped forward, confident, as if born to the
role.

"People of Orissa," he boomed. "I bring you news of the Far
Kingdoms . . ."

The speech he gave that day was praised for many weeks. It
wouldn't have mattered if it had been fashioned of nonsense
words, for Orissa had never known such a hero as Janos
Greycloak. Here was a man of noble family, but exotic birth. He
was also a fighting man, a soldier who knew what it was like to
suffer. Not only that, but it was rumored he was a former slave,
so they were certain he was no stranger to the burdens and toil of
common men and women. He'd also made a fool and a liar out of
an Evocator, and isn't it true to this day that the most amiable
of sorcerers may be respected, but will never be *liked*? Most of
all, he brought them the gift of pride. An ordinary man had
achieved what had been considered impossible a few months be-

fore. Now he promised to better that achievement, to set foot in a magical land that offered promise aplenty for every heart.

As for myself, there were honors and banquets and many people clamoring for my time. Lest false modesty brand me a liar, I will say that I was a hero as well. After all, it had been my Finding that sparked the whole thing, and I walked every step Janos had walked and suffered what he had suffered. But as intent as I had been on instantly gathering up an expedition and retracing our footsteps, now that I was home, my heart did not yearn so deeply for the Far Kingdoms. With my father ill, and considering the mild nature of my brothers, it was up to me to shoulder the burdens of the Antero family fortunes. My brothers had no grounds for quarrel when he made known that I was his choice to head the family. The acclaim I had won for my Finding had removed much of the stain from the Antero name, or at least made it unwise to attack us.

Oh, yes; there *was* one other thing . . . Deoce. She delighted my father, and he was always making excuses to call her into his company. Although his health continued to fail, you would have thought he was young again when she came into his room. No wonder, for she joked and flirted with him mercilessly. To this day I am certain her attentions added to what little time he had remaining. She also held Rali in her thrall—bursting onto the practice field at a moment's notice, asking to learn new tricks of arms, and giving more than a few of her own.

"There isn't a woman in my Guard who wouldn't fight you for her," Rali told me. "The only thing holding them back is that the dear woman is so obviously headlong in love with you."

Our wedding was by necessity a small affair. My new fame would have made any kind of guest list a recipe for insult if it went beyond immediate family. So we planned a simple ceremony at the villa, overseen by our hearthgod. At first, I was concerned Deoce would feel slighted.

"Why should I feel insult?" She shrugged when I asked. "Among Salcae, the marriage is more important than the wedding itself. The truly big feast is held after the couple has survived one complete harvest cycle; every harvest after that, the celebrations get even larger. I think the reverse is so in Orissa because women have little say in your city. So, the wedding ceremony is a poor bone to throw to the girl when she faces a life of servitude. It is practically the only moment in her life when she is the center of everyone's attention, important above all others." I couldn't quarrel, for hadn't I heard Rali bitterly complain about similar injustices?

Deoce took my hand and laid it gently on her belly, which was slightly swollen with our child. We knew it was going to be a girl, because Rali asked the witch who tended her troop's minor troubles to case a divining spell. I laughed when I felt her kick.

"What shall we name her?" I asked.

"We should honor your mother, and mine as well," Deoce answered. "We should call her Emilie, after your mother's clan. And Ireena after *my* mother."

"Consider her named, then. Emilie Ireena Antero ... I like that."

"I want you to promise me something, Amalric," my bride-to-be asked.

"Anything."

"I don't want our daughter to be raised thinking women must behave as they do in Orissa. You can feel from her kick she is going to be a strong-willed child. And at night, when all is very quiet, I can hear her little heart beating. It is a sensitive heart, Amalric, and please believe me when I tell you I know this, although she and I have yet to meet."

"I will hire the best tutors," I said. "And we have Rali to teach by example, as well as training."

"That isn't enough," Deoce answered. "Emilie will see other women shuffle about, ducking their heads in men's company, feeling less worthy because they do not have a cock and set of balls, suffering instead with a function so lowly as only to be the source of all human life."

"What promise can I make to prevent this?" I asked.

"I want my mother to help raise her" was her answer. I was alarmed, for what father would wish to have his child removed from his sight? She saw this and gripped my hand hard. "Please, you must do this for me. If you say no, I will accept it, not as a dutiful Orissan wife, for this I can never be, but because I *love* you, my Amalric. No child can ever be more important than that love. I don't mean she should be sent away, for I could not bear that any more than you. I mean, in three years' time—before bad influences can alter her, Emilie Ireena must visit long with my mother until after the rites of womanhood, when she is sixteen. After that, only personal weakness can affect her thinking. And I promise you, my Amalric, this child will *not* be weak headed."

The more I thought about it, the more I agreed with what Deoce had to say. I was even enthusiastic, seeing the whole thing as a grand, modern experiment: two cultures joining to produce a perfect child, a golden child. I made a formal promise, and afterward we clung to one another as tight as two lovers can cling. I felt her hand slip down along my bare thighs. She cupped me in her hand and bent down to nuzzle and kiss the thick muscle she found there. Then she looked up, dark hair streaming over her face, eyes lighted up with fun. "After all that man-versus-woman talk," she whispered, "I'd better make sure they don't get their feelings hurt." And then she proceeded to soothe them with her hot mouth.

We were wed one week later. My father was too weak to do more than sit in his chair and weep tears of joy. Rali stood in for him, cutting the lamb's throat and letting the blood flow into the god's offering bowl. Janos took the part of Deoce's brother, anointing our brows with the lamb's blood. When it was done, we feasted, and everyone made merry for three more days.

Just before Deoce and I left on our wedding journey, my father died. I like to think he died a happy man: his errant son had proven worth, a triumph had been won for the family he left behind, and the dream of his youth had come true. However, as I contemplate his feelings and sift for the words I am placing in this journal, I cannot help but remember what Janos said on the Pepper Coast: how my father was a better man than Janos because he would be satisfied if his son accomplished what had been denied him. My father *was* a good man, and certainly a better man than either Janos, or myself. But, alas, he was not perfect, and only a perfect man would have died in happiness. Not when it was plain that after the Far Kingdoms, the world he knew would never be the same.

CHAPTER FOURTEEN
The Second Expedition

IT IS NO boast that the funeral for Paphos Karima Antero was one of the largest in our city's history. So many clamored to attend, the Magistrates ordered the Great Amphitheater opened for the viewing of the pyre. Then all Orissa turned out for the long procession downriver to the Groves of the Wayfarers, where we made sacrifice to Te-Date and I scattered my father's ashes to the winds.

Everyone, myself included, was surprised at just how popular a figure my father was. He was by nature a quiet man who shunned honors and large company. But as I mentioned earlier in this journal, he had an uncanny ability to sniff out a deserving man's misfortune and do his utmost to ease that man's pain. He also had a way of conducting his business, so when he came the better of a bargain, he also did not win his opponent's ire. That his great popularity had never evinced itself publicly, however, I can only lay at the feet of the Evocators and the wrong they did Halab; another part of the silent price my family paid for that wrong. Now, however, with my victory so recent, no one feared to display their affection. This time the fear was entirely on the other side, for the panoply of the funeral echoed long after the breeze carried away the last of my father's ashes. Powerful men began striking new bargains, seeking new alliances; the dissension carried into the ranks of the Evocators themselves.

My father's funeral, with all the weeping, hair tearing, and pompous speeches, was an important sideshow to the intense debate that gripped Orissa. The focus of that debate was the second expedition . . . and Janos Greycloak. None of us realized how great an impact the Far Kingdoms had on our lives. Suddenly all the old ways had been called into question. People from the highest on high to the meanest slave believed they deserved a stake in what was to come. All of them wanted change and wanted it now. For the common man and woman; for tinkerer, soldier, and slave; for the young and adventurous; or for just the far-thinking, Janos became the standard bearer.

Greycloak shone under the intense light of his sudden popularity. He attended endless banquets in his honor and then gathered up the rich food and drink left over and distributed them to the poor in the streets. He told the tale of our journey again and again in settings from luxurious villas to impromptu storytellings in riverfront slum lots. Each time he told it, the tale became fresher, and his emotions never played false or stale when he came to the moment when we saw that black-fisted mountain range. Women accosted him on the street and begged to let them bear his child; mothers named their sons after him; fathers stood for hours on the chance he might pass and they could shake his hand. Every one of them had a question. "I've been asked everything from the cost of taxes to the price of tavern wine," Janos told me one afternoon when he had a few moments to spare. "Whether bread rises best when the tides are high or low and if horses with heavy haunches are haulers or runners. A fisherman asked if it was best to lay the nets at the dark of the moon. And a woman, by Butala, even asked if I thought her daughter fair and then pressed me to try her out to see if she would make a good lover." His grin flashed through his dark beard, and he stroked his moustache. "Fortunately, it was no test of my veracity to answer yea to *both* of those questions."

If Janos was bemused by this idolatry, he did not let it affect him. He threw himself into this madness with a single purpose: when he emerged, he would lead the next and, he swore, final expedition to the Far Kingdoms. "I am not a politician," he said. "I have no desire to be Magistrate, or king—if that were this city's custom. Riches are for rich men; let them enjoy their greed if they can. An idea is the only thing of value in this life; and I am beginning to suspect it is the same in the next."

It might seem Janos was the obvious choice to head the second expedition. In fact, it was *so* obvious for a time it looked very much as if it would be denied him. In our naïveté, we also were surprised that the main voice of opposition was Cassini.

Heroism, or at any rate the public recognition thereof, is an odd human trait. A person does not emerge from a great trial with a hero's mark on his or her brow. Heroism must be conferred; others must decree it; still more must accept the declaration and willingly bow in the streets when the hero passes. Once someone has been acclaimed a hero, it is not so easy, we learned, for that mantle to be ripped away. Cassini's supporters, and they were many, were certain he was the victim of injustice. The lies he told were garbled in the passions that followed. Some conveniently forgot the lies; some said his words were deliberately twisted; some said Janos and I had faked our deaths for an unstated, dark purpose. Many of his supporters were only honest fools: if you have shaken the hand of a hero and praised his name at hearth and tavern, it is difficult to suddenly think ill of him, since his heroism reflects on you. Cassini's most powerful supporters, however, had more complex reasons. Influence, and therefore fortune, had been staked on Cassini. To admit his villainy would be to suffer humiliation; and in the corridors of power where battles are won or lost on an errant word, humiliation cannot be countenanced.

There was one other thing in Janos' way: there were a quiet but mighty few who had no desire to investigate the Far Kingdoms. They were content with the way things were. Their coffers were full, their slaves pliant, and they saw only danger to their comforts if there was any change whatsoever.

Malaren, a friend and fellow trader, summed it up well one day. He was my age, and although a bit of a fop, was a hardheaded thinker who masked his talents with an airy, devil-may-care attitude. "Oh, you don't have to convince me, my dear Amalric," he said. "I find it all quite exciting. Quite. But, everyone knows I believe Orissa has become a dreary old hag with a scraggly beard. It is my father, and my father's ilk, you must sway. He thinks Orissa is still a fine beauty. And well he should. He does not have to lift a finger, and gold pours off his ships. He does not care a whit when I tell him his sons and daughters will not have it so easy, and it will be harder still for his grandchildren."

"But he must see that in a single stroke we can vastly increase our city's influence," I argued. "And it isn't just profit and influence at stake. Why, think of all the knowledge to be gained, man! By all accounts the people of the Far Kingdoms have much to offer us. Their very existence amid so much adversity shows that in many things they must be our superiors."

"That is exactly what frightens him the most," Malaren replied. "At the nonce, my father is a large serpent in shallow waters. He feeds at will with no effort. But how will he measure up when he meets his counterparts in the Far Kingdoms? What if they are twice his size . . . or more?"

"But it isn't just up to us," I said. "We cannot make the Far

Kingdoms disappear into legend again by merely turning away. Lycanth, I assure you, will be quick to step into that gap if we do. And then I can guarantee his shallow kingdom will be quickly overcome. His profits, nay his very life, will be threatened. Believe me, the Lycanthians won't be patient enough to allow him to die in dignity and *then* confront his children."

Malaren mused a bit, then nodded. "Your final argument," he said, "has not been stressed enough. Let me take it to him. Then we'll see."

Shortly after that, Cassini's friends staged an elaborate but very private banquet to honor him. No one knew what transpired, so secretive were the proceedings; but the following week, all sorts of rumors attacking Janos sprang up. It was charged that he was in the pay of Lycanth. In fact, he was the son of one of the Archons, and practiced black magic to confound the good people of Orissa.

Janos seemed unconcerned by these attacks. When I urged him to fight back, to reply to these slanders, he refused. "Cassini is behind it all, as everyone knows," he said. "All I can do is repeat what we have already charged: that he is a cowardly, self-serving liar. Unfortunately, I think the more I repeat it, the more chance I have that same charge will be tied to me."

"Then what do you propose to do?"

"Stay the course," Janos replied. "Every day that passes sees another group swayed to our side. Moreover, I have been so overwhelmed by requests to volunteer for the next expedition, I was going to ask you for funds to set up some means to handle them all. I am a soldier, not clerk; but by whatever bloodless god who favors clerks, I swear I shall never malign their breed again. My quarters are overflowing with all sorts of scrolls and documents and whereases and wherefores."

"Consider it done," I said. "I can loan you someone, plus space at one of our offices. However, aren't you a little ahead of yourself? The second expedition hasn't even been officially approved, much less a man to lead it."

"I know that," Janos said. "But I plan to go on as if this could never be in question. Too many people believe in this thing. There's no sense in giving our opponents an opening."

"That is an excellent attitude to take," I said. "However, when you speak of all the people who are opposing your quest, there is one group who are small in number but wield vast influence. And that is the Evocators. They are plainly behind Cassini. I suppose they don't have any choice, since to condemn him would be to risk condemnation of themselves. However, no matter how many in Orissa agree with us, in the end the Evocators can block us completely."

"Do you really think so?" Janos asked, and I could tell he doubted it. "Why, in not much more time, if the great Te-Date himself stood in the way of the common folk, I fear they would rip him apart to get to the Far Kingdoms."

"Perhaps you are right," I said. "Although I think you have much too rosy a view. Still, the Evocators are a powerful force. And they cannot be ignored, or in the end we may lose much more than a second expedition."

It was Rali who proved my fears, although well-founded, were exaggerated. I was relaxing in the public bath when I got the news. It was one of those rare days when I was able to flee the pressures of business and politics for a good workout at the gymnasium, and now I was easing weary muscles in the steam room. It was late in the day, and besides the slave who tended the hot rocks, there were only a few men about. As my tensions eased, and I was considering more personal matters, such as slipping home for a tumble with Deoce, I heard the bath keeper voice loud protest.

"You can't go in there!"

"Get out of my way, you flea," came a booming reply. The boom was unmistakably Rali's.

"Come back tomorrow," the flea responded. "Tomorrow is Ladies' Day. Today is for men only."

"Oh, don't be such a bother. There's nothing in there I haven't seen before."

There was a scuffle, a yelp of pain, and Rali made her entrance. She saw me through the steam and walked over, ignoring horrified looks from the other men. I patted the spot beside me on the stone bench, enjoying their discomfort as my sister once again turned custom on its head. "I've been searching for you all morning, Amalric," she said. She glanced around the room; the men looked quickly away. None of them knew what to do. They believed themselves humbled whether they stayed or fled.

"In fact, I'm so weary from looking," she finally said, "I think I'll join you."

With that, she kicked off her sandals, shed her tunic, and in a wink she was naked and plumping her lovely haunches down on the bench. "More steam," she shouted to the attendant. He quickly complied. Just as quickly, all but two or three of the men fled.

Rali sprawled out, legs splayed wide. One of the remaining

men dared to ogle her. Instead of clapping her legs together and covering her breasts, Rali stared back at him, hard. "It would eat you alive, little man," she snarled. He ran, and before another drop of sweat could fall from my brow, the others had followed him. I laughed until my sides ached.

"Good," Rali snorted. "I need privacy for the tale I have come to tell. But first . . . some wine, brother dear, to slake my thirst."

I poured wine and she drank it down. Then she lifted a big jug of cold water and drenched herself. The water ran over the floor and into the rock pit, sending up a mighty blast of steam.

"Now, what is the news, sister, that puts you into such a state you relish bullying these poor men?"

"Oh, balls, Amalric. It'll give them something to talk about. Spice up their dull lives. If their women are fortunate, I'll have aroused their men so, they'll speed home to prove they are men, after all."

"Quit being clever, please," I said. "The news, if you will. The news." I refilled her goblet, and she plunged into the story without further prompting.

"There is a young woman in my troop," she said, "whose mother has served for many years as a floor scrubber to the Evocators. She has cleaned their halls for so long, they have ceased to notice her. Since this woman was wise enough to see her daughter ought to be steered into our company, instead of joining another generation of stone scourers, I think you will agree the Evocators' attitude was not good thinking. In fact, she so resents it, she has become my willing ear to many of their discussions."

I straightened on the bench; this was *indeed* good fortune. The Maranon Guard was sworn to remain neutral in all affairs of the city; therefore it was necessary for them to have many "ears," as my sister put it, to avoid any hint of playing favorites. "Tell me more, oh wise and beautiful sister," I said.

Rali laughed, gave my arm a numbing clout, and resumed her story. "There was a meeting of the Council of Elders yesterday noon. Cassini was there, as was his mentor, Jeneander. Our floor scrubber found a nice, dirty spot just outside and listened. She said it was plain from the voices—they got quite angry, apparently—the nature of the meeting was a debate, and the subject of this debate was the Far Kingdoms."

"So things are coming to a head," I said, grimly. "They are marshaling their forces against us."

"Far from it" was my sister's surprising answer. "It might be difficult to believe, but the Evocators are as divided as the rest of

Orissa. To the public, they are supportive of Cassini. But only because he is one of their own and many feel they must stand by him. In private, however, the issue has broken into several warring camps. At the moment, those siding with Cassini hold sway; but, from what our brave floor scrubber says, their grip is slippery. For the loudest proponent of all for the expedition *and* Janos is Gamelan himself."

I nearly fell to the floor. "But ... he's the oldest of them. And surely the most hidebound and the most bent on protecting the Evocators' sphere."

"So, I would have guessed as well," Rali said. "However, from his remarks, just the opposite is true ... except for the age part, for there is no denying Gamelan is old. Anyway, he apparently gave an impassioned speech, saying Orissa is threatened by stagnation from within and fierce enemies from without. Not only should a second expedition be launched as soon as possible, but Janos should lead it because its success is so important."

"What about Cassini?" I was nearly sputtering in amazement.

"Gamelan apparently has no use for him. He declared quite openly Cassini has not only humiliated the Evocators, but also undermined the people's faith in them."

I couldn't help but laugh. "Faith? Why, it's more fear than faith."

"Well ... yes. However, the point is Gamelan is on *our* side. I never thought I'd live to see the day when an Evocator supported the Anteros."

"Nor did I," I said. "What was the outcome of the debate?"

"Gamelan lost, of course. Cassini is still their man. However, our hard-working spy said the victory was so narrow it could change at a moment's notice. So it seems to me, all we have to do is find a way to quietly assist that change." I had no quarrel with her reasoning. It was only the how that escaped me. My head whirled, seeking openings we could exploit. "One other thing," my sister said. "There seems to be one very small group that is ahead of the others. Our spy says there has been much mysterious comings and goings in the basement of the hall. Much spell casting and odd noises and smells for even a wizard's lair. It is a very secretive group; and others don't seem to know what they are about."

"What does our friend the floor scrubber think?"

Rali shrugged. "She doesn't know. She doesn't even have a guess. She told me if she did have one, and it was close, then Gamelan and the others would have figured it out as well."

Despite the fact that all things now suggested a swift resolution, the matter stalled for some weeks. Janos took in Rali's information and continued picking away at his opponents bit by bit.

As for myself, I had my family and business to see to. An idea had come shortly after our return to Orissa. It was an idea whose seed had begun to germinate after Eanes' death. I thought I was a fool to harbor such a plan at first, but the more I saw how the folk of the streets reacted to the Far Kingdoms, considering it a possession, a birthright, the more the notion took root. I first broached the subject with Deoce.

"We have been together for only a short time, my love," I began. "But in that time I have found you to be not only a loving wife, a solid friend, but the best counsel among all my advisers."

"Thank you for saying that, my husband," she replied. "But your preamble is entirely unnecessary. For the day you cease asking, *and* accepting, my advice, is the day I book passage for Salcae, where there is no need for a sweet balsam before a woman is asked her opinion."

I blushed, and Deoce laughed and gave me a hug. "Never fear, dear Amalric. If it were even possible for you to treat me as other Orissan men treat their wives, I would have seen it long before. And I would never have slept with you in the first place."

She shifted in her pillows, seeking comfort, then patted her belly, swollen large now with our daughter, Emilie, whom the midwives said would be with us very soon. "Listen well, little one," Deoce said to the swelling. "Your father is about to speak."

I smiled and then said, "I believe I have found the cause for the unease that afflicts Orissa. And it is also the reason why the Far Kingdoms have so captured everyone's imagination. You, yourself, have touched on this ailment, and disease I think it is, many times."

"The status, or lack of it of women, you mean?" she asked.

"That's very much part of it. Women are only one factor, however. In Orissa, everyone is frozen in their roles at birth. A woman can only attempt a few, approved things. The same is true of all the classes in this city. With rare exception, once a craftsman, always a craftsman; a stall keeper will remain a stall keeper; a laborer will continue to toil; and so on. Halab encountered the ultimate barrier when he tried to become an Evocator."

"It is a very difficult city for someone with dreams," Deoce agreed.

"You hit it square," I said. "Dreams are not forbidden in Orissa, but they are certainly not encouraged. Oh, we fool ourselves. We delight in the saucy talk and sassing the common folk give us lords and ladies. But let that sass become more than a charming eccentricity, and that man or woman is done."

"What do you propose to do about it?" she asked.

"I would start with the lowest of the low," I said. "I would free the slaves. Remove that barrier and the flood will start. Then all the dams will give way as each class thunders downriver to come against the next, until ... Well, who knows. Perhaps someday even a slave could become a lord or lady."

Deoce delighted me with a glowing smile of approval that gave me as much pleasure as any feeling I have had in my life. She said, "Speaking as a woman who was almost a slave, and as a woman in Orissa I am all *but* a slave in every place except this house, I heartily agree. Our bold friend, Janos Greycloak, is an example of what a slave can achieve."

"Freeing our own would be a small start," I said. "We would have to be quiet about it at the start, for I fear a loud public announcement would raise so many passions that it would jeopardize the plan."

"That is wise," she said. "If we let it be known to a few at a time, and let that news go from trickle to torrent, it will have a greater effect."

"The only trouble is my brothers," I said. "For the Anteros must free *all* their slaves to make the point. There will be a great family fight."

"Good. It will get their blood going. Your brothers need a shaking up. They've lived off your father's and now your boldness far too long."

My brothers did *not* take it well. The Antero family owned perhaps one hundred and fifty souls, most of whom were either very expensive household slaves, skilled dockside or farm laborers, or educated clerks and managers. By freeing them we would reduce the value of our family's wealth by one fifth. My oldest brother, Porcemus, was the most opposed. He was twice my age and of all of us most closely resembled my father, but with weaker features. "Your plan is insane," he said. "You will beggar us. Who will take the slaves' places? Think of the wages, man! We simply cannot afford it."

I said, "Money is not the question here. If a thing is right, then it should be done whatever the expense. However, if you insist . . ." I took a ledger from the stack before me. "Review the figures I have collected and you will see it is cheaper to employ a man than to enslave him. A free man pays for his own keep.

And he works harder, because he can improve his lot, whereas a slave will always be a slave, so why should he trouble himself?" I opened the document and tapped a column of figures. "See, here, Porcemus. Your orchard production has remained at nearly the same level for fifteen years. Only once did it change, and that season showed an increase." He looked at the figures, frowning. "This was the year when the fever laid all your slaves low," I continued. "We had to hire free men and women to do their work. And the harvest was greater, wasn't it? There was also less spoil, because they worked faster and harder to earn more money."

There were murmurs of surprise among my brothers. Porcemus, however, was stubborn as only a small-minded man can be. "You can't make such a judgment examining only one season," he said.

"I didn't." I pushed the stack of ledgers over for him to study if he wished. "I found many other instances where similar comparisons can be drawn. Over the years our profits are always greater when we pay a fair wage, instead of using a slave. To be fair, I did not include the trade our ships carry, although that is the bulk of our earnings. As you know, we rarely use slaves in the trading business ... for the reasons I just gave. Even the least skilled trader knows there is no greater motive than profit."

"I still say a demon has invaded you," Porcemus said. "Why, if everyone freed their slaves, we would immediately double the number of citizens. Most of our people are already an ignorant and filthy lot. Now, we would have nearly thirty thousand more. Anarchy would reign. It would be the end of Orissa as we know it." He angrily shoved the books back at me. "Hasn't our family suffered enough? First, Halab ... and now ... *you.*"

I had expected an attack on myself; I was prepared for it and planned to be calm and reasonable. It was not strange that my brothers would be jealous that one so young as myself had been handed over the leadership of our family. The attack on Halab caught me by surprise, and I acted foolishly, slamming up from the table, the chair crashing to the floor. "If you were not of my blood," I said, "I would kill you where you sit."

Porcemus turned a ghastly white. My other brothers tried to calm me. But it was not their words that soothed me; it was the sight of Porcemus' frightened face. I was strong in my anger, and I could feel the easy play of my muscles, which had been tempered and tuned for violence during my long journey. What a helpless lot, I thought. Then my anger fled. Ah, well, I thought again. They are a burden, but what of it? They were a burden to your father as well, and he trusted you to shoulder it when he handed over responsibility.

I sighed, picked up the chair, and set it in place. "I am sorry for my anger, brother," I said. "Now, I would like your agreement on my plan. To ease your pain, I propose to repay you the value of your slaves from my own pocket." I turned to the others. "Will that suffice?" There were noises of acceptance all around. Porcemus became very friendly, hugged me, and apologized, and then they all left.

That is how I, Amalric Emilie Antero, became the first to free the slaves in Orissa. It was not a proud moment, for it all still was measured by greed, but at least it was done. I settled back and waited for the reaction. The first was most unexpected. It came from Tegry.

"What have you done?" he thundered.

I was taken aback; slaves do not speak that way to their owners. Then I remembered he was a slave no more. This would take much getting used to, especially with someone I disliked as much as Tegry, whom I had only kept on because of my father.

"Calm yourself, Tegry," I said. "Explain my error, and I will do my best to correct it."

"You ... you ... freed me!"

I am sure my expression resembled a gaping fish. "What is wrong with that?" I sputtered. "I freed *all* of the slaves."

Tegry's eyes filled with hatred. "I have worked all my life to reach my present position," he gritted. "And now it is gone. You have stolen my pride."

"How did I do this? You still have your job, but at a salary. And you are still master of the affairs that were in your domain before."

"I ... I ... defecate on your salary! I've stolen more in a day, as is my right, then you pay me in eight. As for my position, I now have no authority over the servants. No *real* authority. You have freed them, you fool. When I order them to work, they laugh in my face if they do not like my manner. Only this moment I took a whip to a stable hand, and the bastard had the audacity to rip it from my hand. And then he ... he quit. He left. There is no way I can order him back, because he no longer is required to obey."

"You'll just have to adopt an easier manner," I answered. "If you are unhappy with your pay, why, I can raise it. But not eight times. That, Tegry, is more theft than is your right. But I'll double it, and we'll let bygones be—"

"No, you won't," Tegry shouted. "If I am free, then I will not work for such a man as yourself. I warned your father. But he wouldn't listen. Very well, then, if a stable hand can do it . . . so can I. Lord Antero, I resign my position. I will be gone within the hour, and you will be a sorry man that you so abused me." He turned on his heel and stalked out.

Although we did not announce my actions loudly, word spread quickly enough, and there was much hot talk about that "crazy Antero" who freed his slaves. But soon others took my side, especially young businessmen, who could see my point about higher profits. Some of them freed their slaves, and then the profit point took on a tone of morality and civic pride.

"They are saying if barbarians like the Lycanthians can allow their slaves to purchase their freedom," Janos reported with much laughter, "then Orissa can certainly go them one better."

"I only hope it hasn't injured your cause," I said.

"Actually, it has improved it," Janos said. "The same people who support me are the ones most likely to free their slaves. So it turns out we are walking hand in hand again, as if we were back to our trek." Not that all went perfectly. Hot words turned to brawls now and then. Many owners became angry when they were accosted on the street by former slaves who berated them for not freeing the people in their keep.

Then a public meeting was called at the Great Amphitheater. It was announced that a second expedition to the Far Kingdoms had been approved, and there would be public discussion on who would lead it. Once again, Cassini's name was raised. I rode with Janos to the meeting. He dressed himself as a soldier, still favoring the plain, light armor and common sword on his back. But astride his horse, his black beard brushed until it glistened and his big white teeth smiling, he looked like a young king. Outside the amphitheater, we were cheered by a large group of angry young men; among them was Malaren.

"Thank you for the greeting," Janos said. "But what is happening?"

"I will tell you, my dear man," Malaren seethed. "They plan to steal the leadership of the expedition."

"Who is *they*?" I broke in, for Janos was too jolted to ask.

A burly man with thick, calloused hands answered. "Those dog-bitten Magistrates, that's who," he shouted. I saw the mark on his arm—he was a recent slave. "And the damned Evocators're in on it, too."

"Not *all* of them," Malaren said. "But there are enough old men and cowards in both groups to give it to Cassini."

I looked at Janos, his eyes steel and his hand reaching for his sword. He looked ready to kick his horse into a gallop and charge the amphitheater. Someone shouted, "We're with you, Greycloak!" Others took up the shout. "We'll not let them try and cheat you again." Other voices were raised, and I saw many more had joined us. Among them were lords like Malaren and common folk, blacksmiths, and sailors, and yes, former slaves as well. I felt a great stirring of battle coming on.

Abruptly Janos was all calmness. He raised a hand, and there was silence. "We will not behave as rabble," he said. "If you are with me, then come quietly. I want you all to sit together, and I swear that I shall speak for all of you as well as myself."

There were mutters, but Janos' commanding presence prevailed; we readied ourselves to enter. I felt a tug at my breeches, and I looked down and recognized a young servant from my household. Her eyes were wide and frightened.

"What is it?" I asked.

"It is Lady Antero," she cried. "Come quickly. Your child is being born."

Her words pierced me. I was torn by the heat of the moment and fear for Deoce. Janos kicked his horse to my side. "Go," he said.

"But . . . the meeting . . . the . . ."

He pushed me, rough. "I can do this. I will need you more later. Now, go!" My wavering broke, and I swept the servant girl up on my saddle and raced through the streets for the villa. Behind me I heard a great roaring echo from the amphitheater.

The birthing bed was a horror of blood and pain. Two midwives tended my poor Deoce, and not all their medicines and spells could ease her agony. My daughter was coming, but she wasn't coming easily. Deoce gripped my hand so hard, I thought my fingers would break. "I knew you would come," she wept. "They said there was . . . a meeting. The expedition! But . . . I *knew* you would come just the same."

I tried to find words, but they were all puny things beside her pain and faith in me. All I could say was that I loved her and that I would love her until the sands all washed away to sea. She gave a terrible scream, and I thought I had lost my Deoce forever. Silence . . . So thick and heavy after that scream, I can feel it stifle me as I scratch these words. Then I saw my daughter's head emerge between Deoce's bloody thighs. My wife choked back another scream, and the babe came the rest of the way into the practiced hands of the midwife. A moment later, Emilie gave her first cry. My daughter was born.

"Is she beautiful?" Deoce asked in a weak voice.

I looked at the bloody little thing, with her eyes squeezed tight shut. She was howling now, angry for being plucked from warm safety. "Yes, my love," I answered. "She is beautiful." And as I watched the midwives clean her and then wrap her in soft linen to ready Emilie to meet her mother for the first time, I really did believe this so.

OUTSIDE OF A war, the second expedition to the Far Kingdoms was the largest force mounted in Orissan history. This would be no private Finding, where a young man could gallop off wherever he chose, with however many drinking companions his father could afford. Destiny was being gambled for, and every person in the city wanted a place at the table. Fully two thousand would go: troops, horses and their tenders; officers and their servants; camp followers by the score to pleasure the men; cooks, bakers, armorers, bearers; and the simply curious who had influence enough to get their names on the rolls. By unanimous acclaim, the man who would lead this great force was Janos Greycloak.

"It wasn't much of a fight," Janos said that night. "Cassini never even took the stage, although I saw him waiting in the wings, all blown up with his own importance. He was pacing back and forth rehearsing his acceptance speech. If that wasn't enough of a clue for a poor, dim-witted soldier such as myself, the fact all the men on the stage were our enemies was enough to show that someone had filled pips on the dice with lead." Janos shook his head, still in amazed shock. "As soon as I took my place, the whole crowd began shouting like before—'Janos. Janos.' And all that rot." His teeth flashed, and I knew he hadn't found it "rot" at all. "But this time it was much louder, and the voices were so furious, you had to be a fool not to know there was blood in their eyes. Some fellows made so bold as to rush the platform, but fell back when I asked them not to be so rude and to let these worthy gentlemen speak."

Janos gulped down a tumbler of wine, then started laughing. "Oh, I wish you could have been there, my friend," he said. "There's been nothing in your experience quite like it." Janos said Jeneander and his friends held a hurried conference, trying to ignore the boisterous remarks of the crowd. As Janos indicated, nothing like this had ever happened in Orissa, and our enemies were in a panic, flinching under the crowd's abuse as if they were throwing stones instead of words. Someone in the crowd spotted Cassini, and a group charged him; but he managed to flee in time. On the stage a decision was made, but then they began to squabble about who would deliver it to the angry citizens of Orissa. The crowd laughed at their plight, pressing toward the stage again. Then a Magistrate gave Jeneander a hard shove, and he stumbled forward, his image cast large by the magnification spell. He stood quaking next to Janos.

"I silenced our friends, and gave Jeneander my best smile of greeting," Janos said. "I put my arm around him as if he were my brother, and I said loudly, so all could hear, 'No matter what your choice, my friend, all here know that you worthy gentlemen have labored long to arrive at your wise decision.' "

Janos laughed and took another gulp of wine to ease his throat. "Then poor Jeneander began to speak," he continued. "His first words came out a sort of a squeaky quack, as if a mouse had mated with a duck. But he finally got it out, his knees quaking as if we were standing in a wintry breeze. He said, still in that high voice, 'We declare that the leader of the second expedition will be . . . Captain Janos Greycloak.'

"Well, you couldn't hear a thing after that from all the shouting. But no matter, for no sooner had the good Evocator said his piece, he and the others bolted from the stage as if they were rabbits who'd just had a great vision of a bubbling stew pot." I laughed at the scene he painted until tears flowed. I refilled our glasses, and we drank a toast to Te-Date, who had so confounded our enemies.

Then Janos turned serious. "I want you to know," he said, "that no matter what follows in our lives, you could never accumulate enough deeds from me to repay the debt I owe you." I made humbled, nonsense noises, but my heart was full of joy. I heard Emilie cry somewhere in the house, and then the nursemaid's voice lifted in soft song to soothe her. It had been a most remarkable day.

Janos heard that cry as well, and he smiled. "I know it is not possible for you to come with me this time," he said. "You have too many burdens now. But you should know I will sorely miss you."

"That is kind of you to say," I replied. "But, I know that last time I was so green that I was little real help to you. And now you will have a great army, with many experienced, professional men to advise you."

Janos gave his head a hard shake. "Your one real flaw, my

friend," he said, "is you do not realize your own worth. You will be a dangerous man when you do, for you have a natural talent as an adventurer. More important, you have the strength of a firm heart and steady vision. Don't bother denying it, I know you well; perhaps in some things better than you know yourself. We are much alike, Amalric Antero. As alike as if we were twins. But you don't have my dark side, thank the gods."

He peered at me, and I saw from the redness in his eyes he was a little drunk. "I swear to you, Amalric," he said, "when I stand in the Far Kingdoms, I will make sacrifice in your honor. And I shall tell the masters of that place that I bring greetings from my good friend, and twin . . ." His voice stopped in midsentence, and I saw his head had fallen. I plucked the tumbler of wine from his hand before it spilled, and as I crept out of the room I heard his first, weary snore.

One month later the expedition set forth. Every craft that could be spared had been pressed into service to carry that mighty group to the sea. The whole city turned out to see them off. I stood on a hill near the bend as they passed, and am not ashamed to admit I felt a little regret I was not going with them. But when the last ship had gone, and I turned toward home, I thought of Deoce and Emilie, and my step was suddenly very light.

CHAPTER FIFTEEN
The Dark Seeker

WHAT I WRITE next is difficult. I would pay almost any price if I could scrape this time from the scrolls of my life. Orissa had been blessed by the gods for years. Our sacrifices had been rewarded many times over: the harvest bountiful, the river quiescent, soldiers victorious, health excellent, and our children obedient. Then the gods called in the debt.

For a short time after Janos left, my life was nothing but joy. I spent every moment of free time—and robbed my business for more—with Deoce and Emilie. My wife was all things to me: lover, partner, adviser, and friend. She had a head for business and was beginning to come to the docks with me to help organize the trade to the lands Janos and I had opened up. At home she was the delight of the servants—a much cheerier group now that they had been freed—for she relished diving into the work at hand, fearing no dark corners where cobwebs gather deep. And sometimes she would surprise me at my desk and lure me away to a quiet, leafy bower where we made love as we had in the days of the valley of paradise.

Emilie proved to be as delightful a child as Deoce had predicted. She was a merry little girl with plump cheeks, fair skin, and eyes alive with curiosity. My heart ached when I heard her laugh, and the moment she came into my sight, she would cry out with delight and hug me with her chubby arms, and my senses would fill up to the overflowing as her laughter and milky perfume overwhelmed me.

"You are clay in her hands," Deoce would tease. "If there was ever a child who was her father's little girl, our Emilie is that tod-

dler. You had best be wary, my dear, or she will become insuffer-
ably spoiled."

Of course, all was not blossoms under a spring sun. There were
problems: Deoce suffered a sprain, Emilie the colic, and a small
cargo ship from the Northern Lands was lost. Also when Janos set
out, he left our enemies behind. For a time, however, they were
too fearful to do more than whisper foul charges.

There were things, however, that might have given us warning
of what was about to come, but most of us had been lulled into
sweet dreamings of the treasures that would soon pour forth from
the Far Kingdoms. The Kissing of the Stones had gone badly that
season. The criminal the Evocators crushed to bless the harvest
was a starveling turned thief, who produced only a slender trickle
of blood when he was ground between the two ancient stones.
Then we had many days of lightning storms that rent the air with
their hot breath and set the dogs and lizards howling. Afterward
the dawning sun lighted the skies a fierce red, and thick black
clouds swirled about making ghastly images. The rumors also
heated up. There were stories that the second expedition had lost
its way several times, that Janos was quarreling with his officers,
and there was much immoral practicing of black magic whose
only purpose was sexual. And if the tales told on Janos weren't
enough, we received travelers' reports that the Lycanthians were
all astir, drilling their troops and talking of rebuilding the great
wall we had torn down when we defeated them. Still, except for
idle tavern talk, we paid little mind, but just added it all to the
general gossip, such as the odd lights and burning odors emanat-
ing from the citadel of the Evocators. I *did* ask Rali about this, but
her spy could only report that the Evocators were still feuding, except they were keeping their quarrel locked behind thick doors
where even her presence would be suspect.

Then the first members of Janos' expedition returned home and
put voice and person to the rumors attacking him. They charged
that he had become a temperamental leader, who took no counsel
other than his own and publicly humiliated those who opposed
him. They said not only had the expedition become lost several
times, but was still wandering about the countryside, losing baggage and treasure and victims to marauding tribes. Most of this
was believed to be nonsense, for the people who had returned
were notorious sloths and cowards whom we all believed had only
gone on the expedition to win easy glory.

Cassini, however, immediately seized this chance, and began
making appearances again, berating Janos and doing his best to

harm his reputation. His supporters trickled out from under their rocks, and soon he became bold enough to participate in public rites. In fact, he assisted Jeneander in the yearly rain ceremony, tinkling the silver bells that chimed like raindrops, as Jeneander cut the throat of a fat bullock.

The rain came on schedule—but it didn't stop. Hour after hour it fell, and it came so thick you couldn't tell night from day, and all over Orissa we huddled in our homes and listened to the heavy drumming on our rooftops. It was a cold rain, and we all had to keep fires burning constantly in our hearths, and it wasn't long before fuel became scarce. A green mold flourished in the heavy rain, attacking our clothes and spoiling our food. The Evocators rushed about casting spells to rid us of the mold, but no sooner had that abated than ants swarmed by the millions, pouring into our houses through every cranny, and driving us all mad with itching as we swept them off our walls, ourselves, and our children.

All these troubles were minor, however, compared to the sudden fright we all had when the river began to rise. There was no one living who had known it to jump its banks, but there were old scars on the hillsides far from its bed that told an ancient tale of terror and destruction. So when the river became a boiling mass of mud and debris that swept away one of the smaller docks, panic gripped the city. After conferring with the Evocators, the Magistrates fetched a felon—who had slain his wife and children and then roasted them for a meal—from the cells. The whole city was ordered out, and we all made a dreary parade down to the place of sacrifice. We huddled in the rain, miserable and cold, as Jeneander and Cassini—along with a large contingent of Evocators—chanted river-taming spells for what seemed like an eternity. Gamelan was absent, which said much to me. Prevotant, that old thief, was present, which said even more. The ceremony went badly: the incense pots wouldn't stay lighted, and when they tied the felon up, the knots kept undoing themselves. The poor fellow shrieked and moaned and flung himself about, so we knew the numbing potion they'd fed him wasn't working. People were frightened at all the mishaps; no one even laughed when Jeneander took a tumble in the mud while struggling with the sacrificial victim. Some felt sorry for the man; there were mutterings that he'd only been driven mad by the rain; and wasn't that the fault of the Evocators, who should have known better than to order up so much?

Then Cassini stepped forward and clubbed him over the head

with a log. He and Jeneander grabbed him by the legs and arms, and without further ado, flung him into the water to drown. Everyone went home unhappy and angry at the city's leadership.

To no one's surprise, the sacrifice failed—the river kept rising. I rushed about with other men who made their living from the great stream. We emptied the warehouses, hauled up the boats, and sent larger craft away. When I went home late that night, the water was running into the warehouses.

Deoce shook me awake just before morning. "What is it?" I asked, coming up instantly—a habit I'd formed in my journey with Janos, and that I have kept to this day. She stood by our bed in a white gown, Emilie clutched in her arms. Deoce was pale and trembling. Emilie's eyes were wide—in a moment she was certain to cry.

"Listen," was all Deoce said.

I heard a distant thundering—no, it was a roar. Amidst that roar I could also hear the cracking and creaking sounds of large objects breaking up. I jumped from the bed and flung open the window. Even over the scudding rain, the sound was louder; but that rain was so thick, and the night so dark that I couldn't see what was happening. I turned back to Deoce, knowing just the same.

"It's the river."

"Shall we flee?" Deoce's voice was shaking. I had never seen her display fear before; then I realized she'd never lived by a river.

"We're quite safe, here," I assured her. "Besides the old embankment—which the river has rarely reached—there are many hills between us."

I was worried about the docks and warehouses, and I was more worried for the people who lived and worked by the river; but there was nothing I could do. I was no god who could halt a flood. So I pulled my wife and babe back into the bed and held them in my arms. When the morning came, the rain had stopped, and when I awoke the first thought that came to my mind was that Emilie had never cried.

At the waterfront the river was back to near normal. The damage was heavy—but not so bad as I had feared. Some docks had been stripped away, warehouses crushed, boats and ships wrecked, but few lives had been lost. As we gathered to aid our fellow Orissans and dig away the debris, I thought it could have been worse. I looked at the marks the retreating waters had left, and they had reached only halfway to the old scars.

I was one of the few, however, who was grateful. On the way

home I heard bitter grumbling about the state of things in Orissa. I was wearing rough clothing for the day's work and had a cap on my head to cover my red hair, so no one recognized me.

"I hear in the Far Kingdoms the Evocators got spells that keep a river's temper sweet," one man said.

"Won't do us no good," another replied. "You just watch. When Cap'n Greycloak gets back, our lice-ridden lot will do him in. They swear to Te-Date there ain't nothin' for us in the Far Kingdoms ... No matter what the cap'n found."

"Hang Greycloak," an old woman barked. "He's the cause of our troubles. He's nothin' but a blowhard."

"Get out of here with your nastiness," the first man shot back. "Greycloak's the only luck we still got. Him and Lord Antero with all that lucky red hair. Weren't for them we'd have no chance at all."

They began to squabble, and I moved on before I was spotted. For the first time in months I began to worry. I'd always known that much was hanging in the balance with the second expedition. But I'd believed the goal was all but won with such a mighty force to overcome the trials of that hard and distant land. But now I thought of all the twists and turns that had arisen in that first journey. Our sorcery failing, the mysterious Watchers, the deadly terrain, the tricks and traps any wizard who opposed us could lay; and I realized that failure was a definite possibility.

But when I returned home to Deoce's warm greeting and saw my infant daughter's smiling face, I brushed all doubt aside. There had to be a future for such as them; a future much brighter than even my father had dreamed for me. How could the gods fail such a pair—much less, all the mothers and babes of Orissa? It will all be fine, I told myself ... just fine.

The bleak mood deepened as we approached the Month of Harvest. The heavy rains and floods had washed away much of the seed and tender plants that had been set out in the field. Already we were facing lean times and rising food prices. To add to this gloom, all news of Janos and the second expedition ceased. It was as if they had simply disappeared. But I assured everyone—myself included—that it was merely because they had traveled so far that news was much slower in reaching us.

Just at harvest time, no more than a few days before farmers customarily went into the fields—disaster struck again. This time it came in the guise of an unseasonal wind, which swept down from the mountains. It was hot and dry and unceasing. It sucked all life from the furrows, killing most of what the rains had left for our tables. The Magistrates ordered an emergency tax on all households, businesses, and goods to buy grain from abroad. The Evocators took to the fields and chanted and cast endless spells. Still the winds blew, and they kept blowing until one day they died of their own will.

The city was astonished by the Evocators' continued lack of success. For all our lives they had protected us from the evils of the natural world, as well as the spiritual. What had happened? Why were we becoming so unlucky? If things didn't change soon, the Lycanthians would begin to get notions not to our liking.

Some time later, part of the reason was provided indirectly by my friend, Malaren. He came to me saying that one of the Magistrates wanted a private word. The Magistrate's name was Ecco; he'd been a strong, but quiet supporter of our cause, so I agreed without hesitation. We met the following night. Ecco was an older man, but with more wrinkles and gray hair than his age warranted. His eyes and step were young, as were his views. A successful trader before he joined the ranks of the Magistrates, he got quickly to the point.

"If you have had any word from Captain Greycloak," he said, "it would be of great benefit to us all . . . no matter what the nature of that word."

"Honestly, sir," I answered, "I have heard no more than anyone else in Orissa, which is nothing. But there is nothing strange in this lack of news; after all, the Season of the Storms is upon us, and Janos would certainly seek shelter to weather it out."

He stared at me hard for a moment, eyes probing for dishonesty. Finding none, he lowered them and sighed. "Then there is no help there for us."

"What is the trouble, sir? In particular, I mean. For obviously there is trouble of all kinds in Orissa these days."

"You swear to tell no one what I am about to say?" I swore it. He nodded, satisfied, and said, "I fear collapse. Our people are fast losing all faith in us. We have had minor fighting in the streets, as you know, and other trouble that comes from a rebellious mood. And who can blame them? Why, when we can't even get the rains and the harvest right, why should they trust us? Still, I love this city for all its ills, and I would rather die on the rack than see it injured."

"Why aren't the Evocators doing anything about it?" I asked. "You Magistrates meet with them regularly, do you not? What do they have to say for themselves?"

"If you mean Jeneander and Cassini," he replied with disgust, "then they have nothing to say. They come to our sessions and spout empty promises, collect their tithing, and depart."

"What of Gamelan?" I asked. "And the other Evocators?"

"They have stopped coming, or have been stopped from coming—I do not know which. But, I can tell you this, there is a battle being waged in the palace of the Evocators, and anyone who could be our friend is not among the present winners."

"But there must be something more than a simple power struggle," I said. "Jeneander is a fool, and Cassini a liar. But they *are* skilled Evocators. Why can't they help us? I don't think it is a conspiracy, mind you, for they would be damaging themselves as much as us."

"I know of no facts," Ecco said, "and I hesitate in participating in the spread of rumor."

"Hesitate no more, sir," I replied. "Not if rumor suggests explanation."

"You have heard, or witnessed the strange doings at the palace of the Evocators?" he asked. I said I had. "Well, this rumor arises from those odd lights and odors and such. It is said by some that Cassini and his fellows are engaged in wicked magic. For what purpose, the rumors do not indicate. However, what *is* said, is that the practice of that black sorcery has drained the city of its natural magical energy. And this is why all the spells cast in our behalf have failed, or are so weak that they might as well be failures."

"Do you believe these tales?" I asked.

Ecco gave another sigh, long and weary. "No. I suppose I don't. But it certainly is tempting, for it would explain much."

"And it would also relieve Orissa of any guilt that we have somehow offended the gods," I said.

"There *is* that. However, there is no way of finding out, so it is pointless to speculate."

Ecco drained the brandy I had given him and rose to go. "If you hear from Captain Greycloak . . ."

"I will inform you immediately," I said. And he was gone—leaving a long trail of unanswered questions.

There was nothing that could be done but hope. But hope was a mother with withered dugs that year, for the bad times continued without relief. Just before the first frost came the worst blow of all.

It was on one of those idyllic, early winter evenings in Orissa, when it is just cold enough to enjoy a fire, with perhaps a small storm outside to give the windows a gentle rattle and send you to a warm bath and early bed. Deoce and I made sleepy love in the big feather bed; afterward—feeling not a care in the world—I arose to add more fuel to the fire and to fix us both a hot brandy drink. I noticed her face was flushed when I handed her the drink, but thought it was from our lovemaking. As I turned to get my own, she gave a gasp, and the tumbler crashed to the floor.

I whirled back, full of concern. "What is wrong, dear?" She gave no answer, but gripped her head; her face was twisted in pain. "You are sick," I said in alarm. "I'll fetch a healer in a moment."

Her reply was weak. "No, Amalric. Please, there's a storm and you'll get cold and wet."

"Nonsense." I hurried to put on my clothes. She tried to get up to protest again, but then another wave of pain struck her, and she gave such an awful moan that I shouted for young Spoto, the chambermaid, to come and watch her while I rode for help.

The storm had worsened; it had a sharp chill to it, and bits of hail nibbled at my face as I thundered down the road. It was quite dark by the time I reached the healer's house, but I could make out the glowing symbol of his Evocator's license. He was eating a late supper, but came without complaint, and before long we were riding back down that road. This time the storm was driving straight into our teeth, and we had to fight the horses through the hail and sleet. But soon we arrived at the villa, and I rushed the healer to my lady's chamber.

Deoce lay groaning in the big feather bed. I knew the pain must be fierce, for she was not one who complained; preferred, in fact, to ignore her ailments away. She opened her eyes when we came in; they lay large and unnaturally bright in her head. The healer got out his things, and I went to the bed and kissed her; her fever was so hot the kiss burned my lips.

"It's just a winter chill," Deoce said, trying to reassure me. She made a weak smile and reached to pat my hand; but she gave a low cry of pain and let the hand fall. "By the gods of the Salcae, I feel awful," she said. "I ache in every bone and there is a great hammering in my head."

I forced a cheery smile. "There you are, then. A winter's chill, exactly. You will be up in no time, my love, dandling Emilie on your knee."

Deoce looked alarmed when I mentioned our daughter. "Emilie? How is she? Have you checked her?"

"She is well, Lady Antero," Spoto said. "I've just come from the nursery, and A'leen says your daughter is sleeping peacefully."

Deoce sighed relief, then gave herself up to the healer, who had laid out his charms and mixed up a potion for the pain. First he checked her: prodding here and there for tenderness, sniffing her breath, directing candlelight into her eyes. Then my heart leaped as I saw him hesitate . . . as if puzzling. He gave a barely perceptible shake of his head. Then he smiled, and I imagined it as forced as my own, for I was grinning like an idiot to maintain a cheery appearance.

"A winter's chill, as we said—isn't that so, my good sir?" I asked.

Again the hesitation, then, "Uh . . . Yes . . . Yes! Just so. A winter's chill. Now, if you will relax yourself, Lady Antero, and drink this potion. I've put a dollop of honey in it to lessen the bitterness, but you'll still not like its taste. But if you will humor me, please, and drink it all in one gulp . . ." She did as he said, emptying the tumbler as quickly as she could. "Now you may close your eyes, if you will, my lady, and you will soon be asleep. I'll cast my spells, and we'll drive those little demons out. Then, as your good husband prophesied, you shall be well by morning when you awake."

I sat beside her as she closed her eyes, taking her hand to give her comfort. The hand was fiery with the fever, and her finger joints seemed swollen large. Suddenly her eyes opened. "You'll watch Emilie closely tonight?" she asked.

"Of course I will," I said. "And I'll post Spoto by her bed all the night through. And we have a healer with us, so you needn't worry on Emilie's account, if she should catch the chill as well." I kissed her, and her eyes closed again.

"I love you, Amalric," she murmured. I said I loved her, too. "You have been a good husband to me. And a good father to Emilie." I answered by stroking the hot hand I held. She yawned—the potion was taking effect. "You know . . . I think Emilie looks . . . just . . . like . . . you." And she fell asleep.

The healer motioned me back, and I sat in a chair in the corner, while he lighted the incense pots and sprinkled in the ingredients to cure a winter chill. He chanted an ornate set of fire beads to life, then broke them apart and scattered them around her bed. He tossed in more of the special dust, and the dots of lights became a glowing circle. Then he lifted his hands and began to swiftly murmur the spell. But the lights suddenly dimmed, and Deoce cried out, but did not awaken. The healer seemed startled by what had happened. He shook his head, then fetched a box with some other powder and sprinkled the dust into the pots. The beads brightened, and the healer sighed in relief; but *his* relief was frightening to me, for I was forcing myself to believe all was very usual, very routine. As he started his chant again I waited, tense for another cry of pain. None came; instead, Deoce's features relaxed, and I imagined her lips were curling into a smile—a sweet dream, I prayed. The healer droned on and on, and the incense pots filled the room with a heady perfume. Soon he was done, and he got out his little stool, unfolded it, and sat by the bed. He lowered his head in concentration and began to weave another protective spell. I'd seen it many times, even had it performed on me. Yes, it was all quite routine, the usual cure for a common malady. I fell asleep.

It was not an easy sleep, nor was it one I had sought. It was as if a pillow had suddenly filled my head, and I drifted away. The nightmare raged, and I visited with the boatman again ... the ghastly man with the gaping eye socket. Again I climbed those steps and heard the howling and confronted the fate the nightmare carried me to each time it captured me.

When I awoke, the Dark Seeker had come and gone.

Deoce was dead.

I will not desecrate her memory with mewling descriptions of my feelings. I can only write that I have known such desolation, such pain, only one other time in my life. It did not scar me, for a scar does not have a lingering memory to it; it was a ghostly presence, as if your heart were a limb and you could amputate it, but still live.

I do not remember much of what happened next. The healer wept for his failure; but his tears fell on the cold plain of my hate for him. Rali came to give comfort and to see that Deoce's body was properly tended and a preserving spell cast so she would stay fresh until the funeral. I recall my sister telling me others were ill and that all who had fallen ill had died. Her words had no meaning to me, did not penetrate my numbness. It seemed like years passed, but it was not much more than two days. I spent the whole time with Emilie. We played in the garden—she could walk now, in a toddler's fashion, and she could say "Da" and "Mama." I said Mama had gone on a long journey and would not be with us for many a day. Instead of crying, she clung to me more, not for her own comfort, I think, but for my own. Finally I roused myself. There were things to be done, a funeral to plan. But it was like coming up from a second sleep. In the first, Deoce had died; in the second, I awakened to find the Dark Seeker and his minions raging all over Orissa.

It was a plague like no other that had touched our shores. It ravaged through the city, unchecked by any spell the Evocators could conjure up. Rich and poor alike were felled. There was no logic to it. Whole neighborhoods were devastated, but in some, no one was harmed. In others, a single family might fall ill and die, while their neighbors huddled in their homes in terror, but in good health. Sometimes only one member of a household might be stricken, while the others were untouched by anything but grief. The sickness did not produce horrible pustules and sores, but struck out with awful pain and fever. Some lingered ... some died at the first stroke.

The city was crippled by fear. All shops and businesses were closed, the river empty of traffic. The Evocators gathered in emergency session and combed the scrolls for some clue to turn back the plague's wrath. But it raged on without relief. There were no public funerals, for all were too fearful to come out into the open. I buried Deoce on our grounds and made a small ceremony with Rali and the villa's staff.

As the days passed, I kept waiting for the Dark Seeker to return—anxiously peeping into the eyes of Emilie and my servants. Outside, the fever burned on; but still we were spared further grief. I don't know how many died during this time, perhaps two thousand, perhaps more.

On the night of the first snow, Emilie awakened, shrieking with pain. I rushed to her, pushing aside Spoto and A'leen. Emilie cried louder when she saw me, and I pulled her into my arms and held her tightly—trying mightily to force away the pain with my own will. She clutched back, crying, saying, "Da ... Da ... Da." I gave her a potion to make her sleep, and I bathed her slumbering little body in icy water to lessen the fever. It did no good. I held her all the night, rocking back and forth, humming her favorite child songs. I knew it was pointless to fetch a healer, but I was frantic to do something, anything.

Then I remembered Halab's cure when he brought me and my pet ferret to life. I rushed out into the snow, found the home of a vendor of pets, and hammered on the door like a man possessed. I gave him a fistful of coin for a small animal in a cage and rode hard for home. I searched in my chamber and found the ferret-tooth necklace Janos had given me for protection during our journey. I took it, the cage, and Emilie to Halab's altar, where I made a bed for her on the floor. I draped the necklace over her and prostrated myself before the altar.

"Dear brother," I said, "you have helped me before, and I beg you to help me now. Emilie is dying. She is your niece, and you would be proud to see what a brave little Antero she is. Oh, come to me, Halab. Cure her of her pain. Send the Dark Seeker from my door."

Halab's face peered down from the painting. I imagined I saw a great sadness in that face, as if he had been touched by my plea. I took heart and got the ferret from its cage. It was wriggling with life, and its eyes were small beads of curiosity. I placed it in Emilie's sleeping hands.

I looked at Halab's image. "Come to us, brother. Come to us, I beseech thee."

Suddenly the room grew dark. I felt a shadow pass. Emilie moaned, but the ferret stayed quite still, only its whiskers twitching to show it was not a stuffed toy.

A voice came to my ear. "Amalric." I knew it was Halab, and my heart leaped with hope. A light shone from nowhere and settled over Emilie. I smelled an odor of heavy incense.

Halab's voice came again, a whisper. "Emilie . . . Emilie."

Emilie stirred. She opened her eyes and smiled when she saw me. The ferret moved, and Emilie looked down and saw it. She giggled. "Da," she said. "Da."

I wept with relief. "Yes, dear," I said. "It is for you. A ferret, like I had when I was a boy. Ferret. Can you say it? Ferret."

"Ferret," she responded, quite clear, as she added a new word to her small book. Then she closed her eyes and gave a great sigh. Her hand fell open, and the ferret scampered away. One more long sigh . . . and she died.

I roared with grief and pain. I threw myself on her small body, pleading that it wasn't so, couldn't be so. I wanted to die myself; for what reason could there be to go on? All I cared for, all that gave me purpose, had been torn from me.

Then I felt the presence hovering near, and Halab's voice calling, "Amalric." I looked through streaming eyes and saw his form bending over me: cold smoke, wavering, but firm in its shape. The ghost's lips opened to speak. He whispered, but with great effort, "Sorry . . . So sorry." His hand floated forward and touched my face. There was no substance to the touch: it was not cold, it was not warm, it was just there, a comforting breath on my cheek.

The whisper came again. "You must not . . . stop. You cannot . . . surrender."

I wanted to cry out, what was the use? What was the point? The wisp of his touch stroked my face. "Heal, brother," he whispered. Then, "Sleep, Amalric . . . Sleep."

I slept. It was the sleep of the dead, for no one could rouse me.

The servants carried me to my room and put me to bed. They tended poor Emilie, burying her in the garden beside my wife. Six days later, I awoke. The grief was a knot of numbness in my chest. I wanted to cut it out with a knife; but when such dark thoughts came to me, I remembered Halab's plea. I obeyed, but with great difficulty. I ate. I drank. I crept through my sorrow day by day.

Outside in the city there was joy to be mixed with all our sorrows. The plague was gone. The Dark Seeker had fed, and fed well; now he was satiated, and Orissa was safe. But it didn't matter to me, one way or the other. Dead or alive, sick or well, I did not care what fate awaited us.

Then, late one night there came a knocking at our gate. Everyone was asleep, worn out from caring for me and my family, so I went to see who it was myself. I flung open the gate and gave a start. A ragged, injured man sagged against the gatepost. It was Sergeant Maeen.

"Sergeant," I gasped in surprise. "Where have you come from? What has happened?"

Maeen answered, his voice a harsh rusk. "It's all gone to ruin, my lord. To ruin."

CHAPTER SIXTEEN
The Sergeant's Tale

"WHAT HAPPENED," I demanded. "Where is he?"

"In . . . in Lycanth," Sergeant Maeen managed. "In their dungeons. Or, worse . . ." He stopped abruptly, and I turned and saw my servants gathering around, gaping. I quickly led Maeen into the house. I gave orders for food and wine and for no one to repeat anything they'd heard, knowing the last order was in vain. Maeen tried to continue, but I told him to be quiet—unless his story would require action within the hour. Maeen was grim. "Not an hour, Lord Antero . . . nor a day. Perhaps not ever."

I half carried Maeen to a guest chamber where food and drink was already being set out. I had three of my most trusted men keep close attendance on him while he ate like a starveling, drank down a flagon of wine, and then collapsed. Grinding my teeth, trying to be patient, I let the man sleep for four hours, knowing there was nothing to be gained by shaking him awake. I ordered his tattered clothing burned. I also noted he had arrived weaponless and knew something terrible must have happened to separate *this* soldier from his tools. When Maeen awoke he was bathed, massaged, and brought to my study. I poured him a restorative herbal drink, sat him down behind the desk, and bade him tell his story in any manner he saw fit. I expected a barely coherent babble, but I should have thought better of the good sergeant—and of the training he'd received from Janos.

Exhausted, seemingly in shock, Sergeant Maeen reported most succinctly. "Lord Antero, the second expedition to the Far Kingdoms has been destroyed. We were annihilated by sorcery from without . . . and by incompetency from within. The sole surviving officer, to the best of my knowledge, is Captain Janos Greycloak.

He is currently being held in Lycanth as a prisoner. I do not know where or under what charge—he gave me an opportunity to make my escape when we were arrested, and therefore I cannot be more specific."

"But Janos lives?"

"Unless the Lycanthians have executed him, or tortured him to death, I would think, yes. Their soldiery took great pains when they captured us to avoid harming the captain."

Now I told him to begin from the beginning, and tell me everything, no matter how damaging. He did so. Maeen was no bard, who would have begun the tale of the expedition with a doleful statement of purpose, of how the gods turned their faces away before the first sail was set. He did not need to make the point so obvious as he talked about how, from that first day, things had gone wrong. The ships had been overloaded, and once they reached the river mouth and sailed onto the Narrow Sea, it was clear they were of the wrong type. Too many of them were shallow-draft river barges or hastily converted coastal traders.

Bad weather struck, and although it was less severe than the Archons' tempest that had been sent against the *Kittiwake*, the fleet was scattered. The ship the officers were on, which included Janos and Sergeant Maeen, had been one of the first to make landfall, not many leagues from the Shore People's grounds on the Pepper Coast. "That was the only luck the gods gave us," Maeen added.

It had taken several weeks for the rest of the fleet to straggle to the Shore People's village, and five ships were never seen again. The expedition had laboriously unloaded: horses tossed over the side and expected to swim to shore, small boats planked across and used as barges, and even long lines of soldiers used to pass along lighter items from grounded ships to shore. Finally the expedition was on land. By that time there had been several incidents between soldiers and the Shore People: several of their women had been assaulted, there had been a few brawls, and some of the expedition's supplies had been stolen. It had taken all of Janos' diplomacy and Black Shark's reasoning to keep matters from becoming worse. Maeen, heading the guard platoon for the expedition commanders, was privy to most of the meetings. He told me General Versred had said this was so much nonsense— the Shore People were not worth the time.

Eventually the expedition lumbered off, roughly following the same path as my Finding; roughly, since there was no way a host of nearly two thousand men could follow the same paths and trails

we did, or live off the land as we had. Their insistence on carrying luxuries like tents, two commissaries—one for the men, one
for the officers—and full wardrobes also slowed the travel. Their
freight wagons also dictated the route. Maeen told me that five or
six of the officers had brought female "friends" along, and these
friends could not be expected to travel afoot. The horses themselves were an irritant, much more skittish and choosey about
their rations than our asses, and requiring more attention. Men began dying even as the expedition moved through that pastoral,
abandoned land we thought parklike—dying of errors, disease,
and ignorance. Twice the expedition became lost and had to re-
trace its path. This I did not understand—what were their Evocators doing? The sergeant said it seemed their spells were blocked
or sent awry with an even greater severity than Cassini had suffered. I asked about the relict, the scroll from the Watcher. It had
worked just intermittently. The most reliable guide was a copy of
the map I'd drawn. And what of Janos? Janos had become interested in one of the officer's "friends." The officer seemed not to
object to the attentions paid his inamorata. Sergeant Maeen said it
seemed Janos was traveling with only half his mind on the journey, but "perhaps he was reserving his strength for the wasteland." I remembered Janos' lassitude among the Rift Tribe, but
said nothing.

Maeen said the expedition cut a desolate path nearly a league
wide as it went. Like the locusts of his youth, he went on, except
that he remembered locusts traveling more rapidly. They reached
the river's headwaters and moved into the desert. I asked if they'd
been harassed by the slavers or their sorcery. Maeen said they had
not. I asked if the Evocator's powers had returned, and he said not
to any noticeable degree.

Then he looked around the room nervously. "Perhaps, Lord,
you are aware of Captain Greycloak's . . . interests?"

"You mean sorcery?"

"Yes, sir. He had one of the tents set aside for his own use and
spent much time in it. When he did I was ordered to mount a
guard about the tent, and to alert him if any officers or Evocators
approached. It's my belief, sir, the reason we weren't struck by
magic in that place, as we were before, was the captain's doing."
There had been no sign of the Watchers, either.

The expedition had avoided the crater, Sergeant Maeen continued, although he had thought of using it for a resupply base. I
found my teeth on edge, imagining what this horde of soldiery
would have done to the paradise Deoce and I had found. Then I

nearly wept as I realized once more, as if for the first time—as I did every hour of every day—that my love had gone beyond forever. But I showed no expression on my face except interest in Maeen's tale. Janos had changed his mind not from any romantic concerns, but because he feared the crater's spell was too strong, and if death visited that paradise again, it was likely the expedition would suffer awful casualties in repayment. Besides, they had enough provisions and water. There had been no thought of seeking the Rift—there was no way the valley could have supported the expedition, even though there were now no more than fifteen hundred in the party.

The wasteland was a drear nightmare, but it did not bother Maeen since he knew eventually there was an ending to the barren. They'd followed Janos' and my path through the foothills, but now the problem was the season was growing late—autumn had already come on. Perhaps, Maeen wondered, this was where the worst of their troubles were sown. Janos seemed to wake from his lethargy the closer they drew to the pass and behaved as if he were a drover, wanting to physically lash the expedition on to greater and greater speed. Maeen shook his head at that. "I understood what the captain wanted . . . but there wasn't any way to put grease under the ways. Maybe if we'd been a smaller party, carried less baggage, been better trained . . ." He let his voice trail off. "I had the feeling, meaning no criticism of the captain and his ways, he wasn't being listened to any more; that the general and the other officers thought he was ranting like a fishwife. You can only kick a beast that size so much, you know." Janos, General Versred, and his staff *had* determined to force the pass before the first snowfall. Once on the other side, they could seek winter quarters.

"But it never came to that," Maeen said. "We went on, and came to a city, just at the foot of the pass."

I remembered the place. "That must have been where the cavalry came from that attacked us."

Maeen nodded. "That's what the city leaders said, and apologized. All of them spoke the trading language. Said they had terrible enemies beyond, and the commander of the unit had been too hasty. They apologized, as the captain would put it, most profusely." Maeen looked as if he wanted to spit, but recollected his surroundings. "From that day, our doom closed on us," he said.

The city was beautiful, as were its people. "They told the general and Captain Greycloak how much they welcomed our coming." This would mark the dawn of a new day, the city fathers had said, a day when they would make alliance with Orissa, and no longer fear the warriors of the Disputed Lands. They were especially pleased when they learned the expedition's goal. Come spring some of the city's young soldiers might wish to join the party, and march on east, to the Far Kingdoms. The city, which was named Wahumwa, had been, aeons earlier, firm friends with the peaceful savants of the Far Kingdoms.

The sergeant stopped, pulled a tattered roll of cloth from his tunic, and handed it to me. "As proof," he said, "those lying bastards gave the captain this."

I unrolled the cloth and gaped at what had been revealed. It was a banner, suitable for cavalry, and so old the linen was a dirty gray. But the markings were quite clear: set against a jagged sunburst was a great coiled serpent. I remembered the symbol well. My mind quickly flew to the Pepper Coast and the warrior in amber whose ghost we had soothed. The serpent and sunburst had been carved into the leather pouch the dead warrior wore.

Sergeant Maeen said, "They told us that banner had been carried by the soldiers of the Far Kingdoms. And was left behind the last time they came to help them fight."

"What did Janos think?" I asked.

"Oh, he said it was from the Far Kingdoms, all right. And that it must be the crest of the rulers there."

"He was *that* certain," I pressed. I remembered we both thought the crest might signify something like that.

"As certain as when they gave it to him," Maeen answered, "as the day *he* gave it me to hand over to you—if I lived to see you."

I rolled the cloth back up and put it in my writing desk. It sits there to this day. Then I gently prodded the sergeant to take up where he left off. "So, the people of the city claimed friendship with the Far Kingdoms?"

"Yes, sir. That is what those liars told us," Maeen said bitterly. "They told us the city had fought several wars with the barbarians of the Disputed Lands, and had lost contact with the Far Kingdoms. Because of these wars there were vacant apartments enough for all of us and to spare. We need not pitch our tents or sleep on the ground. And as for companionship from the city's many widows or unattached women . . . that too was for the asking." Maeen touched the herbal drink to his lips, then set it down and asked if he might have brandy.

I poured him a goblet, and he went on. "So we moved in, and little by little, what had been a military force crumbled, as the winter storms began. Why need we drill, or even make formation, if we could build our strength beside a fire, with a doxy and mulled wine? I did not like those days. I felt as if I were the butt of a private joke, as if all of us were being made fools, like these people were jesting behind our backs."

I puzzled: surely, when Janos and I had been there, we would have seen smoke from the city's fires by day, or the fire dance reflected against the mountains by night. But perhaps not; perhaps the city had been hidden by a fold in the ground. Maeen told me Janos had attempted to reconnoiter the pass itself, but each time had been driven back by the weather. Finally he resigned himself to being mired in the luxurious trap until the snow melted; and once more returned to his private studies. "Although little good they did him—or us—in the end, I fear."

To celebrate midwinter's eve, the city people announced a feast. It was in a great hall, with long tables, rare foods, and a woman seated beside each man. Servants ran back and forth with platters and pitchers while musicians played and perfume floated through the air from scented tapers. "I do not know why I came armed," Maeen said. "But I did, slipping a fighting dagger into the sleeve of my robe—violating all that I know of hospitality. And the gods be thanked for my discourtesy."

He did not see any signal, but the woman across from him suddenly plunged a dagger into the back of her companion. The hall went mad in a screaming welter of blood and slaughter as swords and knives cut down the Orissans. "My blade slashed before the one beside me could free her own. She fell, then the captain was on his feet, smashing them, using a great candelabra as a club. I knew we were dead men, but it was as if the people were entranced by the blood they'd spilled." He shivered. "I saw a woman, fair and blond, on her knees ripping at General Versred's throat like she was a lioness. And then she . . . and the rest of them . . . fed."

The men and women of the city ravened into the corpses, but seemed to have no interest or concern for those Orissans yet alive. And while this spell lasted, the survivors of the shattered expedition fled, grabbing what weapons and supplies they could, racing out into the storm and the night and the winter. Eerily, they were not pursued by the loathsome people who inhabited the city they called Wahumwa. "Perhaps they had all they needed," Maeen said. I thought just so, and that human flesh was not their real objective, but kept it to myself.

There were perhaps two or three hundred Orissans who lived through the massacre. The ranking officer was Janos; of the officers, only two legates survived. The long retreat began. Now the scythe swung hourly as men dropped from exhaustion, from thirst, or were captured or slain by the desert tribesmen.

"At last there were but thirty or so of us, and Janos the only officer. We had no means of navigation but the sun and the stars, and wandered from our intended course. Finally we struck the sea, but west of the Shore People's land, on a deserted coast. Two of the men had grown up on the water, and knew how to build rafts. We lashed together a crude craft, made a small sail from what garments we could do without, and put our fate in the hands of the gods, hoping the current would carry us to Redond."

They never reached the trading city. Instead, they were captured by a raiding galley. "They claimed to be pirates, but all of them behaved like well-trained sailors. Lycanthian navy, I guessed. Eight more of us fell in that battle. The rest of us were chained in the forepeak of the ship, and the ship sailed for Lycanth.

"Captain Greycloak and I made a plan, and when we were brought on deck just outside that cursed bay of Lycanth, we put it in motion. The idea was for Janos to start a fight, and hope the others would join in. Since I was a great swimmer as a boy, I was to leap into the water, and strike for land. If the captain could break free—he would go after me." Maeen shook his head, shamefacedly, as if somehow he had failed. "But the last I saw was the captain being borne down by guards. Then there were arrows falling all around me, and I had to swim underwater for a space."

Maeen made his way to shore in time to see the galley pass over the great chain that guarded the entrance to Lycanth's harbor. There was nothing he could do for Janos or the others, except carry the tale to Orissa. He told of this final feat most matter-of-factly, as if the wild creatures and the roving Lycanthian patrols were not worth the notice. I guessed, after such a long and grueling journey, they might not have been.

Maeen was finished. I poured him another brandy, and bethought myself as to what should be done next. But matters were taken out of my hands within two hours. Someone—a guard at the gates, someone in the streets, perhaps even one of my household—had spread the word. Orissa wept and rent its garments. There had been catastrophe in the city before. But never before had there been such a disaster. *No* survivors of the two thousand, except for Maeen. All of them either dead, lost in the wilderness, or made slaves: three Magistrates, young but highly respected; General Versred and his staff; other officers, all known for their bravery; all of the Magistrates' Own Guard except the skeleton headquarters staff and one cohort; and heaping over all of it, the hundreds of corpses of common soldiers, some of the bravest, most adventurous young men of Orissa.

Maeen was summoned before the Magistrates and told his story. I had suggested certain omissions, such as any criticism of the late General Versred, the deadly slow pace of the expedition, or of Janos himself. Not that it would have mattered, I realized, as I listened to the anger and wails of mourning. Maeen was ordered to repeat his tale at a city gathering at the Great Amphitheater, and again the frenzy roared up. Orissa was hysterical: rumors, charges, and accusations clamored across the city like flames in dry brush as to what *really* happened. The flames were fed by the Evocators, with Cassini in their forefront. Not only should the expedition have been made solely by sorcerous means, the Evocators casting their presence through spells, but it was foredoomed, being led into a trap by Janos Greycloak. He was a traitor, a double agent in the pay of the Archons. He was worse, a fiend from beyond, not even human. Who, after all, had ever gone deep into the interior, beyond Redond, and found this province of Kostroma? It was Janos who was keeping Orissa from its sacred mission to join up with the Far Kingdoms. Janos' supporters would hear none of this, but their arguments that this tragedy was caused by the Evocators, who wished to preempt the glory of the Far Kingdoms for themselves and sustain their miserable theocracy, were not listened to. Even Gamelan found it politically expedient to withdraw to his retreat beyond the city, there to immerse himself in the wisdom of the Other Worlds before making a statement on the terrible events.

Once again the libels against the Antero family surfaced. We, too, were not really true to Orissa, but gave fealty only to gold coins and silver bars. One night a bravo even chanced, within my hearing, that the noble Evocators had sensed corruption within my brother Halab, which was why he died. I drove the man's teeth down his throat with the butt of my dagger and would have butchered him like a hog if Rali had not dragged me away. She and Maeen were now the only comfort in my life. But even that brawl was one of the few bright colors I remember. It was as if all the world was cast in a gray mist, and that a veil hung between me and life. Deoce and Emilie were more in my thoughts than any of this shrilling and screaming.

It was about this time that the dream returned to me, the nightmare of being a tortured prisoner led by a being I now saw as

Greif the Lycanthian through strange caverns to my destruction, a fate part of me welcomed in the dream.

I caught myself glooming at the river near dawn, watching the dark waters flow out toward the sea, and found myself thinking of how they looked gentle, like a welcoming bed to a tired man. I pulled myself back. My father might have struck me if he had been alive and had known my thoughts. No Antero had ever allowed himself to sink into this kind of self-pity. But I must do something, and do it immediately.

As soon as the thought hit me, I knew what to do. Orissa would do nothing to save Janos, even if the city suddenly came to its senses. Very well, I would; I hastened home. I woke the household and began issuing orders. I told Rali what I intended, and she frowned. "You might be jumping into waters deeper than you think," she said, and I flinched inadvertently at her comparison. "Perhaps Janos is more precious to Lycanth . . . or they've so convinced themselves . . . than we realize."

"I don't see that," I said. "I have never known a Lycanthian to refuse gold. And I shall instruct Janos, before ransoming, to tell the Lycanthians everything he knows. *Let* them mount their own expedition if they wish, and face the desert, the slavers, and the carrion eaters. Janos, as proven by his getting lost in the return journey, has but a faulty map in his mind. No other exists, save what I drew, and what I remember."

Rali shook her head. "You are thinking like a logical man, my brother. That may lead you into trouble. When men concern themselves with the color of their flags, such as both our cities are doing at the moment, and what they see as prestige of race . . . all rationality vanishes. Add to that the insanity a mere mention of the Far Kingdoms is producing these days . . ." Her voice trailed off. "Go if you must, Amalric. But I fear for you."

By dawn the anonymous carriage I had hired was beyond the gates of the city. In it were two chests of pure, soft gold rolls I'd taken from the vaults below our villa. Those would entrance the Lycanthians, even their magic-soaked Archons, if necessary. Not quite a king's ransom, but certainly sufficient for a baron or two. The gold was guarded by six of my best retainers. I wished to take Sergeant Maeen, but realized if the sole survivor to the tragedy left the city headed toward Lycanth, my enemies would find the obvious explanation and have troops after us within hours.

THE JOURNEY TO Lycanth went uneventfully. I ordered the carriage and my men to remain at the last decent inn, just a day's journey from the city, until summoned, and rode to Lycanth alone. I did not notice the weather or if there were other travelers about. I was busily rehearsing my reasoning and the approach I would use to free Janos. I entered the city without incident and rode toward the same inn we had stayed in previously. I planned to refresh myself and then begin investigating in what manner one approached the Lycanthian rulers to seek a boon. I never reached the inn.

It was twilight, and the streets were crowded as the Lycanthian workers made their way home, and I had to force my horse through the throng. Quite suddenly I was alone, sitting my horse on a near-deserted street, the last Lycanthian scuttling indoors.

I heard a baying, had time to remember, and around the corner loped that obscene, hairless hyena with the face of a man; it was the creature that had ordered us to the castle of the Archons, and then called out that young woman to her death. It sat on its haunches and regarded me. Again, it bayed, and the cry echoed across the stone buildings around me.

Then it spoke. "Amalric Antero. You are summoned. You must obey."

I pulled at my horse's reins reflexively, trying to turn my mount away from the caller. But a rank of soldiers doubled across the street behind me, spears leveled. A second line of guards appeared behind the creature.

"Amalric Antero. You are summoned."

CHAPTER SEVENTEEN

The Dungeon of the Archons

I WAS BROUGHT to that great sea castle just at the end of the promontory and escorted through long, echoing, dank corridors, guarded and locked portals, and high-ceilinged chambers. It seemed as if the only beings in this great castle were guards, myself, and that noxious creature that trotted just ahead of me. We reached an entranceway blocked only by a heavy, dark green curtain. The soldiers, without ever a command, wheeled and marched away . . . leaving only the Finder as my guard.

"Amalric Antero. You are summoned," and it went through the curtain. I followed, numb, into yet another bare chamber. Everything in this room was entirely of stone: from the groin-vaulted ceiling, to the stanchions that held flaring torches, to the low riser at the far end of the room. There were two circular pedestals on either side of the riser. The creature positioned itself in front of that stage. I heard, or rather felt, a humming—as if the air itself was moving. The humming grew louder, and then I saw a shimmer atop each pedestal, a shimmer taller than the height of a tall man. The Finder abased itself. I did not.

I suppose I should have knelt. I had and have since knelt in front of many strange gods, kings, and even bandits who have given themselves lordly titles. It matters little and frequently adds to future profit or immediate survivability. It sometimes is just a matter of common courtesy. But here, in the bowels of the Archons' castle, I kept my feet. Perhaps I felt pride as an Antero, or as an Orissan. But I would not kneel to these swirling mists. The humming grew louder still, then changed pitch and grew into an angry bass drone, such as might come from a nest of monstrous wasps; but nothing else happened, and then the drone stopped.

As the silence lingered, a man came out of the darkness behind the pedestals. He was quite beautiful, a term I do not generally use for males; but this man—from his softly curled blond hair, to his boyishly smiling full lips, to his slender body, *was* beautiful.

"Lord Amalric. I had hoped our . . . acquisition of your minion might make you decide to come to Lycanth. I am Nisou Symeon." This then was the man, hardly more than a boy, both my father and Greif had said was the most evil of the Symeons—the clan the Anteros had warred against for three generations. Even though I was in desperate straits, I noted his face and realized once more that only a fool judges good or evil by its beauty or ill favor.

I sorted through my various responses, discarding the obvious ones of fear, surprise, disdain, or even bravura posturing. "Lord Symeon," I finally said. "So you have convinced your rulers that you can seize an Orissan nobleman without heed of any consequences."

"My Lords, the Archons, needed no convincing," Symeon said. "In case you have been buried in your dreams of the past like most Orissans, you may not have noticed there is a new spirit abroad in Lycanth. It is time for us to reaffirm our historic duty and seek our proper place in the sun." I remembered Cassini's harsh verdict outside Lycanth, when he said that we should have obliterated the city and its populace, for fear they would rise once more. Even such a one as Cassini may sometimes glimpse beyond the veil.

"Further," Symeon continued, "even if we were concerned as to any reprisal from Orissa, I doubt if it would be mounted over mischief done to an Antero. Your homeland hardly sings your praises these days." I maintained a stony countenance and made no reply, but he certainly was correct.

"What we require from you," Symeon continued, "is a full and complete description of your route to the Far Kingdoms. It is axiomatic that Lycanth is the only logical power to seek an alliance with the kingdoms—especially considering the catastrophe Orissa, abetted by your underling, managed to produce from the most recent attempt to reach the kingdoms."

"You are quite mistaken if you think Captain Greycloak is in any way my 'underling' or 'compatriot.' "

"Oh? I suppose you have merely come to Lycanth to save him out of pure altruism? And, if he is not your underling, then what?" He curled his lip. "Lover?"

I blinked, not having been aware that Lycanthian attitudes were as backward as their buildings. It was no trouble to ignore what he evidently considered an insult. I managed a cynical grin. "Very well. What blandishments are you prepared to offer for my cooperation?"

"I could be quite foolish," he replied, "and promise you gold, or a high position here in Lycanth. Of course you cannot be permitted to return to Orissa until there is an . . . adjustment between our two cities. But I shall offer you neither, not being a dunce nor thinking you one either. There can be but one prize for you . . . all others are valueless beside it. Actually, I need promise nothing, and my Lords the Archons would think me less than their fullhearted servant if I did. We wish to possess the knowledge you and Captain Greycloak share of the routes toward the Far Kingdoms, from coastal tides to edible fruits to annoying insects to the natives to any and all sorceries you encountered. We are prepared to use *all* the talents and skills of Lycanth in encouraging you to enlighten us, and have no qualms as to how or when these skills will be utilized to convince you. We also are in no particular hurry, since both my Lords and myself are aware of the . . . problems that can be created from an overeager questioning."

"Such as death?"

"That," Symeon said calmly, "or madness; or even, if the inquisitor is insufficiently skeptical, convincement of a deliberate or accidental lie. This, then, is our purpose and intent. Do you wish to comment, or perhaps make a statement of brave rejection we all may savor?" I shook my head. Symeon nodded. "Then that will be all . . . for the moment. All of us will know quite soon when you and Greycloak desire to speak to us once more—desire to speak with all your hearts and souls. So, if you will follow my Lords' messenger to your quarters . . ." Without waiting for a response, Symeon wheeled and vanished into the shadows. At the same instant, the shimmers were gone, and the torches flared, then guttered.

Having no options, I followed the Finder back down the echoing stone corridors. I expected to be taken to a dungeon. Instead, the creature led me to stairs—stairs that wound up and up, and then through more corridors until I guessed we were approaching the top story of the huge castle. At last the beast stopped in front of a huge U-shaped door. The beast's mouth opened; it whined and I was suddenly deaf. It took me a moment to realize that the spell the creature was casting had a secondary element, making it impossible for the listener to distinguish the words. Hearing returned as the door swung open. In front of me stretched the hallway of a palatial apartment. Paintings were on the walls, and the ceilings were hung in silk. I hesitated outside.

"Enter if you are of this world, be damned if you are not," came a cry from within. It was Janos' voice. I obeyed, and the door swung shut behind me. I tried its handle, which turned uselessly in my hand, and knew the Finder had recast the locking spell. I walked down the corridor, toward the room where Janos' voice had come from. On either side were large, high-ceilinged rooms, some fitted with beds, some with couches, some intended for dining or other entertainment. If it were not for the preponderance of that dark stone the Lycanthians are so partial to, and the subject matter of the paintings, tapestries, and sculptures, which ran heavily to the morbid, it was an apartment in which I would not have been ashamed to put up my most-loved friend or most-respected guest and his retinue.

Another surprise awaited me when I entered the main chamber: Janos reclined on a richly upholstered couch. He was surrounded by books, scrolls, and tablets. In front of him was an easel, with a large paper on it that was filled with his scribblings and sketches—all obviously of a sorcerous intent. Behind him were half a dozen large, open windows, and through them I could see the lights of Lycanth and its harbor spread below us. Janos was dressed like a nobleman at his leisure, in lounging robe and silk blouse and tights. He was hardly the picture of a prisoner who had undergone torture, both physical and sorcerous. Then I noticed his face, tight, drawn, as exhausted as it had been when we reached the end of our Finding and returned to the Pepper Coast.

"Welcome, my friend, and friend you have more than proven yourself," he said. He got up and embraced me. "No man could ask for a better partner, although I wish, for your sake, you were more selfish."

"I hadn't," I said with a bit of asperity, "exactly *planned* on becoming the guest of the Archons."

Janos managed a chuckle. "They told me, some hours ago, you were outside the city and would be apprehended shortly. I'd hoped your canniness would have been able to sense their trap." He shook his head.

"How did they foretell my coming?"

"I don't know. They refused to tell me, and what . . . prognostications I was able to cast gave me no clues. Perhaps a warning spell or a creature stationed on the road approaching; or a spy with Evocator's training in Orissa itself, even. You know, I assume, the prime mover in this conspiracy is an enemy of yours?"

"Nisou Symeon. I met him for the first time in my life below-stairs." I told Janos what had happened. He made no comment, and there was none necessary. He offered me wine, juices, or water from a beverage table nearby. I poured myself a goblet of wine, then thought better. I set it down and began to pour juice.

"Have the wine," Janos said. "Or whatever you desire. As far as I can tell nothing has been drugged, and thus far their seeking of knowledge has not required alcohol's befuddlement. Also, I would recommend both of us eat and drink as much as we can hold, because our circumstances will soon be changing."

I poured, drank deeply as I realized how thirsty I was, and re-filled my goblet. I walked to one of the windows and looked out. Our apartment—our cell—hung just over the water, and far below I could see the white flash of breaking surf on the rocks beyond the harbor. "Is there a spell on the windows?"

"Naturally. Not that I think one is needed, unless you happen to have two sets of wings secreted about you."

I turned back and forced a smile. This ordeal, and I sensed it *would* be that, might be slightly more endurable if I sought humor whenever I could. I had questions, and chanced asking them openly. "Should we be cautious as to what we talk about?"

"Yes, within reason. I would not, for instance, be specific about . . . our mutual adventures. But it is acceptable to discuss matters in general. I have conjured up words that should make anyone listening to our conversation actually hear a very dull recital of the religious lessons from my childhood. But thus far they have cast Lesser Spells against me, which I have been able to withstand and for the most part neutralize. I have not sensed Great Incantations more than twice, although who would know if a truly grand conjuration was laid? For instance, it is possible I am now talking to a complete fabrication of the Archons'. And you must wonder whether I myself am but a demon of their powers. But that way lies madness."

"They have allowed you your . . . ah . . . interest," I marveled, using an innocuous term as I had reflexively from boyhood, when I first realized my brother Halab's interest was venturing into the forbidden.

"Allowed? That is not the description. They cannot put a blanket proscript on any wizardry, else that would block their own spells. But they can lay specific wards, so that I cannot quite remember any spell or type of spell that could be used to break chains or bonds, for instance."

"Like the way you and Cassini had your magical memory removed in . . . in another place?"

"Thank several gods their spell is not that complete. But they tried. Forgive me if I seem inattentive, or preoccupied. But . . ."

There came a flicker from the side of the chamber, and it was as if, for just a flash, a door opened to a dark chamber, and I saw men with their flesh being ravaged by black-clad tormenters with nameless tortures. Then there was nothing but the farther wall.

"That is an example of what I've termed Lesser Spells," Janos said. "All of them are intended to wear us down, and to shake our fortitude and stamina. Other spells surround this chamber: sleeplessness, short temper, loneliness, dejection, and various disgusting but harmless physical debilitations—all of which I have kept at bay."

"You have come far in your study of Evocatorial principles since I first realized your secret interest," I said, meanwhile marveling that from somewhere I had the coolness to carry on such an inconsequential discussion while trapped in the coils of a brutal enemy.

"I thank you, but I feel no pride. I should be able to sustain my efforts with no more energy than scratching a mosquito bite takes in the physical world. Or perhaps I am secretly harboring my strength for when they attempt a full scale assault on us."

"You said they tried what you called Great Incantations twice. What form did they take, so I may be on my guard?"

"Both were loathsome. The first and most tolerable was a variation on the succubus, involving a young and beautiful sorceress who entered my dreams, and promised her reality after we had performed various acts of sex magic. All I was to grant her, in return, was some tales of how wizardry was performed in other lands. That I was able to reject without much of a struggle, recognizing that such stories could well provide the entryway into the rest of my soul. When I did, the apparition vanished.

"The second attempt was more dangerous, and began with various Lesser Spells, but ones cast with full power of a Master Evocator's will behind them. I was depressed, angry at everything and everyone beginning with myself. I felt an utter failure."

"Like," I hazarded, "the Lesser Spells you said are around us are designed to produce."

"Not quite," Janos said. "These were a bit different. Behind them was the undercurrent that I deserved greatness, and that the gods and men had conspired, unknowingly, to deny me my full glory." I knew how such a spell would find resonance within

Janos' rationally healthy ego. "Eventually, I determined to end my life. Not from real pain, but to 'show' someone or something, I know not who, what evil they'd done in keeping me from my rightful heritage."

"I see the evil in that spell," I said. "But I do not see how it would produce any information on . . . on a certain subject that is sought. Worse, you would be dead, and their best chance to get that knowledge lost."

"Oh, no. There would have been counterspells laid and perhaps even physical nets hung below these windows should I have chosen to cast myself from them, as well as other protective conjurations around anything I might use to kill myself—like the knives in our kitchen or the draws for the curtains. I also assumed I was watched. But I haven't completely described the spell. As part of my final cock snooking at the world, I would write a full description of what I could have given them, had they but known."

"The Far—"

"Just so, the quest exactly described." I understood and shuddered. That truly was a subtle spell, and I wondered if I could have withstood one as carefully laid to take advantages of *my* multitudinous weaknesses.

I sought another subject and asked why he'd said we should eat and drink well now, because our circumstances would be changing. I could not believe the Archons' and their Evocators hadn't set spells in place to prevent any divination. Or should I not be asking this question? Janos answered, now with a real smile: he had no foreknowledge at all, but what we were being subjected to was standard interrogation procedure, used by everyone from inquisitors to military information specialists to, he added, most likely my mother and father. He termed it good side/bad side. First the prisoner is given fine food and wines and treated kindly, but always with the caution that "others" feel differently about how the captive should be treated, and the prisoner should cooperate instantly to avoid truly monstrous tortures. "Didn't your mother ever suggest to you, as a child, you had best tell her just what sin you had committed to set your tutor's teeth on edge, because when your father came home and found out you were absolutely in for it?" I agreed, knowing what he meant, not saying I had no memories of my real mother.

"So," I said, "what do we do while waiting to see the other side of Lycanthian 'hospitality'?"

"We do what prisoners have always done: we wait, we exercise our muscles and we talk. Talk about everything . . . except what might be important."

This we did over the next several days. I was nervous and afraid, but I sensed I was more relaxed than Janos, even though my nights were made hellish by the repetition of the dream. Over and over the boatman with no face took me into the cavern, and over and over I was led into the chamber by the being on whom I had imposed Greif's face since I'd first met him in this hell city. But dreams can be lived with—I'd lived with this one for years, now.

Janos had not heard of the deaths of Deoce and Emilie, and burst into tears, the great racking sobs of a warrior chieftain when the very bravest die needlessly. But mostly our conversations were trivial and light, as to the best way to learn a language quickly— Janos' theory was in bed, and since he spoke at least twenty-three tongues and ten dialects, I took his hypothesis seriously; whether Lycanthians had their sense of humor amputated at birth or if the gods had cursed them—we settled for divine curse, hoping that would anger those unseen beings we knew were watching us either through cleverly concealed peepholes in the walls or by sorcery; and so forth. Our exercises helped devour the hours of boredom. We did endless rounds of muscle drills and trotted around the apartments like tigers running around the cage of a menagerie. Janos also showed me various techniques he knew with which a man without a weapon need not abandon hope or life even if one or more armed men attack him.

I spent hours pacing in front of the windows, trying to come up with a plan for an escape. Janos, however, seemed to slip into that semitorpor I'd seen in the Rift. Perhaps I might have chided him, but I remembered a tale written by a smalltrader who'd been captured by the Ice Barbarians of the far south and spent several years as their captive/guest before being released. He said he learned there are only two times to escape: the first immediately after capture, before your guards have time to put all their countermeasures in place; or after a long time has passed, when the sentinels have been lulled by your seeming acceptance of your plight. And I knew, when I saw how Janos' eyes blazed when he looked across Lycanth to the hills that meant freedom, that he, too, was familiar with the rules of an evasion and was biding his time.

We were fed well, twice a day—the menus constantly varied. We never saw a warder, however, and I remembered Symeon's words that he and the Archons would know when we were broken and ready to tell everything. But that appeared to be in the distant future. Boredom, anger, annoyance, frustration, worry about what was going on in Orissa, even an increasing edginess that Janos laid to a certain amount of the invisible assaults getting past his counterspells—none of these were enough. I made the mistake of thinking I was unshakable, that Symeon himself would die of boredom before I did.

They came for us after midnight. The outer door crashed open, and cleated boots slammed down the corridor toward my bed-chamber as I woke and stumbled out of bed. I heard shouts from Janos' room, then blows. Six men burst into my chamber, men wearing mail corselets and helmets with face guards. They were armed with iron-bound truncheons and carried long daggers sheathed at their waist. For a moment, I was in wonderment—if this was the beginning of the "bad side," why hadn't they sent the Finder or other creatures from the depths to awe and horrify us? My question was answered when I was hurled to the floor. As I stumbled to my feet, one of the men smashed me in the face with a gloved hand.

"Tha's t' make sure you'll be doin' as we say," he snarled, and I smelled sour beer on his foul breath. In that instant I realized, and have since confirmed, that man can be more awful than the vilest demon of the pits. They shouted me into clothes, chained my hands and feet, and shoved me out of the room. Janos, his face bloody, was slumped against the corridor wall outside; an-other six men and an officer were around him. We were chivied down, down, below the main floor of the castle and far under-ground. The air grew danker, the stones dripped, and the stairs grew narrower and mold covered. The risers were worn down by century after century of men and women who'd been forced down them, and I wondered how many victims had ever come back into sunlight.

"Y're out under th' bay now," one of the guards growled. "Give you somethin' t' think about, lookin' up, knowin' there's no blue sky or green grass above you. 'Specially when the ceilin' starts leakin'."

There were no sentinels stationed at the barred and locked gates, yet they nevertheless swung wide as we approached. Fi-nally we reached the bottom. The stones around us were niter-whitened and very old, set one on another with no mortar showing. The iron gates and torch standards were black and rusty, and the wooden doors and occasional table or crude chair were dark with age. We passed a large cell. Inside were skeletons, some hung from rusty chains, others scattered where the men had died. There was no sign of a door. Had these long-dead prisoners been transported inside by sorcery, and then forgotten? No one seemed to notice the bones except Janos and me. After that, I saw, in the flare of torchlight, a round metal plate in the floor, with a central vent perhaps a foot long by six inches. As we passed over it, I heard, from below, giggles, interspersed with the chitter of rats. The plate appeared to have been cemented into the stone flag-stones when they were first laid.

Now the corridor was barrel arched. To one side, I saw an open door, no larger than that for a baker's small oven. It was the en-trance to a cell, less a compartment than a coffin. There was a stone bench cut into one wall. A prisoner would have no room to stand or stretch. Further on, there was a stain spattered across a stone wall that looked as if someone had cast a bucket of paint and then let it dry. One of the guards saw I'd noted the stain. He tapped his great club and smiled, as if recalling a particularly pleasant memory. I glanced into another room. This was the guardroom. From my glimpse, I guessed the guards were allowed to take prisoners from their cells for whatever purpose pleased them. I looked away.

The corridor opened into a large semicircular chamber. Around the arc were heavy bars between stone pillars that I thought at first were separate cells, but saw was one large holding area. The reason for the unusual design of the dungeon was clear—the pris-oners held in the cell were expected to witness what was going on in the open room across. It was the torture chamber, set apart by two huge iron doors, now blocked open. Perhaps the chamber was the same one I had seen when Janos allowed his counterspell to slip for a moment. There was the paleness of a woman's body, bound to a rack, and beside her a glowing brazier, pincers, and other iron implements red- or white-hot in the coals. Her mouth was open, as if she was screaming, but there was no sound. Per-haps there was a spell cast to prevent screams from disturbing the guards, or perhaps the prisoner was beyond screaming. I also saw, before I forced my eyes away, other doomed prisoners, half a dozen of the black-clad inquisitors, chains dangling from the ceil-ing and walls, and implements of agony, from the boot to the rack.

The guard's officer moved his hands over cell bars, and a door opened. Our manacles were unlocked, and we were hurled into the cell. "Watch the room across," the officer advised. "So you won't think you'll be forgotten forever." His men found this hilarious. They marched out of the chamber, and there was no light except for a torch at either end of the large room, and the glare coming from the horror scene across. I sagged down, onto the muck and filth some long-ago-scattered straw did nothing to sop up.

"Amalric!" Janos' voice was harsh. I straightened and saw them. Our fellow prisoners. There were possibly fifty men in the cell. Most of them stood or lay in defeated abandon, paying but little attention to the latest victims. But not all . . . A group shuffled toward us. I could smell them. I almost thought their eyes glowed, as I have been told the eyes of some wolves glow before the kill, although I've never seen such a happening.

One, somewhat larger, moved in front of the others. "We'll take th' clothes," he said, in a monotone that carried neither threat nor promise, "and th' pretty boy'll serve who we say."

Janos had me by the arm, and we backed toward a wall. The prisoners shuffled after us, unhurriedly. Why not? They had all the time in the world, and probably their game would be all the better for being prolonged. Janos kept chancing glances behind him. I thought we were merely finding cover for our backs. Janos scooped and came up with something . . . something white . . . a stick, and passed it to me. I had time to realize I was holding a man's leg bone when Janos reached down once more, as the prisoners were closing, and his fist came up clenching one cuff of a pair of chained manacles, the bones of the long-dead man who'd been pinioned shattering down to the floor. The first prisoner roared, and leaped toward us, just as Janos swung the shackle like a morning star into the man's face. He screamed like a lanced bear, reared back, blood spurting in the gloom, and fell as another one of them shambled in on me. I slashed with my bone club, the bone shattered like the corpse's arms had, and I lunged, my club now a shard-edged dagger, striking deep into the other's stomach. I jerked it free as one of them pinioned me about the shoulders. I ducked, about to toss him overhead, and Janos came in with the chain. I heard the man's bones crack, and his arms fell away, and I straightened. Another attacker was reaching with strangler's hands, and I remembered one of Janos' tricks, brought both arms up, crossed at the wrist inside the man's reach, snapped them out, flinging the man's arms wide. Without pausing, as Janos had taught me, I kicked the man's kneecap, recovered, spinning to one side, fisted hand crashing into his throat, and he gurgled and stumbled away. Another crash, and a scream as Janos' death dealer landed once more, and then there were only three attackers, backing away, hands held up defensively.

"All right. All right," one of them panted. "But there'll be another time."

"No, there shall not," Janos said flatly. "If there is, you had best kill both of us ... or plan on never sleeping again. Look at me ... *you*." The one who'd spoken stopped his retreat. "I know things you ... and those bastards across there"—jerking a thumb outside the cell at the torture chamber—"cannot even dream of." Before the man could react, Janos dropped the manacles, bounded forward, one hand cupped and reaching out. I swear he but touched the other with his curled fingers in what might have been a lightning caress, but the man yowled agony, and doubled, shrilling, both hands clutching the angle of his jaw. "You will live," my friend announced. "But the pain will remind you of me for a week." The others helped their fellow away, and they found a refuge far across the cell.

"Will they try again?"

"Perhaps," Janos said indifferently. "We will sleep but lightly anyway. I can think of some words that will cause that straw underfoot to crackle like great trees being broken should anyone approach us."

Thus began the second phase of our imprisonment. Somehow, as we dozed, the bodies of the men we had slain were removed from the cell without our hearing. We were not bothered by the coterie of prisoners who ran the cell with their brutality. I saw how they treated the weaker prisoners and wanted to intervene. Janos forbade it. "We've carved our own niche in this little society of the damned. They will leave us alone, so long as we don't interfere with their ... interests." I grudged the probable wisdom of what he said and tried not to listen to the sounds as they indulged themselves. I found I could shut out those noises, just as my eyes could look out beyond the bars into the torture chamber and not see what agonies were being inflicted. Twice prisoners from our cell were taken out and put on the rack. Some of their fellows found this most entertaining.

We could not tell what was day nor what was night. I tried to keep track by our meals, assuming we were fed the stinking gruel and rotten bread once a day. Janos told me not to bother—another common jailer's trick to weaken a prisoner was to feed him at irregular intervals. He might eat three times in one day and think three days had passed, then not at all for three days and think the most interminable day of his life had just gone by. I figured later we were in that foul cell almost a month.

We inquired about our fellow prisoners. Some of them had offended the politics, such as they were, of the Archons or Lycanth; but most were common criminals—of a particularly depraved nature, admittedly, but at least we weren't in the last citadel of the doomed. This was confirmed when we saw one man released from the cell. He babbled thanks, and tears, attempting to kiss the boot top of the guard who opened the cell door.

I knew we were being held here to further weaken our resolve. I guessed that next would come the torture chamber. "Possibly," Janos said. "Or possibly they will seclude us and smash at us with their full magical power." I thought that reaffirmed that we were not in the worst part of the Archons' dungeons, but said nothing to Janos. Neither of our spirits needed any further degradation.

Then came a lift. A prisoner received a visitor! It was a woman, a slattern who claimed to be his wife. She was not only permitted to see him—the torture chamber's doors being, of course, shut during that time—but they were allowed to use the guardroom for a few minutes for their own purpose. A few days later, if days they were, a man's brother came. I noticed they spent most of their time drawing what looked to be plans of the inside of a building and talking in low tones. We asked eagerly for details on visitation rights, and were told that with enough gold, any of the prisoners, except those imprisoned for their beliefs, might be allowed visitors. Depending on the whims of the guard officer. Sometimes there would be a price in addition to money, a prisoner said. The slattern, he rather imagined, would have been required to attend to at least some of the guards' pleasures before seeing her "husband."

"If someone from the outside can enter," Janos mused softly, "then it might be possible for someone . . . two someones . . . from the inside to leave, might it not? Before the third part of the Archons' plan is put into motion."

"How?"

"I do not know," he said. "Let me consider how we can cast for a visitor all our very own." But we did not need a scheme. Shortly afterward, our visitor came to us. Two guards escorted a man into the chamber. He was not tall, but very bulky and misshapen, shambling like a half man, half beast. The guards bellowed for a prisoner, who grunted in surprise, then made his way to the bars. I saw gold glint, and the guards left. The misshapen one said a few words to the prisoner and then the man—a thug who'd been imprisoned for a particularly barbaric murder for hire—came over to us.

"You. He's for you." I gasped, and then both Janos and I recognized the man outside the bars. I should have known him earlier. It was Greif, my nightmare warden and Janos' real-life procurer of sorcerous matter. Again I heard that mellow bass voice curl out from the broken face.

"Lord Antero. Cap'n Greycloak. Looks like th' wheel's come round 'gain, don't it?"

"How did you know that we were—" Janos began.

"Seal it," Greif said impatiently. "Greif gets all that's worth knowin' in Lycanth. I heard, an' bought in, 'cause I know Rolfe, there, so there'll be no s'spicion a'terward."

"Afterward?" I asked.

"You too," he said. "Keep it shut! There ain't *time*! Don't need t' be here, i' one a' th' Archons' Evocators has a spirit look-roun' down here. An' I s'spec' Symeon's got his own wizards castin' warnin' spells aroun' you two, makin' sure you stay where he put y'."

"You can get us out?" Janos had figured out what Greif meant. Greif smiled that twisted smile and nodded.

"I can. An' it'll cost, cost dear. I know an Evocator a' my own. Works th' dark side a' th' street, an' got read out for so doin'. I'll need gold . . . gold enow t' move me leagues beyond Lycanth, an' beyond th' reach a' th' wrath a' Symeon an' the Archons."

"You'll have it," I said. "And you'll have a new life. In Orissa or wherever. How much gold?"

"Half," Greif announced firmly. "Half of *all* th' Antero gold. Figure that for a headprice is cheap, there bein' no Antero's but th' sister with no interest in birthin', an' brothers whose spawn won't stretch beyond th' countin' room."

"You know a great deal about my family," I said.

"This'll be th' one chance I'll have," Greif said. "Enough gold so there won't be no slut, nor boy neither, say nay t' what I pr'pose. Gold so I can tell any watch officer t' shit in his hat, an' he'll do it, clap it on his head, claim it th' latest style, an' parade away with a smile! Knowin' that, I done my studyin' afore I come to see you."

"I have gold . . . a great deal of gold not far from Lycanth," I said. "But it would take much time to convert half my holdings to cash, and then have the gold taken to where you want it."

"And *we* don't have time either," Janos put in. "The patience of the Archons is not known for being great."

"Fact is," Greif assented, "y're for th' Question, I heard, in a few days. First over there—" And he nodded toward the closed doors to the torture chamber, and I realized he did, indeed, know a vast amount about this prison and our dilemma. "—then i' front a three Evocators, in triad. Wi' th' Archons' full powers behin' them. You'll break . . . an' there'll be nothin' left but a couple burned husks fitten for no more'n beggin' in th' streets after, assumin' they'll let you loose someyear."

"So how do I make you rich, then?" I continued. "I don't expect you to trust me to make payment after we're out. Speaking of that, just how will you be able to get us out, anyway?"

"You don't need t' be knowin' that," Greif said. "As t' th' first, I *do* trust you. Ain't never heard tale of any Antero breakin' his bond. But I'll have gifts of y' both, t' ensure. A bit a' blood, a bit a' hair, a bit a' skin, a bit a' y'r juices. F'r insurance."

I looked at Janos. He was expressionless. What choice did we have? Even if the escape attempt failed, what could be done to us? They wouldn't kill us, not until they found what they wanted. So we'd most likely get no more than a beating, be returned to the cell, and our appointment with the inquisitors moved closer. I stuck my hands through the bars, and Greif and I touched palms.

"May m' eyes be stricken, may m' mouth be burned out, may m' ears seal'd, may m' life ended if I break this oath that I'll see y' both beyond this cell, an' walkin' free in th' world," he said. I repeated his oath, changing the last to "if I fail to reward this man as he deserves and heap him with the honor he shall have earned."

"Now. You wait. You just wait," and Greif went back down the corridor, shouting for the guards.

We did. One bowl of gruel . . . another . . . and yet a third. Janos stalked back and forth, unable to eat, unable to sleep. I pretended calm, but wanted to follow his lead.

I woke to the sound of windroar, snapped awake, and saw Greif, pacing into the chamber. He held, level with the ground, a staff of some sort. I could hear him muttering as he approached. The muttering—and windroar—stopped. He whispered, and the bars slid open, the ancient rusted iron moving as smoothly as new-cast, greased steel. Instantly Janos and I were out of the cell. None of the other prisoners seemed to notice either the door opening, our exit, or the door closing. Greif set the staff down, and took two hooded cloaks from the small pack he was wearing. He motioned us to pull them on, then handed us each a scrap of paper. On mine was scrawled: SAE NUTHING. FOLOW ME. WISPER

WORDS ALOTHEM, BERENTA, ALOTHEM. He picked up the staff, and, again holding it level, paced away, toward the stairs and the guardroom, muttering his spell. The windroar began once more. I saw sweat was rolling down Greif's face in spite of the dank cold. We followed him, obeying instructions, whispering the two words of what must have been the spell he'd gotten from the "criminal" Evocator. We passed the guardroom. Half the guards snored, but five or six appeared awake. They did not see us. We started up the stairs. As we approached each of the sealed doors, Greif would touch them with first one, then the other end of his staff, and they would spring open.

We reached the main floor of the castle. Here there were pacing guards, but none of them saw us. I realized Janos had stopped and turned. He was stretching up, reaching to where a pitch-soaked torch flared. He touched it for a moment, then dropped his hand, as Greif turned and impatiently beckoned. Then we were outside the sea castle, in the courtyard, where rain roared and smashed against the stone. I tasted its sweetness and heard the splashing, something I never had expected to taste or hear again. There was a carriage waiting, with four horses, a coachman, and four outriders beside it. It looked as if it might belong to a rich man, just the man who might have very private business with the Archons or their priests at this hour. Greif motioned us inside. He stopped his spell.

"Now. You stay in. Don't look out. This'll take us to th' next step. Then we'll get out of the city. Start thinkin', Antero, how quick you can scrape me up m' gold." He slammed the coach door. The blinds were drawn tight, and it was almost dark inside the carriage. We could see nothing through the blinds. The coach swayed on its springs as Greif climbed up on the step, and then we were moving. I breathed relief.

"Not yet," Janos said. "When we are beyond where their wall once stretched, beyond that and their patrols."

I brought myself back to alertness. "What were you doing, back there with the torch?"

"No bowman carries but one string," Janos said obliquely, "I felt I might need some pitch." He held his fingers up, and began whispering,

"Fire my friend
"Fire you hear
"Fire my friend
"Fire you hear

"Fire you remember
"Fire you hear . . ."

There were other words, in a tongue I did not know. I had no idea what he was preparing, or why. So I concentrated on the sounds outside, the crash of the wheels against cobbled streets, the shouted challenges from patrols or watchmen, Greif bellowing the password, the crack of the whip, the clatter of hooves. The carriage swayed as we turned corners. I tried to figure where we were going, but gave it up, being almost completely unfamiliar with the streets of Lycanth. I asked Janos if he could tell, and he waved me to silence, never stopping his whisper.

I heard the crash of opening gates, and the sound of great hinges as the coach passed through, and I could hear the note of the wheels change from cobbles to smooth paving. The gate boomed closed behind us. The coach came to a halt. We sat in dimness and silence, then the door was jerked open, and torchlight blazed.

"Out!" It was a command. I slid out, blinking. We were in a great courtyard, and the carriage was drawn up near one of the courtyard's high walls. In front of us was Nisou Symeon. Behind him were twenty heavily armed solders. We had been betrayed from one trap into another.

"I welcome you, Lord Amalric Antero, to the somewhat unique pleasures of my house."

The world shuddered and reeled. I wanted to shout obscenities; hurl myself at Greif, who stood not far behind Symeon, a twisted smile of mockery on his face; rip at Symeon even though I knew I would be impaled on the soldiers' spears a moment later. I fought for control, a fight as bitter as any I have waged in my life, and somehow found it, although it might have taken seconds or minutes.

"Why?" I managed. "You had us in the dungeon. Sooner or later, the Evocators or the torturers would have begun. Or do you have some ground wizard waiting? I assume you still wish what secrets you imagine we possess."

"Possibly," Symeon said. "As to why? Circumstances may have changed from a short time ago."

"I see. So you're planning to keep the information you hope to extract from us from your masters?"

Janos walked toward Symeon, moving as if he were some great bewildered lummox. "Why are you going to betray the Archons?"

He had his hands stretched out, as if in bewilderment. One of them brushed the edge of Symeon's robe.

"Get back, you!" Symeon snapped, and one of the soldiers dropped his spear until the point was at Janos' chest. Janos did as ordered. "I do not speak to minions," Symeon went on. "Especially one who is a traitor to the cause he served."

"Traitor, Nisou Symeon?" I asked. "From one who is directly betraying the Archons?"

"I am loyal," he said, "to the master whose oath I have taken! As I have said, circumstances have changed. The knowledge I wish from you has become of secondary import. Enough. You are to go inside, and the soldiers will conduct you to your resting place. It is fully as secure as any of the Archons' dungeons. I will tell you now, this will be your last sight of the heavens, rain-drenched though they be. Waste no time on words therefore, but enjoy them."

I realized Janos was whispering,

> "Fire my friend
> "Fire you hear
> "Fire you burn
> "Remember your brother
> "Fire my friend
> "Fire you *burn!*"

The pitch from the torch "remembered," flickered, and Symeon's robes suddenly caught fire. The flames, built by sorcery as much as by dry cloth, roared up, the rain having little effect. Symeon screamed agony. The soldiers were a shambles of confusion and shouts.

"Up," Janos shouted, and sprang to the doorway of the coach, stretching up for the roof. The spearman who'd confronted him, a bit more alert than the others, dashed forward, ready for a thrust, and I kicked his feet from under him and had the spear. Janos bounced twice on the coachtop, then leaped—fingers catching the edge of the wall—and pulled himself up. I dashed forward, foot on the wheel, about to spring for the coach roof. Hands pulled at me. I lashed backward with the spear butt and heard a scream, louder even than the ones from the living torch that Symeon had become, and was on the coachtop. Lighter, smaller, and more gymnastic than Janos, I leaped, and had the walltop under my elbows, and Janos pulled me to my feet.

I had but one moment to look behind me and saw Greif, staggering backward, howling, hands clapped over his eye. Nisou Symeon was on the ground, soldiers diving to cover him and smother the flames, and then we jumped—chancing the long drop to whatever might lie below.

We landed on cobblestones, recovered, and then we were running, running as hard as ever we had in this life, running into the night, into the rain, and now I praised the gods of Orissa we had torn down Lycanth's great wall. If we could make it through their streets and past whatever night patrols they had, there was freedom. Freedom and home. I knew we would find safety. After escaping from the clutches of the Archons *and* Symeon, there could be nothing but good ahead.

CHAPTER EIGHTEEN
Cassini's Revenge

OUR FIRST SIGHT of Orissa, however, made me certain that "good," whatever it might be, still lay in the distant future. Smoke curled from several places inside the city, and the river was ominously deserted. I could see no sign of activity around the docks. The city gate we approached confirmed trouble. The huge ironwood gates were closed, which never happened except in direst emergency. Above them, on the catwalk, was a full squad of soldiers, dressed not in ceremonial armor but in full fighting gear.

"Who comes?"

"Lord Amalric Antero and Captain Janos Greycloak, Orissans."

There were surprised exclamations from above, a warrant officer's sharp command, and then the gates swung open, without anyone acknowledging us. We entered. The sally ports were also closed, and for a moment, I felt we'd entered yet another trap. Then they opened. The soldiers who'd opened the portals also did no more than come to attention and did not salute either of us as they should have. We said nothing, but hastened toward the Antero villa.

Once beyond Lycanth's wall, Janos and I had chanced going to the inn where I had left my men and gold. The keeper told us they'd returned home, sure of their lord's demise, weeks earlier. Perhaps it was to the good there'd been just the two of us. We were armed only with the spear I'd grabbed in Symeon's courtyard and an evil-looking brush cutter Janos had cozened from the innkeeper. We'd traveled cross-country as much as possible, because the roads and hills were alive with patrols. There were not only patrols in Lycanthian uniform, but cavalry sweeps whose men wore the livery of the Symeon household. "So I did not cremate him as I intended," Janos said. I, too, was disappointed. Supposedly no man should cold-bloodedly wish the death of another, but I knew my life, my family, my clan, my household, and any generation of Antero to come would be in jeopardy until the Symeons were destroyed. I knew I would not be able to mount the blood feud for some time to come. But that would be in the future—at the moment it was enough that we'd managed to slip past all Lycanthian units without problem, and arrived home.

There were many Orissans in the streets, but almost all of them were men. There were a few young women, but no children at all. Their faces were sullen, and I heard shouts and arguments. We saw the root of one smoke plume, the still-smouldering ruins of a building that had burned within the last day or so. It had housed a small counting house used by Evocators to collect duty from any caravan entering the city by this gate. I remembered the estimable Prevotant, in my warehouse long ago, and approved whichever god had sent mischance against this House of Bribery.

We did not know what was going on, but knew we had best hurry for the safety of the villa before investigating. We did not make it. A foot patrol—six spearmen, two archers, a corporal, and a young legate—came out of a side street. All of them wore the Coast Watch breastplates, a unit whose duties normally kept them outside Orissa.

"Halt!" came the shout. Spears were couched and bowmen nocked arrows. Neither Janos nor I moved. The legate took a scroll from his belt pouch. "Amalric, Head of the Family named Antero, entitled by the grace of the Magistrates and Gods of Orissa to call himself Lord?"

"I am he."

"Janos Greycloak, once of Kostroma, once of Lycanth, sometimes using the title of Captain?"

"I will answer to the name . . . and you will answer to the insult one day," Janos snapped.

"Be silent! I mean no insult, but am obeying the commands of the Magistrates as to the manner of address. I have here an order for the arrest of Lord Antero and, if Janos Greycloak is with him, for his apprehension as well."

"On what charge?" I demanded.

"The charge has yet to be made, but will be preferred at the proper time."

"Who laid this open warrant?"

"Evocator Cassini, countersigned by Magistrate Sisshon."

"How can such a warrant be served by the Coast Watch? It is the duty of the Maranon Guard to keep the city safe."

"The Guard has refused service, and been confined to its barracks!"

I couldn't restrain astonishment. What could have happened? Was Rali safe?

"I demand your immediate surrender," the legate said loudly. I looked at Janos. He shrugged—we had no choice, and certainly, as law-abiding citizens of the city, nothing more to concern ourselves with than the annoyance of having to explain our innocence at the citadel of the Magistrates. "Very well," I said.

"Lay down your arms," the legate ordered. "I am further ordered to take you to the palace of the Evocators, and give you into their keeping."

"I will not!" Janos snapped. "Since when do the Evocators control the civil rules of Orissa?"

"Since it became necessary, after the rioting, to declare Emergency Law. As part of that declaration, certain measures were put into effect as temporary measures. This is one of them."

I gripped my spear more tightly. No, I would not go into Cassini's tender care. We had not escaped from two great wolf packs to be devoured by *that* jackal. One of the archers lifted his bow.

"Draw th' string, an' I'll split y'r chest like you wuz a sturgeon!" The shout came from a great barrel-chested woman standing atop a low building. She was one of the river's fishermen, because she held, ready to cast, a long, barbed harpoon. I looked around. The street was packed with Orissans. All of them were dressed shabbily—we were in a poor section of the city—and all of them were armed. From a window menaced a lad with a sporting crossbow. There was a knot of stave-wielding men behind us. Others held clubs or cobbles they'd uprooted. I saw the gleam of unsheathed daggers and kitchen cleavers, and even a few bared swords.

"Ye'll not be takin' Janos t' th' Evocators, sonny," the woman went on. "Nor yet Lord Antero. Goddamned Evocators have ruined enough!" There was a growl of assent, and the crowd surged forward. "Y'll be th' ones t' lay down your arms," she said. "An' there'll be some of us can use th' armor, matters keep heatin' up th' way they've been."

A stone smashed into one of the spearmen. In spite of his breastplate, he shouted pain and went to his knees. Then a shower of rocks and muck. The crowd noise grew, and the soldiers were but an instant from death.

"Stop!" It was Janos, his voice a parade-ground bellow. Everyone froze, for just a moment. "Orissans," he went on. "These men are Orissans as well. Do you want their blood on your souls?"

"Wouldn't bother *me* none," cried someone in the crowd. Yells of agreement followed.

"No! Look at them! I know this legate," Janos said, and I knew he was lying. "I remember when he was sworn in, and I saw his mother and sister weeping for happiness. Do you want to make them weep for another reason?" Mutterings. "Look at the others. They are but soldiers. Any of you might have chosen to wear the uniform at one time, yes? Some of you did take up arms to serve your city. That is what these men are doing. Doing what they see as their duty. Is it their fault they're misled?"

"Damn fools oughta know better," a man shouted, and I thought it to be the same one who said he was not afraid to kill. Janos made no reply for a moment, but then broke into laughter— that great boom of a sound. The crowd puzzled, then snickered, then started laughing, unsure of what they'd found amusing. Janos stopped laughing, and the mirth died.

"I am delighted to hear from a man who Knows Better," Janos said. "When this is over, and the proper order has been returned, come to me, man. I will pay you well, in gold and wine, to make sure *I* always know better." Now the crowd had something specific to chuckle about, but Janos did not wait for silence. He turned back to the patrol. "You. Legate."

The man may have been young, but he picked up on his lead as deftly as any member of a dance troupe. "Yes. Sir." And saluted.

"Take charge of your men, and return to your watch officer. Report to him you were given direct orders by Captain Janos Greycloak, of the Magistrates' Own Guard. He will give you further orders at that time." Again the legate saluted, ordered his soldiers to attention, about-face, and marched them off. They disappeared back down the side street, keeping in formation, even the injured spearman who had to be assisted by his fellows. Janos waited until they were gone, then turned back to the crowd.

"What is the name of this district?"

General shouts, and the blast of "Cheapside" from someone with a set of bellows for lungs.

"Cheapside . . . I thank you. Lord Antero thanks you. I think we owe you our lives. You should be proud to be Orissans. When this is over, Lord Antero and I have a debt to repay. And we always honor our debts."

Shouts of happiness, agreement, disagreement, cries of it was their pleasure, and the crowd began dissipating. Several of them, including that iron-lunged harpooness, wanted to speak to and touch him. "Now," he said to me in a low tone after a spell. "We should have given that jackanapes and his beach watchers time enough to get away." Little by little, through the well-wishers, we extricated ourselves. Then, using back alleys and keeping well out of sight of any of the troops from various units who were patrolling the streets, we reached my villa.

It looked as if it had been readied for a siege. All of the windows on the lower floors were blocked off with the solid oak deadlights my father's father had prepared, part of the gear we maintained and replaced or added to as needed, which was meant for the most extreme emergency.

Sergeant Maeen had taken charge, technically deserting from the army, although no one seemed to care about his action, especially since the Magistrates' Own Guard no longer existed. Helping him keep order was a self-appointed foursome: J'an, the head stableman; Rake and Mose, my sauce chef and storekeeper, respectively; and Spoto, the youngest of the chambermaids. I thought of the two who should have run the household in my absence, Eanes and Tegry, and said a prayer to the memory of them both, one a hero, one a fool.

Rali had managed to slip in from time to time, but no one knew how. I did, but said nothing. She'd managed to get word to my brothers at our estates beyond the city and told them to stay where they were. In fact, the villa *was* ready to be blockaded. Rali had ordered the storekeepers to lay in nonperishables for months, and had both our cellar wells given a sweetness blessing by a trustworthy Evocator. She'd opened the armory and unlocked the weapons racks. Maeen had spent hours teaching the use of them, and J'an, who'd been an eager witness to my early weapons training, assisted. The quartet had paid off any of my staff who were afraid, worried, or felt there might be some merit to the libels against my family. I was honored almost to the point of tears when Spoto said that only three had demanded their wages and gone. Just as Cheapside would be rewarded when peace came, so, too, must I remember each man and woman in this household.

I was tired, hungry, and dirty, but somehow knew I must not waste any time. I had my household leaders—I began calling them my captains—walk me through the house and grounds, telling me all they'd done. By that time, Janos had refreshed himself, and I chanced a quick bath, a gobbled meal, and a glass of wine. I looked longingly at that great feather bed in my chambers, but did not weaken. I went belowstairs and found that Janos, experienced soldier that he was, had made some additions. These included buckets full of either dirt or water placed around in case of an "unexplained" fire. He set a watch on the roof, ordered to sound the alert if they saw or heard *anything* untoward. All doors except the large front one were double barred and spiked and heavy furniture moved in front of them.

Rali appeared suddenly behind me. No one seemed surprised except for Janos—I gathered she had told the staff she'd been given a spell permitting her to enter her home without using the door or some such nonsense. I knew—and later told Janos—how she'd gotten into the villa. Part of the worst-event planning our family's heads had made were two tunnels. One began behind a false bookcase in my father's—now my—office, and ran under the grounds to exit more than one hundred yards behind the villa, and the second went from a trapdoor in the second floor down a false chimney, under the street in front of us to emerge in the rear of a small shop nearby that no one—including its proprietor—knew the Antero family owned.

Rali told us what had happened since I'd slipped out of the city. As I'd feared, my disappearance had weighed the scales against those of us who saw Orissa was at a turning point in its history—a turning point that meant we *must* reach for the Far Kingdoms, that we *must* change to be able to face a new epoch. Many of those who'd bravely stood up against the old guard found it politic to withdraw from the controversy. Those who could afford it, such as Malaren, had taken Gamelan's example and physically left the city.

Words became violence. First was the beating of a particularly hated man who served as landlord for slum tenements secretly owned by some of the richest and most conservative families in the city. One of the night watch's guardhouses had been burned, not far from Cheapside. Then my old friend Prevotant reported to the Magistrates that he and his guards had been set upon by villains in the night, villains who shouted, "Down with the Evocators" and "Lycanth will free us." At this point Rali stopped, raised an eyebrow, and waited for comment. Neither Janos nor I cared to comment on the truth of *that*. Lycanth would free us, indeed. Prevotant was even stupider than I remembered him.

Somehow the Magistrates were convinced to declare Emergency Regulations, regulations that also empowered the Evocators to "provide counseling and assistance in any manner deemed fit to end the current emergency." That, in turn, brought mobs into the streets. Somehow, during the course of a night's protest, two buildings were burned—and seven men and two women, all from the artisan class, "attacked the night watch, intending murder, forcing them to defend themselves with the full force of arms." That was a little too raw, even for the Magistrates' Council, who by now were being almost entirely swayed by the Old Guard.

They called for the Maranon Guard to take the streets and bring peace. But their instructions meant "peace" was to be interpreted as the suppression of those who wanted change, and the preservation of the old.

"We held full council then," Rali said, her face like ice. "All of us, from officers to the lowliest stable hand, all voices to be held equal. It took the greater part of a night, but it was determined that the main reason we are blessed by Maranonia is because we truly *are* the spirit of Orissa. Not Orissa past, nor Orissa to come. For us to choose sides would not only destroy the respect we are held in, but almost certainly incur a curse from the goddess herself.

"We refused to obey, for the first time in the history of the Maranon Guard." Rali looked away, eyes gleaming wet in the firelight. "It was a proud and a shameful moment.

"We were ordered to our barracks, where we remain. We do not know what, if anything, we should do to end this catastrophe that is tearing Orissa apart. We have sought out prophets and wise men and women. A few Evocators, ones we trust, have even visited our barracks secretly. We cast runes hourly. But as yet . . ." She let her voice trail off. "There are times, Janos Greycloak," she said frankly, "I have damned you, and damned the Far Kingdoms as well."

"Change will happen," Janos said. "Whether we will it or not. The best we can do is shape it to our own ends, that will with luck bring the greatest happiness to the most people."

"I know." Rali sighed. "I know. But it is terrible to see the city I love tear itself apart. Now the poor creep out at night to loot, steal, and burn, the Evocators trumpet false triumph during the day, and those who would bring this catastrophe to an end huddle behind stone walls."

She got up. "Word of your arrival reached our barracks within minutes after you came through the gates," she said. "I would suspect matters will come to a full boil now, and we shall learn on which side the gods are smiling."

She ruffled my hair. "Welcome back, brother. I would wager you never thought you and some mountain brigand would lead a revolution, did you?" She was gone before I could recover. Rali—as usual—was correct. We *were* leading a revolution, of sorts. I greatly wished I could tell what its final outcome would be. As I write, I still wish I knew that today.

Guards mounted, both Janos and I retired to our chambers, Sergeant Maeen supervising the first shift. Both of us kept our weapons ready. Janos left orders to wake him in the hour before dawn, when a threat was most likely to materialize. But the threat did not wait until much past midnight. I woke from an utterly dreamless sleep to a shout, a crash, and a scream of fear. It came from the main entrance. Naked, sword in hand, I found myself downstairs at the door as servants hurried up behind me, carrying newly lighted torches. Two of my servants, whose names I shall not mention to prevent shame to their families today, huddled against the wall. At their feet was the huge wooden bar to the entrance. I thought traitors, and readied my sword, then bethought myself as they shrieked for mercy and but a moment to explain. But first things first, and I ordered them to rebar the door. They did, hastily. Janos came pelting down the stairs, his weapon at the ready. "I saw men," he said. "Perhaps twenty of them, armed, waiting across the street. They ran when the commotion began." He realized what had almost occurred with a glance.

"So," he said. "It would have been treason rather than a frontal attack. What gain did they promise you for betraying us," he demanded. The two babbled, and I shouted silence, and bade one of them tell me, slowly, just what had happened. According to the servant, he had gone to bed when relieved from his watch. Then he'd awakened, but it was like he was in a dream and unable to resist, walking toward the door. The other man was waiting. "It was a spell," he insisted. "I tried to fight against it . . . but to no avail."

I hesitated, then lowered my blade, remembering both of them had served my family for years. But I still was not convinced. Nor was Janos. "What broke the spell?" he asked skeptically. "Such a curse, if one was indeed cast, would have had no effect if improperly made, or if powerful enough would have made you carry out the plan completely."

"It was . . . it was a shout."

"From whom?" I wanted to know.

Both men began trembling, and then one pointed—with a shaking finger—behind me. He was pointing to the portrait of my brother, Halab, behind the altar. "It came ... from him. From there."

Now the rest of the servants began chattering, and once more I had to shout for stillness. Both servants returned to their babbling—yes, it had come from the painting, and it could only be the blessed Halab trying to save the family from beyond the grave. I was torn between amazement and skepticism. Janos ordered the two servants to be taken to a storeroom. He said he would find the truth of the matter. "I will hold with no torture," I told him quietly. "No matter what they tried. If you believe them guilty, cast them out. Or else kill them, as is our right, since they have forfeited their covenant."

"I shall not touch them, physically," Janos said. "There are other, better ways." He went for the kitchen, where he could procure certain necessary items. I knew what he intended. Within an hour, he had the answer. The men *had* been telling the truth. Someone had cast a spell from without, a powerful piece of sorcery intended to turn a man into a mindless slave for a space. Even though the spell was intended to work on sleeping minds not on their guard, the sorcerer would be a Master Evocator, working to the peak of his abilities, and most likely backed up by another wizard.

"Black sorcery," I said.

Janos reluctantly agreed, although he did wonder if I would feel the same if the spell had been cast, say, to keep a great villain from harming a good person? Not that we had time for philosophy. He immediately secured other items from our stores and, when the sun rose, sent servants surreptitiously out to what marketplaces would be open to buy other items. He cast several spells that day. The first and greatest was around the entire household. "I cannot prevent another spell such as the one just laid from being attempted, but I can prevent any such spell from taking full hold." He also cast protective spells around each of us, taking great pains over the two men who'd fallen prey to the incantation before. "Just as someone who falls ill of a disease of the lungs must always take care to avoid dampness and low wet places, so a man who's been taken over by sorcery can fall prey to another spell cast by the same person. Or such is my belief, at any rate, even though I have heard it from no Evocators nor seen it in any grimoire."

I asked how the servants had taken it, having words said over them that came from someone hardly a member of the Evocator's class. Janos grinned and said there'd been no problems. "You don't realize, Amalric, there is a whole underworld of sorcery most poor folk rely on. They cannot afford an Evocator, or else they believe certain spells and items their family and friends have used for years have far greater efficacy than anything the Evocators might prescribe. Sometimes that is superstition, but as often as not they are correct. Finally, the things they might want sorcerous help in obtaining, such as a love philter or an enemy to be cursed or an overspell to give them riches . . . any of these might be considered unlawful."

"To them," I said slowly. "But not to me, because I have always had money enough to purchase silence once whatever spell I desired is cast."

"Money . . . or simply the power of the Antero name."

"There is a great unfairness in this city of ours," I said.

"Brilliant deduction," Janos said, not bothering to hide his sarcasm. "When you find a system where that is not true, to a greater or lesser degree, be sure to inform me so that we both can emigrate." I poured him brandy, neat, and told him not to grind it in. Then, very privately, I went to Halab's altar and prayed my thanks. I knew not if he would appreciate sacrifices when this was over, but I promised them anyway. I also swore that his—or his ghost's—doings this day would be told again and again, until the last Antero was taken from the earth.

The next attack came late that afternoon. I heard the blast of a horn and peered out an upstairs window. In the street below was Cassini! He wore the full ceremonial robes of a master-level Evocator. Two other Evocators stood behind him, and there were white-robed lay assistants flanking them. Two of them blew another blast on their trumpets. To their rear were some twenty soldiers.

"Lord Amalric Antero," Cassini shouted. "I summon you to justice." I did not respond until Janos had come into the room. Cassini called for me twice more in the interim. I asked Janos what should be done. He considered. "You may ignore him if you wish," he said. "Or you may speak to him. I see no archers or crossbowmen out there, and I do not sense he has made himself the catalyst for some spell."

I unbarred the balcony doors and stepped out. "I hear you, Evocator."

"I summon you, Lord Antero," Cassini shouted once more.

"By what right? I have broken no laws. And you are hardly a

Magistrate. Not yet, at any rate." I probably should not have added the last, but could not avoid a comment on what our city had become.

"You lie," he shouted back. "We Evocators have sensed someone in and of this household is practicing sorcery. Since there are no known licensed Evocators in this villa, you, and those whom you choose to protect, are accused of this crime against Orissa, against the Evocators, and against the natural order of our land. You are required therefore to surrender to me, as is any person you know of who might be guilty of committing this enormous sin, or aiding and abetting others in committing it. You have one turning of the glass"—and an assistant held the device up—"to prepare yourself, and to bring whatever materials you think might aid in your defense. Heed this summons, Lord Amalric, and yield to our justice. For an honest man has nothing to fear from the Council of Evocators."

"I hear my brother's spirit laughing at that," I shouted, goaded into anger. "And don't waste your time with the glass. Neither I, nor anyone else within these walls, will abandon himself to become a popinjay for the Evocators! If a hearing is necessary, let it be made in the proper manner, and served by Magistrates, not charlatans in robes!"

I saw Cassini smile—he'd known the answer his warrant would receive. He took a long, double-handed dagger from another assistant, a dagger that gleamed gold in the afternoon sun. He took its grip in both hands and held it before him, blade up.

"I have no choice." Another assistant stepped beside him and unrolled parchment. "I, Cassini, gather the power granted by the gods and demons of this and other worlds. I direct this power against Amalric Antero, and all those who serve him, willingly or unwillingly, and declare all of them outlaw and anathema, from this moment until justice has been done, and the outlaw Antero has been brought to bay.

"I curse and condemn both in specific and general, and the curse shall take the following horrible forms, so that the Anteros and all who serve them shall be marked, so that no honest man who fears and respects the gods and their servants will be deceived. The first curse shall—"

Cassini blinked, as a spot of light flashed across the scroll and then his face. He looked up and cried out, the dagger falling into the roadway. He attempted to pull the hood of his robe over his face, but it was too late.

Janos was beside me. He held, in both hands, the great silvered mirror that hung in my wardrobe. He finished whispering the words of a spell, then said, loudly, "Evocator Cassini! I have trapped your image, and the images of those beside you in this glass. I now order you, in the name of the gods of Orissa and the demons of Kostroma, hostage against any further curses or thaumaturgy directed against anyone in the Antero family or service, or anyone who calls an Antero friend. If my command is broken, the image held in this mirror will be sent out into the night, blasted by whatever powers I may summon. Also, this mirror now turns your spell back, away from this house and its people. I offer my own soul to the gods as proof that you, and any Evocator who has taken part in this mummery, are witches! Wizards of the blackest sort!"

Cassini's mouth hung open. I heard a low wail from one of his lay assistants. "This is absurd," he managed. "How can you, no more than an amateur and criminal, claim the ability to cast such a Great Spell?"

"I claim it," Janos cried, "from knowledge and dedication. But more because my powers, and my learning, come from the day, come from the light. And just as day shall always conquer the night, so justice shall triumph over your evil!"

Cassini looked about, realizing his fellows and the soldiers had fallen back. "This is a farce!"

"If you so believe . . . then continue your curse and continue declaring us criminals."

I saw Cassini lick his lips. Then he spun, without answering, and stalked away. The hem of his robe became tangled around his legs, and he almost fell. He recovered, and vanished, back into the city, his minions scuttling behind him.

I heard, below me, the startlement of my servants. I turned to Janos, who was setting the mirror down very carefully. "I did not know," I said, "you have powers *that* great."

Janos forced a grim smile. "Nor did I. Nor am I sure that the . . . ones who are beyond would allow me to cast such a counterspell. I shall not attempt to construct it unless forced by Cassini and the Evocators. Perhaps even conceiving of this makes me guilty of hubris. But I am ready to be judged on that matter."

"So you were bluffing?"

Janos shrugged. "In the invisible world, how can anyone, even the greatest wizard, mark the difference between bluff and inspiration? What matters is that the others, those people who serve us, will be reassured for the moment."

"What if Cassini tries again? Or if he assembles all of the Evocators to cast the outlawing spell?"

"I do not think that will happen. Perhaps I truly have his image caught in my glass, in which case if he tries again, I shall go on the attack. If I do not have him caught ... then all is as before. But at this moment Evocator Cassini *believes* himself in jeopardy, which is enough."

"He won't give up," I said. "Nor will the other Evocators and Magistrates he's enlisted."

"No," Janos agreed. "But I suspect they will try something different. And they will try it very quickly—Cassini is too worried about whether I have power over him to let any time pass at all. All of us must be ready for greater trouble this night."

By dusk I knew Janos was correct, at least in his last prediction. I heard the boom of drums coming, I thought, from the Great Amphitheater, and the roar of crowds from the city. By full dark, torches could be seen lining out the streets. Perhaps we could have fled the villa, but to what end? I knew Cassini would recast his spell, and with a bounty on all our heads, everyone from huntsmen to soldiers would be tracking us. The situation must be resolved here and now.

The night sky was clear, and far overhead shone the cold, hard light of the stars. There was no moon, but it seemed as if a sort of luminescence shone everywhere. Although the night was cloudless, somewhere, not far away, I heard the mutter of thunder.

Janos ordered all lights that could be seen from the outside extinguished. He gathered the ten strongest men together and broke them into two groups, under the command of Maeen. They would be our reserve if, or rather when, we were attacked. The four men who knew a little of archery were stationed on the roof. The watch posts were manned by the youngest servants, whose eyes and ears would be the sharpest of any. Great torches were lighted in front of our gates, at each corner of the villa, and to the rear. Other torches, tied to spears, were made ready. If the large lights were snuffed out, their replacements could be hurled beyond the walls for emergency illumination. Those who wished food were given it, although Janos said he would have preferred no one eat—belly wounds, he told me, were grievous enough without being further corrupted by the stomach's overflow. Also, to prevent filth from being driven into a wound, he had all of us put on clean, dark clothing. Then we waited.

Two hours later the torches began streaming from the center of the city toward the villa. The crowd chants were growing louder. I noted something odd, and brought it to Janos' attention.

"We are, I guess, to be torn apart by a horde angered beyond reason by my scoffing at the gods. Or so our enemies will have it."

"What signs do you have," Janos asked wryly, "that yon throng is *not* your basic mob, wreaking vengeance in the name of all that is good and holy?"

"I see the torches in front and to the sides, moving in lines as if they were being carried by trained soldiers. And the chants sound rehearsed. My guess is they have ordered loyalist elements of the army into civilian costume."

"No," Janos disagreed. "Again, we are opposed by their sorcery. Soldiers would talk, after the event, no matter how they are ordered to keep a still tongue. But men and women, brought out of their homes by a skillfully cast spell, whose skein is finer than a fishing net, will produce the same directed havoc ... and with no guilt or recollection in the morning. History of this night will not be written on a palimpsest."

Within half a glass, the rabble had arrived and surrounded the villa. "Yet another clue as to their organization," Janos pointed out. "A real mob would be centered where things are most likely to happen, which means the front of the villa. Instead, we are now trapped."

"What comes next?"

"Rocks, chants, then a group will chance charging a weak point. We should strike hard, with arrows and spears to drive them back. We must hurt them hard and suddenly any time they make such a thrust. Sooner or later, they will either tire of bleeding without result, or else ..."

I didn't need to ask what the alternative was. "I suppose there is no hope of the Magistrates coming to our assistance?"

Janos shook his head. "Our best chance is that we are still here when the sun rises."

The mob milled and shouted, and rocks and pottery arced toward us. But there was no sign of the anticipated thrust. "Perhaps," Janos wondered, "they are planning the first attack be sorcerous in nature. Look around the crowd, Amalric. Look for their leaders. This mob is definitely led in the person, and not by some Evocator with ghostly hands from their palace. There! See?"

I spotted, at the rear of the throng, several pin lights. "Bull's-eye lanterns," Janos suggested. "The group's leader or leaders, probably being guided since he will be in the throes of his spell working."

"Cassini?"

"Do you think he would allow us to be destroyed without witnessing the event? There is Cassini, and I know if we had a magic glass and could look back to the palace of the Evocators, there would be a great mutter of his fellows chanting like fiends."

Time passed with no further developments. Janos became worried. "They are expecting something, some event that will turn the tide. Or else they would not be keeping the crowd in hand so tightly."

A woman screamed. Screamed from *inside* the villa! "Go," Janos ordered. "I'll watch Cassini and forestall whatever his move is meant to be."

I hurtled downstairs, hearing shouts, and the clash of steel now. Somehow . . . some way . . . the mob had broken into my house. A bent-nosed man, waving a bloody axe, burst toward the bottom of the stairs. I leaped over the banister at him, my sword cleaving. It struck deep into his shoulder, and he staggered and went down, ripping my blade from my hand. I landed, left hand pulling out a duplicate of the long scramasax I'd carried on my Finding. Another villain was on me before I could pull my sword free of the body, his club raised. I went under him and cut his guts out. I had his club in my free hand, and two more were on me. I parried, swung, and they fell back.

I was shouting, "Anteros! Anteros! To me! To me!" and Sergeant Maeen and my reserves boiled out of the side room I'd told them to wait in. The room at the foot of the stairs that led to the main door was a sea of shouting, stabbing, fighting men—they were coming in on us from somewhere. And then I saw him, and knew from where the assault was coming.

Across the room was Tegry! He was one of the few who'd been trusted with the secret of the tunnel, and must have betrayed it to Cassini. He carried a spear and wore some sort of rusty armor. He saw me as well, screamed rage, and cast the spear. It went well to the side, thudding into the wall, and it was my turn. I leaped up and grabbed the torchlike oil lamp from its stanchion and threw—threw with all the anger a body could hold at this ultimate betrayal of not just me and my family, but my father as well.

The flaming lamp struck him in the face, and even over the sounds of fighting I could hear the howl of agony. He fell back, and I lost sight of him as my stalwarts struck again. I heard arrows hum past and saw, at the top of the landing, my archers, sending shafts into the rabble. A shout, then another shout, and the survivors were turning, pushing their way toward the door, back toward the tunnel. Very few of them made it.

The room was a welter of blood. I counted five, no six of my own down, wounded, or dying. I saw Tegry once more. He'd pulled himself up to a sitting position, against one wall. His face was ghastly, black, red, and blistered. His hair and beard had been burned away by the oil as it clung and seared. His blind eyes saw nothing, but he must have sensed my footsteps. He held his hands out, mumbling what might have been a plea for mercy. He received it, dying more cleanly and quickly than the death he had tried to send me and mine.

I heard Janos shouting. I told two servants to block the entrance to the tunnel, recovered my sword, and the rest of us went up the stairs at a run, stumbling now, exhausted, winded. Janos was standing in the balcony, a bow in hand. Methodically he was whipping war arrows into the crowd below. "Now they attack," he shouted. "You bowmen . . . on line. Choose your targets well. Those men there, first. Remember, you cannot hit all of them if you cannot hit any of them."

The mob had secured a battering ram from somewhere, and eight men held its handles and ran back and forth, crashing the bronze-fisted end again and again into the villa's door. The heavy iron-bound oak boomed in defiance at each blow, but I knew it eventually must yield. Bowstrings twanged and arrows sang, but as each man on the ram fell, two more would run to replace him. Either Cassini's sorcery or the crowd's blood lust was very strong. Again the ram crashed against the door, and I heard splintering wood, loud as the door began giving way.

"Back below," I shouted. "Janos. Stand with me. You others . . . rip away the block on that tunnel. We will give you what time we can."

Again we went downstairs into that blood-drenched room. This would be the last moment for the Anteros. Halab's portrait was before me. In a few moments I would be joining him. "You men," I cried. "Your service is finished. Flee, now, down the tunnel, while there's still a chance."

"The hell with you and your orders, Lord Antero," J'an growled, muscles rippling as he readied a great axe, an axe we used to split beef carcasses. "I die when an' where I see fit. There'll be no damn' Evocator or his spawn seein' the back of me this night."

Maeen was beside him and said nothing, but spat on the floor and drew a final line with his foot. I looked about me and realized that more than ten of my servants had chosen to die here, as J'an had. There was a great lump caught in my throat. I looked at Janos. His teeth gleamed white against his beard.

"Now," he said. "Now let there be such a doom of blood the gods themselves will hear the keening and know that Janos Kether Greycloak, Overlord of Kostromo, will be among them." He grinned. "There will be sagas sung of this night, I wager. And I am ready."

Not being gifted at funeral oratory, I forced what I hoped was a death-dealing smile across my lips, said nothing, and lifted my sword and dagger.

The door crashed in . . . and the screams started. From the outside! I heard the keen of pipes, the boom of drums, bowstrings again, and spears thudding into the walls outside, and screams and frenzy. All of us were brought back from that exaltation of death to the real world. We looked at each other, bewildered, as the sounds of a great battle built outside. Janos yanked the axe from J'an, and with three great blows ripped the door away. We ran outside.

From out of the night came three phalanxes of the Maranon Guard. They moved slowly and deliberately forward, spears overlapped, overstepping bodies as they came. Behind the attacking groups were archers and javelin hurlers, casting as they found targets. The Guard's pipers and drummers were crashing a deadly cadence. I saw Rali leading her column, but she had no time to be looking for me.

The mob scattered and ran . . . into the country . . . into the fields, back the way they'd come. I sheathed my dagger and pulled a spear from where it had hurled itself in the ground. Cassini would be fleeing with the rest. It was utterly forbidden to raise a hand against an Evocator, but I had so much blood on my hands, I was not worried about another few drops, whether they came from a sorcerer or not.

But Cassini had not fled. He was not running. I saw him just where he'd been before the mob attacked. He stood in the center of the street. He was all alone—his advisers and assistants must have fled with the rest. I do not know if he was in shock or under some compulsion.

Suddenly he spread out his arms to the sky and began shouting, shouting words in some unknown language. I drew back from my spearcast and then froze. The thunder from the heavens rose, booming, louder than the Guard's drums, louder than an entire army's percussion. Everyone—soldiers, my servants, Janos, the wounded—were as if petrified. White faces looked upward.

The thunder grew louder. Then, from the still completely cloudless sky, a great hand formed of blue flames. The hand reached down, toward us. I wanted to scream, to bury myself in the earth, but could not move.

The hand came down on Cassini. His shouts became shrieks, and then the fingers closed on the Evocator. They lifted him perhaps ten feet above the ground . . . and squeezed, like a gardener killing a worm. The fingers opened and dropped what was left of Cassini onto the roadway. Then flames, hand, and thunder vanished, as if they'd never been.

I turned away. Janos was standing there, still mazed. I walked past him, through the ruins of my door, over the bodies scattered across my anteroom. Outside I could hear shouts and cries as reality—or what we accept as reality—returned.

I did not wish to share my thoughts with anyone at this moment. We had won, yes. But the "war," for that is what it was, wasn't over for me. There was one more battle to be fought, one more victory to be gained, a victory owed to the dead and to the yet to be born.

"LORD AMALRIC ANTERO, and Sir Janos Kether Greycloak, please step forward."

Janos and I were in the citadel of the Magistrates. It was less than a week later, but it was as if an era had passed in Orissa. The Old Guard who'd believed themselves triumphant had vanished from the halls of power. Now Ecco sat at the center of the Magistrates' Bench. Sisshon had announced he was suffering from a rare disease within two days of the battle of the villa, and retired for intensive, private treatment. His supporters had similarly found tasks that generally took them far from the city.

Three days after the battle, the Emergency Regulations had been suspended, and Orissa began working its way back to normalcy. But there were changes—one of the most notable had been the knighting of Janos. He noted, a bit amusedly after the ceremony, that his knighthood would *not* be hereditary. "Evidently they worry about what a half-breed's bastard offspring might bring upon them in the years to come, assuming I have any such issue. But I am well content with this honor, since as we all know the world shall end with my death or transfiguration." He laughed mightily and, in the company of Sergeant Maeen and Rali, drank with his spurs on.

Most important, the Evocators' stranglehold on the city had been broken. Those who'd been in Cassini's camp were no longer to be seen in public. As a matter of fact, none of the Evocators paraded through the city with the same panoply they had in the past. Jeneander, Prevotant, and their ilk were busy trying to determine what the new order would be and how they could somehow control it.

Gamelan had returned and now spoke for the Evocators. For this momentous event he now sat beside Ecco at the bench. We stood at attention as he spoke. Behind us was a throng of our supporters, from Rali to Malaren to, it seemed, half the inhabitants of Cheapside.

"It is the decision of this Council," Ecco went on, "after full consideration and consultation with the proper spiritual forces, that the city of Orissa proclaim a Great Finding, a journey intended to unite the men and women of this city with the fabled beings of that land commonly known as the Far Kingdoms. To this end, we direct all citizens of Orissa, and all residents of lands under their protection, provide Lord Antero and Sir Greycloak with anything they need to successfully complete their task. We now proclaim a crusade, a crusade of peace that will open a new and golden age.

"Lord Antero . . . Sir Greycloak, go forth now. And seek the Far Kingdoms."

The
Last
Voyage

CHAPTER NINETEEN
City of Ghosts

THERE WERE BUT twenty of us, and we were all hard, fit, and young. We had but one goal: the Far Kingdoms; and one rule: never do the expected. It was good that we thought of this expedition as if we were going to war, because from the time we left Orissa following the last winter storm, through our landing on the Pepper Coast, to our journey to the river's headwaters, nothing was either peaceful or normal.

When we embarked secretly at the mouth of Orissa's river on one of my newly built twin-hull fast traders, which was captained by L'ur, all of us could feel strangeness gathering—like fog wraiths collecting around an autumn fire. We made a fast crossing of the Narrow Sea, our intended landing a few leagues below the Shore People. Janos and I planned to visit Black Shark, inform him of our presence in his land, obtain what few supplies we needed, and request neither he nor his people boot our presence about. We unloaded our cargo on a beach and began assembling our equipment as L'ur took his ship swiftly back out to sea, leaving no sign of our arrival. There were two asses for each man, each one ensorcelled so he was voiceless. On them we carried our armory, dried foodstuffs, certain weapons, and rich gifts intended for use when we reached the Far Kingdoms. We intended to treat the animals as if they were treasures themselves: in our company were two hostlers with excellent reputations for knowledge and dedication.

Leaving the unloading in the capable hands of Maeen, Janos and I headed for Black Shark's village. Fortunately dawn broke before we reached it, because we might have passed through its center without noticing—the village and all its people had gone.

The huts had been torn down and burned, but other than that, there was no sign of violence. We searched the shore and the riverbanks; none of their boats remained but one, and that was an old four-man canoe that had sunk unnoticed next to where their dock had been. I asked Janos what he thought had happened. He shook his head, not knowing. Greycloak waded into the river and asked me to help him drag the wrecked canoe out. Puzzled, I did as he asked. He drew his dagger, hacked splinters from the craft, and put them into his belt pouch. We rode back to our party and marched off.

We were moving both fast and slowly, which seems a contradiction, but is not. Janos and I had spent much time discussing this expedition before even soliciting volunteers. Once we had defined our expedition, we put out the word that men were needed. Despite the disaster of the second voyage, half of Orissa volunteered. We took only the young, the fit, the patient, and those with senses of humor as hearty as their muscles. Rali tried to enlist, but I convinced her that at least one Antero must remain behind, if for no reason than to make sure Orissa did not revert to its old evil ways in our absence. She grudgingly agreed. The twenty volunteers we accepted were wildly varied: two had seen service with the Frontier Scouts, for example; one had been a forester; two brothers had, I suspected, been poachers, and so forth. There was even a rather effete teacher of music whose avocation was climbing castle walls without rope or spikes. The final member of our party was Lione. A message was brought to us by his warder. Evidently the man had not improved his ability to live with other people, and was now in a condemned cell. Humorless he may have been, and unpleasant he certainly was, but bravery and toughness counted much in this undertaking. I paid his bloodfine, and he became the twentieth.

On the first day the twenty were assembled at one of my remote country estates, Janos told us we were to behave as if all men's hands were turned against us. He said we must think of ourselves as if we were a band of irregular soldiers or bandits, and all of us must be supremely fit. That was taken care of during the drear winter, as Maeen, who I now realized was a demon in human guise, ran us over rough country until we pleaded for mercy. At that point he would make us do individual exercises, climb trees, or scale cliffs. We also played games—games intended to develop our eye for cover and the country. Hare and Hounds sounds childish, until the rules are changed so that the hare, if captured, is thrown into a millpond. In the dead of winter that penalty is not laughable. When completely fatigued, Maeen would have us draw maps or solve intricate puzzles. Little by little we formed ourselves into a team. The nightmare of the unknown caverns came back to haunt me, but I was so exhausted from Maeen's exercises, it did not trouble me more than twice.

Now, moving through the lands beyond the Pepper Coast, we became skilled in the arts of banditry. We spent long hours in cover, observing open land before we crossed it, especially paying attention to the behavior of the animals and birds. It was another ominous note that we encountered few game animals, and heard bird songs but seldom, as if the land had been hunted out. Or, I thought, as if the animals had sense to flee from a storm gathering to threaten their land. The few villages we'd seen on my Finding were also abandoned, and we never saw any of the hunters or scouts who'd peered at us through cover.

We traveled to the headwaters of the river without incident, although all of us could feel foreboding presences around. But there was one relief—we were not troubled by the minor curses we had been on my Finding. Perhaps, I wondered, our enemies sensed we were beyond such harassment and would prefer to obliterate us cleanly with some Great Spell in the future. We saw Watchers several times, and hid. Since we did not know whether they boded good or evil, we thought it wisest to simply be invisible.

We never moved in a manner that might be expected. Thus, if the easiest route would lie along a valley floor, or on that old, long-abandoned road we had used on my Finding, we never approached it. Nor did we ever use the peaks of the hills for our course. Not only were hillcrests the province of the Watchers, but we could be easily seen from below. We zigged and zagged as we traveled, always keeping within range of the areas we knew from our earlier travels, but never repeating a former route. This expedition was also no endurance contest: we typically traveled for two turns of the glass, then rested for half a turn. Exhaustion, Janos kept telling us, was as deadly an enemy as any ambusher; a tired man, for instance, might stumble up a hill into a trap because his eyes were sweat blinded and his mind intent on his tortured, wheezing lungs. As before, we cooked only at midday, and that with sheltered fires of dry wood. Frequently we did not cook at all and contented ourselves with grain mashed into water and spiced. Twice we netted fish from the river and filleted them, "cooking" them in the sour juice of a fruit native to the region. Despite all the caution, we reached the flatlands in shorter time than my Finding had taken, and in less than half the days it took the massive second expedition to mark the same point. Then we moved with even greater caution, since there was little cover but the copses of trees and occasional folds in the ground.

Four days after passing where I'd arbitrarily decided grasslands had become desert, we encountered the slavers. As before, their outriders appeared and flanked our course. Janos called a halt and drew me aside. "We have a choice," he said. "We can either wait until they attack us, either magically or in person, and then deal with the situation . . . or we strike first. It is my mind to do the latter. I have had quite enough of these skulking nomads. In future days, they or their brothers will harry caravans and travelers to the east, and be a continual plague. I believe we should set a terrible example now, so that in days to come no one will dare trouble travelers from Orissa."

I hesitated, thinking surely there must be a way to avoid such slaughter: we might lose them or find some other means to trick them. Then I bitterly recalled how *kindly* we had been treated on the Finding, and how even more *charitable* the slavers would have been if we had surrendered rather than attacked. Then I thought of Deoce: rage rose red, not entirely directed at these no-mads. "Do what you will," I snapped, and to this day I am some-times troubled by that decision.

"Good. We shall annihilate these hyenas," he said. "But not solely by force of arms. We shall use other, more convincing tools." We changed course, now traveling toward the slavers' out-riders, but directly, not wishing to give even a hint of our intent. Before dusk they galloped off into the distance. But we could see where they were headed—toward another oasis where the remain-der of their party would be encamped, waiting.

"We will take them as they sleep," Janos said. He ordered us to give him our daggers. In the sand he drew a V that was pointed toward the oasis. A second, shallower V closed the open end of his figure, so that it now looked like a spear- or arrowhead. There was no pretense that Janos was not spell casting, or that he was not serving as an Evocator, even though such acts were still for-bidden to all Orissans who were not Evocators. He drew a large circle below the spearhead and placed all of our daggers in it—points toward the center. Next, he took practice arrowheads from our quivers and laid them in the circle in the same manner, their small heads touching the dagger tips. He took a pack from one of the asses, a pack that contained some of the supplies he'd ac-quired in his travels. At the three tips of the spearheads in the sand, he imbedded tiny wooden wedges. He spoke words, and the three wedges smoked and flamed, without ever being consumed. Then he carefully lifted a vial from the pack and unsnapped the two catches holding its lid in place. Ten feet away, the smell from that vial hit us, and I almost retched. The stink was long-rotten meat, from what creature I did not care to guess. Janos laid a bit of this corruption at the center of the dagger ring, then quickly covered the vial and walked back to us. The reek seemed not to bother him.

He considered his work thoughtfully. "A bit of blood would help," he mused. "But not from one of us. That would give a wrong indicator. Perhaps ... yes. You. Lione. Take this measure"—and he handed the swordsman a minuscule gold cup from the pack of sorcerous implements—"and bleed one of the asses. Take no more than is required to fill it." I saw Lione's hand shake as he took the cup. But he obeyed orders without question and soon the ass's blood was sprinkled across the dagger blades. Janos stood behind the circle and began his incantation. As usual, it consisted of unknown words—names of gods, perhaps, or just a foreign, wizardly tongue?— interspersed with phrases I could make out. "This is ... gift ... beyond life ... death ... worm corrupts ... And dies itself ... gift ... The White Peace ... beyond ... Until the jackals come." The small tapers flared ... then went out.

Janos turned back to us. "The spell is complete. Each of you take your blades, and the men who carry bows divide these arrows among you. Under no circumstances, until I cast a counterspell, use either arrows or blades for any purpose; and make very sure—as you value your life—not to cut yourself. We will watch until their camp fires burn down. Then we shall close on them. If they have sentries, I promise you they will not see us as we approach. We will take position on this side of their camp. Each archer is to select a target, and then, on my signal, hit the man with your dart. Then we attack. Do not use any weapon other than your daggers unless you must. You will need but to touch an enemy for him to be destroyed. I will indicate one person in their camp. I will be responsible for him. Do not harm that man, or you shall face my wrath later. Now. We shall eat and rest."

Late that night we crept out from our camp toward the oasis. Again, I thought of Deoce, and my eyes blurred. The boil of anger caught me, and I became nothing but a long knife and a silent shadow. Whether by caution or by a spell, the two sentries indeed did not see us. Janos indicated one to Lione, and he took the other. Both sentinels went down without a sound. We moved on

to the camp. There were no tents pitched, and the fifteen or so nomads slept peacefully, using their saddles for pillows. One man
snored some distance from the others, and this man Janos indicated for himself. The bowmen readied themselves ... and Janos'
hand flashed down. The arrows, little more than toys, arced out.
We shouted once and charged. A half-fuddled man arose in front
of me, trying to fight free of his blankets, and my blade sank
home—body forgetting Janos' orders to but touch an enemy. Another nomad stumbled across my path, shouting pain from a
gashed arm. I prepared to finish him ... and before my eyes he
collapsed. Dead ... and I saw him putrefy. In an eye blink, what
should have taken days or weeks to occur happened—the body
swelled, bloated, burst, blackened, and then the flesh withered,
until there was nothing but a skeleton lying on the sand. This,
then, was what Janos' spell had called the White Peace.

I recovered, looked for another enemy, and saw a slaver bounding toward the darkness beyond. An arrow whispered past and
touched but his arm before ricocheting away. That man, too,
shrieked, died, and rotted. Then there was only one man left alive
among all those foul corpses: their chief, on his knees and writhing in terror in front of Janos.

Janos ordered him tied to a nearby palm. "You speak the trader's language?" he asked. The man nodded. "Look well, then.
This is the fate of those who are my enemies. This ... or worse.
You are permitted a chance to live. Not because I would not love
to see your bones gleaming like the rest of your pack, but because
I wish the tale to be told to all your people of what happens to
those who stand against Orissa. I am the first ... but there will be
others traveling this same route. Remember what happened tonight, and stand well clear of my people. Do you understand?"

The man gabbled understanding. Janos took a small eating
knife from his pouch and imbedded it in the sand about three feet
in front of the tied man. "I shall leave one horse tethered, and one
water bag. If you can stretch far enough, you can reach this knife
and cut yourself free. Then ride off ... and carry the word."

He motioned and we left the camp, after ensuring one mount
was securely tied, the others driven into the night, and all the food
and water, except for one skin, taken for our own use. No one
spoke—less from a desire to impress the slaver than horror at
what we had done. No doubt Janos would have some rationale for
what had happened, but this, to me, was sorcery of the blackest
sort, and there would be a stain on all our souls for this night.

By the time the counterspell was cast that returned our knives and the remaining arrows to normal, it was close to dawn. We forced food down, packed the asses, and started off. We had gone but a sixth of a league when we heard the screams. Screams of a horse, and then a man. We saw great scavengers dropping into the oasis out of nowhere. They were huge, but from this distance no one could tell if they were vultures, eagles, or kites. The screams of the horse and slaver rose, then were cut off. This desert was nothing but death, I thought, never having heard of any carrion eater attacking a healthy man or horse. Janos swore—his example would not be as effective as he wished—and he muttered that the final words of his spell might have even brought these creatures on. This was the first time he had tried that casting.

A bit later we saw a black cloud rise out of the oasis as the scavengers finished their meal. They flew toward us, then veered away. I squinted, trying to see what these monstrous birds were, and gasped as if I'd once more been plunged into that winter mill-pond in Orissa. Others shouted or swore in horror as well. The carrion eaters were a distance away, but we could see they were not birds or even some kind of bat who flew in the daytime. They were human, or at any rate, of human form: each had a manlike torso, legs, and I thought I could discern arms and a head. Their wings were not as large as they should have been, and I wondered if sorcery helped them keep aloft. Maeen strung his bow and sent a war arrow lofting at them. It was a fair shot, into the center of the flock, and they broke formation as doves do when hit by the shafts of hunters. But Maeen's arrow did not appear to have struck their mark. A soldier with eyes keener than mine saw something fall, which I thought to be Maeen's arrow, as the nightmare fliers disappeared into the distance. Some minutes later we came to where the object had come to rest, and one of the men ran over and brought it back, face pale. It was a human hand. I picked up a bit of sand and sprinkled it as we marched away. Not even a slaver deserved to wander as a ghost in *this* desolate region.

Days later we saw the rise of the butte that had been our brief paradise on my Finding. We did not approach, holding to our plan of never repeating our track, but kept it in sight as an aid to navigation. Janos was trying to use magic as little as possible in this area to avoid detection. All of us still felt those watchful presences . . . but no one felt directly threatened as yet. We found the creek that ran from the magical crater and refilled our waterskins.

Janos cast another spell over the party. He used two boughs from the creekside willows to make an arch. He made his Evocation, and a small whirlwind spun up in the center of that arch just to its peak. He ordered each of us to pass through the whirlwind. He chortled as the sand got in our eyes, ears, and hair. He also had our animals led through in the same fashion. They hated it, as much for the sorcery they felt around them as for the dust. When we were done, he explained: the wasteland we were entering was magic-blasted. This was where we would be most likely to be spotted. Anyone looking for us by sorcerous means would, he was sure, now see nothing but a not particularly striking sandstorm or just a succession of whirling dust devils.

Maeen had a question. "What, sir, if some of the Watchers are in our path? Will they see us?"

"I do not know, Sergeant," Janos said. "I am certain my spell will blind any sorcerous vision, but I do not know if the Watchers are physical beings or not, nor even how they 'see.' If we spot any of them, my advice is to make the asses kneel, and cover yourselves and them with your robes. Then attempt to think like a sand dune."

Another question came, this from Hebrus, our music teacher. "Sir Greycloak, have you still no idea who or what is looking for us? I would have hoped by this time you might have found some clues—just as I can tell which of my dullard students is approaching by the tuneless way he thumps his lyre."

Janos shook his head. "I still don't know. Perhaps one, perhaps many. Of course the Archons of Lycanth are our enemies, and have almost certainly set out wards. Nisou Symeon of Lycanth can well afford to send the best Evocators after us. Perhaps, even, someone from Orissa. Not all the Evocators in our city accepted the change." He shrugged. "Mayhap the gods themselves. Or the wizards of the Far Kingdoms."

"I thought th' Far Kingdoms was holy," Lione said. "Not holy, mebbe, but, well, like I grew up bein' taught th' Evocators was. Good. Wantin' to make th' world better. Helpin' folk."

"So the tale is told," Janos said, "and I have no reason to doubt it. But if you were as powerful as the rulers of the Far Kingdoms, would you not post the finest sentries around your riches, and investigate closely any who approached you?" Lione's expression, which had resembled a child who's about to be told fairies do not live at the bottom of the garden, changed, and his relief showed plain.

So shielded, we set out across the blasted land. We encountered no troubles beyond those of a physical nature. The creatures of the pit, now that we were aware of them, were no threat, and I was pleased at our progress. I found myself once becoming just a bit jealous of Janos. He was behaving as if he was the sole commander of this expedition. I stopped myself and turned my mind away—scolding it for giving in to fatigue. This belonged to none of us yet to all of us. If he preferred to walk in front, he had at least as much right as I did. Possibly more, since my rank was hereditary and his, even though it was lesser, hard earned. The mind, when tired, falls prey to many such dark thoughts.

Our intent had been to make a stop at the Rift valley and rebuild our strength for a few days. But either our positioning or our maps were in error. We reached the area of low rolling hills where we should have caught sight of the cleft, but saw nothing. We checked our navigation, both against the stars that night, and the sun's position in the morning, and even recounted the knotted strings used to keep track of the number of paces traveled each day. We should have been within a dozen spearcasts of our friends. But there was nothing. I checked the map I had made on our Finding, and it verified our locations. But there was simply nothing there. Janos and I agreed we must be south of the valley. We chanced two days' travel to the north, found nothing, and returned to our former track. The men were displeased—both Maeen and Lione had told them of the valley and its pliant women. But they were near as dedicated as Janos and I, and we continued on—with no more than wistful thoughts of what we'd missed.

But then all thoughts of disappointment dissolved in excitement when the first man spotted the great mountain range. The Fist of the Gods. Even I felt wonder stir when I saw the pass between the "thumb" and "forefinger" that led through that black range. But caution soon overtook wonder: we were in the dangerous territory; doubly so, since we also knew the city of Wahumwa lay in front of us. We moved most carefully, taking as long as four hours to travel a single league, even though the ground was fairly open. We avoided all ruins, fearing they could be guarded by spells or men.

I called a halt for a council of war when Janos estimated we were a half day's travel from Wahumwa. We had still seen no sign of their cavalry or scouts or even citizens. The problem was that the treacherous city sat athwart the only approach to the pass. After some thought, we determined to get as close to the city as possible during daylight, then go to ground. We would wait and watch, then use darkness to slip around the city's walls and into the mountains. If the approach was that tightly patrolled we would break the party into four groups, as we'd practiced, and each group would have an entire night to make passage. Janos added that I should go with the first group, and set up a forward post. He would go back and forth each night, and guide each of the groups. I thought again of my egoism back in the wasteland and was ashamed to have allowed jealousy of a man volunteering to shuttle like this just to ensure the safety of others.

We journeyed onward, and at last we climbed the last foothill. Beyond lay Wahumwa, Janos said. He went forward with Sergeant Maeen. Maeen would return if the rest of us needed to come up. He should have been back within minutes, but almost an entire glass passed. I could wait no longer; drawing my sword, I went in the direction they had taken, dodging from cover to cover. Perhaps my friends had been captured. I came out of a thick brush and saw them. They stood on the edge of a crest, in plain sight of any one in the valley—and city—below. I feared they had been caught in a spell. I hastened forward, not sure what I would do if they were ensorcelled and turned on me. I came closer—and then saw what had paralyzed them.

"That," I said, incredulous, "is Wahumwa?"

Both men spun—they'd not heard me approach, and Janos' hand was on his sword hilt. They relaxed then. "It is," he managed.

"Or was, anyway," Maeen put in.

There *was* a city below us, but it was in ruins; its great wall had crumbled in many places. Trees grew up, blocking roads both inside and outside the city. There had been tall, monolithic buildings, as great as any in Lycanth, inside the walls. Time and the weather had broken them, and the roofless buildings stretched stone fingers at the heavens.

I started to stammer questions, but Janos just shook his head, very grim. "There was a spell cast," Janos said, almost in a whisper. "A Great Spell, indeed. Call the men up. I will . . . I *must* enter the city."

Sergeant Maeen recovered and ran back for the rest of the party. They, too, stood in amazement, until Janos ordered us to march and for everyone to keep his weapon ready. We went through the gates at dusk. Wahumwa *had* been great once—the gates themselves were iron-bound, solid marble slabs, now broken and hanging from rusted hinges. The cobblestones themselves were monstrous, the size of a charabanc. Now, grass, low bushes, and even some trees grew between them. The buildings would have been lofty, and the avenues broad. Now . . . nothing but ruins. A few hundred yards more, and there would be nothing but rubble. Janos led the way, seeming to know where he was heading. We left the central thoroughfare and went up an overgrown roadway, toward a huge shattered building on a hilltop. Maeen was pale—he knew, and I sensed, where Janos was taking us; but the grip on his blade was steady.

We entered the hall, and men cried out. I had known what to expect, but it was still grisly. The chamber was full of the bones of men, lying amid the rotten ruins of furniture. Skulls were broken, and the bones were scattered, with not a single skeleton being whole. "Vultures, and wild dogs, must have come . . . afterward," Janos said. He picked up a leg bone and showed it to me. It had been neatly split open by a gourmet and sucked for the marrow. "But no wild dog can do this." He threw the bone away, and it clattered on stone. "As I said on the hill beyond, a Great Spell was cast. Cast before the expedition reached the city."

"Everyone we encountered, everyone we lived with," Maeen said hoarsely, "was . . . what?"

Janos shrugged. "Ghosts? Demons, even. Perhaps less than that; perhaps just the details a great sorcerer would add to an enchantment—like an artist would put details in a painting to convince you he really *had* sat at a banquet of the gods."

"But . . . but you've th' talent," Maeen managed. "How could they hoodwink you, too?" Janos had no answer to that, either. I had never heard of wizardry this strong. Compared to this, Orissa's feat of magically tearing down Lycanth's wall was a marketplace curiosity. To first make more than a thousand hardbitten soldiers see a city where there were ruins . . . to fill those ruins with people and animals . . . and for each of those illusions to walk, talk, drink, and even make love . . . and then, in a night of blood, to kill and then eat? Especially when that death meal was nightmare, not illusion? This was an impossibility. But it was.

I shuddered. "We shall not sleep in this city, Janos, nor spend any more minutes than it takes us to flee," I said firmly. "We are leaving immediately. No man is to touch anything he does not have to, nor is he to take anything, not bone, not branch, not stone, from this cursed place."

No one argued. Trying not to bolt in terror, we struck straight through the city to its outer gate, to where the road began climbing to the pass through the Fist above us. None of us, not the soldiers, not me, not Sergeant Maeen, nor Janos Greycloak, dared look back.

CHAPTER TWENTY
The Disputed Lands

THE PASS THROUGH the Fist of the Gods was nearly as smooth as it had looked when Janos and I had first seen it from many leagues. It climbed around the "knuckle" of the forefinger, into the heart of the mountains. As before, and unlike the vision, the Fist was snowless. Remembering Janos had attempted several reconnaissances before, when the second expedition was wintering below in Wahumwa, I asked how far he had gotten before being driven back, by snowstorms, I assumed.

"I did not reach this point," Janos said. "Not by far. However, it was not snow that blocked my way, but gales and driven ice storms. In the winter, hard winds blew across these peaks, so snow didn't cling to the rocks for long."

Our passage was easy: it would not take an athlete to negotiate this defile, I noted with pleasure, since few traders maintain their bodies with anything other than roasts and vintage wine. It would also be simple for heavily burdened beasts, even horses, to cross this range, beasts carrying Orissa's trade goods to the Far Kingdoms. Rock slides had tumbled from the heights, and boulders littered the ground, but since the pass was almost two spearcasts wide, it was simple to avoid these obstacles. There was a small waterfall splashing down, and I saw where someone had laid rocks to make a pool. This route had been traveled before . . . and would be again.

Our path led up and around the mountain. We could no longer see the valley and the cursed city behind us. The way grew narrower. I began to worry that perhaps we were following a blind alley, in spite of the pool we had seen, but was relieved to see the pass widen up ahead.

Janos was walking in front of the column, and I was just behind him, the rest of the party and the animals strung behind. I
spun as gravel clattered from above; one of our archers had a
shaft nocked and was looking up. We saw nothing but bare gray
rocks. Probably it was nothing, but we became more cautious.
Where the pass widened, it also steepened, and I found myself
breathing hard. The track crested ahead, and I resolved we would
pause when we reached that crest, where two boulders sat in the
center of the passage. Eagerness ran through our veins, but as
Maeen had told us over and over again, haste produces only "accidents, ambushes, and wedlock—all of which are to be avoided."
Proof came shortly. Panting, I was paying less attention to anything but my next step when someone shouted a warning. I saw
one of those two huge boulders at the crest rolling toward us. It
picked up speed, crashing from side to side of the pass, as it hurtled down. But the warning had been timely, and we were able to
pull ourselves and our animals out of its way with no damage.
The boulder rumbled into the distance and was gone. I hurried to
Janos.

"Boulders," he said, pointing out the obvious, "do not move of
themselves."

He ordered all archers to string their bows, and put four of
them behind me, each with instructions to scan a particular area
above us. He also brought Lione up, to march as second man in
the party. We moved to the crest, hoping to see the land open out
and reveal the great cities of the Far Kingdoms. Instead, we saw
more mountains and the pass climbing on into the distance.

We examined the ground carefully where that boulder had sat
for so many aeons before choosing its moment. There were no
scratch marks from a lever or pry bar that would indicate a human
agency had sent it careening down. Perhaps purely coincidence or,
I was beginning to suspect, sorcery. Perhaps we'd been located by
our unseen enemies. But none of us, especially Janos, felt any
brush of wizardry. We moved cautiously through the gorge. The
pass closed once more into a deep-V choke ahead, then the defile
opened, climbing toward another false crest. We were just in the
middle of the narrow way when the heavens rumbled. I thought
thunder and looked up at the clouded sky. Then I saw its cause:
an avalanche was cascading down on us. I shouted, one of myriad
cries, and broke into a run, knowing I must escape the trap; I must
flee to where the draw opened again as house-size stones and
monstrous slabs rumbled down. The last of us—Maeen bravely
bringing up the rear—had just cleared the danger area when the

slide crashed across the pass, rocks shattering in demonic cacophony.

Slowly the crashing stopped, the ringing echoes died across the mountains, and the dust settled. Ashamed of my moment of fear, I collected myself and did a fast count. Te-Date be praised—and I determined to make real sacrifice once on the other side of these mountains—all of us had survived, as had all our beasts of burden. The avalanche had been launched a little late. No one was willing to believe in two accidents from above just minutes apart. At least we were safe here—the rock walls that gently sloped up on either side of us were scoured clean of boulders. I was about to ask Janos how we would continue—was there a soldierly plan on moving through passes, as there seemed to be for everything else—when there came a bellow like the mountains themselves were shouting.

That is when we saw the giant. It is common for large men to be called giants, and for any tribe whose height exceeds the norm to be called giants. But this was truly such a being. Even allowing for the magnification from the mountain air, he was three times the height of a tall Orissan, and at least as broad as a man was tall across his chest. At first he might have been taken for some enormous ape, since he appeared to be fur-covered. He was a bit more than a spearcast in front of us. Weapons came up, and the giant ducked behind a boulder. He shouted once more, in his unknown tongue, and it might have been a lonely mountain wind. As we jumped for cover of our own, I found I had recovered my calm.

Coldly, I was considering what had occurred. "I wager," I said, "he is telling us to go back, to get out of 'his' mountains."

Janos nodded agreement and barked orders—of course the military had a procedure for opposed movement through a pass. "There will be more than one," he was telling Maeen. "Most likely they will be up above, providing cover for their comrade."

Maeen nodded understanding as Janos laid out the plan. I said nothing, but listened with half my mind, while considering my first thought; it still made sense. Janos had detailed three men, including himself, Maeen, and the closest thing we had to a mountaineer—our wall-climbing music teacher, Hebrus—for a special duty; and given the others specific orders as to what to do and when to do it.

"We are ready, Lord Antero," he said, reverting to military formality as he not infrequently did when problems loomed and our soldiers were within earshot. "Will you take charge of the main party? The three of us will signal when in position and wait for your reply."

"Janos . . . you may think me either mad, or suddenly stricken with sentiment," I said. "Come aside."

I drew him away and laid out my very different strategy. He frowned. "I do not like it," he said, after he'd given my scheme a polite few seconds of pretended consideration. "If you are attacked . . . all that we have accomplished so far will be ruined."

"No, it will not be," I said. "If the worst occurs, then you are in charge of the expedition and may take any measures necessary. You will not be questioned later. I left such orders with Rali, my brothers, and with Ecco. You not only can speak with my voice, but for the people of Orissa, as well, to as great a degree as I am empowered."

Janos looked away. His voice was thick with emotion. "You . . . you have honored me, and my family, beyond measure. But"— and he turned back— "what happens if that overgrown gibbon up there does harm to you? What an imbecile thing to have happen, when we are this close to our dreams."

"I am not that worried," I said firmly. "I have two good reasons. First, that creature warned us rather than immediately trying to obliterate our party. I also wonder if that avalanche was in fact intended to strike, or was in fact a first caution? Second, I refuse to be terrified of someone who is naked."

There was a third reason I did not mention. The annihilation of the nomads still bothered me. I did not see my mission in life was opening the Far Kingdoms by cutting a wasteland as I went.

"I still think you are being unwise," Janos said.

"Very well," I said. "I am being unwise. Now, what I wish you to do is as you had planned, except you are to wait for a signal from me—or for that creature to attack—before striking. Now it will be even more imperative the three of you not be seen as you move."

"There shall be no problem there," Janos said. "But I must warn you, my friend, if you are killed in this absurd bit of benevolence, I shall speak to you very harshly."

I grinned, clapped him on the back, and set the plan in motion. Janos, Maeen, and Hebrus slid to the rear and then disappeared up a narrow ravine, while the rest of us milled about as a distraction. We waited for nearly an hour. The giant made no further move, other than shouting once more for us to retreat. Beyond that, he seemed content to wait until winter arrived to drive us away. This I found to be another indication that the creature might not be wholly malevolent. I spent my time sorting through various packs, trying to decide what might work with giants, never having dealt with the breed before. I also remembered one immutable characteristic all giants seemed to have in every tale my nurses told, and was further cheered.

At last our keenest-eyed man, who we had set to keep watch on a certain scrubby bush, reported it had moved . . . slightly. I stripped off my coat and weapons belt and rolled up my shirtsleeves, shivering in the mountain wind. I walked forward with the leather case that contained my chosen items. The giant sprang to alertness and shouted at me. I did not reply, but walked very slowly onward. He bristled and wavered, exactly like a house cat not sure whether to flee or not. The closer I got, the less pretty my friend appeared. His thick body hair curled around him like a flea-bitten pelt, and from his constant scratching, I am sure he had them roaming on his body. He was misshapen, with larger hands and feet than even his monster body entitled him to. His head was equally massive and elongated, with a lantern jaw. Yellow teeth, fangs almost, hung over his lower lip. He rose to his full height, brandishing an enormous club. It looked to have been the trunk of a young tree, its branches ripped off and the bark crudely polished off against rocks. I came no closer. The giant was sweating profusely, as if we were back in the desert rather than on these chill heights. He also stank abominably, so badly I nearly became sick. I paid no attention to the pleadings of my overly civilized nose—a trader who dictates social customs to his customers is not only foolish but apt to be handed his teeth as a rebuttal. I set the chest down and opened it, carefully lifting out my articles. My arms were bare, to show I concealed nothing, and I moved very, very slowly. The giant seemed to relax. I sat, legs curled under me, as if I were a common bazaar merchant, and waited. The giant did not move. He *was* a primitive sort.

I chose one item, set it on a flat rock, and depressed the twisted rod that rose from its center. Obediently, the mechanical top spun, its colors flashing brightly against the gray rock. I heard a grunt of interest. Next I picked up a gold necklace, and wincing a bit as I recollected its worth and that it had been intended to hang from the neck of a princess, draped it over my wrist. Then I gently cast it toward my about-to-become trading partner. He drew back, startled. The necklace did not attract him. He crept forward, picked it up, examined it, muttering to himself, then put it on his own wrist. He looked at it this way and that, then chortled in approval at his new bracelet. Next he began looking about him. The fairy tales were correct—giants were no brighter in reality than they had been presented, since it took him long moments to realize there was very little around for trading stock. After considering rocks and even a bit of lichen growing from one boulder, he decided on an item. He set his club down where the necklace had been. Now I was quite sure we were in no especial danger. I shook my head, no, I did not want the club, and motioned that the necklace was a present. He came closer. I saw *his* nose wrinkle in distaste and nearly smiled, remembering my father told me he once traded with men so primitive they *never* bathed or changed the skins they wore until they rotted away, and considered the smell of a clean human being nauseating.

Other items were presented: some he disliked, such as perfumes; others he liked, such as a small silver figurine that I cradled like it was a child. He laughed once more and took the figure. I guessed it would become a doll for his, or another giant's, child. Gold chains were accepted. But the great success was a box of sweetmeats I'd put in as an afterthought. He inhaled the entire box, looking about him warily like any guilty child who was being selfish in not sharing with his playmates.

When all my presents had been accepted or rejected, I stood and motioned to myself, then back at my companions, and then waved my hand toward the track beyond. Fingers mimed walking ... I sought permission to go by. He grunted and then bellowed. From high above came answering shouts. The giant stood, showed me more tawny fangs in a friendly smile, and indicated the way was open. There was but one small other matter. I called out. The giant looked mildly alarmed, then terrified as Janos, followed by Maeen and Hebrus, bows in hand, arrows nocked but not drawn, appeared on the ridge line just above where we stood. Before the giant could snarl betrayal, the three men, following my instructions, set the bows down, ceremonially snapped their arrows in two, and cast them down toward us. Even my less-than-gifted compatriot understood—we could have killed him, but chose not to. The broken arrows were also intended to signify that we had intentions for peaceful passage now ... and in the future as well. The giant laughed, at what I could not tell, picked up his gifts, and bounded up the side of a nearby draw. Janos and his partners slid down from the ridge line, and we re-formed and went on our way. We saw no more signs of the giant or of his colleagues.

That night Janos approached me. "I have learned something," he said ruefully. "A sword is not *always* the best way to untie a stubborn knot." I shrugged it away—success with one peaceful and stupid being did not mean we should in any way lessen our caution. But I did note that Janos had changed. I thought the Janos who had accompanied me on my Finding might just as easily have suggested negotiation instead of bloodshed, but perhaps I was wrong. In any event, we had overcome another obstacle with no loss to ourselves.

One thing of which I am extremely proud is that the "treaty" I made between Orissa and the giants has stood from that day to this. Caravans traveling the mountain route take care to bring presents, or else avalanches threaten or even block the pass. No one has ever seen more than the one giant, if indeed it is the same one I gifted. And his or his tribe's desires have waned over the years. Now all they wish are candies, the sweeter the better. Everything else is rejected by these odd and still unstudied beings.

IT TOOK THREE days for us to reach the central peaks of the great range, and then the pass began winding downward. We journeyed on for two more days before we saw what lay beyond. To our great disappointment, there were no cities of gold below. Instead, there were a seemingly endless number of mountain valleys, reaching in all directions. We were dismayed—could we be on some kind of journey that would go on, and on, and on, until we died of old age on this trail? But we kept marching, following the pass. We would decide which route to take once we reached flat land. But there was no decision necessary—the pass narrowed into a gorge. A spring gushed, other waters cascaded, and we were moving beside a rapidly growing mountain stream. I wondered what would happen when the river now aborning devoured the canyon's floor. When it did, we knew we were still on the right track. A road began, a road cut into the very face of the mountain. It had been sliced into the living rock—a precise groove twenty feet high by twenty feet wide. Here and there were hollows cut deeper into the rock so caravans could pass or camp at nightfall. It followed the river, keeping a stone's cast above the high-water marks. Steps were cut down the rock face so water-skins could be filled. None of us, not even Janos, had seen or heard of such large scale work being attempted by anyone in the lands we called civilized.

It rained frequently, but the rock overhead kept us as dry as if we were walking through a covered bridge. We were almost sorry to reach the valley floor, where we lost our rain blanket, although moving through green and living things delighted the eye and more than compensated for our regular drenchings. Now we followed a stone track that wound through the valley. We debated the wisdom of using the track, but had little choice: to either side grew dense, junglelike brush and trees that would take us weeks to hew our way through, and the sound of our chopping would carry very far indeed. We also slept on the road, having found another danger on our first afternoon. I had instructed the scout to begin looking for a campsite, and he had found one: a small hollow that beckoned off to the side. There was also a pool for drink and bathing, trees we could camp under, and tender grass for the animals. Janos was directing the unloading when I saw the vale move. It was as if the grass had come alive and was on the march toward us. Leaves on the trees waved in the still air. I thought it must be sorcery, and then my stomach turned in fearful disgust when I saw what caused the motion: leeches. I had never seen any so large—these were twice the length of a man's hand. Scenting blood, they were humping toward us like an army of ants at an alarming rate. Other leeches were hanging from the trees themselves—the beckoning "leaves" I had seen. It was a place that turned the bravest hero into a sniveling coward, and we moved on with much haste. We slept in the center of the roadway that night, but only after Janos had cast an aversion spell. Even so, it was necessary to light a small fire the next morning and use burning twigs to sear away a few of the bloodsuckers who had found us and somehow avoided the spell. They were fat and bloated with our blood. When they fell away, the wounds they had caused bled freely and required bandaging.

A few hours later the Watchers found us. The valley had broadened, and the river had shallowed and curved close to where the jagged mountains climbed. The road shot straight across the valley like a javelin cast, and we could see for a long distance. It was hot and still. I remember cicadas buzzing in that lazy mountain summer. Then ahead of us, horsemen came around a curve. From the gleaming armor on both man and horse, I instantly knew who they were. There were at least twenty of them: more than we had ever seen before. They spotted us before we could move off the road into cover. Their leader's lance tip dropped as he couched the butt. I could see gauntleted hands brush over helms, knocking visors closed. But we did not hear the expected clang of the armor, shouts of commands, or even the clatter of hooves against stone as the ghostly patrol broke into a trot toward us.

"Company size," Janos noted. "If they are planning to attack without parlay, their commander will order them to the gallop just after they enter that dip in the road and we lose sight of them."

This was another situation we had trained for. Men pulled specially made spear extensions from the asses' packs and connected them to the iron sockets we had put on each spear butt. Six men knelt at the roadside, spears bristling up at an angle, their shields raised. Behind them were archers and then our animals, with one man to steady two mounts. The rest of us drew our swords, ready to respond where and when needed. Even though we bristled like hedgepigs on the alert, we were not setting up an inevitable confrontation: if they chose, the Watchers could halt or even ride by us without engagement. "Hold your position," Janos cautioned. "Don't worry ... and don't run. There isn't a horse in life or legend who will charge a spear wall. Hold ... hold ..." His voice was as unworried as if this was yet another drill at my estate.

The column trotted into that fold in the ground and was out of sight. "Now," Janos said, "now we shall finally find what intent these men have for us." But we didn't. Seconds became minutes, and the company of horsemen did not reappear from the dip. "How interesting," Janos observed. "There is not even room enough for that many horsemen to rein in without going ass over heaume. Two men! Forward to that dip! Not that you'll find anything."

Just as he had guessed, the two scouts shouted back that the fold was quite empty. "Even more interesting," Janos said, sounding unconcerned. "The first possibility, which I doubt, is that we surprised them by our presence and our readiness to fight. The second is they, or rather whoever orders them, are trying to weaken our resolve. The third, which is only logical, is the commander of that legion is as unsure of us as we are of him. The fourth, which is the one to which I subscribe, is that attempting to second guess a truly great Evocator is like pissing into the wind— satisfying when it begins, but unproductive, messy, and embarrassing as events unfold. Marching order! We move on!" And so we did, with no further excitement. But we journeyed more slowly, wearing armor and keeping our weapons at ready.

On the following day we were ambushed. They had laid the trap well, just where the road passed near a rock formation on one side. On the other, bare ground offered no cover or place to flee, and there was no shelter before or after the site they'd chosen. Their only mistake was that they should have waited until the center of our party was in the killing zone, rather than striking at our scouts. Bowstrings twanged, and two of our men shouted and went down; then spears lofted from the boulders. Someone howled in pain, and our ambushers screamed war cries intended to freeze our blood. We stood, irresolute for a moment, as one of our animals screamed and reared, two arrows buried in its side. I heard Janos shout, "Into them! Into them! Charge, you bastards!" Maeen overleaped one of the wounded men, sword coming out of its sheath, and he ran into the mouth of the ambush. I saw an arrow *chang* off a rock next to him, then he darted behind a boulder. I, too, was running, my blade in my hand, and behind me I heard more shouts, battle shouts this time. I crashed through brush, around a boulder, and a man was there, arm drawing bowstring and loosing, and I do not know where that arrow went as my slash took off his arm. Blood fountained and he cried out. Another man was there, sword up and parrying my cut. I recovered, half falling to avoid his thrust and awkwardly cutting at him. My blade clanged against armor, and I was against his chest, and we swayed together. I forehead butted, smashing his nose, and he reeled back, stumbling. Before he could regain his balance, I lunged into a full bott, my blade burying itself to the hilt in his groin. I nearly lost my sword as he fell, but recovered and put him out of misery. An arrow thudded into the hard ground beside me, and I looked up to see an archer on a boulder just above me; he wore a steel capeline, and his hand was plucking another shaft from his belt quiver and fitting it to bowstring, fingers smoothly drawing back. I saw death in his eyes, death on the tip of that war arrow aimed into my face, as Janos' hurled dagger thudded butt first into his chest. The archer dropped his bow, stumbled back, and crashed down from his boulder. I heard bones snap, and he shouted pain. I was upon him then, and his head went spinning in gore as I cut with all my power.

Then there was no one left to slay. I sagged against rocks and had a short, but quite impressive attack of the shakes. I came back . . . and looked about. Eight enemy bodies were strewn among the rocks. "Eight against twenty," Janos said, with a bit of admiration. "They were not afraid, knowing surprise doubles and doubles once more your force."

He retrieved his dagger and looked at it skeptically. "Why is it," he mused, "in heroic epics when the hero hurls his knife, it always strikes the villain just to the heart? Oh well, at least I hit him. I was quite startled to not impale the boulder itself."

I thanked him. Once again, my life had been saved. Janos smiled and tried to break the tension with a jest. "Actually, the reason I threw that blade was to have the opportunity to discuss that wonderful lunge with which you impaled that first swordsman. It would have scored you a great victory . . . on the mats. If we were in barracks, I would make an example of you for stupid derring-do and put you on the kitchen detail for a week."

"Thank you, Sir Greycloak." I laughed. "You sound like one of my old tutors. Although, come to think of it, he was one of the few who had anything of value to say."

I turned my attention to the bowman and then the swordsman I had killed. I, too, had been hardened by experience, able to evaluate a corpse rather than turn green and then away. "They were well armored, and armed," I said. "All in uniform attire. So they are not bandits. And I don't believe they were the foot soldier's equivalent of our Watchers."

Janos was pale. "I can tell you who they are," he said. "Lycanthians. Look at that man's boots. Or the style of his armor . . . or the hilt on that blade over there. I carried such a sword myself when I first served them."

"But what are they doing *here*? They couldn't have followed us," I said. "They could not have passed us in our journey. Or I do not think so, anyway."

Janos knelt over the swordsman's body and searched it. There were a few coins—Lycanthian—in the man's pouch. "Did you notice," he began, "that even though these men were all Lycanthian, they bore no banner or standard? Nor are there markings on their breastplates." He got up. "Sergeant Maeen!"

"Sir!"

"Have all the bodies stripped. Pile the carcasses. Search their possessions, and bring what you find to me."

"Yes, sir!"

While we awaited the results of Maeen's search, we began the grisly afterwork of a battle. Amazingly, we had lost no one. The first two men struck by arrows would not only live, but quickly heal; although one bled greatly from a wound in his thigh that required several of Janos' spells before it sealed itself, and was then poulticed and bandaged. The other man's wounds were less severe—the arrow had struck completely through his arm, but then blunted itself on his breastplate. The other men who had suffered wounds appeared gory sights, but the sword slashes and a single dagger thrust would quickly heal, especially with Janos' magical art to help speed recovery. The man wounded in the thigh and one other would ride for some days, but everyone else was but walking wounded. The Watchers' appearance had inadvertently prepared us for this ambush. If, indeed, it *was* inadvertent.

My bemused wonderings about the ghostly riders' intent, in spite of Janos' caution against trying to prognosticate a prognosticator, was broken. Sergeant Maeen had found something: it was a small emblem that had been worn on a neck chain. Wordlessly, Janos held it out. I did not need any explanation. I had seen that emblem on the breastplates of soldiers quartering the country outside Lycanth for us. I had also seen it worked in marble in the courtyard of a great estate in the center of that evil city.

It was the house emblem of Nisou Symeon.

THE ROAD LED back to the river and stopped at a series of stone docks intended for small river craft. There were no boats moored there. Janos found a bit of rope hanging from an iron bitt; it was gray and old. It had been a long time since watercraft had harbored in this place. From here we would travel in a manner more familiar to me than this incessant mountain trekking. I was about to order camp set and a working party go out and cut lumber for rafts when I recollected the splinters of the sunken craft Janos had found where the Shore People had once lived.

He was already taking the bits of wood out and preparing his spell. "This is simple," he said as he chalked arcane symbols on the stone landing and drew six closed ellipses next to them. "It is hardly revolutionary to realize anything once part of a whole may become that whole itself. And if the gods smile on my efforts, I shall add a spell of renewal to this casting."

He put a bit of wood into each ellipse and began his spell. I knew what would come next and should have found Janos' skills commonplace by now. But such was not the case. I gave orders to break the animals' packs down into six equal packs, each to contain the same items as much as possible to lessen the catastrophe should a canoe capsize, then returned to the landing to gape like a gossoon. The casting took only a few minutes, then the air shimmered, became hard to look at, and there were six canoes on the dock. But instead of being exact replicas of the gray, waterlogged wreck we'd pulled from the river, these were shiny and new, as if each had just been shaped, sanded, pegged together, and oiled.

This bit of magic, which Janos had dubbed "simple," seemed to awe the soldiers more than other spells had. Janos smiled at this. "Now you see why Evocators perform much of their work in darkness and secrecy. Each witness to my canoe building, once he recovers from seeing the mystic become physical, will wonder why such an event, or others like it, should not be commonplace. Why should his wife, for instance, have to pay a tinsmith to hammer out a new pot when the neighborhood sage could reshape the old one, or even a fragment thereof, with a few words for a copper or two?"

"An excellent question," I said. "Why not, indeed?"

"If you made your living as a tinsmith, or a miner, or a smelter, or a boat builder in this instance, you would certainly know the answer. This might be the conundrum our age may pose—at what point could sorcery, freely available to all, become a force for ill instead of good?"

"Easy answer, sir," Sergeant Maeen said, having approached us quietly. "When we all have magical mansions and live like we're in the Far Kingdoms, we can sit back, order our sprites to open another hogshead of wine, and *then* debate the matter at length."

"At that time," Janos said, amused, "it will be too late."

"Well, sir, then we'll have the answer, won't we? Meantime, we have the loads ready, if you two philosophers are ready to travel."

The canoes were launched, loaded, and we made up crews—making certain someone with water experience was on each craft. The hardest thing was leaving our faithful animals behind. There was provenance enough, and one of the drovers said many of the plants around favored mild weather, so he doubted winter would turn the valley into a frozen wasteland. We had seen no predators that might batten off the animals, and I knew few hunting beasts are stupid or hungry enough to attack the wily ass. Our journey had brought our asses nothing but exhaustion, thirst, pain, and even death. Here, they could grow fat and breed and even bray, as Janos lifted the spell of silence they had been burdened with. But still, when we cast off, and four of the beasts stood on the dockside, gray liquid eyes sorrowing after us, and we heard one great bleat as we floated out of sight, we were silent with guilt.

THE RIVER GREW mightily, as other streams foamed down from their own birthplaces and joined it. Our boats flew downstream, tossing and pitching, spray cascading until sometimes we could not make out our proper course. Again, our speed was both fast and slow. We hurtled down cascades, desperately fending the boats away from knife-deep boulders with our paddles, or sliding down league-long chutes like otters down mud slides. Twice boats capsized, and we spent hours fishing packs and men from the churning waters. By Te-Date's grace, no one drowned.

Sometimes we were forced to beach our craft and laboriously portage them and the packs around rapids or falls too dangerous to chance. Three or four times we had to leave the river entirely, and use ropes to haul our craft up and down cliffs to navigable waters. Despite these difficulties, we not only suffered no new injuries, but our wounded men were becoming as good as new. Then, slowly, as the river grew broader and deeper, it became calmer. Strangely, we still saw no sign of life—not even abandoned villages. Here and there were granite docks such as the one we'd begun this part of our journey from, but the stone roads leading away from these landings were overgrown and forgotten. The country was green and appeared fertile. We could not understand why men had abandoned this land. Then we found both man and a suggested reason for the desolation.

Our ears made the first discovery: first came great booms, as of low thunder. Then crashes, as if we were about to come on a great foundry. Finally, we heard shouts and screams. We rounded a bend . . . and the river turned to blood. A causeway stretched from one bank of the river to a small islet about three quarters of the way across. From the islet a wide bridge arched to the shore. The current quickened, pulling us to that shore; in moments we would be swept under that bridge.

But that was not what we noticed first. First came the bodies. We had happened on the final moments of a battle—a battle that was being waged without any of its combatants taking notice of our six tiny canoes. There were bodies all along the causeway, stacked on the islet, and then high-piled on the bridge itself. Bloody war had been waged across this river. On the far shore, backs against a cliff, the last defenders—or attackers, as they may have begun—were going down into death. I saw a banner so bloody I could not make out its device. There were warriors in a death stand around it. I saw a huge man hewing with a two-handed sword. He had lost his helm or scorned its use, and I could see the white gold of his hair and beard gleam in the sun. A king? A nobleman? Around him were what I imagined the last of his housecarls, and their attackers swept against them again and again, like storm waves on a shore. Then the blond man fell, and his banner swayed and went down, and there were shouts of victory.

Men in my boat were gaping, swearing, groaning, and one or two puking. The water around us was dark, and crimson stained the stonework before us. "Eyes in the boat and on your paddling," I ordered. "Pay heed, or we'll be swept into the abutments. Those with gods, pray we remain unnoticed."

Janos' boat swept up beside mine as the current raced us under the bridge. Above me a man dangled over the parapet, and I saw his eyes stare beyond and his spirit leave just in my single glance. Then we were past. I thought I heard shouts from the bridge, and someone said later that an arrow had been sent after us, but the river slipped around yet another bend, and trees reached up on its banks, and we were safely away.

We sailed on until nearly dark before beaching our craft on a small island in midstream, dragging the canoes well into the brush and out of sight. All of us were fearful and wondering—to see no living sign for so long and then come on such a savage scene.

"Savages is right," Lione put in. "P'raps y' din't see, but there was squads of them, goin' right a'ter th' soldiers, workin' wi' long daggers t' make sure none a th' wounded might want doctorin'. Movin' from one t' another, like they'd been duties off for th' job."

"Soldiers loot," Maeen said.

"They weren't lootin'," Lione said stubbornly. "Just killin'."

"The end of a feud," I suggested.

"Or maybe," Janos said darkly, "these Disputed Lands are well and truly named, if the only victory which counts is that of the worm."

"At any rate," I said, trying to put as cheery a note on the day as I could, "now we know why the Far Kingdoms have not sent out emissaries or traders, if they must travel through lands ruled by butchers like those."

Men brightened at this.

"And now we are reaching some form of civilization, barbaric though it appears," I went on. "The mouth of this river, and the Far Kingdoms themselves, must be very close." I was, of course, guessing at this last.

But a day and a half later, we did find civilization. Or rather, civilization found us. Four long war galleys swept out from an inlet. I counted twenty oars on each side of the green craft, and on their foredecks stood armed men. The prow of each craft had two ballistae mounted, and they were aiming directly at our canoes. We were well and truly trapped. A spade-bearded man wearing armor and helmet hailed us.

"Welcome, travelers," he shouted. "Welcome, guests." His smile was not only mirthless, but quite unwelcoming as well.

CHAPTER TWENTY-ONE
The Wizard of Souls

IT WAS A city like no other: all sound muted, all color unnaturally bright. The dwellings were of pale stone, with only small black holes for doors to mar their faceless features. Red streamers, entrailing down from green-lacquered posts, lined both sides of the eerie avenue.

Our "hosts" had refused to answer any questions as we sailed to the city's port. In fact, they made no comment of any kind and looked away when we addressed them, as if we did not exist. At the port we were handed over to a troop of waiting soldiers, commanded by a dark-visaged captain. Our weapons and other belongings were put on a cart, which followed as they marched us down the city's main thoroughfare. We led the small parade, twenty anxious companions of the road knotted together for strength of spirit. The soldiers flanked around, herding us to our fates. Our new hosts were as silent as the others; except for the drum of their boot steps, dull clank of armor, and the prickles at our necks, you would not have known they were present.

There were few people about, and those men and women we saw moved with no apparent purpose, or stood motionless as stones, staring as we went past. There was no logic to their costumes: some wore rough common togas, others white silk of the rich; mixed in were men in partial soldier's harness, farmers dressed for the field, and beggars in rags. A child looked at me as we went by. I smiled and she smiled back; my stomach gave a wrench, for this innocent had no nose. I began to notice that many others were maimed in some way: an arm missing, or wooden blocks for feet.

I heard Maeen whisper, "There goes an unlucky lot."

Janos leaned close and said, low, "When we reach our destination, follow my lead."

The avenue curved, then ran arrow straight for a tall, blocky building with a huge red chimney on its crown. The chimney belched sparks and black smoke, and a nauseating odor greased the air. As we came closer, I realized the building was larger than I thought. Another lumped in front of it: a structure curved like a hive and with a circular door. A man stepped out of the entrance. He wore a fine red tunic with a small, black badge of authority on his breast. He lifted a hand in greeting; the hand was thumbless and pebbled with finger stumps.

He spoke in a voice accustomed to command. "Good day, gentle wayfarers. My master bids you welcome and kindly offers his renowned hospitality."

"Thank you," Janos said. "And who might your kind master be?"

"Why, his name is known to all," our greeter replied. "It is Lord Mortacious. Ruler of this city, and all the lands of Gomalalee."

"Forgive our ignorance, gentle sir," Janos said. "But we hail from a land so distant, not even your exalted master's name has reached our shores. It will be our honor that we shall be the first to speak it to the multitudes when we return safely to our hearths."

The man replied, "It will be your joy, then, to meet him for the first time. Come. My master awaits at table."

We followed: nineteen silent men, praying for all the gods to aid Janos' wit. I heard the hiss of the great chimney overhead and smelled the foul smoke. Our guide led us to the banquet hall and flung wide the doors. The room was long and narrow and lighted so brightly my eyes were pained. The only decoration was more of those obscene red streamers mounted on the high walls. From one end of the room to the other ran a heavy blackwood banquet table. The table was heaped with many dishes to tempt the palate: roasts of a variety of flesh, platters of whole baked fish, mounds of rich, dark breads, and large crystal decanters of heavy crystal, filled with a red wine so heady its sweet odor filled the room. The food was heaped upon great platters of gold. Forty men sat at this table, and near the entrance there were places set for eighteen more.

At the head of the table, in a green, throne-backed chair, sat a man with the features of a fierce scavenger of the air. He rose when he saw us, lifting his hands so his flowing red robe winged out like that great desert bird. It could be no other than the man who had issued the invitation—Lord Mortacious. He spoke first to his companions of the table. "Gentlemen. We have the honor to host distinguished guests this day." There were murmurs all around: dark or joyous, I could not tell. "Gentlemen, may I introduce you to Sir Janos Greycloak of Orissa." Janos flinched. I felt my own features twitch in stung surprise. I covered, as did Janos. "I believe the man beside him—he of the glorious red hair—is Lord Antero. Also of Orissa." I bowed low, manner calm, mind swirling with fearful questions: How did he know us? What was his purpose?

"We are the ones to be honored, Lord Mortacious," Janos said. I echoed his response. Behind me I heard one of our men cough nervously and Sergeant Maeen's harsh whisper of warning.

Mortacious adjusted the scarf about his neck; it was made of costly black silk. He smiled a smile of lordly benevolence, but his eyes were so smoky and burning with deadliness, I knew him to be a wizard.

"Come sup with us, please," he said, indicating empty seats of honor on either side of his dining throne. "Your men will find places set for them as well by the door." Janos and I walked forward. Behind us, our small party sat where they had been directed. With each step that we took away from our companions, I felt the line of safety stretch thin. Mortacious was most gracious as we took our seats. He fussed with our place settings and poured us each a glass of wine. I murmured thanks and sipped. The wine was so sweet, I nearly gagged, but out of politeness, I forced myself to sip again. This time it was more tolerable, powerful stuff that stoked fires in the belly and smoke in the mind. I vowed caution.

"Tell me, Lord Mortacious," Janos said, "how is it you know of such lowly travelers as ourselves?"

Mortacious chuckled, fingering the black scarf at his neck. "Lowly? I think not. As for my knowledge of you, it is no great trick for a wizard. As ruler of this realm, which many evil men envy, such knowledge is a necessity."

Janos suddenly relaxed; he drank his wine and loudly smacked his lips in pleasure. "To be perfectly frank, my lord, when your men first approached we feared our intentions had been mistook. For we come to these parts by accident, not design. Our purposes are entirely peaceful."

"So you say," Mortacious murmured. "But there is a bloody trail behind you that might indicate otherwise."

"If they had let us pass," Janos said, "they would have lived."

The barbed remark hooked amusement rather than anger. Mortacious smiled. "Exactly, dear Greycloak. Ignorance can be fatal." He topped our glasses. "When I learned of your approach, I was seized with curiosity. I had to meet the men who so ardently sought the Far Kingdoms."

Except for the conversation between Janos and Mortacious, the room was silent. His men made listless motions of eating and drinking; they did not talk with one another, or look this way and that. Down the long table our own friends whispered amongst themselves and shifted restlessly. But I saw they'd had the good sense to help themselves to some joints of meat and bread and were devouring them as if it were their last meal, a thought not far from my own mind as I looked at my still empty platter.

Mortacious caught my look and fussed. "Forgive me, dear sirs, for forgetting your needs. Come, let me assist you in finding a tasty morsel or two."

He carved a thick slab of steaming meat for me, another for Janos, and put them on our plates with much ceremony. A most delicious odor arose to greet my senses and beg me to sup. I cut a long slice and lifted it eagerly to my lips. I paused, confused, as I heard Mortacious give a malicious snigger. Suddenly, the tempting strip became a hissing, wriggling viper; venom dripped from its fangs, searing the table.

"Why, Amalric Antero, you *are* a greedy beggar," Janos said, voice light as a young boy's. "You're always snatching up the best cut. Here—allow me at least *one* bite!" He plucked the snake away with a flourish. "A little undercooked, perhaps," he said. His other hand, fingers arched in a spell-making curve, brushed by the viper's jutting fangs. The snake became a strip of innocent meat again. He popped it into his mouth and washed it down with a glass of wine. "Quite tasty," he said, and cupped a hand in front of his mouth to hide a polite belch.

Mortacious' face turned grim. He plucked at the neck scarf, irritated at Janos' skillful display. But my friend wasn't done. "Why, what manner of dish is that before you, Lord Mortacious?" he cried in mock surprise. He snapped his fingers at the heavy gold plate before our host. Mortacious reared back as the plate became a great golden scorpion, its tail hard arched, sting glistening with venom as deadly as that viper's.

"Come here, my pretty," Janos cooed, and the scorpion sped across the table at a frightening speed and ran up his sleeve. It whipped its sting in anger as he gave it a pat, then became a small, squeaky mouse with soft white fur and a tender pink nose. Janos set it down, saying, "Can't make up its mind, poor thing."

Mortacious hissed and pointed a long, bony finger at the mouse. It gave a sharp squeak and burst into flame; in a moment the mouse had been turned to golden ash. The wizard swept up the ash, then let it sprinkle back down on the table. The particles swirled and then formed back into a plate. I saw that its edge, perfect before, was chipped, but Mortacious was so proud of this final turnabout, he didn't notice. The wizard adjusted the scarf and displayed a wide grin; his teeth made twin groves of yellow gnarled trees. He clearly believed he'd bested Janos.

Janos dipped his head, allowing the victory; but as he made that motion of humility, he slipped his hand into his pocket and quickly out again. "I fear I have no appropriate return," he said with a sheepish smile.

Lord Mortacious reared back and laughed. His breath washed over me; it smelled of the foul smoke outside. "We have had games enough, my friends. Now let us eat and drink our fill. For this promises to be a *most* enjoyable visit." He clapped his hands together; in delight, I supposed, for the mood among his men shifted abruptly. They began to move about, chatting with one another in idle table gossip. I noticed, however, that when they ate it was only a nibble, as if they had supped before our arrival. Here and there I noted features and limbs marred by wounds such as I'd witnessed on the street. Mortacious eyed me, lifted a hunk of bread from his plate, and broke off a small bit. The crumbs tumbled across his robe. He dipped the bread into his wine and slipped it into his mouth. I was suddenly ravenous and fell upon my food like a direwolf. But what was appetizing to the eye was tasteless to the tongue; the meat was dry, and even washed down with wine it remained a hard lump in my belly.

Mortacious gave me a knowing smile, as if he held a malicious secret. "I hope you did not find my jest rude, Lord Antero," he said. He waved at his men. "They make such dull company, I could not resist poking fun at an intelligent man. Your look of astonishment was a rare delight."

"Then how could I take offense?" I replied. "To give innocent amusement to such a gracious host is small repayment for your generosity."

"You are not discomforted in the presence of a wizard?" he asked. He plucked at the scarf, and I saw a brief glimpse of what appeared to be an ugly wound.

"Not at all," I said, wondering if it *was* a wound, what was its cause? "It will make a remarkable tale someday when I relate my adventures to my grandchildren."

Mortacious' mouth stretched into a humorless smile. "If you live to tell it," he said.

"Oh, I fully expect to," I replied. I saw Janos give a slight nod at my correct response. "The gods have been with us thus far in our quest. Although when your men confronted us, I admit I had some doubt." I raised my glass to him. "But once again, instead of trial, the gods permitted me to enter your august company."

Mortacious laughed. "Oh, yes, yes, yes," he hissed in supreme pleasure. "The ways of the gods are a marvel to all, but a blessing to few." He returned my toast, and we both drank. Then he leaned forward, his face assuming a look of great interest. "But do you not fear their wrath, traveling in the company of a man whom some charge has gained his sorcerous skills through blasphemy?"

If he meant to surprise me, he succeeded; if he meant to confound me, he failed. "Why should it, my lord? Was not this undertaking blessed by the Evocators of Orissa—including that aged and holy sage, Gamelan, himself?" Mortacious grimaced and tugged at his scarf, and I could see it was his comfort as well as weakness, betraying emotion he intended to keep hidden.

He turned to Janos, who was busy chewing on his own tasteless repast. "Your friend brings more than redheaded luck to your venture. He brings cool wisdom as well."

"That is what sealed our friendship long ago," Janos said. "More so, even, than his kindly nature and amiable manners."

Mortacious shook his head in mock awe. "A most remarkable partnership for a most remarkable venture. I pray for your sake that it keeps. For when such a friendship sours, it makes a bitter drink." Janos made no reply, but only smiled and sipped his wine. "I have been wondering," Mortacious said, "why you have yet to ask what I know of your goal? You seek the answer to a mystery, but you make no inquiries of the lord whose realm lies closest to the Far Kingdoms."

Janos made his most charming grin; it peeped like a thief from the black thicket of his beard. "I would have, my Lord Mortacious . . . if I thought you would answer."

Mortacious laughed, this time with genuine amusement. "You guessed correctly," he replied. "Few questions are answered with kindness by those who dwell in the Disputed Lands."

Janos shrugged. "It required no crystal gazing, good sir. There were signs of conflict all along the way. And we witnessed a great battle just before your men came upon us. If I lived in a land with as many enemies as you must suffer, I would suspect any questioner as well." Janos made bold, hooked the wine decanter, and poured all around. "There is *one* question, however, that begs an answer, and can cause no harm if I ask it. And that is: why have you called us into your company?"

Mortacious smoothed the scarf. "It is as I said: to satisfy my curiosity."

"And when that has been accomplished?" Janos pressed.

The wizard eyed him, slowly stroking his black scarf as if it were his lover's flesh. The hand was death white against the scarf, fingers, long blind worms. Finally, he answered. "Then you shall pass from my kingdom in safety . . . and with my blessing. But before that hour is upon us, I have questions of my own."

"Ask away, sir," Janos said. "I am but a simple soldier with no secrets but the sweet words I've hoarded to please a maiden's ear."

"If that were so," Mortacious said, "you would not be at my table. And you might have met a different fate at my men's hands." Janos shrugged—point conceded. "I have heard, my good Greycloak," Mortacious continued, "that you were born to wizardry, but have no formal training. Nor were you permitted another sorcerer's company. Yet my informants say you are as skilled as any in the land—and that skill was won solely by hard force of your reasoning powers."

"You were informed correctly," Janos said. "Although my skills may have been overrated. I possess enough to protect myself and my friends . . . and to amuse an amiable dinner companion."

Mortacious brushed this away, impatient with further byplay. "It is your methods that interest me, sir. Others learn by dull rote—you, by testing theory."

"I have had little choice," Janos replied. "No one would give me scrolls to memorize, much less allow entrance to a school for Evocators."

"I have heard of no other mortal man who has accomplished this," Mortacious said.

"That is a fact I could not know," Janos returned. "As you said, no wizard has ever taken me into his confidence."

"Then I shall be the first," Mortacious said. "I have theories of my own. Perhaps they complement yours."

"I am honored, Lord Mortacious," Janos said. He sat back, waiting. His smile was easy, but I saw the wary gleam in my friend's eye.

"Do you think sorcery has some holy purpose?" Mortacious

asked. "A purpose understood only by the gods who give wizardry life? Answer honestly, now. I will not take offense."

"I do not think it holy," Janos said. "I believe magic is as natural as the wind. As common a force as the fire you light when that wind blows cold. And as for the gods—bah. They do not exist . . . except in our minds."

Mortacious frowned. He gave his scarf a hard tug, and once again I glimpsed the wound. "Then why is it when we pray to them, and make sacrifice, those prayers are sometimes answered?"

"Their image helps us focus," Janos replied. "The sacrifice only sharpens that focus. The same with chanted spells. There is no feat of magic I have set my mind to that cannot be accomplished by thought alone. I do not need a god to make a plate a scorpion, or your chanted nonsense to lure it back to its natural state."

Mortacious eyed Janos thoughtfully. "It would be interesting, indeed, to be a wizard such as yourself. No one taught you rules, so you questioned, then made your own. You smash through things that would make others hesitate . . . or turn back. All because you have no fear of gods and penalties; you see no task so difficult that it cannot be accomplished by force of will. Ah, yes, Janos Greycloak. I understand why you alone have come so far."

Janos laughed. "It is a lovely speech, sir, but I detect you heartily disagree."

Mortacious stirred, enjoying himself. "Yes. Yes, I do. I wish it were otherwise, for you do present a pretty view. I admit you have great talent, but it is not so great as you think. As any *true* sorcerer can attest: there are real limits, real fears. I know my Master, and He knows me. We made a bargain, which I keep, and He has granted me powers greater than even a man such as you could dream."

"I assume you make reference to the practice of black sorcery," Janos said. "And you are a servant of one of the gods whose name it is forbidden to speak."

"Does that offend you?" Mortacious asked. He stroked the scarf, features pleasant.

"Not at all," Janos said. "Black or white, it makes no difference in my philosophy. If there are no gods, no holy purpose, what does it matter?"

"Yes. I can see how it wouldn't," Mortacious said. "Marvelous. Simply marvelous. I like how your ideas, no matter how wrongheaded, lead down such a rosy path . . . where we both still meet."

"My own view of the black arts," Janos said, "is they must be practiced with caution. Our beliefs in such things as good and evil have become so deep grained that they present great resistance. I have a theory that when so-called black magic is performed, this resistance causes gradual harm to the practitioner himself. Over time, the sorcerer is weakened, scarred. Possibly even transformed to something not to his liking. Do you find this the case, sir? Are you the same man now as the one who went in that door?"

"Oh, I am better than ever, if anything." Mortacious chuckled. But the chuckle was forced, uneasy.

"Perhaps you take precautions?" Janos asked. "I have thought of a few of my own ... if I should ever attempt such things."

Mortacious gripped the scarf, but feigned lightness. "There are none needed," he answered.

"How enlightening," Janos murmured. His manner was pleasant, but I could see he thought our host a fool who had made a bad bargain. "You said I should speak freely, Lord Mortacious," Janos finally said, "that I would give no offense. Yet, I hesitate to ask the question now uppermost in my mind."

"Have no fear," the wizard said. "Say what you will."

"Your kingdom of Gomalalee lies in a realm of constant warfare. We have seen the wounds your people have suffered. So, I wonder: if your god is so great, so knowing, why has He not given you power over your enemies?"

Mortacious roared laughter. It made a ghastly sound, as if the winds of humor were blowing through that deep cavern where the Dark Seeker dwells. "Oh, but He has, my dear man ... He has." The neck scarf had come loose, and I saw clear the wound it hid from view. It was a putrid, unhealed gash circling his throat. He did not notice my gaze and returned the black scarf to its place. His face was mocking. "What is the greatest power you can imagine, my little wizard?" he asked. "Tell me quick and tell me true."

Janos replied with no hesitation. "To know all things. To be able to lift my eyes from Nature's stitching and see its grand design. I would give all I have—which, in the end, is only my life—if I could have but a single glimpse, one clear understanding."

"Then you *are* a fool," Mortacious said. "For the sum of all things is too large to know. The stitches too numerous for even the gods to count."

Janos made his eyes widen and stroked his beard as if he were in the presence of a great, knowing master. "Then what *is* the answer, my lord? Tell me, please, where my error lies?"

"Why it is as simple as common bread," the wizard said, his

eyes aglow with self importance. "The greatest power a mortal can command . . . is the power over another man's soul."

"I do not understand," Janos said. "Tell me more, pray, to further my education."

But the wizard grew wary, fearing he had said too much. He shook his head, as if wearying of the buzz of little children. He smoothed the scarf, picked up his cup, and drained it. He set the cup down firmly. "I think not," he said at last.

He brushed crumbs from his robe and came to his feet. "I hope you gentlemen have supped well. Now, if you will forgive my rudeness . . . I shall ask you to retire. I pray you find your quarters pleasant, and you sleep an untroubled sleep."

Before he could go, I made bold to say, "Thank you, Lord Mortacious, for your hospitality. I would not want us to overstay it. With your kind permission, we shall depart tomorrow—with deep regret."

The wizard fixed me with those fierce, desert-bird eyes. I did not flinch, but kept a mild look upon my face. "We shall see," he finally said, then swept out. As soon as he was gone, Janos scooped up the crumbs the wizard had discarded and put them in his pocket. He gave me a wink just as the man who had led us to Mortacious appeared. "Come with me, if you please, sirs," he said.

He put all twenty of us in a spacious chamber; it was windowless, and its walls were barren stone. There were cots set up, with soft coverlets that seemed odd amid such barrackslike starkness. There was a large water vessel in the corner, with a dipper hanging from the mouth, and in another corner there was a hole for wastes. As Mortacious' man swung shut the heavy door, Janos signaled us to remain silent. We heard a strong bolt shoot into place; so much for the fiction that we were only guests. Janos crept to the door and ran his hands lightly over the surface. Whatever he learned from the examination pleased him, for he nodded in satisfaction. He turned back to us and made signs there was a listening spell in place. More hand signals sent the men to their cots to feign sleep and brought Sergeant Maeen and me to his side.

"It is as I feared," he whispered. "There is no locking spell on the door. Only the mechanical bar."

"Why is that troublesome, sir?" Maeen asked.

I puzzled with him, for if escape was necessary, or even possible, then the scanty security was in our favor. Then I felt a sudden awful weariness and yearned for the sweet comfort of those soft coverlets. Sergeant Maeen gave an elaborate yawn, and as the uncontrollable urge to ape his actions came upon me, I heard more yawns all over the chamber as our men were similarly affected.

Janos gave Maeen a hard push to jolt him awake. "Fetch some water," he hissed, "and quickly."

As the sergeant stumbled to do his bidding, Janos knelt. I squatted beside him, fighting off sleep. There was no question what had happened: Mortacious had cast a sleeping spell on our food. Janos took the crumbs—the wizard's leavings—from his pocket and spread them on the floor. He leaned close and breathed over them: once, twice, three times. When Maeen returned with the dipper, Janos sprinkled water over the crumbs and made a paste. I saw him struggle with a yawn of his own, as he kneaded the paste into twenty bread pellets. Once more his hand dipped into his pocket, and when it appeared again, I saw his fingers coated with the golden ash from the wizard's plate. He whispered a chant as he sprinkled the ash over the dough pellets, and in dumb amazement I watched the pellets swiftly rise; in a moment they had the appearance and size of small biscuits. Hazy fear enveloped me as Sergeant Maeen sagged down and I felt sleep's dark veil descending.

"Eat," Janos hissed, shoving the biscuit at me. I took it, irritated at being ordered to do anything other than sleep. I bit off a small portion as he demanded, and it seemed so delicious after that awful meal, I had to have more. My mind sharpened with the pleasure of the taste, banishing sleep. Janos raced about, forcing a biscuit into every man's gullet. Soon all were awake and Janos was back by my side. Once more he held a finger to his lips, but this time it was not directed at the sergeant and myself. With that same finger he drew a circle about our heads. He repeated the gesture, and I saw the air begin to shimmer. "Silence," Janos whispered. The shimmer became a swirl. "Silence," he said louder still, and the shimmer became a pale light. Then he bellowed, *"Silence."* But though the shout hammered my ears, it became a dead thing at the barrier of pale light. No echo resounded from the walls or aroused the men, although they watched with anxious interest. "So much for Lord Mortacious and his silly spells," Janos said in normal tones. "Now, we can plot escape in comfort."

"What about the men, sir?" Maeen asked. "Shouldn't they be able to listen as well?"

"The size of the counterspell would alert our host," Janos said. "We must not underestimate this man. He has little wit, but much low cunning, and his powers are as great as any wizard I have encountered. Just because I let him win that little table game, and sniffed out the sleeping spell he cast on our food, it does not mean our continued existence is assured beyond this night."

"It may be difficult, sir," Maeen said, as he put his professional mind to work. "But not impossible. He's got the terrain, and the numbers, I'll admit. However, the demons of surprise are on our side, now. And as for his men—why, most of 'em are walking wounded." he sniffed. "I've never seen such a mangy lot in my life."

But Janos wasn't listening; his brow was furrowed in concentration. Then his skin pearled white. "Oh, what a *fool* I've been," he groaned. "The bastard's tricked me!"

We asked what was wrong. Janos shook his head in fury. "Only try and think of escape, and you'll see for yourselves," he said, voice shaking with emotion. "Think on it hard. Hard as you can. Imagine us fleeing this place. Take it step by step. First the door . . . then into the streets . . . then back down the road they marched us on."

I closed my eyes and followed his directions. The door gave way with ease; soon we were all running along the road toward the harbor. I imagined a likely boat to steal; then just as I had us all aboard and ready to sail, a terrible, unreasoning fear hurled out of some dark corridor in my soul and sank its teeth into my guts. I could not see the beast, but I could smell the mad reek of its presence and feel the hot pain of its fangs burrowing into me. I knew I had only one hope of escape: I fled back down the avenue, back into the building that held us, back into the chamber that was our prison, and slammed that door shut with all my might. I opened my eyes, bile in my throat, panic in my breast, and saw the same terror on Maeen's face.

"Do you see what he has done?" Janos gritted. "I said he had low cunning; but by all the gods I mock, I did not suspect the extent of that cunning." Mortacious had placed more than one spell on the food. One was to make us sleep until he was ready. The other was to prevent us from fleeing once that moment came. We were trapped in this ghastly city, our own fear molded to make that trap.

"There is only one way to break the spell," Janos said. "My own magic is useless. So we must steal some of his."

We did not discuss the how and why of it, for we sensed any lingering discussion would arouse the worm from its lair. We would go at it simply: one step, then another, seizing opportunity as it came. The door gave no trouble, and there were no guards outside. Janos told the men to wait until we returned, then we crept softly away. I cannot speak for my two companions of that night; but if this account is to be as honest as I have sworn, I must admit how thoroughly Mortacious had unmanned me. I did not face the task ahead as a brave warrior, or as the hero of a stirring ode. All along the way I felt the wizard's cold fingers needle my spine and heard his scornful laughter. Despair was my constant enemy, every hulking shadow my final moment. We were only three furtive little creatures, kin to all the dark things that scuttle, cousins of shame.

We moved along bleak corridors, past dark, empty rooms that reeked of pain; the doors to those rooms yawned open, eager to swallow us. Some rooms were barred, and we heard the low moans of their occupants. Near the entrance to the building, I smelled the sharpness of a familiar oil, and the scent of much-used leather. Sergeant Maeen, bless his old soldier's senses, traced it quickly: it was the last room along the main corridor, just by the exit. The room was unlocked, and Maeen cracked it open and disappeared inside. He returned a moment later and managed a small grin through the web of fear. It was an armory, he whispered; and with that small hope to light our way, we moved out into the chill night.

There was no sign of anyone about, although that did not ease our fear. We circled the place, leaping from shadow to shadow until we came to the rear. Across a wide, barren field, the great building with its smoking furnace beckoned. We hugged every pebble for cover as we scurried to it. The smell of the place was overpowering, and far overhead fiery sparks showered into a moonless night. Why we hurried there, I dared not wonder, for any thought beyond the moment would be a black pit from which we would never escape. Perhaps it was a god who pitied us; perhaps it was Janos' lifetime lover, Holy Reason; perhaps it was only the small blind guide that squeaks in the breast of all living things. All I know is, we saw the building . . . and went.

After an eternity of terror, the building loomed up at us, a cliff face of polished stone that stretched deep into the night in either direction. The only feature was the immense black eye of the arched entrance and the twin columns that supported the arch. We stumbled onto the cobblestone road that served the entrance and grasped at the iron gates barring the way. At that moment luck abandoned us with the drum of footsteps and the grind and shriek of heavily ladened wagons. As we stood there, helpless orphans of fate, torchlights flared at the curve of the road. Then a long procession ribboned out of the night in our direction. We ducked behind one of the columns and prayed luck would relent and shield us from our enemies' probing eyes.

Our hiding place gave us a clear view of the procession's approach. There were more than twenty large wagons, and instead of beasts to draw them, there were people laboring in chain and harness, men and women, barely covered in filthy rags. Large men with whips moved among them, lashing anyone who faltered. I jumped as the iron gates beside us suddenly rumbled into life, rolling open on oiled runners. We huddled back into the column's slender shadow as whips cracked and the wagons moved through. A charnel smell wafted over us as they moved past, and I saw with horror that the wagons were heaped with bodies. There were some still living among them, for I saw movement and heard desperate pleas.

As the third wagon was dragged by us, one of the women faltered in her chains and fell to her knees. Her rags were clotted with dried blood. They came open as she fell, and I saw a gaping wound in her belly, and the glistening of entrails. She looked up, and for a moment our eyes met; but hers were as blank as an oxen's. A whip snaked out, cutting a bloody furrow in her cheek. She did not show pain or emotion, but only rose dumbly to her feet and gripped the chain to labor on.

As the last wagon moved through, Janos hissed for us to follow. We leaped on the back and clung there, struggling for a grip on gore-soaked wood. The gates rumbled shut, and we were inside. I looked back and saw with numb acceptance that there was no one to operate the gates. Moments before the wagon was jerked around a turn, I spotted an odd shadow near one of the gate's huge hinges. The bars there were bowed and twisted from some accident. I risked my grip and nudged Janos, and he saw it, too: a gap just large enough for us to squeeze through. We jolted along a dark passageway. Somewhere in the wagon a man groaned ceaselessly; then I heard a child cry, and almost wept. But the cry had stirred my anger and that anger pierced a hole in Mortacious' black sorcery. It was only a small hole, a pinprick at best, but it was enough to allow a slender light of courage to peep through. I still feared Mortacious: my flesh still flinched under his spell's cold net; but if he came upon us now, he would find a man—not a scuttling rodent. A big door boomed open, and light flooded down the passage. As we leaped from the back of the wagon, a wave of intense heat followed the light. It seared the lungs and turned the roots of my hair into small, hot needles. But

I still had sense enough to catch Janos' signal: we ducked under the slow-moving wagon and used it as cover as we crawled the rest of the way on our hands and knees.

We were in a vast chamber of pain and death. The floor and walls were mirror smooth and blazed with reflected light and heat. The most ghastly scenes and demonic creatures decorated that surface and were granted locomotion by black wizardry, so they swirled and flowed from place to place, making an obscene nightmare of fang and talon, rack and tong, cracked bone and severed muscle. One-third of that chamber was filled by a monstrous open furnace. An unholy fire raged, with blue flames taller than a man shooting up to arc and curl and writhe like serpents driven mad by intruders in their nest. The flames were stoked by huge bellows with great clanking chains that moved to an invisible will; with each stroke the bellows gathered in a torrent of shrieking air; with the other, it expelled the air as a howling wind. An endless belt, such as would turn a carpenter's lathe, but as wide as a city lane and made of meshed metal, was suspended over the roaring fire, driven by thick-toothed gears commanded by sorcery. Far overhead, rising like a hollow mountain, was the great chimney. Its interior was a gaping red maw, with long, white fangs nestled about its entrance. It was a grotesque idol to a dark god, a demon master. All we looked at—chamber, furnace, fire, belt, and chimney—was the engine of Mortacious' black powers. We hid behind the wagon load of gore for more minutes than I now care to ponder, and watched what fed that awful engine, and what it produced.

The men with whips commanded their ragged slaves to empty each wagon. The corpses were slung on a bloody pile by the belt. If any emerged from the wagon still alive, the whip men drew short swords from scabbards at their belts and corrected the error of stubborn life. When the butcher's heap reached a certain size—I did not calculate their grisly measurement—the slaves were ordered to toss the bodies on the moving belt. The flames leaped higher in hungry contemplation of their meal. The bellows shrieked and howled in demon song. I turned away as the first body crossed into the heart of the fire, but Janos bade me to turn back and witness Mortacious' evil. The corpse leaped as if in agony when the blue flames arched to embrace dead flesh; it writhed and bent this way and that. Then the body burst into flame, and sparks and black smoke rose up and filled the room with that wretched, greasy odor we smelled when we first arrived in this terrible city. The smoke curled into a thick column, with sparks leaping and dancing about in its belly. The column lifted up and up and was greeted by the chimney's red maw. My stomach lurched as I saw the huge fangs had come to life, gnashing and clicking together in ghastly appetite. I heard the obscene sound of a giant, invisible diner breaking fast, slurping and sucking with delight as the smoke, laden with a life's hot cinders, passed into the night.

Janos gave me a nudge, and my eyes jolted back to the belt, where I saw the corpse complete its hellish journey. I heard Maeen gasp, as he took in what my own disbelieving eyes were witnessing. Instead of a blackened mass of burned meat and bone, the corpse looked exactly as it had before. In fact, the only marks on it were the bloody wounds it had suffered when it was still a man, with a life to win or lose. But disbelief was followed by complete confoundment when the belt delivered the corpse to the other side. As the body flopped to the floor, one of the whip men stepped up and gave it a mighty kick. He kicked it again and again, as if death were not sufficient to satisfy revenge. Then my mind screamed for some kindly god to deliver me from this place, as the corpse twitched into life. Three more of the whip men joined the first, lashing at the man who had come back from death. They tormented him to his feet. He shambled about, a hulk given purpose in pain. For the first time I saw him clearly. Their victim had long, white-blond hair, matched by a still-longer beard of the same color. I remembered the battle we had seen before being captured and realized this man was the chieftain whose death we had witnessed. Now he stood before the whip men, alive again.

I heard fire burst from another body; above, the slurping of the godly diner. Janos leaned close and whispered, "They're not alive. They're still dead." I shook my head; what could he mean? But this was not the place for a full answer. He signaled to Maeen that it was time to withdraw, and we slipped out of the chamber. "Mortacious doesn't bring the dead to life," Janos said. "He *commands* the dead! He told me so himself, when he said he had the power over men's souls. What we just witnessed was his power at work. He fed the souls of those poor devils to whatever it is he calls his Master. In return, his Master feeds him the sorcerous powers he lacks; and it gives him the corpses as his slaves." Far down the corridor, we heard another soul being sucked from its shell. Janos shook his head. Even in this city of horror, newly gained knowledge made him marvel.

"Why, there has not been a person we've seen since we were

captured who is alive. They're all dead! All of them, except Mortacious."

I suddenly remembered the gaping wound beneath the wizard's scarf and his pains to hide it. There were *no* exceptions. Everyone was dead, including Mortacious. The beast in the chimney was the only master of the realm, with a dead wizard as his chief slave. I told Janos this, and once again I saw the hungry gleam in his eyes as he added new secrets to his understanding.

"But what of us?" Maeen said. "May the gods forgive us for ever coming to such a place, but how do *we* avoid the furnace?" The wizard's plan was obvious. In the morning we would join the dead who populated this city as slaves. We would be walking, laboring corpses; and I did not say it, but I wondered if that state were to be favored over what would become of my soul?

"The solution is back in that chamber," Janos said after a few moments. "If we pass through that fire as living men, we will have stolen his sorcery. It is only the souls of the dead that our Lord Mortacious can claim." I quaked in horror of his logic, but fear of what I had seen drove me to accept his reasoning. "There is still one great danger remaining," Janos said. "When all twenty of us pass through that fire and gather at the other side, Mortacious will know in an instant. A few—the three of us, for instance—might escape unnoticed. But all of us challenging him will be as loud a jangle to his senses as any bell that has ever been cast."

Once again I was confronted with one of Janos' peculiar hesitations. I knew my friend's imagination had raced beyond this place and was set on the road to his obsession. The Far Kingdoms were calling him again, a wanton song that tested all his bonds. But this was no time for doubt's ungracious mewlings, whether his or mine.

"The only way to get to that furnace is to kill the men who guard it," I said, using reason as bait, instead of emotion. "It will take *all* of us to accomplish it."

"Even then," Maeen broke in, "the odds are slender. And they get more slender still once we reach the streets."

Janos nodded. "Let's do it then," he said. "Besides, I am weary of this wizard. He marched the twenty of us in like whipped dogs. But now it's time for the twenty of us to go out; and we'll do it as fighting men . . . as soldiers."

We went back for the others. It was difficult to reenter Mortacious' palace, even though once more we saw no guards. Janos told the men what to expect, and I was amazed no one balked at the horror to come or questioned what we had seen. Perhaps being in this city of dead souls inured us all to terror. My courage revived somewhat when we stopped in the armory Maeen had found, where our confiscated weapons were held. My sword's steel was reassuring, although I wondered how effective it would be against the already dead.

IF PANIC IS Fear's sister, it was she gave us strength that night, while her brother fired our blood lust. We fell on them unawares, those poor soulless men with whips and short swords forged only to cut a compliant path for final release. They were silent when we came howling into the chamber, and silent they remained during the furious fight. We cut them down and pierced them where they fell. But as we moved on to reap their brothers, they rose up and came at our backs. We were killing men who were dead when we slew them, then killing them again, and again. We cut off their limbs, but they still had teeth to bite; and the lopped-off arms, attached to hands that still gripped swords, snaked across the floor in blind search for us. So we severed every joint, chopped off every head, and gutted the flopping trunks that rolled about to knock us from our feet. We were twenty butchers, half-mad with fear, wading through a slaughterhouse of meat no man could eat, grappling with poor beasts who did not cry out when we maimed them, and fought with only the wizard's hate to hold them up.

Finally, we were done. Our clothes were blood-drenched uniforms, our faces gory masks. We turned away from the demons our slaughter had conjured. All of us knew the blood would remain even if we bathed in whole rivers of pure water. The shame was undeserved, but fairness is a great stranger to life. There was nothing we could do but swallow ugly fate and get on with it.

The furnace waited, and above the furnace was the demon who fed on souls. Janos stood by the moving belt that clanked across the unholy fires that roasted those souls to the demon's taste. He urged us to hurry, and we shambled to him as if we were already one of Mortacious' slaves. I looked across the great belt and saw the blue flames leaping through the grate, and I heard the demon's gnashing teeth above. On the far side of that soul conveyer, Janos said, was rescued life; on this side, eternal slavery. He said he would go first to prove his theory, and warned that we must follow quickly, for he sensed the wizard was wakening. I would go last, he said, to make certain the pace did not slacken.

Then cold, cold Reason tapped me on the shoulder. I turned, angered by his unsummoned presence, and asked what it was he wanted. But I saw the answer in the hard mirrors of Reason's eyes. Janos' plan was sound enough, but it must be turned from tail to head; for if Janos was wrong, and error plucked him from us, we would all be helpless before the wizard's wrath. I must go first, Reason demanded, and Janos last . . . if I survived. Then the mirrors melted, and I found myself gazing into Halab's sad, knowing eyes. He whispered words of courage and warmed Reason's chill message until it was easier to hold. Halab stayed with me as I went to Janos and stopped him as he was about to mount the belt. When I presented my logic, Halab grinned in encouragement. Janos argued, but at last he admitted I was right. Rare emotion nearly overcame him. I saw tears well, and as he turned to hide them, saw the tremble of his beard. Then he embraced me and whispered that I was the only one who had believed him from the beginning. He called me friend and brother and thanked me for my faith. I let him keep that lie as my gift, knowing that when he put it in the chest he kept to hold such treasures, my gift would find little company. For all the time I knew Janos, I never heard him call another man or woman friend. I see now that Janos was a man who liked but never loved, save once, and his curse robbed that of any value. So I let him believe the lie of my faith: but when he reached out, it was Halab's hand I grasped; and when he led me to the clacking belt, it was Halab, not Janos, who whispered my redheaded luck would confound the soul eater. Finally it was Janos who stepped away, while Halab crouched beside me as the conveyer swept me toward the flames.

I was hurled into a heat that had form and substance. It stole the air before I could breathe it, sapped my strength before I could gather it. The heat was a hammer that cracked me like an egg with its first blow; with its second, it crushed me into a trembling mass that knew only pain and fear. Fire spat and roared, and I was swept into a tunnel of blue-flamed serpents that struck from every side. I felt my flesh peel away so the flames could attack naked nerve; and when they were ash, the wizard's furnace boiled off my blood and cracked my bones to sear the marrow. Everything that made me, even my screams, was slowly consumed by that fire. At last, all I had left were eyes to see the demon's twitching maw, ears to hear the clatter of its fangs, and a mind whose only thoughts were painful present and fearful future. Then Halab leaned over, blocking the demon from view. He sang a song, the song I favored most as a child, and banished all the sounds I dreaded. He stroked my tormented body, and I felt bone and blood and flesh reform. Then he told me there was only a little way to go . . . a small bit of pain to endure . . . and we were done. I felt a great easing, and a familiar sense of self returned. With that return I realized my soul had left me for a time. We gave it a joyous welcome, my body and I. A moment later, I leaped off the belt, as strong and fresh as I have ever been in my life. I shouted to my friends across the great fiery expanse to hurry to me; we had a wizard to fight.

Sergeant Maeen was next; then the others came one by one. But as each passed through the furnace, under the hungry demon, I saw no sign of the suffering I had experienced: they lay immobile, as if in peace. Later they said they'd felt the same torment and fears as I, but a ghostly presence joined them on the belt, easing their passage and curing their pain. They said the ghost looked much like me. Then it was Janos' turn. He vaulted onto the belt and rode it standing up, his legs braced wide, arms crossed on his chest as if in defiance. But I saw his face creased with deep concentration and knew brave posturing was not what he was about. Suddenly, his whole body gave off a golden light. The blue flames stirred higher and hotter, and the demon shrieked from frustrated hunger; but they were powerless against the golden glow. Then the flames drew in, withering into decreasing smallness until they were embers . . . and winked out. Above us, the demon was silent, teeth frozen in death's grimace, red maw still and turning to gray. Janos, now a great thief of magic, bounded off the grate when he reached the end. But before we could rush up with congratulations, a voice large enough to fill that vast chamber seared the air with its fury.

"What have you done, Greycloak?" It was Mortacious. The sorcerer had wakened. The voice boomed again. "Wait for me, little wizard. I'm coming to you."

Janos did not wait, nor did we. We ran from that place as fast as we could into the cold night. We raced down the cobbled road, weapons ready. Behind us I heard an explosion. I looked back and saw the door to the wizard's palace had been blown away by some powerful force. Through that smoking portal came an enormous ball of fire as blue as the flames in that furnace. The ball shot jagged lightning and exploded the pebbles on the road as it passed over them. The wizard's voice cracked out at us from inside that fiery ball. "Run, little wizard, run." Laughter followed, cackling and crackling at our backs.

If his words were a command, we had no quarrel; added strength surged, and I ran even faster than before. We sped down the avenue they'd marched us along, past the one-eyed dwellings, with dead men for occupants. Our pace began to slow as our limbs wearied from the mad pursuit. Mortacious' gleeful laughter grew wilder as the gap narrowed. The fiery ball he rode cast our shadows far ahead of us; and oh, how we ached to be those distant, fleeing shadows. I heard Janos' labored breathing beside me; he seemed to stumble, but only bent to scoop up a pebble. Then he was gone and I turned back, thinking he'd fallen. Instead he was standing in Mortacious' path. As I ran to his side, he drew his sword and knocked the pebble against the blade. A spark leaped from the ringing metal. He struck again, and this time the spark he drew was longer—arcing toward the fireball that raced down on us.

Mortacious cried out, "I have you, little wizard." But the third time Janos struck, the spark exploded off the blade. As it arced outward, it exploded again and became a great shower of jagged stars that rained across the path of our hunter. Then they were falling on the ball, and it burst apart with a thunderclap, hurling Mortacious from its center. He tumbled end over end, then crashed onto the road.

The wizard was still for a moment, his robe a red puddle around him. If it had been a moment longer, he would have had us, because we were about to charge and finish him off. The robe jerked, then ballooned into immense red wings. We wheeled and ran as the wings carried Mortacious aloft, and he loosed a howl that shattered the air like glass. It was a call to the hunt, and as we sped to catch our comrades, the call was answered. Out of the one-eyed dwellings poured the wizard's slaves. They sniffed our living blood and bounded after us. We rounded the last turn before the harbor with that voiceless wolf pack at our heels, their winged master soaring overhead, urging them on. Our comrades were struggling to free boats to carry us away. But they stopped when they saw us racing down the hill with the horror at our backs. It was too late to do anything but fight.

I heard Sergeant Maeen bark orders as Janos and I plunged into their ranks to momentary safety; and I felt the shock as our friends absorbed the fury of the first wave and drove it back. We formed a battle line across one of the docks, forcing our enemies to attack in small groups. In the night sky, Mortacious circled, gathering his slaves for the final assault. It would be a repeat of that fight in the chamber, but against these odds there was no hope of an identical result. We hauled tar barrels out of a caulking barge and fired the docks as they came for us. It was a fire of *this* world, not the next, that met their charge. Fueled by tar and old, dry wood, instead of spells, it became a fast-moving inferno that rushed down on them like a raging river. It burned their legs from under them and melted their weapons in the ashes of their remains. With no will of their own to heed pain's warning, they continued to advance; each rank waiting in patient turn for the others to be hurled against our fiery shield and be consumed. Above them, Mortacious cursed their ashes and called more of his warrior slaves to take their place.

The shore bristled with their numbers, and still more hurried down the road to them. Mortacious was building a bridge of their ashes and fire-burst bones. Soon there would be enough for them to scramble across and take us. But they would have to hurry, for this fire had no master to command it: on one side it was our shield, on the other it was our enemy as well, feeding on the dock we stood on and driving us into the sea. Mortacious sent men into the water, swimming along the burning dock to come up at our backs. The wizard drifted closer, mocking our hopeless folly with his laughter.

A hand reached up through broken boards to grasp Janos' foot. I leaped forward with a shout of warning and cut off the hand with my sword. Janos saw it, flopping on the dock. Mortacious cackled and swept down at us. Janos plucked up the writhing hand, pressed his sword grip against the twisting fingers, and they held firm. He threw the blade upward with all his might. With the hand gripped hard on its hilt, the sword made an eerie spear: a phantom seemed to guide it as it hurtled toward Mortacious. His laughter stopped in midcackle as it took him in the eye. He plummeted out of the sky, howling angry pain, and splashed into the water. We saw him sink beneath the waves, but the sight gave us small pleasure as we turned back to face his men. They were scrambling over the bridge of carnage up the burning dock. We knew as we braced ourselves that their master would rise from the sea again to urge them on.

I made peace with the gods who formed me and sent a last thanks to Halab. A smoking brute plunged out of the fire, and I raised my sword to meet him.

Then the fates blew in from the sea to save us. The deep, clarion voice of a great magic bell rang across the waves. The tone was of such immensity, all other sound fled as it rolled over us, then spread to fill night's dark vault. The bell sounded again, and we felt peace wash over us. The peace was a melodious blanket that smothered the fire. It was a clear, ringing song even dead men could hear: they stopped, turning their heads to listen. As the last echo of the bell crept away, Mortacious' slaves dropped their weapons, wheeled, and shambled away.

Out of the darkness came a wondrous ship, with glowing sails and cheery lanterns dangling all along the sides. It was more graceful than any ship we had ever seen, and it sped toward us on enchanted wings, for there was no wind to fill those billowing sails. I heard Janos gasp, or maybe it was my own ragged breath of surprise, as we saw the crest emblazoned on the sails: a huge coiled serpent, set against a sunburst.

As the ship came on, a graceful swan against black waters, I realized all we had faced before had been a test; and Mortacious had been the greatest test of all. I thanked the gods we had passed it.

A voice called to us from the deck. "Hail, seekers." The voice was as melodious as the bell. On the deck I saw the speaker: a handsome man, dressed in glittering white. He called out again, "We bring greetings . . . from the Far Kingdoms."

Janos gripped my arm in joy, and around me I heard the men cheer. As the ship dropped boats to carry us away, my own joy overcame all, and I was cheering as loudly as the others.

And that is how we came to discover the Far Kingdoms.

CHAPTER TWENTY-TWO
The Far Kingdoms

EXPECTATION CAN BE a fickle goddess, but knowing that is no protection once she fires the lights of her shadow show. Promise is her most alluring plot; the more she keeps it dancing just ahead, the more willingly you follow. I have mourned as she danced away entirely at the end; but I have also known the greatest joy when she relented and I came into her arms. It was Expectation who drew me to the Far Kingdoms, and it was Expectation—multiplied many times over—who offered bright promise to those who awaited me at home. It was their dreams I carried, and they lay close as we danced across sparkling seas to those shores.

I had often wondered what vision would first present itself. Sometimes I thought I would see a city of dazzling gold, with graceful towers and swooping minarets. Sometimes I thought it would be rich fields and sweet meadows, with peaceful hamlets and white-walled villas abounding with flowers. However, no matter what form it took, in my mind's eye I always saw it from some great height: a jagged peak, perhaps, or some vaulting promontory. But I came upon our goal in a fashion more befitting a citizen of Orissa; just as it was upon the river of my birth I began the journey, it was another river that bore me to the end.

As we left the sea that had borne us away from Gomalalee's evil, the great ship's bell tolled our arrival. The main sail billowed, displaying the serpent crest of the Far Kingdoms. As we approached the river's wide, graceful mouth, another bell answered from far beyond. We pressed against the rail, eager eyes probing for the first view of the goddess who had called us here. But she teased by drawing a veil, a pale blue mist, across her features. Then she let it lift before our white ship, blue wisps rib-

344

boning across the sails. A breeze wafted, polishing the view; our seduction was complete.

The first thing I saw when I entered the Far Kingdoms was an emerald tower rising out of the river. The tower had been artistically tapered to a slender point. A wondrous mirror spun on that point, showering the ship with butterflies of light. I felt a pleasant tingle as one alighted on my face, then a gentle, sorcerous sniff at my intentions. It hesitated when it found the protective spell Janos had cast over each of us after we boarded the rescue ship, but took no offense and fluttered on.

The first thing I heard when I entered the Far Kingdoms was a melodious song from the throats of a thousand or more birds. They flew out of a forest of tall, shapely trees that smelled of mint, and swooped back and forth over us—a cloud of color as glorious as the song. When I looked closely, I saw the birds were the size of hunting eagles: metal fighting spurs winked from their talons; their beaks were heavy and hooked for tearing. The banks of the river were lined with a tumble of floral bowers; to our delight, one of those bowers broke off and became a floating, sweet-smelling island. As it passed under our bow, a voice called from the thicket of purple, trumpet-shaped flowers; when our captain answered back, I saw the tips of spears needling out.

The first thought I had as we passed through those gates was that the hand extended to us in welcome wore a velvet glove to cloak a steely fist. I shivered as the second thought prickled my spine: I was glad these people called us friend instead of enemy. As we rounded a high-hilled bend, all thought melted before the splendorous view those hills curtained. The river was deeply curved, winding like a glorious serpent through misted fields and blue-green forests. Far inland, like a beacon, rose a graceful mountain as blue as the river that so bedazzled us. Beneath that mountain, we had been told, was our goal: the city of Irayas, where the great King Domas held court over all the realms of the Far Kingdoms.

We traveled for days on that river, and each day presented a multitude of wonders. On the first, we sailed past a bustling port city three times the size of Orissa. Boats and ships buzzed about the docks, unloading and loading all manner of goods and foodstuffs. The port was amazingly clean and free of foul odors. The buildings and dwellings we saw had no common design, except to please the eye with a variety of shapes, sizes, and colors. Captain Utorian, our host and the king's emissary, said the port was the center of all trade within the kingdoms, which he said spread out from both sides of the river, and stretched ahead, beyond the mountain beacon, for many a league. He told us King Domas' realm was composed of eleven principalities, each ruled by a prince who swore allegiance to the king. Scattered about these principalities were seventy great cities, and many minor ones as well. Grandest of all, he said, was Irayas, the seat of final justice and power. He said the entire realm, what we called the Far Kingdoms—was named Vacaan, in honor of the supreme god of the Old Ones, who had ruled this land with great wisdom for more than a thousand years, before they mysteriously departed. He said their ruins could be found all over Vacaan: there were remains of a city near Irayas, and ancient altars on the mountain's crown.

Utorian was a most congenial host: he took pains to answer as many questions as he could; those that made him hesitate he urged us to ask when we reached Irayas. After he hauled us off the smoking docks at Gomalalee, he went to much trouble to see that our wounds were treated and that we were availed of hot baths and comfortable quarters. The only words he knew of our language were those he had called out when he came to carry us away from Mortacious' soulless city; but no sooner had we boarded than one of his officers presented us with transparent sponges and bade us by gesture to lick the moisture from them. As soon as we had done so, we were able to fully speak and understand their tongue. I fear our excitement made us spew such a great racket they must have been very sorry we did.

It was during those first few hours that Janos cast a protective spell over each of us. Although the captain and his crew seemed to be kind and pleasant men, Janos reminded us we had only just come from being honored guests, and had best be cautious lest our hosts held similar intent. We needed little urging. Janos drew on new power gained from his encounter with Mortacious to forge the guardian spell. He said it would not turn aside an assassin's knife blade, but would warn us when grave danger lurked. After the alarm, it would be up to us to hide, fight, or run for reinforcements. The spell was a wise precaution, but after a short time in Utorian's company, I forgot I carried it, remembering only when we encountered the tower's inquisitive lights.

After we had refreshed ourselves, Utorian called Janos and me to his cabin, where we chatted over mugs of hot brandy that had a tangy, soothing aftertaste that lessened the horror we had just experienced. His cabin was sparse, but artistically so, with cozy seats touched with just a little color on the soft fabric coverings and a table that remained steady in any sea. The wood that enclosed the cabin was rich with strongly knitted grain that formed interesting patterns a man could ponder for days. On the broadest wall was the cabin's only decoration: a silk banner, bearing the blue, coiled serpent, set upon a golden sunburst, that was the crest we had sought for so long. Utorian wore a similar crest on his white uniform. Besides his small bunk in the corner with a coverlet that matched the seats, the only other furnishings were an empty chart table and the locked cabinet that held his instruments and maps. There was one other thing: a golden rope dangled through a hole in the ceiling. Utorian said it led to the bellhouse; it operated the enchanted instrument that caused Mortacious and his horde to flee.

Before we deluged him with questions, Utorian begged our indulgence and explained his presence. He told us King Domas and his younger brother, Prince Raveline, had followed our progress with great interest. He made no secret of how this was done, but said—besides a few sorcerous devices beyond his small abilities—the information came from a few well-placed spies, and from the mysterious riders we called the Watchers. He said the Watchers were not subjects of the king, but a nomadic tribe of wizards who spurned mortal company and restlessly roamed the land for purposes of their own. The kingdom had made a pact with them long ago, trading magic goods they needed for whatever information required to guard Vacaan of unwanted visitors.

Then he said, "You must know, that until I received orders to retrieve you, all visitors have been considered unwelcome. To the best of my knowledge, you and your men will be the first outsiders to visit our land since we raised it out of the ruins of the Old Ones. I cannot say why our king has had a change of heart; but as a free and loyal subject, I can assure you without fear of contradiction his intentions are honorable, and once you have spoken to him, no one will bar you from returning safely home. Although I was not told his reasons, I can guess them. It is no great court secret King Domas has been pondering that perhaps we have begun to grow stale after all these years of shunning contact with the outside. And I believe your thirst for knowledge and single-minded pursuit has further sparked his thinking."

The captain said we would have complete freedom of the ship until we arrived in Vacaan. We could ask anything of anyone and go anywhere we chose. The only exception, he said, was that we would be required to remain in our quarters when he took sightings. He apologized most profusely for this and said he was forbidden to let us see his charts or instruments, nodding at the locked cabinet, because their nature was a closely guarded secret. He said, however, once we met the king, he suspected many of those secrets would be revealed.

Utorian refilled our mugs, and the three of us toasted the promise of a bright future for our peoples. But I could tell by his manner he believed that if change was to come, it would be Orissa that would benefit most. This was a belief shared with nearly all the people we met in the Far Kingdoms. They had little curiosity about the world we hailed from. The only thing that stoked excitement was the journey we undertook to reach them, and they were always pressing us for details of our adventures. But then their curiosity stopped. The reason became obvious: Vacaan was a land of more marvels than I have linen pages to number. The people were blessed with bountiful harvests; there were few ills their Evocators could not cure; they had a seemingly endless variety of pleasures and possessions. In fact, they considered themselves so superior to all other people, it was impossible for them to imagine those people had anything of value to offer. If I remarked on a feat, original thought, or artistic accomplishment that was a source of pride to Orissa, they hastened to mention something from their own land they believed made ours pale by comparison. I thought it minor at the time, a small irritation, or source of amusement. Later I could see it was a more serious flaw than I had imagined. Having said that, I cannot deny that as we sailed upriver, the wonders I witnessed outshone nearly all I had ever encountered. One of the wonders was the river itself. I have compared it to a great serpent, and that description is apt, since that is what the snake signified on the Far Kingdoms' crest, while the sunburst stood for the sorcerous wisdom that guarded the land.

Imagine that serpent, with its lustrous blue coils close together—not quite touching—with only the head and neck extending from the twists. Now make that serpent a river again, its head the mountain we traveled toward, and you will see that although the distance was great for the ship, a bird would make short work of it. But I would not have bargained our sails for speedy wings, because as we tacked first in one direction, then doubled back to the other, the river let us see close up nearly all the marvels of the Far Kingdoms.

The river rose tamely through Vacaan. When we moved to a new height there was no lock to compel the difference. There was only a shimmer in our path, then we moved on serene waters to the higher level. Utorian said their wizards had mastered the river long before and bent it to common purpose. He showed us the amazing absence of flood marks on the banks and said they had mastered the weather as well, requiring the storms to replenish the river, but no more. They could also command the river to fold in and out at any point, making it easy for the farmers to irrigate and ensure bountiful harvests. The crops that made up those harvests, he added, came from blessed seed that always bore fruit and repelled disease and insects. I thought of our own hard-laboring farmers as we blew past unimaginably rich fields and orchards; I remembered with pain the ruinous flood and famine we had just suffered. I prayed our journey might ease that labor, and rout suffering from our hearts.

We saw forests thick with game, hills laden with veins of malleable metal and valuable gems, and pastures bleating and lowing with fat herds and flocks. We saw people of every variety: from farmer, to laborer, to merchant, to lord and lady. They were a calm, graceful people given to easy laughter, which we heard floating across the water. The men were handsome even to great age; and the women were pleasing to look upon, with time only touching their features with wisdom and dignity. Their children seemed the happiest of all: they appeared to run and roam at will; and it was their shrill laughter we heard most frequently.

Utorian said all their children had some schooling, and the ones with the best minds or talents were picked out for special attention. No avenue was closed to them after that; they could rise to nearly any level of society. When he said it, I thought of Halab and mourned that he hadn't been born in such a land.

We gazed on the many cities that nestled against the river. All of them were a marvel to behold. Some delighted the eye with variety, such as the port we sailed by on the first day of the river voyage. Some were all of a kind: made of carved white marble, or richly painted timbers, or of strong, gleaming metal. Their design ranged from low-built structures blending with the forests that framed them, to swooping towers connected by delicate spans, to cozy domiciles, with high-peaked roofs, and cheery fires glowing through the windows at night. Each city we viewed dazzled us in some way, and just as we thought there could be nothing more to amaze us, a new marvel would be revealed as we rounded the bend. Then at last we came to Irayas: it was the most glorious city of all.

We came upon it without warning. The channel spilled east— away from the mountain for the final time—and suddenly flared; the banks retreated before our eyes into distant ribbons of greens.

The river made a lake, and out of the lake floated Irayas. Our senses quivered in the spell it cast, willing strings under the hands of a master harpist. Irayas was a place of light and water. The setting sun was at its back, and the city was ablaze in full glory. Color shimmered through crystal towers and leaped off golden domes. The river flowed beneath, a molten mirror in the sun's dying light. The air was musical with chimes and bird song, scented with dusk's blooms. Small boats wisped through that beauty, timid supplicants of a goddess queen.

Visions such as this make a wanderer's wine: once he has tasted it, there is little he will not suffer to drink from that vine once more. We sipped until we were drunk, then night fell, and we were left groaning in darkness. But Irayas had a trick for that thief, and we gasped in renewed amazement as light sprang up over the city. The glass towers became bright fountains; the gold domes glowed from within. The canals that served as thorough-fares were illuminated by long strings of small, lighted globes. The sounds of a busy city continued, and I realized the Evocators of Irayas had extended productive hours long past the close of day.

We slept aboard the ship that night. My thoughts were so fired, I believed rest would be impossible, but exhaustion took all of us early. I was awakened once by wild music and tavern shouts. Isn't it a wonder, I mused, that wherever there is a waterfront, no matter how grand the city it services, you can always find a place for strong drink and raucous play? Then I fell back into dreamless sleep.

The next day Utorian took us to meet the king. His palace spread over more than half the ten islands that formed the center of the river sprawl that was Irayas. The grounds were a marvel of well-tended lawn, trees, and beds of flowers or exotic plants. There were gentle animals and songful birds to please the heart, artistic statuary to delight the spirit. The palace was a many-domed wonder, all cast from precious gold. The columns and arches were of gold alloy, and the exterior walls were a kind of glass that could be darkened for privacy or to shade the sun's glare.

Soldiers in gold and white tunics and breeches guarded the corridors of the vast palace, but Janos noted that their spears and sidearms were clumsy, gaudy, and seemed mostly ceremonial in function. We entered a courtroom so immense it shrunk all purpose other than the king's. It was made to seem even larger by the vaulting glass walls. Some were clear and emitted a plenitude of light; others were mirrored, reflecting the multitude who had gathered to seek the king's attention or tend his business. It was a curved, three-tiered chamber, with many steps leading to each level. The bottom tier where we entered was the most crowded, and the dress was that of common folk; the second held a smaller group, with costumes and manners superior to the first; the last was nearly empty, reserved for wizards and other men of high authority. They strolled the edges in wise conference. Rising above all this busy splendor of state was a broad platform, bearing a great golden throne, with a high arched back that displayed an immense royal crest.

King Domas sprawled across that throne in easy boredom. Even from a distance, he was a man who was not diminished by size of chamber or throne. He idly twirled his crown—a plain, gold band I saw later in closer view—about his finger as he listened to advisers; and where their speech was smothered by the noisy crowd, his tones rumbled over all of it. Then I lost sight of him as Utorian hurried the twenty of us forward. His importance was apparent by the way the throng stepped respectfully aside. Mildly curious stares tracked us until we came against the rail that marked the edge of the third level. He told us to wait and craned his head this way and that as if looking for assistance. We pressed against the railing, gawping like farmers fresh from field to city. But our gawping was downward, as a yawning, golden-throated pit seized our eyes before they could rise and marvel at the throne.

The depression filled most of the third level; there was a path around it for strolling officials, and another that wound to the bottom. Floating there, like a huge eye, was an enchanted simulacrum of the Far Kingdoms. Every detail—from snaking blue river to city, farm, and field—was revealed in exact, living scale. You could see boats on the river, and I imagined little moving dots of people and animals. Even more amazing was that the sky itself had been duplicated and brought to life; I conceived flights of birds slipping in and out of the clouds I saw floating in the winds. As we watched, wizards and officials walked down the curving path, discussing and observing the simulacrum. Several wizards fixed their attention on a cloud bank, swollen and black with storm, and commanded it to move to a different place, where lightning suddenly flashed and rain fell. I had no doubt that real-life subjects of that parched area were being blessed by the storm that raged before us in miniature.

A kingly bark of disagreement broke through, and I raised my eyes to see Domas up close for the first time. His advisers were knotted about him in heated debate. Whatever had tested the king's patience must have been resolved or no longer held his interest, for I saw him politely cover a yawn and resume twirling his crown about his finger. The king was big—a head at least over Janos—and his plain white tunic stretched over a body quarried of stone blocks. His hair and features were fair. So plainly was he dressed that other than the crown there was no indication this fellow ruled such a powerful realm.

There was another man to the side of the throne. He was as big as Domas, and in fact, looked quite like him in features and blocky form; but where the king was fair he was dark. His costume was of richly embroidered gold, with a princely emblem on the breast. He seemed to favor heavy, ornate jewelry and rings, and his long black hair was held by an emerald band that shouted he was royalty as well.

"Prince Raveline," Janos whispered. I had guessed the same. Janos leaned closer; his whisper edged with excitement. "He's a wizard. A *most* powerful wizard." I had guessed that, too: his dark eyes held the inner gleam of an Evocator, and my skin prickled unpleasantly. I studied him closer, seeing that despite the glitter of Raveline's appearance, his manner lacked Domas' self-possession, and if you stood them together there would be no mistaking who was king, and who was a merely noble brother.

There was a stir along the rail, and I saw a little man with a most unremarkable appearance slipping toward Utorian. His breeches were a badly washed white, and his tunic was worn. Dangling absently from the tunic was a tarnished gold crest. However, there was no mistaking the little man's importance: the captain bent quickly, but with stiffened back to hear his whispers. The little man had to rise on his toes to make his lips reach and showed no concern some might think his posture clownish. As he spoke, and Utorian nodded, his eyes flicked to us; then made quick jabs at Janos and me as he guessed our identity from among the twenty. This may be a mouse, I thought, but it is a bold little mouse with quick wit and no fear of kitchen cats, because *this* mouse dines with the king. The little man dropped off his toes, ducked under the rail, and scurried around the pit and up the steps to the throne. Utorian motioned frantically for us to make ready. We did so, and as the king swiveled to smile greetings to his little favorite, there was much clothes tugging and hair smoothing among us.

Domas waved, sweeping back the clump of advisers, and the

little man repeated his whispered performance, except this time he clutched the king's robes for balance. The king's features lighted, boredom falling away as he listened. He boomed reaction. "You don't say? How long have they been here?" The voice was big as the man, easily reaching us and beyond. He frowned as the little man's whispering continued. Then, "Why didn't you tell me before, Beemus?"

I was taking his measure as quickly as I could, sniffing that big voice for clues. Domas formed his words heartily, strung them on short necklaces, and carelessly flung them to the crowd for anyone to catch. Beemus whispered reply to the king's question; he accompanied the answer with a shrug I am sure made some incompetent a sorry man for ignoring us. If he was watching, he would have been sadder still when he saw Domas' brow furrow in anger and his fair skin redden. But this king was bored with anger just now, and the incompetent would have sighed in relief as excited interest cleared his features again.

Domas smiled hugely and gave Beemus a pat, saying, "Never mind that. I'll get to the bottom of it later. You just go fetch them for me, Beemus. Quickly, now. We've been rude enough." Beemus jumped down and made the long scurry to do his bidding.

The king turned to his advisers, saying, "Enough! We've tracked through this mud before. It's time for *new* business, sirs. New business, indeed." He rubbed his hands together in anticipation. Prince Raveline moved lazily to join him, at some pains, I thought, to avoid an appearance of haste. I switched my attention back to Domas, taking a last measurement before we were called to such confusing splendor. He was a forthright man, I theorized, blunt in purpose and deed as well as word. He had no care what anyone thought of him: I am King Domas, his bluff manner said, and I can be who or what I please. My trader's instincts were chiming as Beemus reached us. Such confidence, I thought, was the mark of a man who would at least listen if the bargain was presented logically and without decoration. Then we were being hurried to him, and in a moment the twenty of us were drawing up in formation before the king. We started to bow low, as we thought proper, but he stopped it with a wave. "None of that bowing business," he said. "A good rigid and respectful posture will do." He turned to his brother. "There's all too much ceremony in this court," he said. "All that bowing makes me dizzy."

Raveline laughed, hearty and full, but it was heavy with mockery. "Just order us all to stop," he said, "and then you'll see how much you miss it."

Domas gave him a mild look. "You're being clever again," he said. Then he sighed, as Raveline answered with more mockery by bowing, very slowly and very low. "I don't feel clever today," the king said. He looked at Beemus. "Think of something clever for me, Beemus. Something that'll cut him good. You're good at that." Beemus whispered a promise, and Domas turned his attention back to us. "So these are the fellows who have caused such a fuss," he rumbled. But he said it with a smile. Then he studied us thoroughly, the smile growing broader still. "A fine-looking lot," he said to his brother. "Don't you agree?"

Raveline was doing his own bit of studying: his wizard's eyes roaming here and there, finding me, where they paused, then Janos, where they lingered for a much longer moment. "I do indeed," the prince said. His voice was nearly as loud as the king's. He was smiling as well, but his lips stretched thinly over his teeth. Like a hunting dog's, I thought, when he returns with the scent of his prey.

The king rose from the throne and with Beemus scampering at his side, strode down the steps to view us more closely. Janos and I tensed, thinking we would be the first to be examined. Instead, the king strolled casually around the formation. "What a sturdy group of men," he boomed in admiration. "You can see why they made it. And none the worse for wear, to boot."

"A little lean, perhaps," Raveline quarreled. "And battered a bit."

"Who wouldn't be," Domas replied, "after coming so far to find us?" He looked down at Beemus. "Are you still thinking?" Beemus said he was. "Good," the king said. "Make it nice and sharp and wounding, please."

More studying and nodding followed. Then Domas suddenly whirled and waved to the chamber, shouting, "Friends! Friends! Your attention, please." His bellow filled the great chamber and rolled back without the aid of magic. Others took up the cry, quite unnecessarily, saying, "The king is speaking! The king is speaking!" The crowd looked up expectantly.

"I want you all to meet these fellows," the king bellowed. "You've probably heard I'm interested in them, and here they are in flesh. They're all brave adventurers. And what adventure it's been! They've come all the way from far Orissa. Daring deserts and bandits, and all sorts of other terrors." Domas resumed his stroll, talking to the crowd as he went, with patient Beemus trotting at his side. "Let's talk to a few, shall we? And see what makes such spirit." He paused, hurling a great stone of a frown at the crowd. "A spirit many of you sadly lack." Then he returned his attention to us, and a smile replaced the frown. His smile was quite unlike his brother's: it was wide and generous and its path was smooth from much use.

The king looked us over again, until his gaze fell on Sergeant Maeen. "You, sir," the king roared, pointing. "Tell us your name."

Maeen purpled with embarrassment. The purple deepened as confusion caught him between a salute and a bow he recalled had been forbidden. Domas rescued him with a commander's salute for a soldier. Dilemma solved, Maeen snapped his best brisk reply, saying, "Sir! I am Sergeant Maeen! Sir!"

The king shouted to the crowd, "Did you hear that? Sergeant Maeen, he says. I guessed his rank. You can see by the cut of him that he's a sergeant."

"Thank you, Your Majesty," Maeen said.

"Tell us, good sergeant, what do you think of us now that you're here? How do you find Vacaan?"

Maeen's features glowed, and he struggled mightily for the proper response. Finally, he blurted, "Marvelous, Your Majesty! It's just marvelous!"

Domas roared laughter. "Do you hear that?" he bawled. "He thinks we're ... marvelous!" More laughter. Then, "Good plain soldier's talk. We need more of that around here." Maeen blushed.

Then the king asked, "Is there anything you don't like? That isn't ... marvelous?"

Maeen gave it his honest consideration, puzzling until he found a small blight. "It's the food, sir," he said.

"The food?" Domas thundered. "What don't you like about our food?"

"Oh, I like it fine, Your Majesty," Maeen said. "But, begging your pardon, sometimes I think it's somewhat ... rich."

Domas was absolutely delighted with this. "I think so, too, Sergeant," he said. "They're always putting glop on nice fresh stuff and ruining it. Next time, tell them to scrape it off. Of course, I do that all the time, and it does me no good. And I'm their damned king!"

Prince Raveline broke in. "I think you have found a friend in my brother, Sergeant," he said. "And I can see why. You're just his style of fellow."

"Thank you, Your Majesty," Maeen said.

Domas held up a hand. "You shouldn't call him 'Your Majesty,'" he admonished. "It's like confusing officers with sergeants. Only kings are majestic. My brother's a prince. And princes are . . ." He paused, searching, and a sudden glow lighted his features. He shouted for all to hear, "Princes are . . . *less majestic*." Then he laughed until the tears flowed, the crowd laughing with him. Raveline made his smile that was a sneer. Beemus whispered to Domas, who nodded, then said, "It *was* clever, wasn't it. But you keep thinking, Beemus. I'll be needing more soon enough." He shot his brother a look and snorted. "Good old Less Majestic."

Still laughing, he thanked Maeen and strolled on, picking out several more of our men, introducing them to his subjects, and praising each in turn. Finally, he came back to the front where we stood.

He caught my red hair first. "You, sir. Don't tell me your name, I know it. It's . . ." He frowned as it escaped him. Beemus whispered, and Domas grinned. "Antero, that's it . . . Amalric Antero."

"I am honored, Your Majesty," I said.

Domas puzzled at me for a moment, then he said, "You're the merchant?" I said I was. "Merchants aren't usually the daring sort. All they care about is profit." I told him that profit was certainly not my goal. The king studied me further, and I could see he believed me. He tapped Beemus. "I want to speak with him further," he said. "Make a bit of time in the next day or so." This request drew a furious bout of whispering from Beemus. "I know, I know," the king said. "But do it for me anyway, and there's a good fellow."

That done with, he turned to Janos. "I know your name right off," he said. "It's Janos Greycloak, soldier and wizard."

"Thank you, Your Majesty," Janos said.

"Which are you the most of, Greycloak, soldier or wizard?"

"It was both that helped get us here, Your Majesty," Janos answered.

The king was impatient. "No avoidance now. I've made this court an open court. All are commanded to speak their minds. I do. So does my . . . less majestic brother." He chuckled in memory of his fun.

Janos braced up, even firmer than before. "I have been a soldier all my life," he said. "But during that time, there was only one banner that drew me. The Far Kingdoms have been my dream, sir. Now I am here, if you will permit it, the study of magic is what interests me most."

Domas eyed him, gave a slow nod, and said, "Why not?" He turned to the crowd, shouting, "That's enough. I want some privacy now. You all go back to whatever you were doing. Wasting my money, I suppose. Oh, yes. These fellows will be visiting a while, and I want you to show them the utmost courtesy. Is that understood?" Rumbles from the crowd and friendly faces showed it was. Then the crowd turned away as he'd demanded, and Domas went back to his throne.

He thought for a moment, then, "I said before, I liked your looks. I liked them better when I looked closer. But only time can tell how right . . . or wrong, I am. So here is what I am going to do. Beemus, here, will find you places to stay. As honored guests, I suppose he'll come up with a palace for Antero and Greycloak. And something . . . not so rich"—he grinned at Maeen—"for the rest of you. Now, if I've forgotten anything, or you have trouble of any kind, ask Beemus and he'll take care of it."

We murmured our thanks; the king nodded, accepting them. "Now, here's the rules. Be on your good behavior, but not so good you spoil your fun. Besides, I want to see what you're *really* like, and I can tell you now, I don't like tight-arsed fellows."

He looked at Janos. "You, sir, wish to study our magic. I'll see if any of my wizards will take you under their wing." He shook a warning finger at Janos. "But don't go dabbling with the black sort. There's no demons allowed in my realm. And I intend to keep it that way."

Janos dipped his head in acceptance; his eyes were alight with pleasure. Just then, Raveline stepped forward. "I'd be glad to take him on, brother," he said. "I hear he has amazing talent."

"I thought you might," Domas said. "And that is fine with me." He looked back at Janos. "Prince Raveline is my chief wizard. Damned good one, too. Although not as good as he thinks. Fact is, I could best him with a little practice, but wizardry and ruling do not go together in Vacaan. We've kept them separate from the start and always shall in the future."

"I also do his dirty work for him." Raveline laughed.

"And you're damned good at that as well," Domas said. "Too bad you enjoy it so much." Then, to us, "I know he practices the black arts in that palace of his. And he knows that I know, and all that circular rot. Unfortunately it's a necessary evil. We have many enemies outside. With only his filthy work to keep them at bay."

"Such admiration, brother dear, is overwhelming," Raveline said.

The king ignored him. "So there's no confusion, you ought to know what all my subjects know: I dislike my brother intensely. As much as he hates me. The only reason we haven't killed each other, as everyone in Vacaan *also* knows, is that it was forbidden from the beginning. If one of royal blood kills another, or causes one of our subjects to kill, then our dynasty is ended."

The king chortled. "My less majestic brother has greater need to kill *me*. You see, he wants more than anything to be king, but I have ten royal children in line for the throne." He laughed again at his brother. "You'll be dead ten times over, oh less majestic one."

Raveline returned his laughter. "Then I shall have to be happy with my dirty work," he said. More words were fired back and forth, and we tried not to show discomfort at this display of long and bitter rivalry or show signs of taking sides, although I easily chose mine. I studied Raveline as the two royals engaged one another. Utorian had said the prince was the younger brother. I would have guessed otherwise: while Domas seemed to be in the early part of his fourth decade, Raveline had the look of a man knocking hard on the door of his fifth. His forehead above and below the crown was deeply channeled; his eyes were pouched and edged with fishnets of long conspiracy; the lips were knowing and sensuous from practiced decadence. I heard his laugh again: it was rich and deep, but it came too easily and was touched with the love of mockery. His brother the king roared laughter in reply, but this mirthful boom rang sincere. Domas was a man who relished the very act of laughter—even when it jeered.

My dislike for Raveline did not grow slowly from the bitter ground of later experience; it rooted and leaped to full maturity at first sight. If I had written his description a minute after we met, my quill would still have lusted for poisonous ink. His description, I realize, paints a man with masked features that hid sorcerous connivance and twisted purpose. In reality, he worked hard to match his brother, keeping his face open and allowing emotion to do as it pleased with position and complexion. He made his speech blunt, and he rode it down the short road to direct points. But I had my father's eye for sizing up a customer, and this was one I did not trust. However, distrust can catch a bargain as well as its pretty sister; so I made it into a coin for further use. I glanced at Janos and worried when I saw how he was weighing Raveline's every word. Ah, well, I thought, he's practiced in taking care. Besides, knowledge was his purpose now, and what harm can knowledge be?

The brothers ended their quarrel, and I saw my chance. I caught the king's attention and asked, "If I may ask a question, Your Majesty?"

"Ask away," Domas said.

"That *we* have much to gain from this experience is obvious. But, I wonder, sir: what benefit are *we* to *you*?"

Domas was startled; he pulled his head back and peered at me for a long moment. Then he laughed and turned to Beemus. "Remember the time I asked you to set aside? So Antero and I could talk?" Beemus whispered that unfortunately, he did. Domas said, "Well, make it longer." He spread his hands apart quite wide. "*Much* longer."

His broad face swiveled back to me. "I'll tell you then," he said.

With that, our audience ended.

CHAPTER TWENTY-THREE
The First Veil Parts

A KING'S PROMISE is not the same as other men's. My word *must* be my bond; only a fool would trade with me if it were not. But a king can renege when he pleases and suffer little, if at all. His business is unique: there is no other source for such promises; and if only one is granted out of ten, there will still be ten more supplicants elbowing through the crowd to win the king's favor.

Two weeks after King Domas had given his promise, we were still gnawing on that doubtful coin to test its worth. I had not heard from Beemus about that "time" the king had promised, and there had been no answers from the palace to my many queries. Janos was particularly worried, for he held the "less majestic" promise of a prince, and his equally numerous messages to Raveline had also gone unanswered. Adding to Janos' woes, Prince Raveline had done nothing at all beyond that first gesture, while Domas had made good on at least part of what he had promised. Our men were well cared for, enjoying an easy life at a villa near the main docks, where there were many entertainments and awe-stricken women to beguile them. Janos and I had each been given a palace for quarters and luxuries aplenty to soothe time's passage. But the abundant and glamorous present was perched on the crumbling edge of the future, and each second of our wait had become an agony.

"I almost wish Raveline had stayed out of it," Janos said one day. "With the prince claiming me as his student, no one with any *real* knowledge dares do more than wish me a good morrow."

My distrust of Raveline made me glad, but friendship prodded a sigh of sympathy. "Both our royal hosts have become as unreachable as that mountain," I said, indicating the holy summit that graced the view from my balcony. Actually, it was one of many balconies I could claim in the palace I had been given; but the great blue Holy Mountain reflecting in the river had made this one my favorite. "I keep telling myself to be patient," I continued, "but when patience is your *only* choice, such reminders are little help."

Janos gave his beard a tug and laughed. "You are a good friend, Amalric," he said. "But I am *your* good friend as well. So I know you hide your true feelings just now."

I shrugged and laughed with him. I had told Janos my poor opinion of the prince, and he had brushed it off as sheer speculation, which it was. "When I speak to the king," I said, "I will be sure to press him for a . . . shall I say . . . more available tutor."

"*If* you speak to the king," Janos said, the laughter quickly gone.

I sighed again, this time, heartfelt. "Yes . . . *If!* I have grown to despise that word. Whenever I have a thought there is always an *if* leaping out to trip me. *If* only I could see the king. And *if* once I saw him: *if* only he would listen. And *if* he listened: *if* only he would find favor with my proposals. And *if* he finds favor: *if* only—"

"I take the point," Janos said dryly. "Too well, in fact. The word will haunt my dreams . . . *if* I should ever sleep again."

Laughter returned to lighten our worry. I eased back in my soft, gilded pillows and wondered again at the Holy Mountain. I thought of the altars of the Old Ones Utorian had mentioned, and the ceremonies they once held to honor the wisest of their Evocators after the Dark Seeker had taken his due. For a moment I imagined the smoke rising from their ashes on the flaming stone, and I imagined the wind carrying the smoke away. To the east, Utorian had said. "Why to the east?" I murmured.

"East of what?" Janos asked.

"Nothing," I said, embarrassed by my rude reverie. "A bit of silliness, which forced idleness seems to encourage."

Janos had other things on his mind as well. He waved at the river, which flowed past in commanded peacefulness and beauty. "They think they are such a superior people," he said, "and show us grand marvels, such as that tame river, to prove it."

"It seems a marvel to me," I said.

Janos snorted. "Only the scale is a marvel. The principle is as plain as honest soap. We routinely calm small areas about our own ships, when conditions are right, just as we call winds from bags we buy on the market to fill our sails. It is only a bit of wind, but there is no difference between the logic applied to that wind, and what they surely must do to bend the weather to their will."

"Could you do it?" I asked.

Janos shrugged. "With experiment, yes, I could crack their methods. But I would also have to figure out where they get all the energy required. Even with a thousand Evocators focusing all their powers on a single purpose, only a tenth of the energy needed would be produced."

"But our Evocators are weaklings next to theirs," I said.

"Nonsense," Janos replied. "Oh, I admit these fellows have more knowledge, and a few, such as Raveline, possess great natural power of their own. But I have as much as he, and am capable of far more." I knew he was not boasting, but making a statement of fact. "Still, even if all of their wizards were as great as Raveline, the power would still be lacking. Therefore, they must get it elsewhere. And when I know where, so shall I."

"But we have seen more than river and weather," I said. "There is wondrous magic wherever we look."

"Toys and tavern tricks," Janos scoffed. "Once again on a larger scale. There are written rules for all the spells we have seen. If—that damned word again—I am allowed to see the scrolls of the ancient wizards, I will perform those tricks as well."

"Is there nothing that impresses you?" I asked Janos.

"Oh, to be sure," he said. "Otherwise I would despair. I have seen many things that I ache for knowledge of. To name one: did you know they can transmute common elements into gold?"

I laughed. "What do you care? Gold has never been something you fancied, except as a means to an end."

Janos remained serious. "Forget the value. Although any ordinary element will do, they make it from sand, as that substance is the most plentiful; and they do it with such ease and in such quantities, they use gold in common construction. They even prefer jewelry of gold alloy, which they can only get from manufacture, because it is not so soft. It is the doing that excites my interest."

"I saw you change a scorpion into a mouse once," I said. "And Mortacious made the mouse a gold plate. Why is sand to gold a greater feat?"

Janos thought for a moment, searching for a means to explain a complicated thing to a man who was less than a novice. "I did not *change* that scorpion into a mouse," he said at last. "I *put* the scorpion away. Into another . . . place, is the only word I can think of to describe it. I did not see that place, but I felt it with my mind. And with my mind I fingered an opening, then . . . *put* the scorpion through that opening. I got the mouse the same way. Although it was not from the same place. Perhaps it was in Mortacious' kitchen, poor thing. Or perhaps, it wasn't even of this . . . world." He looked at me to see if I understood. I was ignorant enough to think I did, and nodded.

"Good," Janos said. "So, you see it was only an exchange of sorts. The gold of Irayas is a different matter. They actually manipulate the sand, somehow. Actually, they manipulate what makes the sand, sand."

"Why, the smallest thing that goes into making sand," I said, "is a grain of the same material."

"Not at all," Janos said. Then he stopped himself. "I shouldn't sound so certain when I am not. It is a new theory I have. It came to me when I considered what they had accomplished, and how it could be done. I think, now, that all we see about us—the table we sit at, the balcony it rests upon, that mountain we view, even our own bodies—is made of particles so small the very grain of sand we consider is a mountain itself in comparison. And I think they somehow move those particles about, rearranging them, if you will, until they have the same form as gold. In fact, it *is* gold, and no longer whatever the material they chose to make it from."

I blew out a long breath. "I have followed you as far as I can, my friend," I said. "But I fear you lost me where a single grain of sand was revealed to be not one, but many grains, and those so small I have not vision enough to see them."

"If you understand only that," Janos said with a smile, "you understand all. Right now that makes you as wise as me." Gloom returned to darken his features and make him worry at his beard. "Do not misunderstand my scoffings at these folk," he said. "I did not mean to diminish their accomplishments. I was only putting them into perspective. There are many secrets worth having here. Many, indeed. And I am sure there are many clever fellows about, if only they would let me meet them."

I exploded laughter as that fearful *if* raised its head again. Janos caught it and joined in. Then he looked past me, and I heard footsteps pad out onto the balcony. I turned to see one of my servants, a message fluttering in his hand. "What is it?" I asked, reaching for it.

The servant shook his head, saying, "Pardon, my lord, but it is not for you. It is for Sir Greycloak."

Janos frowned as he grasped the message, absently muttering thanks. The frown turned to glee as he read the message. "Who is it from?" I asked.

Janos waved the paper at me, victorious. "Prince Raveline," he cried. "And he wants to see me immediately!" He jumped up and gave me a hug. "At last. One of those clever fellows. Now we shall see what we shall see."

He made a hasty good-bye and rushed out, hurling promises over his shoulder that he would tell all when he was done. I sat, moody, watching as Janos ran out of the palace and rushed across the sprawling grounds to his gondola tied to my palace's main dock. My mood was laced with jealousy as well as suspicion of Raveline's intentions. I saw no humor when I resumed that bitter roundelay: If only the king would see me. And if he should see me: if only he would—

The circle broke abruptly as I saw Janos' boat cross paths with another. This boat was smoothing toward the docks he had just left. It carried the royal crest on its sides. When it stopped, a man hopped off before it had been properly tied to a bollard. I leaned over the rail, anxious for a better view. I saw a little man with a most unremarkable appearance, and as he scampered to my palace door, I knew he was Beemus, coming to fetch me to the king.

I WAS TAKEN directly to the king's private chambers. I noticed little grandeur on the way; my mind was too full of speeches quickly devised and just as quickly discarded. The long wait, coupled with suspense, had scattered my previous plans into confusion. I barely noticed the huge doors we stopped before, or the absence of guards. I only saw the doors as an obstacle and raised a hand to push them open. A whisper from Beemus stayed that presumptuous hand. He put his finger to his lips for silence, then cupped his ear, bidding me to listen. As we stood there, I heard the strains of the most wonderful music wafting through the closed doors. The notes were faint, but still formed the body that makes melody, and the ghostly snatches I heard made me yearn to hear more. Beemus motioned to follow him away from the doors and down a long, narrow corridor that circled the king's chambers. We came to a small door, which we entered, and I found myself in a curtained vestibule. The music swelled louder, more wondrous than before. Beemus parted the curtains and led me through. The chamber was dim, but in front of me I could see a hulking presence that could only be the king. He was seated, and his back was turned, but there was no mistaking that big head resting on a brawny arm. Beemus pushed me forward, and I stumbled against a chair beside Domas. The king didn't seem to notice the stumble, the scrape that followed, or the sigh of the soft pillow when I sat next to him. Beemus' shadow flittered to the other side and flowed up into the vacant seat on the king's left. I was tense in Domas' silent presence, then I saw that his eyes were closed in soft concentration, and there was a small, delighted smile on his features. Then the music teased tension from its nest, and I turned to listen and see who could make such lovely sounds.

I saw her shadow first, cast large on the wavering curtain that framed her. She was turned to the side, arms uplifted in a piper's classic stance. The shadow arms were long and slender, the wrists gracefully tilted, the fingers arched in dance on the pipes. A smooth brow bent low, but I could see the flutter of lashes and the quiver of upper lip as she kissed the notes and blew them through the pipes. Then I looked down and saw the shadow's mistress, small in the light that bathed the platform where she sat. She wore a simple white robe, belted with a gold sash. Her arms were bare to the shoulder, and the robe cut a modest circle about her slender neck. Her features were sharply defined, as if chiseled by a sculptor, but softened and blended to a more artistic whole, as if that sculptor had spent the remainder of his life polishing the work. Her hair was dark in the light, but when she shifted to form another stream of notes, I saw a gleam of red tresses, red like my own.

I heard the king whisper, "Isn't she lovely?" His whisper seemed to snatch my own thoughts, but his eyes were still closed. The question had been directed inward, and it meant the music, not its maker. I turned back to open myself more fully and let the music wash over me. I had always loved music over all the arts, but this was music that turned boy's love to mature worship. The piper dusted the air I breathed with precious notes, then made them a gale that swept me away. I was a ship of the sky in that melodious storm, and peered over the rail to see wonders that made all others hollow. I had never felt so free with that fresh wind beating at my back, and I wanted to stay on this ship forever.

The music shifted smoothly, and I was back in the chamber, listening to the pipes make a different song. A strange feeling caught me, then, as if I knew what was about to happen next. Somehow I knew the piper would lift her head, and as I saw her do so—her lips never leaving the pipes—I also knew her eyes would search for mine. The thrill I experienced when they met was even greater for having known it would come. I believed I saw a similar shock hit her, and then I was bending forward as her music made a question. The notes were eager, but there was a shyness as well: trepidation that comes with past hurts. The music must have found an answer in me, for it was suddenly very glad.

Gladness swelled in me in return, and I saw her eyes glisten, and I felt the caress of love's familiar fingers. Then suddenly, Deoce's image jumped up, and the fingers burned with guilt's sting. I fled that musical joining as if it were a fanged demon and retreated to the numb loneliness of the cave where I had dwelt so long. The woman's eyes showed shocked injury, and her body sagged as if she had suffered a heavy blow. Then she steadied, and the pipe's notes lifted, grasping for angry stones to hurl at the woman's betrayer. But as I forced my eyes away, I saw her give a sudden nod, and the anger turned to a sweet completion of the song.

Silence draped the chamber for many long moments, a silence that honored great artistry. I heard the king whisper appreciation. The piper rose, bowed thanks, and vanished behind the curtain. But just as the lights bloomed up, the woman gave me one last look; regret stabbed, then she was gone. I turned to the king, shaken, but determined to regain strength of purpose. He was looking at me, a bit oddly, I thought; then the look shifted as he grinned.

"That was Omerye," Domas said.

I pretended idle interest, but felt the thrill of recognition once more. "Thank you, Your Majesty," I said. "Now I know whose name to praise when I tell my friends of that wonderful music."

Domas laughed and struck my knee. "Come now, you were more taken than that. And it wasn't just the music, I warrant." I stuttered denial, but it only gave Domas greater delight. "Never mind," he said. "I won't press further. But I shall tell you this, as one good man to another: Omerye is no courtesan, as you might be thinking. She's one of my kingdom's finest artists, and can choose, or reject as she likes." More stuttering as I thanked him for information I really didn't need. But the king was bored with matchmaking and turned quickly to his reasons for the meeting.

"You want to open trade," Domas said, blunt as usual. "And I will tell you straight—without hints of this and that and the other—I am considering approval."

"I am honored and greatly pleased, Your Majesty," I said. "But what can I tell you to turn that consideration into a contract?"

Domas nudged Beemus. "This fellow keeps growing in my estimation," he said, jabbing a thumb at me. "If he weren't a merchant I'd make him an adviser. Did you notice how he tossed that right back in my lap? Causing no offense, in doing so?" Beemus whispered that, yes, he'd noticed. The king returned to me. "My advice," he said, "would be for you to answer that question you asked *me*, when we first met. I asked Beemus to recall the words exactly."

Beemus knelt in his chair and whispered in the king's ear. Domas was his trumpet, sounding my own speech back to me. " 'That *we* have much to gain from this experience is obvious. But, I wonder, sir: what benefit are *we* to *you*?' "

The king pulled away from Beemus. He said, "Answer that. And answer it well."

I had to laugh, for the king had done what he'd accused me of doing, and so there I sat, my own lap full to overflowing with what I had hoped to heap in his. The laugh came without thought of the king's presence; the grin that was his appreciative reply made me glad I'd reacted so openly. Then I said, "Very well, Your Majesty, I shall attempt just that. I won't dress up our needs by extolling my city's abilities as traders, with a wider area of commerce than any other land. Nor will I boast of my family's achievements, and its reputation for honesty. You know these things, or I would not be here; and even if I were, you would not involve yourself in such a discussion." The king nodded. Encouraged, I pressed on. "Profit is not my motive, sir. And profit was not the motive of my people when they sent me to seek your favor. Here is what I want, sir. And I will put it plainly to you as I know how."

I told him about Orissa, and the good people who made it a city, rather than mere structures scattered by a river. I told him of our dreams and hopes, and our evils, as well. I retraced our recent suffering, lingering, as honesty demanded, on my own losses and sorrows. Then I confessed how I had viewed all the wonders of Vacaan as I traveled up the river to his court, and coveted them to enlighten and protect my own people. I spilled it out, never hesitating to check the flow, praying the king was not viewing me as a young fool for my honesty. When I was done with this preamble, I sat back for breath, and to take measure of what effect, if any, my words had worked.

Domas was silent for a long moment, and I believed he might even have been moved. He said, "Now I truly understand why you came, Amalric Antero. Why you were willing to chance your life, and more. And your reasons do not shame my kingdoms as a goal. They touch on *my* feelings for my own people. Although sometimes I think they forget all that I do, I do for them." He rumbled self-mocking laughter. "Of course, I am not so altruistic as I'm making out. I'm a king. Kings are selfish by nature. We also must do cruel things, which is why my brother's about, instead of locked up in some tower. He's my hellhound. He makes certain my selfish nature, which wants all my people to praise my name, is kept reined in when there are troublemakers among us."

He stopped, as Beemus whispered in his ear. He nodded, muttering, "Yes. Yes. I *was* coming to that." He turned back to say, "Beemus reminds me your speech, while pretty, is shy of the main point. I admit I feel sorry for your people, and their troubles. But, Amalric Antero, what is any of *that* to *me*?"

"It is everything to do with you, Your Majesty," I replied, "for without *our* desires, you would have little of value to entice the trade I seek."

"Show me your goods, then, trader."

So I rolled out my blanket of imagination, and set all manner of things upon it. I told him of the porous stone from the north that the people there carve into singular idols that weep perfume just before it rains. I told him of the lovely, painted cloth the women of the south weave, and how each bolt is different from all the others in design and feel, and flow on your body when it is made into a costume. I told him about the great variety of fruit and grain and drink that flowed to us from all the lands bordering our sea. And I said, although I had seen great bounty in the Far Kingdoms, I noted there was a gray sameness to it as well; which is why, I supposed, his cooks went to so much trouble to disguise that sameness with rich sauces and gravies. I talked at length, and he never wearied as I spun my trader's tale of exotic kingdoms and peoples and odd wonders as distant to him as his land was to mine.

As I rolled my imaginary carpet back up, I closed with this, "I claim no talent as a seer, Your Majesty, when I say that I believe you have become bored with your protected land of plenty. And I have heard you yourself say you fear your people have lost spirit, and are growing stale: The goods I have offered in trade have three qualities of singular value: the excitement of strangeness, the stir of wonder at the unknown, and the spice of adventure renewed." I sat back, charged with the excitement of my own sales talk. "That, Your Majesty, is why I believe you have just as much to gain in this bargain as we have. That is why I am certain, that once struck the contract will be of such immeasurable value to us all."

King Domas' eyes reflected my own excitement. He nodded to himself, once, twice. I believed I had won the day. Then a king's caution took hold; the excited glitter dulled. "The trading could not take place in Vacaan," he said. "Outside influences, as my brother continually warns, can make our people discontent."

"We could easily choose a neutral port," I said. "A place convenient to both of us."

"Yes, we could," Domas said, but his tones were sailing for neutrality as well.

So I spread my hands wide, helpless, saying, "What *else* can I say to convince you, Your Majesty? I have run out of what little wit my father knocked into my thick head."

Laughter returned to the king. He hurt my ears with his bellow, but I didn't mind: I saw reborn excitement in his eyes. "Nothing more, my good fellow," he finally said. "You've done a good job for your city, and you have nothing to be ashamed of. I like your proposal. I like it enough to accept on the spot. However . . ." He stopped as Beemus whispered, then went on. "However, as Beemus says, we must consider the details closely before we put seal to agreement."

"I think that is the wisest course, myself, Your Majesty," I said, rising, for I knew without prodding it was time to depart. "As my father said, 'All bargains glow when first struck, but most become cold lumps by the time you put them in your pocket.' "

"A wise man," the king said.

"Thank you, sir. He was. Now, if you will permit me, Your Majesty . . ." I began to withdraw. Domas hastened it with a gentle wave of his hand, and Beemus jumped down to lead me away.

"How did I do?" I asked when we reached the corridor. Beemus whispered that I had done very well, indeed. With that reply I also knew I had the little man's support; it was easily big enough to carry the day.

I TOLD JANOS every detail of the meeting, only holding back the music and . . . Omerye. When I was done I saw he had noted some omission: Janos had the twin of that odd look the king gave me. Normally Greycloak would have pressed, and I would have confessed, although to what, I was not certain; he had news of his own to convey, and the moment passed. But first he had to examine my efforts for flaws. Finding none, he praised them and said I was sure to bring the work to a happy conclusion.

When I asked him how his own meeting had gone, he became so charged with enthusiasm, his words kept stumbling on confusion as he tried to describe all the wonders Prince Raveline had revealed. He stopped after his last effort: a spell from the scrolls of the Old Ones that caused water to crystallize into ice.

"It was *manipulation* again," he cried. "Like sand to gold, but not near as complex, because water is . . . is . . ." Light dawned and he struck his head a great blow. "By the gods, now I see it!" he shouted. His mind raced, grasping for an elusive prey. Then he shook his head in frustration as it escaped. "Gone, now, dammit!" He looked and saw an ox's ignorance in my eyes, and laughed.

"Never mind," he said. "It will come." He poured us more drink. "Raveline has invited me back tomorrow, and the morrow after that. So there will be *much* more."

"Did he show you his demons?" I joked.

But the jest went awry, and Janos flushed dark. "No . . . He didn't." The flush was of disappointment, and it made me glad. I worry for nothing, I thought. The king forbids it. Even his brother would not dare to defy him. Then I thought: *especially* his brother would not dare.

Janos raised his cup in nostalgic toast. "To the Far Kingdoms."

And I raised mine in that old echo of reply. "To the Far Kingdoms."

ALL WAS GOOD for a while as we plunged into the life that was Irayas. The meetings with Domas and Raveline opened a flood of invitations: we ate and drank at noble tables, we learned new dances in grand ballrooms, and an embarrassment of honors and gifts were showered on us. At night we sailed the silvery lanes of that great lighted city, roaring songs with new friends clutching our shoulders. By day we strolled through wonderful gardens and even more wonderful galleries where the arts of Vacaan were displayed. I saw Omerye once: she was studying the statue of a great harpist. The mysterious bond between us tugged hard, and she began to turn her head in my direction; but the wound Deoce's death had caused gave a sudden ache, and I quickly backed away before she saw me.

The jolt she had given me roused awareness, and I began to worry again. I could no longer ignore that weeks had gone by, and I had yet to meet again with the king. I could have paved a small road with all the messages I sent, asking what progress had been made in the trade agreement. Some went unanswered; most drew the mild reply of: You must understand, these matters are complex. And we praise your patience in advance for bearing up under these unfortunate, but necessary, delays.

As I worried over these oracles from dry authority, I suddenly noted a great absence of Janos. A second worry now gnawed as I realized it had been some time since I had seen him. And before that, his presence had become rarer with each passing day. I also remembered recent messages I had sent to his palace: they met the same fate as those I had sent the king. His servant, Gatra, always answered with regret that his master was busy with the prince and could not be disturbed. Perhaps another date? But each date we set became inconvenient when the time drew close.

Finally I went to the tavern our men favored. It made an unruly sprawl along the freight docks. After so much time amid the perfection of Irayas' wealthy neighborhoods, the ramshackle buildings along the docks and the noisy chatter of common folk was refreshing. I suppose I was homesick for the docks of Orissa, with their tantalizing sights and smells, and the feeling that here, every person, be he fisherman or monger or My Lady fingering the quality, was equal.

Sergeant Maeen and the others were delighted to see me. Lione begged me to put my money away and bought a round for the whole tavern in honor of my visit. As we drank and exchanged gossip, I looked around and saw the men were doing well for themselves. There were plenty of eager young women in their company, and they were *good* women, daughters and young widows of workers and stall keepers. I expected many marriages to come out of this, and idly wondered who would stay and who would go when the time came for us to depart. The other men in the tavern, many of whom had become friends of Maeen and the others, were also a sturdy, hard-working lot; and among the clientele I saw only a few who wore the twisted smile of small larcenies. The sergeant asked how Sir Greycloak was getting on.

"I was hoping you could tell *me*," I said. "I have not seen him about for some time."

Maeen frowned, then forced cheer. "You know how Sir Greycloak is at times, my lord," he said with a laugh. "He gets that mind of his after a badger in his den, then dives right in after it. Don't worry. He'll show up for some fun with his old mates, by and by."

"Have you heard *any* news of him?" I asked.

Lione leered. "Oh, he's not *all* learnin' and business, my lord. Sir Greycloak's as randy as most." He gave me a nudge. "Some say, even more so."

Maeen cut him silent with a glare. To me, he said, "Pay him no mind, lord. Sir Greycloak might have been to a few parties, or so. Just to get the kinks out. But it's all in good fun."

"Did these ... uh ... *parties* ... have anything to do with Prince Raveline?" I asked, knowing the answer, but hoping I erred.

Maeen's long hesitation told me I had not. Then he said, "Well ... I suppose, they did, my lord." The frown returned to channel his brow. He sighed. "They were pretty wicked too, I hear." He gave a nervous laugh. "But there's no call to worry, my lord. It's only a man's passing fancy. And when all is said and done, Sir Greycloak is easily the match of Prince Raveline."

A drunken shout broke in. "What's that dog's name I hear? Prince Raveline, is it?" A big, red-faced fellow followed the shout by lumbering into our group. "This is *my* tavern, sirs. I'll not have that name blacken its premises."

I eyed the landlord, curious at such hate. Maeen and the others had pulled away; some were muttering nervously. Duty drew Maeen back to give the landlord a warning. "We're only here for a friendly drink, man. If it's politics you want, we'll take our commerce elsewhere."

The tavern keeper bleared, angry drunk and near violence. "If I want to call that prince a dog, I'll *call* him a dog, damn you! And it's shaming a dog to do it for all the harm that man has caused!" Before he could continue, friendly patrons grabbed him. He struck out and wrestled a bit, but was finally hauled away: two women, daughter and wife, I guessed, dragged him through a door and slammed it. The whole time the landlord blistered the air with curses on Raveline and his doings.

We were left uneasy by his outburst, but Maeen seemed most troubled of all. He looked nervously about, checking the villains I had picked out before. But where I had seen twisted smiles, there were only bad masks of bland disinterest. "We'd better find another tavern soon," the sergeant muttered to Lione. "That landlord is set on bringing trouble." Lione vigorously nodded agreement.

"I admit he's an uncouth fellow," I said. "But what trouble can he bring? His words may be unpleasant, but the king does not discourage his subjects from speaking their minds. In fact, he demands it. You heard him say so, himself."

Maeen stirred, uncomfortable. He leaned close and spoke low. "The king may *say* one thing, my lord; but that is not how it works down here." He patted the table for emphasis. "And from what I've heard, my lord, it does not always work that way above."

"Tell me more," I murmured.

Maeen shook his head. "It's not wise to linger on it too long, my lord. There are *ears* about." He indicated one of the blackguards who was slipping closer to us. "But I will say this. Mayhap the king's good intentions are being spoiled by another. And that other fellow, if you know who I mean, seems to take offense real easy, like. Dark things have been known to happen when his name is abused."

I wanted to ask more, but the slippery one was nearly at our table, his back turned in studied unconcern, but you could see his ears swivel to listen. So I said, loudly, "Here, now. Let me buy the next round. And we'll all toast our royal hosts." There was much overloud compliance to my proposal, and after a time of broadly innocent fun, Maeen tipped me the wink that I should depart now, so they could casually follow after a suitable period.

I returned home in great alarm. I wondered at those "parties," as Maeen called them, that were hosted by Raveline. Orgies, I supposed, sexual tricks and frenzy stoked by magic. I remembered well the great appeal such things had to Janos. And I had just seen for myself that all was not wondrous light in Irayas. But then I thought of the important negotiations with the king. I *knew* Domas was not lying about his interest, nor was he hiding some dark purpose. Hope sprang again with the reminder that I actually had *seen* nothing, I had only heard. I did not distrust Maeen's word, but he himself had it by third or fourth hand. Not only that, I self-chided, but wasn't I letting my dislike of Raveline flaw my view? After all, what did I have to base that dislike on? The prince had certainly not done anything to deserve it.

While I still had that clumsy ball of yarn tied up with such dubious knots, Janos reappeared. He burst into my palace, full of energy, wit, and high spirits. "I've missed you, my friend," he roared, slapping my back. "I've been buried in dusty old scrolls for too long, and my ears are so stuffed with spells, I fear I am growing deaf from not hearing normal talk."

"Then your studies go well?" I asked.

"Damned well," Janos said. His manner had always been blustery, but I suspicioned a touch of aping of our bluff-mannered hosts. Suspicion faded as he clapped me on the back again and said we ought to see how the men were doing, and swap a drink or three. We found them at another tavern, just as large and soundly working class as the first. With Janos we were twenty again; the reunion was noisy and glorious. Much drinking followed, and perhaps a tipsy tear for fond memories of shared adventures. But just before we were all taken by drink, Maeen came to me. "Remember that talky landlord?" he asked, low.

"At the other tavern?" He nodded. I looked about their new favorite place admiringly. "You were well to be shed of him, I suppose. And you chose the replacement well."

"We weren't shed of him," Maeen said. "We hadn't time. He disappeared that night, and no one has seen or heard from him since. And the tavern was ordered closed."

"By whom?" I asked.

"He wouldn't put his name to it," Maeen said. "But everyone says it could be none other than Prince Raveline."

CHAPTER TWENTY-FOUR
Omerye

ANY RENEWED BROODING over Janos and Raveline was cut short the next day when Beemus showed up at my palace. He said, in his whispered shadow-speak, the king was engaged in important business, but assured me it was only slightly more important, in Domas' view, than the business he had with me. Barring unforeseen emergency, our trade agreement was next in line.

"Can you give me some hint which way the king is leaning?" I asked. He replied with a shrug, but accompanied the shrug with an upward tilt of one corner of his mouth, making, for Beemus, a grin of encouragement. "When will he decide? Can you guess?" Another shrug; the mouth line remained straight, meaning, he wasn't sure. "Can you at *least* tell me this: will it be very long?" Beemus thought a moment, then shook his head: no, it would not be long.

After he had gone, I faced the day with brighter hopes. I sent a message to Janos, thinking we could discuss our prospects. But when I saw Gatra's familiar scrawl on the reply, I knew without reading that, once again, Janos was not available and had returned to Raveline's side. This was not enough to spoil my cheer, so I called for my boat and set out for a lazy day viewing Irayas.

The water has always brought me peace, and I spent several enjoyable hours alone with my boatman that day, cruising the river. It was late afternoon when I came to a district I had never seen before: it was an older area, near the center of the city. The canals were narrower and heavily shaded in the arch of thick-branched trees; the water reflected trunks twisted into forms and faces long past maturity. The homes, although certainly not poor or common, were smaller and steered sharply away from sameness. I smelled fresh paint, the dust of newly cut stone, and woolen yarn, dampened to greet the loom. As we moved through the maze that tied the district together, I saw bright color in the windows of the homes. They were paintings, I realized, and lovely tapestries, as well; all were art in the making, for I also saw limners and weavers at work. The boatman took me past one large, open yard that held a delightful litter of sculptures in all stages of development. We turned into a pleasant bywater, and I eased back to enjoy the song of a bird piping from a tree not far away. Then I realized, with a cold pang, it wasn't a bird making that music. The single note was followed by a gentle stream on the air. The delicate signature was unmistakable: it was Omerye's. I hoarsed for the boatman to turn back, but he was so intent on the music himself, he did not hear and only drew harder on the oars. Then it seemed the pipes had caught my presence, for I recognized the same notes of sudden interest I'd heard in Domas' chamber. More music followed: gentle sniffing all about me, then a joyous cry of familiarity. Low-dipping branches parted, revealing a small dock, and on that dock, feet dainty, bare, and trailing in the water, sat Omerye. As the boat drew up she played a final note; it was one of glad greeting. Then she lowered the pipes and looked at me. Her red hair made a lustrous frame about her pale features, but in the light I saw it was not as close to mine as I thought: it was a deeper red, and softer. She was dressed in a white tunic cut short to mid-thigh, and it clung close to her lush figure. The smile she wore was shy, but it made me glow, and then that glow made me sad, for I knew I must leave.

"I knew you would come." Her voice was as light and musical as her pipes. There was no artifice in it: she *had* known, and, somehow, so had *I*. She pointed the pipes at a white cottage with a slanted roof of weathered blue: her home. "Please?"

There was only one answer I could give, but when I forced it out, it turned on its head and I heard myself say, "Yes. I would like that very much." I clambered onto the dock, trembling when her hand touched my shoulder to help steady me. We stood together, close, almost touching. She was tall, and I found her eyes with no trouble: they were blue; then her chin tilted up, and they were green; the chin tilted higher still, and now they were gray. Her lips were slightly bruised in color and swollen from her piping. They would be easy to kiss, I thought. She stepped away and took my hand and led me to the cottage. Behind me, I heard the boatman chuckle and the scrape of wood as he pushed off, and I almost turned to urge him to wait, for I would not be more than a moment. I heard the splash of oars as he pulled away, and I entered the cottage. It was dim and hung with old, thin tapestries of artful design. The main room was spread with pillows of muted color. They made a circular pattern about a small stool. Omerye sat on the stool and patted one of the nearest pillows. I sank down, so full of questions and confusion, I only had strength for silence.

It was broken by her musical voice. "Do you understand what this is about?" I shook my head, no. She raised the pipes. "You are the *one* I play for," she said. I still did not understand. She raised the pipes higher, until they nearly touched her lips. "Since the first moment I played," she said, "I saw a person in my mind. And it is that person I make my music for." She stopped, the pipes drooping lower, and shook her head. "No. That isn't right." She pressed the pipes tight against her breasts. "I make music for *me*." The pipes came up again. "But I play the music for . . . *you*. You are that person in my mind." The pipes were closing on her lips again. She said, "And you have been there, since . . . since . . . well, always."

She commenced to play. In my mind the music formed the image of a small, pale child; she was silent and serious and given to dreams. When I write that I *saw* her, imagine my ears were my eyes, and the notes created form and color better than any light. The child loved all sound, whether shrill bird cries or the knock of dry wood against a dock. I saw her make sounds of her own, using common things to produce uncommon notes. I saw her form those notes into a first whole song. She always played to a mirror, and in the mirror I saw an image I couldn't quite make out. The vision blurred, then I found the child grown into a girl with swelling buds for breasts and hips flaring into womanhood. She sat before the mirror, red hair spilling downward as her head bent over new pipes. She made a lovely song, but you could tell by her hesitation, she was testing new ground. I saw her glance into the mirror, as if seeking approval. At first I thought I saw her own reflection there; but the red hair that shone back was of a slightly different color, and the features smiling approval were not hers, but mine. The music carried me onward: I saw the girl become a woman, saw her music lift above all heights, saw that woman play before important and approving people. But always there was one person whose approval Omerye was really seeking, and that person was me.

The song ended, and I opened my eyes to see tears in her own, but there was gladness in the tears. "Now, here is the first song

I ever heard in my head," she said. "But, I could never play it . . . until now." She lifted the pipes once again, and melody swirled about me. Each note was one I had never heard before, but the refrain haunted close, oddly familiar. The song found secret places, and each place was happy to be revealed. Omerye's pipes swept me away, and she and I were discovering new things together: fresh vistas of mountains and rivers and rolling seas. The pipes stopped, and as the last notes drained from the air, I realized the song had been made only for me.

"*Now*, do you understand?" she asked, trembling, anxious.

As I began to answer, a black pit opened, and she became a small, distant figure across the wide gulf. Bitter memories of Deoce and little Emilie flooded out, washing over me. Grief struck and became hard, dry sobs rattling in my chest. I was locked in mourning, and as I mourned I knew I would soon suffer another great loss. For how could I ask Omerye to live with such specters?

Halab heard me and took pity. I felt his presence, and his whisper rustled in my ear. "You will find them there," he said, "if you will only look." I did, and when I raised my head, the pit had vanished. Omerye's face was close, and I looked into her eyes and saw Deoce and Emilie reborn. Omerye's love joined theirs and became the whole. "Do you understand?" she asked again.

"Yes," I said. "I understand." I swept her from the stool, and she came into my arms with a cry of delight. We fell into the pillows, aching for want of the other, all hot hands and twining limbs. My fingers opened her tunic with ease, as if from much practice. They caressed softness that was at once mysterious and familiar. I heard myself say, "I love you, Omerye." I heard her whisper back, "I have *always* loved you, Amalric." And then, except to repeat those words, we did not speak for many hours. We made love until dawn, and in the chill morning, Omerye played that song once more. She played and I listened, and we were complete.

They say time passes swiftly for new lovers, and as if in a dream. Only the last was true for us: we spent the following weeks in a trance, drunk with one another, but each week seemed more like years and heaped together they made a lifetime. There was much to know, but there was also much *known*, and before very long there it was understood that any future the gods allowed would be lived in the other's company. The only question was where, and that was settled the first time I broached it. "Shall I speak to the king?" I asked. "And ask to become one of his subjects so I can remain here with you?"

"Only if it pleases you," Omerye said. "But don't make the mistake of doing it to please *me*."

"Wouldn't you rather remain with your own people?" I asked, thinking of Deoce and wondering if fate would have cast different dice if we had returned to her tribe. "You are much admired here. I fear your art would suffer in Orissa."

"Admiration has never been my goal," Omerye said. "Only freedom to make any music I choose."

"You would have that in Orissa," I said. "And admiration as well. But I do not think art is as great a treasure as it is in Vacaan."

Omerye's face darkened. "It is not so wonderful as you have been led to believe," she said. "The king may *say* all is encouraged for art's sake, but in practice it is another thing. In Vacaan there are unspoken boundaries that limit all the arts. If you go beyond it, certain . . . things . . . happen. The least of which is you are suddenly without patrons, or audience of any kind."

"But how can that be?" I asked. "Why, in Vacann, artists are paid the greatest of all compliments. When their work is complete, a spell is cast so no one can duplicate it in any manner. And each is preserved, so the work remains in all ways unique."

"Uniquely tame . . . and therefore not unique at all," Omerye replied. "When you have been here longer, you will see nothing is allowed that stirs public questioning or debate. An artist can only dare with form, or color, or tone. But we can never challenge authority. Much is made of our system, because authority goes to great trouble to sniff out our talents when we are young. Then we are given the best of training. But along with that training a very subtle message is imparted: do this, and no more."

"What happens to those who don't listen?" I asked.

She shivered. "One day," she said, low, "they simply fail to appear." The twin of the chill that had touched her, touched me, and I thought of the missing tavern keeper . . . and Raveline. "We all know better than to ask what happened to them," Omerye continued. "And we take great care we never mention their names again." She nestled deeper into my arms for comfort, sighing. "At least *I* had *you*," she said. "That alone is what kept me content."

It was decided she would return to Orissa with me. The decision tumbled me out of love's trance, and I became anxious to complete my business. Omerye moved into my palace, and I resumed skirmishing with the king's officials. Along with awareness came fresh worries about Raveline and Janos. The old nightmare of the ruined city returned to haunt my sleep, but this time I had Omerye's sweet music and love to lessen the torment. The gentle balsam she spread made it easier to think. Ideas leaped up and became theories that only needed testing to become solutions. Finally, I sent Janos a firm message that I must see him. A day or so passed before I received a reply: Greycloak agreed to meet with me . . . immediately.

I found him hard at work, deep in the bowels of an old building that smelled of parchment dust and the stale sulfur of ancient spells. His eyes widened in surprise when he saw me, and I knew our meeting had been forgotten. "Amalric, my friend," he shouted, jumping up from a writing table and spilling old scrolls on the floor. "What a happy coincidence. I was just thinking of you." His clothes were in absent disarray, and he was covered with so much dust, it fell in clouds when he bounded over to me, and made him sneeze.

"You look like one of my old tutors," I laughed, "and sound like him, too. He was always going about with a snuffling nose and absent air. It was a pity my father had to let him go. The old fellow never knew what I was up to."

Janos smacked his forehead. "How stupid of me," he said. "That's right, I *invited* you, didn't I?"

"If you insist on being absentminded," I teased, "I suggest you form some other habit of abasement. A few more knocks on your pate, and you'll be permanently addled."

"You're right," Janos said. Still lost in his studies, he raised his palm to give his head another knock. His wits returned as the hand reached eye level. He stared at it a moment, then laughed. "You are right, twice!"

I looked about the big room: from floor to vaulted ceiling, and from wall to distant wall, it was filled with scrolls of every shape and size. On Janos' desk I saw one scroll held open by small weights. The writing was not in any language I knew, but was colorfully illuminated by geometric patterns painted in the margins. "These are the archives of the Old Ones," Janos explained. "As far as I can tell, it is a complete record of all their spells—all the way back to their beginnings."

"You must have made an even greater impression on the prince than I thought," I said dryly. "For him to trust you with such ancient secrets."

"Yes. Yes, I have," Janos said, so lost in his studies he did not note my mocking tone. "Although I am not certain he sees real value in these archives." He sank back into his seat, picking up a scroll and studying the inscriptions. "For the wizards of Vacaan," he said, "these are much picked-over leavings. But they were a treasure of immeasurable value when the king's ancestors first settled here . . . on the very bones of the Old Ones."

I eyed the long walls of knowledge. "It is a pity we were not so blessed in Orissa," I said.

Janos slapped the scroll down, excited. "You have it exactly," he said. "Domas' people came here as ignorant as any barbarian. Raveline admits it himself. All they have accomplished are refinements of what was once a great art."

"I see you have not yet met the smart fellows."

Janos glowered. "Not a damned one. I am coming to believe there are no *smart* fellows. Not anywhere."

"Not even your mentor, Prince Raveline?"

"Oh, he thinks he is," Janos said. "But I'm learning more looking over his shoulder than listening. What I get from a thing, and what he says is happening, are often opposites."

I indicated the scrolls. "What about the Old Ones? Were there any smart fellows among them?"

Janos sighed. "I know you'll think I'm a boaster," he said. "But I must answer honestly. No. There were not."

"Did any of them stumble on the trail you are now following?"

"A few might have. But for some reason, they never continued." Janos snorted. "I suspect those were the wizards the Old Ones honored on the Holy Mountain." Another snort. "Although what they were honoring remains a mystery I doubt is worth unraveling."

"So that leaves only you," I said.

Janos gave me an odd look, whose meaning I could not decipher. Then he said, firmly, "Yes . . . Only me."

"But only because the others have been blind, or abdicated," I said.

"Whatever the reason . . . No one has even come close to what I see. All of them kept going in greater and greater circles, from one generation to the next. They were doomed for never asking a single question: why?"

"Do *you* know the answer?" I asked.

Janos gave his head a mighty shake. "No. But I am close, dammit! Close. I already see things no one has even dreamed of looking for." Janos' excitement intensified. "You remember when I told you about the trick with the scorpion and the mouse? How I *put* the scorpion away in one place, and *took* the mouse from another?" I nodded that I did. "Well, now I know the how and why of it. There are many worlds, my friend, that exist alongside our own. Each world follows its own rules. A demon has his. We have ours. When we summon the demon, we also summon the rules of his own existence, and with knowledge we can manipulate those rules to our ends. Just as he can manipulate ours if he is the superior in the bargain."

"Like Mortacious?" I asked.

Janos' face darkened. "Yes. Like Mortacious."

"How does one assure himself he will always be the superior?" I asked.

"By knowing that no matter how different those worlds appear, no matter how different the rules seem, there is really only one law that commands everything. The differences that so confuse us are merely many manifestations of that single law."

"Do you know that law yet?" I asked.

Janos' eyes glowed with the passion of his hunt. "No. But, as I said, I am close, my friend. *Very* close."

I breathed a sigh of relief. "Good. Now, listen to me, Greycloak. All is not as it seems in Vacaan. It can be a dangerous place if we tarry much longer. I think all of us should leave as soon as I complete my business with the king."

"Leave?" Janos said, astounded. "I couldn't leave now. I told you . . . I am *very* close."

"The terms of my bargain should keep much of that knowledge coming," I said. "And I have a plan that can offer much more, besides."

"What is that?" Janos asked; his tone was as if he were addressing a child.

I ignored it. "When we return to Orissa, I shall fund a great school of wizardry. You will be in charge. Think of all the eager assistants you will have to carry out any experiment you like. If you all hammer at it jointly, why, soon the wall shall fall, and you will have all you seek."

Janos frowned. "But . . . then . . . *others* will know!"

"Exactly," I said. "That is the beauty of my plan. If everyone knows then all of us are equals. Together we can accomplish as much, or more than they have in Vacaan. And without the blinders you constantly bemoan, we can do it more quickly."

"That could still take a lifetime," Janos said. "*My* lifetime."

"What of it? You will still have the satisfaction of knowing someday it *will* be done."

Janos coughed and busied himself picking up the scrolls and

sorting them. "I fear you are making a complex thing too simple," he said.

"Oh, come now, Janos." I laughed. "You are always the one to insist on the opposite. The simple is made too complex out of ignorance, or, more likely, the desire of the wizards to appear wiser than they are. Why, from what you have told me already, and remember, I am a simpleton when it comes to sorcery, I could put a right-thinking Evocator from Orissa on the same trail you are on. If I told Gamelan, for instance, that business of many worlds, side by our own; and added your theory that one law commands all forces, seen or unseen; why, even that old brain might begin to glimmer. Who knows where that glimmering would take even Gamelan?"

Janos gave me that odd look again. "Who knows, indeed?" he murmured.

"You see my point?" I asked.

"Yes, I suppose I do," Janos said.

"Then you agree to my plan?" I pressed.

Janos twisted and untwisted his beard. He picked up a scroll and stared at the inscriptions, absently, at first, then with more and more absorption. I could see his thoughts racing away. "Janos," I prodded again, and louder. "Do you agree?"

He looked up, that charming smile of his flashing through his unruly beard. "Why, of course, I do, my friend. Of course, I do. Come and see me when you're done with the king. And we'll talk again."

"What is there to talk about . . . if you agree?"

Janos shrugged. "Oh, I am hunting a thing just now, and if I cannot find it by the time you are done . . . Well . . . There might be a small delay. A very small delay." I had to be satisfied with that, for his eyes were glazing over, and his lips were muttering aloud the strange words he was reading in the old scroll. I wished him farewell, got an absent whisper in reply, and left.

I fretted over our conversation for an hour or two, then, from the lazy comfort of Omerye's arms, I took another look and fretted less. The more I thought about it, the more sound my plan appeared, and after a while I believed it so sound, I knew my friend—he who worshipped reason—could not help but see it, too. So there was only the business with King Domas to conclude, and then we would all return to Orissa bearing even more than what we had dreamed when we first set out for the Far Kingdoms.

The next day a royal invitation came. But the summons was not from the king; it was from Prince Raveline.

CHAPTER TWENTY-FIVE
The Servants of Corruption

AT THE APPOINTED hour, a gondola pulled into the dock of my mansion. It was large and could easily have carried twenty as well as one. I was the only "guest" aboard. There were four other men to be seen: a steersman at the rudder, a serving man in the luxurious glass-windowed cabin, plus two men in the bow with long trumpets to warn other craft out of the way. The gondola carried eight oars on a side; the rowers were hidden belowdecks. They might have been human, but if so had been trained to perfection: the oars bit, feathered, and stroked as if they were run by clockwork. The trumpeters were not needed, for any gondolier who saw Prince Raveline's red, gold, and black house colors blazoned on my craft would scuttle away like water spiders fleeing a crafty old pike when it comes up to the shallows to feed.

The boat turned off the main canal into an untraveled waterway that led beyond the city toward the Holy Mountain. It was odd to be moving by water through green, rolling countryside that was as carefully manicured as an athletic field. There were no farms, no farmers, nor did I see houses, roads, or even paths. The canal curved in a series of eye-pleasing bends. Far out in the country it ended in a circular pond.

A low, sleek carriage waited; it was drawn by six matched, blaze-faced black horses. Four footmen led me to the carriage and bowed as I entered. They mounted to their stations, and without a command from the driver, the horses moved away. Despite my apprehension, I peered eagerly out the carriage windows, curious as to what Prince Raveline's estate would look like. I was not disappointed—but neither was I enthralled with splendor. The road we traveled was made of stone blocks, each block stretching from one side to the other of the roadway, which was easily five times the height of a man in width. Each was precisely fitted to its fellow. I expected the road to come to a huge wall, with elaborate gates, but there was none. The perfectly manicured countryside rolled on around me, with trees and ponds as precisely laid out as if a master gardener had been at work for aeons. As inviting as it appeared, I felt that if I had come on this preserve knowing nothing, I would have found it cold and foreboding. The longer our journey on that peaceful lane, the more my dread grew; I did not know whether the dread came from a protective spell, or if it was merely because I *did* know the identity of the estate's lord.

I saw the first guardians—there were two of them, standing on either side of the road. They were nearly one hundred feel tall and carved from dark polished stone. Each statue was of a woman, holding a naked sword vertically before her. I knew no earthly being had served as a model for the sculptures—the women were impossibly beautiful, but hard, cold, distant—the faces as pitiless as a chieftain's from the ice fields of the south. After we passed, I looked back at the forbidding monoliths and drew in a sharp breath. Each statue had a second face, looking to the rear, and that face was a leering, malevolent, fanged demon. I hoped for his sake that the sculptor had worked merely from his imagination, but from what I'd heard of Prince Raveline's interests, I suspected not.

I regained my composure and saw movement through gathering gloom. I thought it would most likely be a roving cavalry patrol, and once again was wrong. From behind a copse trotted a pack of direwolves. There must have been a dozen of them. They came directly for us, and I swore for not having dared to bring a weapon. These huge shaggy killers would bring down the horses in an instant, and I doubted if the six of us could stand against the beasts for more than a few seconds. Each of them stood about eight feet at the foreshoulder, and their dreadful fangs gleamed long and blood hungry. I braced, waiting for the horses to see the wolves and bolt. But they did not. The wolf pack split around us, as if they were, indeed, escorting cavalry. They trotted on either side of the carriage. I could hear the scrape of their nails against the roadway. One of the beasts was beside my window, and it looked in. I vow its gaze was nearly human and wholly baleful. Overhead there was the whisper of great wings, and I saw a patrolling flight of those spur-armed, monstrous eagles we'd observed coming upriver to Irayas. Raveline's castle was well guarded, indeed, I thought as the fortress came into view. It was a huge hexagon with round towers at each angle, and it sat in the center of a perfectly flat field. I estimated each wall would have stretched nearly a third of a league. I thought all the castles I had ever seen, including that sea castle of the Archons, could have been fitted into this edifice's keep. I saw no sign of guards either on the battlements or patrolling around the structure.

One man waited outside a yawning portal—Prince Raveline. There were no other guests, no welcoming servitors. Now I was truly afraid, my fear enough so I felt I could taste its metallic aridity. The coach drew to a halt in front of him, and the footmen sprang down and bowed to their master. He nodded acknowledgment, strode to the door, and opened it himself.

"Lord Antero," he said. "You honor my presence."

I slid out, bowed deeply, and touched my lips to the hand he extended. "It is you who honor me," I said. "I have never been invited into the home of any prince, let alone one so great as yourself. Nor personally handed down from my carriage by the prince himself."

"There," Raveline said. "Now we have both dispensed with the required niceties. I plan no other ceremonies, and if you have speeches or clever compliments ready, we shall take them as given and returned." He smiled, but his eyes were cold, cold.

He took my arm and led me into the castle. "I pondered long as to whether I should invite others. I did not . . . do not . . . want you to think you are being slighted by not being surrounded with panoply and courtiers, but we have matters of import to discuss— matters I would rather none of those who dance attendance around my brother would witness." He made a mirthless smile. "I cannot," he continued, almost to himself, "order the tongue cut out of *every* loose-lipped sycophant in the Great Court. Much as that would prove a blessing."

I hoped my face showed no response as I realized Raveline must have seriously considered the option before reluctantly rejecting it. We passed into the heart of his castle. He apologized for not giving me the full tour, but said that would take several days and might serve for our mutual amusement at another time. "Besides," he said, "I am not entirely sure even *I* can find my way about."

For this reason, I cannot go on for page after page of the marvels of this Black Prince's abode. I shall mention but a few things of note. One was each wall and floor appeared to have been hewn from a single slab of stone, polished to a mirror glaze, then hand fitted to its mate. Another was the warmth. I know of no way to keep castles from dankness and chill, but in this one I was as comfortably warm in every room and hall, without being scorching, as I am at this moment writing in my study with a peat fire glowing. I gaped at the treasures, from tapestries glowing with inner lights, to furniture shaped and polished until it whispered like the finest silk to my fingertips, to paintings ranging from realistic to bold bursts of pure color that sang to my heart. There were other things I noted and turned away from hastily, things that sometimes still appear in my dreams, that I will not, must not describe.

Raveline led me through the great hall, where relicts and battle flags from his dynasty's reign hung below the shadow-buried gambrel roof, into a smaller chamber. In the center of the room was a table. On it were half a dozen covered dishes. There were only two places laid, and each of the utensils and plates had been turned or cut from a different-colored block of jade, from red to translucent to various greens to white. To one side was another table, this one laden with a dizzying assortment of bottles and decanters, containing the liquors of many lands.

Prince Raveline asked me what I cared to drink, and I suggested I would be most content with whatever he chose, although I warned him I would most likely offend by not showing proper appreciation by draining my glass. "For it is a custom of my people, especially with me, who has a weak head, to avoid the grape until business has been concluded. Since you said outside you had some matters of import to discuss, I would be deeply shamed if I woke tomorrow and found all the wisdom I'd spouted had been filtered through dregs. After I have heard your ideas, and determined how best we Orissans can implement them, well, then we can pour it down by the hogshead if Your Highness wishes." Raveline smiled, poured two glasses, but said nothing, neither acknowledging my flattery nor reprimanding me for it.

We sat down and, without preamble, he began. "You know of course that your journeys toward our lands were watched, from the first day you were first wrecked on the Pepper Coast until we provided rescue on the wharves at Gomalalee."

I kept a bland countenance and answered that we had been told of the Far Kingdoms' interest, but not that it had reached back to my Finding. "A question, my lord. You used the words *Pepper Coast*. I thought the people of Vacaan had but the smallest interest in what lies beyond their own borders?"

"Mostly correct," Raveline said. "But there are exceptions. I am one such, which will be a topic of conversation in a few moments. But holding to the subject at hand first: you were not only watched, but you were tested at times. For instance, in Gomalalee."

"Of course, if we had failed to respond as you deemed fit . . ." I said, and let my sentence trail off.

"Then, you would hardly have been worthy of being the ones who *did* achieve Vacaan." I felt anger flash, remembering dead men, injured men, sick men, and desperate men facing death from thirst or sorcery, but repressed it. I did, however, allow a touch of sarcasm to color my next sentence as to how pleased we were to have been found worthy.

"Now to return to the earlier matter," Raveline said. "I am sure you're aware that, at present, the interest the kingdoms of Vacaan have in your western lands is minor, and shall probably extend to no more than allowing some of our knowledge or goods to be exchanged, at a point beyond our borders, for whatever crafts, artifacts, or perhaps people of pleasure we might find amusing."

I felt a slight thrill—despite his use of words meant to diminish my hopes, this was a clue from the king's brother himself that my efforts might meet with success—and smiled approvingly. Needless to say, I set aside any reaction to the proposal that I might be interested in pimping for the Far Kingdoms.

"You look pleased," Raveline observed. "I, myself, think such a boon would be a paltry return for how much you and your companions, especially Sir Greycloak, have endured over the years. So what we will discuss, after we eat, is how much closer a relationship between the lands of the west and these kingdoms might be, should circumstances . . . alter."

With that, he lifted one of the dish covers and began to serve our meal. I do not remember what viands we consumed, other than they were perfection—each bite sending a different explosion through the senses. What impressed me was the manner of serving. At no time did a servitor appear, but whenever Raveline lifted the cover from a dish, a different course would be exposed. I heard no sound of pistons or hydraulic mechanisms from below, so I presumed the platter change was done magically. Similarly, our plates were always kept fresh and clean. I would eat all I desired of a particular dish, look away or laugh at a bit of Raveline's wit, and somehow sensing my satiety, the plate would be clean and bare. I wondered if Raveline preferred to dine in this manner at all times, with never a smiling servant or maid to be seen or a beaming cook to compliment and reward. It seemed sterile, but I thought it *would* prevent anything discussed over a meal from becoming fodder for the city's gossips.

I do not recall what subjects we chatted about, but they had nothing to do with anything bearing on trade, Orissa, or even our presence in Raveline's kingdoms. Most of his talk concerned various court intrigues, the details stopping just short of being salacious. We also talked of the arts and music of Vacaan. As he spoke, I realized he knew of my love for Omerye, and that he was telling me, most subtly, she should now be considered as much a hostage to fortune as Janos, myself, or any of my men. Do not think I became angry, or even felt threatened—Raveline merely ensured I was aware there was now one more factor in the equation for me.

When we finished, he led me into another room. There were couches arranged about the room, and when I sank into one of them, it welcomed me as softly as a lover's arms. Another drink table was next to us, and both Prince Raveline and I sipped a fruit liqueur. The couches were in a semicircle around a tall, highly polished mirror that hung from a stand as if it were a gong. I knew the glass was sorcerous and wondered what Raveline intended to show me. Before sitting, he touched the surface of the mirror, and it sprang to life. I was looking at a small party of men walking beside a river. I was observing my own Finding as we marched through the fertile, abandoned valley above the Pepper Coast. The perspective must have been from one of the Watchers.

"You were not jesting about having observed my entire career," I managed.

And Raveline replied, "Each time you've entered our lands, or those lands bordering them, our Watchers have been there. I will confess, however, that your recent expedition was mounted in a most clever manner. You were not seen—although seeing is not the correct word—until you had crossed the pass beyond Wahumwa and entered the frontiers of Gomalalee."

He motioned, and a new image swam up on the mirror. Now I was looking at Orissa, as if seen from an invisible tower a thousand feet tall, in the center of the city. A great wave of homesickness swept across me, doubly strong as I realized the image before me was Orissa at this very moment. It would have been just before dawn, I observed, but there were still lights showing. I could make out the Street of the Gods, the citadel of the Magistrates, and the palace of the Evocators. I tried to locate my own home, without showing such interest to the prince.

"As I said, I take more interest in the west than most of my people," Raveline said. "Which is one reason, after a certain period of what I shall politely call skepticism about you and Janos Greycloak and your intentions, I became your most fervent supporter. I have realized Vacaan must look in new directions in the future . . . beginning with Orissa and Lycanth."

"What form," I asked carefully, "do you think Vacaan's interest should take?"

Raveline sipped at his drink. "I am not sure I care, nor am I sure I am able, to answer your question in the fullest detail. Suffice it to repeat that, if certain imbalances within the court were corrected, in a short time there would be a much closer relationship with Orissa." His expression hardened, as did his tone. "This is an opportunity I shall *not* allow Vacaan to miss. We must, and shall, seize the moment. That is why I requested your company this evening. I propose to throw the full weight of my power behind a plan to open the doors to the west." His voice became calm once more. "When this is accomplished, I shall require representation—personal representation—in your lands. I offer such a position to you, Lord Antero."

"As a merchant?" I asked. "I was told you have nothing but scorn for the mechanics of business."

"I would not express my feelings for those who predicate their lives around profit that impolitely, although I personally have always preferred another sort of coinage. But the answer is no. Your trade is secondary to your title, your obvious vision, and the respect you are given in Orissa. I want a man whom I can trust, a man who will sit in the highest councils in your . . . palace of Magistrates. You would speak with my voice in Orissa and, it is not inconceivable, Lycanth as well."

I could not allow Raveline to read my expression, so I stood and paced away from him. It was obvious to me what the prince thought Vacaan's interest ultimately would grow to become—conquest. I would never preside over the destruction of my homeland, least of all as some wizard's toady. As quickly as the thought struck, I forced it away, not sure if the spells swirling around me could include mind reading. Now knowing Raveline's intent, I had to choose my thoughts, words, and actions with exactitude. Not just because it appeared I was one step from opening the gateway to the Far Kingdoms, but also because rejecting Raveline's offer out of hand might mean I would find out just where the disappeared ones went.

I sought and found a ploy and turned back to the prince. "I am honored," I said. "But, frankly, my ambitions have never been quite that lofty, assuming I understand your offer . . . and I think I do."

"Those who reach, grasp," he said. "*Someone* in Orissa will fulfill this function for me. Why should it not be you?" So Raveline's plans were far advanced, and my co-option would not be the scheme's linchpin.

"Someone?" I suggested. "Why not my friend, Janos Greycloak?"

"I have several reasons. The first and least important is I doubt your people would accept a half-breed as even their de facto ruler. I shall add that sort of foolish intransigence can be dealt with. You have passed several times through a great wasteland on your journeys. That land, as I am sure Janos' divinations have told you, was once green and storied. But its people stood against Vacaan. That was aeons gone, in the days of the Old Ones, or so the legend says. But to this day there is nothing but barren ground and sharp flints, and thus it shall serve as an example to others until time itself comes to an end!"

Raveline lowered his voice. "The second reason is because Sir Greycloak has ambitions and plans of his own, ambitions that fit most comfortably with my own desires. Greycloak has impressed me immensely. He wishes to learn all . . . to know everything that has been thought since the earth itself hatched sorcery. Where else can he learn such wisdom, but here in Irayas? I propose to enter him into my household services, given, of course, your willingness to release him from whatever oaths he swore to you. As he progresses . . . as he learns . . . he will not only win honors far beyond those Orissa has grudged him, but I plan to give him real power, power only just less than what I myself wield. I have heard my brother the king refer to me as his hellhound. Such is the role I propose for Janos, soon to be Baron Greycloak. He shall be *my* hellhound!"

I drained my glass, began to refill it, then deliberately looked about the bottles until I found a brandy decanter. I wished to appear as if I might be sealing a potential bargain. I poured my glass half-full and turned back to Raveline.

"This is all most new, Your Highness. I assume you do not require an answer this moment."

"I had hoped for one," Raveline said, and a scowl touched his face.

"Forgive me, but I cannot give it, Your Grace. I have spent long years striving to reach your kingdoms, all of which was spent in the company of a partner. I must confer with him. And,

I should add, that Janos owes me no oaths or fealty beyond those of friendship and a once-common goal."

Raveline started to say something, then bethought himself and painted on an agreeable smile. "Ah. Yes. I forget that in the west the lines of authority are not as clearly delineated as they are here. A man may be considered a subordinate, but his opinion and rights given as much weight as if he were an equal. Very well. Consider our conversation. Discuss it with Sir Greycloak thoroughly. Of course, I would prefer this meeting to be considered sub-rosa for everyone but Janos."

"Of course, Your Highness," I said. Raveline refilled my brandy glass and poured one of his own; he raised it in a toast. "There is a peasant proverb, which predates our taming of the Serpent River: 'The wise man, caught in a spring flood, allows himself to be swept downstream to new riches. The fool struggles and is drowned.' To the wise."

After that there was little else to be said, and I made my excuses, saying I was so excited by the ideas presented by Prince Raveline, I wished to discuss them this very night with my friend . . . if he was yet awake.

This amused the prince. "He does not sleep, Lord Antero. I shall order my servants to take you directly to his palace."

The coach was waiting, and as it drew away, I looked back. Lord Raveline was still standing outside the entrance. In spite of the distance, in spite of the night, I felt as if his eyes still burned at me. I leaned back against my seat, trying to puzzle out a plan. But I wasted invaluable moments by cursing myself, Janos, and every Orissan from Ecco to the peasants of Cheapside, and especially the bazaar tale tellers and nurses who had prattled their stories to me as a child. None of us, not one, had ever considered the not-unlikely possibility that a nation as magnificent and powerful as the Far Kingdoms might not be overflowing with the milk of kindness, waiting only for one Orissan to dance up, so they could bless us with the knowledge that would allow us to return to the Golden Days, when each man was a king and his rulers the gods. I even allowed myself a moment of self-pity, wishing I had never met Janos Greycloak and that my Finding had consisted of one long orgy of whoring and drinking through the lands of the west. But then I would never have met Deoce. Nor Omerye. Let alone the other things that had stretched me much beyond the callow youth I had been to whatever I was now. For better or worse, I preferred what was to what might have been. That was enough wasted time. My paw was firmly stuck in the honey jar, and I had best consider how to get it out.

I glanced out as we passed those two huge stone guardians that bordered Raveline's immediate grounds. I pulled my head back into the carriage with a shudder. It was quite dark, and I was certainly overwrought. But I swear I saw the heads of those two monstrous furies turn and look down at me.

RAVELINE'S PREDICTION THAT Janos was still awake was borne out as the gondola tied up to the floating dock that led up to his water-girded mansion and I saw lights blazing within the manse. Two of the footmen were escorting me up the steps toward the mansion's deck when I noted something unusual: tied to a piling, half-hidden in the blackness, was a small boat. I might not have noted it, but every sense was now atingle for treachery or danger. I heard the sound of soft crying. I ordered one of the footmen to hold his torch high so I could see more. In the craft was a bundle of rags; then the rags moved and I saw that they clothed a woman. She was the first poorly dressed person I had seen in Irayas. The footman was about to challenge her, but I tapped his shoulder and shook my head. We had no time to waste, and she was oblivious of our presence.

We went up the stairs and across the deck to the mansion's entrance. The second footman touched a small brass plate, and I could hear the resounding of a huge gong. He rang twice more before a door set within the main gate swung open, and four guards appeared, flanking the mansion's castellan. It was Gatra, the maker of Janos' many excuses.

"Lord Antero," he said. "My apologies for the delay, but there must have been an error. We were not anticipating the pleasure of your presence."

"I am not expected," I said. "I must speak to your master immediately, on a matter of the greatest import."

Gatra hesitated. "Sir Greycloak retired to his studies earlier, with the expressed desire he not be disturbed. But ... since it *is* you, my lord ... excuse me for a moment." The door closed, and the castellan was gone for long minutes. The portal reopened and he bowed me in. "Again, my apologies for making you wait," he said smoothly. "You are, as always, most welcome. Sir Greycloak is in the tower."

I dismissed Raveline's footmen and followed the man inside. Then I bethought myself. "Gatra, there is a small fishing skiff tied below, with a woman aboard who is crying as if she has just lost everything. Is this of concern to you or to this house?"

The castellan's face showed a flash of anger as he snapped, "She made a fair bargain. And the woman came to us in the first place." Curiosity overcame my preoccupation with greater matters, and I lifted an eyebrow for details. "A few days ago, we sought to augment our staff, even considering applications from country folk. Since the proper training takes much time, we required such prospective servants to be less than ten years of age, and of course, unsoiled by the world. One of them was that woman's daughter. She was here but a day before she stole something and managed to escape from the mansion into the city. I have no idea why the woman chooses to lament her spawn here. It isn't as if she cannot breed more. After I take you to Sir Greycloak I'll have her driven away."

I wondered at Gatra's knowledge of every detail of this enormous household, down to the honesty of the lowliest scullery-maid-to-be, but said nothing. As he turned to lead me onward, I noticed that he had a ribbon sewn to his tunic's lapel. It was red, gold, and black. Gatra led me through the mansion's winding corridors toward the central courtyard. I wrinkled my nose, smelling something untoward.

Gatra saw me. "This has been a night full of the unusual," he said so smoothly I knew he lied. "Not an hour ago we had a kitchen fire, when some lamb fat being reduced for a marinade blazed up, and it took a bucket brigade, and even a spell of Sir Greycloak's before the fire was out . . . and I fear its reek still permeates the mansion."

The stench grew less noticeable as we came into the courtyard. In the center of the courtyard was the tower Janos had chosen for his private apartments and study.

"If you would go on up, milord," Gatra said. "Sir Greycloak said you should not be escorted into his presence, since he is just finishing his night's work, and any presence beyond yours might destroy his concentration. He will be in the uppermost chamber." I thanked him and went up the stairs that climbed along the inside of the tower wall. As I opened the door that led into the observatory, I heard a deep bass humming, a sound yet not a sound that resonated through my body and the stones around me.

"Come in, but do not speak," Janos said. "My guest is skittish."

I had not noticed it before, but the upper room's roof was hinged and was now open to the clear night and the stars. There was a single taper burning on the large desk to one side of the room. Janos sat behind the desk, his face silhouetted like an un-hooded hawk in its mews. There was something else in the room. It was a swirling, hard-to-look-at cloud of utter darkness, with myriad red pinflashes scattering through it. Janos did not further greet or even look at me; all that existed for him was that eddying cloud. I was afraid, without knowing why. I found myself moving backward, my lips curling in a silent, feral snarl.

"You are in no danger," Janos said, again without looking. "My friend is pinioned within the pentagram, and has already been given what he sought." Now I noticed the design Janos had de-scribed, deeply etched into the stone floor. The figure had strange curlicues in and around it that might have been a foreign tongue or signs beyond any language I knew. In the center of the penta-gram guttered three small candles, and between them was a large brass bowl filled with a dark liquid. As I watched, the liquid swirled, then lifted toward the cloud—exactly like a waterspout I had once seen off the docks of Orissa. The cloud was absorbing—"drinking"—that carmine-appearing fluid. The bone-touching hum grew louder. In seconds, the bowl was empty. The cloud grew and the flashes within became brighter as it spun more rap-idly. Janos stood and held his hands in front of him—first palms down, then facing the cloud, then turned up. The cloud blurred upward, like a dim red shooting star seen in reverse, and van-ished. The humming was gone.

Janos motioned around the room, and other tapers flared into life with not a match or sparker required. Another motion, and the roof hatches silently closed above us. Now the chamber, if the pentagram on the floor was ignored, looked no more ominous than the paper-, book-, and scroll-littered study of a savant.

"Friend Amalric," Janos said. "This night I have reached deep into the unknown. That being comes from beyond, and now I have given him what . . . he most desires, and he will come again at my beckoning."

"What manner of creature is he?"

"I do not know yet," Janos said. "But I found suggestions as to his existence, the spells to attract him, and even a dark hint as to the bargain he requires in Vacaan's archives. The information was on a scroll, and its crumbling wax seal held a symbol I knew to be terrible without understanding why. The scroll looked as if it had been untouched since the time of this land's Old Ones. No one—not even Prince Raveline—seems to know of this being, nor the learning he offers. As I said days ago, there is knowledge beyond what anyone in this kingdom has learned. Knowledge for he who dares. Tonight I have begun walking that path."

Janos came out of his exaltation and looked shamefaced. "I have been boasting, my friend. And Gatra said your voice told him some catastrophe was pending."

"I fear so."

"Will wine lessen the calamity ... or make it worse?" I managed a rueful smile. Janos opened a cabinet, took out a decanter and glasses, and without ceremony dumped papers from a chair so I might sit down. "What has happened? When we last spoke, you said nothing of any pending quandary."

I began at the beginning, and as soon as I had mentioned the invitation from Prince Raveline, Janos' face darkened. He said nothing, so I continued. Several times in the course of my narrative, he almost blurted something, but held his tongue until I was quite through.

"Is that all?" Janos asked. I ran the events past my mind's eye again and nodded. I had described what had happened as completely and as impartially as I was capable.

"Damn that—" he began.

I interrupted. "Janos! Remember what I just said? He knew you were not sleeping nor absorbed with your concubines. Be wary of your tongue."

"We shall see about Prince Raveline and his spying," Janos muttered, went to his desk, and found a flask. He scattered powder from it around the room, quickly muttering a spell. "Now, if our Black Prince is listening, he will hear nothing but the repeat of a drunken conversation you and I had about whether there would be profit in opening a restaurant serving the food of Vacaan back in Orissa."

"Won't that be a signal clue to Prince Raveline, and make him suspicious?"

"That man drew suspicion in with his first breath," Janos said. "Nothing that we do can make him more wary. Now, let me return for a moment to where I was. Damn that man! When he first broached the subject of what he saw Orissa's future to be, I told him you could not be tossed a bribe as casually as if you were some greasy Evocator at a customs shed! Not even when the bribe is a kingdom!"

I felt my temper rise, but held it in. "You are saying you knew of Raveline's scheme some time ago, but did not say anything to me?"

Janos' expression flickered. "I did, my friend. I suppose I

should beg your pardon for not alerting you when I first was told. But there was a reason."

"Which was?" I demanded, and I knew anger was in my voice.

Janos studied his wineglass, then drained it. "I must choose my words carefully, Amalric. Do you promise you will hear me until I'm finished before you speak?"

"I . . . yes. I'm listening."

"Let us assume the worst—which I am not prepared to do— and accept your somewhat hysterical assertion that Raveline intends to rule both Orissa and Lycanth with an iron fist. Even if that's true, I have met harsher masters than Raveline, and can name some now in power in lands we both know. I understand him a bit better than you, Amalric. Raveline is a man who shall *never* be king here in Vacaan, and this has embittered him. When he realized this, it was like a yet unforged bloom of iron being hurled into a quenching bath. In a sense it shattered him rather than turning him to steel. Raveline is a creature of enthusiasms, moving from one great project to another as his interests wax and wane."

"He has been interested in *us* for quite a number of years," I said.

"I asked you to hear me out. Please! So he is infatuated with our lands, and has been, as you say, for a period of time. I believe this is simply because they have always been beyond his grasp, in the same sense a child desires a sweetmeat different from the one he sucks. Once the umbrella of the Far Kingdoms has overspread Orissa and Lycanth, he will find another enthusiasm. Perhaps it will be further exploration, perhaps it will be his harem. But he *will* look away, I promise you. By then we Orissans shall be as rich as anyone here."

I waited, but Janos said nothing more. I took a chance. "He wants us to serve him. What are the penalties if we should displease him? I do not know if he has the power to duplicate that great wasteland he said came from the Old Ones, but he made it very clear to me he would happily dispense such a judgment on anyone, and I use his words, who dares stand against Vacaan. Which means Prince Raveline. Further, he said he tested us, but did not elaborate. I wonder what those tests were . . . precisely? What Evocator cast the spell that rebuilt Wahumwa? Was it his sorcery that destroyed the finest soldiers Orissa could field?"

"No!" Janos said loudly, then stopped. "Well . . . I must be honest," he went on, in a calmer tone. "I'm not sure. I don't think so. But what if he did? Would we Orissans have taken measures if a great army tramped steadily toward our borders?"

"Not before we found out their intent," I said.

"I wonder," Janos said. "I wonder. Let us consider something else, as long as we are talking about Orissa. We—you and I—won a victory not long ago against the Evocators and their stranglehold on Orissa. They represented the long-dead past, and they used that past to diminish today's life and tomorrow's dreams. Do you think *all* of those hidebound fools vanished with Cassini? I know they will try to impose their choking tradition again, most likely within a short time after we return to Orissa and inform them the old ways are doomed. And what of Lycanth? I *know* those people. I know their Archons. They are talking even now of rebuilding their damned monstrous wall. How long before they begin increasing the size of their army? And once that is accomplished they will cast covetous eyes on Orissa."

"What of it?" I wanted to know. "We defeated them once, we can do it again."

"I am not sure of that," Janos said. "I have not seen men in Orissa recently with the mettle people like your father and his generation showed. No, Amalric, we *need* Raveline. I beg your pardon, let me be more exact. We need what he represents. We need the knowledge that this city and these lands hold. I sneered at those dusty archives and their librarians, but there is more knowledge on one cobwebbed shelf than in the entire citadel of the Evocators. With this knowledge, with these powers, we *can* bring about a Golden Age, a Golden Age such as man passed through before, and then was found unworthy to live in. In a few years we shall have all the wisdom these lands possess, and then we can step beyond them. We are a young people, and they are old, tired, and set in their ways. I see Vacaan, Irayas, and Raveline as a false dawn, a harbinger of a new, fresh age, an age beyond gold."

"Well said," I replied. "But this is not the time for a battle oration. Consider reality. Do you really think Orissa could rise up against the rule of the Far Kingdoms? I look about me at all these happy, contented faces, like so many purebred cows who do not realize their sole purpose is to breed more cattle and eventually grace their master's table. Do you think these people of Vacaan will ever revolt? And if they do, what would their chances be? Do you want to see Orissans, the people you've taken as your own, become like these cud-chewing cattle?"

"Would they be worse off?" Janos asked. "Do not answer hastily. Think of that slum we walked through when we returned to Orissa. Cheapside. Have you seen anything near its poverty since we've been in these lands? And Cheapside is far from the worst in Orissa. I shall not even mention Lycanth's seething tenements. I believe that if you offered most Orissans a choice between the golden chains of this land, and what they now live with ... they would loudly be shouting for the blacksmith, his hammer, and shackles."

I held my angry retort, poured wine, and forced myself to sip. Then I became even angrier. "I remember, years ago, in the desert, when we freed Deoce and tried to free the other slaves the nomads had taken ... and how furious you were at those who chose to return to their chains. So now you think it acceptable wisdom to seek out the slaver? Hold, sir. I have another statement. You said most Orissans would chose to be ruled by the Far Kingdoms if they were richly rewarded. What of the others—those you think to be a minority? What of men like Ecco, Gamelan, or even Maeen and the other soldiers here in Irayas? They'll think it a capital jest when we tell them what their pains have produced. And what of the women? What of that little chambermaid, Spoto? What of my sister, Rali? And Otara, her lover? Or the other Maranon Guards? Do you think they will cheerfully invite tyranny? What will Raveline do with them?"

"All kings have laws to support their rule," Janos said, a bit weakly. "Is Vacaan's law, where those who rebel simply vanish, more evil than the Kissing of the Stones? Or even the Archons' Calling?"

"As to the first," I said, "yes. No one is executed in Orissa without an open trial. As to Lycanth, I cannot answer. Especially since I have not spoken to anyone who has been disappeared, and know not what agonies were connected with their going."

"Perhaps," Janos said slowly, "we should summon such a spirit and ask him. Although I warn you the dead speak in awful tongues." Then he made a slight shift in course. "Say you are right in your doom crying. What plan do you have?"

I took several deep breaths, again to calm myself. "I have but the beginnings of one, and welcome your additions—or even an alternate proposal," I said. "I would suggest both of us temporize with Raveline. Make vague promises such as any merchant does when a shipment is overdue. It was my impression that King Domas has already decided to allow some trade to commence. Now, since you say Raveline is a creature of momentary enthusiasms, perhaps we should use that agreement as a way for us to return to Orissa. Once in our homeland, I think it absolutely imperative we immediately put my plan of a few days ago into action. You, Janos, must take the entire Evocators' Guild in hand, and begin preparation. But not for an immediate war, nor for war at all. I am thinking aloud as I speak, admittedly, but I cannot see how Raveline could mount an attack, either magical or physical, against us, when his people have no interest beyond their own noses. Further, I agree that these Vacaanese are terribly hidebound. I think we should trade with them, and learn everything we can. I think you should be in charge of synthesizing this knowledge." I suddenly ran out of words and slumped back in my chair. "Beyond those thoughts . . . no, I have no precise plan, especially since Raveline, in fact, has not even proposed attacking our lands."

"But he will, in one form or another," Janos said firmly. "However, in the end, it shall come to naught." He pulled me to my feet and led me across the chamber to a circular mirror. "Look in this glass, my friend. Look at us. When we met, you were a boy, and I was a youth whose greatest responsibility was a company of spear throwers. Now we have reached the Far Kingdoms, and in our grasp is all the power, all the wisdom, the gods which do not exist are reputed to hold. All that stands between us is one person, someone I *know* can be dealt with, *at the proper time*, and I cannot make my point too strongly. If we cock a snook at Raveline now, and flee for the border . . . I doubt we shall even make it as far as the Pepper Coast. So we die in some wasteland . . . and Orissa returns to its unchanging obstinancy. Amalric Antero, we were chosen to bring Orissa into a new age, and you must realize it. If we must temporize with this Raveline for a space . . . well, so be it. We are both still young, and there are years ahead, and the times change."

I started to respond, then really looked into the glass. At the moment I looked anything but young: my face was lined by the miles and the pain and all the deaths, my hair no longer flamed as red as it had, and my eyes looked beyond, as if I'd seen too much and my soul needed time to recover in peace and green. But I looked like a swaddling babe compared to Janos. He was but a few years older, but now, in this light, he could have passed for the father of the man who had rescued me from that dockfront bar. His thinning hair and beard were striped with gray—a yellowed gray, as if Janos had recently risen from a sickbed. Time's scars slashed furrows across his face, his complexion was jaundiced, his cheeks had begun to sag, and I could see the beginnings of wattles where his beard ended. But it was the eyes that held me. They were red rimmed and set deep in their sockets. Their haunted gaze had experienced ... and welcomed, horror. I had seen eyes like that recently, and recalled where: at Lord Mortacious' banquet ... when I first met the wizard's death stare. I repressed a shudder and pulled away, angry once more.

"You actually believe that we can stand against a man who can create a nightmare city like Wahumwa?" I said. "Not only stand, but in time destroy him or render him impotent? Janos, wake up. If I agree to his plan, he will permit me to exist just so long as I follow his every desire, his every wish, as if it were graven on my soul. Pawns are not permitted to debate with the master. But there is something more important than the role I would play in Raveline's new world. Janos, I cannot believe you think *you* can somehow subvert this man to your ends. Frankly, I am not entirely sure he even *is* a man. Prince Raveline has spent his entire life playing royal games of death and power. He will eat you for a light lunch!" My voice was loud in the postmidnight silence.

Janos, too, was angry. "You think I am that weak?"

"I think you are that foolish!" I snapped. "You are dancing attendance on Raveline, just as I did on that whore Melina. Not only do I see no Captain Greycloak to come to *your* rescue, but in the end you will prove yourself an even bigger dunce than I was."

"How dare you," Janos hissed. "You ... a merchant's son, barely a man, who never had to fight a real battle. Whose most difficult decision was the markup on a bolt of cloth. You ... preaching wisdom to me, Janos Kether Greycloak, whose line has led a people since the beginning of history. How dare you?"

My fist was clenched and drawn back before I could find control. Words danced on my lips about how I had finally learned what he thought of me, and then I saw myself in the glass, face as red as my hair, and instead of striking out I dug my nails deep into my palm. I was panting as if I had run a footrace. Calm, of a sort, came back.

"This is foolish of us both," I managed. "And produces nothing. We will continue this tomorrow. When we have both learned to behave ourselves." Janos managed a jerky nod of agreement. He began to say something more, then clamped his mouth shut. Without farewell, I turned and hurried out of the chamber and down the tower steps. In the courtyard I began shouting for Gatra and a gondola.

* * *

IT WAS VERY late when I returned to my palace. I did not know what to do. I shed my clothes next to the lotus pool, dived into the cool water, and swam three times across it, trying to make my muscles broaden my mind's reach as they themselves stretched. I pulled myself out of the pool, the before-dawn wind chill on my skin. I felt a bit better, but no wiser.

Politeness dictated I should have waited, but I could not. Something told me that every moment was important. I must discuss this with the one who appeared the only person in this land who was still sane. I went to a kitchen and made a pot of tea without rousing the dozing attendant. I took it to our chambers, intending to wake Omerye gently and then tell her what had happened. But she was fully alert and standing at a window. I set the tray down and took her in my arms, wanting nothing more than to be able to start eternity at this moment and never have to leave her embrace. After a while, she pushed me back.

"Was it that bad?"

I told her what had happened, both at Raveline's palace and with Janos. When I had finished, it lacked but two hours before dawn. Omerye poured two cups of the now-cold tea and drank.

"There are those in Vacaan," she began, "who would find it humorous, and no more than what should be expected from a halfman outlander, that a musician should be consulted for wisdom."

"There is no one else who knows me better," I said. "No one that I trust as much, including myself."

Omerye kissed me, then she said, "Very well, then. Shall we start with your friend? Consider this: if someone came to me, as Prince Raveline evidently has to Greycloak, and promised I could know all chords, all fingerings, tunings, and pitches of all instruments of this day and the time of the Old Ones, and be able to use that knowledge to build a music of the future . . . perhaps I myself might be blind to the failings of that gift bringer. Besides, there is some truth to what he says. Not that Raveline's great evil can be transmuted to good as easily as base metal becomes gold. But he *can* be turned aside."

I felt a bit of hope. "How? Should I go to the king?"

Omerye gasped in horror. "Do not even *think* that, my love. If you went to King Domas, and told him all that had happened, he would indeed summon Raveline, and chastise him severely. He might even require the prince to exile himself in a far-off estate, saying the sight of him sickens decent men's eyes. And you would be rewarded for your honesty. But Raveline would be welcomed back to Irayas in a few months, and you would be gone.

Even though the brothers hate one another . . . no one is permitted to embarrass the royal family. No one. Besides, in Vacaan, matters are handled more delicately. A way we might deal with the situation is for me to have a word with some friends who are considered wise in the eyes of the king. And for those friends to chat with *their* friends. These discussions would be held most privately and most quietly. In time—perhaps a week, perhaps a month, we can also have a word with Beemus. Then a whisper will float past the king's ears. He will have his most subtle chamberlains investigate, most privately, and most quietly. Once he learns the truth, and he will learn it all if he wishes, then Prince Raveline might be reined in. He will suddenly be ordered to mount an expedition against the bandits to the north, perhaps."

I was incredulous. "Just like that, the situation will return to normal, and Orissa's and my problems be solved?" I was quite incredulous.

"As I said, Raveline has been brought to heel before, and in matters that we, at least, consider more important than the fate of two barbarian cities far to the west. Forgive me, Amalric my love, but that is how Vacaanese think."

I knew that nothing, especially the vagaries of prices, could be guaranteed. But Omerye had offered the only real plan that made sense. On the morrow, I would return to Janos and we could resolve our argument. I was still angry, having seen the raw steel of his ambition. But I told myself none of us are perfect, and the Far Kingdoms had been his obsession much longer than mine. But still, I knew as I lay down to rest that our friendship would no longer continue on quite as easy a basis as it had.

I WOKE AN hour later with a scream trapped in my chest. It boiled up violently and tried to prise open my lips, but still it would not come. Omerye tossed and turned uneasily beside me. It was as if I was awake and at the same time deep in a fever stupor.

Two things blazed through my mind. The first I already knew, at least in principle: a black wizard will feed and batten off pain, fear, and death. If Raveline were to carry out his plan, Orissa and Lycanth would become chaos. Armies would clash and sway across our lands, armies degenerating into bandits and murderers. In time, we, too, would be nothing more than bloody wasteland like the Disputed Lands, and I could imagine Raveline's face hanging high above those gory wastes, smiling at the destruction that was as mother's milk to him.

If Raveline were to be allowed to carry out his plan . . . and

then I recollected what Raveline had said about wanting Janos as
his hellhound. And I thought: hellhound? Or assassin? Janos was
not under any ban preventing him from conspiring against the
House of Domas. Mistake me not—even in this waking nightmare
I did not vision Janos skulking through the king's palace with a
drawn and poisoned blade. But could Janos mount, lead, and ex-
ecute a coup? To then be cut down in his moment of victory by
a newly crowned king, sorrowing for his brother's murder? No.
That was too fantastic. I dragged myself out of my mind's maelstrom. I looked out the window. Even though it was still dark, I
could hear the sleepy chirping of birds in my garden. Once more,
I should not have been able to sleep, but did. I do not remember
my head striking the pillow. All I can recollect is my thought that
the morrow would be a very different day indeed.

CHAPTER TWENTY-SIX
The Cavern

I WOKE INTO nightmare. Torches flared on either side of me. I lay on cold, wet stone. The reek of mildew filled my nostrils, and I tasted the hard iron of blood in my mouth. I knew where I was: I was still in the dungeon of the Archons, far below the great sea castle of Lycanth. I was awakening from one of those marvelous dreams where half a lifetime passes, and every moment is perfectly detailed. Janos and I had never escaped this dungeon, had never fought the Evocators for the soul of the Orissan people, had never journeyed beyond the Pepper Coast and the haunted city to enter the Far Kingdoms. I remembered the dream woman named Omerye, realized she never was, and my eyes welled. At least the gods had sent me a moment of imaginary happiness in that long and frequently dreadful dream.

I awakened more, my mind still wandering the maze of that intricate fantasy. I remembered not only escaping from this dungeon, but just *how* we escaped. That brought me to full alertness. I looked about the condemned cell for Janos. I would tell him my dream, particularly that part dealing with this Lycanthian dungeon, and perhaps we could build on my illusion to prepare a real escape.

A voice grated, "Up wi' ye, Antero! Th' spell's had more'n enough time to wear away."

And I was *not* back in the Archons' dungeon. I *was* in a sodden stone cell, but it was small and cramped. There was no one else around me—no guards, no torturers across the way, no fellow prisoners, and no Janos. I was alone ... except for one other: Greif. He sat curled on a heavy bench against the far wall. He was smiling. I forced myself to my feet.

"Lord Antero," he mocked. "Y' wake. Shall I send in th' wenches to draw your bath? Servants t' lay out your silks? P'raps that fine-titty musician you been futterin' t' play a tune? Woulda like to have brought that along, an' let you watch *me* pleasure her f'r a bit. But 'twarn't permitted."

My mind a whirligig, I said nothing. Nor could I move further from where I stood. Greif got up and strolled to me. I saw his gaping eye socket, black and oozing corruption. My thrust with the spear butt had indeed put out one of his eyes. Greif knew what I was staring at, and his muscle-knotted fist smashed into my stomach. I gagged and went to my knees, breath driven out.

He booted me over onto my back and stared down. "Aye," he said. "You put out one of my glims, you did. But I found a better way to see. M' masters give me . . . somethin' t' spy with. Gi' me a bit of their power, t' look at men, an' see some' at of their intents." Greif tapped his empty eye socket, then laughed, very hard, and his mirth echoed around the stone room.

At that moment, I saw, in that empty socket, a red fire, *a tiny, red, writhing fire.* And I realized I was entering the reality of that nightmare that had cursed me for so many years. It was not meeting Greif in Lycanth that made him my nameless torturer, boatman, and escort. I had been permitted, for good or evil, a glimpse of the future. I wished desperately I would have realized my nightmare was clairvoyance and cut Greif down when I first met him, standing below me in the courtyard of the Lycanthian inn.

"I c'n see you're still mazed, an' wonderin' where you are now. Somewheres in Irayas. Somewheres far, far under th' ground, where there's nobody to hear you scream, which you will do in a bit. Y' know, first thing I learned, first time I was grabbed by th' thief takers, is you start breakin' someone with words. So . . . You was duped. Played false by th' man you thought y'r friend. Th' man who cast th' protective spell you believed w'ld keep you from harm also lifted it, so's me and my assistants could slip in, an' winkle you out."

Despite my efforts to keep control, my face must have twisted from my heart's distress. Greif laughed once more and spat into my face. "Get up . . . an' look about you. See th' fine toys I've got waitin' to play with. Th' prince gimme all day t' fun myself with you. All he said is I can't kill you or send you mad. Oh yeah, an' I can't maim you nor break bones neither. Guess th' prince's got his own games he wants t' play wi' you later on. Wager his games might be even better'n mine, though I've had time to think on what I wanted t' do t' you, an' time t' remember what others done to me. 'Sides, th' limitations he put on, ain't restrictin' to a man who's spent time in th' service of Nisou Symeon."

My only consolation was that Greif could not have any knowledge of my nightmare, or else he would be even more gleeful as I contemplated the horror that was to come. But even as I faced this, that agony was not as great as learning of Janos' betrayal.

"First," he said. "Lift up y'r hands. There's manacles hangin' down. Clamp 'em on y'r wrists." He chortled as I found my body obeying. "Ain't the spell th' prince's man gimme somethin'? Gonna be a boot, seein' you actin' as my assistant."

A spell had stolen my will, and I could not resist the order; I clamped the shackles on my wrist. Greif cackled and went to the wall where a rope hung from a bolt in the ceiling and ran down to support the cuffs. He untied the rope and yanked until I was lifted almost clear of the ground, my toes just touching the flagstones.

"Y' dislocate anythin', there'll be time enough t' snap th' bone back in, afore we . . . take our trip," he said. "Now, I'll just let y' dangle for a few, 'cause I'm sure you got some questions t' ask. An' I'll answer 'em all, 'cause th' answers'll just make th' last few hours you got worse." He went back to his bench and waited.

I did not want to give him any gratification, but there was one thing I had to confirm. "You still serve Nisou Symeon?"

Greif laughed that foul laugh of his and nodded vigorously. "He thinks I do . . . an' I take his silver so long's his wishes match mine. Ain't never left his employ, if that's th' question, an' this marks th' second time I've snared you. Three times, if y' count th' time I cut th' guts out'n your slave, back in Lycanth, tryin' t' get y'r relics for Symeon's incants."

Of course he'd been the murderer of Eanes, and I tried to make myself believe I would avenge that death and put his spirit to rest before I, too, became a ghost. Hope flickered but dimly in my chest.

" 'Course," Greif went on, "mebbe ye c'd question who m' real master is, since Lord Symeon's sworn obeisance t' th' prince."

Again, my intuition had been confirmed. The thought I'd had some hours ago must be true: Raveline *indeed* planned to turn our lands into slaughterhouses, setting each against each.

"How did he . . . and you . . . get to Irayas?"

"Lord Symeon ain't here," Greif said. "He's back in Lycanth preparin' matters for th' move against Orissa. He's ne'er been t'

Irayas, neither. When y' have a lord as powerful as th' prince, man don't have to be standin' there in body t' kiss his ring. Symeon's been servin' him f'r . . . damned if I know how long for cert, since he ain't exactly my bed partner an' sharin' secrets, but for a long while, I'm guessin'. I on'y found out 'bout th' wheels wi'in wheels couple, three months ago. As t' how I got here?" Greif looked momentarily troubled. "Can't speak on that, neither. Lord Symeon gimme orders t' serve th' man I'd see when I woke, e'en i' death or th' fires'd take me, put a spell down, an' th' next thing was I woke here, in that six-sided castle th' prince has, out'n th' country. Not that I'd need any threats hangin' t' obey him. I know *real* power when I sees it . . . an' what he's tasked me for, I'd be likely as not to pay to do as a priv'lege."

He rose and strolled around the cell. It was littered with instruments of pain: ropes, ringbolts, lashes, pincers, fire, water, and vises. He picked up, then set down, first one, then another. "Hard tellin' what t' start with," he mused. "But there's been enough words. Ain't but one more thing, Antero, my friend, my prize"—his voice growing thick as anticipation and passion of a sort rose within in him—"f'r you t' think on. Y' c'd a' had it all, y'know. If y'd but bent knee t' th' prince . . . y' could've been Lord Symeon's flunky when things shake out, an' y' could'a had all Orissa bow an' scrape afore ye, near as much as f'r Symeon himself. But y' had t' let th' pride show. Y'll be regrettin' that. Now . . . an' f'r etern'ty t' come. I got the feel th' prince ain't plannin' to allow you th' real death."

He picked up a scourge and ran its thongs over his hand. "E'en if that's what y'll be beggin' for," he hissed, and the lash came down on me.

THERE IS NO point in soiling these pages with the details of my torture. Those who wish to know more on the subject are advised to find the nearest wineshop to any prison and purchase drink for a warder to have their curiosity satisfied. Suffice it to say that Greif had paid close attention when *he* had been the tormentors' subject, so he was quite skilled in plying the various instruments of agony.

There are only four things to note: The first is that a bond is formed between torturer and his prey. It is neither sexual nor nonsexual, and I am not sure how to describe it. Others I've known who spent a longer time in the grasp of inquisitors have told me that eventually the victim becomes a near-willing slave of his afflictor as his soul is ground away by the endless pain. The second is the red delectation that comes as a tittering observer to pain. This feeling, too, is complex, partially nerve propelled and from close to the same source as sex, or so I'm guessing, but more from the challenge to preserve a bit of your soul, a bit of your own, against the invader and his fire and the agony. The third thing I learned was that Greif's desire outran his performance. A skilled torturer, I have learned, never allows his victim the pleasure and relief of unconsciousness. This was Greif's greatest error, and possibly my salvation. Three times that blessedness washed over me and allowed my inner being to rearmor itself for Greif's next assault. The final thing was the most valuable: All things come to an end . . . eventually. As did that day.

But then the *real* nightmare began.

I RECOVERED CONSCIOUSNESS as I was dragged down stone steps, half carried by two men. In front of me, lighting the way with a lantern, was Greif. I knew him by the scars of the lash on his back. He wore naught but a pair of black breeches. The stairway was old, and I could see white niter outlining the stones around us. It ended abruptly in a pool of water where a small boat . . . the black boat of my dream . . . was moored. I was slung aboard, and Greif's two helpers left, with never a word being spoken. Greif untied the boat, stood at its tiller, and a current caught the craft, sending us rushing into and down a tunnel whose roof curved but a foot above his head.

In bare minutes we were swept into open waters. It was night, and there was no moon, no stars. We were moving along a canal that seemed familiar to me. We were in the heart of Irayas, but I saw no other gondolas or watercraft. I was neither chained nor fettered and should have leaped out of the boat; failing that, I should have shouted for help. But I could do neither. I suppose I was ensorcelled, although it is equally probable I was simply in shock from the abuse. In fact, the latter is more probable, because events were as vague and as hallucinatory now as they had been before in the dream.

What I remember from that passage are but fragments. We traveled at a speed as great as I had on the river that had brought us down from the mountains when we entered Gomalalee. The canal entered the Serpent River, and now I knew we were powered by sorcery, for the boat flew upriver against the current, without aid of oars or sails. As we passed beyond the city's outskirts, I saw the Holy Mountain on my right, then we sped past it into the range beyond the Old Ones' peak. I next remember being in a deep gorge. The hissing river beside the boat's gunwales looked as if it were no longer water, but a dark, thick, oily fluid.

Greif did not touch the tiller, but suddenly the craft bore sideways, about to crash into the rearing cliff. Instead of meeting stone, however, a cavern's mouth yawned, a cavern the river's currents had carved over centuries. Inside the cave a stone dock waited. Greif tied up the boat, clambered out, turned, and beckoned. Every piece of my soul that remained mine fought, but I followed, stepping awkwardly across the boat's thwarts and then lunging upward to the slime-thick dock carved from the living stone. My feet dragged as my mind screamed: Strike out. You can not go up those stairs. You must not. But I did.

Greif took one of the torches that guttered on either side of the arched passageway, and beckoned once more. I heard the baying and knew what was above: there was a great, ruined, cursed city on the gorge's plateau. Far above me, far outside this river-dug cavern, in the city, in the shattered amphitheaters, in the gods-hammered stones, the creatures sat in patient rings. Up there in the dark of the moon the creatures that bayed like hounds bore no semblance to anything seen on this earth. The thought came to me they might have been men, once. Men who had struck a dark bargain.

I followed Greif. My mind, moving as slowly as if I were drugged, told me no victim had ever come back down these steps, and desperately tried to devise a strategy. I found none. The thunder of a great drum began. We entered a great chamber, with its arches lifting into blackness. I heard a gong resound, and as Greif turned I saw that wormlike fire writhe brightly in his dead eye socket. I heard him say words about my desire, this was what I wanted, this was my weird, and he laughed. The laugh boomed loud, louder, joined by the baying from the creatures beyond, laughter of joy in pain and death, laughter rising to cacophony, and Raveline was there. Silence dropped across the chamber and above among the damned creatures like an axe blow. Greif became a statue, and considering Raveline's words, I believe was under a momentary spell of paralysis. The prince wore bloodred pantaloons and a black, full tunic with gold lace showing at his wrists and neck. He wore an ornate dagger on a belt. He might have been dressed for a casual court affair.

"So we reach the end, Antero," he said. His voice was calm. "Do you wish to know your doom?" I said nothing. "In bare moments, I shall obliterate your physical being. Most of your soul will be scattered to the winds when I take you in my embrace.

But you will be more than just a hapless wandering ghost like your brother or that slave this brigand killed. I shall keep a part of you in my own soul, and it shall witness, through my eyes, the great changes that are to come on this world. Witness them, but without ever being able to do more than scream in mute horror as they happen."

"An honor," I said sarcastically, determined to at least die with a bit of dignity.

"Not at all. I want to keep a fragment of you close as a reminder of failure, and a caution against vainglory."

"It would hardly appear that you have failed," I said.

"Quite wrong. My failure with you and yours has taken several forms over the decades. Many years ago I sensed the presence of your bloodline, far away and very faintly. I paid no heed, thinking, like most Vacaanese, that the doings of barbarians beyond our kingdoms were meaningless. But then I felt the presence more strongly. I allowed my senses to follow the trail, and discovered your brother."

His words jolted me fully alert, fully awake. I do not quite know how to explain, but for some reason one sentence of the dream Greif had spoken had never properly impressed itself on me: . . . *This is what your brother could not embrace* . . . I have talked about this with savants, and have heard the phenomenon is not uncommon: that a man may suddenly swear everyone around him is speaking in a foreign tongue when they are not. One described it as the familiar become strange.

"I allowed my spells to flow out and around Orissa," Raveline continued, "and learned I was being warned, like a jungle beast senses the hunter when he first enters the jungle. Your brother, untutored and with no family tradition of sorcery, was potentially a wizard greater than any land I know has conceived for time beyond memory."

Even in my agony and death moment, I felt a thrill of pride, and rage took me. "And so you killed him."

"And so I killed him," Raveline agreed. "I laid my trap carefully. Halab was no more a perfect being than you or I are, so all that was necessary was to cast a small spell encouraging him into the slightest bit of hubris. I sent a larger one against those fools your city respects and calls Evocators, although not one of them then or now has talent enough to divine water if he were drowning. They were to feel threatened by Halab, and to send against him, when he asked to be examined to become an Evocator, their most lethal devices. Your brother was tested. He easily stood against those paltry sprites the Evocators hurled at him, and was about to be victorious. Here was my first failure—I *still* had not properly measured his greatness.

"I cast two mighty spells then. One to make time have a stop, which gave me moments to summon a being whose nature and name I must not even think of. The creature's price was high: a township of innocents was sacrificed afterward. I killed Halab, or rather my creature did. But even then, my success was not complete. Rather than being blotted out from this and all other worlds, Halab managed to leave his ghost behind, like any man who met death unshriven or -avenged. At that time, I should have sent doom against all you Anteros. It was foolish to believe Halab was a sport, a freak. All of your family has a bit of the talent. Your sister has a fair amount of it, made greater in that she has not married, bred, nor coupled with a man. You, too, have a bit, as you of course are aware.

"Ah," Raveline said, having noted the flash of startlement that must have flickered. "You did *not* know. It is not great, but has been sufficient, over the years, for you to sidestep hostile magics without being aware of them. Men call such a trace of the power luck. I shall, by the way, make sure the Antero 'luck' disappears, by extirpating your entire line within the next few weeks." He amused himself with my agony for a moment, then, "I will return to my confession. I must admit I am quite enjoying this, since there has never been anyone in my life I was foolish enough to confide in, nor shall there be anyone again. Unless, perhaps, if I choose to evoke your spirit from time to time and permit it an audience. *That* might prove amusing.

"To go on. After Halab's death, I let my guard slip, like a wine-filled sentry drowsing on his battlements in the noonday sun. The next I became aware of the Anteros was when you had partnered with Janos Greycloak. Another wizard of remarkable, if unschooled power. Your family attracts sorcery like honey does flies, it would appear. Again, I determined to take action, but again I chose maltempered steel, from the Archons and their much-vaunted tempest, which was but a zephyr compared to the powers I wield, then fools such as Cassini. At least, when I failed I had the pleasure of wreaking personal vengeance. Then Nisou Symeon, whose merits I shall severely reevaluate when I am finished with you. At least I have learned not to allow time to pass when a problem presents itself, and that a great problem must be dealt with directly. And I do have Janos Greycloak now. You know, in some ways, Janos might have been greater than Halab, since Halab would have been no more than an inchoate, if great, force for what you groundlings label as good. Janos, with his determination to measure, catalog, and analyze magic into a system could have shaken this world, and perhaps some of the ones beyond, to their roots. It is fortunate for me that greatness describes his vices as well as his virtues. Janos Kether Greycloak is quite comfortably defanged now."

Raveline held out his hand, fingers up, and closed his talons. "Until two days ago, he was not quite secure within my grasp. But after you left his company after babbling all—oh yes, I listened, in spite of Greycloak's puerile attempts at casting a blocking spell—he notified me of what had occurred. I told him what he must do . . . and he obeyed! *He obeyed!* And now he is mine."

"And yet you still fear him," I said.

"I fear no one," Raveline said boldly. But his eyes darted to the side as he spoke. He recovered and snapped, "Enough of this. The conversation has ceased to amuse. Now it is time for me to clasp you to me. Come, Amalric Antero. Come to your doom."

Raveline opened his arms and smiled. I felt his power, in crashing waves. My own arms lifted. I took a step forward. Raw red anger rolled over me, and his spell shattered. My hands came down. Raveline was taken aback.

"You have more power than I thought. Greif! Bring him to me!"

Greif came out of his paralysis and sprang forward, his hugely muscled arms pinioning mine, and he lifted me free of the ground, crushing me in a grinding chestlock. But then it was easy, and his hold sent my muscle memory flashing back to oiled bodies grappling on mats, shouting judges, and desperate tricks old wrestlers taught while admonishing us never to use them in sport. I back kicked against Greif's knee, and he yelped, grip loosening enough for my right fist to smash back into his genitals. His arms came loose as he shrieked, finding agony beyond awareness of this chamber. I turned into him, my fists joining and lifting high above my head and hammer striking at the base of his neck. Greif was probably dead at that moment, but as he fell to the stone floor I had a fistful of his greasy hair in one hand, my foot on his neck, and I jerked sharply upward. His neck snapped like a rotten limb.

I thought I heard a whisper, a voice I had not heard since I held a dying man in my arms in the streets of Lycanth: *"Now I am truly free . . ."*

I came back into a fighting stance, ready for Raveline's attack. But he had not moved, and now his smile was a bit broader.

"That rubbish," he remarked, "shall go unmissed. This becomes interesting. Now it shall be what latent power you Anteros have, against my tested, developed skills. Again I order you. Come to me, Amalric Antero!" This time his fingers wove a spell, and he whispered words that even though I could not make them out, sent a wormcrawl through me.

The chamber grew darker, until there was nothing but Raveline's presence, and then nothing but his eyes, beckoning tunnels that ordered me forward . . . drowning pools of evil pulling me like a maelstrom. My mind swirled and was drawn in, and there was but a moment for my thought, and perhaps I called Halab's name, not even hoping for a miracle in this evil cavern. And it was as if a layer of gauze transposed itself in front of Raveline's basilisk gaze. The room brightened, and in that instant I was free, free to leap forward, without grace, without intent, as a goalkeeper deadens a ball before it can score. I crashed into Raveline and sent him stumbling back and down.

I scrabbled toward him, trying for a grip, hoping I might seize his dagger before he brought me under his spell once more. But Raveline's abilities were more than sorcerous. He snap rolled away like a tournament wrestler and was on his feet, hand drawing that dagger as sinuously as a serpent bares his fangs. Its blade glittered, and I knew it to be ensorcelled. But this time I did not allow time for the snake to gaze on the rabbit, for in that light that had appeared as I called for Halab's aid, I saw an archway behind where Raveline had stood, and I was running as hard as I could. But as I ran I heard that monstrous mocking laughter of Raveline's and heard his words as clearly as if he were standing next to me. "You wish to play this out? You shall have your wish. They say the prey's flesh is made sweeter through terror and pain. Go, Antero. My hounds are already on the scent. We shall meet shortly, when you have been brought to bay."

I paid no mind. I had escaped the first trap, and would face the next when it was sprung. I ran on, taking every stair that led upward. Above me was the ruined city and its creatures, but there was also the sky and the night and the air. My lungs seared air, and my tortured body begged for mercy, and I paid neither the slightest heed. I found two gates, gates that reached high into the gloom above. They were locked with a crossbar as thick as my body, just at the height of my shoulders. I looked for a windlass or lever, but saw none. I shoved at the bar vainly, knowing it would take a squad of soldiers to muscle it free. But the crossbar silently lifted, and the gates were unlocked. I but touched those gates, and they swung open, exquisitely balanced either by construct or magic. Moonlight gleamed through the doors. The clouds had washed away while I was in Raveline's death chamber. Outside the gates were huge toppled stones, broken pillars, and the shattered pavings of the cursed, ruined city.

I ran out into the cold moonlight. I hoped to find a negotiable ravine or slope that would lead me either down to the flatlands or to the river. I was willing to chance my luck swimming those viscous-looking waters through the rapids to seek safety downstream. I took a moment to get my bearings from the stars, frigidly indifferent as they stared down. I picked a direction I thought the quickest route to the plateau's rim would lie, and having recovered a bit of my wind, trotted off. I heard the first howlings from Raveline's creatures. I so dub them, even though I do not know if they were his creations or merely maleficent beings whose vile desires paralleled the prince's. The baying grew louder, and I broke into a run. I came into a broad avenue. Down the center of the boulevard lay the remains of toppled statues. I wasted a glance as I ran past. Each statue's face had been effaced, as if a mason had chiseled each countenance away after the statues were brought down. The statues were of men, but men not as we know them, nor had the models been giants or dwarfs. I do not quite know how to describe them, except the proportions were not as they should have been. I had no more time for observation, as the first of the creatures broke from a side street toward me. The moonlight delineated him—it—well. Imagine a large man, almost a giant, running on his hands and feet. Further conceive that this man's arms and legs had been broken repeatedly and reshaped so that it became a bit easier for him to travel in this fashion than it would for a normal human. Stretch a skull face until it is twice as long as a man's, add fangs, elongate and slant the eyes a bit like a wolf's, although that noble creature should not be compared to this beast, finish with a pale, rotted skin like a leper hides from the world, and you have a fairly accurate picture. Its claws clattered against the stones as it closed on me. Its baying rose into triumph, then became a howl of surprise as I scooped up a fist-size chunk of rubble and threw it with all my strength full into its face. The creature reared and fell, writhing in blind agony and astonishment. Perhaps the prey it had hunted previously had never struck back. I fled on. Behind me I heard more howling. At the end of the boulevard I looked back. The monster's packmates had joined their crippled fellow. But they were not chasing me. Instead, they took the moment to feed on their crippled brother. I chose another street and ran toward where the ruins, and the highland, should come to an end.

Something smashed into me, knocking me spinning. I back flipped reflexively, and saw yet another of the beasts, just as it landed, spun back toward me, and leaped. Another of Janos' trainings flashed to mind, and as the beast's jaws gaped, and I smelled its putrescent breath, I fed it my left forearm, smashing the limb sideways against the back of its throat. I felt the fangs tear my flesh as my other arm went behind the back of its neck, clenched, and I brought my left arm sharply upward and my right in toward me, and the beast's neck broke cleanly. I let its weight turn me, and brought the creature down, falling with my knees against its chest and heard ribs crack like withies.

I regained my feet and sped on. I hoped the pack would appreciate another morsel, and that the beast's fangs had not been poisoned. Just at that moment my second wind came, and pain fell away. Now I could run all night if it were necessary. I heard a roar and thought it to be the river below. I must be near the edge of the plateau. Ahead of me the ground dipped into a natural amphitheater the builders of this city had used to build their own arena, one far vaster than Orissa's Great Amphitheater. Stone steps led down a hillside to the stage, which had been protected with a stone canopy. Some of the columns that had supported the canopy were still standing, with fragments of the dome hanging on their capitals. And beyond was a vertical cliff edge. I must skirt it until I found a ravine I could use for my descent.

In that moment the beasts trapped me. The pack streamed out of nowhere—from the earth itself, as if the ground were vomiting them. I ran toward the stage, leaping from step to step. I jumped to the stage and put my back to a column. I grabbed two more chunks of stone for weapons. The creatures encircled me, and, snarling and yapping, began closing the ring. I knew they would not be allowed to kill me, but imagined Raveline would permit me to be thoroughly savaged before he pulled his hounds off. One creature chanced a lunge, and I crushed his skull as a bravo's reward. Now the ring was tighter as the pack came in on me. I ventured a look behind me, and confidence flowed. I would die here, I knew. But I would not perish either under the fangs of these brutes nor from Raveline's magic. When the end became inevitable, I would choose the quick clean death of the long fall to the river and rocks below.

And then my ferret returned. I did not know what he was at first, but I heard a hissing, a whistle, and liquid death flowed through the amphitheater toward me. It was almost thirty feet long, sleek light-colored fur, and red-glowing eyes, and I knew not its nature until I bethought myself of a mink, and then knew better, seeing the black mask around its face just as the huge ferret took the first of the creatures from the rear, nipped once delicately at its spine, and cast the corpse aside. The pack howled dismay at this new and unexpected attack and turned to savage the new-comer. But the ferret was here, there, nowhere and everywhere, and every time its fangs snapped, one of the nightmares yapped its last. One of Raveline's creatures bounded free and bayed a command. The others broke away from the battle and scuttled up the steps, trying to flee, but being slaughtered as they fled. Then they were gone, and the great animal reared back on its haunches, snakelike head seeking new quarry, and in that moment I knew not only what, but who the being was, as my memory cast the picture of my long-dead pet, scenting the wind just before it slid after a rabbit. He came back toward me, his long tail whipping, whistling a greeting as he had done years and years ago, and even in that moment of the greatest danger I found myself choking back sobs.

The air shimmered next to my pet, and a manlike form appeared. I knew it to be Halab's ghost and opened my mouth for a greeting, and then ferret and shade were gone. As was the moon, the stars, and all of the amphitheater. It was if a black dome had been dropped down. From its middle shone a dim ghost light. All that existed in this world was the stage, the columns that had held the roof . . . and Raveline. He held his dagger ready.

"Most clever," he snarled, and now there was no pretense of being casual. "And I have just made my last error with you, when I estimated you had but little of the talent. I did not sense at any time you had any spirits watchdogging you. Very clever indeed. Why did you not call on your brother or whatever that beast is for rescue back in Irayas when Greif abducted you? Or were you setting a trap for *me*?"

Raveline stopped and shook his head in wonderment. "The double cunning that sorcery brings. But it does not matter whether you hunted me, or I you. This dome, this shield, is one of my proudest spells. It utterly seals us. We are beyond the reach of any power I know, earthly or supernatural. I prepared it years ago, when my brother and I were first struggling over which one our father, damned may his soul be, would choose to rule over Vacaan. It is, perhaps, the ultimate version of that protective spell Janos cast and then lifted over you. It is proof against all, and will only vanish when I will it ... or I die. Its only limitation is the spell disallows the use of magic by anyone, including myself, under the dome.

"So here it is, Antero. You have your wrestling skills ... and I have mine. And I have the knife. Now without the powers my magic gave it, but still razor enough to cut your guts out. I am truly sorry your skills have defeated my attempts to make your demise more complex, but so be it. At least your ghost shall never be avenged, and shall never know peace in its wanderings. This time, Antero, I shall come to you." True to his words, he shuffled toward me.

I have never considered myself either a fully skilled soldier or back-alley brawler and know little about knives other than the most sensible thing is to flee with great rapidity anyone waving a blade about. However, Janos had tutored us what to do when faced with various assailants when unarmed. There were ways to disarm and destroy a man who held his knife like an ice pick, like a candle, or one who waved his knife wildly in front of him as if a blade provided a magical shield. As for a man who moved like Raveline, who shuffled in slowly, moving crablike always toward your weak side, keeping his blade well back, against his thigh or nearly touching his side, with his other hand extended for a block ... Janos had smiled grimly and told us there were but two options: flight or death.

I, too, shuffled to *his* weak side ... away from the knife ... keeping my hands well out, hoping Raveline would strike wildly and I could seize a wrist, or perhaps kick his legs from under him. As I'd learned, I watched nothing but my enemy's eyes, knowing I would sense any movement of the blade as it began. He slashed once, then again on his backhand, but my stomach was not there. Once more his dagger marked air, and I chanced a blow. The razor edge of his knife sliced the inside of my arm open, but fortunately he'd missed any blood vessels. I ignored the wound ... and we circled on. He changed his tactics slightly and moved closer, forcing me back and back again. Eventually he would trap me against the dome and pin me like a butterfly to a wall. My back-reaching foot touched rough stone, one of the columns, and I momentarily lost my balance. Raveline lunged for my heart, and I sidestepped quickly, his knife scoring my chest, but my fist smashed his face. He yelped pain and stumbled back. His nose was broken, and blood gushed from his nostrils. But he still kept his fighting grip on the knife.

"How long has it been since you've felt pain, Lesser Majesty?"

I said, deciding a man who loved the sound of his own words as much as Raveline did might also fall victim to the words of others. "How long, princeling-that-shall-never-be-king? Perhaps you feel faint. Perhaps you wish to cry."

His lips drew back in a soundless snarl, and he short stepped toward me, keeping one foot held back, like a fencer. He would lunge in an instant, and I held my mind ready for his attack, not allowing tension . . . willing my muscles to seek their own response.

The lunge never came. I heard, from above, a slight scraping. Raveline glanced up, then stared, eyes widening, mouth opening, and the great rock, once part of the stage's canopy, whose mortar had held it to the column's capital for aeons and aeons, crushed him as a boot crushes a scorpion. He was dead before he could scream . . . and the black dome was gone . . . and once more the ruined city was about me in the moonlight. Stunned, I looked up toward the top of that column. The air shimmered above me, and I dimly saw the form of a man. "Halab," I gasped.

I heard, more in my mind than anywhere, the soft voice. *"The prince knew not all the rules of all the worlds. Even a ghost may move the real . . . If the call is great enough."*

There was silence but for the rush of the river below, then Halab's voice again, *"I am revenged, and my ghost will wander no more. I go now, following the path you opened to Eanes a short time ago."*

I bowed my head. "Good-bye, my brother."

I heard Halab for the last time.

"Good-bye, Amalric. There is one task left. I cannot be with you . . . cannot be of aid. But it is one which must be completed. For you, for the family, for Orissa, and for all of this world. I make you a final gifting. May it serve you well."

I felt emptiness. Something was gone . . . something I realized had been not far from me all these years, since the day my father returned from the palace of the Evocators with the tale of Halab's death.

I took a deep breath. Yes. There was a final task to be performed.

CHAPTER TWENTY-SEVEN
The Last Voyage

NOW THERE WAS little to fear either in this cursed city or in the catacombs below. I took the poniard from beside Raveline's body and went back through the streets to where the entrance to the Black Prince's burrow yawned. I took no wrong turnings, nor made missteps, as sure of my direction as if I were in Orissa. I followed the stone steps as they went down, down, down, and knew I was the first of Raveline's victims ever to do this. I passed Greif's sprawled body and bethought whether I should find some dirt to sprinkle, then decided otherwise. His ghost had much evil to atone for; he deserved to haunt those caves for an eternity.

The black gondola was still moored to the dock. I untied the boat and boarded it. Using the rudder as a sweep, I turned the boat toward the cavern's mouth. As I came out of the cavern into the dark river that poured down toward the flatlands and Irayas, the current sent the boat speeding down the canyon. The craft obeyed my unspoken and undefined desire as well as it had Greif's.

I could see dawn's promise as I neared the city. Perhaps I should have made the enchanted gondola take me to my palace, where I knew Omerye agonized. But I also knew I must confront Janos *now*, not just for the sake of my people ... but for all who live as wizards' slaves. To this day I honestly do not know what end I foresaw when I finally did confront him. For my soul's sake, I pray my intent was pure and untainted by desire for revenge.

As Janos' mansion bulked out of the calm waters, I dropped Prince Raveline's dagger into the river. Through the remnants of the night I saw its jewels and sorcelled blade spin until the

419

knife—my only weapon—vanished. I tied Raveline's boat to a piling under the main deck where that sobbing woman's skiff had been lashed. I had planned to climb one of the pilings to avoid the guard that should have been on the landing, but there was none. I crept up the stairs and noted with greater surprise that one of the edifice's entryways yawned wide. Perhaps, I thought, this was the gift Halab's ghost had promised; I slipped within. I did not know how close I would be able to come to Janos before his own watchdog spell would clamor him awake, but I continued onward, quietly as a questing ferret. The torches and lamps that illuminated the huge building were guttering low, but I needed no illumination as dawn's light grew steadily around me. My wonder grew, because I saw never a sign of sentry, factotum, or servant. At last I entered the courtyard and approached the tower where I knew Janos would be. I went up the stairs toward his bedchamber, which was just below the study he used for incantations.

Janos lay sprawled in the middle of his huge bed. He was alone. He wore but a silken loincloth. He slept deeply, so deeply I thought he had been enchanted. At that moment my resolution vanished and I stood, as if mired, at the foot of his bed. Then I spoke his name. Janos' eyes snapped open, and as I saw awareness dawn, he rolled sideways and was on his feet, graceful and deadly as a startled leopard.

He knew instantly what had happened. "You killed him? You killed Raveline?" His voice was incredulous. "And I sensed nothing? How could that be?"

I did not answer—I only stared at Janos in shock. Only two days gone I had marveled at how he had aged. Yet now it looked as if decades had passed since we looked at each other in the mirror abovestairs. Where jaundiced gray had striped his hair and beard before, it now discolored it in patches, and his face was as raddled as a rich old degenerate. But he looked worse than any of those debauchees, because there was a brooding evil in his appearance, evil like I'd seen on Raveline's face . . . and yes, Mortacious'. Janos' eyes had changed as well. Once they held the fierceness of the eagle, but now held the hard glare of a carrion eater. Most telling of all was the necklace he wore about his neck: the dancing girl from the Far Kingdoms that his father had given him. She had been "healed" by our journey, and when last I saw her, she had been a glorious, seductive work of art. Now she was tarnished and broken at the hips . . . just as she was the first day Janos showed her to me at the wineshop in Orissa. I knew at once that although I had been the one who had been tortured, hunted, and savaged by beasts on four legs and two . . . Janos had paid a heavier price for betraying me.

I had said nothing since calling his name and had no words prepared. I held Janos' eyes with my own for a moment. He looked away . . . it was the first time he had not been able to face me. "What were you promised?" I asked, and noted there was no anger in my voice, even though all the years of companionship should have caused me to seethe rage. "How much silver and gold was offered for your reward?"

Now anger grew on his face. "There was no price named," he hissed. "What I did . . . was needful. You would have destroyed . . . you *have* destroyed everything."

I maintained calmness. "What is this *everything*, Janos? By luck," and I recollected what Raveline had told me luck was, "I am still alive. Now Raveline's darkness will not be able to destroy our lands. And now we have the measure of the Far Kingdoms. And even if King Domas expels us as the price for his brother's death, what of it? We will still be able to achieve what they have gained . . . and more. Is that everything? Or is everything the ruin of your own ambitions . . . and the loss of your black guide?"

"We needed Raveline," Janos said. "*I* needed him. He was my stepping stone. He would have been my tool."

"For what end? So you could become more evil than he? So you could reach deeper into demon worlds than he has? So you, in the end, would be able to rule with fire and the lash in a manner that would make people remember the Black Prince as a kindly benefactor?"

"Words, words, Antero," Janos barked. "You still use words that you do not know the meaning of . . . or that have no meaning at all. Evil . . . good . . . We stand at the threshold of another age, an age beyond all of the petty considerations of prattling parents and teachers. Men say that once there was a Golden Age, when we were all like gods. That age never existed. All there has been, since this world formed itself from the slime, were flounderings; sometimes a bit toward the light, sometimes a slip back into the abyss. Raveline would have helped me split the clouds and let the radiance shine for all eternity. Men would have been, not gods, but beyond gods. Except for your doing. Except for one small-souled peddler who can see nothing but profit and some sort of mythical woolly-brained benevolence in a world where there is nothing but predator and prey. There was but one chance for all of us. Can't you see? Chance, which is the only real god to worship, created one brief moment for this change to begin, for man to step up and beyond."

That was quite enough. "Gods," I said, and there was anger in my voice as well. "You claim I use meaningless words. Well, this peddler is having trouble with some of *your* words, and gods is one of them. Another is this new age you mention. If we are to be gods, my pardon, more than gods, all of us small-souled beings should now look at the face of Janos Greycloak, and see the awful halo of the future he promises. Look at yourself. Your face mirrors what you have become, man! You're nothing but a degenerate who prattles drunkenly of the morrow's blessing while he cheerfully plunges into the gutter with the swine. Janos, can't you see? I recollect a time when you spoke of what gains *we* could bring back from the Far Kingdoms . . . gains for everyone. Instead, what is your goal, now? You told me to look at one grain of sand and see a myriad within it. I cannot. All I see is that poor woman in her boat, sorrowing under your mansion. What did you give *her*, Greycloak? Did you make her . . . or her children . . . more than gods? Look at yourself now, my once friend. And answer this simple merchant's question: why, if your quest is for the heavens, do you now have the face of a demon?"

Janos did not look away. His obvious scorn grew, and I realized why he was letting his anger build. "Knowledge . . . power . . . exacts its own price," he said. "You would know that, if you were anything but a child."

We stared at each other for a long moment, and in that moment, Halab's final gift showed itself. I knew what must be done, and my heart shriveled as it realized that just as there had been no possibility of Janos' redemption, my duty was now equally graven in stone. I fought the revelation, but knew its truth.

The second part of the gift followed. I was suddenly watching the room with two sets of eyes, as if one brain controlled two beings who stood apart from one another. Images of everything doubled and overlapped. Everything—except for Janos. His eyes gleamed brightly as they became lamps, their glow not dissimilar from the light that had shone from Greif's blind eye.

"Could have," he murmured, "and still shall be."

Without looking away, without a change of expression, he swooped to one knee, seized a long blade that had been lying on the floor, and slashed at my midsection. But I was not there. The third, and last, part of Halab's gift was now mine. I had "seen" the knife, fully as long as a sword, just before Janos' hand found it—and realized his plan. Time came to a stop as he cut at me, and it was most easy to step back beyond its reach.

"No, Janos," I said. "You do not need to do this. Neither of us needs to die." I said the words, but they were hollow. They were not a deliberate lie, but came from the last part of me that still fought against the onrushing end to this tragedy. He did not answer, but attacked once more. His knife gleamed, glowing as if it had been carved from a single jewel, and each facet caught the dawn's sun and reflected a thousand thousand shimmerings across the room. He lunged . . . and his thrust went past my side as I slipped out of the way.

He recovered as my right hand found the grip of the sword that, without looking, I had known would be there. I drew it from its sheath, which hung on a bedside chair. The blade I held was either the same, or a duplicate, of that plain, slender soldier's blade Janos had used to save me from Melina's pimp. As it snaked out, Janos cut at me again, this time for my face. My blade rose, parried his strike with a crash, and the knife jewel, if that was what it was, shattered like dropped crystal.

Its pieces still hung in midair as my blade finished its semicircle; then I lunged, every muscle, every nerve, every part of my body and soul in that swordpoint. It took Janos in the lungs and drove through his body until I "saw" nearly six inches of crimsoning steel emerge from his back. Halab's final gift, a gift that carried a curse to my heart, disappeared then.

There was no movement from either of us for what seemed forever. Janos' eyes showed enormous surprise, like those of a seer whose vision had proven faulty. He opened his mouth, but instead of words or a scream, blood gouted. He swayed. I released my grip on the sword. Janos took one step forward, then sank to his knees, both hands coming up to grasp the blade buried in his chest. He collapsed on his back, the sword standing above him. His eyes were closed, and then they opened, and looked up, past the swaying guard of the weapon, into my face.

"When . . . the blade comes out," he said, in a harsh whisper, "my soul comes with it."

I nodded. My eyes were blurred once again, but not from magic. My face was wet.

"I . . . remember," he said, "once telling you, outside that tavern where first we met . . . that to meet a red-haired man was . . . was a lucky omen." He forced a smile, and there was a harsh gasping as his body fought on for life. "At least . . . at least we found . . . found the Far Kingdoms," he said.

"We did," I said. Then, more strongly, "*We* did."

Pain struck Janos then, and he writhed. "Take ... take the blade out now," he said, and his voice was a command. "Before I dishonor my pride."

I pulled the blade free. And as it came out, a soul fled into the embrace of the Dark Seeker.

Janos Kether Greycloak, Prince of Kostroma, Captain and Knight of Orissa, unanointed Baron of Vacaan, seeker of the Far Kingdoms, and, yes, a man who had once been my friend, was dead.

CHAPTER TWENTY-EIGHT
The Holy Mountain

I COME TO the end of this journey now; and as I write these lines, I can feel Janos' weight sag in my arms when I lifted his body from the cart. My rheumy eyes look through younger ones, and I see clear the path we dragged that cart up to reach the crown of the Holy Mountain. Sergeant Maeen and the other men step forward to help me, but I harshly order them away. I must do this myself.

I shift my burden and turn toward the great pocked ruins of the Old Ones' altar. I stumble toward it, weak with present age; and I am weary, so weary I pray for that youth's strength so I do not fall. My quill trembles with effort as I lift Janos to the stone. I lay him out and take a panting step back so I can see the man who led us here.

Ah, there you are, Janos. I know you now, Greycloak. I see your naked flesh on the stone, and the scars of your great failure mark that flesh. But I am not done yet: thought must wait as I complete my labors. Maeen puts the flask in my hands and I pour oil over Janos' corpse. Now I must pray, but I do not know the Old Ones' words, so I merely say, Farewell, Janos Greycloak.

I light the fire and stumble back from its angry flare. I see the flames attack, furious strikes all along his body. They strike the hardest at the sorcerous scars; then the scars vanish, and I see Janos transformed, young and handsome as when we first met in innocence.

Now there is a moment for those thoughts I held back before. You were my friend, Janos Greycloak, and you betrayed me. Ah, but I have hissed those curses before. I did not begin this journal to open old wounds, but to banish those scars, like the altar fire banished Janos'. There were two journeys intended in this ledger: one for those who read my scratchings, the other for myself. We accomplished a great thing, Greycloak and I. We found the Far Kingdoms. But Greycloak traveled farther alone. And our world will never be the same for his discoveries. It was *I* who carried them back, however; and it was *I* who was given some of the credit. But I did not lie, Janos Greycloak. I did not betray, like Cassini. My quill is eager to expunge those self-inflicted wounds. And I think: what did you do to me after all? What I have seen, and all I did later, was because of you. You set us free, Janos. You stole magic from the secret hearths of the wizards and made it a common tool for common men. And my beloved Orissa now basks in peace and great bounty. Shouldn't those gifts be enough for forgiveness?

Very well: I forgive you, Janos, and I forgive myself as well for not knowing enough to rescue you that final time. You were not a good man, Greycloak, but you were a great man, and it was your greatness that slew you in the end—not I.

With that understanding—and forgiveness—I am anxious to get to the finish, but I will see it with new eyes now. I hear Maeen and the men paying their final respects to Janos. And I feel Omerye's soft presence beside me. She lifts her pipes to play a song of sweet regrets. The fire leaps, and the body is transformed once more—this time into dark smoke. I feel the east wind hush past and it lifts the smoke into the sky. The smoke pauses overhead, and swirls about as if it had commanded the wind to wait.

I wipe wetness from my eyes . . . and look again. Suddenly I see a vision of great clarity. Far to the east, across dazzling seas, where they say no man lives, a trick of light lifts a mountain range above Horizon's curve. The range looks like a great clenched fist, and between thumb and finger I see the glitter of a pure white blanket of snow. The mountain fist exactly fits the vision I saw when the Evocators cast the bones that began our quest.

The vision pulls hard now, as I write. But I cannot go, I cannot go.

I look up at the smoke that was Janos and see it suddenly give way to the eastern wind, then sail eagerly across the vast skies to meet the vision.

I whisper after it, Farewell, Janos Greycloak. Farewell, my friend. May the gods speed you on this final journey—to the Far Kingdoms of our youth.

Return to the world of The Far Kingdoms
with Amalric's warrior sister, Rali,
in a brand-new epic fantasy
of awesome magic and sea-going adventure:

THE WARRIOR'S TALE
by Allan Cole and Chris Bunch

Published in hardcover by
Del Rey Books.

Coming to bookstores everywhere in
November 1994.

Turn the page for a sneak preview!

CHAPTER FOUR
The Wizard's Heart

THERE HAS NEVER been a victory feast as great as the one that came after the fall of Lycanth. It didn't matter that one of the Archons and Nisou Symeon had escaped. It was enough, when the new day dawned, that soldiers saw the Orissan banner flying from the highest point of the Lycanthian seacastle. Now they could creep out from their tunnels and walk freely about under the looming battlements that had spat death at them for so many months. The soldiers were drunk with joy, shouting, singing, whirling about in mad dances. All of our gods were hauled out and bedecked with garlands, looted finery, and jewels. The seacastle was sacked, and real drink found, and the celebration grew wilder still. Beeves, fowls, pigs, and pups were sacrificed to the gods. Just knowing there'd be life the next day and the day after that was so soul-filling that all discipline was swept away in that joyous storm. Wisely, we officers made no attempt to stem their antics, other than making sure no civilians or prisoners suffered.

My women celebrated as wildly as any of the others. Polillo tromped into our encampment with a keg of looted brandy on each shoulder. She broached them with her ax, and the amber li quor flowed into my sisters' throats. Corais and Ismet stayed reasonably sober, keeping watch on their comrades tempers. Such extreme happiness, mixed with brandy, can be a powerful elixir for the unwary, and the demons of anger are always ready to pounce on the smallest insult. Many a lovers' quarrel has been settled with a blade after a battle.

We had blood enough on our hands.

As for me, I suddenly found I had become that oddest of

creatures—a hero. The young recruit dreams of such a thing, weary muscles trembling in their sleep after a day of shouting sergeants lashing her from one absurd task to the next, a dream of one day standing tall but humble as thousands of voices shout her name; while old soldiers speak in hushed tones when she passes.

I dreamed such dreams when I was young. But when hero's garland really was bestowed on me that day, I did not find it so pleasant. The fast ship that carried news of our victory to Orissa also bore flowery descriptions of my deeds and the deeds of the Maranon Guard. The battle-blasted landscape echoed with my praises. Wherever I walked, crowds of soldiers parted before me. Some reached to touch my tunic as if it were sacred cloth instead of a rough soldier's weave. Gifts were heaped before my tent, and the mound grew so quickly I had to post a guard to politely turn their bearers away. There were marriage proposals by the scores. Men begged to father a child with me. Women—even those who'd once turned their noses up at me—left intimate things in my path, and whispered hot entreaties from the shadows to share my cot. It was said a day would be named in my honor, with all the special sacrifices and ceremonies that sort of thing entails.

I did not find it pleasant, Scribe. I still do not. It is a false thing, a deadly thing, that can turn a happily common mortal into a demon of vanity. Heroes belong in the grave. It is the only place they can be safe from themselves—and their worshippers.

The worst thing about my sudden leap to sanctity was that Jinnah's hatred deepened as he saw himself being robbed of the hero's crown he'd coveted. Somehow word leaked that Jinnah had been forced by Gamelan into carrying out my plan. Within hours after the last Lycanthian surrendered, there were jokes being made at his expense. The long, bloody siege was being dubbed "Jinnah's Folly," and there were those who cursed him bitterly for letting the fight go on so long, and for so many addle-brained decisions which, they charged, had cost thousands their lives.

To be fair, the Lycanthians had been the toughest of foes, and the Archons so powerful they nearly bested our own Evocators. Still there were many things Jinnah would have to answer for, not here, but when he returned to Orissa and stood before the Council of Magistrates. It was apparent that some god would have to take a sudden and very great liking for Jinnah if he was to save himself from a shame that would last into the ages.

Jinnah's luck, however, changed that very night. It rode in on a furious storm that sank our encampment in a sea of mud. The rain was blinding. The seas raged high, crashing over the rocky shore in waves three times the height of a tall woman. Then Jinnah sent word that I was to come to him—immediately. Not to his tent, but to the seacastle and to the Private Chamber where I'd killed the Archon's brother.

As I entered the vast room I could not help but grip the little amulet Gamelan had given me. I took comfort in the absence of the awful odor that had betrayed the Archons' presence. As I looked about, shielding my eyes from the white hot glare of sorcerous torches rekindled with Orissan magic, I saw with much surprise that there was no sign of the struggle that had taken place just hours before. Everything seemed to have been put back into pristine order by Gamelan and his Evocators. I saw white-sashed novices sweeping up the last bits of broken glass. The shards were given to yellow-sashed apprentices who shook sweet smelling smoke on them and whispered enchantments, and the bits re-formed themselves into jars, or vials, or crystal bowls, etched with sorcerous symbols. Other wizards and their helpers were moving quietly about, replacing things on tables and benches and hand-carved shelves. The whole thing was being directed by several red-sashed senior wizards, who seemed to be working from parchment maps of the room that Gamelan, or an assistant, had used spells to recreate. To one side, near a large golden urn, I saw Jinnah and a knot of aides. They were watching Gamelan, who had set up an odd apparatus on a portable altar. He was making some adjustments, but no sooner had I entered than he looked up—his yellow eyes darting about until they found me. He made a signal—as if in warning. Before I could make clear his intent, Jinnah saw me.

"Ah, Captain Antero," he said. "The hero of the hour." There was venom in his tone. "Come here, if you please. We have need of your assistance."

I knew jealousy and hatred had mated in Jinnah's breast, but as I joined the group I was startled to see a look of pure delight in his eyes. I wasn't sure what to make of it, but the look reminded me of our old kitchen cat when she had a rat at her mercy.

"General," I said. "What is the trouble?"

"It seems we may have won the battle," Jinnah said, with odd relish, "but not the war."

"Well put, sir," his toady, Captain Hux, said. Then to me: "We fear all your bold actions may have been for naught."

I looked at Gamelan. "The Archon?" I asked.

Gamelan nodded, grave. "The general sent Admiral Cholla Yi after him," he said. "But the Archon raised the storm we are now

431

experiencing, and forced him to give up the chase." He continued making adjustments to the apparatus, which was a complicated thing, with spidery tubes and wires and glass retorts filled with multicolored liquids set to a boil by some magical force. Colored steam issued from them, but there was no odor.

I shrugged. "It can't storm forever. We'll catch him soon enough. No land will take him in, now that he's lost his armies and his homeland. Our spies will soon ferret him out." But as I said this, I felt a chill at my spine, and involuntarily touched Gamelan's amulet.

The old wizard caught my motion and nodded. "We can't risk our future to chance and spies," he said. He made a wide gesture, taking in the vaulted room. "We've re-created every detail of this chamber at the moment before you so boldly entered, down to a cockroach that had just investigated the contents of a wizard's pouch."

Gamelan lifted up a small, leather bag. The leather was rich and scored with symbols. He undid a gold tie, pinched out a bit of dust, and held it over one of the glass retorts. "This was one of the ingredients for a spell. It's made of ground bone and the stalk of some vegetation. But it is bone and plant life that none of us have ever encountered." He dropped the dust into boiling liquid. Then he corked the retort and pushed a piece of copper tubing through a hole. The tubing ran into the maze of tubes and glass that made up his apparatus. Gamelan spun the blades of a small prayer wheel set up next to the device. We heard the faint sound of bells, as the wheel began its automatic chant. I knew little of magic then, but had no doubt the machine, linked somehow to the prayer wheel, was born from my brother's and Janos Greycloak's discoveries in the Far Kingdoms.

Gamelan made no explanation. He turned back to us as if the apparatus had nothing to do with our conversation.

"Tell her the rest," Jinnah urged. "Tell her what you have learned."

Without preface, Gamelan said, "We have found unmistakable evidence that the Archon and his brother were only days away from creating that weapon we all so feared. What's worse, the Archons had prepared for possible defeat by making duplicates of all their equipment and notes. Those things were placed in special trunks that cannot be penetrated by any natural or sorcerous force. When our friend fled on Lord Symeon's ships those trunks went with him."

My innards gave a lurch. I turned to Jinnah, angry. "Storm, or no storm, we should be out there right now hunting him down. What possessed Cholla Yi to turn back? Symeon didn't have much of a start on him. And I've no doubt that pirate has faced worse tempests before."

"Admiral Cholla Yi did his best," Jinnah said. "But he did not have the means to press the chase."

"He wanted more money, I suppose." I did nothing to disguise my disgust.

Jinnah nodded. "Naturally. We fight for ideals. He fights for coin. Besides, he needs more ships, supplies, and a greater force, so that when we catch the Archon, we can finish the job."

It suddenly came to me that the general was being altogether too casual. What was the purpose of this meeting? Why was he wasting time telling me all this? I was but one of his officers. Instead of telling me his plans, Jinnah should have been issuing the pertinent orders. An expedition needed to be mounted immediately. The greater the distance the Archon and Symeon put between us and their ships, the more difficult it would be to capture and defeat them. As we spoke, an Orissan commander of sea-experienced soldiers should have been readying his men to board Cholla Yi's ships to resume the chase, just as I should be putting my women in motion for a quick march home to take up guard in case the Archon somehow found the means to threaten Orissa. All the talk of doomsday weapons and slippery wizards reminded me of the Maranon Guard's historic duty to keep Orissa safe. Then it began to dawn on me what Jinnah had in mind. Before the realization was fully formed, he said, in the most oily manner imaginable, "You'll be pleased to know, Captain, that I've decided the Maranon Guard should have the honor of this most vital mission."

"That's foolishness, sir," I retorted. "My soldiers are more battle-weary than any others in our army. Or are you forgetting today's battle?."

"Of course I haven't, dear Captain," he oozed. "It was your courage and theirs I had uppermost in my mind when I made my decision."

I knew instantly what he was about. He was as transparent as any courtesan's dancing veil. With me out of the way, Jinnah would be able to shift the glory my Guard had won onto his own shoulders. As well as a jackal pack's worth of the booty from our defeated enemy.

"Yes, indeed," Jinnah continued. "This is a mission of such im-

433

portance that only one woman is suitable for it. The Hero of Lycanth. Captain Rali Emilie Antero."

I knew I was lost, but I tried one more sally. "I'd be glad to oblige, General," I said, as smoothly as I could. "And we all thank you for the singular honor, but the Maranon Guard's duty is at home. As a matter of fact, I was going to come by in the morning and ask you for my orders."

"You can have them now," Jinnah said. "But you won't be going home. As I said, this is a task for a hero. And a hero it shall have. As, no doubt, the Magistrates shall agree when I toast you at the victory feast in Orissa a few weeks hence."

Hux and the other aides sniggered.

Jinnah's next words came in a growl of command. "You and your women will join Admiral Yi at first light. Your orders are to pursue the Archon. You will find him and kill him. You will spare no effort, no cost, no life, until you find him and kill him. What's more, I order you to not return until that goal has been accomplished. Do I make myself clear?"

It was like banishment, as if my women and I were being punished for our success—which we were.

You seem as stunned as I was, Scribe. The histories that have been written of those events make no mention of Jinnah's motives, do they? Welcome to the side of the world that women dwell in, my friend. It's quite cramped, for men require—and command—a great deal more room than me and my sisters. It's quite cold over here, as well, Scribe. The fuel for our fires have been rationed, you see. It has been deemed that we need only enough to warm childish pride in our looks, the ability to win a bed mate, and to keep hearth, children, and kitchen clean. And it's quite gloomy. You don't need much light when you're a mere reflection of man.

I stared long and hard at Jinnah after he had spoken. I tried to will him to call back his words. But I wouldn't, and perhaps from his view couldn't, retreat. I wanted to shout that the Guard was a land force, and had been so since its inception. We had no experience with the sea. I wanted to curse him for trying to steal the glory that only an hour before I had disdained. I wanted to plead with him—not for my life—but for my sisters' lives. How many now had a hope of returning to Orissa's blessed shores? But I could not do any of those things. Orders had been clearly given, no matter how insane.

But I did not give him the least satisfaction in seeing my turmoil, my fears. Nor did I click my bootheels and fire off my crispest salute. For he did not deserve this respect. And respect was all I could deny him.

So I merely nodded. And said, "Very well, sir. But if I am to do this, I must insist on one thing."

"What is that, Captain Antero?" Jinnah sneered. He did not dare retort that I could insist on nothing. After all, the general himself had called me the Hero of Lycanth. How can one deny a hero?

"I want complete command of this expedition, sir. Cholla Yi is to be told in no uncertain terms that my every whim is to be instantly obeyed. Obviously, I will not misuse this, sir. I will leave to him matters of the sea. But in the hunt, itself, and in any conflict, it is my word that must rule."

Jinnah laughed unpleasantly. "The Admiral and I have already discussed these things, Captain," he said. "I made quite clear what role he is to play."

More sniggering from Hux and the other aides.

"Sir, I request that you repeat all that I have said in a formal conference with the Admiral."

"If you think it's necessary, Captain," Jinnah replied, "I shall be glad to do so." He turned to take leave. "I'll call a meeting within the hour."

Then I heard Gamelan croak. "One moment, General."

Jinnah stopped. He looked at the old wizard, a frown of worry creasing his too handsome features. Was Gamelan going to somehow interfere? I had such wild hopes myself, but Gamelan quickly dashed them.

"An Evocator will need to be assigned to this expedition," he said.

"Choose whom you please," the general replied.

"Oh, I shall," Gamelan snapped, making certain Jinnah realized the Chief Evocator's choices were his and his alone to make. "And I choose myself."

Jinnah gaped. "But that's—but you're—"

"Too old?" Gamelan snorted. "That's the very reason why I shall go. The work that remains to be done here would best be dealt with by younger wizards. And, I dare say I am more of a match for my sorcerous cousin, the Archon, than any of my fellows. No, I believe this expedition will have a better chance if I am along."

I saw delight in Jinnah's eyes: two enemies with one blow. He could not have hoped for more. "May the blessings of Te Date be upon you," he intoned.

Gamelan did not answer. He was fussing with his apparatus again—acting as if he'd already forgotten the general's presence. After a long, somewhat embarrassing moment, Jinnah shook his head and departed, his aides crowding around his heels as rock lizards just out of the egg scurry after their mother in case father come home to make an early dinner.

I remained behind. I was beginning to get an inkling of the old man's ways. "Thank you," I said.

"For what, my dear Rali? For burdening you with someone with years as long as his beard?" He stroked the unkempt mass at his chin. Gamelan's eyes were a warm yellow, like a cheery hearth. Crooked teeth laughed through the gray thicket.

"Just the same," I said, "until you spoke up, I thought this whole thing hopeless."

"You doubt your ability to carry it off?"

"Not really," I said. "If the odds were even. But I do not think my commander intends for me to return. I believe he's more worried about his own reputation—and fortunes—than the safety of Orissa."

The yellow hearth of his eyes burned hotter. "That was my opinion as well, Rali," he said. For the first time I took note at how familiarly the wizard had begun to address me. As if he saw friendship in his future. At that instant, I welcomed that offer. Although, as an Antero, I was nervous about it. My family has not had good fortune with wizards. But we did not speak of such things then.

"My distrust," Gamelan continued, "was the reason I insisted I go along. We can give the Archon no peace, or he will complete that weapon. It will take him longer than if he were allowed to remain untroubled in his chambers. Also, he does not have his brother to assist him. But we dare not let him rest in one place, or the victory here will be hollow indeed."

As I pondered that danger, Gamelan laughed. It is an odd thing to hear a wizard laugh. I have met many in my travels, and that human thing we all do so naturally does not come easy to them. Some shriek like a witch. Some croak like a mating frog. Some howl like direwolves greeting the moon. When he was happy, which I later learned was a rare thing in Gamelan's life, Gamelan hooted—like a great hunting owl. For the first time since we had met, I rather enjoyed that sound.

"I have another reason," he said. "I must confess that it is quite selfish."

"And what is that?" I asked.

436

"I remember the day when I gave permission for your brother and that rogue Greycloak to seek the Far Kingdoms. I sat on my throne of office, feeling like a little boy, instead of a wise old Evocator of much responsibility and power. I tell you, I would have traded that throne and every speck of knowledge and authority, if only I could have gone along."

Now it is my turn to laugh. "Adventure? Is that your poison, wizard?"

Another hoot from Gamelan. "I was born to it, Rali," he said. "But fate intervened. I was unlucky enough to be cursed with sorcerous talent. But that is another story, which I shall be delighted to bore you with on our voyage."

He shook his head and twisted his beard in great delight. "Imagine. To speak of such things ... storytelling, and voyages, and adventures. Why even now I feel quite like a youth again." Indeed, he seemed to have dropped years in the few minutes that had passed since our conversation had begun. His cheeks above his beard had a rosy hue. His eyes were brighter, his form straighter. Why, he almost looked handsome. If my women were of a different bent, I dare say several of them would have been ready to come to blows for a chance to trip that old man up on a hearth rug. I swore to myself that sometime during our journey, if the moment presented itself, along with a comely woman who liked the company of men, I would guide her to the wizard's cot.

Gamelan gave a start. "See, I am too old," he said. "I'd almost forgotten the work I was at." He hurried back to his apparatus, sniffing the odorless steam, turning little petcocks to let one liquid drip into another, talking as he went about his tasks. "Thanks to you," he said, "I have the means to arm ourselves against the Archon with a secret weapon of our own. It may not be enough to defeat him in the end, but it will certainly weaken him. And it will make our job easier to hunt him down."

He put an ornate box on the table. It was ebony black, with rich inlayed colors. There were no seams, no sign of a means for entry. Gamelan passed his hands over it, whispered a few words, and pressed the sides with the thumb and forefinger of each hand. It sprang open. I looked inside, and nearly retched at what I saw there. It was a large hunk of flesh with the brownish purple hue of an internal organ a few hours from rot.

"It's the heart of the Archon you slew," Gamelan said. He lifted it out with the ease of a man comfortable with offal. He placed it under a large copper spigot that protruded from the machine. He turned the petcock. Thick, oily drops of liquid—a glowing green in color—dripped onto the heart. The liquid flowed over the organ, coating it with a thin sheen of green. Gamelan chanted:

> Heart of stone,
> Brother to fear:
> No love
> No tears
> No pity!
> Heart of stone,
> Brother to hate:
> No joy
> No warmth
> No beauty!
> Hate to hate,
> Fear to Fear,
> Stone to stone:
> Brother find brother!

The heart began to shrink, and change form and color. It got smaller and smaller, slowly at first, then I blinked, and it had gone from the size of a fist to that of a bird's egg. Then it was as smooth and black as the ebony box. Gamelan lifted it gingerly with crystalline tongs and placed it in the box. Once again he pressed the sides and whispered a chant. The box snapped shut. Gamelan picked it up, holding it between flattened palms. He bowed his head, squinting in concentration. Then he nodded and looked up, those gnarly teeth gleaming thorough his beard. "It works," he said, quite pleased, as if he had been in some doubt.

He offered me the box. I drew back.

"I don't want to touch that thing," I said, as skittish as a new blooming maid.

"I don't blame you," Gamelan answered. "After all, we do know where it's been. Still . . . To please me, if nothing else."

I took the box and held it as he had. Instantly I felt a tingle. A vibration, like a stringed instrument that had recently been strummed.

"What's happening?" I asked.

Gamelan made that hunting-owl hoot of his. "Why, it's telling us that its brother is still quite near. And now we only have to follow it, andù."

Then excitement at his victory caught the wizard. Gamelan

threw back his head and gave a shout that rolled and echoed across that great Chamber of the Archons:

"I've got you, you bastard! I've got you!"